Flavia, *Sendara* of the Graelands, is desperate to find the hero who will save her Labyrinth World from Ab'addon, Lord of Desolation. According to the Prophecies, that hero is Oliver Medley, who possesses the one Gift that can defeat Ab'addon's dark forces. But Oliver is middle-aged, overweight, and shy, and is completely oblivious to Flavia's existence. He also has no clue to what his Gift might be. Only when formidable Great-Aunt Belvedine crashes into his quiet life and sweeps him off to the Labyrinth World does he realize he's in the adventure of his secret dreams. Sent on a Quest to rescue Flavia, he encounters Dwarvians, Wraiths, Ab'addon's Garden of Smoke and Mirrors, and more terrors than he has ever imagined. But he must persist, for he has pledged his fealty—and his life—to the *Sendara* Flavia.

Saint Amber's Rose is a story of high fantasy, deep magic, and the soul's journey to reach its greatest potential.

Saint Amber's Rose

a novel by

Charleynne Gates

What you have inside you, if you bring it forth,
what you have inside you will save you. What
you have inside you, if you do not bring it forth,
what you have inside you will destroy you.
--The Gospel of Thomas

Cover art and illustrations by Kathryn Nance.

First Printing

A RED MOONS PRESS PUBLICATION

ISBN-13: 978-0-9847324-0-1
ISBN-10: 0984732403

Printed in the United States of America

Set in 11-point Times New Roman

"Be Thou My Vision," words attrib. Dallan Forgaill, 8th cen. Trans. Mary E. Byrne, 1905; versed by Eleanor H. Hull, 1912. Music: "Slane," Irish tune.

ACKNOWLEDGMENTS

My heartfelt thanks to Jessica Maxwell (author of *Roll Around Heaven*), founder and leader of the Red Moons writers support group; members of Red Moons for critical feedback; Dr. Kay Porter (*The Mental Athlete*), who first read the whole manuscript; Dr. Tom Titus (*Blackberries in July*), who supplied biological taxonomy for the Sunder stonecritter; Cliff Scovell (*Prison Earth*), for computer expertise; Alice Adams and Sandra Boynton, who each read an early draft and saved me from embarrassing errors; Greg Nance, who produced the CD of my reading of Chapter One; Kathryn Nance, who designed the cover art and illustrations and gave me a great critique; and the staff of the Eugene Public Library, who patiently coped with my bouts of computer-induced panic.

DEDICATION

to Saint Amber

Ever in my thoughts,
as I am in hers.

TABLE OF CONTENTS

Part III. Ancient Paths

Part IV. The Way of the Rose

Part I

The Summons

I think there are things that are real--more real than we are--but mostly we don't cross their paths, or they don't cross ours. Maybe at very bad times we get into their world, or notice what they are doing in ours.
--A. S. Byatt, "The Thing in the Forest"

Prologue

Et in Arcadia ego. I also was in paradise.
--The Serpent

The Servant of the Desolation crouched in a corner of the old wall at the end of the garden. Thorn-laden shrubs grew in front of the weathered stones. Their stubby trunks, so near the ground that only an inch or two showed, were harder than iron, harder than steel, harder than human hearts. The blade had not been forged that could sever them. Fire would not burn those bushes, nor poison kill. Time itself did not change them, for they had been there long before the present owner occupied the property, and that was longer ago than he could have imagined.

Between the shrubs and the scarred wall was an irregular patch of soil in which nothing grew or had ever been planted, for sunlight could not reach it and the air was dank and still. Beneath the surface, the earth was full of jagged rocks. Most living creatures avoided the place.

The Servant liked it fine. It was an excellent place to hide--and to wait--for as long as necessary. Time had no effect upon the Desolation.

.

Chapter One

The Visitation

We all need to create a paradise to escape into.
--Azar Nafisi, *Reading Lolita in Tehran*

How true it is that we can choose our friends, but our families come ready-made! For some people, this fact evokes feelings of comfort and connection. For others, a visit by a particular relative makes them cry aloud, like the Lady of Shalott, "The curse has come upon me!"

The looming Curse of the Medleys was not apparent to Oliver Medley on that lovely bright day in late June. Given his penchant for avoiding the uncomfortable and ignoring the unpleasant, it wouldn't have been, because Oliver Medley disliked Change.

And the Curse was precisely about Change.

A young snail (*Helix aspersa*) crept up a rose cane, apprehensive at the magnitude of his task but determined to carry out his mission. The honor of his regiment depended upon it. The snowy petals of the rare Don Quixote variety nodded above him, blotting out the sun's disk and protecting him from its withering rays. A few more inches... He was almost there...

"That's not the right place for you, little gastropod," he heard someone say, though the language was unknown to him, and found himself sliding down the metal surface of a gardening trowel. Before he had time to panic, he was borne across the lawn to the other side of the garden where a white picket fence bordered a vacant lot. There the trowel touched ground, and the snail was encouraged to descend into a bed of feral thyme.

The owner of the trowel, Oliver Medley, returned to the center of the garden and sat on the deacon's bench by the sundial to rest. He removed his gardening gloves and stroked the fur of a tabby cat (*Felis domestica*) curled next to him. At his touch the cat settled her head on her paws and began to purr.

The scent of roses in bloom enticed a breeze that danced around the bushes and set blossoms nodding on the tallest one, a Knight-Errant in apricot blush. Oliver smiled at it and felt a swell of contentment around his heart. Here on this perfect afternoon were beauty, peace, order--a refuge from the tumult of the world outside his garden. A sense of gratitude washed gently over him. He closed his eyes and breathed in fragrance.

His personal paradise. *My little Eden.*

Not that paradise was without a few flaws, for no human life is perfect. Oliver's might have been closer to perfection had there been a Significant Other, but there wasn't. His ideal love had never appeared except in his daydreams. Regrettably, she wasn't likely to appear anywhere else, for whenever the specter of real-life Romance reared its head, Oliver shrank into a shivering, damp-handed, incoherent caricature of his normal self. And then he fled.

The only other factor in his life that he might have changed if he could was an ever-present feeling that he had missed his proper era. Stuck in the twenty-first century as he was, he had accommodated himself to its rush and clangor as best he might—to the incessant deedle of electronic gadgetry, the calculated offensiveness of postmodern media. No, it was his father's era he pined for, or even his grandfather's, when (as he imagined), things were quieter, and time moved at a more decorous pace. The Edwardians, possibly, would have made him feel more at home, and what he wouldn't give to have seen Paris in the Twenties or Berlin in the Thirties...

But those days were entombed in history. Oliver knew he had much to be grateful for in the present day, and saw no point in repining over what he could never have. His life was a comfortable one, and he took a quiet pleasure in what he had: music, books, good friends, his garden. If Youth had flown, he did not regret it. If he now trod the broad terrain of Middle Age, at least it was solid under foot. Being still distant from the desert of Decrepitude, he anticipated many more pleasant years to come. Thus had Oliver Medley walled himself away from everything that might have disturbed his tranquil life and sent him tumbling into misery--or happiness.

Saint Amber's Rose

"Yoo-hoo! Ol-i-ver!" His next-door neighbor, Aurelia Dawn, hailed him over the garden gate. "I've got something for you! I'll just let myself in and bring it over."

She did so, skimming in sandaled feet across the grass. Oliver repressed his irritation and arose at her approach.

"Oh, you don't have to get up for me! You've been working hard in your gorgeous garden. You need your rest."

Aurelia was his senior by fifteen or twenty years and tended to treat him like a small boy or an invalid, but he managed to smother his natural feelings of resentment and look anticipatory.

"Something for me?" he inquired.

"Just look!" She waved a large, ivory-tinted envelope in front of him. "It came *Special Delivery* yesterday, and our new mail carrier brought it to my house by *mistake,* and I knew you weren't *home,* so I told him the name on the address was *really* 'Olivia', it was *practically illegible* anyway, and I signed for it. I *knew* you'd want it *right away*, so *here it is!*"

She presented the envelope with a flourish and a grin, displaying her excellent bridgework. Sunlight glinted on her tight, brassy curls, the result of her latest attempt at home coloring. The breeze, fascinated by this exotic intruder, came over to investigate and ruffled Aurelia's gypsy skirt.

Oliver took the envelope with murmured thanks. "But, Aurelia," he couldn't help adding, "today is Sunday."

"And isn't it a *beautiful day*!" she said happily.

Oliver tried again. "That is, ah, if you'd have let me know about this a little sooner? It might be important. Not that I don't appreciate--"

Aurelia's eyes rounded between their mascara'd lashes; her expression became serious. "Of *course* it's important! It's *Special Delivery!* Oh, I get it!" She flapped a hand and laughed. "You mean I *should* have brought it over *yesterday*! But you were *out* all day, and *I* didn't get home til the *wee hours myself*, and *you're* always in bed by *ten-thirty*. Besides, I wanted to draw a *Rune* to find out *when* I ought to give it to you." Her voice darkened with undertones of mystery. "It came out a *Five*, the *Wild Ox*, the *Rune of Terminations* and *New Beginnings*."

She resumed her cheerful aspect. "So I knew that *today* would be your *best* time for *new beginnings*, being *Midsummer Day*. You *don't* have to *thank* me! That's what neighbors are *for*. *Well!* I have to get back to work on my *new book*: '*Secrets* of the *Cauldron* for *Wiccan Wenches*,' forthcoming from *NewHarpy Press*. It's a *cookbook, see!* Isn't that a *clever title*? Ta-ta!" She danced back across the lawn to her own house, ear-hoops bouncing, bangle bracelets clashing like wind chimes in a hurricane.

Oliver sat down heavily on the bench, his tranquil mood a distant memory. Aurelia had been their next-door neighbor for decades and a close friend of his late mother. He had always been dubious about Aurelia's trade--astrologer, Tarot card reader, writer for New Age publications--but Tolerance was his personal motto, and he tried to live up to it. Occasionally, as in Aurelia's case, it was a bit of a strain.

He examined the ivory-tinted envelope, noting the spidery penning of his name (as Aurelia had mentioned, it was half-obscured with an inky smudge), the blurred return address in the upper left corner, the stamp of elaborate design and unknown provenance. At least it was unknown to Oliver, who had had an extensive stamp collection in his younger days. Also, this one didn't appear to have a cancellation mark, although mistakes do happen even with computerized processing.

Oliver had a foreboding feeling that he knew the identity of the sender, and reluctantly turned the envelope over to verify his suspicion. There they were, in a blob of purple sealing wax: the letters P B M M de M interwoven in curlicues.

Oh, no. Great-Aunt Belvedine! "You've not met Great-Aunt Portia Belvedine Medley Makebold, Countess de Montfort," he remarked to the sleeping cat. "Consider yourself lucky."

The cat flicked an ear and ceased purring.

Great-Aunt Belvedine was the only other extant member of the Medley family since his mother had passed away last winter, leaving Oliver bereft of close kindred. According to family gossip, Belvedine de Montfort led a Bohemian life that didn't bear close examination. As a young woman, her carryings-on were said to be a considerable embarrassment to the Medleys and de Montforts. (The Makebolds, the entire clan of which resided in a late Victorian mausoleum, were presumably beyond embarrassment.)

Oliver had met her only two or three times in brief but memorable encounters, recalling that as a child he had been quite terrified at her sudden appearances. "So this is the heir to the Medley name?" she demanded at her first visit. He had tried to hide behind the dining-room door, but she fixed her steely eye upon him. "Come here, boy!" she commanded in a voice that promised doom to the disobedient.

He would have run from that formidable presence had not his father put a kindly hand on his shoulder. "Aunt Bel's harmless," Mr. Medley whispered. "She won't bite."

Despite his father's reassurance, Oliver suspected her of being a sorceress of some kind, like Morgan le Fay in the Arthurian legends he was reading at the time. True, she always dressed like the late Queen Mary, in loops of pearls and fulsome hats, rather than like a legendary sorceress, but the feeling was there. Later, when he began reading science fiction, he realized that she might well be a time traveler. Nothing ever arose to disabuse him of that notion, although he wasn't comfortable thinking about it and indeed ceased to do so as he grew older.

He decided he ought to wash his hands before opening the letter, but before that, he might as well finish tidying the herbaceous border at the far end of the garden. Picking up a corner of the envelope between thumb and forefinger, he took it to the back porch, placed it carefully on the seat of the swing, and went back to his gardening.

After he had neatened the border and cleaned his trowel, he returned to the house to wash up. It was a beautiful place, the ancestral Medley home--buttercup yellow with white gingerbread. There he had lived companionably with his widowed mother for many years.

The phone rang while he was drying his hands. "Why, yes, Dr. Mornington," he told the dean of the local chapter of the American Guild of Organists, of which Oliver was a member. "I'd be glad to substitute for you. The last two Sundays in August? Prelude, offertory, and postlude on the new pipe organ. Certainly. Enjoy your vacation in--where was it? The Amazon River. Observing the anaconda in its natural habitat. How... interesting."

He hung up, wondering at people's sometimes peculiar hobbies. Dr. Mornington taught medieval music at the university and was a fine organist, but his rather eccentric passion was the study of herpetology, particularly the larger snakes. Oliver did not pretend to understand such an affinity, but he was pleased at the assignment, which gave him something to look forward to during the doldrums of late August.

That business concluded, his attention turned to the creation of dinner: chilled wild-caught Pacific salmon with a salad of red oak-leaf lettuce and fresh strawberries in cream for dessert. Then he listened to an Oregon Bach Festival recording of Haydn's *The Creation*, turned to the thirty-seventh chapter of Ezekiel for his nightly Bible reading, and went to bed.

In the night the swing on the back porch rocked back and forth--there was no wind--and creaked a bit in its old bones. Oliver heard it in his dreams, but didn't awaken. In the hour before midnight, a raven landed on the swing, picked up the ivory-tinted envelope in its beak, and flew away.

In the morning he awoke with no memory of dream or letter. He dressed in a three-piece summer-weight suit with his old prep school tie, ate a bowl of organic oatmeal with local blackberry honey and rBST-free milk, and drove his father's Buick to the University of Oregon library, where he worked as an archivist.

Some years ago a wealthy alumnus had willed to the university his collection of ancient music, maps, and manuscripts from all corners of the world. The Willoughby-Smythe Collection was unique in size, content, and age, and was the envy of many a museum. Dr. Willoughby-Smythe, a friend of Oliver's father, had made certain stipulations to his bequest, one of which was that the archivist of his collection be hired and paid by the Willoughby-Smythe Trust, although the collection itself would be housed in the university library. In effect, this proviso made the archivist of the collection independent of the university employment system, a fact greatly irritating to the Head Librarian, a martinet who resented the fact that one particular area of the library was not under his control.

"Good morning, Professor Finbiter," Oliver greeted the Head as they passed each other in the lobby.

"Rrrm," growled the Head, his usual response, as he charged onward without a sideways glance.

Unbeknownst to his colleagues, the Head had applied for the position of archivist of the Willoughby-Smythe Collection. When Oliver Medley received the appointment instead, the Head never reconciled himself to his defeat. The idea that Medley's meticulous scholarship was superior to his own didn't enter his mind.

Saint Amber's Rose

Oliver was aware of the Head's animosity towards him, but never guessed the reason. In the absence of any motive to do otherwise, he continued to behave in a uniformly courteous manner to the Head and to everyone else he met.

His life, if placid, was a pleasant one, and he assumed, without thinking too much about the matter, that the serene ebb and flow of his days would go on unchanged until they ended.

Until that day.

Oliver took the elevator to his solitary fifth-floor office and prepared for another day of cataloging the Willoughby-Smythe material. All that morning he sat at his desk, tabulating, indexing, and cross-referencing, until at one o'clock he broke for lunch at the Collier House Faculty Club.

His guest that day was Mrs. Winifred Shorter Hills who, half a century ago, had earned a tidy fortune writing lurid romance novels under the pen name of Rosalind Fairwood. Her late, unlamented husband had gambled away nearly all of her money, and she now lived in reduced circumstances in a shabby residential hotel. She kept on typing romantic sagas on an old Royal portable, but they were written in a style so dated that no publisher would take them.

"I'm not worried at all," she declared with determined optimism as her life and resources steadily declined. "My books will be back in fashion one of these days. I know I have a public; they just don't realize I'm still here. Romance, Oliver! Romance and High Adventure! Brave Hearts and Noble Deeds! That's what people really want." The long pheasant feather on her outmoded chapeau nearly stabbed him in the eye with the force of her conviction.

Privately Oliver agreed with her, for although Romance for him might be an impossible dream, how often, as a boy, had he not longed for a life of High Adventure! He had found vicarious adventure in reading Tennyson's *Idylls of the King*, but it had been a very long time since he had opened a volume of the verse he used to love.

Mrs. Shorter Hills (she preferred "mrs." to "ms." unless someone addressed her as "Miss Fairwood," which flattered her immensely) had known Oliver's mother, and in her memory he was pleased to invite the authoress to luncheon from time to time. He admired the lady's spirit, if not her prose, and looked upon these occasions as a privilege rather than a duty.

Their meal concluded, he put Mrs. Shorter Hills in a cab and paid her fare home. She smiled brightly at him, chin high, and waved as the taxi pulled away. Oliver strolled back to his office, glancing idly at reflections of himself in the back windows of the Art Museum.

In appearance he favored the paternal side of his family, for his face, like theirs, was round and clean-shaven, and he wore rimless glasses over mild brown eyes. Because the day was warm, he had worn his straw fedora, the only one on campus. Conservative in dress, he had had some of his father's suits tailored to fit him, not to waste good wool and fine lines. Some of his colleagues murmured among themselves that Oliver was a walking anachronism, but a good man all the same.

I have to admit I've grown a trifle stout lately. I've even started a little paunch--but the men in Father's family tended to be of stocky build, so it's only natural. Nothing to worry about. After all, I'm not going to be climbing mountains any time soon!

Back in his office, he worked steadily at his current project until, glancing at his pocket watch, he noted that the hour was exactly twenty minutes before four o'clock. He tidied a batch of papers, tucked them inside their manila folder, and reached toward the desk drawer where he kept his tin of Earl Grey tea leaves. All of a sudden the door to his office burst open and banged against the wall. A spider-shaped crack appeared in the center of the opaque glass and radiated to the edges like a giant cobweb.

A whirlwind swept into the room, bringing with it a scented cloud of mingled white gardenia, Turkish coffee, wet sheep's wool, and frying bacon. Open-mouthed, he rose to his feet and stared in dismay at the apparition towering before him. Over six feet in height, turbaned and gloved in purple, dressed in a tea gown of paisley silk with a pashmina shawl draped around her shoulders, Oliver Medley's great-aunt, Portia Belvedine Medley Makebold, Countess de Montfort, stood in the exact center of his private office, one hand resting on her bony hip and the other gripping the handle of a gold lame' umbrella whose sharpened tip tapped menacingly against the tile floor.

Oliver stifled a groan.

"Well, Medley? Are you going to stand there and goggle at me in that fish-eyed manner or are you going to invite me to sit down?"

Oliver gulped. "I beg your pardon, Great-Aunt Belvedine. Please do sit down. What a pleasant surprise. I wasn't expecting you."

Saint Amber's Rose

He scurried out from behind his desk and pushed forward the only other chair in the room. Unsure of its cleanliness, he whipped out his pocket handkerchief and dusted off the seat as inconspicuously as possible.

Great-Aunt Belvedine ignored the chair. "What do you mean, you weren't expecting me?" she snapped. "Didn't you receive my letter? Don't you realize we have a family crisis on our hands?"

Oliver stared in horror at his tall relative. A snarly feeling in the pit of his stomach warned him that he ought to have read that letter which, he remembered with a guilty start, remained on the porch swing at home.

"You didn't read it, did you!" Great-Aunt Belvedine accused, narrowing her eyes to focus on him like a marksman on a bull's-eye. "I'm positive Aurelia Dawn handed it to you personally. Oh! What a muddle we're in now! All the information I had about this dilemma was in that letter, along with directions to The Rendezvous. Brambles and thorns! I suppose what can't be cured must be endured."

"I--I might go home and try to find--" Oliver ventured.

"It's too late for that!" retorted Great-Aunt Belvedine. "We'll just have to do without it. There's not a second to waste. Get your hat and come along! We've a mission to accomplish!" With this enigmatic pronouncement, Great-Aunt Belvedine turned on her heel and strode toward the doorway.

Sucked into the vortex of her energy, Oliver made a flying clutch at his hat from the coat-rack as they shot out of his office and into the echoing corridor.

What family crisis? The only family I have left is Great-Aunt Belvedine! What can she mean?

"We'll take the stairs," Great-Aunt Belvedine announced over her shoulder. "Faster than the elevator and better exercise. I can see you're not getting enough exercise. You've developed quite a paunch."

Oliver exerted himself to his fullest extent as they fled down five flights of stairs to the main floor. Never before had he connected the word "flight" to the manner in which they descended, but he was certain they had the elevator's best time beaten hands down.

"I want to tell you, great-nephew," she continued with no slackening of speed as they clattered down the stairwell, "how much I regret that I was unable to attend your mother's memorial service. I knew Edwina better than you realize and admired her immensely. I trust you are keeping your spirits up. Edwina could never bear to have dismal people around her. She would be most displeased if you made yourself dismal on her account. Hurry along now."

Too breathless to reply, Oliver ran on in Great-Aunt Belvedine's wake and reflected that he had become dismal in recent months.

No one seemed to notice them as they dashed through the lobby and out the main entrance. When they skipped down the outside steps past one of the stone lions, the fringe of Great-Aunt Belvedine's pashmina shawl fluttered across its nostril. Oliver was almost positive that he heard a muffled sneeze and thought he saw the lion's huge paw rub its nose. But he couldn't stop to check, and chased doggedly after his venerable relative, whose pace would have astonished the Oregon Track Club.

Great-Aunt Belvedine charged across a grassy field to the parking lot beside the School of Music, where the Buick rested in its customary space. "Get in!" she ordered. "Hurry!"

Oliver unlocked the front doors, and they piled into the seat and buckled themselves securely.

"Forward!" commanded Great-Aunt Belvedine.

Oliver backed out of his parking space and paused. "Where are we--"

"If you'd read my letter, you'd know!" retorted his formidable kinswoman. "Follow Corax."

"I beg your par--" Oliver began.

Just then a remarkably large raven landed with a thump on the hood of the car and eyed him through the windshield.

"Him!" ordered Great-Aunt Belvedine. "Follow *Corvus corax*! The raven, Medley, the raven!"

What? Follow a raven? Why?

But unable to formulate a coherent reply at the moment, he put the car in Drive and drove. The raven levitated off the hood and flapped away. Oliver followed, by mischance hitting three red lights in succession. While waiting, he surreptitiously studied Great-Aunt Belvedine's profile. That lady had lapsed into a brooding silence as soon as they pulled out of the parking lot, and he didn't really care to venture a question. Out of the corner of his eye he observed her strongly-chiseled face, the half-hooded eyes and high-beaked nose giving her a profile like a predatory bird. ("We have had some unusual forebears," she once remarked to Oliver's father while sipping an old brandy. "We have," replied Medley senior, "and some of them are best forgotten.")

How odd of her to pop up like this. I wonder if she might actually be a time traveler, as I used to think when I was a boy. Nothing about Great-Aunt Belvedine would surprise me. I hope this little errand of hers, whatever it is, won't take too long. I don't mind humoring her, but I do have work on my desk.

Despite the warmth of the summer afternoon, Great-Aunt Belvedine pulled the pashmina shawl closer around her bony shoulders, sank into its cowl, and ignored Oliver completely. Oliver, keeping a judicious silence, could only guess at her thoughts.

Oliver Medley is not the man his father was, he imagined her thinking, and went on with this unrewarding theme. *Now my nephew, Arthur Medley--there was a man worthy of emulation! Polo player, fencer, poet, explorer, world-class violinist. Entered the Foreign Service with a perfect examination score. Appointed at an impressively young age as ambassador* in camera *to a little-known but diplomatically crucial nation.*

Great-Aunt Belvedine (in Oliver's imagination) recalled Arthur's falling in love with the beautiful Edwina Greylight, whose parents were in attendance at Court. The Medley family, including herself, had had a few qualms about the match, for although Edwina was exquisite in person and manner and cut a dashing figure on the polo grounds, her family had a strain of wildness running through it, and people whispered that the Greylight origins went back to the Age of Faery. Of course that was merely base rumor interwoven with envy and superstition, and the Medleys had quickly embraced Edwina as one of their own.

It was after her marriage that Edwina had spoken of certain mysterious things to Great-Aunt Belvedine, secrets of wisdom passed down through the women of the family, and Belvedine's eyes had been opened to the splendor of forgotten days.

Yes, Edwina was the perfect match for dear Arthur, Oliver continued. He had gone from them too soon, leaving as his only scion young Oliver, who seemed to have inherited neither the outstanding abilities of his father nor the brilliance and beauty of his mother.

Great-Aunt Belvedine permitted herself a small shrug of resignation, which Oliver incorporated into his mental drama. *She wasn't to blame, whatever happened.* It hadn't been *her* idea to bring him into this situation. She had warned them about Oliver Medley's exasperating meekness, his total lack of the qualities of a hero or an adventurer. And those were the very qualities that would soon be needed--desperately so.

Great-Aunt Belvedine squared her shoulders. *Oliver Medley is completely inadequate to the task ahead of us. I knew that, but I made a promise. I have set my foot on a perilous path, and I will tread it to the end. And Medley is going to tread it, too. And that is that!*

Resigned to the perils put before him by his dolorous flight of imagination, Oliver returned his attention to the road ahead.

When the third traffic light permitted him to move again, Oliver wondered if he had lost sight of the raven, but no, there it was, waiting on top of a street sign. As the Buick pulled even with the sign, "Turn right," Great-Aunt Belvedine ordered. He obeyed, getting on to Interstate 5 far more rapidly than he had thought possible.

They sped north along the freeway straight between the lush green farm-fields of the Willamette Valley. Great-Aunt Belvedine said not a word, nor did Oliver, even when he noticed something inexplicable in his rear-view mirror. There were no green fields to be seen behind them, although he saw them plainly through the front windshield. Instead, in a horrifying apparition, the whole valley floor behind them seemed to be disappearing under a tsunami of concrete rushing directly toward the car. Trees toppled before it, wild creatures fled in vain. With terrible ferocity the concrete wave bore down and crushed everything in its path to nothingness.

Oliver slammed the accelerator to the floor and leaned into the wheel, desperate to outrun the monstrous wave. Nothing happened, even though he stomped on the pedal repeatedly. The Buick continued at a lawful speed, neither faster nor slower than anyone else on the road. Other drivers didn't seem to be bothered by the advent of the concrete mass, almost as if Oliver were the only one seeing it. But that was impossible. The thing was real.

The tsunami caught up with them and arched over the car. Oliver's mouth opened in a silent scream. But the wave divided and passed their vehicle on both sides, disappearing as it swept in front. In its wake, a grid of tall buildings with mirrored black surfaces arose like hammered spikes, and after the buildings a new shopping mall--Vanity Fair, it was called--sprang up, running parallel to the highway, on and on as if it had no end.

Stores with glittering windows appeared magically on the concrete graveyard. Shoppers rushed from one to the other, ants to sugar, trampling unaware and uncaring over buried meadows and choked streams, buying trinkets, gadgets, toys, stuff: things they purchased with irreplaceable hours of their lives, working jobs they did not like in order to buy things they did not need.

"Medley! Have you seen enough?" demanded Great-Aunt Belvedine, bringing Oliver abruptly back to the frightening realization that he had driven several miles while fixated on the scene in the rear-view mirror. "Do you understand what you saw? Turn around."

Without knowing how it was done, he found himself back on Sixth Avenue. As he pulled even with the street sign where the raven still perched, Corax lifted off and flew straight down the avenue, obliterating its normal curves. Hands white-knuckled on the wheel, Oliver followed, doing his best to avoid other vehicles and keep an eye on the bird at the same time.

What is happening? Is Great-Aunt Belvedine doing all this? Or am I having hallucinations? Something isn't right here.

"We will drive past the Owen Rose Garden," ordered Great-Aunt Belvedine. "Corax will fly over it. You'd best go around."

Oliver considered explaining that they couldn't very well go past it, inasmuch as its farther boundary was the Willamette River.

"Don't contradict, Medley," said Great-Aunt Belvedine, divining his thought.

To his silent surprise, when they drove by the rose garden he found himself not in the river but in a neighborhood with which he was completely unfamiliar. The numbered avenues went from First to Zero, then Double Zero, then Triple Zero (he hadn't realized avenues could be numbered in the zeroes), and the cross-streets had names he didn't recognize, like Mugwort and Mire. To their right loomed Skinner's Butte, the hill overlooking the city of Eugene on the north. It was the last landmark he was to recognize for a considerable time.

Corax glided ahead. The paved street became a dirt road, then narrowed to a one-way lane bordered by trees whose branches grew so closely together that their boughs interlaced into a single canopy overhead. The Buick went on in deep shade even though the sun shone in a cloudless sky.

The raven alighted on the car with a thump and faced front like a gothic hood ornament. Unable to see clearly through the bird's unnaturally large body, Oliver thought of a) applying the brake or b) honking the horn--shuddered as a light finger of ice touched the middle of his shoulders--thought better of both options, and slowed to four miles per hour. He wished, as they crawled along, that Great-Aunt Belvedine would break her silence and inform him what this business was all about, because he was growing really indignant about having had both his person and his automobile commandeered in such a high-handed manner.

It's all because I didn't get around to reading her letter. Evidently I should have: It might have explained this escapade. But it is the middle of a workday, and I ought to be getting back to the office.

"We are now entering the Blackberry Labyrinth," Great-Aunt Belvedine announced as they inched into a winding corridor of thornbushes so tall and tangled that they made solid walls on either side of the car and twined overhead, turning the last remnant of daylight to dusk. Oliver automatically reached to turn on his headlights, but such a chill ran up his spine that he didn't touch the knob after all.

Corax began to give directions by pointing with his left or right wing where Oliver was to turn.

A mist gathered inside the thorny corridor as they crept along, rapidly forming a dense white vapor which completely blocked his view ahead. All he could see, and not very well, was the raven on the hood, signaling with his wings.

It was as if they had been swallowed by ghosts.

Deprived of forward vision, Oliver rolled down the window and leaned out. At once wicked little blackberry thorns reached out to pinion his jacket sleeve and snatch at his hat. Hastily he drew back inside and rolled up the window, but not before thick, milky fog swirled inside and tickled the back of his neck with icy fingers. He shivered despite the summer day.

The fog twisted itself like a scarf and wound around the shoulders of Great-Aunt Belvedine, who ignored it. Out of the corner of his eye he thought he saw the fog assume an impossible shape, like an inhuman face. He wanted to turn and look directly at it, but didn't dare take his eyes off the raven's semaphore signals. Instead, he gripped the wheel harder and scowled at the whirling mist. Trying to stare through it was making him lightheaded.

"We're nearly there."

Nearly where? he was about to ask.

"Ravenhome," stated Great-Aunt Belvedine, and Corax on the hood spread out both wings so that Oliver had to slam on the brakes. The Buick stopped short with a crunch of dirt and gravel.

"We're here, Medley," said Great-Aunt Belvedine in an irritated tone. Oliver hastened to extricate himself from the driver's seat and run around to assist her out of the vehicle. "That will do, Corax," she said, unfolding herself to her proper height. "We shall require your services again soon, I'm sure."

"Nevermore," quoth the raven, and took off. Oliver was not at all certain whether he had actually heard the raven say anything, or if he had simply imagined the quotation.

"That's the corporate motto of the Raven Express Messenger and Guide Service," Great-Aunt Belvedine remarked off-handedly. "He doesn't mean it literally. Come along."

She began striding farther into the labyrinth, and Oliver was obliged to walk as fast as he could to keep up with her. Within a few steps they reached an immense wrought-iron gate set into the blackberry hedge. The gate was twice as tall as Great-Aunt Belvedine and had an intricate design of the letter R alternating with ravens' heads. In the lower left-hand corner was a circle with the initials T & T entwined around a rose. He tried to peer through the interstices, but saw only more white mist on the other side.

Great-Aunt Belvedine approached the gate without hesitation, took a deep breath, and began intoning words that made no sense to him. "Andiron emeritus," she chanted *sotto voce*, as if she were warming up her voice. Then "*Ad astra per aspera*," she sang in a strangled soprano. "*Jacta alea est. Nil desperandum.*"

Oliver backed away. Great-Aunt Belvedine was the only truly tone-deaf person he had ever known, and she was blithely unaware of the fact. To Oliver's sensitive ear, Great-Aunt Belvedine's singing was second only to cat claws sliding down a windowpane.

Charleynne Gates

Mercifully, her song quavered to a halt as Oliver, mentally translating from the Latin, wondered what she meant by "to the stars through obstacles," "the die is cast," and "do not despair".

After several seconds of silence, during which Oliver was acutely conscious of the lub-dub of his own heartbeat, they heard the shriek of unoiled iron scraping against itself. An inconspicuous wicket gate set inside the larger one opened reluctantly, as if it hadn't opened in a very long time and didn't particularly want to do so now.

When the wicket gate had parted to its widest extent, Great-Aunt Belvedine stooped and stepped through it to the other side where the fog was so thick that Oliver couldn't see her at all.

"Great-Aunt Belvedine—" he began before she could vanish. "I think you really need to tell me where—"

"Come along, Medley," rasped her disembodied voice.

Once through the wicket gate, he headed after the crunch of her footsteps on the carpet of thorny twigs and dead leaves. With a screech and a bang, the wicket gate clanged shut behind him. Oliver turned, but saw nothing through the fog. *I hope she's still sound of mind—not that I was ever convinced of it in the first place.* After all, Great-Aunt Belvedine *was* getting well up in years, even though it seemed as if she hadn't aged a day in the past few decades. She certainly outpaced him with embarrassing ease.

At last the fog dissipated into thin, dreamlike shreds, and he caught up enough to see her marching ahead. They were now on a level road that might have been a carriage drive at one time, but had been overtaken by weeds long ago. He trotted around a ragged rhododendron and almost crashed into Great-Aunt Belvedine, who had stopped in front of a verandah stretching across the width of a house that appeared quite suddenly out of the woods--a rambling, three-story structure painted as black as the inside of a coal mine.

What in the name of all the Mysteries is this place?

Dark trees whose boughs drooped over the gables like mourners made the house virtually invisible until they came right up to it. A flagpole jutted out of a turret window, and on the flagpole hung a banner with a device of three ravens on a field of silver.

"Dear Ravenhome!" Great-Aunt Belvedine said. "How I have missed you!" She fished a lace handkerchief out of her reticule and dabbed at a tear in the corner of her eye. Oliver took a handkerchief from his vest pocket and patted away drops of perspiration that had formed on his forehead. Jogging in a three-piece suit, albeit a lightweight weave, is a warm affair.

Great-Aunt Belvedine remained where she stopped, gazing nostalgically at the multitudinous black gables. Oliver thought that he had never seen so many gables on one house in his life. Atop each gable sat rows of ravens, all as black as the house and as silent as epitaphs. They stared at him with their black-bead eyes until he became self-conscious and looked away.

"Why is it painted bl--" he inquired in a whisper.

"Because it's a portal, of course," Great-Aunt Belvedine snapped, as if the fact ought to be self-evident. "Come along." She clutched her skirts with one hand and her umbrella with the other and climbed the steps.

"Now, just one minute, please, Great-Aunt Belvedine," Oliver tried again, following her up the rickety steps. She ignored him.

They crossed the verandah to the front door, as black as the rest of the house. On the door was a brass knocker in the shape of a raven's head. Great-Aunt Belvedine seized its beak and rapped three times against the plate. Oliver heard the echo, faint and hollow, inside the house.

While they waited for a response, Oliver peered around the verandah. It was wide enough to accommodate several bone-colored rocking chairs from which paint was peeling in shaggy patches. The chairs were empty and quiet, as if they were sleeping, but as his glance passed over them, he thought he saw the baby rocker at the far end rock once.

Another chair rocked, as if in reply.

The first chair rocked again, then another, and another after that. Then more chairs began rocking, some slowly, some faster, one with such energy that it jumped up as high as the railing, and one or two others actually skipping forward, as if they were trying to rock off the verandah and down the road. The chairs rocked furiously around the two humans, enclosing them in a clattering circle. Oliver struggled to think of a rational explanation for the phenomenon--was sure there was one--wished he knew more about the engineering of rocking chairs. Most likely it was the vibration of their footsteps that had set them going.

Great-Aunt Belvedine paid the chairs no attention.

After an interminable wait (or so it seemed), during which the baby chair scooted behind Oliver and nipped his heels, the black door opened.

"Down, Death! Back, Doom! Mordor, be quiet!" commanded a bodiless bass voice out of the darkness.

Oliver couldn't see anyone in the doorway, but Great-Aunt Belvedine apparently did, because she spoke a few unintelligible words and strode across the threshold. Oliver needed no encouragement to hasten after her, for nothing would have induced him to remain outside with that pack of madly rocking chairs whose gyrations rose to a climax of creaks, cracks, rattles, and rolls.

The door swung shut behind them. Silence was sudden and absolute.

It took a few moments for Oliver's eyes to adjust to the umbral gloom. He followed a step behind Great-Aunt Belvedine as they processed down a high-ceilinged hall with a carpet runner in a design of dark-green leaves and vines. He thought he caught a glimpse of an impish face half-hidden in the carpet foliage, but when he blinked and looked a second time, the face had vanished.

The walls, paneled in dark wood, bore imposing oil portraits of men in powdered wigs sitting at desks covered with piles of parchments, quill pens, and books. Next to them, a formidable-looking lady in purple velvet, with a nose the twin of Great-Aunt Belvedine's, sat sidesaddle on a handsome black hunter with a white blaze on its forehead.

Your ancestors, Medley. Pay attention! Oliver thought he heard Great-Aunt Belvedine fling the remark over her shoulder as she forged ahead, but then wasn't certain that it hadn't originated inside his mind. He halted for half a second in front of a niche where stood a marble statue of a Roman aristocrat in a toga with senatorial stripes, and marveled that the serene nobility of its countenance greatly resembled that of his own father. But the crook of Great-Aunt Belvedine's umbrella caught him above the elbow, forcing him to hasten onward.

A few yards farther down the hall, he passed a full suit of iron armor, complete with belt, sword, lance, and helmet, poised as though standing guard. As Oliver hurried by, he fancied that the knight's visor lifted, revealing two keen black eyes that glared at him.

Saint Amber's Rose

It's only my imagination, of course. It's been over-stimulated by these unusual surroundings. All the same, I believe I'll make an appointment with my optometrist when I get home.

By degrees he became aware that they were heading toward a rectangle of glowing greenish light in the distance. Great-Aunt Belvedine continued marching toward it, following the invisible person ahead of her.

They stopped abruptly before the green rectangle, and Oliver realized that the light came from two french doors. They opened inward to a vast conservatory filled with a jungle of plants. Some towered to the ceiling with huge spreading leaves like giants' hands, while others were tiny, in clusters of flowerpots. Everywhere, flowers in rainbow hues bloomed in profusion. He felt no draft, yet the leaves and petals moved gently, as if a breeze stirred them. The sound of trickling water in the midst of verdancy hinted of a hidden fountain.

Great-Aunt Belvedine kept moving along a winding path through the greenery until at last she halted in front of a tall screen woven of feathery ferns. "That will be all, Grimtread," she said to their invisible guide. A presence Oliver sensed more than saw glided past them back into the house.

"Great-Aunt Belvedine, I need to be getting back to my off—"

"Stay!" she hissed, and stepped around the fern-screen. "My dear!" she said to someone on the other side in a voice so tender, so different from her usual tone, that Oliver wondered mightily about the cause of such a transformation.

Another voice, soft, gentle, and low, answered. "Dearest Belvedine! How long it has been!" Oliver felt as well as heard the second voice, as if it had caressed him.

"Much too long indeed," replied Great-Aunt Belvedine. "But let me come directly to the point. As you requested, I have brought the person who may be able to help us in our dilemma: my great-nephew, Oliver Medley. Medley!" she said sharply, her tone reverting to normal.

Hearing his cue, Oliver made his way around the fern-screen and stood beside Great-Aunt Belvedine, his vision dazzled by a radiant silver light.

"Medley, I have the privilege of presenting you to the Lady Flavia Caliburn, *Sendara* of the Graelands," Great-Aunt Belvedine announced. "Your seventh cousin seven times removed."

-- 21 --

Charleynne Gates

Hat in hand, Oliver blinked, bowed in his old-fashioned manner to someone he couldn't quite bring into focus... and rose to face the glory of his life.

Chapter Two

Ravenhome

"Cousin Oliver."

Her voice, cool as dew, soothed his ear and his feelings. The bright light softened and settled around a woman seated amid clusters of green fronds and white-blossomed branches. She extended a slender hand, and he stepped forward to take it in his own. Her clasp was as light as thistledown.

"You are welcome here! You shall call me Cousin Flavia, and we will be friends from this moment," she said, smiling into his eyes.

Oliver's heart bounded like a young gazelle, and he flushed to the roots of his hair. He murmured some conventional response, but never afterward had any recollection of what he actually said.

When he recovered, he was sitting in a white wicker garden chair to one side of Cousin Flavia. Great-Aunt Belvedine perched on an identical chair directly opposite. Flavia's chair was shaped like a silver throne, its back curving in a high arch with a leaf-and-briar design twining around the edge. At the top of the arch was the relief of a single rose in full bloom, tinted in the colors of a summer morning.

In a daze, Oliver heard Great-Aunt Belvedine speaking emphatically, but as if she were very far away, and he didn't take in a word of her discourse. Not until much later did he realize that she was speaking in a language unfamiliar to him. All he desired at that moment was to sit mutely where he was and drink in the beauty of his new-found cousin.

Flavia's complexion, fair as pearls, was smooth as the cloud of petals that nodded and swayed around her. She seemed young, but Oliver found that he couldn't begin to guess how old she was, for she might have been anywhere from twenty to infinity. There was an ageless quality about her, an aura of serenity and wisdom that does not often come to the young in years. It might have had something to do with the play of light on her face and on the corona of her wonderful dawn-hued hair. Encircled by an emerald-green browband, it curled and waved and spilled over her shoulders and down her leaf-green gown like a mantle afire with the meaning of her name: light. Oliver's mind entangled itself in those tresses as he gazed, mesmerized, at the swift changes of expression on her face.

Her eyes looked black at first, their irises unfathomable. *When she turned her head just then to look at Great-Aunt Belvedine, I saw they really are as gray as river water... or as blue as a lake in the woods. But when a tiny beam of sunlight illumined them directly... Now they are the color of the deep green sea.*

A long-forgotten memory surfaced in his mind. When he was a boy camping in the forest with his father, he came upon a small pond among the evergreens. Twilight touched the treetops reflected in the shining water, and in a lilac sky the first summer star twinkled. A solitary stag appeared on the other side of the pond and bent down to drink. The scene was so still, so full of peace, that he didn't dare move lest it vanish. After a while the deer raised his antler-crowned head, silver drops of water falling from his mouth, and looked directly into the boy's eyes. Oliver wanted the moment to last forever, that feeling of numinous magic... And then it was gone.

Great-Aunt Belvedine paused, and Flavia began to reply, but Oliver didn't hear her any more than he had Great-Aunt Belvedine. He watched Flavia's hands drawing patterns in the air. On each hand she wore a silver ring set with a winking gem: on her left a deep blue sapphire, on her right an emerald. As she spoke, the beautiful hands rose together like a prayer, then spread apart as she leaned forward in her rose-crowned chair and brushed aside the foliage around her.

Oliver's heart thumped once, very hard; the breath in his lungs stopped for an instant that felt like eternity.

Flavia was in a wheelchair.

The shock of this discovery brought him back to reality just at the moment when a person of indiscernible aspect manifested--more or less--behind a thicket of potted hedge-plants and announced, "My Lady, the company are gathered in the library," in a voice of deep gloom.

"Thank you, Grimtread," said Flavia. "It will be a great pleasure to have you dine with us, Cousin Oliver."

"Pleasure... all mine," he managed, and blushed as he heard himself speak with a gasp, as if he had been running hard instead of sitting quietly. *Dine? Why was Great-Aunt Belvedine so melodramatic about a simple dinner invitation? And why haven't I met Cousin Flavia before, or even heard of her? How beautiful she is! But why is she in a wheelchair?* And his heart melted with pity.

"Now where is Mildrith?" Flavia continued, unaware of Oliver's internal monologue. "Ah! There you are." A dark-haired woman who, he observed with satisfaction, could look Great-Aunt Belvedine straight in the eye, came to stand in front of Oliver, who stood up at once.

"This is the newest member of our clan, Oliver Medley," said Flavia. "My friend and companion, the *Foressa* Mildrith Antara." The tall young woman identified by the unfamiliar title took his hand in a firm grip, proving that she was as strong as she was tall.

"I'm Flavia's gallowglass," she said in a pleasing contralto. "Call me Mil."

Gallowglass. Oliver pondered the word. An old Irish term, he recalled, and it meant... Mildrith—Mil--was Flavia's bodyguard! As she shook his hand, he was surprised to feel her fingers press two different points on the palm of his hand, but so quickly that he wasn't sure he had actually felt anything. If he had, then he would have guessed it was some secret sign of identification. He hadn't belonged to any societies with secret handshakes since he and Timmy Hornbeam invented their own two-member Knights of the Pendragon when they were ten, so perhaps it had been his imagination. Mildrith may have expected some occult word or gesture in response, but she didn't so much as quirk a black-winged eyebrow as she released his hand and returned to her place.

In her black jodhpurs and long-sleeved white tunic with a blue plaid scarf draped from her shoulder to the wide belt around her waist, the *Foressa* gave the impression of great physical strength under the absolute control of her will. He thought that he had never before met anyone with such an air of elegance and athleticism combined. He wondered—briefly—about the significance of the bright orange brooch she wore on her scarf. Tiny coruscations of light flashed from its star-points at intervals like some kind of signal.

The *Foressa* (*Was that a military rank of some kind? Or an aristocratic title?*) returned to Flavia's chair and began pushing it down a winding path of greenery.

"Come along, Medley!" Great-Aunt Belvedine took Oliver's arm in a raptor-like clutch and propelled him rapidly after them.

They threaded their way through a labyrinthine library furnished with red leather armchairs and black writing desks. Bookshelves stretched across the walls and from floor to beamed ceiling, filled, Oliver guessed, with many a volume of forgotten lore.

I would enjoy having a few hours with the literary treasures in this room.

"Pay attention, Medley," Great-Aunt Belvedine whispered sharply, and let go of his arm.

Mildrith wheeled Flavia's silver chair to the center of the room. At once they were surrounded by a crowd of guests who had been waiting for them--at least Oliver had the impression it was a crowd. They seemed somehow indistinct, a bit blurry in outline. What little he could see of them was confusing, for they all appeared to be wearing garments of an earlier era, men and women alike. They might be actors coming from a performance of *A Midsummer Night's Dream* or something similar.

Perhaps Flavia is a patron of the theatre.

The guests gathered around her, sometimes glancing curiously toward him and whispering among themselves. Most of them held glasses from which they drank as they conversed.

"Have a cocktail, Medley," said Great-Aunt Belvedine. Oliver was about to say that he seldom drank alcoholic beverages, and then only a little wine for his stomach's sake, but she ignored him. "An infusion with bay leaf would be good, I think," she mused, examining a tray with a selection of vegetable fluids and selecting two glasses of green liquid. "Bay leaf is said to bring victory. And luck. You'll need that. Don't you agree, Grimtread?" to the astonishing individual presenting the tray for her inspection.

Oliver blinked and stared. He reminded himself that staring is rude, but it was difficult not to gawk at the large, inconstant shape, butler-like in form but transparent in substance.

"Indeed, madam," the individual murmured. He gave Oliver an inscrutable glance and bore away the drinks toward the other guests.

Oliver rubbed his temple. "Great-Aunt Belvedine--" he began.

Saint Amber's Rose

"Grimtread is a Wraith," she interrupted, handing Oliver one of the green glasses. "They make the best sort of butler. Ravenhome would be unmanageable without him."

Oliver shook his head to clear it, but the butler still looked exactly like a Wraith, the kind he had read about in stories. It was an impossibility, of course, but there was the evidence, right before his eyes. If there wasn't something wrong with his eyes. If he wasn't starting a migraine. If any of this was real at all. If--

"Come along, Medley," and Great-Aunt Belvedine took off.

So rapid was Great-Aunt Belvedine's determined progress down the long room that Oliver was left behind for a moment or two. Struggling to keep her in view, he was startled to hear Grimtread's Wraith-ish whisper close to his ear.

"If I might have a word, sir?" the butler inquired. Oliver turned toward him, inadvertently looking straight through the Wraith to a musician plucking a lute on the other side of the room. Embarrassed, he hastily refocused.

"My three brothers and I," the Wraith continued, "were unfortunately separated during an incursion of the engines of mass destruction. Our eldest brother, Gall, is a friar at the Abbey, and Dour, our middle brother, is in the service of a Mage. It is our youngest brother, Gloom, who has the rest of us worried. We've heard nothing of him in a considerable time. On your journey, sir, if you would be so kind as to take notice of any sign of him, any rumors, things of that sort, we'd be--"

"Medley!" Great-Aunt Belvedine summoned sharply. Oliver, thoroughly confused by Grimtread's plea and its unexplained references, excused himself and hastened to her side. They approached an excessively slender, brown-skinned man with sleek dark hair and a gray-streaked goatee who stood in a corner formed by the bookshelves, running a long finger over the gilt-encrusted binding of a book.

"Dr. Sepulchra!" Great-Aunt Belvedine hailed. "How is your research on the morphology of the sinister-spiraled fireworm going?" The man in black inclined his head and smiled sadly, not attempting a reply for which she made no pause anyway. "Medley, you have read of Dr. Antonio Bernardo Sepulchra y Salamanca's illuminating conclusions in his field? You must do so at your first opportunity. I can't think why you don't take more interest in real research. It would do you good to get out of that ivory tower of yours."

A round, red-cheeked man in a dun-colored robe and a natural tonsure hurried toward them. "Friar Ablejohn! About time. I have something to say to you--"

But Friar Ablejohn brushed past Great-Aunt Belvedine to greet Oliver warmly and shake his hand with both of his own. "I've heard your name, of course," he exclaimed with a trace of Gaelic lilt in his voice. "An honor to meet you, I assure you! Might I be permitted to hope that you have come to assist in the cataloging of our Ravenhome library?"

"Well, I hardly--" Oliver began, but Friar Ablejohn ran on. "I would rejoice in the fact, my dear sir, positively rejoice! I've done my poor best to keep it in some semblance of order; it is part of my duty, but truthfully, I'm more of a scholar of arcane lore, and half the time, no, more than that, to be perfectly honest, a great deal more than that, I start out with the best intentions of putting all our materials to rights, and then I stumble upon a fascinating bit of obscure information and I start to follow the trail of literary clues and the next time I look up--well, it's lunchtime and the morning's fled away!" He threw up his hands, smiling ruefully. "You know how it is, I'm sure!"

Oliver did know how it was, and said so.

Friar Ablejohn became serious. "Unfortunately, even with the constant encouragement of our Sendara, I've been unable to discover a remedy for her condition thus far, even in our oldest and rarest manuscripts." He paused, looking reflective.

Oliver wanted very much to ask what the condition might be that had confined her to a wheelchair, and what hope existed that she would walk again, but reluctant to intrude into matters of a delicate personal nature, he kept silent.

"It's in the secret of the rose, I'm almost certain," the monk went on, frowning a little. Then he brightened. "After dinner I'd be delighted to show you around our library. There are one or two items of incunabula that I'm sure you would--"

"Friar Ablejohn!" Great-Aunt Belvedine interrupted. "Medley can find his own way around a library. That's his day job. We are here for a different purpose entirely."

Saint Amber's Rose

"Dinner is served, my lady," Grimtread announced in a *basso profundo*.

"Will you take Cousin Oliver into dinner, Mil?" Flavia asked, distracting Oliver from further reflection. "Belvedine, shall we two lead the way?"

With a nod (a rather icy one) to Great-Aunt Belvedine, the *Foressa* Mildrith relinquished her position by Flavia's chair and took Oliver's arm. "Don't be surprised, Cousin Oliver," she remarked in an undertone as they trailed behind the others, "at anything that happens here." She leaned a little toward him, turning eyes of a startling blue in his direction. He noticed a faint white line bisecting one cheek and wondered how she had acquired it. If it weren't so unlikely in this day and age, he would have guessed the mark to be a dueling scar.

"I'm assuming," she continued, "that Belvedine filled you in on the details of this venture. She--no?" Mildrith exclaimed softly as Oliver shook his head. "Do you mean she's told you nothing about why you're here?"

"Not really," he replied. "Actually, nothing at all. I hadn't seen her in years until she appeared in my office and ordered me to come with her. She said something about a family crisis, but I didn't know I had any family left other than Great-Aunt Belvedine. I--I had never met Cousin Flavia before."

Mil made a slight sound deep in her throat that Oliver would have called a growl if the word had been applicable to someone of her gravitas. "That woman," she muttered more to herself than to him. "She was supposed to explain everything before you got here. As if we didn't have enough to worry about already."

They took a few steps in silence, passing through a hall lined with crystalline mirrors, as the *Foressa* brooded over the perversity of Belvedine. Then, "You do fence, don't you?" she asked Oliver, who shook his head.

In rapid succession she named several martial arts, of which he admitted no knowledge. "Archery? Javelin? Caber toss? You ride, of course?"

"I'm afraid not," he replied, recalling a particularly humiliating incident in prep school and wondering why she asked.

"Combat training? Marksmanship? Heavy artillery? Espionage?"

Charleynne Gates

"No, not at all."
"Ah." Mil ceased speaking and frowned.
Oliver opened his mouth to ask the reason for such a battle-oriented line of inquiry, but after a glance upward at her forbidding countenance, the question died unspoken.
I'll ask later.
Oliver glanced around, trying to gather more information about the nature of the mysterious house. This corridor, like the one leading from the front door, had a green carpet runner with a leaf-and-vine design. Oliver looked down, half expecting to glimpse another impish face peering out at him, but he saw nothing of the kind. Instead, as he looked at the myriad mirrors lining the dark-paneled hall, he saw not only his own reflection multiplied ad infinitum, but also Mil's. Her reflection wasn't clothed the way he saw her in person, but in a suit of silver armor, close-fitting and supple as fish scales, with a sword in its scabbard swinging at her side and a battle helmet crowning the blue-black sheen of her hair. Deep in the mirror behind their two reflections were other misty forms impossible to discern clearly, but whose attention seemed to be centered on him. *Like a cloud of witnesses*, he thought fleetingly, and knew not why.
The dining hall was a long, high-beamed room with a heavy oaken table placed exactly in the middle. A cavernous fireplace with burning logs warmed the air, which was rather chilly for a summer's day, or perhaps it was merely drafty in here. Hanging on the walls were great tapestries, one of a formidable mountain rising above a wave-tossed sea, another of a shadowed forest whose trees touched the stars, and in the center, directly behind the High Seat at table, one of a single rose tinted in the colors of an autumn sunrise.
An iron chandelier with a score of blazing wax candles was suspended from the ceiling over the table. The brilliance of its light made deep shadows in the far corners of the room. The scene was hardly what Oliver would have expected, given the exterior of the building. This room seemed more like the Great Hall of a castle.
They were about to follow the company to their places at table when Mil leaned down again and addressed him. "Never mind," she murmured in a confidential tone. "Not everyone needs to be a warrior. You were brought here for a reason. It will come to you."

Saint Amber's Rose

The idea of being a warrior of any kind had never entered Oliver's head, at least not since he was fighting enemies of the Round Table. He puzzled over what Mil might mean.

Great-Aunt Belvedine wheeled Flavia's chair to the head of the table. *Wheelchair!* he repeated to himself, and wished he knew why his cousin was confined in such a manner. *Why did Father and Mother never tell me about her?* He'd always thought that the three of them were a close-knit family, with no secrets worth the keeping. These unexpected revelations disturbed his equanimity, and he didn't like the sensation.

Mil stopped at Flavia's chair, bent down to the bright hair, and murmured something. Without intending to eavesdrop, Oliver caught a word, "Pavarr," perhaps a name, but meaningless to him.

A gong sounded the hour in nine measured strokes, and the company standing round the table fell silent.

"Friar Ablejohn," said Flavia, "will you give us grace?"

The friar beamed all over his plump countenance, lifted up hands and voice, and sang (to the tune of *Tallis' Canon,* a favorite of Oliver's):

> *Grace be with all, and grateful be*
> *For earth and sky and sun and sea.*
> *In grace may all be fitly fed,*
> *And blessing be with cup and bread.*

Other voices joined the friar's song--many more, it seemed, than could be accounted for by the number of guests.

"Blessed be," Flavia said when the song ended.

"Blessed be," echoed everyone else.

"Blessed be," Oliver added belatedly. He had never heard this particular grace before meals, but decided he liked it very much.

Conversation began immediately as dinner was served, apparently by invisible hands, because Oliver couldn't detect how the leaf-patterned tureen of steaming-hot vegetable broth, whose delicious aroma teased his nostrils, had appeared on the table. The courses following were subtle and varied in flavor, as good or better than he himself could have prepared. The wine, a vintage he hadn't tasted before, seemed made not with grapes but with music. He sipped, and discovered his awareness heightened rather than dulled. His customary reticence in unfamiliar company slipped from him and vanished altogether.

How beautiful she is. Her hair is the golden hue of an autumn sunrise.

Oliver's mind filled with the near presence of his cousin, and his heart opened to a dream he didn't dare believe.

Firelight and candlelight from the iron chandelier grew brighter. Shadows in the further reaches of the room elongated and crept forward... Oliver glanced down once or twice, vaguely aware that the shadow nearest his chair was closer to him than when dinner began. He also thought he noticed, in his peripheral vision, other forms, not of shadow but of light, that encircled their table and seemed to be keenly interested in the flow of conversation. One of the light-forms swayed toward his chair, and the shadow quivered and drew back. Or was it an illusion created by flickering flames?

Oliver moved his attention back to the general discussion.

"Weather," Mil was saying in answer to a question of Friar Ablejohn's, "is not well understood in the Maze World. They have tracking systems, to be sure; they even grasp the concept of patterns, but the psychology of Weather as an emotional expression of the Earth is not yet considered. The dynamics of inter-arboreal communication are completely unsuspected. If their climatologists would simply listen to the intonation of the wind in the grasses--"

"The *Foressa* was trained in the sciences at the Citadel of Secret Mountain," Dr. Sepulchra, next to him, said in an aside to Oliver. "They're expert Weather interpreters, you know."

Oliver had no idea what Dr. Sepulchra meant, but was fascinated by what Mil was saying. He got that impression that weather —or Weather--was of crucial importance to the guests at table, not only in regard to daily events of sunshine and rain, but as somehow intimately entwined with the fate of the Graelands (a name associated with Flavia, Oliver recognized, but whose import was entirely mysterious to him). To the company of Ravenhome, Weather seemed to be a song of many voices sung by the Earth itself--a symphony of Nature.

He glanced down at the compote of fruits and edible flowers that had been placed before him by invisible hands. Were they being served by spirits? The Wraith-butler Grimtread was present somewhere in the hall, Oliver was fairly sure, and directing the service of dinner, but somehow he couldn't quite locate that remote individual in any one spot.

Either the butler is in fact a Wraith or else he has learned to move faster than the human eye can follow. This place is really quite out of the ordinary. I wonder why Cousin Flavia is in a wheelchair. Ought I to ask, or would it be too personal a question? I wish someone had told me about--

"--roses," remarked Dr. Sepulchra, and Oliver became aware that he was being addressed. "I have heard that you are an expert on the cultivation of roses."

"I'm only an amateur," replied Oliver modestly, "but they are a passion of mine."

"Mine also," returned the dark-browed doctor, whose face had so little flesh as to resemble a cadaver. "I keep a small rose garden here at Ravenhome. The *Sendara* enjoys their perfume. She says it soothes her when she feels most ill." He paused and took a sip of wine.

Once again it was on the tip of Oliver's tongue to ask what injury or illness had placed his new-found cousin in a wheelchair, but again, he didn't.

Dr. Sepulchra went on. "I have endeavored for many years to persuade a Don Quixote variety to take root in my little plot, but to no avail. Perhaps you've heard of it?"

"I have a Don Quixote in my garden at home," Oliver replied, "planted by my late father. The bush is now taller than I am. I'd be pleased to give you a cutting if you would like."

Is that why I'm here, then, to give advice about growing heirloom roses or the cataloging of antique books? He hoped his disappointment didn't show on his face. The prospect of getting further information out of Great-Aunt Belvedine appeared to be fruitless, and he didn't quite like to ask Cousin Flavia the reason he had been brought here lest he inadvertently cause offense. If there was a reason other than rose cultivation or book cataloging.

Dr. Sepulchra bowed his thanks. "I wonder if you'd care to see my rose garden, Mr. Medley. That is, if you'll be staying on?"

"He will NOT," Great-Aunt Belvedine interrupted. "We shall be leaving almost immediately. We--"

But Great-Aunt Belvedine stopped in the middle of her sentence and sank back into her chair. Oliver half-rose from his seat, thinking that she had had a seizure of some kind, then saw that Cousin Flavia had raised her hand slightly. Without a word spoken, Flavia had silenced Great-Aunt Belvedine! Oliver resumed his seat and hid his amazement.

"Grimtread," Flavia spoke above the table conversation. "We are ready for our *semera* now."

The Wraith-butler exited foggily into the kitchen. Oliver's eyes followed the butler's disappearing back. Difficult as it was for him to comprehend, it really did seem as if the butler of Ravenhome was--well, transparent.

He had no opportunity to consider the question further, for Grimtread returned almost immediately, bearing in his misty hands an ornate silver samovar, which he set on the sideboard. He proceeded to mix together several ingredients--leaves and twigs, it looked like--and poured them into the appropriate area of the samovar. As the instrument began bubbling, Grimtread took his place on one end--or possibly it was the other--of the sideboard.

The *semera* (whatever it might be) brewed; the diners gradually ceased their conversations. The room filled with silence except for the occasional snap of flame and crackle of log in the fireplace and the constant mutter of the samovar.

After a time, Flavia gathered the silence and gave it order. Then with uplifted hand she wordlessly commanded and was obeyed. The shadows outside the border of fire and candlelight retreated; the light-forms around the table drew nearer until their soft white radiance illumined all those seated there.

"Cousin Oliver," Flavia began, and it seemed that the even the air currents in the Great Hall stilled to listen. "You have been brought here by the will of another, for a purpose you do not know, to be with people of whom you have never heard! You are brave, Cousin, and I am glad that I have met you at last. Thank you, Grimtread."

The Wraith-butler had filled delicate demitasse cups with the fragrant brew and served them around the table. Oliver puzzled how the butler, having no discernable vertebral structure, could manipulate material goods with such ease, but decided that it didn't really concern him. His only concern was Flavia, being near her and gazing into her gray-green eyes, changing like the sea under sunlight, under storm.

Saint Amber's Rose

"I asked Belvedine to bring you here, Cousin Oliver, because we of Ravenhome and the Graelands find ourselves facing an overwhelming danger, one which will be, if it is not averted, disastrous to the Maze World also."

"The--the Maze World?" asked Oliver. "I don't quite know what you mean."

"Hush, Medley," Great-Aunt Belvedine interrupted. "You'll find out in due course."

"Belvedine," Flavia said calmly, "Cousin Oliver has a right to know everything we can tell him before he makes his decision. *You* are from the Maze World," she went on, addressing Oliver directly, "the world without Magic. It is the place you left when you came through the Blackberry Labyrinth. Ravenhome is a portal to another dimension, one connected with yours but not identical to it. Where you are now is the border of the Labyrinth World. We are not bound by time and space in the same way as the Maze World, and we still have High Magic, of which Merlin of Camelot was the great master."

Merlin... Camelot... King Arthur! Long-forgotten names from Oliver's childhood. A chill whispered down his spine, and the little hairs on the back of his neck stood up. The air in the hall seemed charged with mystery.

Flavia lifted her cup to take a sip of the fragrant *semera* when all at once two hectic red spots appeared on her cheekbones. She leaned back in her silver chair and closed her eyes.

Dr. Sepulchra came swiftly to Flavia's side. Taking out a gold pocket watch, he counted her pulse as she lay back, pale as starlight except for the unnatural flush on her cheeks. After a full minute he snapped the lid back on the watch-case and released her wrist. "The *Sendara* needs to rest quietly for a few moments," he announced. "Belvedine, you'd better continue."

Great-Aunt Belvedine sighed, either from relief or impatience. "All right, Medley," she began. "This will have to be brief, so listen well. The Graelands, where Flavia reigns--"

"Guards," Flavia murmured audibly, her eyes still closed. "I am their Guardian, not their ruler, as you know, Belvedine."

Great-Aunt Belvedine inclined her head toward Flavia. "I stand corrected, *Sendara*. The Graelands is the jewel of our world, the source of our life and a sanctuary of peace. It lies far from here, surrounded by the Mountains of Zund, which were once thought to be impassable from the outer world. Recently we have discovered that they are not. A thing of evil has crossed over the boundaries that were erected in the Dawn Age to keep us safe. That evil is poised to invade the very heart of our world. If it cannot be stopped, it will kill every vestige of life in the Graelands. And if the Graelands die--"

"If the Graelands die," Dr. Sepulchra continued as Great-Aunt Belvedine pressed a handkerchief against her lips, "then all the Labyrinth World will die, slowly, horribly, in full consciousness of its own destruction. And if the Labyrinth World dies, Mr. Medley--"

"Then will your Maze World also die," Friar Ablejohn spoke in his turn. "The evil that is here will be able to go through the portals without restraint. It will invade your world, and everything that is green and living will die. And there will be nothing ... nothing... that can bring it back to life. There would be no hope. No hope at all."

"But this is terrible!" Oliver exclaimed, shocked to his soul. "What--what evil thing is it?"

"We do not name it," Dr. Sepulchra resumed, "except to call it the Ashes of Waste. The term refers to a small, dry, colorless scale about the size of a snowflake. It looks like gray sand or frost from a distance, but it never melts, and whatever it touches dies: green plants, animals, fish, insects, the soil itself. All that is left, when the Ash passes over the land, is desolation. It kills whatever lies beneath it, down to the center of the Earth itself."

"How is that possible?" Oliver asked. "Where did it come from? How is it spread?"

"It is spread by agents called *wyrga*," said Friar Ablejohn. "*Wyrga* are not created beings, but slaves manufactured to do the bidding of their masters."

"One master, Friar," Mildrith interjected. "One master only."

Oliver wanted to ask many questions; nothing came out. He was having trouble with his breathing. The wax candles in the chandelier burned lower; the room grew darker.

"What 'master'?" he managed at last. "Who is their 'master'?"

No one answered for a while. Outside, the whisper of the evening breeze had grown to a wail of wind around Ravenhome's gables. For a fraction of a second, he thought he caught one of the shadows at the end of the hall inch toward Flavia's chair--of its own volition. *But that's impossible! An optical illusion.*

Dr. Sepulchra took breath to resume his narrative, but just then Flavia inhaled deeply and opened her eyes. The hectic red spots in her cheeks were gone, but her face was pale as ivory.

"No, Doctor," she said gently as the physician stood to attend her. "I shall be well enough now. Cousin Oliver," turning to him, "your question is one that I alone must answer."

"And only because of your impertinence, Medley," interjected Great-Aunt Belvedine. "Have you no consideration for Flavia's health?"

"Hush, Belvedine," said Flavia, and this time her voice was less gentle. "The answer to your question, Cousin Oliver, is--the Destroyer, whom we know as the Lord of Desolation. His true name is... *Ab' addon.*"

The name meant nothing to Oliver at that moment. He had expected to hear of some amoral global corporation trading lives for profit, or a terrorist cell dedicated to the false martyrdom of destruction. Then he remembered that those were things of his own world, and he was now in a different dimension entirely--or so they said. He was not yet completely convinced. What they were telling him went against what he had always known as rationality. But as he listened, a flicker deep in his mind began to bring an idea to the forefront of his consciousness.

Flavia went on. "We do not often speak his true name here, lest the echo of it draw him near. Dr. Sepulchra, please go on." Violet shadows spread stains under her eyes. Once more she leaned back in her silver chair.

"At great peril to herself," the physician continued, "our *Sendara* has journeyed from the distant Graelands here to Ravenhome, at the edge of the Labyrinth World. As you now know, Ravenhome is a portal, one of those places where the barrier between the two worlds is thin, and passage may be made between them. It is here that we have gathered to await--but I have gotten ahead of my story."

Great-Aunt Belvedine made an impatient sound halfway between a snort and a sigh, and looked pointedly at the watch pinned to her lapel. Dr. Sepulchra ignored her.

"You see, Mr. Medley," he said, choosing his words carefully, "the fact is that Flavia, our Guardian--*Sendara* in the Old Boreal

-- 37 --

tongue--holds in her own person the vitality of the Graelands. Flavia and the Graelands are really one being, joined in spirit. I understand the ancient kings and queens of your own world were joined to their lands in the same manner. An injury to Flavia, in body or spirit, is a like injury to the Graelands. Should the *Sendara* decline and die before her proper time, which should be many Ages hence, then the Graelands will fall before the Lord of Desolation, as have countless other lands and worlds before us." He took a sip of wine to ease his throat. Oliver was speechless, scarcely able to credit what he heard.

Friar Ablejohn took up the burden of the tale. "Our *Sendara* has been infected by an illness. A traitor whose identity we do not know slipped through our defenses and put an Ash-derived poison in her bath, so that before we realized the danger, she had already absorbed the toxins. As yet her illness is held in check, but every day her strength declines. The progress of the disease is inevitable. She must die--and soon."

"No!" Oliver shouted, and sprang up from his chair. "No! That can't be! There must be some medicine, some treatment! Cousin Flavia, let me take you to--to my world. We have the finest hospitals, the latest technology--" He fell silent before the expression of infinite sadness in Flavia's eyes.

"I cannot leave the Labyrinth World, Cousin Oliver," she said softly.

Oliver sat down slowly.

"There is, however, one possibility," Dr. Sepulchra added.

"One hope," said the friar.

Oliver looked eagerly toward the physician.

"The *Sendara* must go to the Abbey of Saint Amber, where lives a community of holy sages trained in the highest arts of healing," said Dr. Sepulchra. "My knowledge of medicine does not begin to equal theirs. Only at the Abbey is there a chance to save her life—if Saint Amber's Rose is found and restored to her."

"The Abbey of Saint Amber?" Oliver repeated slowly. "Where is it?"

"A far journey from here," replied Friar Ablejohn. "It is situated high on the Great Mountain of Zund, on the edge of the Fathomless Ocean."

Saint Amber's Rose

"The way there is very dangerous," remarked Mildrith, speaking for the first time in a long while. "Full of terrors you cannot even imagine."

Oliver sat still for a moment, processing the information. It was overwhelming. He was in another world (or so they claimed), another dimension of time and space. People he had met for the first time tonight seemed to know all about him. And Great-Aunt Belvedine: *What is her role in all this?* He couldn't say he was well acquainted with her, given the infrequency of her visits over the years. *I'm not sure I trust her intentions.*

The tiny thought that had begun a while ago deep in his unconscious mind seeped into his consciousness, took form, at first vague and cloudy, then clearer, as if it were a light dimly seen at the end of a dark and terrifying tunnel.

"Why--?" he started to ask, but the tension in the room pressed heavily upon him, and he couldn't quite put together what he wanted to say.

Flavia opened her eyes and gazed at him with an expression he couldn't interpret. "Cousin Oliver," she said, "I asked Belvedine to bring you here to Ravenhome so that I could request a very great favor of you.

"In our most ancient scrolls there is a prophecy that one will come to us who brings a special Gift. This Gift will be the saving of the Graelands--and me. The difficulty is that no one knows what this Gift is, not our wisest councilors or our oldest writings. It may be that even the Gift-Bringer does not know."

"But--" Oliver began as a shadowy suspicion twined itself around his mind. "What... If... Who...?"

A calm like great bells tolling in the distance enveloped them. The light-forms around the table shone out with a clear brightness.

"*You*, Brother Medley, are the Gift-Bringer. So say our ancient prophecies."

Friar Ablejohn pronounced the words with measured solemnity, and Oliver felt them drop like hot stones into his stomach.

"I? But I'm not... That is..."

Great-Aunt Belvedine shot him a scathing glance. "Be quiet, Medley! Pay attention."

Her countenance perfectly serene, Flavia smiled at him. With infinite courtesy she held the silence as he tried to grasp what had been told him.

Then she spoke again. "Cousin Oliver, I can tell you no less than the truth: If you choose to come with us on our journey to the Abbey, the danger will be great, as Mil told you. It may be that none of us will reach our destination--or return from it. But if you are with us, our councilors assure us that you can save us in our hour of greatest need--if you *will* to do so."

It was on the tip of Oliver's tongue to protest that he had no "special Gift" that he was aware of; that there were many librarians and rose growers of more prominence back in the Maze World, and although he would be only too happy to do anything for Flavia that was in his power, he couldn't begin to think how he could help in their situation. He wasn't much of an athlete; he had certainly never contemplated mountain-climbing. The *Foressa* Mildrith had already established, to her satisfaction and his own, that he was incompetent in any martial art known to man. Beside that, he was middle-aged, overweight, nearsighted, introverted, and otherwise totally unsuitable for the role of heroic adventurer.

He had never felt so useless in his life.

A sudden gust of wind blew open the double doors at the end of the Great Hall and scattered a shower of leaves over the threshold. Friar Ablejohn sprang out of his chair with an agility surprising in one so rotund.

"There!" he exclaimed, and pointed toward the leaves. "Oak! Ash! Thorn! The warning signal! Our defenses have been penetrated! The *wyrga* will be at Ravenhome within the hour. *Sendara,* I beg you to hasten your departure!"

Mil and Great-Aunt Belvedine stood up at the same moment. The *Foressa* went to stand by Flavia's chair as Great-Aunt Belvedine spoke urgently. "Flavia, my dear, we must leave now!"

But again Flavia lifted a restraining hand, and Great-Aunt Belvedine fell silent. "Cousin Oliver," Flavia resumed, "the decision must be yours alone. Freely choose: Will you come with us on our perilous journey? Or will you return safely to your own world?"

A confusion of thoughts blew fitfully around Oliver's mind like strands of spider-silk not yet woven into a web.

Then his heart told him what to do.

He stood and did not hesitate. Unaware of what might lie ahead, he looked directly into her gray-green eyes. "Cousin Flavia," he said with a confidence that he had never known before, "I will serve you with all my heart as long as I live, even unto the world's doom."

The words were out of his mouth and flown to every listening ear, and he could not call them back even if he wanted to. Not that he could imagine wanting to do such a thing. Certainly not then.

A delicate flush tinted Flavia's cheeks, but she smiled at him and sank back against the cushions in her silver chair. Great-Aunt Belvedine sniffed at his audacity but said nothing more, because all at once there was tremendous activity everywhere, and no more opportunity to say anything.

Chapter Three

The Mort-Mire

Everyone (except Oliver) moved rapidly and silently, as if it were a precision drill rehearsed many times. Great-Aunt Belvedine stepped beside Flavia's chair, took a silken scarf from invisible hands, and draped it carefully over Flavia's shoulders. Mildrith disappeared from the hall. The costumed guests vanished unnoticed. Grimtread came to stand like mist behind Flavia's chair, and at her nod wheeled her away from the dining table and out a small door at the end of the room.

Great-Aunt Belvedine beckoned impatiently, and Oliver made haste to follow her down a narrow corridor that twisted and turned until it opened to a stable converted to a garage, where a large automobile stood waiting. Oliver recognized it from his father's collection of classic cars: a vintage 1915 Rolls Royce Silver Ghost, tended as carefully as a thoroughbred racehorse. Lanterns along the walls reflected their yellow lights in the polished silver sheen of its coat.

Beside the vehicle stood its attendant chauffeur, proud as the head groom of a premier racing stable. He was at least as ancient as his charge, but though lean as an alder stem, his posture was ramrod-straight. His white hair was slicked back under a Glengarry cap that matched his spotless gray-green uniform. As the wheelchair approached, he stepped forward, opened the rear passenger door, and bowed. "My lady," he said in a voice that creaked like a forgotten gate.

"Old Auldie," Flavia replied tenderly, and for a moment laid her hand on his sleeve. "My cousin, Oliver Medley."

"Sir," said the chauffeur, touching his cap.

"Mr. Auldie," said Oliver.

"Old Auldie will do for me, sir," responded the man with a Highland burr. "Like my father and gran'ther before me."

Saint Amber's Rose

Grimtread lifted Flavia in transparent hands, placed her in the middle of the back seat, folded the wheelchair and deposited it in the rear compartment of the car.

Guided by Great-Aunt Belvedine's imperious finger, Oliver hastened to seat himself beside Flavia via the opposite door. Great-Aunt Belvedine scrunched her inches into the seat on Flavia's other side. Grimtread handed Great-Aunt Belvedine a thick woolen robe to cover Flavia's lap and shut the car door. Flavia closed her eyes and was so still that she seemed to have left them.

Old Auldie took his place behind the wheel. Oliver wondered where the *Foressa* Mildrith was, but on the instant the warrior dashed into the garage from another door. She had changed into a black field uniform, with her dark hair under a beret and a bandolier looped over her shoulder. But the bandolier, Oliver saw, did not hold bullet cartridges. Instead, it seemed to be a sling-carrier for a small black rectangular object so ultra-thin in profile that it almost disappeared against her clothing.

Could it be a weapon? An explosive device? A shiver went up Oliver's back that made his hair-roots tingle. *Where are we going, and what have I gotten myself into? Should I have brought along Father's old revolver, or at least a toothbrush? Great-Aunt Belvedine really ought to have given me more information!* He fully intended to have a word with her when this expedition, or whatever it might be, was over.

Mil slid swiftly into the passenger seat and shut the door with a firm click. She belted herself in and opened the black rectangle, which turned out to be a laptop computer with an odd-looking keyboard and a screen with shifting colors that wriggled and shook and formed fleeting symbols. Oliver became lightheaded watching it.

Mil's fingers began dancing across the keyboard, and the screen shuddered and cleared as mathematical calculations interspersed with Egyptian hieroglyphs scrolled down. The speed of the scrolling symbols made him feel rather ill; he stopped watching and turned his attention to the view outside his window.

He couldn't see anything. The lanterns on the garage walls had gone out. Oliver unconsciously hunched his shoulders and returned to watching the computer monitor, now their only source of light.

Mil stilled her hands for a moment and looked back at Oliver. "Cousin Oliver," she said in a low but audible voice, "I shall caution you before we start. As you were told, Ravenhome is on the border between your dimension and ours. At this moment, you may yet choose to leave us and return to the Maze World. If you hold to your vow to Flavia and go on, then you must realize that it is possible that you will never return. When we enter fully into the Labyrinth World, everything you believe you know will change. You will keep some memories of your personal history, but you will begin to forget names and places familiar to you now. For the second time of asking: Will you come with us or will you return to your home?"

For half a minute--and that only--Oliver considered the matter. Aurelia Dawn would take care of his cat and his garden until he returned... or even if he didn't. His will was on file with his attorney. His job would go to another qualified person. What was there, really, to hold him to his ordinary life? Had he not always secretly dreamed of High Adventure? And was this not his opportunity to have one at last?

Take it! his conscience urged him. *This is your chance to Make a Difference!*

Oliver straightened his spine and squared his shoulders. "I'm quite ready to proceed," he said, having no concept of the extent of his unreadiness.

Mil faced front again. "Engage engine," she ordered quietly.

Old Auldie started the car's engine.

"Remove barriers."

The garage's double doors slid aside, revealing an iron portcullis that might have belonged in a medieval castle. Mil pressed a few more keys, and her computer screen cleared its calculations to reveal a view of galaxies and nebula in deep space, with the superimposed image of an hourglass. Grains of sand trickled through its narrow waist.

Unconsciously Oliver held his breath as Mil watched the screen, her fingers poised above the keyboard. Grain by grain, the moments fell into the bottom of the hourglass. "Three... two... one," she counted. On the screen a star exploded in a supernova, and the last grain of sand plunged to its doom. It was precisely midnight.

"Go!" she ordered, and the Rolls-Royce shot through the portcullis as if it were smoke. Oliver saw the iron bars whiz past him but felt no sensation at all.

They were on the road. Above them the constellation Pegasus, the flying horse, sped along a star-strewn path through the cosmic night.

Inside the darkened House of Ravenhome, a skeletal hand drew back the heavy draperies on one of the clerestory windows overlooking the carriage drive. Dr. Sepulchra frowned thoughtfully at the automobile as it vanished into the fog and rain. "He didn't ask the Question, did he," the physician remarked.

At his side, Friar Ablejohn sighed gently. "No. No, he didn't, the poor man."

"I fear he must travel a dark road before he reaches the Abbey," said Dr. Sepulchra.

"Yes," nodded the friar. "A long and terrible road. I pray for their safety--and his courage. May he have the heart to bear his heavy burden!"

"So be it," responded the physician.

"And blessed be," added Friar Ablejohn solemnly. Lifting his hand, he traced a sign in the air over the departing travelers.

Dr. Sepulchra consulted his watch. "Seven more minutes, and the enemy will be here."

"All is in readiness," the friar replied.

The two men remained in front of the tall windows. The friar silently fingered a string of wooden beads fastened to his cincture while the physician stood with his hands behind his back, peering into the darkness like a brooding heron.

"Look there!" the physician exclaimed, extending a long forefinger toward the window. "*Wyrga!*"

"I see it," answered Friar Ablejohn.

At the edge of the feral gardens a shadow darker than the night crept toward the house. Other shadows joined it, moving forward like a miasma.

A single ray of starlight pierced the mist and illumined a patch of lawn. The shape of something neither quite animal nor fully human passed through the light, hunched over in a limping run like a hyena. Metal gleamed along its torso and flanks, and its head was encased in heavy iron bars. The face, as much as could be glimpsed inside its cage, was a grotesque distortion, a foul relic of forgotten nightmare.

The friar inhaled sharply. "The poor thing!"

A ring of *wyrga* advanced toward the house, near, nearer...

Dr. Sepulchra studied his watch again, waiting until the minute hand joined its fellow. Somewhere in the house, the soft chime of a grandfather clock sounded twelve measured strokes.

The last tone faded away.

"Time!" announced the Wraith Grimtread, hovering behind physician and friar.

Like a fading sunset, Ravenhome dislimned and vanished entirely, leaving nothing but bent stems of grass slowly righting themselves as a great weight lifted from them. The *wyrga*, milling around in the empty space where the house no longer stood, shrieked and howled their rage to an indifferent moon.

So it begins, said a Voice inside a Mirror filled with wavering tongues of smoke.

The Fool's journey begins...

The Rolls Royce fled into the storm-whipped night. Trees tossed their boughs like witches' wands, and the wind lashed about angrily between ominous rolls of thunder. Flurries of rain clicked like pointed fingernails against the windshield of the automobile, and Oliver could not control a sudden shiver that crept down his spine. Once he stole a glance at Flavia, but she lay back among the cushions with closed eyes. The slight rise and fall of her bodice indicated her respiration; otherwise, he would have been hard-pressed to say that she was alive. He wanted desperately to touch her hand, to hold it, to transfer to her some of his own energy, but he did not dare. He also wanted to ask where they were going in such inclement weather, but again, he did not quite dare.

Great-Aunt Belvedine sat folded into herself on the other side of Flavia, scowling like a hawk diving for prey. Not a word had she uttered since the beginning of their journey, not even when a lightning bolt struck close to her window. One hand flapped idly at it, as if brushing away an insect.

Oliver fell into contemplation of the eccentricity of Great-Aunt Belvedine and of the unusual characteristics of his entire family. It seemed he didn't know nearly as much about his progenitors as he had thought, and now he had neither parent left to ask.

Saint Amber's Rose

How could I possibly have lived all my life in the same geographical region as Cousin Flavia and not been acquainted with her? Why? he asked himself, unable to come up with an answer. Hadn't his parents trusted him? They surely must have known about her.

Other memories came back to him as the Silver Ghost sped along an Old Straight Track through dense woodland, memories of signs and clues that might have had more significance than he realized. What of his mother, always his best friend? What of those mysterious letters in the long, green envelopes she used to receive once or twice a year by special messenger? They had the most fascinating stamps on them, but he never could persuade her to give them to him for his collection. Every other stamp from her vast international correspondence was his for the asking, but not those on the green envelopes.

"Someday, darling, you'll have them all," she told him, smoothing his cheek, "but not just now." And she had locked them away in her morocco letter-case.

Oliver still had the morocco letter-case packed away in one of his mother's trunks in the attic at home, but he had never opened it. He hadn't thought about the green envelopes for years, and now his initial curiosity revived. Why wouldn't she tell him who sent them or where they came from?

Secrets... Family secrets. A void had appeared in his recollection of their happy life together, and he did not understand it.

A terrific crack of lightning sounded, striking closely enough to light up the whole interior of the automobile. A long roll of thunder followed. Despite himself he shivered again, not entirely because of the lightning.

If this is High Adventure, he said to himself, *it certainly isn't anything like the knightly quests I read about in my youth. I'm not sure that I ought to be here. There must be someone better suited for this job--this Gift--whatever it is. Mightn't it be better for all concerned if I ask to be let out at the next bus stop? But I did promise Cousin Flavia I'd go with her, and I won't break my promise.*

The track ahead was so narrow that trees on either side scratched against the automobile's windows with twigs like clutching fingers, as if they were desperate to get inside. Once or twice Oliver's head jerked involuntarily toward his window. He was almost positive he'd glimpsed a face... But it was gone. He returned to his musings.

Charleynne Gates

Maybe this is the kind of High Adventure I always wanted. After all, the knights of old didn't venture forth in comfort and safety along a modern highway with service stations at regular intervals. No, they rode into the pathless wilderness armed only with sword, lance, and a brave heart. Whatever came to them they accepted as their destiny and met with courage.

And here was Cousin Flavia, who had appealed to him personally for his assistance. Nothing in her could be evil; he knew it in his heart.

In an act that had surprised him the instant he opened his mouth, Oliver had pledged fealty to her, even unto yielding up his life. He had given his solemn word, and he would not go back on it.

It's only a storm. Nothing to be concerned about.

All at once the car screeched to a halt as Old Auldie stomped on the brake. Directly in front of them the headlights shone on an enormous oak blown down by the storm and lying right across the road. There was no getting around it.

Oliver was about to suggest that he get out and see if the tree might be dragged aside so the car could edge past it, but at that point Great-Aunt Belvedine's head emerged from the folds of her shawl like a turtle from its carapace.

"The *wyrga!*" she uttered in a doom-laden voice. "They've found us out!"

Flavia sat upright, her eyes wide open and focused on the massive wreck in the road. "No," she said softly.

In the front seat, Mil kept tapping at her keyboard. "No sign of *wyrga* that I can find," she reported.

"But there must be!" Great-Aunt Belvedine protested.

"I cannot sense them," Flavia said. "This is from Nature." She sank back against the cushions again and closed her eyes. Even in the fitful light Oliver could see that she was in pain.

"Shall I take the other road, my lady?" quavered Old Auldie. "Or return to Ravenhome?"

"Surely not the other road, Flavia!" exclaimed Great-Aunt Belvedine. "The other road leads to--"

"I know where it leads, Belvedine," Flavia replied calmly, "but we have no other choice. Ravenhome is gone by now. The Mort-Mire Road, please, Old Auldie."

Saint Amber's Rose

Mort-Mire? thought Oliver. *"Death Swamp"? I've never heard of it. Is it close to--* He recalled that he was no longer "close to" his own city... or state... or country, if it came to that. Supposedly he was in a different world, and he had no idea how far from home that might be. Or how he might get back.

Best not to think about that right now.

Great-Aunt Belvedine muttered something unintelligible and pulled her head back into the cowl of her shawl. Old Auldie reversed the car about ten yards and turned off to the left, onto a road even narrower than the Old Straight Track where they had just been. It was hardly a road at all, rough, rutted, overgrown with weeds as it was. Peering through the windshield, Oliver couldn't tell how the chauffeur managed to find it, let alone follow it.

Between gusts of wind and cracks of lightning, Oliver heard the crunch of small stones and dead leaves as the wheels rolled over them, then the splash of puddles and a thunk! chunk! as the car dipped into potholes and scraped its axles. Low-hanging branches scritched across the hood of the car. *Like claws,* Oliver thought, and realized that drops of perspiration had beaded on his forehead. He wiped them off surreptitiously with his handkerchief.

The limousine went slower and slower. Gradually its headlights dimmed. Old Auldie had to roll down the driver's window and lean out to see where they were going. Finally the car stopped altogether. Its headlights died.

The chauffeur tried to coax the engine back to life, but gave up after several fruitless attempts.

"I do beg your pardon, my lady," Old Auldie said, his voice faltering. "I don't know where we are. And I--I can't get the automobile started again."

"It isn't your fault, dear Old Auldie," Flavia said gently. "It is the Mort-Mire itself."

"'What enters the Mire, ends in the Mire,'" said Great-Aunt Belvedine hollowly, quoting an old saying.

"Don't be so negative, Belvedine," Mil cut in. "It's just another obstacle."

"Mil is right," Flavia said. "We are being tested. You might as well turn off the engine, Old Auldie, while we think of what to do next."

The chauffeur disengaged the engine, and the night sounds of the swamp enveloped them. Drifts of white mist arose around the car, obscuring most of their view. Given the Stygian darkness, the view hadn't amounted to much anyway. After a minute Oliver thought he heard a curious kind of chomping sound, as if something out there were eating with its mouth open.

Mil kept typing rapidly on her keyboard, apparently little concerned about their predicament. Oliver wished he knew more about internal combustion engines. Probably wouldn't have helped in this case, given the antiquity of the vehicle.

Will-o'-the-wisps began to appear, bits of bright drifts like snowfire. They flitted beside the windows, peered in, and darted away as suddenly as they had come.

"I'd better take a look outside," said Old Auldie, and at Flavia's nod detached a lamp from inside the car and got out, shining the light around. Oliver saw that they were at the edge of a vast breeding ground of *darlingtonia californica*, and the flower-heads seemed to be in motion. The pale, bulbous cobra lilies, being meat-eaters, had lured their prey inside their hoods with the deceptive promise of nectar. Now they were in the process of masticating their dinners, crunching up rodent bones like carrot sticks.

Oliver felt rather nauseated. He hadn't known carnivorous plants dined in quite that manner--or so loudly.

Old Auldie returned to the car and put his head in at the driver's window. "There's no road at all, my lady," he said. "It just runs out. It's been a long time since I came this way, and I don't remember the Mire being so extensive."

"The Mire is much larger than it used to be," Great-Aunt Belvedine asserted. "It was not nearly so close to Ravenhome in my day. Encroaching Ash is changing the entire terrain of the Labyrinth. We'll have to take another route. We can't possibly get through this way."

"That is for Flavia to decide," Mil remarked from her position in the front passenger seat. Her fingers continued to speed across the keyboard.

Oliver couldn't contain himself any longer. "Where is it we were going?"

"That's none of your concern, Medley," snapped Great-Aunt Belvedine.

"Belvedine," Flavia reproved softly. "Of course you must know, Cousin Oliver. Forgive me for not explaining more fully as we drove, but Dr. Sepulchra insists that I rest as much as possible--"

"As you should be doing now," muttered Great-Aunt Belvedine, and pulled her shawl closer around her bony shoulders.

Flavia paid her no attention. "We are driving to an inn at the border of Threshold Forest. We must reach it by midnight; we have no other option now. When we left Ravenhome, which is ensorcelled, we left our protection."

Ensorcelled? thought Oliver. *Does she seriously mean that Ravenhome is under a spell? And wasn't it midnight when we started?*

Old Auldie's head emerged from under the hood of the car. "I can't find anything wrong here, my lady. She just won't start. It's got to be this place. The Mire. The dampness of it seems to have gotten right into her bones. I believe I'm going to have to go for help, my lady."

"Perhaps there might be a telephone in the vicinity?" Oliver ventured. "I'm afraid I didn't bring my cell phone—"

Great-Aunt Belvedine cut him off. "Those things don't work here."

"It's true, Cousin Oliver. They don't," Mil said. "You're between worlds, remember. Our electromagnetic fields aren't exactly the same as yours. My computer is especially adapted for passage through the portal, but it will only work until we reach the inn."

"Old Auldie will have to walk out," Great-Aunt Belvedine said flatly.

"You can't go alone," said Flavia to the ancient chauffeur.

Oliver's heart swelled: He heard his cue! Here was his opportunity to perform a service for his Lady! He opened his mouth to volunteer to go anywhere, in any world, at her slightest wish, but Mil said firmly that she would take her laptop and go along with the chauffeur. They would find the road faster that way, and she would make a weather envelope for them as they walked. Cousin Oliver, she added, ought to stay with Flavia and Belvedine for safety, and before she left she would set up a protective shield for them. "But stay inside the car," she warned, tapping out instructions on her keyboard. "My software program has no effect on the Mort-Mire itself."

-- 51 --

Charleynne Gates

Oliver didn't understand what she meant, but his chest puffed with pride that he had been asked--or directed--to remain with Flavia. And Great-Aunt Belvedine, of course. With some reluctance, Flavia agreed to this plan, and Mil and Old Auldie set off to find their way through the Mort-Mire and walk to the inn, where assistance would be available.

Flavia, her cheeks drained of color, lay back and closed her eyes again. Great-Aunt Belvedine sank into her shawl and brooded. Oliver stared out the window into the eerie night. Will-o'-the-wisps appeared again, whirling around the car as if they were disembodied eyes.

Oliver pondered the situation. He had a vague feeling that he ought to "take charge" in some way. It was his knightly duty to protect Fla--er, the ladies. Just sitting here in the dark wasn't doing them any good as far as he could see.

More of the dratted will-o'-the-wisps spun past the window like tops. Their constant motion made him lightheaded. It almost seemed as if they were being deliberately provoking... *That's irrational. They're just specks of phosphorescence blowing in the wind from the swamp. Although I can't see any leaves being blown around... I'm sure it doesn't mean anything.*

He wondered where Mil and Old Auldie had gotten to by now. *Where could they possibly find another road? Old Auldie was very old, after all; he wouldn't be able to see things in the dusky Mire the way a pair of younger eyes could. That must be the real reason Mil went with him.*

He stared out the window, squinting past the will-o'-the-wisps. There was a small grove of trees over there beyond the darlingtonia. If he stared hard he could almost make out individual shapes of tree limbs through the brooding darkness. For a second he thought he saw a face in the drifts of mist, a human-like face between two trees on the other side of the darlingtonia patch. At least it might have been a human face. He saw it for an instant--was positive he had—and then it was gone. Whatever it was, he had the fleeting sensation that it had been staring directly at him.

There it was again! And it was staring at him! What's more, he could feel its eyeless visage projecting some kind of energy toward him —sharp and hard, like shards of glass. This kind of thing—psychic projection--was exactly what Oliver firmly, though tacitly, had always denied whenever Aurelia Dawn brought up the subject; now, he wasn't so certain. The face—if it was really there—wanted him to do something, and whatever it was, wasn't good. He didn't know how he knew that, but he couldn't deny the fact.

The invisible energy intensified.

Oliver, ambivalent, squirmed in his seat. *I ought to get out and confront the creature, whatever it is. If it's human, then it's got to help us. We can't just sit here all night in the cold and dark! Who knows what might have happened to Mil and Old Auldie?*

Stay in the car, Mil said. She must have had a good reason. She knows the area, and I certainly don't. But... I ought to be doing something. I should be protecting the ladies. But how? And from what?

The energy from the face stretched out invisible tentacles toward him as more specks of *ignis fatuus* danced maddeningly in front of his vision. Oliver tried his best to ignore them.

I need to get to the bottom of this. I need to stay inside the car. I need to find out if that face across the Mire is human or not. I need to stay with Flavia and Great-Aunt Belvedine.

The dark energy increased, focused, drew him without his conscious knowledge.

It can't hurt to get out and have a look. I'll just be a moment.

He made his decision and turned the handle on the car door.

At that instant two things happened: Great-Aunt Belvedine's head popped up from the folds of her shawl. "Medley!" she hissed, but he ignored her. The door swung open.

"There's someone out there!" he explained firmly. "I'm going to get out and find him! Whoever he is, he's got to help us!"

"Don't be ridiculous, Medley!" Great-Aunt Belvedine ordered. "Stay where you are."

At the same time Flavia said, "Cousin Oliver, please! You mustn't go outside!"

But Oliver was determined, and angry as well. There *was* someone out there. He would find whoever it belonged to or--! He grabbed the lamp and slid out of the car seat onto the spongy ground. He took a few steps in the direction where the face had been and lifted the lamp to shine as much light around as he could through the thick air.

Turning completely around, he looked in every direction, but saw only scraggy trees with carnivorous flowers beneath them.

"Hello!" He gathered his courage and shouted into the night, advancing toward the darlingtonia patch. "Hello! Is someone there!" He listened, straining to hear any sound other than the soggy night noises of the Mire.

A single flake of snow fell, settled on his sleeve, and melted. Then more flakes fell, and more, and quickly became a snow-shower. Oliver thought he glimpsed the face again through the whirling snowflakes and took a few steps toward it until his shoe touched the sucking Mire-muck. As he did so, the snow fell even harder, turning into a blizzard. Even though he was only three or four yards away from the automobile, he suddenly realized that he couldn't see it any more.

On the verge of panic, Oliver began running to and fro in the snow accumulating in drifts at his feet, calling for the face to show itself. "Help!" he cried again and again. "We need help! Come out, whoever you are! I know you're there!"

Great-Aunt Belvedine pushed open the door on her side and bellowed, "MEDLEY! COME BACK HERE AT ONCE! YOU DON'T KNOW WHAT YOU'RE DOING!"

But Oliver heard her only as a faint, unintelligible buzzing. Determined to find the person he thought he saw, he kept on stumbling through the snowdrifts, first one way, then another, shouting vainly into the icy wind.

As quickly as it began, the snowstorm stopped, and the drifts piled high on the ground melted away as if they had never been. Oliver saw that he was much farther from the car than he realized, and the passenger door on his side was wide open. On the other side of the automobile but some distance away from it stood Great-Aunt Belvedine, gripping her umbrella and glaring at him. The door on her side was also fully open.

An awful fear struck him. He gulped for breath in the dank air and hurried back to the car. Raising the lamp, he saw by its light that the middle passenger seat was empty. Only a silken scarf lay across the cushions.

Flavia was gone. There was no sign of her at all.

Chapter Four

Castle Mormorion

Far to the east of Ravenhome, on the borderland between Threshold Forest and the Great Waste, the Prince of Taraman sat astride his horse, waiting. Both of them, horse and rider, were absolutely still. Not an eyelash of either one flickered; not a breath disturbed the air. In front of them huge, ancient trees, hoary with mosses and lichens, shielded them from view. Unseen, they observed the Waste from the top of the Bordering Cliffs, noting everything that moved on it. The prince, an expert scout and tracker, automatically registered minute changes in the landscape, but his innermost thoughts were elsewhere.

Beloved, are you thinking of me now, as I think of you? Are you still waiting for me? I will come for you, I promise. But this I must do first so that we may have our life together, and our children live in health and peace.

At last their patience was rewarded. Across the monotonous distance of the desolate flatland, a long line of ungainly machines lumbered toward the forest, heading for a gap in the high, bare boundary cliffs that enclosed the Waste. Even as far from them as the prince was, the machines looked unnaturally large. Closer up, they would be monstrous--engines of mass destruction, as he knew only too well.

"Rumor was right this time, Firemark," he whispered. The stallion's ear flicked, but otherwise he didn't move a muscle. *The wyrga have broken ground into the Labyrinth, carrying the poisonous Ashes of Waste with them, and now Ab'addon's war machines are following them into the Labyrinth farther and faster than anyone anticipated. And I should have done so. He is hiding the information in ways I do not understand.*

The stallion tensed. The prince felt it immediately; he waited for the horse's lead before he made a move. They had been together so long and knew each other so well that theirs was a partnership of equals rather than of master and mount.

Firemark made a low sound deep in his throat. The prince at once lifted his head to scan the sky, spotting potential danger. A vee of black objects flew through the gray glare over the Waste, heading in the same direction as the advancing line of engines.

"*Gnaarx*," muttered the prince. "I've never seen them so near the border. Something's going on. I wish I knew--"

Quite suddenly a young doe darted out of the forest and ran past them in a panic. She crashed through the protective foliage, leaped headlong down the rocky path, and ran out onto the Waste. The predator that had been chasing her stopped abruptly, too experienced to venture outside the bounds of Threshold Forest, but the doe kept running for several more steps until she stopped, bewildered at the change from forest floor to hard-caked ash.

The vee of black objects overhead at once gave forth harsh cries. They veered from their course and dived toward the confused animal, who didn't think to look up until they were almost upon her. *Gnaarx* they were indeed: airborne attack machines with metal-boned wings and narrow heads set with unblinking eyes, red as burning coals.

Without hesitation the prince and Firemark broke cover and dashed out to defend the terrified animal. The prince's whip cut down two screaming *gnaarx*. Rearing, Firemark beat two more out of the sky and trampled them to ground, but the other *gnaarx* dodged and circled and dived again, seeking for vulnerable places on human- and horseflesh where snap of fang and clutch of talon would be most deadly. The doe, at last collecting its wits, ran back into the forest, but its defenders found themselves in a pitched battle.

The beat of great wings, strike of hooves galloping on air and over cloud! Two white horses swooped out of the sky and struck the foul *gnaarx* from the rear, their attack swift and sure and fatal. The *gnaarx* couldn't sustain a fight against the crushing teeth, the powerful kicking legs and hard hooves of three battle-trained steeds. In less time than it takes to tell, the remnant of the *gnaarx* streaked away, retreating across the Waste and out of sight.

The winged horses touched ground lightly beside the prince and Firemark, and together the four sped back to the forest cover, not stopping until they were far enough inside to be securely concealed.

"Many thanks, Friends," said the prince in the equine tongue. "What have you seen?"

"The whole of the *wyrga* force on maneuvers," replied Sornor Star-Rider. "Never before have we seen them in such great numbers, or out in the open. And many *gnaarx* together in bands. He's been making more of them. The ones that attacked you were new, only partly trained, or we wouldn't have chased them away so easily."

The prince frowned and bit his lip. "I must meet with the Owl Guard--and quickly. They may have been able to estimate the enemy's numbers. Do you return to the inn?"

"Yes. The High Council of Threshold Guardians gathers in three days," said Sornor. "And we have heard that the *Sendara* has left Ravenhome with the one foretold in the Prophecies."

"The one who brings the Gift!"

"The very same. They are expected at Council, as are you, Prince."

The prince looked away, glanced up at the canopy of overlapping leaves. "I know--but that depends on what I learn from the Owl Guard. I will have to go into the Icewode before the Council."

Beghed, mate to Sornor, shook her head. "It is not wise to go there alone, Prince, not in these troubled days."

The prince smiled wryly. "Danger is not only in the Icewode, O Daughter of the Wind. It's all around us, and will be until he is driven back to his domain. Because of Her--"

All at once a raven flew down from the forest canopy and landed on the prince's sleeve.

"Hail, Prince of Taraman!"

"Hail yourself, Uriel Corax! What message from the Raven Express?"

"Catastrophe!" said Uriel, and reported what had happened in the Mort-Mire. The three horses conferred intently with urgent small whickers and gestures, while the prince frowned, pondering the news.

Flavia abducted! Who would dare? The Lord of Desolation? I hadn't realized he had advanced so near to Ravenhome. His interests went in another direction, or so I thought. Did some unknown entity simply take advantage of an opportunity? What should I do now?

The Mort-Mire lay a considerable distance away, several days' journey at least. Even if Pavarr went there, it was likely that all traces of the *Sendara's* party would have been obliterated by now. Nothing that entered the Mire ever emerged from it, said the old tales, for Miremuck swallowed everything that trod heedlessly upon its sucking surface.

Not Flavia! She couldn't have--

The prince's leg muscles unconsciously tensed. Firemark felt it, tossed his mane, lifted a hoof in readiness. Sornor and Beghed waited for the prince's decision.

Pavarr made himself relax his thigh-grip. "I cannot go back and track the *Sendara* from the Mort-Mire. I'll have to go on, for time presses. The High Council must have more information if the Labyrinth World is to be saved from the Ash," he said to the raven perched on a nearby branch. "Tell the *Foressa* Mildrith that I'll meet the Questors at The Rendezvous. *Va'in 'a moru'*!"

Making hasty farewells, the four separated, departing in opposite directions, and Pavarr and Firemark soon disappeared in the forest's thick undergrowth.

"But first," Prince Pavarr spoke softly into Firemark's ear, "I have to answer the summons from Castle Mormorion."

The prince lapsed into the kind of communication he and the horse had long employed, a code of small movements, flexing of muscles, shiver of skin, wordless murmurs. Together they flowed through the forest, and as they approached the fortress of the Lord of Desolation, gradually became less and less visible. *Fadingweaven*, an entrancement-spell requiring great concentration, ran down one's store of energy, and Pavarr carefully conserved his. Not until they had sighted the sinister battlements on the far plain did he speak the last spell of thinning visibility and cast it like a mantle over the horse and himself.

They halted at another edge of Threshold Forest, where the Great Waste spread out before them like an arid sea. There the prince dismounted and shouldered his knapsack--not that any equipment he possessed would do much for him once he entered the castle, whose potential hazards were unknown. But pure water he might need, and the means of making fire, and his Dwarvian-made dagger. Fresh food he dared not take because of its scent, but Pavarr was accustomed to fasting for many days when necessary.

Saint Amber's Rose

Firemark whickered as lightly as snowfall, but Pavarr shook his head and stroked the muscular neck. "No, Friend, not this time. You could not enter undetected where I must go. If you stay here, the *fadingweaven* will wear off and leave you vulnerable to *gnaarx* attack. Go back to Keeper's Inn, and if I do not return... *Va'in 'a moru'*."

Firemark, having a high degree of intelligence as well as common sense, did no such thing. Staying silently where he was, he watched his companion maneuver almost imperceptibly through the underbrush and emerge onto the vacant flatland of the Great Waste, heading for the shadow-shifting fortress that was the bastion of the Lord of Desolation. As soon as Pavarr was out of sight, the horse turned and picked his way through the forest to a spot on the opposite side of the Bordering Cliffs, much closer to the fortress. There he found a shelter under autumn-clad trees, well concealed from airborne *gnaarx*, where snow had not yet penetrated and where sufficient grasses grew to furnish several meals. There he waited, keeping close watch on Castle Mormorion's murky outline.

Pavarr hiked steadily toward the shadowy dwelling of the enemy, maintaining his semi-visible *fadingweaven* cover. It wasn't easy to focus the necessary energy for that long a time without a break, but the results of letting down his guard would almost certainly be fatal, so he kept his concentration at peak. He had no fear of his footprints being traced as he trod upon the hardened ashes, for as soon as they were imprinted, they vanished as if the ground had swallowed them. The plain of the Great Waste tolerated no trace of any living creature upon its surface, and the prince did not linger lest he come to an unthinkable end.

From his vantage point back in Threshold Forest, Castle Mormorion had seemed to be many *kephan* in the distance, but now it suddenly seemed to be so near that he could have reached out and touched its walls. No outside observer had ever been able to pinpoint its precise location, for the mere sight of it distorted the perceptions of the viewer. Its towers and battlements appeared to be fashioned of billowing smoke, with coils and currents of flame and darkness winding through it. In one instant it might seem to be close to one of the Bordering Cliffs; in the next, at an unimaginable distance across the boundless reaches of the Great Waste. Knowing this, the prince had planned his route with the remote assistance of an informant inside the castle.

In these troublous and uncertain times, with the Labyrinth World under greater threat than ever before, accurate information about the Lord of Desolation and his plans had become crucial to the Labyrinth's defense. The only problem, Pavarr reflected, was recognizing which piece of information was true. The High Council's secret agent inside the castle, an individual not personally known to Pavarr, was loyal to the Labyrinth, or so the High Council believed. Whether their belief matched reality was about to be put to the test.

Finally, as the *fadingweaven* began to wear off, Pavarr approached his destination. As he did so, the billows of smoke hardened into high, black iron walls, smooth as window glass and unmarked by chink or scar--unclimbable. But he kept on until he reached a place where two irregular projections of black wall came close together but did not quite meet. There he found a narrow, jagged opening, invisible until he stood directly in front of it. As per instruction, Pavarr slipped cautiously inside the opening and stopped, letting his eyes and ears become accustomed to the cancellation of visible light.

All senses on high alert, he frowned. *Too easy. Why is there no guard at the opening? Am I walking straight into a trap?* Without a whisper of metal against leather, he unsheathed the Dwarvian dagger at his belt and sank into a half-crouch, ready to run, dodge, or fight. And he waited.

The mysterious informant did not appear, not that Pavarr expected it. He would have to go farther inside before he met anyone, but he had no idea how far.

At first he heard nothing but the slithering of air currents along the castle's massive iron blocks, but soon the echo of his breathing told him that he was in a small passageway. It also told him that the passage made an abrupt right-angle turn an arm's length from the entrance.

As soon as his eyes had adjusted to the darkness enough to make out the shape of the wall's angle, he began following the passage into the fortress. Slowly, cautiously, he advanced, pausing at each turning.

An odor drifted under his nostrils, a sharp, acrid stench. He knew what it was--the toxic waters of the Saurian River, which cut its heavy course from the outer reaches of the Great Waste, circled near the Boundary Cliffs, and doubled back to tunnel underneath the fortress. The water stank of what it contained: the liquefied remains of ancient reptiles pressed to annihilation under millions of tons of rock. Saurian blood and bones had made the river, and the river stank of death.

The odor grew thicker as the prince pushed farther into it. He pulled up the scarf around his neck so that it covered his mouth and nose and filtered out some of the noxious haze.

The prince scanned every bit of the passageway carefully, but he didn't discover any branches off the main corridor. After a while he became conscious of a low, deep thrum of hidden engines vibrating the floor and walls of the passage--a sound almost beneath the level of human hearing. As the worn rock under his feet descended little by little, the thrum grew louder.

Pavarr's footsteps became slower and slower, and he halted often to take his bearings as best he could. He must be getting closer to the river: The odor alone told him that, as well as the downward incline of the passageway.

The High Council of Threshold Guardians, which had sent him on this mission, had long suspected that the present invasive evil in the Labyrinth World had its origin somewhere inside Castle Mormorion, but no one outside the Lord of Desolation's realm had any means of entry. Until now, that is, when the High Council had received an urgent message pleading for someone to come. The unknown agent whose code name was "Dweller in the Smoke" was both a servant of the Lord of Desolation and a spy for the High Council, but the agent's identity was secret from all but the Guardians.

The malodorous mist made his head swim and his eyes water. He stuffed more of the scarf into his mouth to muffle a cough and realized that he couldn't go on at this rate. Someone was bound to hear him. What if he went back to the entrance, sought another way inside? There must be other passages that led to the interior. The message he had received had told him only where he was to enter the castle, so the prince had assumed that once he was inside, the Dweller in the Smoke would find him.

He turned around to find his way back up the passage... but there was no way back up. The solid iron walls had closed silently behind him so that he could not even tell where the opening had been.

He had been led into a trap!

Inhaling foul fog from the underground river was sickening him with every breath he took. He understood the effects, but pressed on. Even if the passageway finally took him to the place where Ab'addon's engines of mass destruction were hidden, the prince reasoned that there'd have to be another exit, at least one for the machines themselves.

He continued stealthily along the passage. Looking over his shoulder, he saw that the walls continued to close behind him as he advanced. When he halted, they halted; when he started forward, so did they, in eerie silence, without the slightest scraping of metal against metal. He felt his way around the next angle--and froze in his tracks, stifling a sharp outcry before it escaped him.

The prince had reached the underground core of the castle. The passage he followed ended abruptly on a ledge high above a huge open pit. Beneath him the floor was covered with the menacing assemblage of the Lord of Desolation's factories, and he barely saved himself from plunging headfirst into it.

When he recovered, he glanced around the pit walls. They were honeycombed with numerous dark openings like the one where he stood. He took a step back, making sure he was in shadow. As far as he could tell, there were no guards in the other openings.

Far below him in the bottom of the pit, a square pool of Saurian fluid roiled around a dark metal object. The object, a domed cylinder, spun around as it pumped up and down, up and down. As it worked, it sent out currents of thick fumes. The low thrum was louder here.

No *wyrga* guards or slave-workers were in sight, but on the opposite side of the pool were three groups of cages. Straining to see through the gloom, Pavarr made out the shapes of human mortal forms in the one farthest away from him. They appeared to be naked, with no protection whatsoever from the swirling fumes. All of them wore iron collars locked around their necks. The cage was filled with them, some climbing the bars in an apparently desperate attempt to find a way out, others lying supine on the floor. Some clung to one another, shaking with fear, and others wandered around like sleepwalkers, aimlessly, stepping on or over bodies that lay in their way.

Pavarr recognized what the humans were from old rumors he had heard for years but never quite believed: They were the raw material from which the Lord of Desolation made his inhuman slaves.

-- 62 --

Saint Amber's Rose

The three groups of cages held subjects in various stages of transmutation. The farther cages held human mortals captured from lands outside the Great Waste. Their terror streamed invisibly from them; Pavarr felt it even at a distance. His heart ached for them; he would have helped them escape from their prison if he could, but the situation was impossible. *Wyrga* guards came and went at random, sometimes shoving more human victims inside the padlocked cages. Their captives made no outcry, for they had been tortured into complete dullness and were now nothing more than passive, limp forms, drugged and insensible. Only later, when they had awakened slowly into half-consciousness, did some of them sense what had happened. The luckier ones remained in a daze.

The second group of cages held those pitiful creatures that had begun to go through their terrible change. They were close enough that Pavarr could see their faces dimly through the turgid atmosphere--faces devoid of humanity, eyes empty of expression, glittering like glass pebbles. They were gray-skinned half-*wyrga*, prepared for their final transmutation. They walked around and around the cage in slow circles like automatons, mindless, never blinking, never touching one another for comfort or compassion's sake. Their souls had been cut out of them.

The third cage was empty.

"Prince," came a whispery breath on the back of his neck.

Pavarr's skin turned to ice. Not an instant too soon he realized who the whisperer must be and controlled his instinctive response, which was to spin around and slash upward with his double-edged dagger.

"If you'll come with me, sir," continued the voice. "And hurry, if you don't mind." Trusting the speaker because he had no other choice, the prince took a careful step backward and made a quarter-turn so that he saw both the cages in front and the entity behind him. The speaker wasn't a solid presence, but resembled a kind of whitish fog with human features.

The entity led him back toward the solid iron wall and walked through it. Seeing no door, Pavarr stopped an inch away from the wall. The entity, with an expression of chagrin, returned at once, grasped the prince's sleeve with a misty hand, and pulled him through.

"If you wish, we may converse now, Prince," the entity informed him when they reached the other side. "In this state we are invisible and inaudible to *wyrga*--and the others. And Lord Ab'addon is absent from the castle at present."

"How was that done, passing through an iron wall?" the prince asked, unable to contain his amazement as they walked swiftly through empty corridors, away from the dreadful pit.

"Quite easily, sir," replied the entity. "The atomic substrata contain a vast amount of empty space. We simply passed through the space, taking precautions to avoid solid particles."

"Ah," said the prince. "I should have known. I assume you are my informant?"

"Yes, sir," answering the last question. "Not at all, sir," answering the first. "I am a Wraith. We Wraiths, being of soluble substance, learn this method of travel at our mother's knee. My name is Gloom, Prince, also known as "Dweller in the Smoke". I am an indentured servant of the Lord of Desolation. I serve here under contract."

"You--contracted yourself to Ab'addon?"

"I was deceived, sir, wickedly deceived! But I did sign a contract. I passed my word of honor--"

"Then it's a fraudulent contract!" interrupted the prince. "Deceptive intent renders a contract invalid in any realm of the Labyrinth World!"

"Yes indeed, sir. But when a Wraith passes his word, under whatever circumstances, nothing can alter it. I assure you that my own brothers would tell you the same."

"Your brothers?"

"Grimtread, Dour, and Gall, of Ravenhome, Keeper's Inn, and the Abbey, respectively. I have not seen them since the last Age."

"The last Age!" exclaimed the prince. "That's over a thousand years ago! How long does your contract run?"

"Seven years, per the standard articles of indenture," replied the Wraith.

"Then--"

"Time does not run in this place as it does in the rest of the Labyrinth World, sir. Castle Mormorion is not even precisely *here,* even though it can be seen in the Desolate Lands, or the Great Waste, as it is called in the Labyrinth. Castle Mormorion is *out of time.* Lord Ab'addon commands time in this place, slowing or otherwise altering it at his will. Thus, only half my period of indenture has passed. I will not be free until the contract is fulfilled--or Lord Ab'addon defeated."

So speaking, they hurried through a maze of corridors, all identical, until even the prince, with all his tracking skills, wasn't sure that he could find his way out again. He hoped that Gloom wasn't planning to betray him. He reminded himself--again--that the Dweller in the Smoke was one of the Guardian Council's most trusted secret agents. But here, inside the fortress of the Lord of Desolation, Pavarr wondered what temptations--or threats--beset the long-indentured servant.

"Be very careful now, sir."

The darkness of another chamber opened like an abyss before them, and here the Wraith halted, barring Pavarr from entering. "Lord Ab'addon does not know that we are here," he whispered. "I thought it needful to show you this secret chamber first, for here is where he worships that which brought him into being. It is the source of his energy. Behold the Abomination of Desolation!"

The Wraith moved aside, and the prince looked beyond him into the enormous cavern. Its vault reached to an unguessable height, as if it were inside a hollow mountain. Currents of darkness swirled inside it, moaning like unquiet spirits. After a while, Pavarr made out a shape of something even darker, an immense, enthroned figure raised high above the floor. *A statue? No, an idol!* An idol made of gold--gold that glinted, not with light, but with a denser darkness. Its face had the semblance of humanity, but distorted, demonic, as if all that was bent and distorted in human nature were condensed here. And the face was the mirror-image of Pavarr's!

He couldn't tear his eyes away from it. Even though the thing radiated evil, it was, at the same time ... fascinating. . .

Pavarr hated the thing... *needed,* with every part of his being, to fall on his face before it, to abase himself utterly, to worship it, worship... himself!

The Power! The Dark Power!

Pavarr sensed the idol's awareness of him. It knew he was there, knew him, body and soul, better than he knew himself!

Is this how the Wraith planned to entrap him, give him over to the Enemy? The prince tried to take a step backward, away from the thing's influence, but found, looking down, that he had instead taken a step forward into the vaulted room. He stopped, frozen where he stood, wanting with a frightening intensity to crawl to its feet and embrace the monstrous thing, but prevented by a will greater than his own.

"You understand now, sir. Come this way."

Startled, then steadied by the feathery voice of the Wraith, Pavarr found himself pulled away from the chamber. Great drops of perspiration stood out on his forehead, and he panted for breath as if he had just run a long way, harder than he had ever run in his life.

"That thing... has *my face*," he gasped.

"It takes the image of anyone who looks upon it," replied the Wraith, hurrying them onward. "The Lord Ab'addon worships himself... and the adoration of one's own self makes monsters of us all."

"No one," added the Wraith when the shrine of evil was well behind them, "but the Lord of Desolation and his *wyrga* bodyguard have seen that abomination in the vaulted chamber. The High Council of Threshold Guardians does not know of the source of his power. I asked the High Council to send you here so that you may see for yourself what awaits all created beings if Lord Ab'addon is not stopped, driven back to his domain and sealed inside his fortress. Now I will show you how captured human mortals are made into *wyrga*."

"I have seen *wyrga* before--too often," muttered Pavarr, wiping his brow.

"Yes, but not how they are made. Do you realize that they are forged of human flesh, Saurian fluid, and iron?"

"I didn't until I saw those cages," replied the prince. "I had heard only rumors."

"Most rumors of Lord Ab'addon's doings are true," stated the Wraith, "but the truth is more terrible than any rumor. Here we are."

They stopped abruptly in front of another solid iron wall, impenetrable by ordinary means, but Pavarr now realized the Wraith's skill at maneuvering through sub-molecular structures.

"We will be invisible to the workers in this chamber. Their senses after full *wyrga* transmutation are very keen, unnaturally so, but they cannot detect activity at our vibratory level."

The Wraith put his filmy hand against the iron wall. Slowly the wall became transparent, as if the iron were changing first into liquid glass, then into air. A myriad tiny points of light darted and shimmered where the wall had been, or continued to be, and the prince understood that he was seeing what human mortals had only been able to imagine by means of mathematics: the atomic structure of solid objects. It seemed that the Wraith could not only see and traverse the space between atoms, but also was able under certain circumstances to transfer this ability to non-Wraiths.

"Now," said Gloom, "you may see how their transmutation takes place. Of all the evils the Lord of Desolation has generated, none is more ruinous than this. Look below!"

They stepped forward, standing invisibly on a high balcony overlooking a factory filled with gigantic machinery whose upper parts resembled dragons' heads. Dark, oily smoke circled around the room, bringing with it the same acrid odor Pavarr had smelled in the chamber of cages. Tanks of swirling black fluid separated one machine from the next, and each machine plunged its fanged mouth into the fluid at intervals, as if drinking from the tank.

A door opened on the opposite side of the room. Two *wyrga*-guards took stations beside it, and other *wyrga* behind them brought in a line of naked, gray-skinned human mortals--prisoners. Their faces were dull, expressionless, even though they must have seen what lay ahead of them.

The guards prodded the prisoners with iron-pointed sticks. Their prodding drew blood which trickled in small rivulets to the floor, but the prisoners seemed to feel nothing. They neither cried out nor tried to fight back.

The *wyrga*-guards herded the line of prisoners toward the dragon-heads. As each prisoner approached, a dragon-head bent down and opened its massive jaws. The prisoner walked forward into the monster's mouth; the jaws closed; the prisoner disappeared.

Every muscle in the prince's body tensed; his fingers gripped the handle of his Dwarvian-made dagger. He felt the uselessness of the gesture, for it was obvious that there was nothing to be done. He wished fervently that he had his Taraman warriors with him to destroy this place, free the prisoners, raze the castle to the ground... but all he could do was watch in horror.

"Wait," murmured the Wraith beside him. "Worse than this is coming."

After a moment a fitful reddish glow lit the dragon body from inside, and out of it came a scream like nothing the prince had ever heard before. It was agony in its purest, cruelest intonation. The excruciating torment in that cry leached the strength from Pavarr's muscles. Only by sheer force of will did he make his legs keep him standing.

"Why not kill them outright?" muttered the prince to himself. "Why torture them like that?" He clenched his jaw in rage.

The Wraith, well aware of the prince's revulsion, leaned toward him and whispered, "That is the last pain they will ever feel. Now they will be refashioned so that they are invulnerable to most weapons. Only to the Four Elements are they vulnerable, or to the severing of the single vein that pulses at the base of their skulls. Or to the Lord of Desolation himself, if he wishes to destroy what he has made."

Below them the misshapen dragon-head turned to the side. The cavernous jaws opened, its iron tongue extended, and something was spat out onto the uplifted hands of four entities, each masked and clothed in black from head to foot. The limp form looked like the corpse of the prisoner the machine had swallowed, but now the body was crushed, its bones broken, its spinal column shattered. And yet--it lived... breathed. Pavarr saw its pitiful, deformed chest rise--not much, but enough to signal life.

The four entities received the body and swung it onto a flat surface, anvil-shaped. Two more black-draped figures ranged themselves on either side of the body. One of them punctured an artery in the curve of the body's elbow. Blood began to flow into a trench along the side of the anvil, then into a system of pipes that led away from the dragon-heads. The other figure inserted the tip of a glass coil into a vein on the opposite wrist. Black fluid snaked into the body as red blood drained out.

When exsanguination was complete, two more cloaked and masked figures began to flay the skin and peel it back, then did the same to the musculature. Quickly they came to the splintered bones, which they extracted at unnatural speed. They replaced the bones with a metal endoskeleton and layered muscle and skin back over the helpless form. Then the two figures took up an iron exoskeleton glowing red with heat, and by some process that wasn't clear to Pavarr, welded it fast to the gray skin of the victim.

Now Pavarr realized why the Wraith Gloom had led him here, to the heart of the Lord of Desolation's domain. By some unnatural means Ab'addon had discovered a process of forcing an unholy marriage of intractable iron and human mortal flesh.

Two *wyrga* came to the anvil and roughly assisted the victim to stand and walk between them. They disappeared into the shadows where Pavarr could no longer see them. The dragon's-head spewed out another hapless prisoner, which the four slaves caught.

"Have you seen enough?" inquired the Wraith. Pavarr, sick with loathing at the sight, nodded.

"The process continues day and night, in this and many other places," said Gloom as they walked back through the sparkling wall and continued through sharply angled corridors. "New *wyrga* are made without ceasing--thousands of them. These new ones will be returned to the chamber of cages until the trainers are ready for them. Then they will be taught to obey, fight, and kill as slaves of the Lord of Desolation.

"Ab'addon has forged an army far larger than the Guardian Council realizes. He has sent numerous patrols past the Bordering Cliffs into Labyrinth lands. They are small patrols, and can keep themselves well hidden. Wherever they go, the Ashes of Waste go with them, making the earth they tread forever desolate.

"I cannot escape my servitude here, but you, Prince Pavarr, can return to tell the High Council how *wyrga* are being made. The Labyrinth realms must raise a matching force! They must push the Lord of Desolation and his armies back to the Great Waste, or every mortal being in the Labyrinth will face the fate of those unfortunate captives.

"Lord Ab'addon will be back soon," concluded Gloom. "I sense all his movements. Be cautious in your going, for he is quick to discern the traces of an intruder, even the least remnant of heat from a human mortal body. Prince Pavarr, I ask you--I beg you--tell the High Council what you have seen, or the Labyrinth World is doomed!"

"I will do so," promised the prince as Gloom led him to an arrow-slit between two walls on the other side of the castle, too narrow for any human mortal to pass through it.

"And," added the Wraith, "if you meet any of my brothers, would you be so kind as to mention that you've seen me?"

He touched the sleeve of the prince's shirt and gave Pavarr a slight push forward. The iron wall dissolved into black space beset with darting points of light. Pavarr slipped between the lights and through the arrow-slit, and was gone.

-- 69 --

Outside, the terrain was exactly as on the other side of the palace: flat, empty, colorless. But here, Castle Mormorion appeared to be closer to the Bordering Cliffs than the place where Pavarr had left the forest. As soon as he was safely out of the palace, the prince began to cloak himself in *fadingweaven*, for there was no cover in the Great Waste, and he would be in utmost danger until he reached the shelter of the trees.

He had started for Castle Mormorion in daylight--if day it could be called, for the sky over the Great Waste was a continuous, unremitting gray glare with neither cloud nor glimpse of sun. Now it was night, unmarked by stars or moon. The gray glare simply darkened until the Waste was black. Guided only by his keen internal sense of orientation, the prince alternately walked and ran in a zigzag pattern toward the nearest cliff and began to climb up its broken side.

He had taken only a few steps into a narrow defile when a soft word arrested him in his tracks.

"Sir! O sir!" pleaded a voice, tremulous and desperate.

A woman, surely, and nearby!

"If you are human and mortal, help us!"

The prince spun around, hand to dagger, eyes searching the darkness. "Who's there?" he demanded. "Show yourself!" *Who could have seen me in the dark, under* fadingweaven?

"Here, sir," replied the voice. Pavarr peered at the base of the cliff. Gradually, two human forms took shape, sheltering beside a heap of boulders. One, a man, was lying on the ground; the other, a woman, knelt beside him, cradling his head in her arms. Both were naked, with no scrap of cloth to cover themselves and nothing to protect their feet from the sharp-edged grit of the Waste.

"How did you come here? Is your man hurt?" Pavarr spoke more sharply than he intended because he was angry with himself for having been caught off guard.

"He--he is badly hurt," said the woman, with a catch in her voice. "They did it--the *wyrga*, at the castle. We are supposed to be gray-skins, the second stage of transmutation, only they made a mistake with Vord, my husband, and didn't finish changing him into *wyrga*. They threw him out into the Waste, as they do with all the captives they ruin, but the Wraith helped me escape to be with him. We ran this far, and then Vord collapsed. He--he needs water, or he'll die. We'll both die. Please, sir, help us--"

The woman had moved closer to Pavarr, begging him on her knees, and now she bowed down, touching her head to his foot in supplication. Her long, tangled hair covered her back, and her wasted body shook with sobs.

Pavarr had no lack of compassion, but as a seasoned warrior, he was wary of any unexpected occurrence. He made no move to touch the woman, but unhooked the water flask from his belt and cautiously put it down beside her, waiting to see what she would do.

With a startled outcry she grabbed the flask and scuttled back to her husband, who in her absence had begun to moan weakly and turn his head restlessly from side to side. The woman put the tip of the flask to his lips and let a few drops trickle out to moisten the man's mouth. As soon as the water touched his parched skin, he opened his mouth for more. Little by little she gave him the water, to let his body absorb it gradually. Only when the flask was nearly empty did she take a drink herself. Then she looked up at Pavarr, eyes shining with gratitude.

"Grace be with you, sir," she whispered.

Pavarr remained where he was. He was beginning to believe the woman's story, but his instincts told him not to get within reach, at least until he found out more about them. Keeping his eye on them, he searched in his knapsack and found a few dry crumbs of elven-made journeybread. He held them out to the woman to see if she would take them, for according to elven-lore, any being with a devious heart would be repulsed by an elven-made wafer.

She crawled forward again and eagerly received the wafer crumbs in her cupped palms, then returned to her husband. She fed them one by one to the man, whose mouth moved slowly as he ingested them. Soon one of his eyes opened--the other was a mass of dried black blood--and looked back at the prince with an unfathomable expression.

"He saved us, Vord!" the woman told him, her voice filling with excitement. "We can go home now, back to our people!"

"Help... up," gasped the man, and his wife put her arm around his back. He leaned against her and struggled upright. The prince took a step toward them, but held himself back, his years of experience tempering his natural impulse.

At last the man stood straight, gripping his wife's arm to keep his balance as he swayed on his feet. His body was gray-skinned, but he had terrible slash-marks where the skin had been partially flayed from his body. Bloodstains running down his torso and legs looked black as swamp-oil in the shadow of the cliff.

"My thanks, Prince of Taraman!" he rasped, the breath rattling harshly in his lungs.

Pavarr tensed. Even though the two people before him seemed unlikely to do him any harm, his hand stole toward his dagger.

"How do you know who I am?" he demanded. "And how can you see me?"

"When they make us into... gray-skins... they give us vision that... penetrates *fadingweaven* spells," the man replied, panting for breath between words. "I knew you for... the Prince of Taraman... by the... light... around you."

"Hush, my love," the woman interrupted him urgently. "We have a long way to go. You must save your strength."

But her husband pushed her away gently until he stood alone, struggling to keep his balance, but with an odd, determined expression on his ruined features.

"Prince, I beg you... do one more thing for us... Take my wife... to our home village... in Threshold Forest... It is not far."

"Vord!" protested the woman. "Not without you!"

"Ildranna, you must... go!" the man said, and put his hand up, motioning her away from him. "You carry... our child!"

"I will get you both out," said the prince, his voice softening. "We will find a way."

"No!" said the man in as close to a shout as he could get. "Understand this, Prince: The *wyrga*... took me further through their... deadly process... than they took my wife . . . She can... recover. I... cannot. Please... take Ildranna with you... and kill me!"

"NO!" screamed the woman, and reached toward her husband. "No! I love you! I won't go without you!"

Pavarr took another step toward them. "Both of you," he said firmly. "I will take you on my back, Vord."

The man seemed all at once to grow bigger and heavier. Thick black fluid streamed from his empty, crusted eye socket, his head drew down between his shoulders, and he sank to a half-crouch.

"I am... *wyrga* now," he growled. "Save her, Prince... and kill me... or I will kill you!"

Vord sprang at Pavarr, his open mouth revealing rows of sharp fangs. He struck at Pavarr's jugular vein, but the prince sidestepped like lightning and drew his dagger at the same instant. The half-*wyrga* snapped at the prince's shoulder, tearing a great red wound in the flesh. Blood poured out. The monster clawed wildly at his enemy's body, but the prince held him off.

In a flash it was over. The half-*wyrga* tired almost at once and collapsed heavily against the prince. Pavarr sliced his razor-edged dagger through the pulsing vein at the base of the other's skull, then pushed the half-*wyrga* away.

Vord fell backward onto the Great Waste. His life fled. With a shriek of utter despair his wife rushed to him and flung herself across the supine body.

In shock, the prince staggered back against the cliff face. Dizzy from loss of blood, he wondered how he could manage to bury Vord's body. Vord deserved no less from the Prince of Taraman.

He did not wonder long. As he tore a piece of cloth from his shirt to staunch the bleeding, he spotted long, undulant lines in the distance under the surface of the Waste, slithering rapidly toward him. Horrified, he realized that he couldn't move fast enough to get away, not at the speed they were traveling. Between one breath and the next they would reach him...

Only they weren't heading toward him, but toward the body. The lines stopped, and two monstrous, pulsating heads lifted out of the ground. They were Ash-*vrom*, wormlike beings of the Great Waste, so rarely seen that their very existence was in dispute. It was rumored that they were implacably hostile to mortal creatures, and their function was to rid the Great Waste of any living thing that ventured upon it. Only by constant movement was it possible to avoid detection by the *vrom*, who responded to minute changes in temperature and pressure in their vast dwelling-place.

The two eyeless *vrom*-heads stared at Pavarr, and their probing energies swept across him. Trapped, he held his breath and didn't move--but for only an instant. Forcing his remaining strength into one motion, he dashed to Ildranna and pulled her back with him to the shelter of the cliff.

Charleynne Gates

As suddenly as they had materialized, the *vrom* dived back into the Waste, leaving a deep hole behind them. Vord's lifeless corpse slid into the hole and disappeared. Undulant lines serpentined back across the Great Waste.

Pavarr realized he might be very near death, for the half-*wyrga*'s fangs had bitten deeply into flesh and muscle and likely carried poison. He could not stay here; he had to move, to get out of this place lest the *vrom* come back for him. And now he had to take the woman with him, who in her grief and fatigue sagged against the cliff. She made no outcry but shuddered in every limb, moaning softly, her hair covering her face. Using his one good hand, Pavarr dragged his blood-spattered mantle from his shoulder and gave it to her.

With an effort he turned again toward the cliff, searching with dimming vision for a way up the defile of tumbled boulders. Looking back at the Waste for signs that the *vrom* might return, he saw, out of the corner of his eye, a glimmering of light in the shape of her husband as he once was--a fully human mortal. The light danced above the place where the body had disappeared--and then it was gone.

"Vord!" breathed the woman, seeing it too. Her eyes shone with mingled anguish and joy. "Farewell, my love!" she whispered. Then she stood up straight and turned to go with Pavarr, and never looked back.

The prince didn't remember afterward how they managed to climb up the cliff together, but somehow they made their way under the cover of Threshold Forest before he collapsed. Firemark found them there, exactly where the horse had anticipated. Nosing his friend's prone form, Firemark scented violence, blood, toxins, and the unfamiliar essence of creatures he could not identify. Tearing some dark brown leaves from a nearby bush, the horse chewed them until they were mashed, then let the wet pulp drip onto the prince's wounded shoulder.

At first, seeing the great horse coming up to them without hesitation, Ildranna backed away and crouched at the base of a tree. But then she realized what the horse was doing and edged closer to Pavarr. A skilled healer among her own people, she drew back the torn cloth from the prince's wound and smoothed the pulp across it expertly. Then she bandaged his shoulder with the ragged strips and covered him with a blanket from Firemark's saddlebag. The horse watched her with calm brown eyes, understanding that the woman was helping his friend.

-- 74 --

Saint Amber's Rose

Blood stopped flowing from the wound. Pavarr did not regain consciousness, but his body relaxed and he passed into a deeper sleep. Ildranna clothed herself in some of Pavarr's spare garments, then, wrapping another blanket around her shoulders, she lay down beside the prince.

Firemark whickered; a breeze wove through the trees above the prince and Ildranna. Yellow and crimson leaves showered over them, keeping them warm and camouflaged as Pavarr and the woman succumbed to utter exhaustion. The horse stood guard, grazing occasionally, using his inborn skills to melt unobtrusively into his woodland surroundings.

Firemark blew out a long breath and shook his head. He was as devoted to the prince as Pavarr was to him, but he sometimes wondered at the propensity of human mortals to venture into hostile environments. Life with the prince was never dull, but at times it seemed they sped from one hazardous situation right into another. Horses had more sense.

Once in a while Firemark wished his friend would settle down, give him some little princes and princesses to bounce on his broad back. He would teach them how to ride as well as their father.

But that would have to keep. For now... sometimes all a friend can do is stand by and be patient.

Charleynne Gates

Chapter Five

The Black Mirror

A branch deep in the wood around the Mort-Mire cracked loudly under the weight of a nocturnal animal stepping on it. The iron bands that Oliver Medley thought were shackling his arms and legs suddenly snapped. His lungs, which had refused to function in the first seconds of shock, released, and he inhaled a wheezing gasp of swampy air. He broke out of his frozen posture and began to run in tight little circles beside the car, frantically calling "Cousin Flavia! Cousin Flavia!" but the Mort-Mire smothered his cries in its dense atmosphere.

At last his spurt of adrenaline ran out. He stopped, panting with the unaccustomed exertion. Vapor from his breath condensed into a cloud. A sudden silence descended, in which only the sullen trickle of muddy water through the marsh could be heard, with the occasional soft belch from a darlingtonia that had dined too well.

With an exasperated sigh, Great-Aunt Belvedine re-folded herself into the automobile. "You might as well stop that nonsense, Medley," she said in disgust. "Flavia's gone. Get back in the car."

But he didn't hear her, for a belated thought struck him. He ran to the rear compartment of the car and threw it open. There, neatly folded, was Flavia's silver chair.

Oliver stared down at it. Flavia couldn't have gotten out of the vehicle by herself. If she had fallen out, they would have found her somewhere near the car. She wouldn't have been able to move very far without her chair.

A horrible realization came to him. The only possibility left was unthinkable, but it had to be the solution.

Abducted. Flavia had been taken against her will. Somehow, in that blinding freak blizzard, a malefactor had managed to get into the car by the door that Oliver had opened despite Great-Aunt Belvedine's warning. Great-Aunt Belvedine had made the same mistake: They had inadvertently left both passenger doors open. Neither of them had been able to see or hear anything while the wind was howling and snow was piling its drifts as high as the car doors. That was when Flavia had been taken by someone or something unimaginable. And now the snow had melted into the ground, taking with it footprints or clues of any kind.

The weight of a grim gray mountain of guilt descended on Oliver's shoulders as his newly-acquired self-confidence crumpled like rotten scaffolding. "*YOUR FAULT!*" his conscience accused. "*IT'S ALL YOUR FAULT!*"

And it was. Scarcely an hour ago he had solemnly pledged his lifelong loyalty to the Lady Flavia, and now he had proved himself worse than useless at the first sign of trouble, leaving her alone and vulnerable to a fate he couldn't begin to comprehend. Bowed with shame, he trudged wearily back to the automobile and climbed into his seat.

"Medley! What do you think you're doing?" demanded Great-Aunt Belvedine. "Sit in front!"

He stared at her uncomprehendingly.

"You're going to have to drive!" she stated.

"Drive?" he sputtered. "What about Cousin Flavia? We can't just leave her here in this swamp! Besides, the car has broken down! We can't go anywhere!"

"Medley," Great-Aunt Belvedine said sternly, "you must face the fact that there is no use our staying, because Flavia is not here. And the longer we remain in the Mire, the greater the danger to ourselves. We must go on to Keeper's Inn. The Keepers will know what to do. It's our only chance of finding her alive. Now get in the front seat and start the car!"

Unwillingly but without further protest, Oliver took the driver's seat and began to examine the unfamiliar dashboard. "It won't work," he muttered rebelliously. "It's dead. It can't work." But after a minute he figured he might be able to start the engine if it still had any life. Great-Aunt Belvedine sounded so authoritative, he thought the thing just might turn over.

He tried the ignition, expecting no response, but at once the automobile purred into life as if nothing had been wrong with it at all. Its headlights shined straight into the patch of pale darlingtonia.

Following Great-Aunt Belvedine's directions, Oliver managed to turn around in the confined space with the merest maximum of jerks, stops, and starts. At last they faced the road that had led them into the Mire, really only a couple of ruts in the mud. Cautiously he proceeded back along it, craning his head over the steering wheel to follow it as best he might.

The ruts ran out after a few yards, and once again they were left in darkness. *Now what?* thought Oliver. *We're still in the Mire. I don't know how to get out.* On impulse, he strained to see out the opposite window if the face might still be visible across the darlingtonia patch. It wasn't.

"Great-Aunt Bel—" he ventured.

"Don't expect any help from me," she rasped. "If you'd done what you were told in the beginning—but of course you wouldn't listen to me. Now look where we are!"

This blatantly unfair piece of criticism fired Oliver with an unexpected spurt of rebellion. "Now *you* look, Great-Aunt Belvedine," he began in a tone of voice utterly foreign to his normal mode of address. The desired effect was rather spoiled by the fact that in turning around his elbow inadvertently hit the horn, which gave forth a trumpet blast that could have raised the dead, had any been lingering in the vicinity. At once a legion of Mire-birds arose from their roosts and fled, screaming, to the skies.

"Now see what you've done," Great-Aunt Belvedine commented acidly.

Suddenly a very large raven separated itself from the terrified flock and landed on the hood of the Silver Ghost. It glared through the windshield into Oliver's face. It did not look happy at having its slumber so rudely interrupted.

"It's a Guide, Medley," said Great-Aunt Belvedine, "from the Raven Express Messenger and Guide Service, by its badge. You'd better follow it if you ever want to leave this malodorous swamp, in which you have caused nothing but trouble."

Oliver could not think of an appropriate reply. He tried the engine again, found that it turned over, and followed the bird meekly. It led him in an entirely different direction from where they had come in, over a route that meandered, dipped, climbed, and meandered again until Oliver was even more disoriented than before. But in only a short time they arrived back at the Old Straight Track, well beyond the fallen oak. It looked like a broad highway compared with the ruts into the Mort-Mire.

Here the raven left them. "Nevermore!" it signed off, sounding about as disgusted as any bird could.

Great-Aunt Belvedine said nothing for a while, for which Oliver was thankful. He became accustomed enough to the controls that he could let part of his mind revert to the central problem: How could Flavia have disappeared in the space of only a minute or two in that howling blizzard?

As if she had been reading his mind, Great-Aunt Belvedine spoke up. "Mildrith will know what happened to Flavia, Medley. I hope you realize that Mildrith did not cause the snowstorm in the Mort-Mire."

"Mil!" exclaimed Oliver. "I never thought she did! How could the *Foressa* have caused a blizzard like that?"

"Mildrith does Weather," replied Great-Aunt Belvedine. "One of her fields of expertise--she has many--is the design and implementation of software for the control of Weather in the immediate environment."

"'Control'?" Oliver echoed. "You don't mean 'control,' do you, Great-Aunt Belvedine? You must mean 'forecast'."

"I meant just exactly what I said, Oliver Medley," retorted Great-Aunt Belvedine. "I always mean what I say and say what I mean. It is a trait which you would do well to emulate." She shut her large jaw with a crocodilian snap.

Oliver retreated back into silence and thought about many things as he stared into the path that the headlights made through the darkness.

Back at Ravenhome, and as he sat beside Flavia in the Rolls Royce, he had accepted everything that was happening to him as perfectly plausible. When Flavia was near, he desired only to believe in the reality of her world, but now, alone except for his disagreeable relative, reality seemed to be receding. The idea of anyone being able to control weather with a laptop computer was a little too fantastic for him to swallow.

But every thought led him inexorably back to his overwhelming sense of guilt. If he hadn't opened the car door, hadn't run out into the Mire looking for a face he was sure he had seen, leaving the door wide open and Flavia vulnerable... He was relieved that the interior of the automobile was so dark that Great-Aunt Belvedine couldn't see the flush that began at the back of his neck and spread over his face, or the single tear that trickled from the corner of his eye.

It was *my fault.* How could he have failed, so easily and so soon in their acquaintance, the Lady to whom he had promised his loyalty, his life, and--unbeknownst to her--his love?

For who could know Flavia and not love her?

Great-Aunt Belvedine said nothing further until the vehicle caught up with Mil and Old Auldie, who were walking steadily eastward. Old Auldie matched Mil's long, strong stride step for step, showing no sign of fatigue at all. Mil had her laptop slung on the ammo belt and tapped at it occasionally with one hand. Even though the night was densely dark and a fine mist of rain drizzled steadily down, the two of them seemed to be walking inside a shell of some kind, for a dim light glowed around them and they appeared to be perfectly dry.

Oliver surrendered the controls to Old Auldie with considerable relief. Mil slid into the front passenger seat again, and the chauffeur put the car in gear.

"Do not blame yourself, Friend Oliver," Mil told him. "There are things going on that you do not understand." She was about to face front again, but stopped and looked at Oliver. "Flavia is in great danger, but she lives."

They knew! Somehow, they knew what had happened without being informed. The fantastic idea occurred to him that they might even have expected it. *But how is that possible?* Was this some kind of conspiracy with which he had innocently become involved?

He wanted to explain, confess, accuse--he didn't know which, but when he opened his mouth, Great-Aunt Belvedine caught his eye and gave him a piercing glance. He held his tongue.

No one said anything further. Old Auldie drove ahead. Mil continued to tap her keyboard. Great-Aunt Belvedine stared out her window into the midnight forest. Oliver huddled into as small a corner as he possibly could and pressed his forehead against the cold window glass. *Is Flavia out there alone in the dark? Is she in the hands of her abductors? Or--despite what Mil said--her murderers?*

He felt sick.

Saint Amber's Rose

After what seemed like hours, the automobile emerged from the wood bordering the Mort-Mire onto a road that sloped upward by gentle degrees onto a level plain. The sky was clear above them; by starlight Medley made out a broad valley of open land punctuated by dark trees in orchard rows. Little lights winked at intervals across the valley floor, probably from farmhouses. In the sky was a pattern of stars he did not recognize.

"That constellation's called the Watcher," Mil informed him, reading his thought. "It's a signal: The heavens mark what is done here. Never doubt it."

Shortly afterward their vehicle drove through a crossroads, on each side of which was a pillar of about Oliver's height with its top carved into the likeness of a helmeted head. The headlights showed wreaths of fresh flowers twined about each pillar.

"Those are Herms," Mil commented. "Very old. The folk round about drape them with flowers, or garlands of holly in the winter, to keep away *wyrga.*"

Does it work? Oliver wondered, but did not ask.

Soon they passed through an avenue of tall poplars, then under a stone archway. A looming dark mass in front of them resolved itself into a compound of buildings. *Keeper's Inn,* the sign creaking in the breeze proclaimed. A silver key inserted in a lock of antique pattern was painted under the name.

"I wish to say one more thing," said Great-Aunt Belvedine, abruptly breaking into Oliver's thoughts. "And then I shall be silent on the matter. I disagree with you, Mildrith. This entire situation IS Medley's fault. IF he had read the letter--which I sent him by special messenger, mind you--WHEN he received it, and had acted upon its instructions, then we might have left Ravenhome long before the storm forced us into the Mort-Mire. The *Sendara* would be safe with us, and the complications we are about to encounter could have been avoided altogether."

Oliver wished that darkness would cover him, or that he could hide in a small cave somewhere and never come out.

Mil shook her head. "Some things are meant to be," she said calmly, and shut her laptop with a decisive click.

Old Auldie pulled the Rolls Royce into a cobblestone courtyard in front of the inn and disengaged the engine. At once lanterns blazed

Charleynne Gates

out in the darkness, and a cluster of attendants ran smartly up and opened the car doors. The chief attendant assisted Great-Aunt Belvedine to dismount, while Mil slid smoothly out of her seat and Oliver hastily clambered out the rear door.

Mil bent down to the driver's window and whispered something in the chauffeur's ear, of which Oliver caught only "Alert the--". After an attendant removed Flavia's chair from the rear compartment, Old Auldie steered the automobile to its berth in the stable, surrounded by admiring grooms.

What is this place? Oliver wondered. The night air was quite cool, and a draft whisked inside his shirt collar and down his spine. He shivered and tried to pretend that he hadn't.

The massive main doors of the inn burst open, and a crash of light and noise spilled out to the courtyard. A gigantic silhouette, black against the background of yellow light, emerged from the building and ran toward them like a bull in full charge--a huge, thunder-footed man, with a beard as thick as a thornbush and arms like tree trunks. His heavy boots pounded on the paving like drums.

I'm going to die now, thought Oliver, irrationally but understandably, realizing that there was no time to move out of the giant's way before the impending crash.

But the man stopped short in front of Mil, muscular arms akimbo. He grinned broadly, showing dazzling white teeth in the middle of the black beard. "You are welcome, *Foressa*," he said in a voice amazingly gentle to be issuing from such a rough-hewn body. "And Madame de Montfort," bowing briefly to Great-Aunt Belvedine, who nodded back.

"Keeper," she acknowledged stiffly.

"And you, Friend," the man added, looking at Oliver. "You are welcome to my inn." His black eyes seemed to stare right through Oliver in a most disconcerting manner.

"This is my great-nephew, Oliver Medley," Great-Aunt Belvedine pronounced. "Medley, our host, Jon Keeper. This is his hostelry." Oliver bowed, but Great-Aunt Belvedine went right on before he could reply. "Amatilda is here, I trust? She knows what has befallen us?"

Saint Amber's Rose

The innkeeper's smile vanished; his face became solemn. "Aye. She awaits you now. Come in, if you will. It is best that we not stand outside to speak of these matters."

With a gesture of his brawny arm, the innkeeper indicated the broad double doors, which had shut again. Oliver saw a woman standing on a stone step in front of the doors. She held a candlestick with a flaming taper, and by its light he saw that she was tall and slender, with smooth golden hair bound back under a white cap and a pale, oval face. Her expression was neither sad nor smiling, but her presence radiated serenity, and Oliver felt reassured before she had spoken a word.

"Merry meet," the woman spoke as they approached her. "Fear not the night, but come in quickly." Then she turned as one of the great doors opened behind her, and led them inside the inn. Mil followed first, then Great-Aunt Belvedine. Oliver hesitated for half a second, wondering--doubting--where this strange excursion was to take him next. If it were not for Flavia... and his vow...

The heavy doors began to swing shut. Oliver took the last step with a little bound, reaching the opening just in time. Holding his breath to make himself smaller, he squeezed into the narrowing space and stumbled across the threshold. Behind him, the doors closed solidly. A heavy oaken bar fell into place across them, and he was locked inside.

But there was no time to think about that, for no sooner had he crossed the threshold than his senses were assaulted by a burst of light, heat, noise, and delicious aromas of roasting and baking. They had entered a great hall, an enormous room as long as the inside of a cathedral and as broad as two barns put together. He couldn't even see where the room ended because steam from hot food drifted over innumerable wooden tables and benches. People crowded around them, dozens, perhaps hundreds of people laughing, talking, eating, drinking, and singing at the top of their voices. The sudden tumult smote Oliver's ear like an orchestra of cymbals clashing together at the same time.

Perspiring servitors in medieval garb scurried among the tables, bearing trays laden with foaming pewter tankards, bowls of hearty stews, plates of round brown loaves of bread with chunks of golden butter melting down their sides, and baskets of leeks, onions, radishes, turnips, rutabagas, and other winter vegetables. Every table had heaping displays of crimson apples, yellow pears, roasted acorns and chestnuts, purple grapes ripe to bursting, berries gleaming like jewels of the night, and stoneware pitchers from which thick cream poured like folds of satin.

A cavernous fireplace that a man could walk into and stand upright held a roaring fire under three huge black cauldrons all bubbling busily, and spits upon which roasting fowl turned slowly and dripped hissing hot fat into basting pans. Oliver inhaled it all and discovered that he was extremely hungry.

But they had no opportunity to stop for refreshment, for the tall woman led them at a rapid pace, threading among the tables over the rush-strewn floor. Surprisingly, only a few of the revelers seemed to notice their passage.

The cacophony of sound gradually revealed itself as a drinking song sung by tuneless but cheerful voices. Over and over they belted out the words of a refrain punctuating a string of verses. The terrific din, made even worse by the singers keeping time by banging their tankards on the tables, made it difficult to understand what was being sung, but after the eighth or ninth repetition Oliver managed to catch most of it.

> *Pass the cup and fill it up!*
> *St. Bran and St. Amber and lay me down under!*
> *Give us a bite and a bone to sup!*
> *Remember St. Amber and sever the Sunder!*

"It's the Eve of Saint Bran of the Ravens," the tall woman called over her shoulder as they progressed through the tumult of revelers bellowing for more food for their trenchers and more brew for their tankards, and the spark and crackle of the hearthfire as logs split open and crashed into the grate. "They're singing an old riddle song," she continued, "part of a much longer saga, mostly forgotten now. No one knows what it means any more, but it's always sung on Saint Bran's Eve."

Must be a theme restaurant, Oliver thought as he caught glimpses of the inn's clientele. In fact, the place might well have been a movie studio, for he saw costumes of many different historical periods and national entities. At one table three men stood up and saluted their hostess with elaborate flourishes of their plumed hats. They were dressed down to the last detail in seventeenth-century French military uniform. *Gascon musketeers!* Oliver thought he recognized D'Artagnan--or was it Cyrano de Bergerac?

Across the room a party of four knights in armor clanked in, followed by their retinues of squires and pages, and lowered themselves creakily onto a bench already occupied by two Iroquois sachems who stared silently into the distance and puffed meditatively on long pipes. They took no notice whatsoever of their knightly neighbors.

At the next table, seated across from three silk-clad Mandarins, were two powdered and pompadour'd ladies with décolletages so low it was scarcely worth the bother. They gossiped intently over their fans. Absorbed in scandal, they did no more than glance at the party as they passed, but in those glances the measuring eye gathered all the information necessary. When Oliver passed by them, they saw him; he felt their stares go through and through him. For one unforgettable instant he met their brilliant, experienced eyes and knew an undeniable shiver of attraction coupled with an acute sense of danger. *Aristocracy of the Court of Versailles!* Women of power whose lightest word breathed in a royal ear could raise a man to dizzying heights of favor or plunge a nation into war. The nearness of that pair of peeresses made him very nervous. He hastened after the others.

At last, to his relief, their leader reached the opposite side of the room and entered a darker corridor. Immediately they were enveloped in gloom as they went under heavy beams darkened with smoke from torches, now unlit, fastened in sconces on the stone walls. Only their leader's taper candle let them see where they were going, but its elongated flame also made trembling shadows on walls and ceilings-- shadows that seemed to reach out for them, then scurry away.

Fortunately for Oliver's nerves, their hostess soon ushered them into a room totally dark except for a faint gleam that came from high, narrow windows. She closed the door behind them, abruptly cutting off the racket from the Great Hall.

Mil, Oliver, and Great-Aunt Belvedine stayed in the entry as Amatilda went swiftly around the room lighting candles, after which she went out the door again. As each candle burst into a tiny flame, Oliver saw that the room was a large library. Bookshelves lined the walls, each filled--untidily, he was sorry to see--with piles of books, most of them looking quite antique. Unable to help himself, he went to the shelves and wandered along their rows. The book-lover in him yearned, but he doubted that he'd have a chance to examine the volumes. Given his recent experience, he figured they'd soon be hurrying off somewhere else.

As the candles illumined the room, Oliver realized that it held not only books but also many curiously-carved birds of prey made by some unidentified artistic genius. They were painted in such a lifelike manner that he thought at first they were alive until he saw that their intimidating poses were frozen in place.

One carving, a great horned owl (*Bubo virginianus*), perched in the most natural manner upon a wooden rod above a large porcelain cachepot filled with white-spotted foliage. The owl had incredibly minute detailing, from the tufts of feathers above its half-shut golden eyes to the black talons that gripped its foothold. Fascinated, Oliver went to examine it more closely and observed that the bird was painted so perfectly he was almost certain he saw its chest feathers move as it breathed.

"Whooo are you?" said the bird softly, opening its eyes to their full-moon extent. Oliver gasped and stepped backward.

"Medley!" Great-Aunt Belvedine interrupted her low-voiced conversation with Mil. "Where are your manners! Hera Vespasia," she addressed the owl, "may I present to your notice my great-nephew, whose disastrous sense of propriety has brought us to this pass. Her Excellency Hera Vespasia, Great Chief of the *Norrengild*, Medley, of which even you have no doubt heard."

Oliver had no idea what a *Norrengild* might be, but thought it best not to say so under the circumstances. He removed his hat and bowed to the owl, who slowly lowered and raised her eyelids. "How do you do?" he managed through dry lips.

"Quite well, I thank you," replied the Great Chief in a feathery voice.

"Stop dawdling and come to the table, Medley," commanded Great-Aunt Belvedine. "Sit down. Amatilda will return directly. We shall have to make our plans as we eat; we have only a few more minutes of midnight left to us. Ah! Here is Amatilda. Medley, stand up."

Saint Amber's Rose

He obediently stood up as Great-Aunt Belvedine performed a perfunctory introduction. "Sit down, Medley. Why must I tell you everything?"

Mistress Keeper smiled serenely at him and nodded at the two servitors who followed her. One of them set three cups of hot soup, three thin slices of brown bread barely scraped with butter, and three small glasses of red wine before the travelers. The other servitor went with a covered tray to the owl's perch.

"I know you must be hungry after your night's journey, but I can serve you only this slight refreshment until we have looked into the Black Mirror. A heavier meal would dull your senses. Grace be with all," she ended, and sat in the fourth place at table.

"Grace be with all," replied Mil, Great-Aunt Belvedine, and Hera Vespasia together.

"Grace be with all," Oliver murmured last of all. The two servitors left the room with their empty trays.

For the next few minutes the three occupied themselves with sipping and crunching. The delicious, if miniscule, portions of soup and bread warmed him and relieved the tension he had unconsciously borne since Great-Aunt Belvedine's dramatic appearance in his office back in... . The name escaped him, doubtless due to travel fatigue.

Once--and only once--he glanced at Hera Vespasia, but quickly averted his eyes as the owl consumed a whole roast field mouse laid out with a decorative sprig of thyme in its mouth. Regrettably, he didn't turn away fast enough to miss the view of the rodent's tail dangling out of her beak. The sight reminded him that no matter how human-like an animal may seem, in the end the animal usually prefers to follow the customs of its own kind.

"We discourage our young from attempting to imitate human nature," Hera Vespasia later explained to him. "We feel there's no future in it."

When they finished, "Friends," said Amatilda, her voice like light shining through crystal, "Hera Vespasia told us this morning what her Owl Guard has discovered. I think we ought to hear this before we make further plans."

The owl spoke from her perch on the back of Amatilda's chair. "Threshold Forest has been penetrated."

Mil and Great-Aunt Belvedine froze in place, Mil with her wineglass halfway to her lips, Great-Aunt Belvedine about to take the last bite of her bread. "No!" Great-Aunt Belvedine whispered.

"I did not know they had come so far," said Mil, and downed the remainder of her wine in one swallow. "We must make even greater haste."

"Captain Ferronce spoke with Pavarr," the owl resumed. "He says that *wyrga* have made two inroads on the western border of Threshold Forest. Seventeen of the Alconta trees were cut down, and marks of Ab'addon's engines were found in the area. The trees were crushed where they stood, useless to anyone and disastrous for the shade-loving plants beneath it. He told the captain to bring us the news immediately."

"I cannot believe it!" Great-Aunt Belvedine gasped. "Not the Alcontas? Unmatched for beauty! Where were the border guards?"

"Pavarr believed they were lured away, possibly killed, and their bodies thrown to the *vrom* in the Great Waste," Hera Vespasia replied. "He found no sign of them."

"Where is Pavarr now?" Mil asked, an edge to her voice.

"He will be with us when the Council is held, three nights hence," answered Amatilda. "The journey from Taraman is... more difficult than it used to be."

Maybe it was the wine that sparked his courage, or the fact that he understood none of the conversation. However it was, Oliver could contain himself no longer. "I beg your pardon--" he began.

"Be quiet, Medley," replied Great-Aunt Belvedine.

For once he did not subside. "If I might inquire--" he tried to continue.

"You may not," said Great-Aunt Belvedine. "These are matters beyond your understanding."

Oliver stood his ground. "I think not, Great-Aunt Belvedine!" he said firmly. "Obviously there are things I don't understand, but how can I possibly contribute intelligently to this expedition unless they are explained to me? It's my right to be told! Remember, I bring the Gift!" Where that bold statement came from he had no idea, but once it was out of his mouth, he felt an implicit confidence in it. The only small difficulty was that he had no idea what the Gift might be.

"Indeed you do, Friend Oliver!" Mistress Keeper looked kindly at him.

"And, Mistress Keeper," he said, ignoring Great-Aunt Belvedine, who glared at him from the other end of the table, "no one has mentioned the Lady Flavia since we arrived here. Has everyone forgotten about her? She vanished when we were stuck in the Mort-Mire, you know--"Mistress Keeper nodded--"and I'm very worried about her. Is someone out looking for her? Because I think someone ought to."

"We have already sent out searchers," said Mistress Keeper softly.

"But why is everyone sitting here calmly when we don't know where Cousin Flavia is? She might be a prisoner somewhere, injured, maybe even--" He couldn't finish the thought.

"Your kind heart does you credit, Friend Oliver," said Mistress Keeper, "and you have the right to know everything about this situation that we know." She glanced at the ornamental hourglass on the mantelpiece. "But I ask your patience for a few moments more. First we must prepare the Black Mirror, for the farther edge of True Midnight approaches. Do you agree, Mildrith? Belvedine?"

"Agreed," the *Foressa* said crisply.

Great-Aunt Belvedine chewed and swallowed her last tiny square of brown bread, brushed away a miniscule crumb, and frowned. "I suppose I must concede the wisdom of your words, Amatilda. I am refreshed now. I shall make myself ready for the Ordeal of the Black Mirror."

Mil, who had removed to a nearby desk where she jotted down calculations with a quill pen on sheets of parchment, shot her a derisive glance. Great-Aunt Belvedine ignored her.

"You weren't the one I was thinking of, Belvedine," Amatilda replied mildly. Great-Aunt Belvedine's eyebrows arched practically up to her hairline, but Amatilda continued in her lovely, calm voice. "Friend Oliver," she said, turning toward him, "please call me Amatilda, for I hope we shall have a long and pleasant association. You must realize that you have traveled to a dimension entirely different from your own, and have now entered fully into the Labyrinth World. More I cannot tell you, for I am unschooled in the structures of time and space as they exist in the Maze World. Later you might speak with our resident Mage, who understands cosmological matters. Our *Foressa*"--she nodded toward the black-clad warrior immersed in her writing--"also knows of these things, but we cannot spare her from her labors at present."

Great-Aunt Belvedine pointedly examined the small, jewel-rimmed watch pinned to the lapel of her dress. "True Midnight approaches. Amatilda, we must open the Black Mirror now!"

"Will you come with me, Friend Oliver?" Amatilda rose from her chair and led him to a space between two bookshelves where a painting in oils hung. As Amatilda lifted up her candlestick, Oliver saw that it was a portrait of a great vulture, shining black wings outspread. The background was a desert of unrelieved gray, with a solitary, sinister-looking tower rising in the distance.

Amatilda pressed a particular spot in the ornate rose-and-key border of the brass frame. It swung open, revealing a cube-shaped hole in the wall. Inside the hole was an object swathed in a black veil.

"If you would, please, Friend Oliver."

Oliver lifted the object, surprisingly heavy for its size, and bore it back to the table. At Amatilda's direction he placed it in the center.

Amatilda snuffed out her candle and placed the smoking taper upon the table. At the same moment every other candle in the room went out, and the hearthfire sank to glowing embers.

Mil put down her quill pen and stood up. "Seventy-two hours to nadir," she announced without explanation, then left her calculations and returned to sit at the table.

Great-Aunt Belvedine consulted her watch again. "We must hurry!" she declared in an ominous tone.

"Friend Oliver, are you familiar with the phenomenon of *overlooking*?" Amatilda asked.

Oliver's mind began to race and his palms to sweat. He hoped fervently that no one was reading his thoughts. *Overlooking was... It was on the tip of his tongue... Of course! Remote viewing! Clairvoyance! Extra-sensory perception!* Terms that belonged to the field of psychic phenomena. He had read about scientific experiments involving *psi* forces, but this was hardly a scientific laboratory, was it! Rather, it seemed to be exactly the kind of thing his neighbor Aurelia Dawn did, psychic readings and Tarot cards and so forth, and he always felt acutely uncomfortable when she talked about her trade.

Saint Amber's Rose

A qualm of unrest stirred in the pit of his stomach. *What's going to happen now? Table-turning? Emanations of ectoplasm? Spirit trumpets badly played?*

"Don't be ridiculous, Medley!" Great-Aunt Belvedine intercepted his thoughts. "Amatilda never uses questionable methods. Stay in your seat."

Oliver hadn't stirred from his chair, but the impulse had formed in his mind. He had always been leery of attempts to communicate with spirits who ought to be left in peace, as they had heretofore left him in peace. On the other hand, he couldn't discount the aura of essential goodness that emanated from Amatilda, who now lifted the black veil from the object in the middle of the table.

The object--no wonder it was so heavy--was a black cube apparently made of solid glass. It collected all available light in the library, but instead of reflecting it, as one would expect, the cube swallowed it.

"It is called the Black Mirror," Amatilda explained, "because it was made from a single piece of black rock that burst from the Mountain of Flame when it destroyed itself eons ago. We are waiting for True Midnight, when Today stands poised upon the edge of Yesterday and Tomorrow. Things far away and long ago or still to come can be seen in the Black Mirror then."

"But--" Oliver puzzled, "--but we left Ravenhome at midnight. We were on the road for more than an hour, not counting our time here at the inn. I don't understand--"

"Ten," Mil announced in a businesslike voice. "Nine. Eight. Seven."

Oliver felt the hairs on his arms rise and tingle. He sensed that something of tremendous import was about to happen; he sensed also that in the instant before whatever-it-was began, he was being given a last opportunity to get out of there and drive back with Old Auldie to that rambling, multi-gabled house they called Ravenhome. He could then return to his own familiar world.

As for Great-Aunt Belvedine, who had dragged him willy-nilly into this situation: She was a woman of infinite resource and could jolly well make her own arrangements for transportation back to--to whatever world she chose to inhabit. *I wouldn't put it past her to use a broomstick.*

Charleynne Gates

"Six. Five. Four."

The moment hung in the air, ripe with the possibility of retreat.

"I invite you, Friend Oliver, to look into the Black Mirror. You have given your word of honor to the *Sendara* Flavia, and by the binding of your word you have received the power to *overlook* her. You may be able to discover where she was taken."

Oliver, absorbed in his doubts, became aware that Amatilda was speaking to him.

"It is your choice," she was saying. "To look or to leave us, as you will. For the third and final time of asking: What is your will?"

The image of Flavia in her silver chair arose in his mind, Flavia in her shimmering green gown with her cascade of sunset hair, her lovely face with deep violet shadows under eyes changing like the sea under sunlight, under storm: green to gray to black.

Dear Cousin Oliver, it must be your free decision...

Her image faded. Again he recalled his vow of fealty, given, perhaps, without sufficient consideration, but given with his whole heart. *Lady of the Graelands*, he silently repeated his promise, *while the world stands, I am your liege man, to serve you all my days.*

"By my word freely given, I will not rest until the Lady Flavia is safe," he said aloud, and meant it with his whole soul, even though his voice was not quite steady.

"Three. Two."

A sharp rattle of dry leaves whipped against the windowpanes; a gust of wind moaned under the eaves of the inn. Time flew toward that magical instant when the energies of Today are vanishing into Yesterday, but those of Tomorrow are not yet manifest. Invisible channels into other dimensions opened around them.

"One," Mil finished.

"Time!" said Great-Aunt Belvedine.

Oliver could barely make out the dim shape of Amatilda on the other side of the black cube, but he heard her draw in a deep, unhurried breath. Then she began to sing in a clear, soft voice:

Open, Mirror, let us see
World and Time that may yet be.

Saint Amber's Rose

Nothing happened for a long moment. Then he blinked, unsure of what he was seeing. Maybe his eyes were dazzled by staring fixedly at the glass cube, or Black Mirror, as Amatilda called it. He imagined that the inky surface of the Mirror, at least the side facing him, had folded in on itself and was rearranging its parts in different ways that it couldn't get quite right.

Amatilda sang the song again. When the last note faded away, the surface of the glass cube shuddered--there was no other word for it-- and gradually cleared to a pristine transparency. The light of a bright sunny day beamed out at him from within the mirror.

Oliver's jaw dropped open. The Black Mirror had become a kind of window. Through it he discerned a landscape with a broad, purple-hued valley leading to snow-capped mountains under a brilliant blue sky. No camera in the Maze World had ever recorded details so fine and sharp, colors so true, or perspective so precise, and all of it three-dimensional, as if he were really there. Surely no human hand had made this cube of black glass! Beads of sweat broke out on his temples and inched damply into his collar.

Because suddenly he knew what was happening, knew it down to his bones, beyond all doubt or denial: This was Magic.

No one spoke. The room, bereft of hearthfire, grew chilly. Oliver shivered and stared into the Black Mirror. At last he understood that no evasions, no rationalizations, were possible. He really had crossed into another dimension where the familiar rules of the Maze World did not apply, at least not in the same way. And he realized that he couldn't imagine how, or even if, he would ever return home. It might be his destiny to remain in the Labyrinth World forever.

Oliver felt a cold stone of foreboding drop into the pit of his stomach. Icy crystals of fear formed in his veins, but he steeled himself and stared into the Black Mirror. The bright light inside it softened, and a new scene came into view. He saw it from a great distance, from high above, and then he was inside it, like a bird balancing on the wind. Lightly he floated down...

He was above a narrow dirt road running through a purple valley. A tiny dot moved along the road. He wished to see it more clearly, and immediately the image in the Mirror turned so that his viewpoint descended. The shadowed mountains bordering the valley appeared higher and more forbidding, the trees beside the road taller and shadier. He could even make out separate leaves on the branches.

When he swooped over the moving dot, he saw that it was a horse-drawn wagon with a house built on the back, a gypsy caravan painted canary yellow with neat red and black trim. A patient chestnut horse drew the wagon, nodding to itself as it ambled along, in no hurry to get anyplace in particular. The caravan made a pleasing picture beside the woodlands decked in autumn colors, scarlet and orange, gold and brown.

With a flick of his will Oliver swooped closer to the moving wagon, near enough to pick out details like milk cans and copper cooking pots and iron skillets hanging from pegs on the sides. They clashed together like wind chimes to the rhythm of the horse's pace.

Oliver's breath caught as he realized he was hearing as well as seeing the image in the Mirror. He heard the lazy crunch of the wagon wheels over the dirt road, birdcalls in the wood, whispers of leaves as the breeze wove through the trees, and he inhaled the breath of an early autumn day: clear air, leaf-scent, earth-scent, little puffs of road-dust stirred up by the horse's hooves.

Did they hypnotize me in some underhanded fashion? Beneath his lashes he stole a glance at the other three, which he surely couldn't have done under hypnosis. Mil, Amatilda, and Great-Aunt Belvedine were all looking in the Mirror, not at him. They must be seeing the same thing he was! Mysterious forces were at work here, forces beyond anything in his previous experience.

Oliiver Medley didn't want to miss a minute of it!

He returned his attention to the Mirror and wished he could see the driver of the caravan. The Mirror obligingly shifted focus to the front of the caravan, to a swarthy man with an enormous black moustache who held the reins slackly, letting the horse take its own pace. He looked exactly like a gypsy in a picture-book, with wide black trousers and a pair of black boots. He wore a white shirt with flowing sleeves, a red bandanna tied over his head, and a small gold earring in one ear. He whistled to himself now and then, a kind of tuneless tune repeated over and over.

The gypsy glanced up, looked straight into Oliver's eyes, grinned broadly, and winked!

Saint Amber's Rose

Startled, Oliver drew back, then remembered that he wasn't really in the scene at all but only viewing it remotely. He didn't understand how the gypsy could have been conscious that he was being overlooked, but as people kept telling him, the physical laws in this world were different from his own.

Oliver began to enjoy himself. There was an exhilarating kind of freedom to this remote viewing thing, a sensation of bodiless soaring above the earth without the restraints of gravity. He decided to explore its limits and willed himself to fly above the caravan, as high as those dazzling-white puffs of clouds far above.

The whole panorama of the valley spread itself beneath him. Breathtaking!

He spotted a black dot a great distance away, coming toward him. A bird, of course, a kindred spirit of the sky. Oliver smiled to himself and awaited its approach. *Is it a hawk? An eagle?* Or, judging from the wide wingspan, a vulture with sunlight glinting on its feathers?

It was none of those. As it flew closer, he saw that it had iron-like wings, a long, angular head with flame-red eyes, and reptilian feet with extraordinarily long talons. And a narrow beak ending in a needle-sharp point!

It was heading straight for Oliver and flying fast, faster than he thought any bird could fly.

Its beak opened, revealing cruel, sharp fangs.

It dived toward him...

For the first time in his life Oliver Medley fainted, falling sideways out of his chair.

Chapter Six

Dwarves, Dwarvids, Dwarvians

Oliver came to himself in a place so full of darkness that he wondered if he had died. He didn't feel dead, exactly, not that he would know what being dead felt like. He didn't really feel much of anything; he just lay there and waited for something to happen.

After a while he became aware of enormous shapes in the darkness, ink-blot shapes folding in and out like the ones he had seen in the Black Mirror before it became a window. The shapes moved around him, making a tunnel of black inside blackness. Impelled by a force he did not understand, he floated upright, the way one does in dreams, and began walking forward heavily, as if he were wearing weighted boots at the bottom of the ocean.

He didn't know how long he moved like that, but at last he saw a patch in the distance that seemed a little lighter than the surrounding darkness. The patch became gray as he moved toward it, then dully luminescent.

A shadowy landscape formed ahead of him, and soon he made out the silhouette of a small stone building in ruins. It might once have been a temple or shrine, but now its door and most of the roof were missing. His dream-self went over to it and peered in.

The temple (if it was that) had only one room, completely bare of furniture except for a marble bier in the center. On the bier was a human form. Oliver went toward it with an eerie foreknowledge of what he would find.

Flavia lay there, as if in sleep--or death. Her eyes were closed; her hands rested across her breast. In contrast to the red-gold hair fanned in an aureole over a satin pillow, her face was absolutely without color, white as the stone beneath her. Oliver leaned over her motionless figure and saw no sign of respiration, but in some way he couldn't fathom, he sensed that she was alive.

At the head of the bier stood a shining sword with its hilt upward, forming a cross. Sparkling lights coruscated up and down the blade, as if it were a sentient being standing guard over her.

He sensed something else, too, an inchoate presence accompanied by a sharp, dry odor that burned his nostrils, but which he was unable to precisely locate or identify. The presence seemed to be trying to envelope the bier, to nestle itself next to Flavia, but couldn't penetrate the invisible shield around her. Oliver couldn't locate the presence; he simply knew the thing was there. And that it wanted Flavia, and meant her harm.

At once he thrust out his arm across her body, trying to push away the presence that darkened the air around the bier as Flavia lay helpless and unaware. He felt something give way before him; something wavering and insubstantial, like thick smoke. It dodged away, returned, whipped past him, whisked itself beyond his reach. He flailed uselessly in the air, unable to grasp it.

He redoubled his efforts, hitting out at it, and for one brief instant saw the thing that endangered her. It had a face, a face like the one in the Mort-Mire that he had glimpsed distantly between stunted trees. But before he could get a clear focus, it rapidly became a pair of fanged jaws. The jaws yawned widely and lunged toward him.

"NO! NO!" he shouted. Desperately he grabbed for the sword above the bier, but it fell between his awkward hands, stabbing his ear with a searing pain.

"Friend Oliver! Friend Oliver!" His name was called gently. "You are dreaming. Awaken!"

Oliver awoke suddenly and completely and sat up with a jerk, shaking and gasping, the sheets all a-tangle about him. Amatilda Keeper was at his bedside with a servitor behind her bearing a tray piled with covered dishes. His right ear stung; he automatically clapped his hand on it. It came away smeared with blood. Then he noticed that above him sat the great horned owl Hera Vespasia, gripping the brass bedstead railing with curved black talons and staring at him with golden eyes. She clicked her beak twice, and he understood how he had been recalled from his nightmare.

Mouth agape, Oliver blinked and peered around. He was tucked in a bed in a cozy room full of daylight, with rays of warm sunshine streaming through bright chintz curtains at the windows and making patterns of light and shade on the floor. A dresser with a blue-and-white ewer and basin stood against the far wall, a wardrobe reached to the beams on the ceiling, and a round rag rug in a cheerful jumble of colors lay in the center of the room.

Looking down at himself, he saw clean homespun sheets under a buttercup-yellow quilt, and found that he was wearing a long-sleeved nightshirt which he didn't remember having put on. In fact, he didn't remember how he had gotten there at all, or what had happened to him before he awoke. Except for his ear, he seemed to have no injuries.

"I asked our physician to examine you," Amatilda told him as she anointed his ear with a salve which instantly removed all pain. "You startled us when you fell off the chair! Dr. Mortibus said to let you sleep, that you would be quite well when you awoke. Murg here"-- she indicated the servitor, who had set his tray on the table and stood waiting with folded arms. On being introduced, he bobbed his head--"put you to bed here and stayed to watch if you needed anything during the night."

"Thank you," Oliver said to the muscular servitor, his voice croaky from disuse. Dimly, for his senses were not yet fully alert, he wondered why a person of such obvious physical strength would have been appointed to watch him, for Murg was built like a wrestler. *What happened to me? Did I need to be restrained?*

He looked at his wrists: no sign of ropes or handcuffs. He wiggled his feet under the covers: no shackles around his ankles.

"Friend Oliver," said Amatilda, "we will leave you to your breakfast now. Your clothing was stained with Mire-muck, and Murg has taken it away. You will find other garments in the wardrobe. In three days we will hold a Council to study the meaning of the vision you saw in the Black Mirror. Until then, go freely wherever you wish in Keeper's Inn. You are a welcome guest."

Amatilda smiled at him again and opened the door into the hall. "Only be careful," she added, "not to go beyond the inn-yard into Threshold Forest. It can be... deceptive if you don't know your way about. Grace be with you in your rising and in all your doings this day."

Then they were gone, and he was suddenly aware of the delicious aromas emanating from the tray on the table. Lifting the cover, he found hot cereal made of a grain resembling oatmeal, with pitchers of wildflower honey and cream and slices of amber-skinned pears and crimson apples on the side. Not until he had finished did it occur to him to wonder how they knew his preferences in breakfast food. He didn't wonder long; it didn't seem important at the time.

His appetite satisfied, he washed in the basin of warm water on the dresser and looked into the wardrobe for something to wear. It was amazingly roomy inside, with dozens of little drawers and dividers, hooks and nooks--a regular warren of hiding places if you happened to be a mouse.

A suit of clothes, evidently intended for him, was hanging neatly on the rod. He took it out and after some study donned the various articles, then inspected himself in a mirror inside the wardrobe door.

"Oh, my!" he said to himself in wonderment. "I look like... like... Well, I can't imagine!"

His reflection wore nut-brown leggings, a long-sleeved, dark-green tunic, a wide belt, a cloak tied with strings, and a pointy-rimmed hat with a white owl's feather stuck in the band. On his feet were boots which fitted perfectly. He thought that was rather an odd coincidence because he had an irregular foot-shape inherited from his father and normally had to have his shoes custom-made.

Examining his belt--tooled leather with an incised design of leaves and vines--he discovered a small scabbard appended to it and a slender dagger inside, sharp as a paper-edge. Oliver took it out and examined it carefully, admiring the workmanship. While not a weapon-carrying person, he had no fear of knives, and possessed a complete set of the highest quality chef's knives for use in his own kitchen. Turning the blade so that it flashed in the light, he discerned letters graven in delicate script on the metal: S-e-v-e-r-n-e-t. *Severnet. Must be the brand name.* If so, it was new to him. Or... The thought struck him that it might be the name of the blade. In olden times, swords and daggers were often given names as a way of bestowing upon them those particular qualities, like *Sting* or *Dragonslayer.* Or *Excalibur.*

For an instant a puzzling thought flashed across his mind, but then it was gone like lightning in the night, and in the next instant he had forgotten about it.

He gazed and gazed at his reflection, fascinated with his transformation, and turned around to view himself from as many angles as possible. *I do believe I cut a rather jaunty figure. I look like someone about to have an Adventure!* A pleasurable shiver of anticipation danced up his spine until he remembered why he was here.

What has happened to Flavia? What are these people going to do about it?

Sobered by this recollection, he looked around for his wallet, watch, and keys, and found them placed neatly on the nightstand. He distributed these impedimenta of civilization about his person and considered what he ought to do next.

The Great Hall of the inn was almost empty when he came downstairs. Gone were the revelers whose songs and laughter had rung to the rafters the night before. Tables had been pushed against the walls, and servitors went about quietly and efficiently scrubbing floors, sweeping aside dusty cobwebs (taking utmost care that no arachnid lives were lost), and arranging candlesticks on mantelpieces over the four fireplaces. Darts of light danced on rows of polished copper and cooking implements. Toasting forks, slotted spoons, and long-handled ladles hung on the wall above the huge kitchen hearth. Only a small fire burned in it now, just sufficient to keep a kettle simmering on the hob.

A traveler or two leaned against a bar near the hearth, sipping hot drinks from pottery mugs. The innkeeper stood near them, one foot on the brass railing, conversing with the white-capped chef.

"Friend Oliver!" Jon Keeper called to him. "Good to see you looking hale this morning. We were a bit concerned about you last night."

"Thank you," Oliver answered, flushing pink. "I'm much better now. Sorry I caused a bother."

"Think nothing of it," Jon Keeper replied. "You know how women love to fuss over us men when we're under the weather, not that we'd want them to stop doing it."

"No, certainly not," Oliver agreed. A large mug of steaming liquid appeared on the bar in front of him.

"Chef brewed the dark-roast *mekhash ban* this morning," continued the innkeeper. "Good for warming your bones." Oliver sipped the aromatic drink and felt the strengthening heat down to his marrow. It reminded him of something similar back home, but he couldn't quite recall the name.

"You might as well come on rounds with me this morning," said the Keeper. "It'd be good to learn your way around the inn, so you'd know your boundaries." He stopped to sip his own drink. "I take it my wife warned you about staying inside the inn-yard?"

Oliver assured him that she had done so, and ignored the little flicker of wariness that made his fingertips tingle momentarily.

A servitor came in and spoke quietly with the innkeeper. Oliver politely looked another way so as not to overhear their conversation, but he inadvertently caught the word "Pavarr". It was the second time he had heard it; he didn't know what it signified.

He was about to ask about it when the innkeeper put his empty mug on the counter and said, "We'll start with the stables. You'll want to see the Sky-born. They're not a common sight these days."

Oliver trotted along beside Jon Keeper as they passed through the double doors into a morning of bright sunlight in a cloudless sky. The inn-yard was much bigger than he had realized last night, as big as an outdoor stadium back in--back in the other place, what was it, where he had come from... He blanked on the name for the moment. The whole yard was surrounded by a dark green hedge, and beyond the hedge were dozens of trees with leaves like--

"Fire!" Oliver exclaimed. "Mr. Keeper! Those trees! They're on fire!"

The Keeper stopped, glanced in the direction Oliver indicated, and chuckled in his deep voice. "Aye, they look like it, don't they," he said calmly. "But they're not. Those are fire-trees. They call them that because in Leaf-Fall they turn scarlet all at once, and with the sunlight on them and the leaves pointing up, they look like a bonfire. By the way, I'm just Keeper. Or Jon."

The Keeper strode ahead toward the stables on the opposite side of the yard, and Oliver hurried after him, one hand holding his new, owl-feathered hat firmly on his head. He saw fire-trees dotting the landscape all around the inn-yard, interspersed with other trees whose autumn leaves flashed and glimmered in the sunlight.

Now wait: Didn't Great-Aunt Belvedine appear in my office in June, on Midsummer Day as a matter of fact? Wasn't that yesterday? What happened to the rest of summer?

Oliver's steps slowed as he pondered the implications. Somehow an entire season in his home world had passed, or else the familiar four seasons worked differently here. If he cast aside his preconceived notions about how the universe operated, then hadn't

Midsummer Day been regarded as magical as long as human memory? Think of *A Midsummer Night's Dream*. The Bard of Avon must certainly have known what he was talking about!

A light breeze tickled the back of his neck, and he came to himself to find that he had inadvertently wandered into a circle-garden in the center of the inn-yard, a plot of earth crowded with chrysanthemums, zinnias, dahlias, asters, and other autumnal flowers. Far ahead of him the innkeeper strode toward the stables. Oliver, greatly embarrassed, extricated himself from the flowerbed and broke into an awkward run to catch up.

He became aware of new noises nearby, rhythmic clashes of metal against metal. Glancing to the side, Oliver saw two helmeted figures fighting with broadswords inside a ring of compact, muscular individuals with swords and shields at their sides. A coach or referee dodged around the two fighters, apparently directing the match.

The fight looked in deadly earnest. Neither warrior appeared to be winning, for they seemed to be identically matched except for unequal height. Then the taller one--about Mil's height and build-- missed a footstep and stumbled backward. The opponent didn't press his advantage quickly enough, and the tall one recovered and resumed attack.

She (if it was Mil) gave her opponent a mighty thwack with the flat of her sword and knocked the other warrior to the ground. The referee declared victory. The victor extended a hand to help the other up, and both removed their helmets as the circle of warriors applauded by thumping their sword-hilts against their shields. It really is the *Foressa* in that suit of mail! Oliver went on with renewed respect for that redoubtable young woman.

On the far side of the combat ring five or six stalwart men took turns tossing the caber (a log the size of a telephone pole in the Maze World), while beyond them hammer throwers hurled their weapons with blinding speed, and steenstossers flung immensely heavy stones at marked distances. Oliver recognized the activities as typical of Highland Games and assumed that that, or an upcoming Renaissance Faire, was the reason for the intense preparation. That would fit the medieval theme of the inn.

In the distance the innkeeper disappeared through the stable opening into the dark interior. To Oliver, panting to catch up, it seemed that Jon Keeper had been swallowed in darkness... but the thought was fleeting, and he had forgotten it by the time he reached the stables.

They were gigantic, stall after stall in an endless line. All the stall doors were open, as if the occupants were free to come and go just like any other guest in Keeper's Inn. Oliver thought--no, imagined--that he saw a large, scaled tail trailing outside one of the stalls, and from another, three separate tails which all seemed to belong to the same animal.

In the shadows under the high roofbeams, horns--single and double--and antlers rose above the stall enclosures. Cattle or goats or... *could that possibly be a unicorn?* His eyes must be having difficulty adjusting to the dusky stable after the bright light outside.

Overhead, two little barn owls perched on a rafter stared sleepily at him. He wondered if they might speak, like Hera Vespasia (his ear tingled at the memory), and prepared himself to be startled, but they said nothing.

"Here we are," said the innkeeper as they approached a stall where a groom was giving a rubdown to a magnificent stallion who looked (to Oliver) almost as tall as an elephant. Even in the twilight shadows of the stables, the animal's coat shone like moonlight. "That's Sornor Star-Rider," pronounced the innkeeper, "of the sons of Pegasus. Not as many of them as there used to be," he added in an aside.

The barn must have had quite a lot of dust in the air because the Keeper made a sound between a snuffle and a snort which echoed through the building. *Must suffer from allergies*, Oliver thought sympathetically, being troubled with seasonal allergies himself.

When the Keeper made that curious sound, the groom stopped what he was doing and said something Oliver couldn't catch. Jon Keeper frowned and bent to pick up the horse's hind foot. He examined the hoof carefully and finally took a small tool out of his pocket, which he used to extract a tiny foreign object lodged in a tender place. Then he let the hoof gently down and raised the offending item into a pencil-thin beam of sunlight, where it glittered wickedly.

The Keeper inspected it closely. "*Fffrhynn*," he said. The stallion nodded his great head several times and uttered a long, rolling whicker to which the Keeper listened intently. "*Hmmmnnn*," he said when the horse had finished, and with the utmost care put the miniscule object in the pouch on his belt. Then he lifted the injured hoof again

Charleynne Gates

and drew a chain out of his shirt. A small medallion was attached to it, engraved with a spiral design. Its curving lines enclosed a central image or symbol Oliver couldn't quite make out. But he saw that on the reverse was--of all things!--a keyhole almost too small to be seen.

Jon Keeper blew softly into the keyhole and the back of the medallion opened, revealing a miniature vial. He held the medallion over the injured place on the horse's hoof, and a drop of liquid half the size of a dewdrop squeezed out of the vial and onto the spot where he had removed the foreign object. The horse shuddered visibly, and its skin rippled from neck to withers, but the leg didn't quiver in the Keeper's hand.

The Keeper set the hoof down again and murmured deep in his throat. The horse nodded; the man spoke again in that curious mode of communication which sounded remarkably equine. The stallion replied in kind.

"Forgive us, Friend Oliver," the Keeper said, standing up, "but we had a bit of an emergency. All's well now. Captain Sornor of the Winged Horse Cohort, Friend Oliver Medley."

Winged Horse! Really? wondered Oliver, with pardonable doubt, but he removed his hat and bowed with as much composure as he could muster. He had never been formally introduced to a horse before, but at least had the sense not to offer a handshake.

The great steed turned his head to see him more clearly. In its luminous dark eye reposed wisdom beyond anything Oliver had ever seen in an animal--or a human, for that matter. The horse solemnly returned his bow, then turned to his feed-box and began pulling hungrily at the hay.

"The Lady Beghed, Daughter of the Wind, mate to Sornor," continued Jon Keeper. The mare in the next stall nodded a greeting.

"Now, Friend Oliver," said the Keeper, clapping him on the shoulder in a friendly way. Oliver staggered under the blow, but recovered and tried to pretend he hadn't. "We'll go across the yard and see the brothers who work the smithy. They make or fix everything around the inn-yard, from shoeing horses to rescaling stationed dragons."

Oliver, hastening a step or two behind, thought he heard the Keeper say "reselling station wagons," and assumed the smiths also had a business in pre-owned automobiles.

-- 104 --

"Automobiles, too. Good thing they found what was wrong with the Silver Ghost, or it would have broken down again before Old Auldie got back to Ravenhome. If you ever want to do any repair work yourself, just come down to the smithy. They have every tool you can think of."

Oliver was at a loss to imagine what use he could make of a non-gardening tool, considering the infantile level of his mechanical ability, but he tried to appear reassured.

As they exited the gloaming of the stable, he glanced over his shoulder for a last glimpse of the majestic stallion. As he did so, an errant sunbeam struck Sornor's shining coat, and Oliver saw with unmistakable clarity the outline of a great wing folded across his back.

I must be hallucinating. Flying horses are mythical. I'm almost sure of that.

The smithy looked dark and bright at the same time, for a forge stood in the middle of the room, and all kinds of implements in various stages of repair crowded against the walls and hung from the rafters. The forge blazed away energetically, and two short-statured smiths labored over it in postures of extreme concentration. They wore metalworkers' helmets as protection from the flames, and between them they held a wad of glowing iron in giant pincers. After a few knocks and taps with their hammers, they swiftly transferred the metal to a nearby anvil and began to shape it into something whose ultimate purpose Oliver could not begin to guess.

Jon Keeper advanced into the smithy and selected a solid wooden pillar to lean against, waiting until the smiths had finished the task at hand. With a nod he indicated a broad-backed sawhorse, and Oliver promptly sat thereon.

The smiths worked quickly, putting down and taking up different kinds of tools as they needed them until the metal began to cool into the desired form, a finely-shaped, scale-like piece of black iron. One smith grasped the piece with a pair of tongs and plunged it into a tub of water. A hiss like a fairy-tale dragon's issued from the tub's bowels, together with a cloud of steam.

"Medered Blacktongue lost another primary last week," remarked one of the smiths without looking up.

"Eh," responded the Keeper. "Getting on in years, isn't he."

Charleynne Gates

"Over seven hundred," replied the smith. "Led a hard life. Too many tournaments."

"Retired undefeated," said the other smith. "Awarded the Corona Dragonis. First time in the history of the games."

"We won't see his like again," said the innkeeper after a pause.

"Eh," agreed the smiths.

The cooled iron was removed to the anvil, where a few more taps here and there rendered the piece to the smiths' satisfaction. In another minute one of them glanced at the Keeper and nodded.

"Break time, Brother," he said, and laid down his tool. The other one followed suit.

"So," the first smith said. "This the Gift-Bringer?"

"It is," said the Keeper. "Now I've got rounds. Friend Oliver, I'll leave you with the Whackitts. That's Tipp. That's Tapp. They'll fill you in before you leave."

With that enigmatic pronouncement, the Keeper left. One of the inn-yard cats, black as a burnt ember, strolled into view. It gave him a straight look out of its yellow eyes as it passed, then disappeared around the corner of the smithy.

Tipp wiped his face with a large polka-dotted handkerchief. "Friend Oliver, I suppose you're wondering about the Labyrinth World. Must be a sight different than where you're from. Where are you from, if you don't mind my asking?"

"Not at all. I'm from, originally from... from... I can't seem to remember the name of it right now," he apologized.

Tipp regarded him kindly. "Never mind," he said. "Happens to most of our guests at first until they get seasoned--accustomed to our Labyrinth World, that is. You remember, Brother, when that last fellow came, the one who said he was on a pilgrimage to some place in the Maze World, but got off his bearings and ended up here instead. Now when was that?" he mused, rubbing his chin.

"1176 by their reckoning." Tapp said rather abruptly.

But that's almost a thousand years ago! How could they have known the man personally? I must have misunderstood.

"Ah, yes," said Tipp. "That was it."

"It was," Tapp insisted, scowling as if someone had made an objection. "Just ask the Mage." He squinted at Oliver's right ear and nudged Tipp. "See that?"

Tipp followed Tapp's glance and nodded. "Looks like Hera Vespasia put a hole in your earlobe, Friend Oliver. We can fix that for you."

"Mistress Keeper put a salve of some kind on it," Oliver said, touching his ear gingerly. "It doesn't hurt now."

He felt cool metal slide into the hole in his ear and wondered what it was, but only for a second before Tapp showed him his reflection in a square of shiny copper. *An earring? Good gracious! I never thought I'd have my ear pierced! Whatever will they think of me back in... wherever I came from?*

"You won't be able to see it, but your earring has a design of the Lock and Key," Tipp informed him. "It's the symbol of Keeper's Inn. Hera Vespasia has marked you as one of us."

"Won't come off, either." Tapp added. "Whatever happens," he muttered.

A bell began ringing from the inn, interrupting the explanation and leaving Oliver mystified.

"Midday meal!" Tapp exclaimed happily. He took off his tool belt, and put it down on a worktable inside the smithy. Tipp did likewise.

"We'll be eating outdoors on a fine day like this," Tipp remarked. He stretched and grinned, sniffing the air appreciatively. "Frottlefish chowder and fresh-baked quackerbread or I miss my guess. Best come with us, Friend Oliver," Tipp invited. "You'll be needing a good hearty meal, considering what's ahead for you."

"Amatilda's homemade pickles!" Tapp exclaimed, cutting off the possibility of a reply. He hurried forward toward an arbor of grapevines sheltering a long trestle table and benches. The table was already groaning beneath a plethora of trenchers, soup tureens, baskets of quackerbread, bowls of fruit, and platters of greens. Servitors and inn workers sat on both sides, laughing and trading good-natured jokes.

"Hold on. Take a look over there, Friend Oliver," Tipp said, indicating the other side of the main building. "You see that tall turret on the north side of the inn?" Oliver looked in that direction and saw a cylinder-shaped projection attached to the main building. It was constructed of irregular brickwork with a pointed cap of some material that seemed to absorb, rather than reflect, all the light that reached it. "That's where the Resident Mage lives," Tipp continued. "You ought to visit him while you're here. He knows everything about this and other worlds, information you'll need when you leave."

"Leave? When am I leaving?" asked Oliver, newly bewildered. "The Keeper said that too. I don't understand."

But the two smiths were already greeting co-workers at the table, and Oliver didn't have another opportunity to ask.

The company sang grace, the same one he had heard at Ravenhome, then fell hungrily upon soup, bread, pickles, and a dressed salad of herbs and vegetables unknown to Oliver. *Roup, zalat,* and *krus* is what the leafy greens were, he was told. They were delicious, whatever they were.

Curiously, he saw no sign of Amatilda Keeper or Great-Aunt Belvedine, but he did notice the *Foressa* Mildrith sitting at another table, deep in conference with warriors from the outdoor combat ring. They were noticeably below the minimum height requirement for military personnel, as far as he knew. He couldn't imagine how they could drill in equal combat with opponents as statuesque as Mil, but at least one of them had.

Tipp noticed the direction of his glance. "Dwarvids, those are," he muttered to Oliver. "Ferocious fighters. You wouldn't want to meet one in a dark alley!"

"Dark alley!" Tapp repeated around a mouthful of quackerbread.

"Dwarves?" Oliver questioned.

"Not Dwarves." Tipp swallowed a spoonful of soup and enunciated more clearly. "Dwarvids. Related to the race of Dwarves." Warming to his subject, he continued between bites of roup dipped in mustard sauce. "You see, there are three main branches of the Dwarf peoples: Dwarves, Dwarvids, and Dwarvians, each differing in occupation as well as physical type. Now your classic Dwarf--the original tribe, as they like to remind the rest of us--your classic Dwarf takes to mining and cave-work as if he was born to it, which in a sense he was. Take a Dwarf away from his mountains and mines and he's as likely to pine away as not."

"Most of 'em do," agreed Tapp.

"Dwarves are the shortest of the three clans," Tipp went on, holding up his index finger in a professorial manner. "They adapted themselves to small spaces in the mines many Ages ago. It was easier for their work, digging for minerals and precious stones. They use stones like that in their architecture. Someday you might see for yourself the wonderful things they built, like the Great Hall of Diamonds under the Icewode--"

"Hsst, Brother," Tapp said, and right away Tipp changed the subject, as if he might have said too much.

"--and next are the Dwarvids, like those with the *Foressa* Mildrith over there. They're taller than Dwarves, having branched off from the original tribe Ages ago and emerged from the mines into the sunlight. They lost interest in mining when they discovered that they liked wielding metal better than welding it, as we do, or digging for it. They can fight with any weapon made of iron--sword, dagger, spear, mace, anything."

"We make 'em; they fight with 'em," Tapp put in.

"The Dwarvids are the military?" asked Oliver.

"In a way," responded Tipp. "Not exactly like your world."

"A national guard, perhaps," suggested Oliver.

"When necessary," said Tipp, scooping another spoonful of chowder.

"Mercenaries, then?"

"They don't like to talk about it," Tipp said in a low tone, not looking at Oliver. "So we don't ask. There're things that happen off-world that no one wants to know about. But we've been wondering why so many of 'em are here at the same time."

"Combat drills," muttered Tapp. "Maneuvers. Patrols, lots of patrols. Never seen so many before."

"Rumor has it that--" Tipp was about to add something, but just then a fierce-looking Dwarvid reached between them for a plump yellow pear. Tipp changed the subject at once and spoke louder.

"And we're Dwarvians, Tapp and I. Our clan ancestors also came out of the mines and got to like living under sunlight and blue skies. We don't go in for mining, like Dwarves, or fighting, like Dwarvids. We're artists. We work with metals in the forge, preferin' hammer and anvil to the miner's pick and the warrior's sword."

"We were apprenticed to Wayland Smith himself," said Tapp, speaking a whole sentence for the first time. "He was our mentor."

"Still is," said Tipp. "But we shouldn't boast," glancing at Tapp, who ignored him in favor of a bunch of purple grapes. "I suppose you've heard of Wayland Smith, Friend Oliver?"

Oliver was about to say that he hadn't, but all at once recalled that he had: Wayland Smith! Mysterious figure of myth, magical ancestor of all who work with hammer and anvil. Far too ancient for these two Dwarvians to have studied with him. *In any case, Wayland Smith is purely legendary!* And yet he believed them and knew not why.

He had an unwelcome thought. "Do you ever make firearms?" he asked. "Guns, if you know what they are?"

The Dwarvians looked at each other, then at Oliver.

"No," Tipp answered. "We know of them, and could make them if we wished, but we don't wish."

"A bad thing happened," said Tapp. "Very bad."

Tipp nodded his head slowly. "It was long ago. After it happened, the High King of the Labyrinth made a solemn decree on the Hill of Binding, standing bareshod on Earth, facing the Wind, holding Fire in one hand and Water in the other, and no firearm has been made in this world since that day."

"Even our culture hero, Arkon, didn't use them," said Tapp, shaking his head. "And he had more adventures than you can shake a stick at. Why, he could send an arrow into a bull's-eye from a thousand paces and seven arrows after it to split the first one in half. He could hurl a stone with a slingshot as high as the eagle flies and faster than a lightning flash. He tamed the wild dragons of Verindar, he--"

"That's what comes of sending you to technical school," Tipp interrupted crossly. "We sent Tapp here through the portal to the Maze World. He was supposed to study Extremely Advanced Welding Techniques at one of your colleges. What does he do instead but take a class in how to produce your own comic book! I don't know what came over you, Tapp."

"Arkon is the ultimate action hero," Tapp rejoined. "He deserves his own comic book."

"Through the portal? You mean you go back and forth between dimensions whenever you like?" Oliver asked, a beat behind. "And-- college? You attend our, ah, educational institutions?"

Saint Amber's Rose

"Many of us visit other dimensions," said Tipp, twirling a stem of roup in melted cheese. "People there can't see us."

"Some of 'em can," Tapp insisted. "I've seen 'em see us. But they forget right away. It's built into their genetic code."

Oliver said nothing more for a while. He had a great deal to think about.

The dinner bell pealed again. Everyone seated at the benches rose, bused their own tables, and left the grapevine arbor. Another group came in and sat down for second serving. As Oliver and the two smiths strolled back in the direction of the forge, Tipp stopped.

"Friend Oliver," he said, "Tapp and I must return to our work, for we have many orders to finish. You're welcome to wander about as you wish, but I caution you not to go beyond the inn-yard. You'd have a hard time doing it anyway, for the gate is guarded and the boundary hedge lets no one pass but small animals and birds. The window in your chamber has a full view of Threshold Forest, but if I were you I wouldn't look out of it any more than I absolutely had to."

Oliver promised he would remember.

Calmed by his nourishing meal, he meandered toward the circle garden, idly observing the life of the inn. Ducks paddled around the sparkling blue pond. A little breeze made the yellow heads of sunflowers nod and sway. A row of ravens perched on a branch of the nearest fire-tree, and a squirrel on the next branch chattered at them.

Dwarves. Dwarvids. Dwarvians. Oliver shook his head in mingled wonder and disbelief. *And dragons. I mustn't forget dragons. Or flying horses. I suppose they have elves and fairies here, too. And unicorns, of course, and pixies, trolls, and leprechauns for good measure. How can they think that I believe in such things?*

And this whole business of traveling to another dimension... I don't know. Either I'm having an unusually vivid dream or someone's playing an elaborate trick on me. If it weren't for Flavia... Flavia! I have to believe in her. She's real; she can't be otherwise. I--I would know it. Somehow I would know it. But where is she? Is she alive? Will I ever see her again? Oh, I wish I were back home in my own garden! If only Great-Aunt Belvedine hadn't come crashing into my office and upsetting my nice, comfortable life!

Oliver looked down. The big black cat that had glared at him in the smithy sat on its haunches in front of him and stared coldly into his eyes.

"Pretty kitty," he said, and tried to coax it to him. He liked cats; they usually purred when he talked to them.

The cat growled and switched its tail in a markedly hostile manner. Oliver backed away. "Beg your pardon," he said to the beast, and for prudence' sake strolled in the opposite direction.

"What do you make of him?" asked Tipp as the smiths walked back to the forge.

"Odd little man. Slow on the uptake," said Tapp.

"Cautious, I imagine," Tipp amended, "which isn't a bad thing."

"Cautious or slow," returned Tapp, "he'll need to figure things out faster than he's doing right now. Doesn't seem to know why he's here."

"We shouldn't judge before we're better acquainted," Tipp reproved.

They walked on for a minute or two.

"He's in love with Her," said Tapp.

"So are you. So am I," retorted Tipp. "Who isn't?"

"Anyhow, he looks pretty useless to me," Tapp insisted. "I'm guessing somebody'll have to look after him all the time, rescue him from situations he stumbles into. Put the rest of us at risk. I vote we don't take him along."

"It's not a voting matter, Brother," said Tipp, and opened the half-door of the forge and went inside. The half-door shut behind the smiths, revealing the woodburned design of a circle enclosing the initials T&T entwined around a rose.

Alone for the first time since beginning his adventure, Oliver returned to his room, deciding that what he needed was just to sit and think about everything that had happened to him since Great-Aunt Belvedine whirled into his office. *Speaking of Great-Aunt Belvedine, why hasn't she made an appearance this morning? Where is Amatilda? And Old Auldie, the chauffeur--has he already driven back to Ravenhome?* If so, then his one means of return--or escape--had truly vanished. *Not,* he reminded himself, *that I would have used it.*

Saint Amber's Rose

He sat down in a cozy rocking chair and rocked back and forth several times, trying hard to summon all his powers of memory. That proved to be more difficult than he had anticipated. *Didn't someone tell me that I'd start forgetting things as soon as I got into the Labyrinth World?*

After concentrating for a while, he remembered awakening in that very bed, now crisply made up with its flower-wreathed quilt smoothed under the linen pillowcase. A brown earthenware pitcher filled with yellow chrysanthemums stood on the nightstand.

He had awakened from a nightmare. And Flavia had been in his dream! But what had frightened him so terribly about that dream? *Something about a tomb? No, a temple or a chapel, in ruins.* And inside it was a bier, a marble bier beneath a stained glass window. There was a picture in the window, but its outlines were fuzzy, and he couldn't make out what it was. *If only I could remember what was lying on that bier...*

Absently, only half aware of what he was doing, he moved toward the balcony window beside the bed and gazed at the fire-trees standing like flaming sentinels against the forest of dark evergreens. *How thickly the trees grow in that forest! How does anyone get through them?* Maybe no one ever did. The forest trees, much taller than those bordering the inn, swayed in the wind like waves in the sea, a heaving ocean of green vast as the sea itself.

A face between the trees looked out at him, a face he was startled to realize that he recognized. "Oh yes!" he murmured. "I remember you! You're... We met when... I've never forgotten you. Wait! I'll come to you."

Somehow the double windows had opened, although he wasn't aware of unlatching them. How lovely it was to look right into the heart of Threshold Forest, into those whispering masses calling to him to plunge into their depths, to be pillowed on those soft waves, to dive into deep, green peace, all his worries melting away. Oh, to surrender! To be embraced in those reaching arms...

In another wing of the inn was a small, book-lined study, tucked out of the way of the main corridors. Its narrow door was shut, locked on the inside with a silver lock of strange pattern. A couple of portly grandfather chairs with hassocks upholstered in crimson velvet stood in

Charleynne Gates

opposite corners of the room, and heavy draperies of the same velvet were drawn across the windows, barring all outside light. An oval table of black wood was set in the middle of the room, and on the table a single white candle burned in a silver candle-holder. Its steady flame was the only source of illumination.

Four persons sat around the table, engaged in an intense discussion: Amatilda Keeper, Great-Aunt Belvedine, Mil, and another person whose face could not be clearly seen because it was in the shadow of a hood. The candle flame picked out only the curve of a chin, the tip of a nose, and the long, slender fingers of hands folded upon the tabletop.

"But he hasn't been initiated!" Great-Aunt Belvedine insisted, as if objecting to some remark. "He's not entitled to know anything!"

"His ignorance may prove more dangerous to us than premature knowledge would be," rejoined a quiet voice in the shadow of the hood. "The matter of initiation will be taken care of presently. In the meantime, what does he know about--"

With a gasp, Amatilda looked up, her gaze fastened on something she saw beyond the close confines of the little room. "Oliver! He's in danger! He needs help at once," she said urgently, turning toward the fourth person.

"Yes, I see it," said the low voice matter-of-factly. The long, slender hands unfolded themselves and unhurriedly made a subtle gesture in the air. "Azar-Azriel, incarnadine!"

Pain stung the back of Oliver's leg as if he had been whipped by a cactus branch. "OW!" he yelped, and found himself balanced perilously on the narrow windowsill outside his room, four floors above the ground. Suddenly wide-awake, he stumbled backward into the bedchamber and whirled to find out what had attacked him.

There sat the black cat from the inn-yard, its paw upright, blood dripping from its extended claws onto the rag rug.

Oliver's blood.

"HHHT!" the cat reprimanded. Oliver backed into a corner. The cat stayed where it was, scowling.

Oliver wiped blood off his calf. That beast of a feline had sneaked up behind him and attacked him viciously, for no reason at all!

Then he remembered where he had just been--standing outside on a high windowsill with nothing to break a fall. And the forest wasn't close at all; it was actually far away, much too far to be able to distinguish a face between the trees.

That cat saved my life.

"Thank you," he said respectfully, cautiously keeping his distance. The cat cast him a glance of cold contempt, reminding him vividly of Great-Aunt Belvedine, and stalked out the open door.

Oliver collapsed onto a chair and thought hard about many things, being very careful not to look at the window at all.

After a while the idea occured to him that his conduct so far hadn't been anything to write home about. He had blamed Great-Aunt Belvedine for getting him in this situation, but the truth was, when she whirled into his office, something started to come to life inside him that he hadn't experienced before.

He could have put a stop to this escapade at any time and returned to his own life. Three times he had been asked if he wanted to continue, and three times he had said Yes. Wincing, he recalled that he had come dangerously close to forsaking the promise he had made to Flavia. Did his word of honor mean so little to him, that he could so easily forget his vow when things got unpleasant?

Cowardice. That's what it is. And that's what I am—a coward.

Before now, he had felt secure in his comfortable life, believing that he was safe from disturbances. Safe from challenges that he might not be able to meet. Safe in his garden, his personal paradise. *My little Eden.*

Only no one anywhere is ever really safe, and Oliver Medley knew that. He acknowledged at last that the winds of Change were blowing into his sheltered world, and he understood that the quiet pattern of his days had been transformed forever.

Do I have the courage to open myself to those rough winds, tempests though they be?

Chapter Seven

The Labyrinth

A memory like a lost echo surfaced from the depths of Oliver Medley's mind, a remark made by someone in the Maze World. It began to make sense now. *True Love* and *High Adventure*, the lady was saying. And something else... *Noble Deeds*. Oliver even recalled who had proclaimed those sentiments: Dame Rosalind of the Fair Wood, Lady of Wisdom in autumn-colored robes and a crown of pheasant feathers, who spoke of the world she knew intimately, the enchanted realm of Heart's Desire.

High Adventure? Like it or not, he was in the middle of one now. True Love? Although his love for Flavia would never be requited, and he would never speak of it to another living soul, he had found the star of his seeking. He only dared love her silently from afar, of course. He understood that.

And Noble Deeds?

Let's not make excuses, said his conscience disdainfully. *Please.*

So he didn't. Thus far, his only approach to a Noble Deed had been to profess his allegiance to Flavia. And that was on the spur of the moment, when he was dining safely at Ravenhome, and danger seemed unimaginably remote. His vow, given in the first flush of starry-eyed Romance, thus hardly qualified as a Noble Deed. And at the first sign of difficulty, what had he done but fling to the winds every warning he had been given, thereby causing Flavia to be lost in the Mort-Mire! He had as good as abandoned her.

Oliver felt sick. His chest contracted; his shoulders hunched. He bowed his head; one hand shaded his eyes as guilt overwhelmed him.

And yet his vow, freely given out of the fullness of his heart, had placed him solidly in the company of her defenders and set upon him the obligation to give his life, if need be, to protect her from enemies known and unknown.

But for practical purposes, what can I actually do to help in this situation? They--Flavia, her physician, her chaplain, and the *Foressa* Mildrith--had intimated that he possessed some kind of Gift, but either no one knew what it was or wouldn't tell him. It definitely wasn't physical prowess! There was no point in going down to the combat exercise ring and hacking about with a broadsword, if he could even lift one. *I'd probably only hurt myself.* The *Foressa* had established back at Ravenhome that he didn't have the makings of a warrior.

He frowned, thinking deeply. There was one thing he could do, and do very well. He did it every day back at... back in... back home. The correct place-name was on the tip of his tongue, from whence it refused to emerge, but he ignored the annoyance. What was crucial was that he remembered clearly what he did there: *I'm a librarian, and I know how to organize information.*

What he needed first of all, then, was a way to acquire information. In the absence of computers or even card catalogs, he was evidently going to have to do it the old-fashioned way: by hand. *I need to find someone who knows how things work in this world and is willing to talk to me.*

Where was such a person?

Tipp had pointed out a turret on the north side of the inn and said that a resident wizard or sage--no, Tipp had called him a Mage--had his office there. Amatilda Keeper had mentioned him also.

Oliver was not accustomed to keeping company with mages, sages, sorcerers, witches, warlocks, or wizards, but now, he decided, was not the time to be squeamish. The mysterious person in the turret might be his only means of securing the information he needed.

Accordingly, he heaved himself out of his rocking chair and went in search of the north turret. He found it after an hour or two of perambulating a series of randomly interconnected corridors.

The turret door was painted black with gold specks all over it. They looked like constellations of stars in the night sky. Oliver thought he discerned the Horsehead Nebula on the lower right panel, but when he bent down to examine it, the specks shifted until they formed a different pattern.

There was no doorknob or handle, but affixed to the door was a sign with one word in gold letters which, as he looked, changed rapidly from one language to another and another and another. "MAGE" he read as the same word translated itself into Latin, French, and German (all of which he understood); Transylvanian, Ugarit, and Sanskrit (all of which he didn't). Then came Arabic, Hebrew, Chaldean, and a host of others whose origins were unknown to him.

This must be the place.

He raised his knuckles to knock, but before he had the opportunity, the door flew open, revealing a small vestibule whose farther end had a filmy gray curtain hanging from floor to ceiling. Oliver thought that he must be facing the door-opener, but he couldn't quite bring the person into focus. There was a kind of mist in the way.

The mist took a step backward, opened the door to its widest extent, and gestured foggily for Oliver to come inside. Behind him the door shut with a firm click.

"If you'll follow me, sir," whispered the misty form, and pulled aside the gray curtain--woven of cobwebs, Oliver observed, and tried to avoid getting stray strands on his clothes as he passed through them.

At first, so thick was the blackness that he had to wait for his eyes to adjust before moving forward. As he waited, he became aware of a muffled noise, like an enormous cat purring. It sounded both remote and near at hand, and he wondered nervously whether it had been fed recently.

At last his eyes began to adjust, and he saw shadows against the darker background. One of them became clearer: the profile of a great stag with antlers which grew as he watched until they became a tree whose branches reached to the heavens. Then it faded out, leaving him doubtful that he had seen anything at all.

Light gradually increased, coming from two tall, narrow windows in a far wall. Uncurtained, they revealed a night sky dotted with stars whose twinkling gently illumined the entire chamber.

Oliver stared, thoroughly confused. *Surely this can't be a small, cramped room in a turret!* Not this vast space crowded with furniture and an immense glass dome for a ceiling. Through the dome he glimpsed more stars, planets, and constellations swimming in a vast midnight ocean. He recognized Sagittarius, Orion, Cassiopeia... ringed Saturn... gigantic Jupiter... red Mars, god of war.

Saint Amber's Rose

He came to himself with a start, realizing that he couldn't possibly be seeing them so closely. Each of Saturn's rings stood out distinctly. And the canals on Mars... It was like reading a map!

The enormous room lightened gradually to a crepuscular shade of blue, revealing laboratory tables, desks, and cabinets scattered randomly about. Atop every surface were pieces of alchemical equipment: scales and balances, alembics and abacuses, mortars and pestles, urns and uraeuses. Every few feet around the walls stood articulated humanoid skeletons, uncannily presenting the appearance of a palace guard. Bookshelves lined the room behind the skeletons, filled with papyrus scrolls, clay tablets, and books so old they looked as if they would crumble into dust at a touch.

"Sir, the Mage awaits you," breathed a vaporous voice quite close to his ear, impelling Oliver out of his trance. He followed the vapor through the maze of furnishings to a clearing beside the tall windows.

A telescope was aimed out the open window toward a distant galaxy that might have been the Milky Way except that its characteristic swirl was positioned at a different angle. A high desk stood next to the telescope; upon the desk a tall blue candle burned in a silver candlestick. In front of the desk, hunched over a scroll upon which he was writing with a quill pen, was a slender individual with dark hair cropped short, wearing a robe of indigo whose cowl hid the rest of his profile, for he was sitting with his back to them.

"Mr. Oliver Medley, Your Excellency," announced the door-opener.

The writer put down his quill pen and turned toward them. Whatever Oliver had expected, it was not this. In place of a white-bearded wizard wearing a conical hat and wielding a magic wand, was a man neither very young nor very old, with a keen, thin, angular face, beardless and olive-skinned, with eyes as golden as a cat's.

"Friend Oliver," the Mage said, and Oliver felt that the golden eyes were seeing clear through to the back of his skull. "You are welcome here. I am Dandriel, Mage of Threshold Forest." The slim brown hand took Oliver's with a firm grip, held it a second, and let it go, leaving him with an impression of immense energy.

"This is Dour, my personal assistant," said Dandriel, waving one hand toward the misty form. "Please move up a chair for our guest, Dour; that one'll do."

A long silence ensued.

Oliver felt he oughtn't to speak first, and waited for the Mage to say something. Anything. Once or twice he fidgeted in his chair, uncomfortable in the prolonged quiet, particularly as the other's unblinking eyes gazed steadily at him all the while. He didn't feel the Mage's stare was offensive; rather, it seemed as if Oliver were being inspected thoroughly and impersonally.

Just as Oliver thought someone really ought to speak, the Mage said, "So you have come to us at last."

The point seemed incontestable. Oliver couldn't think of a suitable reply, so he sat up straighter in his chair and smiled nervously.

"I imagine," Dandriel continued, "that you were expecting someone rather different. Older, perhaps? More 'wizardly', with a white beard, a conical hat, and a magic wand?"

"I suppose I was," Oliver admitted. "More traditional, at least, like Merlin."

"He is a member of my order," said the Mage, nodding. "The Order of the Wise. Some call us Magi; others, the Wyrd" (he pronounced it with a slight breathiness at the end, as if the word were Gaelic), "which implies that we have greater powers than any created being ought to have. In fact, what powers we possess derive from our unceasing communication with the heavens. And your work is with the Willoughby-Smythe Collection. Is that not so?"

"Yes, it is," Medley replied promptly. He cleared his throat unobtrusively, not wanting to appear vain of his prestigious position.

"Interesting," mused the Mage. "You may not know that Erasmus Willoughby-Smythe was a frequent guest here. He spoke highly of you."

"Did he?" Oliver responded, startled. "I--I didn't know. That is, I didn't know he had traveled here. He was a friend of my father's."

"Yes," said the Mage. "I knew your father well. Do you still have his key?"

An unexpected catalyst of memory transported Oliver back to his boyhood, and he recalled his father's last days with a case of viral pneumonia straining a weak heart. A short time before he died, Oliver's father called him to his bedside and pressed into his hand a tiny silver key.

"Son," he said, breathing with difficulty, "Keep this with you... always. Don't use it... until your hour... of greatest need. You will know... when..."

Oliver kept the key in a pocket of his billfold, but assumed that his father's mind was wandering a bit toward the end and that the key was merely to one of his father's collections of antique miniatures. He carried it with him because his father had asked him to, but seldom gave it any thought. Now his hand automatically felt for his billfold before it occurred to him to wonder how the Mage knew about the key.

"I do not need to see it," said the Mage, answering his thought. "I am pleased that you keep it on your person, even though you do not understand its significance." He paused, then went on before Oliver gathered his wits enough to ask what its significance was. "Before we continue, Friend Oliver, I must tell you that it is my task to guide you through the Labyrinth of Initiation, for otherwise you will not be able to continue on the Quest."

The questions Oliver wanted to ask flew out of his head.

Quest?

"Yes," said the Mage, again interpreting his unspoken thought. "You and others have been appointed to find the *Sendara* Flavia and to escort her safely to the Abbey of Saint Amber."

"Appointed to find her?" said Oliver. "But I'm the one who lost her! I don't know where to start looking! Aren't there people out searching for her?"

"Oh, yes," replied Dandriel. "The search began before you reached the Mort-Mire."

"Before? But she wasn't lost then! How--"

"Friend Oliver," said the Mage, "you realize by now that the dimension of the Labyrinth World and the dimension you normally inhabit are very different from each other. We may speak of this when you return. At present we are in a surge of time and must catch the moment.

"Your initiation into the Mysteries of the Labyrinth ought to take at least three years. We have one hour. In that hour I shall show you how our world began. You will need to know something of this matter so that you may better understand your appointed task.

"It is no coincidence that you have become entangled in our great trouble. What the end will be, no one knows. But I feel it coming, and it may mean the end of our world as well, for much that is good may be consumed in the destruction of evil.

"Consider all that you have experienced since you entered this world. Do you wish to proceed?"

"I do," answered Oliver, sensing that their conversation was passing into another, entirely different, realm of reality. The atmosphere in the room tightened; charcoal shadows under the roofbeams bent toward them. A draft of cold air slid down his back, and he shivered.

"Then I shall ask you three questions," said the Mage. "Whom do you seek?"

"The *Sendara* Flavia."

"Why do you seek her?" Dandriel continued.

Oliver had no intention of telling anyone, not in this world or any other, what he had confessed to himself in solitude. It would be too humiliating. The idea that he, Oliver Medley, dared to dream of the *Sendara* Flavia! Unthinkable! A declaration of love from a middle-aged librarian with unremarkable features, to the Guardian of a great land far beyond his ken? Sheer arrogance! Better to keep his emotions locked firmly--and secretly--in his heart.

"Because I love her," he said simply.

The Mage did not react indignantly to this arrogant avowal. He simply continued to regard Oliver in silence.

"You gave the *Sendara* your pledge of fealty, did you not?" Dandriel continued after a brief pause.

"I did," Oliver replied, and cringed mentally as he remembered how many second thoughts he had had since then.

"Yet you have wavered in your loyalty, have you not?" Dandriel went on calmly. "You have wondered if another might perform your task with more skill and authority than you. You have thought about taking the opportunity to return to the Maze World because you have been disturbed by things you have seen. You desire Flavia's welfare, but you hesitate to believe those who have guided you in the Labyrinth World.

"The truth of the matter, Friend Oliver, is that you are sitting on a fence! You have given your word of honor to the *Sendara*--and I believe you are, in your heart, a man of honor--but without fully committing yourself. As they say in the Maze World, you have 'kept your options open' because you do not believe that you are capable of the noble deeds of your highest dreams. Is this not true?"

Oliver's face went white, then flushed red. He sat motionless in his chair, stiff with shame. How could this Mage person know about his internal dialogue? It wasn't possible! But he did.

"It is true," Oliver whispered through tight jaws.

"Why, then, do you hesitate to follow what is true and worthy of your love?" The Mage's unblinking golden eyes stared straight into Oliver's mild brown ones.

Oliver swallowed convulsively. Those eyes demanded from him everything he knew about himself, the whole truth from the place where his soul dwelt.

He told the truth then, the whole truth, and throughout, Dandriel's golden gaze did not waver.

"I am unworthy of a greater life," Oliver finished. "I am not my father's equal: I have always known it. I never quite fit into the world in which I was born, and now it seems that I lack the courage to live in this one. But--" he protested, leaning forward in his chair "--I do, truly, want to be of service to the *Sendara*. It's my fault that she was abducted. People keep telling me I have a Gift of some kind, something that will help her, but no one will say what it is."

"Nor shall I," said the Mage, "for I do not know. But you are no coward, Friend Oliver! You need not doubt yourself. *Commit* to the task before you, set your *will* on your intention, and *believe* that you will succeed! Come!"

Dandriel sprang up from his stool, and Oliver hastily rose from his chair. Unwilling to be left behind, he followed the Mage on a winding path among the crowded furniture to the glass double doors leading out to Threshold Forest.

"Be steadfast, Oliver Medley!" the Mage admonished, and gestured toward the forest, tenebrous and menacing. "Fear not the terror by night, nor the arrow that flies by day."

The glass doors, reaching from floor to ceiling, flew open; a dark wind blew into the room.

"Come!" the Mage said again, and walked swiftly into the night as Oliver hurried after. He knew not how far they went into the forest, for he could see almost nothing before him except the Mage's dark-clad figure moving very fast. Oliver did not dare to fall behind in this midnight wood where he heard only the brushing of branches, the snap of twigs, the stirring of grasses. Once or twice he caught the gleam of unblinking yellow eyes as creatures of the night stared at them.

The Mage halted when they reached a small clearing. The pale full moon gave illumination enough to make out separate shapes of trees encircling the glade and a pattern of white stones in the grass. The stones formed a circular shape that filled the entire clearing. Other circles lay within the larger one, forming patterns that twisted, turned, and spiraled toward the center. Oliver recognized the pattern: It was a labyrinth, a spirit-path of transformation sacred from the most primeval memory of human mortals. At his feet was a space where a few stones had been taken away, leaving an opening.

The Mage strode directly up to the opening, turned to him and spoke. "Friend Oliver, do you know the difference between a maze and a labyrinth?"

Oliver shook his head. He tried to form the word No, but no sound came out of his throat.

"A maze is an illusion," Dandriel continued. "It is designed to mislead and entrap those who enter it. Weary are its meanderings, for a maze has no center; its paths lead nowhere. Many are the turnings of a labyrinth, but all who tread that path arrive at the center. And here I tell you a great mystery, for the center of the labyrinth is the center of your own soul.

"Friend Oliver: Is it your will to enter the labyrinth?"

"It is."

"Then learn of the Graelands, and of the part you are to play in its unfolding destiny. *Trust your soul's leading.*"

Dandriel moved aside, and Oliver faced the opening in the outer circle of white stones. Cautiously he put his right foot across the threshold. Immediately he felt a sensation like an electric current pass through him, only there was no spark, no jolt, and no pain. The sensation was not on his skin but deep inside him. He brought the other foot up to join the first, and began to tread the ancient path.

He turned to the left as the path directed him with its white-stone outline, and as he did so, a veil of mist passed across his eyes. He blinked once or twice to clear his vision and saw, when the mist disappeared, another scene entirely. The voice of the Mage came to him as from a remote distance, and as Oliver listened, he saw the story unfold.

"Long and long ago, longer than you can imagine, when the Earth was without form and covered by the great waters, the spirit of Chaos dwelt in uttermost darkness. In perpetual rage it stirred the waters into a furious tempest. Even when the Creator divided the waters from the dry land, that restless spirit would not be quelled. As soon as creation was in place, the dark spirit began to destroy it. All that the good Earth brought forth, Chaos sought to kill, to wound if it could not kill, to infect with despair if it could not wound. In everything that was bright and beautiful, Chaos--the Dark One--insinuated its terror.

"When human mortals appeared in the Earth and learned to understand something of the Noble Way of life, the Dark One made war against their souls and sought to lure them from the Labyrinth into the Maze. Some humans kept to the Noble Way, but others--many more, I fear, than those who were steadfast--allowed darkness into their minds and made war upon the Earth out of greed, for their love of gain.

"But the Creator also made a sacred space, a refuge, in the heart of the Earth. Its name was different then; now it is called the Graelands. There all was beauty and peace. Wolf and lamb played together; lion and leopard lay down while deer grazed nearby. None were afraid; none went hungry. Men and women lived there also, pledged to be Guardians of the Graelands forever. They were the first *Sendars* and *Sendaras*, and they gathered friends about them--the Companions of the Noble Way. They have watched over the Graelands always.

"For an Age, and two Ages, and three Ages, the Dark One attacked the Earth, seeking to destroy all that was good upon it. The Companions of the Noble Way prevailed against it, though at great cost to themselves.

"Finally the Dark One grew strong enough to attack the Graelands directly, and a terrible war was fought, lasting many epochs. Neither one side nor the other gained the victory. But in the waning of the Third Age, the Dark One developed a new evil, a thing made, not created, that had never before been seen in the Earth.

"We know it as the Ashes of Waste, and we have no defense against it.

Charleynne Gates

"On the last day of the Third Age, the Dark One unleashed the Ash against the Graelands. We were not prepared for such evil, and nearly all the Companions of the Noble Way perished. So many friends lost to us! Well-loved faces not to be seen again until the ultimate end of all things.

"In desperation, the High Council of the Labyrinth gathered in the Graelands with those few friends who remained. By our combined powers a tremendous energy was raised, and with it the Labyrinth was sundered from the rest of Earth, hurled into another dimension, so that the Graelands might not be overcome by the Ash. The Sundering strained our resources of power and wisdom to the utmost, but it made the Graelands safe--for a time.

"We had no wish to abandon the Earth, but our losses were so great that we had to create a place of refuge where we might regroup. We needed to develop a plan whereby the Graelands could be defended in the Last Great Battle to come. Only a few secret portals were left between the Earth--your Maze World--and the Labyrinth World. Ravenhome is such a portal.

"It took us many centuries to recover from the losses we suffered. Now we are well into the Fourth Age, and we are nearly ready to face the enemy again. The Dark One has come close to mastering the Maze World, but the defenses of the Graelands remain fast.

"But Chaos, that old serpent, still seeks to find a way into the Graelands. Until recently, our patrols have kept the Labyrinth World clear of contamination from the Ash, but lately something has gotten through, looking for a way into the Graelands. The *Sendara* herself became infected with an Ash-derived poison during one of her visits to the outer portals. Because of her illness, she cannot return to the Graelands until she has been healed, lest the contagion spread there. If she does not return soon, the Graelands will die, for she is its heart and soul. If the Graelands die," the voice went on, echoing what Oliver had been told the first evening at Ravenhome, "the whole of the Labyrinth World will follow. And after the Labyrinth, your world, Oliver Medley, will also die—unless you can find and recover Saint Amber's Rose. For in it is hidden the secret of the Labyrinth, the secret that will restore the Light and heal the world.

-- 126 --

Saint Amber's Rose

"The third question is this: Will you seek to discover your Gift, to find Saint Amber's Rose, and to save the *Sendara* Flavia, no matter the cost to yourself?"

A cold wind blew against him, chilling him to the bone. He shivered, and his consciousness returned to the present. Once more he stood at the entrance to the labyrinth, but now he faced outward, having traversed the whole encircled pattern without realizing it.

"But what can I do?" he whispered desperately. He lifted his hands to his bowed head, as if he might press from his brain a solution to the dilemma in which he found himself.

"Take heart, Friend Oliver!" Dandriel said firmly, appearing by his side and startling him considerably. "You have been entrusted with a Gift greater than yourself. Help will be given you in your hour of utmost need. Ask! You will be answered."

"But what--" Oliver protested. "I don't--"

The deep tone of a bell reverberated through the forest.

"The High Council of Labyrinth Guardians meets tonight," said the Mage. "They expect you. Dour--" to the Wraith who had semi-materialized nearby--"will you escort Friend Oliver to the Council chamber?"

"Wait!" cried Oliver. "I-I need more information! What am I supposed to--"

But Personal Assistant Dour had already interposed his transparent self between Oliver and the Mage, and with a gesture indicated that Oliver was to follow him.

The Mage remained beside the labyrinth, watching Oliver disappear into the gray mist. Then he lifted his face to the night sky and blew out the moon like a candle-flame.

Darkness descended; at once a ring of lambent eyes appeared around the labyrinth. Hands hidden in his sleeves, the Mage stood before the opening, barring all entry.

"Ab'addon! Come forth!" Dandriel called into the darkness.

One pair of yellow eyes detached itself from the others and approached the Mage: the form of a mortal man cloaked and hooded in black, his face in deepest shadow. "Mage." The hood bowed slightly.

"What do you want here?" asked the Mage.

Charleynne Gates

"I want Medley. And the Rose."

"The Rose will never grow where you would confine it. And remember: You may not touch Medley while he stays in Keeper's Inn," replied the Mage.

"And when he leaves?" questioned the man.

"Then he will be under the Protection," stated the Mage.

"Protection!" repeated the man with a low laugh. "Against the Powers I hold? I think not. When he leaves the inn, he will be open to me, and I shall lead him by hidden ways to my realm. There I will take his Gift for myself."

The Mage made a swift sign in the air between himself and the shadow-man. "Ab'addon, beware! Threshold Forest is not your domain. You cannot harm him here."

"I know well who guards the forest! But by covenant with the Guardians, I roam freely within its borders. And I will take him, Dandriel, Medley and his Gift, when and where I please!"

"Your time has not yet come," replied the Mage. "Begone!"

The shadow was no longer there, nor the ring of lambent eyes, nor the circle of white stones. Threshold Forest closed in, obliterating the Labyrinth.

In deep contemplation, the Mage paced the pathway back to the inn.

Oliver stood in the small side entrance where Dour had temporarily left him. He marveled at the changes in the inn's Great Hall, now dimmed to dusk. Not a single candle had been lighted, nor were any torches blazing in their sconces. The fires in the four hearths had been banked to an outline of glowing embers, providing warmth but little light.

Even so, it was obvious that the room had been transformed. No longer was there any resemblance to a busy inn, where last night a motley gathering of travelers had consumed quantities of food and shouted from one end of the room to the other for more ale. Now it seemed more like the sanctuary of a great cathedral. The roof, supported by flying buttresses, seemed to have grown upward to a great height, and none of the furnishings of a tavern were to be seen. The floor had been cleared of crowded furniture; in its place was a long, narrow table in the center of the room, covered in cloth of silver.

Crystal goblets set with precious gems were placed evenly down its entire length.

Despite the ringing of the bell, whose reverberations echoed faintly in the shadowed corners, no one appeared in the hall--not a traveler, not a servitor, not a soul. The entire space was full of a whispery silence in which invisible currents of anticipation darted about.

He stared at the long table and saw at its head--so far away from him that it was barely visible in the distance--a chair quite different from the others: a high-backed throne surmounted by a golden circle enclosing a cross. He wondered who would occupy it.

Why didn't Great-Aunt Belvedine tell me about this in advance? I could have packed my evening clothes. Too late now! The garments he'd been given seemed more suitable for hiking in the woods than attending a formal dinner party, but they'd have to do. No others had been forthcoming.

"May I assist you with your vestments, sir?" asked a watery voice near his left ear.

Oliver jumped a little and spun around. Dour's wispy transparency hovered valet-like at his side.

"Oh! Please do," he said, trying to calm his thumping heart. "Is this really where I'm supposed to be?"

"Yes indeed, sir," responded the Wraith, adroitly stepping in back of Oliver and whisking a clothes-brush over his garments. "The Gathering of the Grand Council will take place quite soon. I note with interest, sir," Dour went on, busying himself with minute adjustments to hang of tunic and fold of cloak, "the depiction of a caravan in the coat of arms shown on your place mat."

Coat of arms? Caravan? Oliver opened his mouth to ask, but Dour continued without pausing for questions.

"I wondered what model of vehicle it might be? I am personally saving up for a Paragon 7-ZX, but my lady friend, actually my fiancée as of last Wednesday fortnight, prefers a Lavender Dreamwagon. More room for the future little ones and their accoutrements, is her reasoning."

Oliver had no idea what Dour was talking about, but he felt it polite to murmur agreement. Unaware of his incomprehension, the Wraith went on.

"The caravan on the seal of your realm--wherever it might be, sir; I was not informed--bears a close resemblance to the Paragon 7-ZX.

If I might have your confirmation of that fact, then Undine (my intended) might be more inclined to support my purchase of a Paragon 7-ZX rather than the Lavender Dreamwagon, which has a pudgy appearance and cannot pretend to the torque of the Paragon. My Undine is most impressed with your visit, sir, and a word from you would... I have a picture of the Paragon with me, if you wouldn't mind just taking a look for purposes of comparison."

Dour tucked the clothes-brush under his arm, whipped out an advertising brochure from the area where a fully-visible person's inside jacket pocket would be, and eagerly presented the particular page for view.

Peering at it, Oliver also saw that on the table just beneath where they stood was a mat of finely woven linen in dark blue. A place card had his name on it, spelled creatively as "Owlyfur Meedle." Oliver squinted at the design on the table mat. It was a circle in gold, and inside the circle was the outline of a covered wagon traveling across the horizon against a background of the setting sun. It was an exact replica of the design of... the design of... something that was very familiar to him, if only he could remember in what context.

Dour was right: The Paragon 7-ZX on the brochure was very like the covered wagon on his place mat. And it did look like a caravan... a gypsy caravan. Now why did that association tickle his mind with a wavering image like smoke in a mirror? Smoke and mirrors...

The Black Mirror of last night! I saw a gypsy caravan inside the mirror! What was the connection? And why had Dour suddenly become conversationally inclined? Was it because he was away from the Mage's presence?

Oliver admitted to himself that he wouldn't have guessed that a Wraith like Dour had a "normal" life, with a fiancée and a burning desire to possess a vehicle of a certain status, just the way someone in his home world would have a girlfriend and prefer a jaguar over a minivan. With a stab of shame Oliver realized that he had unconsciously been guilty of a kind of racial profiling, and reproved himself sharply.

He mulled over this uncomfortable realization as Dour twisted, tucked, straightened, and scrunched various items of his apparel. At last, satisfied with his handiwork, the Wraith gently but firmly whirled his charge around to face a mirrored panel on a nearby column.

Oliver stared at himself, astonished beyond words. Not only had his woodsy attire been brushed free of the odd mote of dust, but also had been magically altered into a more formal, elegant garment. He couldn't help admiring his reflection. It seemed so lifelike.

"Begging your pardon, sir," Dour interrupted Oliver's moment of narcissism. "The High Council is about to gather. This way, sir, if I might be so bold." He led the way to a concealed alcove near the mirrored column. Oliver followed meekly.

The alcove was just secluded enough to shelter him and Dour from casual view but allow him to see most of the Great Hall. He had misunderstood the Mage, of course. He wouldn't actually be seated at that grand table; he wasn't of sufficient standing to grace such an event. The card with his name on it must have been misplaced, or else it was meant for another person whose name was actually spelled in that unusual way.

"Oh no, sir, you will sit at table with the High Council," Dour hastened to explain, intuiting Oliver's train of thought. "It is simply that visitors are not permitted to witness the Gathering of the Labyrinth Guardians, which takes place before the Summoning of the Guests. I took it upon myself to assume that you might be interested in seeing the Gathering. It's quite memorable. My old master hid me in here to see a Gathering back when I was an apprentice Wraith. There hasn't been a High Council since that time.

"The Labyrinth Guardians don't like to be observed, but in this little alcove no one will notice us. You understand, sir, the Guardians aren't like us. They don't see things the way we normal people do."

"They can't see?" Oliver exclaimed.

"Oh no, it's not that. Indeed, they see further and deeper into most things than we do. It's simply that in descending to Keeper's Inn, they must pass through a portal connecting many dimensions, and the energies involved in that process could be extremely dangerous for the Labyrinth World. No telling what might happen. And, sir, if you don't mind my asking another favor--"

"Not at all, if I'm able to do it," Oliver replied.

"My three brothers and I were separated during a cataclysmic event in the Labyrinth. Brother Grimtread is at Ravenhome and Brother

Charleynne Gates

Gall is the apothecary at the Abbey. We three can communicate, but it's our little brother, Gloom, who worries us. We haven't heard from him since the event. If you should happen to hear anything of him during your Quest, anything at all, we would greatly appreciate a word. The Raven Express will always find us."

Quest? That word again! Oliver wasn't sure what Dour meant, but he agreed to keep on the lookout for a Wraith named Gloom. He was about to ask what "Quest" Dour was talking about, when--

"Back, sir!" Dour hissed in his ear. "Stand well back! Here they come!"

By now the Great Hall was almost completely enshrouded in darkness; only the silver tablecloth glimmered in reflected light. He tried holding his breath, straining to hear the least noise in the eerie quiet, but nothing moved. Not even a mouse skittered in the wainscoting. Silence was absolute.

And then... a horn called in the distance, immeasurably far from Keeper's Inn. Three times it sounded, and faded into nothingness.

Music never heard in Oliver's world began, solemn and reverent. Illumination increased sufficiently for him to see the famed Owl Guard of Threshold Forest process with measured steps along the walls of the Great Hall. He had caught glimpses of one or two before as he passed through the corridors of the inn, but now he saw them clearly. So tall were they! Two heads or more they towered above him: warrior-women half human, half owl, unearthly beautiful in their melding. Wide wings gleaming in the dusk, soundless as snow they paced, feathered hands holding bannered lances, moonlike eyes gathering and reflecting light. Like rows of marble carvings they stood at their posts, sentinels of the High Council.

Then did shadows thicken in the corners of the Great Hall and condense into cloudy forms moving up the nave in slow-paced lines. They were almost indistinguishable in the dusk, but he saw them clearly in his mind, the people of the Elder Ages: knights and foresters, shepherds and kings, queens and maidens, beasts of wood and wild, tree-walkers, stone-riders, river-dancers. They emerged from their hidden realms, no tread sounding upon the floor, and like a dream, one by one they passed by the alcove where Oliver and the Wraith hid. Never did those otherworld beings appear to notice him, but, half-fearful, half-marveling, he felt their awareness of him as his skin

-- 132 --

prickled with expectancy. Slowly the grand procession filled the Great Hall.

Then that happened which, of all wondrous and unbelievable things Oliver had seen, was the most incredible of all. High above him the vaulted ceiling opened to the midnight sky. There in the heavens, unimaginably remote yet coming closer and closer, were the star-woven constellations: Cygnus, Pegasus, and the signs of the autumn zodiac-- Libra, Scorpius, Sagittarius. Immense, walking in beauty to the music of the spheres, they descended from deep space into the hall and proceeded to their places at the high table.

Inside the curtained alcove, Oliver filled his vision with that holy radiance, scarcely able to breathe for the wonder of it. Tears stung his eyes and ran down his cheeks. He would have sunk to his knees had not Dour grasped his arm firmly and propped him upright.

"No, no, sir," he admonished in a whisper. "We mustn't kneel to them. They wouldn't want us to. They're created beings like us."

Oliver didn't fully comprehend what Dour told him, but he remained standing, filling heart and mind with the glory of the heavens come down to earth.

Only one chair remained empty, the throne at the head of the high table. The company of constellations turned toward it and with one accord bowed in its direction, as if to a Power superseding them all. To Oliver's view nothing was there, but even in their narrow nook he felt a tremulous pressure in the air, and he sensed that what was about to appear was beyond all imagining.

Motes of stardust drifted down from the vault of midnight. Down and around the Great Hall they swirled until Oliver became dizzy and shut his eyes against the tumult of light. When he opened them again, the throne was filled with stars in the shape and form of the Oldest of All Old Things: ancient Presence, implacable Power.

Thus the High Council of Labyrinth Guardians convened, Oliver wrote later in the "Chronicle of the Rose". *We knew that it was the final Gathering, for when its last great task is finished, the Guardians must depart forever. For this is the Threshold of the Last Age.*

"LET THE QUESTORS BE CALLED."

The voice came from the throne. It was neither a human nor an animal voice; it was deeper by far than any sound the earth can make.

Oliver marveled that he was able to understand what was said, for the Guardians spoke in the long-vanished language of Old Boreal. In that tongue, it was said, thought flew to thought, mind sang to mind, and no deceit was possible when no desire could be hidden.

Straining to peer through a tiny gap in the curtain, Oliver saw the Mage Dandriel advance to stand beside the throne. Opening an enormous book resting upon a lectern, he began to read aloud. Later, Oliver wished the book had been far longer, indeed, had never come to an end. Or had never been written.

"The *Foressa* Mildrith Antara."

The massive oaken doors of the inn opened, and Mil strode inside, clad in silver armor that covered her like scales, supple and serpentine, exactly as Oliver had seen in the hall mirrors at Ravenhome. With a salute to the throne, she went to a place near the end of the table.

"Portia Belvedine Medley Makebold, Countess de Montfort."

Oliver had to stuff the edge of his cloak into his mouth to keep from shrieking with laughter as Great-Aunt Belvedine appeared, clad in an antique black battle costume with a bouffant riding skirt. Three white plumes nodded from her burnished helmet as she made her reverence toward the throne. Her ever-present umbrella, sticking out of its scabbard, just missed whisking up the hem of her skirt. She looked so much like an ostrich that tears of suppressed mirth ran down Oliver's cheeks.

"Tipp and Tapp, the Brothers Whackitt."

The Dwarvian smiths came in, doffed their caps to the Presence, and took places opposite Mil and Belvedine. Only two empty chairs were left, one at the foot of the table and one adjacent to it.

"Hera Vespasia, Great Chief of the *Norrengild.*"

Down from a flying buttress swept the great horned owl. She landed on the back of the chair at the end of the table, folded her wings, and opened her luminous eyes to their fullest extent.

All at once Oliver became aware of a feeling in the pit of his stomach as if a bottomless chasm had opened inside him. He wondered if there was a back door to the alcove which he might use to escape without being noticed.

"Oliver Medley, Ph.D."

WAIT! Oliver thought he shouted, but his mouth was so dry that no sound came out.

Saint Amber's Rose

Be steadfast! he thought he heard Dandriel whisper in his ear, but the Mage remained at the distant head of the table.

"Sir, they're waiting," muttered Dour, and gave him a respectful shove.

Hesitantly he took a step out of the alcove, then another, and another. Imitating the others, he removed his hat, bowed toward the throne, and peered helplessly at those he knew. Mil gave the slightest of nods toward the one place left beside the Whackitt brothers, the one set with the dark-blue linen mat and the card with his name. He took the chair as unobtrusively as possible.

"Pavarr, Prince of Taraman."

No one answered to the name.

"Pavarr, Prince of Taraman," the Mage repeated.

Again no one answered or appeared.

A third time the Mage called out, "Pavarr, Prince of Taraman."

No one came forward to bow to the throne or to claim the empty seat.

Who is he? Oliver wondered, with a flash of irrational jealousy. *A friend of Flavia's?* Or-- Of course someone so beautiful as she must be married or at least betrothed. Why hadn't he thought of that before?

His heart turned to ashes.

Whatever this Pavarr person might be to Flavia, where was he? Unavoidably detained? Or not coming at all? *Did he abandon her—as I did?*

Oliver's heart turned from ashes to stone. If Pavarr, whoever he was, had hurt her in any way whatsoever—

There being no response to his call, Dandriel turned again to the book before him and continued to read from its pages. As he spoke aloud the words therein, it seemed to Oliver that the voices of the constellations joined with the Mage. Whatever may have been the words that were read, what he heard was a letter to his own world, left so far behind.

"Children of the Maze World, do you truly believe that you are the only living beings in all the Cosmos? We, who are the substance of the stars, tell you that you are not. Will you listen to us or will you turn away from the truth, as you so often have before? Your philosophers, your scientists, your artists, musicians, and poets, aye, your prophets themselves, have told you in countless ways that you are *not* the center of All That Is. Even when you realized that the Maze World is a dot at the edge of a minor galaxy whose real name is not yet known to you, still you could not rid yourselves of false pride in the chains and shackles you forged for yourselves, believing them to be wings.

"Do you not understand that all the creatures on your planet, even the sands of the sea and the rocks from which they come, have life? That everything in your world has will and memory—and a soul? You have forgotten this truth—forgotten the necessity for humility and respect, and by so doing you have separated yourselves from the Great Circle of Creation. You believed that you gained the mastery over those who share your world, but you have only learned to manipulate and to destroy. Greed and Pride have led you to the secrets of Destruction, not of Creation, as you suppose.

"Children of the Maze, you will soon have the potential to destroy other worlds in the same way you have ruined your own. At this moment your powers are not mature, but if they are not checked, if you refuse to understand the evil you are about to do, then you will start a tidal force of destruction that will not cease until it reaches the farthest boundaries of the Universe.

"And that cannot be permitted. We, who dwell in the star-woven Womb of the Universe, have descended to this world to warn you.

"Even now you have lost the Light of the Graelands, and that by your own doing. Find Her; find the Light and live within it or be condemned to Darkness, to Chaos, forever."

A deep and awe-filled silence ensued, or so it seemed to Oliver, who had gone as pale as a corpse-light. *How can I be responsible for every human misdeed? On the other hand—I did lose the Light of the Graelands. I have to rectify that—to redeem myself. But I don't know how--*

"GIVE THE QUESTORS THEIR CHARGE," said the Presence.

"Without Prince Pavarr?" Dandriel inquired respectfully.

The Presence inclined its diadem of stars.

The Mage gripped the staff of his office. "Questors!" he called. "Stand in your places."

At once Mil, Great-Aunt Belvedine, Tipp, Tapp, and (after half a second) Oliver arose from their chairs.

Saint Amber's Rose

Dandriel lifted his staff and intoned: "You will seek the *Sendara* Flavia by wood and by water, by earth, air, and fire, by day and by night, until she is safely returned to the Graelands. For she is the life of the Labyrinth and its hope until the end of the Age."

He struck the end of his staff upon the floor. The sound of it echoed in the great space like a boom of thunder. "Speak, Questors," he continued. "Before these witnesses, say you, one by one, if you accept this charge."

"I do," said Mil immediately.

"And I," said Great-Aunt Belvedine.

"And we," said Tipp and Tapp together.

"I also, in the name of the *Norrengild*," Hera Vespasia replied with a sharp click of her beak.

"And--and I," said Oliver Medley last of all.

"Be valiant," Dandriel admonished them, "and faithful to your task. Find the *Sendara*, for the hope of the world."

The Mage struck his staff once more upon the stone tiles, and at once the company around the table raised their crystal goblets. Finding one in his hand, Oliver did the same.

"Grace to the Graelands!" Dandriel called.

"Grace to the Graelands!" responded that mighty Gathering. All drank of the cup, and it seemed to Oliver that the wine therein was made of starlight.

"Now GO!" thundered the Presence in a voice like many mountains, and at once the massive double doors of the inn blew open with a tremendous rush of wind and banged back against the walls.

"Wait! Wait!" cried Oliver, finding courage for one last protest. "I need more information!"

"It's too late now!" snapped Great-Aunt Belvedine. "This way!"

She clutched him by the sleeve of his tunic and dragged him along as their little group of six ran pell-mell toward the doors. Oliver glanced back over his shoulder as they crossed the threshold, still hoping for a last-second explanation. But to his horror, he saw not the Great Hall with its starlit company, but stones and beams and buttresses tumbling inward as the ground beneath their feet shook and split apart. The earthquake opened deep cracks in the earth to either side of them, and clouds of dust billowed as they fled, obscuring his view.

"No!" he cried out, and struggled to escape from Great-Aunt Belvedine's iron grip. "We have to go back! We have to help them!"

"Run! We have to get away!" someone shouted, and Mil's hand grabbed his other sleeve. Between them, Mil and Great-Aunt Belvedine pulled him down a narrow path toward the dark inn gardens.

But he managed to glance over his shoulder once more and saw, rising above the dust and tumult, the face of the Presence on the throne, the Oldest of All Old Things: Ursa Major. The Great Bear. And a sudden terror of things that were light-years beyond his understanding shook him to the depths of his soul.

Then he ran with the others as hard as he was able.

Part II

The Sundering

This is the trouble with new adventures: They take you
to unexplored territory of the soul as well. You find out
things about yourself you'd just as soon not know, things
you don't have to face when you stay home.
--Dorcas Smucker, "Letter from Harrisburg"
The Register-Guard, July 8, 2007

Chapter Eight

The Destruction

"There! Through those trees."

Ildranna, mounted behind Pavarr, peered over the prince's shoulder into the distance, then pointed toward a birch grove off to their left, where a narrow path made a shallow groove in the leaf-strewn ground. The mark was so faint that it was nearly indistinguishable unless you knew where to look. To Pavarr, it seemed to be nothing more than an old deer trail.

"That trail leads to Centerpole--my village. Hurry! Oh, please hurry!" the woman urged him, but the prince signaled Firemark to stay where they were.

"Wait," he said over his shoulder. "There may still be *wyrga* around. Weren't you and Vord captured nearby?"

"No, no, we were much closer to the Bordering Cliffs, gathering *fearn*-spores for medicines. We didn't expect--we didn't know the *wyrga* had come into the forest. Please go on! I must get back to my mother and sister."

But the prince shook his head firmly. "Best to be cautious. No telling how far the *wyrga* have penetrated."

Despite her urging, Pavarr refused to move directly onto the trail, and instead went several yards off to the side, weaving their way slowly through close-crowded birches. Firemark walked as quietly as he could, making almost no sound at all. Pavarr warned Ildranna not to say anything, lest in her eagerness to reach her home she alert an enemy.

After a while Firemark stopped, although the prince had given him no signal. The horse took in a long breath and flicked one ear. Taking the cue, the prince sniffed the air and detected the faint, sweetish odor of a fire gone cold.

"What's wrong?" whispered Ildranna, then caught the scent herself. "Oh, no!" Her eyes grew wide with fear, and she covered her mouth and nose with the edge of the blanket wrapped around her shoulders.

Slowly, cautiously they went onward until at last the birch trees gave way to a clearing where Ildranna's village stood--or what remained of it, for there was nothing but charred timbers left from a conflagration. Burnt ends of logs and planks stuck out of the ground like grave markers, and debris lay strewn across the open space--debris covered with layers of gray ash.

There was no one alive in the whole place. No villagers lay where they had fallen, either wounded or dead. Even more mysterious, there were no bodies to be seen anywhere.

Firemark halted at the edge of the trees, still inside their cover. Pavarr quickly scanned the area, but sight and hearing told him nothing. Whoever--whatever--had destroyed this place had struck and vanished.

Behind him Ildranna smothered a moan of anguish. Then, before Pavarr could hold her back, she slid down from the horse's back and ran straight into the ruined village. She stopped in the central space beside a tall carved pole that had been broken off halfway and partially burned, and began to turn around slowly, her face a mask of horror.

Pavarr dismounted, whispered to Firemark to remain where he was, and crept toward the woman, watching keenly for indications of an enemy returning, or any alien movement at all. Once, keeping an eye on the distraught Ildranna, he knelt beside a tumbled pile of burned wood that must once have been a family's dwelling, and put his hand on the blackened embers.

They still held a faint warmth.

No more than two days ago, the prince thought, and felt under the ashes, where the embers were warmer. He touched something, dug deeper, brought it out. It was part of a silver chain whose torn links indicated that it had been broken off from something larger. Absently he fingered the intricate links, working out in his mind what must have happened to the village.

Yesterday. The hour before dawn, while the people were asleep. They were peaceful, so didn't think to set a night watch for an enemy. The palisade around the houses was to keep out nocturnal animals.

He peered around the devastated area. *Where are they? Why are there no bodies? Were they all captured?*

Then he saw the thing he suspected might be in the vicinity: the mark of the *wryga*. A narrow trail of disturbed earth began at the west side of the village and led toward the fields where the people raised their crops. The earth looked as if frost had passed over it, as if crystals of ice had turned black and scorched the ground.

Ashes of Waste.

He had seen it before.

Wherever the Ashes of Waste touched, nothing would grow again. Even if the people returned to this place, the fields where they had grown corn and beans and green vegetables, their orchards and flower gardens, were ruined forever.

More than a hundred generations must have lived here, but the people of Centerpole Village could never come home again.

He guessed what had happened: A *wyrga* raiding party came after human slave material to make into more *wyrga*, as he had seen them do inside Castle Mormorion, and as they had begun to do to Vord and Ildranna. But the prince had not seen *wyrga* invade this far into Threshold Forest before.

The Lord of Desolation was extending his realm, casting his shadow wider over the Labyrinth lands.

And the *Sendara* of the Graelands, the ultimate defense of the Labyrinth: Where was she?

Pavarr frowned, piecing disparate bits of information together in his mind. He no longer saw the devastation before him; his thoughts ranged over the borders of the Labyrinth lands to the Great Waste itself.

Ildranna gave a small moan, as if she had no strength left, and fell to the ground in a faint. Stuffing the chain hastily inside his shirt, Pavarr got up and ran to her. Kneeling, he put his arm beneath her shoulders to try to revive her.

A black-fledged arrow sang through the air, passing no more than an inch from his face, and buried itself in the carved pole. In one motion, Pavarr laid Ildranna down again, whipped out his dagger, and took what little shelter was possible behind the pole's base.

"Come out, *wyrga*!" came the rough command--from a young voice, one barely out of childhood. "I want to see your coward face. And stay away from the woman!"

"I am no *wyrga*!" the prince called back. "I was bringing this woman home. I have never been here before."

"Who are you, then?" demanded the voice, hidden inside a dark patch of brush at the edge of the village. "How do you know her?"

Pavarr hesitated for an instant, then made up his mind. The voice probably belonged to a boy from the village, one doubtless known to Ildranna.

"I am Pavarr of Taraman. Come out yourself, and so will I. The woman needs help. Do you have any water?"

For a moment the brush didn't move. The speaker was being cautious, thinking it over. Pavarr silently approved. The boy had sense enough not to trust a stranger right away.

Then a slender, hooded figure emerged from the shade of trees and underbrush and cautiously approached Pavarr, who had moved back to Ildranna's side. The boy had his bowstring drawn and another arrow fitted in the notch, ready to let fly at one suspicious move from the prince.

So--he has courage! Pavarr decided, despite being in danger of instant death. He kept perfectly still, watching both the boy and Ildranna's supine figure. *There's a lad I'd like to have on my side.*

"Here's water," said the boy. With a quick, practiced motion he transferred the bow and arrow--still notched--to one hand, unfastened a leather flask at his belt, and tossed it to the prince. Before Pavarr caught it, the boy had drawn his bowstring back to full tension, with the arrow pointed at the prince's heart.

Pavarr sheathed his dagger, surprising the archer, and knelt again to sprinkle a few drops of water on Ildranna's face and pat her cheek gently. After watching for several seconds, the boy evidently decided that Pavarr intended no harm. Hesitantly he came closer to where Ildranna lay, close enough to see her face.

"Ildranna!" the boy exclaimed. "Ildranna!"

Forgetting Pavarr completely, he put his bow and arrow on the ground and knelt at her side. Taking her hand, he began to stroke it urgently.

"Sister! Sister!" he pleaded, his voice high and near to breaking. "Wake up! It's me, Andis!" The boy's hood fell back, and the prince saw his face in full light.

The archer was a girl! Thirteen or fourteen at most, with a slight figure and short dark hair that looked as if someone had chopped it off with a hatchet. The face had the same oval shape as Ildranna's, and the same eyes. In a few more years, Pavarr noted, the child would grow into a striking beauty.

After a while--too long, Pavarr decided, and wondered how or where he would find help for her--Ildranna opened her eyes. A faint blush of color came back to her cheeks, and she looked at the two figures bending anxiously over her.

"Andis! Is it really you?" she whispered. "Are you... all right? What... happened to our village?"

Andis opened her mouth to answer, but "Wait," Pavarr said. "We have to get under cover. Is there any shelter left where I can take her?"

"This way," said the girl. Grabbing her weapons, she stood up and led the way out of the village center toward a path on the opposite side.

Pavarr lifted Ildranna and carried her after Andis. Ildranna protested feebly, but soon fell silent, too exhausted to speak any more.

He followed Andis through birch groves and across one or two small streams until they came to a small hunter's cabin built of logs and pebbled mortar, well concealed among the trees. The single room inside was immaculate and efficiently arranged, with a bench, two rough-hewn stools, a table, and a low bed against one wall. Weapons and hunting equipment hung on the walls--quivers of arrows, coils of rope, snowshoes, axes, every item a hunter would need. At one end was a fireplace with a full kindling box on one side and a cupboard on the other.

Pavarr laid Ildranna down on the low bed, which had a neatly-made bedroll spread on it. Andis found a blanket and tucked it around her sister.

"You need something to eat," said the girl, and went to the cupboard. Opening it, she took out wooden trenchers and spoons and containers of dried and preserved food. She built up a fire with quick, compact movements and began to make dinner in the small cauldron in the hearth while Pavarr gave Ildranna more water from the girl's flask.

Experienced in hunter-craft, Pavarr thought. *Someone taught her well.*

The fire would produce some smoke, he knew, but Andis had evidently decided to risk detection. An intuitive understanding of when to take risks: That was the mark of a good hunter... or a warrior.

Saint Amber's Rose

Three bowls of steaming venison stew with root vegetables and a basket of bread were soon on the table. Andis was about to go to Ildranna's bedside to help her up when a sudden scrunch of leaves and dry twigs outside made Andis's hand flash to her hunting knife. She darted to the shuttered window, flattened herself against the wall, and peered out a miniscule slit in the shutter. Pavarr, absorbed with his soup, didn't bother to look up. Ildranna glanced toward her sister and Pavarr. Seeing that Pavarr seemed unconcerned, she moved to the table, cupped her hands around her bowl to warm them, then tentatively dipped her spoon in the broth.

"It's a horse!" Andis whispered. "The biggest one I've ever seen!"

Pavarr stopped eating long enough to reply. "That'd be Firemark," he said. "He'll be wanting food himself." He drank the broth in the bottom of his bowl and left the room, stepping outside so unobtrusively that only the most observant spy would have noticed him.

The prince removed saddle and gear and dug out the horse's feedbag. Before he attached it, the two friends exchanged vital information in the equine tongue lest there be hidden listeners.

"You saw no sign of *wyrga* war-bands," the prince repeated, "except their tracks where they came through the forest to raid. And left the same way they came, with the captured villagers? So."

The horse murmured something more.

"A dead *wyrga* at the edge of the forest, with an arrow-wound in the great vein at the back of his skull. Probably the sister, Andis, killed it. She must have seen the raiders leaving. She's a good marksman, almost as good as a Taraman archer.

"I want to find out why the *wyrga* attacked this particular village. There must be other settlements closer to the bordering cliffs. Was it a random raid or were they hunting Ildranna and Vord specifically, to take them to Castle Mormorion?"

But Firemark did not know the answers to these questions.

Inside the hut, Andis left her listening post and rejoined her sister at the table. "That man didn't say anything I could hear," she complained in a whisper. "But the horse seemed to be actually talking to him. It's as if they understand what each other is saying. He's beautiful, that horse," she added under her breath. "I'd like to ride him."

Charleynne Gates

She recollected herself and ladled broth into her sister's bowl. "You must eat more, Sister, and build up your strength. Now," she continued as Ildranna sipped spoonfuls of nourishing stew, "tell me about him. He says his name is Pavarr of Taraman, but who is he really? Can we trust him?"

"I think so. He's been good to me," Ildranna insisted. "He was wounded down on the Great Waste, but he took me with him after Vord... after Vord--" She hesitated, then told her sister everything, including Vord's death.

"Grace be with him," Andis said simply, and covered her sister's hand with her own. After a moment, "Sister--did Vord ever find our father's medallion?" she asked hesitantly. "Was he carrying it with him?"

"I don't think so," Ildranna answered, one hand rubbing her forehead. "The *wyrga* took everything away from us, even our clothes. We had nothing when we escaped from the castle. If he found it, he never told me. And he would have, I know. It belonged to our father. He wouldn't have kept it from me. O Vord! Andis, I miss him so terribly! We're going to have a baby, and now he'll never see his own child."

What medallion is that? Pavarr wondered, eavesdropping without shame. Not that he doubted their courage: Ildranna and he together had helped each other climb up the steep, treacherous bordering cliffs, and it was only because of her and Firemark that he had been healed of his injury. And the girl had been ready to put an arrow through the prince to protect her sister. But why did she ask about a medallion? It seemed to be important enough for Andis to mention it even as her sister grieved for her dead husband.

"Is Mother all right?" Ildranna asked when Pavarr came back into the room as silently as he had gone out. "She wasn't taken away, was she? Is she hiding? I want to see her so much!"

"Oh, Sister," Andis began, and gulped back tears. "She's gone. No!" as Ildranna half-rose from her stool. "Not with the *wryga*. She-- she died. It was the week before the raid. You knew she was ill, even before you... left. The medicine women could do nothing more for her. She always believed you'd find a way to return to us, and wanted to live long enough to see you one more time, but--"

"Better that she died before the *wyrga* came," Ildranna said, with bitterness in her voice. "At least she was spared that."

-- 146 --

"What about your father? The other men in the village?" asked Pavarr, joining them at the table.

"Our father was killed years ago when I was ten and Andis was only a baby," Ildranna replied. "We have no brothers."

"Everyone in the village was taken away two days ago," said Andis. "The *wryga* set fire to the houses and drove the people out before them. I knew it was the *wyrga* because I saw another village after a raid, and they left their stench, like gases burning in the marshlands. I was away in the forest hunting deer when they came to Centerpole. I smelled the smoke and raced back here, but too late. No one was here, and everything was destroyed. But one *wyrga* stayed after the others. I found it digging through the burning embers as if it were looking for something. I put an arrow through the vein that holds its life."

"You are brave," nodded the prince. "Not many would have returned after a *wyrga*-raid. What was the *wyrga* looking for? Do you know?"

"No," said Andis quickly, looking at her sister, not at him.

"Gold, maybe," Ildranna supplied hastily, "but no one in our village had anything like that."

"Where will you go now?" asked the prince, changing the subject deliberately. He was curious about what the *wyrga* was searching for, but he didn't want to make the two sisters aware of that. "You can't stay here. I'll take you to another village."

"I--we--" Ildranna faltered, and covered her face with her hands. The numbness of her initial shock was passing, and the full impact of what had happened to them and to their village struck her like a blow from a mailed fist. "Oh, Andis! Mother... Vord... all our neighbors, our friends--gone!" She tried to stifle her sobs, but they wouldn't be held back any longer.

Andis came swiftly around the table and took her sister in her arms. Together they mourned their dead. Respecting their sorrow, Pavarr quietly went outside again to think and plan.

The forest was thick here, out of sight of the village. The prince listened carefully, but heard only the nocturnal sounds of prowling animals, nothing unusual. Firemark waited as his friend circled the cabin slowly, letting his vision become accustomed to the settling night.

Pavarr finished his circuit of the little cabin and returned to stand beside the horse, pondering what to do next and how far he could trust the two women. They seemed to be exactly what they were, villagers who had lost everyone they knew save each other, but he sensed they were holding something back from him. But then, he thought wryly, they were being wary of him as well, exactly what he would have advised a friend of his to do in the presence of a stranger.

The full moon rose above the forest, its light filtering through interlaced branches to dapple the cabin in light and shadow. Firemark stirred and lifted a hoof off the ground. Pavarr, aware of the horse's every motion, waited for Firemark to indicate whether he needed to take cover or draw his dagger to defend himself.

Firemark stepped away from the hut to a nearby patch of thick brushwood. There he struck the ground with his hoof--once, twice-- making very little noise. The prince came swiftly to his side and carefully examined where Firemark indicated. The moon's light dimmed above the forest canopy, but not before the prince noticed the outline of a small, square trapdoor underneath a layer of dirt and old leaves. A cellar for storage? A hideaway? Whatever it was, it had been opened recently, for Pavarr saw signs of disturbance.

Working noiselessly, Pavarr brushed away dirt and twigs and exposed part of the trapdoor. He tugged at the iron ring; it came up easily, confirming that someone had used it not long ago. Peering into the space below the door, he saw several crude steps cut into the earth between twisted tree-roots. And at the bottom of the hole, a packed dirt floor led off to--what? A bolt-hole?

The moon found a clear space in the foliage long enough for his eye to catch something else--the tinsel glitter of metal dropped on the ground directly beneath the trapdoor. He climbed down the narrow steps, reached for it, and brought it into the light... and marveled at the confluence of destinies whose evidence he held in his hand.

It was a medallion, scorched silver on a broken and twisted silver chain of a peculiar pattern. On the medallion was engraved a coat of arms, one with which he was intimately familiar: a circlet of oak leaves enclosing three stars. Below the circlet were three runic symbols. It was the device of his own noble house, the ZorDain of Taraman.

The moon's light faded away, but the prince had seen enough. The question that puzzled him was--how did it get here? He took the other fragment of silver chain out of his pocket and compared its broken links to those on the medallion. They matched perfectly. Pavarr put chain and medallion back in his tunic and returned to the cabin.

Andis had gotten her sister back to bed. Ildranna slept heavily--exhausted, no doubt, from her deluge of grief. Andis, banking the fire, put a finger to her lips as Pavarr came in--an unnecessary warning, for he moved like a cat.

He went to sit near the hearth, waiting for her attention. When she finished making everything fast for the night, he asked her softly what she and her sister intended to do.

"Ildranna needs to go where we have family," Andis whispered back. "There is another village of our clan to the west. It's called Seventree. My uncle--my mother's brother--and his wife live there. They will take her in." Pavarr noticed the slip but said nothing, and Andis went on. "I think she'll be safe there, if--" She didn't finish her sentence; she didn't need to.

"She--she'll want a good midwife in the spring. Ildranna is going to have a baby," she added unnecessarily.

"I'll see that she gets to her aunt and uncle," said Pavarr. "And you. You're going with her, aren't you? She'll need you."

Andis didn't reply for a moment, nor did she meet Pavarr's eyes. Instead, she glanced at the bed where Ildranna lay huddled beneath a blanket.

"I have to see to my sister," she mumbled, and went toward the bed.

Pavarr didn't pursue the matter. The girl was very young, and had been thrust unexpectedly into a position where she had to make life-and-death decisions for two people. But she was strong, no question about that, physically and emotionally. And in spite of what Ildranna had probably told her sister about Pavarr, Andis was right not to give him her complete confidence. Not yet.

Andis pulled the blanket up over her sister's shoulders, then lay down on a bedroll on the floor beside the bed.

Pavarr took his blanket to the corner by the hearth and soon slept--lightly, as he always did, ready to awaken at the slightest disturbance.

He awoke before dawn, all senses on full alert the second he opened his eyes. He heard the quiet, even breathing of the two sisters, felt the chill of early-morning air. He waited, tense, holding his breath.

A low whicker came from Firemark, calmly cropping grasses outside the cabin, and Pavarr knew that nothing unusual had disturbed the horse. The prince eased himself out of his bedroll and went outside. He took a keen look around, but found nothing to cause alarm.

"We're in a dilemma here," he murmured in Firemark's ear. "We ought to have been at Keeper's Inn for the Calling of the Questors. Too late now. We've got to take Andis and Ildranna to their clan relatives; can't leave them here on their own. After that, we'll have to cut through the Icewode to get to The Rendezvous in time."

Firemark twitched a muscle in his shoulder.

"You're right--the Icewode's no place to be without an armed escort, especially not now. But we'll have to take our chances. I'd like to find out what that *wyrga* was looking for before we get to this other village, Seventree. Do you think it was a medallion on a chain?" he mused, not expecting an answer. "But why would a *wyrga* be looking for such a thing?"

Why indeed? The question gave Pavarr much to ponder as he saddled Firemark and made ready to leave.

They left the cabin as dawn was lightening the world, with Ildranna riding Firemark. She had protested, insisting that she was perfectly well enough to walk, but Pavarr and Andis overrode her objections and told her that she needed to ride at least part of the way.

"I'm used to walking all over this part of the forest," said Andis, chattering nervously, pacing beside Pavarr as they proceeded slowly along the path back to the ruins of their village. The loss of her home and the responsibility of caring for her older sister was beginning to sink in, and she needed someone to talk to, even a stranger like Pavarr. He let her run on, not simply out of compassion for a bereaved young girl. Some information of value might come out, possibly answers to questions he hadn't yet asked.

"My clan uncles taught me to hunt, and I've been bringing meat home for my mother and sister since I was young. Ildranna has a gift for healing. Mother trained her to be a medicine woman like she was. Me, I never could stand to stay indoors all the time, studying old books and things like that. Vord--" Andis lowered her voice so that Ildranna, half-drowsing on the horse's back, would not overhear--"Vord was a potter. He had his kiln at the edge of the village. He made the most beautiful things! Ildranna and Vord used to go collecting plants for her medicines and dyes for his pottery. They often went into the wildest part of Threshold Forest, as far as the bordering cliffs. Vord said there was a special kind of leaf-mold that made a dark-blue dye. That's where they were when--"

She swallowed hard and was silent for a while. Pavarr didn't press her.

They were about to pass the blackened pyre of ruined houses where families had once dwelt in peace. Ildranna draped her shawl over her face, unwilling to see the wreck of her old home, but Andis stopped before they went by.

"You go ahead," she said to the prince. "Ildranna mustn't see any more of this. It might mark the baby. I just want to--to take a last look around. I'll catch up with you."

Pavarr was about to explain--gently--that babies couldn't be "marked," when Ildranna sobbed once and turned her face away. Firemark started walking again, and the prince went with him, looking over his shoulder at Andis. Once inside the forest, Pavarr and the horse stopped behind a double-trunked tree, out of the girl's sight, and the prince crept closer to the village again, keeping a close watch on Andis.

The girl didn't move. She stayed where she was, peering at the burned houses. Then, with a quick glance toward the place where Pavarr and Firemark had vanished into the forest, she hurried to the pile of embers, dropped on her knees, and worked her way through them, patting the floor with her hands.

Pavarr watched her from the edge of the wood for several minutes as she crawled farther into the place where their house had been. She was searching for something, for she made her way to the remains of a fireplace and began removing debris from it. She worked quickly and soon uncovered the hearthstones. She dug at them with bare hands, smearing herself liberally with ashes in the process, until she found a loose stone. Pavarr saw her trying to tug it out of its place and repressed the impulse to break cover and help her.

Best let her find it herself, whatever she's looking for.

At last, as tears of frustration streaked through the soot on her face, she worked the stone free and put her hands in the hole beneath it. Pavarr saw her scrabbling around, but the hole must have been empty, for the girl's shoulders sagged in dejection. She clenched her hands into fists and pressed them against her forehead, as if concentration would reveal what she wanted to find.

Quietly Pavarr came up behind her, the blackened silver medallion dangling from his fingers. "Looking for this?" he asked.

With a gasp, Andis scrambled upright and grabbed at the chain, but the prince held it away from her and put it back in the pocket of his tunic.

"Where did you get that?" she hissed at him, remembering just in time to keep her voice low. "It's mine! Give it to me!"

"It might be," Pavarr replied calmly. "We'll talk about it. Right now, we'd better get back under cover." And he turned and headed for the wood without looking back. After a moment, Andis followed, furious but unable to make any noise for fear of what might be lurking nearby.

"One more thing," Pavarr said before they rejoined Ildranna. "What happened to that *wyrga* you shot? Where was he when you shot him? In the ruins of your home?"

Andis gave him a quick, angry glare. "How did you know?" she demanded.

"Someone dragged a heavy body off to the underbrush," Pavarr replied calmly. "The trail through the ashes, from your house to the forest, is pretty obvious. Did you do that?"

The girl's mouth fell open. "Yes! That monster was in our home! Our *home*, where my family..." She swallowed. "I wouldn't let that filth lie there! I dragged it to the edge of the wood. I meant to come back and bury it, but then I thought I heard someone coming through the forest, so I ran away and hid. When I came back later, you and Ildranna were here."

"Is the body still where you dragged it?" Pavarr asked.

"I guess so. I didn't move it anywhere else."

Pavarr veered toward a patch of broken brush, where something heavy had been awkwardly dragged.

Nothing was there.

"But--" Andis protested. "I left it right here. Where did it--? It wasn't an animal that took it," she concluded, checking for signs of a predator. "I don't understand. I know I put an arrow in its neck!"

Pavarr didn't understand either. A dozen explanations flashed through his mind, all of them equally plausible. A forest predator might have taken it away--but leaving no tracks? The *wyrga* might have recovered enough to drag itself a little way, but they would certainly have found the body. And Pavarr had never heard of a *wyrga* surviving an injury to its great vein, the one vulnerable place in its body.

Did one of its monstrous companions come back and carry it off? Possibly, but the wyrga *are mindless slaves of their master. They have no will of their own, and make no bonds with other* wyrga. *If one falls in battle it is left where it lies, with no care to retrieve the body. The wounded are abandoned with no attempt at rescue.* These matters had long been known to the prince.

Could the old information be wrong? Have the *wyrga* started to bond with others of their kind? *If they have...* Pavarr considered the implications and found them overwhelming. What he had seen of the factory under Castle Mormorion, where human mortals were made into *wyrga*, their souls ripped out of them, their minds broken, their bodies hideously altered by the Lord of Desolation's servants... Could one *wyrga* have acted independently for a purpose of its own?

"Let's go," said the prince, but the girl continued to search in vain for some sign of the dead or wounded *wyrga*. The prince saw two places in the surrounding mat of undergrowth where something had stepped and stumbled, for the bent grass stems were starting to rise again and resume their former shape. He marked their location in his memory and said nothing. The three of them weren't prepared to face a single *wyrga*, let alone the possibility of more.

If the *wyrga* had begun to act as individuals, making their own decisions, then Pavarr would have to think very carefully about what that meant.

"I can't find... I don't..." Andis said, pacing aimlessly about.

"We'll figure it out later," said Pavarr, walking back toward Firemark. "Let's go!" he ordered. To her own surprise, the girl obeyed. "When we get to a stream, you'd better wash your face," was his last comment for a considerable time.

Following a trail whose signs were so subtle that even the prince was hard-pressed to spot them, Andis led them to a swift-running brook, a tributary, Ildranna said, of the mighty Sunder River many leagues to the west. Pavarr decided they could rest there a while, for Ildranna told him the water was pure, spring-fed and icy cold, and by now they were well beyond the place where the raiders had emerged from the forest to attack their village.

Ildranna insisted on preparing their simple lunch, for she "felt much better," and intended to walk along with them afterward.

"But Sister, you need more time to recover," said Andis. "You're just coming back from being a... I mean, you weren't really, but--I mean, I didn't mean--"

"I know you didn't, Andi," Ildranna soothed the girl. "But I never was close to being one. It was only Vord... Vord..." Her voice trailed off, and she rose from her place and walked a little way from them, leaning against the trunk of a white birch tree.

"I didn't mean--"Andis began again, her voice breaking. She was about to run to her sister, but Pavarr stopped her.

"No," he said. "She needs to be alone for a while. You and I will talk about this," and he brought out the silver medallion. "Where did you get it?"

Andis made an impulsive gesture toward the chain, then let her hand fall into her lap.

"It belonged to my father," said Andis. "He always had it with him, my mother said. I--we never knew where he got it."

"Mother knew," said Ildranna, returning to them. "She told me the night before my wedding, in case anything happened to her. How did you come by it, Prince Pavarr?"

"Prince!" Andis exclaimed. "Why do you call him 'Prince'?"

"Vord called him the Prince of Taraman," replied Ildranna, turning to Pavarr. "It is true, isn't it? Vord said he saw a light around you."

Pavarr nodded a little reluctantly. "It's true, but let's forget about the title for now. Might be dangerous to let it be heard in these parts. 'Pavarr' will do. Now I'd like to know more about this medallion."

Andis frowned. "I'd like to know more about you first, and why our father's medallion is so important to you. And if you're really a prince, what were you doing wandering around in the Great Waste? I don't think you look much like a prince!"

"Andis!" Ildranna reproved her. "Pavarr saved my life--and my baby's!"

Pavarr smiled. "Not to mention that you saved mine as well. But your sister's right, Ildranna. I think it's time we trusted each other a little more. I'll go first."

He paused, thought a moment. "This medallion"--he laid it on a flat stone between them--"bears the crest of the House of ZorDain. My father's family. As to why I'm 'wandering around': Before we assume the burdens of stewardship in my country, it's our custom to go on a FaringYear, to become acquainted with other lands and peoples in the Labyrinth World and to serve where we find a need. Which is what I'm doing now."

"But why were you in--" Andis began, with a suspicious look on her face.

"My turn," Pavarr interrupted. "How did your father come to have the medallion?"

"Mother said he had it when they were married," Ildranna explained. "What you're saying... Do you mean he had some connection to Taraman, to your family?"

"Do you know how he got this?"

"I remember he wore it around his neck sometimes, but not often. One day he buried it under the hearthstone. I saw him do it, and he told me never to tell anyone about it. Mother said he told her if we were ever in great trouble, to take the medallion and go to Taraman, and they would help us. But Taraman is so far away! What did he mean?"

"It means," said Pavarr, "that you and your sister can claim my protection and my service--which I willingly give." He closed his hand over the medallion and looked into the distance. Then, abruptly, he made his decision.

"Andis," he said, "Firemark needs to be groomed. Would you like to do that?"

The girl's face lit up. "Oh, yes! He's so beautiful! Do you think he'd mind?"

"He'd probably like a change from me doing it all the time," Pavarr replied. "There's a currycomb in the saddlebag."

Andis was off in a flash, a child with a golden opportunity to be with a horse.

The prince waited until she was out of hearing. "Now," he said to the older sister, "we need to speak plainly. This medallion proves it can't be by chance that we met in the way we did. Something unseen has drawn us three together, but the purpose is not yet clear to me."

Ildranna nodded, staring at the chain in the prince's hand. Haltingly she told him what she remembered of her father. Little enough it was, but Pavarr understood that her father had once been a knight of Taraman. Wounded in a skirmish with a *wyrga* patrol, he had been nursed back to health by Ildranna's mother, Liora, a famous healer of her day.

By the time he was well, he had fallen in love with Liora and had chosen to stay in the village with her, becoming a noted hunter. "He used to try to organize the men into some kind of unified defensive force, but they just couldn't see the need to train as warriors when we'd lived in peace for so many years. If only they had!"

"How did he die?" Pavarr asked.

"A hunting accident," Ildranna replied. "That's what Mother and I told Andis when she was old enough to hear it. We said he was buried in our village cemetery."

"But it wasn't true," said Pavarr.

"No, it wasn't. I saw it happen, and I was old enough to remember."

"A *wyrga* raid?" asked Pavarr.

"Yes. They--took him captive. We never saw him again," said Ildranna. Her head drooped low, and her hair swung forward to hide her face.

Pavarr veered to another subject. "Did anyone beside your parents and you--and Andis--know about the medallion?"

"Oh, no," Ildranna said quickly. "Father made us promise to keep it secret. He thought we might not be safe if anyone else found out. We were only to take it in a time of great trouble. Where did you find it, Pavarr?"

"Someone dropped it in the cellar outside the cabin."

"What?" Ildranna exclaimed, but "Hush!" whispered Pavarr, and glanced quickly at Andis. The girl was happily occupied with Firemark, who let her groom and chatter away to him to her heart's content.

"I don't know how it could have gotten there!" said Ildranna.

"Did you know about the cellar?"

"Yes, it's the end of an old tunnel that ran from under the hearthstone of our house to the hunter's cabin. Father cleaned it out and enlarged it in case we ever needed to escape from the village, but no one's used it in years. I had almost forgotten about it," said Ildranna, frowning. "How--"

"I don't know," replied the prince. "But about that *wyrga* your sister shot: She said it was trying to find something, and it was digging in the embers of your house. If it knew about the medallion... How could a *wyrga* possibly know about it unless..."

Ildranna stared at him for several moments, wanting desperately not to understand, but unable to deny what was becoming obvious. "You mean--they tortured my father to make him tell them where it was? But he wouldn't have! And how would they know about it in the first place? You don't think . . ."

"I don't know what to think," Pavarr responded. "But I've never heard of a *wyrga* surviving an injury to the great vein in the back of its neck. And I've never known a *wyrga* to act alone, independently of the others. They're made so that they can't--" he broke off, not wanting to describe what he had seen inside Castle Mormorion.

Ildranna wasn't listening. Her mind was absorbed in the realization that the thing Andis believed she had killed might have been their father.

"Father?" she murmured. "Did you remember your home? They couldn't turn you completely, could they!" Her voice became fuller, choked with tears.

"Shh... shh. Wait," cautioned Pavarr. "Don't tell Andis, not yet. We can't be certain, and we don't know what really happened to the *wyrga* back there. Look: When we get to the other village, I'll put the chain back together again. Then be sure to keep it with you, and don't let anyone else see it. Just know that you have a claim on the House of ZorDain through your father. The runes on the medallion tell me that he was a Knight-Commander of a legion known as Companions of the Noble Way. There is no higher service in all the Labyrinth lands. But I think--" helping her stand up--"we ought to be on our way. We don't want to stay in the same place too long."

After two days they came to Seventree, another village of the sisters' clan. During the whole journey, Pavarr couldn't keep Andis away from the horse--or from him. Ildranna felt strong enough to walk more often, and now that immediate danger appeared to be past, Andis begged to ride the stallion from time to time. She also talked constantly to Pavarr.

"You could stay there, too, at Seventree. There'd be plenty of room, and they can always use an extra hand. My uncle would be glad if you stayed, and so would my sister. And I'd help you take care of Firemark!"

"I am pledged to a Quest," Pavarr told her in as many tactful ways as he could think of. And that was all Andis learned from the Prince of Taraman.

Ildranna and Andis's aunt and uncle welcomed them with tears and embraces. "We heard what happened to Centerpole," said the aunt, Joti, a young matron with small children hiding shyly behind her skirts. "I'm thankful you're safe. And I see you'll be needing my services in the spring, Ildranna. So. Something good will be born from your distress. Come, my dears," and she swept the two sisters into her house.

"Sir, my thanks for your protection and care for my nieces," said her husband, Darvad, a burly man with the arms and torso of a blacksmith. "One of the Owl-Guard scouting the borderlands told us about my sister's village. The *wyrga*! They've terrorized us for years. Someday--" He stared down at his boots and shook his head. "Someday we'll have to do something about them. I've got children. They need to be safe. But--" He looked up at Pavarr and spread his hands in a gesture of helplessness. "What can we do? Where is the army that can fight *wyrga*? The Lord of Desolation sends them. We have no weapons against him!"

The prince was silent a moment, noticing a small tattoo on the smith's powerful arm: three stars inside a crown of oak leaves. After an exchange of glances and a swift sign, Darvad led the prince into the shadows of the nearby smithy. Briefly, Pavarr informed the blacksmith of who he was and how he had met Ildranna and Andis. Darvad's expression grew more somber as the tale proceeded.

"I suppose we'll have to pack up and leave Seventree," he said. "Where will we go? All the other clan villages in Threshold Forest are in as much danger as we are, and soon the clans outside the forest will be affected, too. Our situation seems hopeless."

Pavarr took note of the intelligence in Darvad's eyes and decided to trust him further.

Saint Amber's Rose

"They say--" he began, first looking around to be certain they weren't overheard. "They say there's someone coming--a Gift-Bringer. They say his Gift has the power to drive the Lord of Desolation out of the Labyrinth World."

"We've heard that rumor for as long as I can remember," replied the man. "But if it's true, where is he? If he's ever coming, now would be the time."

"He is already in the Labyrinth World," Pavarr told him. To Darvad's puzzled frown, he added, "and moving toward the Abbey of Saint Amber on the Great Mountain of Zund. I cannot tell you more now, but it would be well for you to forge weapons for the people of your clan. Mix them in with the farming tools that you make, and let them not be seen openly. I believe the *wyrga* have spies in the Labyrinth lands, so trust no stranger who speaks fair to you." He smiled wryly. "Even one like me."

Pavarr and Darvad talked late into the night, not noticing the darker shadow hidden in a far corner. Before they both turned in for a few short hours of sleep, Pavarr put the medallion and its broken chain in the blacksmith's hand. Darvad squinted at it, made out the design, glanced at Pavarr in surprise--and suspicion.

"Tirgon--the girls' father--used to wear this. Where--?"

"I found the chain in the embers of their house when I brought Ildranna back. The medallion was in a cellar by the cabin in the forest. I don't know how they got where they were, but I can tell you this." And he explained what the medallion meant. "Can you re-forge the chain?"

"Aye, though the pattern is intricate. But--"

"Give it to Andis when it's finished," said the prince. "I have a hunch she'll be the one to wear it. Can you get word to Taraman that I'm on my way to the Icewode?"

The blacksmith nodded. "The Raven Express often flies through here. One more messenger won't be noticed, even if there are *wyrga* nearby."

Very early the next morning the prince mounted Firemark and left the village as inconspicuously as possible. "I'll get away before Andis tries again to persuade me to stay!" he said to the blacksmith, and bade him farewell. "Now to the Icewode!" he murmured in Firemark's ear. "Let's hope we get out of it alive!"

He did not see the slender figure of young Andis slip out of the house and watch him ride away, her child's face set with a determination beyond her years.

You can leave, Prince Pavarr of Taraman, but don't think I'm staying here! I'm going to go and fight wyrga *with you. . . And nothing's going to stop me!*

Later that day the blacksmith dispatched a Raven Express messenger and watched as it flew eastward over Threshold Forest. Darvad did not see the messenger fall in mid-flight, brought down by a *wyrga*'s deadly *thringa*-weapon. He never knew that the *wyrga* took the raven's body back into the shadows.

Chapter Nine

The *Forbeodan* Tunnels

Snow was falling as the six Questors ran into the kitchen garden behind the Inn. Snow--soft, silent, powdery, the kind that blankets the ground layer upon layer, sleep-inducing, deadly. In his youth Oliver had delighted in falling snow because he liked to capture snowflakes on frozen slides and examine them through his microscope. The beautiful crystalline shapes, no two alike, fascinated him for hours.

But that was then, and this was now. Snow flew into their eyes and slicked the ground under their feet as they dashed along a narrow path between patches of withered vegetable foliage. Mil took the lead while Great-Aunt Belvedine, her white plumes tossing, followed closely behind. The Whackitt brothers sprinted to keep up with Great-Aunt Belvedine's long stride. Tipp took a firm grasp of Oliver's jacket so that he was borne along without a choice in the matter. Hera Vespasia gripped the gold epaulette on Great-Aunt Belvedine's battle uniform with her talons and leaned into the wind.

They came to a little gate set among the stones of the garden wall, a gate that had been locked for more than an Age, or so it seemed, for the huge padlock fastened through an iron loop was mottled with rust. Dry brown stalks of tall grasses barricaded the gate; bare sticks and vines made a lattice across its face. The opening had been so well-hidden that Oliver wouldn't have noticed it at all if they hadn't stopped right in front of it. He panted from the unaccustomed exertion, steam rising from his overheated face. Numerous questions came to his mind, but he had no breath left to ask them.

"No one's gone through that gate since the Second Age," stated Tipp, peering keenly at the padlock. "They say it was locked by a Mage's spell. Not Dandriel. Someone before him."

"Spell or no spell, we're going through," declared Great-Aunt Belvedine.

They all moved back as she drew her umbrella from its scabbard and assumed a fencer's *en garde* position. "*Ouvrez!*" she commanded, and tapped the padlock sharply with the tip of her umbrella. The ancient iron lock promptly disintegrated, falling into reddish fragments on the snow. They looked like drops of blood. Oliver shivered involuntarily, whether from a premonition or the wintry air he didn't know.

Great-Aunt Belvedine sheathed her umbrella. "Forward!" she cried, and Mildrith led them at a trot through the opening and into the field beyond.

Oliver followed as fast as his feet would move, for Tipp had let go of his sleeve and he was desperately afraid of being stranded in a slippery no-man's-land between Keeper's Inn behind them and the forbidding Threshold Forest toward which they ran. He had an equally desperate impulse to glance once more at the inn, for he was worried about the kindly people he had met there, Jon and Amatilda Keeper, Murg, Sornor and Beghed, and all the other servitors and travelers and animals. But he needed all his energy just to keep up with the other Questors, and he didn't dare look away from Tipp's broad back bouncing ahead of him.

On they ran, threading their way over furrows and gullies, ditches and drainages, past wood-piles and brush-piles and dried, broken cornstalks. Oliver was hard put to keep his feet under him, trying not to stumble and perhaps sprain an ankle, as well as following Tipp. All the while the snow fell faster and faster until the air seemed filled with cotton, and Oliver had difficulty keeping Tipp in view. He saw Tapp dimly, bounding ahead of Tipp, but the rest had disappeared in veils of white.

Suddenly Tipp stopped in his tracks, crouched down to the ground, and began crawling forward. Oliver had no idea what Tipp was doing, but he quickly followed suit, dropping on hands and knees in the slick snow layer and crawling forward as Tipp did. Within a couple of yards he found himself crawling in mud and wet gravel instead of snow.

Lifting his head in surprise, he bumped against a low ceiling. *A culvert*, he surmised, and hoped the stream or creek-bed didn't choose this moment to fill with snow-water and wash through it.

Oliver's guess appeared to be correct, for in a few more yards they were surrounded by snow again. Just before Tipp stood up, he

Saint Amber's Rose

turned and snapped, "Keep down! Run as fast as you can! And don't show your face, whatever you do!" Before Oliver could ask why, Tipp stood up and ran forward. Oliver followed, trying to keep his shoulders hunched over and his face hidden in the hood of his cloak.

But all at once he couldn't see Tipp any more. The snowfall had turned into a swirling blizzard, and snowflakes struck hard against his face until he became disoriented. Panicked, he stopped, stood up straight, and began to look wildly around. The hood fell back, exposing his face to the icy wind. Then a hand grabbed his ankle and yanked hard, and Oliver found himself tumbling onto the dirt floor of a shallow cave in a hillside.

"What'd you stop running for!" Tipp hissed at him.

"I couldn't see you!" Oliver hissed back. He started to get to his feet, noticed that the rest of the Questors were huddled together along the back wall, and decided he'd better join them. Wrapping his sodden cloak about him as the others had done, he squeezed into the last space left along the cave wall and tried to control his ragged breathing.

For a long while no one said anything. They sat facing the cave opening, where snow fell steadily against the night sky. Gradually it piled higher over the cave mouth and banked on the ridge above them until the two crests of snow almost met. Oliver wondered why they were sitting in a cold, dark cave, apparently waiting to be completely snowed in, but some instinct told him to stay quiet. After a few minutes his breathing calmed, and he saw that the snow had ceased to fall. Staring out of the last tiny gap in the opening, he beheld a sight that was to haunt him for the rest of his days.

The gibbous moon, clear of clouds, shone directly down on Keeper's Inn... or its remains, for the whole sprawling structure--inn, turret, yard, and stable--was now a heap of lifeless ruins blanketed thickly with white.

NO! he screamed, but the sound was only in his mind. All those precious people buried under stones and beams with no one to help them! He began to struggle to his feet. *We have to go back! Someone might still be alive!* Again he thought he shouted, but no sound escaped.

At his movement Tipp, next to him, thrust out a restraining arm. "Have no fear for them at the inn," he whispered, not unkindly.

Mildrith glanced over at them, but Oliver, suddenly bereft of energy, subsided in his place again. Something in Tipp's voice quieted his anxiety. He couldn't have said how or why, but a spark of hope kindled inside his grief. With hope came resolution, and he determined not to make his own sorrow a burden to the others, whose loss must be even greater than his own. He began to think that one day he would discover the reason for the fearful destruction they had narrowly escaped.

Then a cloud drifted across the moon and snow fell again, faster and faster, until the opening of the cave was sealed from the outside world. At first the cover was thin and allowed a grayish light to filter through, but then snowflakes packed the opening solid, and they were left in deepest gloom.

Oliver's teeth began to chatter.

"Now," said Great-Aunt Belvedine decisively, "I think we might have some light, Mildrith."

Mil nodded, got up from her place nearest the cave mouth, and crept back to the rock wall, crouching because of the low ceiling. Kneeling, she moved her hands across the stone next to Oliver. She must have triggered some kind of hidden spring, because a ragged, rectangular section of the wall began to slide away. Stepping through the opening thus revealed, she disappeared into the cleft.

At once they all got up and scuttled after her, Great-Aunt Belvedine in the lead. She had to bend almost double because of her considerable height, but her movements were amazingly spry, considering her probable age. Tipp and Tapp, because of their Dwarvian stature, could stand nearly upright. Hera Vespasia deserted Great-Aunt Belvedine's epaulette for a perch on Tapp's shoulder.

Oliver, with panic-induced foresight, thought to grab the hem of Tipp's cloak so that he wouldn't be left behind, and followed the Whackitt brother through the small opening into yet another cave, so utterly dark that Oliver couldn't tell if his eyes were open or closed. Quicksilver darts of light in kaleidoscopic colors flashed across the insides of his eyelids as they did sometimes when he was lying in bed waiting to fall asleep. He wished he was asleep and only dreaming this adventure, but he wasn't, and there was no use wishing it so. He gripped Tipp's cloak more firmly.

Saint Amber's Rose

They stopped short. Oliver's nose bumped into Tipp's back. Behind them came the faint whish! thunk! of the stone panel sliding back into place.

He heard a different kind of click ahead of them, like the knocking of one stone against another. Again came a click, click, and a tiny spark burst into life and died. Click, click, and another spark appeared. This time it caught on the wick of a candle set in a small depression in the stone floor. The flame lighted a small circle around itself, and within its halo Oliver saw Mil, with the hood of her mantle pulled over her head, kneeling next to the candle, and Tapp crouching across from her with two flintstones he had used to make the spark.

Mil made circling motions with her hands over the flame, and as she did so the cave seemed to grow a little warmer. The tension in Oliver's back and shoulders relaxed as light and temperature increased, but he kept his hold on Tipp's cloak just in case.

"We will sit down now," ordered Great-Aunt Belvedine. Oliver marveled that she managed to be imperious while speaking in a whisper. All of them (except Mil, who paced around the circumference of the cave securing a perimeter) sat in a circle around the candle, spreading out their wet cloaks and hold them in front of the candle-flame.

At least it's warmer in here, Oliver thought. *But I wish I knew what's going on, and what happened to the people in Keeper's Inn.*

"We need to decide what we're going to do, Mildrith," resumed Great-Aunt Belvedine as Mil returned to the circle. "We ought to plan our immediate and long-term goals. Develop a strategy."

"Say," interrupted Tipp. "Who's running this show? You or the *Foressa*?"

"Why, Mildrith, of course!" returned Great-Aunt Belvedine huffily. "I never suggested otherwise."

"Better let her do the talking, then," grumbled Tapp.

They fell into an uncomfortable silence. Oliver wondered at the ability of the Whackitts, or anyone else for that matter, to put Great-Aunt Belvedine in her place. He wished he knew their secret.

Mil paid no attention to their momentary skirmish. She knelt again before the candle-flame, hands hidden beneath her cloak, her eyes focused on the mote of fire in the floor. Just as Oliver was beginning to feel sleepy, she spoke. "We will stay here until false dawn, then we will move. We have to use the *Forbeodan* Tunnels as far as we can to escape any spies that might have seen us leave Keeper's Inn, then we will risk going through the forest."

"Surely it would be safer to stay in the Tunnels all the way," Great-Aunt Belvedine remarked.

"We cannot," returned Mil firmly. "We would bring the Earth-dwellers into danger long before they would meet it in the course of Nature. Eventually we will have to go aboveground to The Rendezvous, and then we have no choice but to go openly and visibly. We must find a way to communicate with Pavarr before we get to The Rendezvous. He does not know the way of the Tunnels."

That name again: *Pavarr*, thought Oliver, and the name was like a pinprick in his heart. "Who's Pavarr?" he blurted out. Five heads turned in his direction.

"Medley! You do not need--" Great-Aunt Belvedine began.

"He might as well," Mil interrupted. "He has to learn of these matters sooner or later."

"Sooner is better," Tapp grunted.

"Prince Pavarr is heir-elect of Taraman, eastern neighbor to the Graelands," Mil went on. "He is a royal cousin to the *Sendara,* and her close friend. He was supposed to be present for the Calling of the Questors. We do not know why he did not come. I fear-- but there is no use fearing when we have no information. We will simply have to count on meeting him somewhere in Threshold Forest before we get to The Rendezvous. Until then--"

"Ahem," said Hera Vespasia with a feathery cough. Everyone turned toward her where she perched on Tipp's shoulder. Mil bowed in her direction.

"As I told you, Captain Ferronce spoke with Pavarr when the Owl Guard was patrolling the borders of Threshold Forest," said Hera Vespasia. "The captain said that Pavarr intended going deeper beyond the Great Waste, even as far as the Desolate Lands."

"The Desolation!" exclaimed Mil and Great-Aunt Belvedine together.

"Pavarr said that there was something he had to find out," the owl continued, "and could do so only by going into the Desolate Lands, and afterward to the Icewode. He wanted to do this before the High Council met. He must have expected to return in time to give his report and receive the Questors' charge. Captain Ferronce did not know what it is that Pavarr sought, but after the prince left, the captain talked with one of the vultures who patrol the Desolate Lands. The vulture said he saw Pavarr riding toward the Realm of the Stonemen."

"Is there really a Realm of the Stonemen?" asked Tipp. "I thought that was just an old story."

"Oh, it's real enough," replied Mil, "a place of deadly peril."

"There is no more terrible place in the Labyrinth World," added Hera Vespasia.

"Why?" whispered Oliver.

"Because," Mil answered, "in the center of that Realm stands the Tower of the Black Flame, and beside that Tower is the City of Dead Souls, and in that City is Castle Mormorion, where dwells the Lord of Desolation--Ab'addon."

"Hush!" said Great-Aunt Belvedine. "Do not speak his name! He has spies everywhere."

"In that case," said Mil wearily, "he already knows about us. But it is only the *Sendara* he wants, so he might not consider us important enough to be worth his notice. Pavarr may have tried to lay a false trail to divert suspicion from our Quest, lest we inadvertently lead the Lord of Desolation to Flavia. It is useless to speculate. In the *Forbeodan* Tunnels we have no way to communicate with Pavarr or anyone else. We can only continue to The Rendezvous and wait for him."

Tipp and Tapp nodded in agreement.

"But--" Great-Aunt Belvedine started to object.

"We will sleep now," Mil commanded, and at once Oliver felt his eyelids droop. Comfortably warm from the heat of the candle, he curled up in a hollow in the stone floor as the others were doing, wrapped his dry cloak about him, and despite his misgivings, was soon fast asleep.

He was running in a vast white space on thick layers of snow. The horizon stretched infinitely ahead of him. He was looking for someone but couldn't remember who it was. He ran on and on before he noticed a black dot in the white glare of the sky. The dot flew closer and closer, growing larger and larger, and became a raven, black wings outspread, circling and circling. Then it dived down and landed on the snow directly in front of him, right where he was running. He crunched to a stop. Vapor from his breath rose into the cold air.

Charleynne Gates

The raven, a full head taller than Oliver, fixed him with its knowing eye. His dream self stared back, waiting. The raven seemed to want to communicate something. "Braan! Braan!" it croaked. Oliver strained forward, trying to comprehend...

"Hey!" said Tipp, sitting up to avoid Oliver's flailing arms. "Wake up, can't you?"

Oliver woke up, gasping for breath.

"Were you dreaming, Friend Oliver?" Mil asked in a whisper. "Do you remember your dream?"

He didn't. It had vanished as most dreams do when the dreamer wakes.

The candle in the center hollow had burned low, and some of the chill had crept back into the cave. The other Questors awakened and readied themselves to continue the journey.

Mil took five small black stones out of the pouch at her waist. Bending over the last flicker of flame on the candle-wick, she passed each stone over the fire in a spiral motion, murmuring unheard words. As she did so, the stones began to glow with a curious green light. When all of them had been passed over the candle, she gave one to each Questor. Oliver examined his closely, wondering how the green light in the stone came to be there, and concluded it probably worked on a couple of double-A batteries.

Next, Mil brought out a little silver-colored flask. Without a word, Great-Aunt Belvedine, Tipp and Tapp brought out cups from their belt-pouches. Oliver opened his own pouch, felt around, and found a cup. Mil poured one droplet of a golden liquid into each of their cups and two into her own. "Drink," she told them. "It is all the refreshment we will have until nightfall."

Oliver wondered why she had given herself two drops, but he raised his cup with the others and licked the bit of liquid out of it. Instantly he tasted a delicious cool fire on his tongue, sweet as honey. It ran down his throat and into every cell of his body, and he felt more awake than he ever had in his life. He saw everything around him more clearly, even in the darkness of the cave.

Looking up, he saw veins of minerals running through the stone ceiling, and sprinkles of quartz and mica sparkling in the walls. To his astonishment, he heard the tiniest of noises made by unseen burrowers, worms, beetles, and other bugs scrabbling their way through the dirt.

-- 168 --

Saint Amber's Rose

He felt tremendously energized, was positive that he could walk great distances, run without tiring, swim turbulent rivers, climb high mountains, for days on end. And yet he didn't believe he was hallucinating. His mind was keen, his wits securely about him. A quality of courage--even of daring--was awakening within him which he had never realized he possessed.

He looked around their circle with new vision and discerned an oval of faint light around each Questor. Great-Aunt Belvedine's was scarlet; Tipp's was sky blue; Tapp's was indigo; Mil's silver, and Hera Vespasia's had streaks of gold. How beautiful they all were! Oliver wondered if he had one also, and what color it might be.

Hera Vespasia dipped her beak into Mil's cup and drank the second droplet. "I don't particularly care for tunnels, *Foressa*," she said. "In fact, this cave is making me feel claustrophobic. I will fly back to the entrance, then to the farther exit, and wait for you. We of the *Norrengild* can move more freely than you two-legged walkers, you know. You're taking the north-by-north passage, I assume?"

"Yes. It's the only one I can navigate by memory."

"You realize the passages have shifted," said the owl.

"Shifted?" Mil queried. "I didn't have that information."

"It's because the Lord of Desolation has meddled with the natural courses of the Earth," responded the owl. "He's been doing so for some time now."

"I know--but what happened to the passages?" asked Mil.

"I'm told by my underground contacts that some of them close behind travelers when they pass through," replied Hera Vespasia.

"'Some?'" repeated Tipp. "Which ones? The north-by-north only or the others as well?"

"Unknown," said the owl. "The rumors are vague. Certain of the tunnel passages shift direction at random, and certain others close in and become solid stone after travelers have gone through. Thus, the passage becomes impossible to retrace should the necessity arise. As it well might. You recall, I am sure, the Terror of the Tunnels."

The Terror of the--! Oliver thought with a shiver of trepidation, and was about to ask what such a dreadful thing might be and if there was a way to avoid it entirely, but Mil frowned and continued.

"I do recall the legend," Mil stated, "but we have come too far to return. All is destroyed behind us. Going back is more dangerous than going ahead."

"Quite so," said Hera Vespasia.

"Then--" said Tipp.

"Exactly," said Great-Aunt Belvedine. "We must go right on. *Nil desperandum.*"

"We will go on, then. Grace be with us all," Mil pronounced, and the others echoed, "Grace be with us all."

The owl returned to the first cave, brushed away the lip of snow covering the opening, looked around carefully, and flew away on silent wings.

"Come quickly!" said Mil. "Follow me closely. There are dozens of passages branching off each other in the Tunnels, so do not lag behind. Getting separated from the group could be fatal. And remember: Make as little noise as you can!" She hastened toward the back of the cave, where another narrow cleft led into a wider tunnel with a higher ceiling.

The rest of them followed, each holding a black stone with the greenish light in its center. As they plunged into the darkness, the glow increased enough for them to see the path ahead. Oliver, bringing up the rear, did not hesitate or stumble, nor did he need to clutch the hem of Tipp's cloak.

They veered off into another tunnel almost at once, this one with a ceiling of dirt instead of stone. Other openings led off this new one--some as small as gopher-holes, others large enough to accommodate a bear. He wondered about them, where they led, as they jogged quietly past. Perhaps some day, he mused, he would return here, explore those mysterious, dark openings with the newfound courage that the golden droplet gave him.

But his daydreaming had made him fall behind the others. The light inside the black stone flickered and dimmed, and Oliver stopped and shook it. Shaking didn't seem to help, so he figured the problem must be with the batteries.

"Oh, dear," he said aloud, looking up into blackness. "Tipp!" he called as loudly as he dared.

No answer. He cocked his head to one side, held his breath, listening hard. No sound came back to him except his own heartbeat.

Saint Amber's Rose

He was alone.

The green light diminished to a pinpoint. "I will not panic," he whispered to himself. "I will not. I will not."

He took a cautious step to the right--or left, he couldn't really tell which, and at once the green light went out.

Suddenly a hand yanked at his sleeve, and he stumbled forward, almost falling as Tipp's rough fist pulled him back on course. The green light in his stone shined again as Oliver caught up with the others. The Dwarvian smith made no comment, but Oliver resolved to stay alert in future.

At length the Questors slowed down after passing hurriedly through a long expanse with many corridors branching off the main tunnel. Mil led them to an alcove where a hidden spring made a clear trickle of water down the wall before disappearing through a hole in a round stone in the floor.

"Must be one of the underground springs that feeds the Sunder," muttered Tipp.

"Let me drink first," Mil commanded, and held her cup under the trickle. She sniffed it, tasted, sipped warily, and closed her eyes, analyzing the water before swallowing. "It seems safe," she said. "Drink, for we shall not find water again until we are out of the Tunnels."

One by one they advanced to the trickle of water, caught it in their cups, and drank until their thirst was quenched. (The golden droplets had energized them but did not quench thirst.) The water was clear, clean, and cold, and tasted of nothing but itself, as water ought. Oliver wondered why Mil insisted on drinking first. *Does she think the water might be poisoned?* But he didn't ask.

"We cannot tell how far the agents of the Desolation have advanced into the forest," said Tipp, answering Oliver's unspoken question, "or if they have managed to pollute groundwater or springs beneath the earth."

"Let's go on," said Mil, and they all put their cups back in their belt-pouches. Tipp took Oliver aside. "Look, Friend Oliver," he said firmly, "you've got to keep up with us. You almost delayed us back there, and we cannot lose an instant. If you get lost again, we'll have to leave you behind, and there's not a soul ever went into the *Forbeodan*

Tunnels alone and came out alive. They say the Terror of the Tunnels gets you, and you go mad."

Oliver, duly impressed, felt a chill creep up his spine. "I am very sorry indeed," he apologized. "It was this flashlight." He showed Tipp his black stone. "I think the batteries died."

Tipp frowned. "Bat trees? I know not what those might be. Bats in Threshold Forest live in caves. Hmp. I suppose I'll have to explain how a finding-stone works." He took the black pebble out of Oliver's hand and thought for a moment. "I shouldn't have spoken sharply, Friend," Tipp said gruffly. "This is a time of great change and disturbance in the Labyrinth World, and we forget you wouldn't know the ways we learned as children. Now see," and he brought the stone up where Oliver could see it closely, "this green light shines brightly now because it's near the other stones. It's not a light-source in itself; it's a finding-stone. The light grows dimmer the farther away it is from the other finding-stones."

"Ah!" said Oliver, comprehending. "It's a navigational tool!"

"Now that I understand!" Tipp replied, pleased with his pupil. "Navigation! That's it!" He put the black stone back into Oliver's hand and became stern again. "Finding-stones are very rare and precious. There used to be a good many of them around, but most have gotten lost, and we don't know where they came from originally, so don't lose this one. And don't fall behind again. We won't stop another time until we're almost out of the Tunnels." He emphasized the point by poking a broad finger against Oliver's chest. "Above all, don't talk while we're in the Tunnels! Any noise could put us all in peril!"

Tipp returned to his brother, who cast a quizzical glance at Medley and muttered something in Tipp's ear.

Mil put the hood of her cloak over her head again. "Come, we must keep going," she said quietly, and walked rapidly ahead into the tunnel at the far end of the trickle of water. Great-Aunt Belvedine, Tapp, and Tipp followed immediately, and Oliver was so careful to keep right behind Tipp that once or twice he trod upon the Dwarvian's heel.

The next part of the Tunnels was even more convoluted. Oliver could tell that Mil kept bearing left, but he had no idea of the direction, whether north or south, east or west. The tunnel entrance, as far as he could figure out, had been east of the inn; the first passage seemed to have borne southerly. But after turning and turning, reversing, angling, and spiraling, he was completely disoriented.

"I feel something menacing in the atmosphere of this tunnel," Great-Aunt Belvedine grumbled to Mil at their next rest break. "It's all Medley's fault that we have to be here at all. If he had read my letter in the first place--"

"Never mind, Belvedine," said Mil firmly. "What's done is done. The Tunnels will get us where we need to go--eventually."

"Let us hope so," said Great-Aunt Belvedine. "I'm sure I detected a tunnel shift at the last turning, exactly as Hera Vespasia warned us. The path positively quivered under my feet."

"I felt it too," replied Mil patiently. "It's an aftershock from the earthquake."

Great-Aunt Belvedine grumbled again under her breath, but Oliver didn't catch what she said. Probably just as well, he thought.

They hiked on. Occasionally he glanced at the finding-stone in his palm. Its little green light remained steady. Oliver didn't even want to think about what might happen if it faded again and he were left behind.

From time to time Tipp whispered a word of warning over his shoulder to Oliver. "Pothole!" he hissed so that Oliver could avoid it and not risk a sprained ankle, and "We're coming up to a crevice in the path. Have to jump it." Once, crossly, "Look out! You've stepped on my heel again!"

"Ssh!" whispered Tapp, ahead of Tipp. Oliver tried to leave Tipp room to walk without kicking the Dwarvian's heels, but he was fearful of falling behind.

"Crevice again!" Tipp warned. "Pretty wide this time. Better take a good run at it." Suiting action to word, Tipp started off at a run. Oliver saw his silhouette leap, sail across a wide space in the path, and land in a crouch on the other side. "Hurry up!" he called softly to Oliver, and jogged to catch up to the others.

Oliver Medley had never been much of an athlete. For years his exercise had consisted of a daily brisk walk and a swim once or twice a month at the YMCA pool. Being put to the test, he gathered his courage and sprinted forward. At the appropriate moment he launched himself awkwardly into space. Luckily he landed on the other side, realizing as he did so that what he had heard Tipp say as "crevice" ought to have been "crevasse". Stumbling over a loose pebble on the touchdown, he lost his balance and fell hard on hands and knees.

He must have had a dizzy spell for a minute or two, because when he came to himself he thought he had landed in a crypt, so dark was everything around him. And his finding-stone? Panicked, he felt around the floor, afraid that it had gone to the bottom of the crevasse. *What if I'd tumbled in there myself? I'd never see daylight again!* The next party of cave explorers--if there were any--would find his desiccated skeleton and puzzle over how he came to be there.

"Ahoy!" he cried feebly, hoping the Questors were still near enough to hear him. "Ahoy! Hoy! HOY!" But no reply came. No pounding feet ran back to help him.

Calm. Keep calm. Keep on going, Oliver repeated to himself over and over. *You'll catch up eventually. Keep calm. Keep moving.* "*Calm. Keep calm*," he muttered aloud to ward off panic. Carefully he rose to his knees and began feeling around the floor again, searching for the finding-stone. And there it was! "Eureka!" he exclaimed as his fingers closed around its smooth shape. Almost weeping with relief, he clutched it tightly, expecting to see a glow of greenish light, but the thing was as dead as mutton.

He put it in his belt-pouch anyway in case it might be revived, and stood upright before he remembered: He had no idea which way to move. Away from the crevasse, obviously, but how could he be sure he was moving away from it? People lost in the woods, he had heard, tended to walk in big circles until they eventually came back to the place where they started. Better stay on his knees and crawl forward. That way he could keep feeling the floor ahead of him and not accidentally tumble into another crevasse. *Stay low and slow. Low and slow. No need to panic.*

He inched forward cautiously, or at least in the direction he hoped was forward, sweeping his hands across the path before him as he crawled through the cold tunnel, breathing dank air. Hand over hand, hand over hand, he crept along blindly, muttering to himself.

Keep calm. Keep calm.

After a while, the words changed imperceptibly to something like a prayer.

Help me... Help me... Let me find a way out... Help me... Help me...

Saint Amber's Rose

He thought he detected differing currents of air from branches off the main tunnel, but he couldn't be sure. Once or twice he had to sit and rest. How he wished he had a drink of that good water back at the spring! Maybe there would be another one soon... No, Mil said that was the last water until they're out of the Tunnels. He might die of thirst before he found the way out, or before they noticed he was gone. *When they do, surely they'll come back for me.*

Won't they?

He crawled onward interminably. Eventually he sat down again to rest his sore knees and the bruised palms of his hands. He no longer had any idea where he was or how long he had been crawling in the dark.

Old Sal dozed peacefully, as she had for the last several Ages, stirring only to stretch and rewind her immense coils. "Salamandra-Anaconda *Eunectes murinus*" had been her given name, but she was so very ancient--born in the First Age--that no one remembered it any more, and she had almost forgotten it herself.

She slept and dreamed. Her dreams never varied; they were always reminiscences of meals--delicious morsels of rats, mice, other snakes, rabbits, small deer, the odd goat. Over and over she relived the excitement of the hunt, the capture, and the ensuing feast. Her imagination reveled in the hot saltiness of blood, the lick of bone, the interesting tastes and textures of skin, scales, and fur. Her pleasures were simple, and she never tired of dreaming about them.

Once, long ago, soon after she had taken up residence in the cave, some obnoxious little two-legged creatures had appeared. She hadn't invited them; they simply invaded her domicile one day. They made loud hammering noises that disturbed her domestic tranquility. She hadn't liked them at all, even though she had taken the trouble to catch and ingest one just to show an interest. What a disappointing dinner it had made! Tough, stringy, no flavor to it at all.

To make matters worse, they had brought fire, which she hated above all things. They showed no consideration for a lady's feelings, so she gathered her dignity about her and pointedly ignored them. Her strategy must have been effective, because she hadn't sensed them around in a while.

Charleynne Gates

Her heart gave one slow beat, as it did every so often, and she took a breath of mold-scented air, the only one she needed that week.

Oliver crouched on the broken-stone floor of the tunnel, knees drawn up close to his body, making as small a mass of himself as possible. He shivered, and his breathing whistled raggedly.

Nothing in his life had prepared him for this. He realized that all the other times when he'd thought he was afraid amounted to very small potatoes. This, right now, was the genuine article: FEAR. It poured into his mind like black water.

They've abandoned me. I'm going to die here.

A review of his life scrolled before his mind's eye like a reel of film on double-fast forward. He'd always thought of himself as basically a good human being, but now everything he'd ever said or done flashed before him, and he saw how much there was to regret: a host of little nastinesses--complacency, vanity, cynicism, condescension. Greed. Stubbornness. And, too often, unacknowledged envy. Hot tears inched down his cheeks as he was forced to confront all that he had been and done up to this moment, the bad mixed in with the good... and more of the bad than he wanted to admit.

Worst of all was realizing how casually ungrateful he had been for all that had made his life not only possible, but also, more often than not, beautiful.

Deeply ashamed of himself, he dived down below his fear and said in his heart, *I'm sorry. Forgive me. Thank you.*

Then, worn out with exhaustion and despair, he sank into oblivion.

When he awoke, he found that it was no use even opening his eyes, for the darkness was as thick as ever. To distract himself from hovering panic, he took the finding-stone out of his belt-pouch and waved it around. To his surprise, he thought he spotted a pinpoint of greenish light inside the stone. But it couldn't be. He must be seeing flashes on the inside of his eyelids.

He stared at the finding-stone. *There it is!* A definite glow, a little larger now, the size of a drop of water. He must be near another finding-stone.

The Questors are coming back to get me!

Saint Amber's Rose

Carefully he aimed the stone in every direction, trying to find where the green glow was strongest. He crawled forward, propping himself on one hand, holding the finding-stone in the other and waving it in front of him. *They're coming! They'll find me! I'll be all right!*

"I'm here!" he shouted, but his throat was so dry that only a croak came out.

After a few mistakes, he found the direction where the light grew stronger as he advanced, and followed it as fast as he dared. Suddenly the small glow expanded hugely, bursting on his sight like the headlight on a locomotive. He rose up on his knees.

He was in a cave! The others must have passed through here, and not long ago!

Hope flared in Oliver's heart, and he struggled to his feet, lifting the finding-stone high so that the whole chamber was illuminated.

And hope died.

The light from his finding-stone sparked reflections from a thousand places in the chamber--a myriad black stones glowing greenly. Stimulated by each other, the lights bobbed and danced so brightly that Oliver was almost blinded, and had to shield his eyes by pulling his hood over his face.

At last his eyes grew partially accustomed to the light, and he was able to look around again, blinking and squinting painfully as his worst fears were confirmed. His finding-stone had erupted in light because it was near its own kind. This cave must have been where finding-stones were originally formed.

The other Questors had never been here.

Then Oliver spotted something at the far end of the cave, and his heart gave a leap. Hope sprang up again. A miner's forgotten pickax leaned against the cave wall. He wasn't alone! People had been here, people who might--would!--return!

"Ahoy!" he shouted, partly in relief, partly to see if anyone answered. No one did, except for the echoes bouncing off the walls. "Oy-oy-oy-oy-oy," they mocked him.

But he couldn't be discouraged now. If the cave was a mine, then there must be a mineshaft leading to the surface. What was on the surface was another question entirely, one he would consider when he got there. His immediate task was to find the mineshaft.

There, near the pickax. *Yes!* There was a shaft that went up and up and up to a square opening, as if human beings had carved it out. A small patch of dark-blue sky showed through it, and a tiny winking star.

But on the opposite side of the cave was a similar opening. Perhaps he ought to investigate that one, too, in case it had easier access to the outside world. He advanced toward it, noting that two of the black stones inside it emitted a particularly intense green glow.

What's that? The delicate sensors in Old Sal's long, nimble tongue activated, sent subtle signals to her reptilian brain. Sensing an alien presence, she awoke from her slumber and taste-tested the moldy air. *Who's gotten into my cave?*

He thought the two stones moved a little as he went cautiously toward the opening, but that must have been because his eyes were still dazzled.

Flessh! That's human flessh, that is! Why, it's been Ages since I ssampled human flesssh. Not since—let's ssee... that prince, what's-his-name. SSmelled good. A nice tasty chunk of meat, I thought. But he hurt me with his ssssword. I hope it'ss not him again.

He came closer. The two stones moved again. He was certain of it. *But they can't be moving by themselves, can they?*

The two greenish lights glided out into the glittering cave, and he saw that they were the unblinking eyes of a gigantic serpent coming to investigate the interloper in her home. The snake's huge body eased out of her cave-boudoir, coincidentally blocking that potential exit. Her forked tongue flickered in and out, taking the measure of the intruder.

Oliver froze, staring into the mesmeric eyes.

It's not moving. Nice to know I haven't lost my touch. Those endlesss hours I spent taking hypnosis classes has certainly paid off over the years. I'm glad now that Mother nagged me about practicccing.

The forked pink tongue touched Oliver's cheek as lightly as a leaf, and there wasn't a thing he could do about it.

Hmm. Round and ripe. I wonder if I have any of that mole sauce left? Or—wait a minute. There's ssomething wrong here. Let me just taste him again— EEUW! EEUW!

She arched her tremendous coils to the ceiling and swung her great head back and forth, trying to spit out the mere touch of his skin.

Saint Amber's Rose

The creature's from the Maze World! I've heard they eat all kinds of trash over there, with additives they don't even know how to ssspell. Mother always said you could poison yourself if you ever ate flessh from the Maze World. I'd better crush this little monsster before I forget and eat it.

The snake's head bent down past Oliver's face, followed by her coils. They slithered over his shoulder and around his neck.

Va'in 'a moru', Sendara! Va'in 'a moru' rang in his mind as if someone else had spoken. He did not realize that he himself had shouted it before the breath left him.

"What'ss that?" The suffocating pressure released abruptly; the coils dropped away. Gulping deep breaths, Oliver plopped down on the floor like a flat stone. Both hands grasped his throat, feeling his windpipe to make sure it was still intact.

"What'd you ssay?" Startled, Old Sal rewound her coils and contemplated the intruder with very little pleasure. "Did I jusst hear you invoke the *SSendara*?" she said in Common Tongue.

Oliver wheezed, unable to utter another syllable.

"Well! If I hadn't heard it with my own ssense organs, I wouldn't have credited it. The day a mortal from the Maze World gets into my private residence and nobody detects it and then it invokes the *SSendara*... I don't know what the Labyrinth World is coming to, I really don't. SSessamisss!"

"Yes, Mama!" A much smaller serpent poked her nose through a crack in the wall. "You hissed?"

"I certainly did! And where were you, I'd like to know? Out playing hide-and-seek in that old sarcophagus again, weren't you! I've told you a hundred times not to go there by yourssell. You were ssupposed to be watching while I took my nap."

"Sorry, Mama. What'd you want?"

"Go call a Raven Messenger to find that Prince Whosis—"

"Pavarr, Mama! Prince Pavarr. I've got his posster up in my room."

"Just have the raven tell him one of his Maze World friends is stuck in here. I won't touch the thing, but I'd like the prince to remove it as soon as possible. It might contaminate our food stores."

"But Mama, the last time a raven came, it ate my brother Hugo!"

"Oh, sso that's what happened to him. I did wonder. Well, just keep out of the way of its beak and you should be all right. Go on, Ssessamiss! SStop dawdling!"

The small snake backed out immediately.

Old Sal settled her coils again and scowled at Oliver. "Now I remember: I've heard about you. Rumor is, you're the one who's going to find Saint Amber's Rose, not that you look like you could, barging in where you're not invited and upsetting decent folks in their naptime. But if the *SSendara* wants you to, then you'd better try. I can tell you this much, you piece of Maze World trassh: You'll *have* to find it if you want to get out of the Labyrinth World alive!" She lowered her triangular head toward him again, green eyes blazing with indignation.

Oliver did not wait upon ceremony. Long before his mind formed a rational thought, his leg muscles propelled him in a giant leap backward, and he landed where the pickax leaned against the wall.

The shaft happened to be the main entrance to the mine, abandoned for an Age. It was actually of considerable interest to archaeologists of the Labyrinth World, but Oliver didn't really care about such academic matters at the moment. The only matter of importance to him was that the shaft possessed a series of ladders. He clambered up them with a speed unimaginable in his ordinary life, climbing well beyond the reach of any cave-dwelling reptile.

Suddenly he was out! He shot through the mineshaft opening like a comet, only stopping when he realized he was in grayish daylight and snow was falling, snow like thick wool, and the air was icy cold. And he had no idea where he was. Nothing was visible but falling snow, glimpses of gray sky, and a wilderness of dark trees everywhere he looked.

His body remembered its thirst. He tipped his head back and opened his mouth, letting the soft flakes fall onto his tongue, then bent down to the snow and ladled handfuls of it into his mouth.

Finally his parched throat was eased. He stood again, wiping snowflakes from his face.

What now?

Pavarr let Firemark pick his own way through the icebound forest. The horse knew the path as well as the prince or better, given the reserves of instinct and memory inherited from a thousand equine generations.

Wrapping his cloak about him against the windless chill, Pavarr set himself to thought.

What happened to Flavia? He had no information, no evidence, no hint how she had disappeared. *Did Ab'addon abduct her? If so, how had he done it?* Flavia had left Ravenhome under all the protection they could muster at the time. *Protection!* Pavarr mused wryly. *One ancient chauffeur; one acid-tongued old lady; one total stranger to the Labyrinth World.*

Mil had escorted them, and her warrior-strength and cunning was beyond reproach, but would it have been enough against Ab'addon? Pavarr held no illusions about the overwhelming power of the Dark Lord's forces. He had met them more than once—and survived. *So far.*

The scar around his wrist began to throb—a scar that looked like the mark of a constrictor's scales. It was the remnant of an old wound, one that bound him forever to the enemy he had once fought to a draw. Each had struck the other nearly to the death, but in the end had come to a truce: They would spare each other's lives (which were close to the ebb anyway) and grant each other their own territories. Pavarr promised not to intrude again into her innumerable caves and caverns, and Salamandra agreed to confine herself therein and not seek to enlarge her domain aboveground. In addition, with grudging respect for each other's prowess, they devised a signaling system by which, in case of emergency, they might render aid, one to the other.

The prince gently massaged his scale-scarred wrist and looked up in time to spot a Raven Messenger land on a branch in front of him.

Oliver turned around and around where he stood, straining for a glimpse of a landmark of any kind, but nothing gave him a hint of where he was. The mineshaft--maybe he ought to go back and climb a little way down, just enough to get out of the snow. *But where is the opening?* He had stumbled away from it when he emerged, and now everything he could see was blanketed with snow. Even if he had been able to force himself to go back down the ladder and face that snake, he couldn't have found the shaft.

He was marooned in an ocean of snow.

-- 181 --

Fatigue washed over him like a wave. He had to find a place to take shelter and rest. He knew sleep was dangerous, but he didn't care, right now, if he ever woke up again.

To his left was a small hillock with a ledge of overhanging rock. Maybe he could get out of the falling snow under there. He dropped on hands and knees, crawled over to it, pushed away some of the snow, and found a hollow space underneath the ledge. It was big enough to get out of the wind, but not much more than that. He might be able to get a bit of rest there and wait for the snowfall to stop.

He brushed away more of the snow-cover--and something quite close to him growled. He glanced up and found himself staring into the disgruntled countenance of a gray badger (*Taxidea taxus*).

But Oliver Medley, traveler from another world, was simply too tired to care. Muttering an apology for disturbing the occupant, he curled up in the opening of the badger's den, faced the falling snow, and waited. For what, he did not know.

"Flavia," he murmured, and despite himself, fell asleep.

A hard blow struck the snowpack near his face, startling him to consciousness. His eyes flew open, and he peered up the long legs of a black horse with a wild eye in its tossing head. In the saddle sat a man whose dark, amused face stared down at him.

"Friend Oliver Medley! Couldn't you find a warmer bed this winter night than Brother Badger's den?"

Caked with snow from top to bottom, Oliver scrambled to his feet, gawking at the rider. "H-how did you know my name?" he stammered, then had a sudden flash of intuition. "Are you--?"

"Pavarr of Taraman, at your service," replied the rider, and reached down a hand to pull Oliver up behind him.

Chapter Ten

The Icewode

Two ravens flew through the gray sky, swooping low over the forest. "Braan!" said the first. "Mwk!" answered the other, who had something in his mouth, and at once they separated, the second flying ahead, the first landing on a bare branch and peering keenly at signs of movement on the snow-blanketed ground. In the sky, a sudden swirl of snowflakes blotted the second raven from view. He flew steadily onward, bearing an ivory-colored object in his beak.

"We'll take a break now. Not long," Mil said, and the Questors sat on the ground and huddled together.

"How much farther?" panted Great-Aunt Belvedine, and patted her forehead with a large purple handkerchief.

"About a *kephan*," Mil replied. "Or a little more."

"Why not go on, then?" urged Great-Aunt Belvedine. "The more ground we cover--"

"Do you have to argue about everything, Belvedine?" grumbled Tipp.

"I don't know what to expect when we come out of the Tunnels," Mil said quickly, forestalling a quarrel. "I want us rested and ready for whatever happens."

"Good idea," grunted Tapp.

"Is the pace too fast for you, Friend Oliver?" Mil inquired. "I could have called a break more often, but our need for haste is imperative."

No one answered.

The Questors turned to look next to Tipp, where Oliver ought to have been. No one was there. With one accord, they pointed their finding-stones in the direction where Oliver was not, and saw nothing but the empty passage stretching back into the Tunnel.

"Where is he?" demanded Mil, rising to her feet.

"I don't know!" exclaimed Tipp, swinging his finding-stone around. "I thought he was right behind me."

"He's dawdling again," snapped Great-Aunt Belvedine. "Deliberately delaying us! He has no consideration for others!"

"He's not here," said Mil, ignoring her and shining her finding-stone into the passage where they had emerged.

"Shall I call out for him?" asked Tipp.

Mil shook her head. "Better not," she advised. "Can't tell what we might awaken."

"I'm positive he was following me!" Tipp insisted. "I know he was because--"

"Yes?" Mil prompted.

"I heard him breathing," Tipp replied. "Puffing and blowing like a, like a--"

"Whale," Tapp finished.

"He kept treading on my heels, he was so close behind me," said Tipp. "About every fifth step or so, I'd feel a kick from his boot. I whispered to him once or twice to stay back a little, but he never did. I was about to give him a piece of my mind when we--"

"He didn't follow us here," Mil stated.

"But he was coming after me!" Tipp insisted. "The last time he stepped on me couldn't have been more than a few minutes ago."

"No sense of direction, that one," said Tapp.

"We'll have to go back and look for him," Mil decided. "We cannot leave him alone in the Tunnels."

"I told him if he fell behind, we wouldn't come back for him," said Tipp, his brow furrowing. "I only meant to scare him enough so he'd keep up with us."

"Let's go," Mil ordered. "We can't lose him; he is the Gift-Bringer."

Four finding-stones flashed together, making streaks of eerie light in the gloomy cave. Cautiously the Questors advanced into the darkness, searching the narrow dirt path as far back inside as they dared, swinging their finding-stones from side to side to illuminate every possible branch where Oliver might have wandered off and gotten lost.

"He wore journey boots," Mil told them in a low voice, "those that the elf-kin make. Look for his footprints. Their mark will be on the boot-sole."

But they saw only four sets of prints coming out of the Tunnel: Mil's in the lead, then Great-Aunt Belvedine's long, thin riding boot with

Saint Amber's Rose

its absurd dress heel, then Tapp's sturdy work boot, then Tipp's. And
nothing more.

Suddenly Mil stopped short. She lifted her finding-stone so that
its glow illuminated a sheer stone wall blocking the passage through
which they had come.

"Hold!" she whispered, and the others stopped in their tracks.
"This wall is new! The tunnel has closed behind us!"

"Hera Vespasia said it would," muttered Tapp.

"It's cut us off from Friend Oliver!" Tipp exclaimed, horrified.

Great-Aunt Belvedine gasped and stretched a long finger toward
the lintel of a stone arch over the blockage. "Look there!"

The others caught up and peered where her finger pointed.
There on the lintel was an image chiseled into the stone: a gigantic,
black-scaled serpent coiled and ready to strike. Its eyes glittered greenly
in its triangular head; its mouth opened, exposing wicked yellow fangs.
Even as they stared, the innumerable coils seemed to writhe and twist,
the head to lunge toward them. The Questors instinctively jumped back.

"The Terror of the Tunnels," Tipp breathed. "It got him."

Without another word, the four Questors turned around and
silently retraced their steps.

"I was absolutely positive he was right behind me," Tipp
mourned as they came back to the place where they had discovered
Oliver's absence. Then a thought struck him: "Who kept treading on
my heel, then? And breathing down my neck?"

But no one knew the answer, and ice crept into their bones as
they pondered the question.

"We have to go on," Mil said decisively. "We cannot lose any
more precious time searching for the Gift-Bringer, for we have a task to
accomplish. Now it depends entirely on us to find Flavia and escort her
to the Abbey of Saint Amber."

"But the Gift!" Tipp interjected. "Friend Oliver said he didn't
know what it is, but the Prophecy says his Gift will save the Labyrinth
World!

I never put much stock in that old story, Tapp thought but didn't
say. *Don't really know what use Friend Oliver is going to be, when all's
said and done.*

Mil shook her head slowly. "I know--but we must go on. If the
Labyrinth is to be saved, it will have to be done in some other way."

Charleynne Gates

Three deeply depressed Questors trudged behind Mil to the north-by-north exit, where they were to reconnoiter with Hera Vespasia.

"Wait," said Mil, putting out her hand to hold them back. "We need to take precautions. I'll go out first and make sure it's safe."

"*Foressa*," said Tapp, who spoke so rarely that everyone looked at him in surprise. "Let me be the first one out. With your dark clothing, you'd make too good a target against the snow. If anyone's out there, they won't be expecting a Dwarvian."

Before anyone could object, Tapp dodged around Mil and approached the exit autiously, keeping well behind the jagged opening to get a clear view of the landscape. He saw a wilderness of white punctuated with black tree-trunks whose scraggly branches were draped with knife-edged icicles. Nothing moved except for the wind-blown skitter of ice crystals across the frozen snowpack.

"Here goes," he muttered, and wriggled through the opening and stood warily upright.

Whoosh! At once a shower of black arrows fell around him. One struck him in the shoulder, and he staggered back into the tunnel.

"Tapp!" exclaimed his brother, and rushed forward to drag him away from the opening. Mil and Great-Aunt Belvedine ran to them and bent over Tapp, whose face had turned deathly white.

"*Wyrga!*" Tapp choked out. "They know we're here! Don't bother about me. Get away!"

"Not without you," said Tipp. "We can--"

Another volley of arrows striking against the stones of the entrance interrupted him, and the Questors shrank back, shielding Tapp with their bodies.

"If we can get you back a ways, we can cut the arrowhead out," said Tipp. "Sorry, Brother, it's got to be done."

"Protect yourselves first!" Tapp said hoarsely.

"We don't have sufficient weapons," said Mil. "We can't fight them in the open. We'll have to carry Tapp farther back into the tunnel and hope they won't follow us."

"If we can't return fire, there's nothing to stop them," said Great-Aunt Belvedine.

"I'll hold them off with my sword," said Mil. "That may buy us some time."

"Help me up, Brother," Tapp gasped. "I can walk."

-- 186 --

Saint Amber's Rose

"Lean on me," said Tipp, and levered his brother to a standing position. With Mil and Great-Aunt Belvedine covering their backs, the two staggered down the tunnel past the first turning. Tipp lowered his brother to the ground with Great-Aunt Belvedine's help, while Mil kept an eye on the opening.

"I can't hear any more arrows," she whispered. "They may be coming for us!" She drew her sword and put her back against the wall, ready to defend them as long as possible.

The tunnel was absolutely quiet; no one moved or spoke. The four listened intently for any sound of *wyrga* crawling through the narrow opening.

"If they come, leave me and run," Tapp rasped.

"Don't be silly, Brother," said Tipp. "We've always stuck together. Not going to quit now."

"I see them!" Mil whispered. "Get ready!"

Just then the earth beneath their feet rumbled and shuddered. Mil slipped and fell to the ground. Tipp threw himself across his brother to protect him, but after the initial quake nothing happened except for a few loose pebbles rolling down the wall.

Mil pulled herself upright, retrieved her sword, and looked toward the tunnel opening. "Aftershock!" she exclaimed. "It was another aftershock from the earthquake, and it's caused an avalanche outside! The exit's blocked with rocks! The *wyrga* must have been buried underneath. The rest of them can't get inside now, and we can't get outside, not by this exit!"

The rockfall gave them a respite, and they turned their attention to Tapp. Mil brought out a tiny vial on a chain around her neck, opened it, and poured a drop of the precious fluid inside it on Tapp's wound to disinfect it and ease some of the pain. The medicine stung, causing Tapp nearly as much pain as his wound did, but he gritted his teeth and refused to let the least moan escape. Then Mil cut out the arrowhead with her Dwarvian dagger and removed the shaft, covering the place with a makeshift bandage from her kit.

"Can you walk at all, Tapp?" Mil asked. "We dare not stay here longer."

"'Course I can," Tapp insisted, breathing hard. "Help me up."

"Where will we go now?" demanded Great-Aunt Belvedine. "Hera Vespasia expected us at this exit."

"I'm sure the Great Chief will figure out that we have to go to another exit," replied Mil.

"Do you know of one?" asked Great-Aunt Belvedine.

"No," said Mil. "Do you?" which silenced Great-Aunt Belvedine for a whole minute.

"I do," said Tipp, looking up from his brother. "I know of at least one not far from here."

"You're familiar with these tunnels, then?" asked Mildrith.

"We Dwarvians know more about tunnels in general than we like to tell," replied Tipp. "This seems like an appropriate time to use our ancestral memory."

"Lead on," said Mil, and followed Tipp and Tapp about half a kephan to another exit, this one no larger than a crawl-through at ground level.

"This time I go first," said Mil firmly. She dropped to the ground and wriggled through the opening, going slowly to survey the territory. The other Questors watched her disappear until only the soles of her feet were visible, and then they couldn't see her at all.

The land around this exit was free of any tracks of *wyrga* as far as Mil could see. In fact, the only sign of life in the black-and-white landscape was the owl, Hera Vespasia, sitting on a high branch in company with a raven. Spotting them, Mil raised her hand and made a swift sign in the air. The raven left its perch and landed on Mil's arm.

The warrior-woman bent her head to its ear and whispered "Vladir. *Sleidh*!" and launched the raven into a gray sky.

Hera Vespasia next dropped down and gripped Mil's shoulder. "Farduran Corax saw everything," she said softly. "He arrived just as the avalanche started, and filled me in as soon as I got here. The *wyrga* ran away. They didn't even try to rescue their comrades buried under the rubble. I believe you will be safe from them now, if you proceed with utmost caution."

"We have one Questor wounded," Mil told her. "Tapp caught a *wyrga* arrow in his shoulder. I removed it, but don't know if the arrowhead was poisoned. I didn't tell the others, but the point dissolved into a black mist and disappeared as soon as it came out. Typical of their vicious weapons! We can't risk taking Tapp overland; we'll have to continue through the tunnel until we get to an exit where Vladir can pick us up. Tipp says he knows another way--the Zemora passage, he called it."

Hera Vespasia frowned, thinking. "I know of that one. It comes out at the big lightning-struck oak. I'll wait for you there. But be careful, *Foressa*! The Zemora passage hasn't been used for a thousand years. They say something lives there that hasn't seen sun, moon, or stars since the First Age."

"You mean the Terror of the Tunnels?" asked Mil. "We have seen its warning sign, and we think it may have taken the Gift-Bringer."

"What!" exclaimed Hera Vespasia.

"We lost him," said Mil. "He didn't come out with us. We went back as far as we dared to look for him, but found nothing, not even a footprint, and the passage we came through had closed behind us."

"This is disastrous!" said the owl, shocked to the core.

"But we have to go on," said Mil. "We have to keep looking for Flavia. And the Gift-Bringer has to be kept secret from the *wyrga*, if they don't know about him already. The fact that he's now lost can't be told, either, not until we meet with Pavarr at The Rendezvous. Then we can decide what to do."

"I agree," said the owl. "I will meet you at the lightning-struck oak." And she flew away.

The four Questors turned away from the exit, Mil in the lead, Great-Aunt Belvedine bringing up the rear. Guided by Tipp's ancestral memory, they picked their way toward the Zemora passage, this time without further incident. Tapp leaned heavily against his brother, doing his best to stifle his groans. If Tipp worried about the strange, guttural words mixed in with the moans of agony that did escape--indications that the arrowhead had indeed been tainted with *wyrga* poison--he did not let his brother know it.

The afternoon wore on. Grayish daylight faded imperceptibly into early twilight. The great horse seemed tireless, walking steadily forward through the powdery snow with never a misstep.

Oliver slumped behind Pavarr, wearing the prince's spare cloak in place of his own soaked mantle. Exhausted, he half-dozed, half-awoke over and over again. When he awoke, he clutched fistfuls of Pavarr's tunic in his hands, fearful of falling off. When he dozed, his hands loosed their grip and he swayed to one side or the other, in imminent danger of losing his seat.

Pavarr stopped once to anchor his passenger firmly to the saddle with a loop of rope. Thereafter, Oliver felt more secure in his dozing. His head fell forward against Pavarr's back and bobbed as he continued his interrupted slumber. He did not waken when a winter-furred fox (*Vulpes vulpes*) darted deliberately in front of the horse and stopped beside a fallen tree on the other side of the path. The fox turned its sharp little face toward horse and riders before disappearing into the forest. Pavarr's eyes followed its passage, but he said nothing about it to his passenger.

They rode on under glass-gray skies turning darker, through sparsely falling snow. All around them were leafless trees whose branches were festooned with icicles glittering dully in the fading light. Moving onward at a pace that ate up miles, the horse obeyed the lightest touch of the reins as if he and Pavarr were one person. Oliver slept and dreamed, his head bouncing gently against Pavarr's back. Years afterward, he was to describe his life in the Labyrinth World as an interminable series of short naps and long nightmares punctuated by episodes of incredible beauty.

"Whoa, Firemark," Pavarr said softly, and the horse stopped to let his rider dismount. Oliver woke up and peered around at the monotony of white snow and black branches angled across each other. *Like prison bars*. They must have come quite a distance from the mineshaft from which he had emerged. *But where are we going? And what will happen to me when we get there?*

He shuddered. Nothing ahead could possibly be worse than the ordeal in the *Forbeodan* Tunnels, coming face to face with that overweight serpent who might have taken a notion to swallow... *I won't think about it any more.*

Oliver yawned widely and inhaled a lungful of frosty air. His gaze idly followed Pavarr, who had gone toward a huge lightning-struck oak to the side of the path. Its upper half had been sheared off, leaving only the mighty trunk and a few jutting branches as a stark reminder of the power of the sky.

Pavarr stopped in front of a hole in the tree, inserted his riding quirt into the hollow interior, and cautiously poked around inside. A small fuzzy creature emerged, chattering crossly, and flew away on stubby, fur-tipped wings.

"A *djarmil*," Pavarr remarked over his shoulder. "They'll eat anything. I hope it didn't--"

Just then a raven, its feathers disheveled and travel-stained, landed on a branch of the oak. It held an ivory-colored envelope in its beak. The bird gave the envelope to Pavarr and sat back, looking put-upon and resentful.

"Double overtime," it muttered. "Hazardous duty pay. And I'm talking to my shop steward on Monday."

"Many thanks, Friend Gorboc Corax," Pavarr said courteously. "Raven Express messengers have no equal in any dimension."

"Nevermore," croaked the raven, somewhat mollified, and flew off.

Pavarr glanced at the superscription, put the envelope inside his tunic pocket, and remounted.

Having slept the edge off his exhaustion, Oliver woke up fully as Firemark began walking again. Nothing changed in their monotonous surroundings for several *kephan*. Black trees, white snow. Black trees, white snow. Oliver became bored with the scenery and refocused his thoughts internally.

So this was Pavarr, Prince of Taraman, the man whose rope held him fast to the saddle. Pavarr was some sort of cousin to Flavia, as Oliver was himself. Pavarr had nothing on him there, though Oliver wondered just how near their kinship was. His own relationship-- seventh cousin seven times removed--was so remote that it had been a great kindness on Flavia's part to accept him as one of her extended family. *Cousin Oliver* she had called him. The memory made a warm glow around his heart.

He admitted grudgingly that it had been decent of the prince to rescue him from what would have been a frozen grave if he'd remained outside the badger's den much longer. The thought came to him-- reluctantly, but there it was--that Pavarr had not only rescued him, but also seemed to be protecting him, as if Oliver were incapable of protecting himself. Which, of course, was exactly the case: He was utterly incapable of defending himself in this world (or, truth be told, in the world from which he had come).

Charleynne Gates

The realization pricked his ego; on the other hand, he was alive. He ought to feel extremely grateful to Pavarr, and he'd better swallow what little pride he had left and be grateful. In any case, he reflected, gratitude is a good thing, and easier to swallow than pride.

The next question concerned the matter of who or what so endangered Oliver that he needed Pavarr's escort. Why hadn't Pavarr shown up at the High Council when the Questors were called? And what was this "Rendezvous" place where the Questors were to meet Pavarr?

He felt strongly that someone ought to have explained these things to him, but he supposed no one had thought of it in all the rush. The Mage Dandriel could have done so, perhaps, if it hadn't been for the necessity of hurrying him through the Labyrinth. There were definitely large and troubling gaps in Oliver's understanding of this strange new world.

Not that he had any intention of quitting the Quest, despite his regrettable lack of information and his terrifying experience in the *Forbeodan* Tunnels. Not when there was the smallest chance that he could help Flavia (and redeem his heedless mistake that had caused all the trouble in the first place). He had pledged himself to her service. He may have backslid once or twice since making his spontaneous vow, but it was only in thought, not in action. Nothing in this world or any other would prevent him from fulfilling his promise, even the presence of a rival like Prince Pavarr.

Thus by degrees he got around to the question that puzzled and hurt him deeply: Why did the other Questors abandon him in the Tunnels? He'd almost begun to think of them as friends, but now it seemed they hadn't liked him after all. A depressing sense of betrayal overwhelmed him.

Was I wrong about them?

Were they wrong about me? Have they discovered I'm not anyone special after all?

The afternoon wore on. The last remnant of daylight melted into a gunmetal gloaming. The great horse, Firemark, seemed tireless. Oliver wished he could drift into sleep again, but although the scenery was repetitive, even mesmerizing, the horse's pace rhythmic and gently rocking, he couldn't make himself doze off although he was physically and mentally fatigued. His physiology had not yet adjusted to a foreign world with its different weather, water, air, and food.

And his secret dream of High Adventure wasn't working out in reality quite the way he used to fantasize. In fact, this Quest business was more of a strain than he had anticipated. He needed time to recuperate from the unanticipated shocks to his system. He yawned again, then gulped as he caught a glimpse of something out of the corner of his eye. Quickly he looked aside to see what it was, but it disappeared when he refocused in that direction.

It's eye fatigue. I've been staring at the same identical landscape for too many hours. There it was again--a flash of shadow between those two trees over there. *No, there!* Ducking down behind that fallen log! *Is it another hallucination?*

He blinked and stared, but nothing else appeared. A crick developed in his neck, and he turned toward the other side. There it was again! Whether it was man or beast, he couldn't tell. In one glimpse it seemed tall, attenuated, like a quaver of smoke; in another, squat and pale as a toadstool. Then there were two at once, shadows long and rangy, running on all fours from tree-trunk to tree-trunk, visible only against the snow. There again--more of them! Emerging for an eye-blink, then vanishing like vapor before he could get a good look.

"Prince Pavarr!" he whispered. "Did you see those--?"

"Yes," was the quiet reply. "They won't harm you if you pay them no attention." Oliver took note of the "if" and faced front resolutely. Only his eyes darted from side to side as he tried to pinpoint the elusive creatures.

"They are Twilight People," Pavarr explained later. "They live only in dusk and are invisible by night and in daylight. They are bound to no country; they answer to no authority. They perceive everything that goes on in the Twilight World, and they may tell you things--if you know how to ask. You can trust what they say, but be careful. They are implacable foes of treachery and deception."

A short while later, an indeterminate obscurity appeared between two black oaks. Pavarr passed by with a glance and a nod, but in a few more steps he brought Firemark to a halt and dismounted. He left Oliver on the horse and walked back to the ice-mantled oak grove. There he seemed to be holding converse with the obscurity, although Oliver couldn't hear anything they said.

Charleynne Gates

Oliver sat and shivered, waiting for Pavarr. The air was even colder here, but it wasn't a matter of temperature. Maybe there was less oxygen than there ought to be, because there was a kind of deadness in the atmosphere. As if the whole Icewode, locked in ice and snow, were coming to the end of its life.

He dared to look around, but saw nothing more or less than he had seen all day--snow, ice, black trees.

Wait! What was that? Over there, opposite to where Pavarr was standing. A swirl of snow--or no, a swirl of something with a dull metallic glitter. Oliver couldn't quite make out what it was because brownish smoke, possibly from a nearby campfire, drifted across it like a veil. With the smoke came a choking odor, a stench which smelled far worse than any other kind of burning.

He squinted, tried to peer through the smoke... and thought he saw Death itself.

Man-tall, motionless, it stood between the trees, no more than ten feet away. It seemed to be wearing some kind of iron cage, as if it were an exoskeleton. Inside the iron was a being in vaguely human shape, but its form appeared to melt and congeal, melt and congeal over and over again, as if it were made of thickened sludge rather than human flesh. Its surface glistened with rainbow colors, but the colors were all, somehow, terribly wrong.

And the face... the dreadful ruin of a face stared back at him. In its eyes was implacable rage mixed with unbearable sadness.

Oliver didn't move. He didn't breathe. His brain refused to work. Transfixed, he gaped at what he could not believe.

And then it was gone. Firemark, who sensed the thing before Oliver did, stamped a hoof in the snow and sent a low call of alarm to Pavarr. The prince returned on the run, dagger drawn. But the apparition, whatever it had been, was no longer there, with no trace left behind but a faint, nauseating odor.

Pavarr, after a long look around, sheathed his sword and conferred with Firemark in the equine tongue. Remounting, he said to Oliver, "So now you've seen your first *wyrga*. And it was alone. Why didn't it attack?" he continued, more to himself than to his passenger. "Even one *wyrga* might have overwhelmed the three of us. There's something here I don't understand."

He turned in the saddle and made a swift sign to the gray obscurity back in the frozen oak grove. "Later, Old One," he muttered. "At The Rendezvous."

They went on at a faster pace than before. Oliver puzzled over what he had seen--or hardly seen, for the apparition had lasted but a few seconds. He wondered mightily why he hadn't felt afraid of it, even when Pavarr told him what it was. In fact, he recalled a sensation altogether different from fear, although he couldn't put a name to it at the moment.

After a while, he realized that although the thing was horrible to look at, he couldn't forget the pain in its eyes. He found himself wishing that its pain might be lifted, for its burden of agony seemed to be greater than even such an unnatural being ought to bear.

Thus, by degrees, the soul of Oliver Medley began to grow up.

Night descended, and the Twilight People faded from sight. The sky became black, and the first, second, and third stars glimmered. Firemark came to a halt before a snow-covered mound surrounded by prickly scrub-brush. Pavarr dismounted and gave his passenger a hand down, smiling at Oliver's efforts to control his rubbery legs. Cautioning Oliver not to say anything, Pavarr took the horse's reins, and the three of them ducked under an overhang of crusted snow and, surprisingly, through a hidden door and right into the mound itself. Oliver staggered inside and found himself in an underground shelter.

It was a circular room, much larger than he anticipated, with an open horse-stall at the front end. Pavarr quickly removed the saddle, tended to Firemark with currycomb and blanket, and gave the horse grain in a feed-bag as Oliver tramped around in a wobbly circle, trying not to complain about his aching thigh muscles. Pavarr returned to the entry-way and surveyed the darkening countryside with a keen eye. Then he took out his dagger and traced a runic symbol in the fresh snow outside the threshold.

With no comment about what he had just done, Pavarr went to the firepit in the center of the room, knelt, and with flint and tinder made a fire, using dry wood stacked nearby. He kept the blaze low, but even so, its light was heartening and its warmth welcome. Oliver crouched as close to it as he could and spread his hands to gather in the heat.

Cold, so cold. I've never been cold like this. It's not just the temperature; it's something else, something... hostile. What is this place?

Pavarr unrolled two blankets near the firepit, then dug out a pan and some packages that looked like (Oliver hoped they were) food. At the mere thought of something solid to eat, his stomach rumbled like a drum roll despite his efforts to stop it. Pavarr took no notice.

Soon the pan was propped over the fire, and a stew that looked and smelled delicious was bubbling inside it. Pavarr took out two bowls from his saddlebag, filled them, and handed one to Oliver. "Grace be with all," he said.

"Grace be with all," responded Oliver, pleased with himself for remembering the spiritual etiquette of the Labyrinth, but rather embarrassed because that was all he knew.

They ate, and the stew warmed Oliver to the tips of his toes. He began to feel almost comfortable, but that feeling disappeared as soon as he remembered the Questors. *Where are they now? Did they go back into that* Forbeodan *place to look for me?*

Pavarr finished the last of the stew and went to the entrance to fetch snow in the pan. Heating it over the fire, he washed out the cooking utensils and returned them to the saddlebags.

Huddling next to the firepit as he watched Pavarr's efficient movements, Oliver felt waves of sleep wash over him. His head nodded; he looked longingly at the bedrolls Pavarr had laid out.

"Not yet, my friend," said Pavarr. "We have matters to discuss."

"Oh yes, of course," Oliver replied, shaking himself awake.

"Go get a breath of cold air. That'll wake you up. Just don't cross the threshold. You don't want to be seen."

Oliver obeyed, flapping his arms around to energize his circulation. Returning to the entrance, but not a step beyond, he inhaled a deep lungful of winter night and immediately wished he hadn't, for it re-chilled his whole interior. Rubbing his arms briskly to warm himself, he returned to the firepit.

"So tell me," said Pavarr. "How did you come to be in the badger's den?"

Oliver drew in a breath and prepared to risk confiding in his rescuer, but before he could utter a word, a long, quavering wail stopped him. The sound grew higher, was joined by other wails. They filled the ice-entombed forest and spiraled up to the moon.

"What's that?" Oliver gasped, his face drained of color.

"The White Wolves of the Icewode," replied Pavarr, unconcerned. "They are guardians of the forest. Tonight they hunt."

Oliver shivered. "I didn't know there were w--wolves in Threshold Forest," he stammered.

"We're not in Threshold Forest any more," Pavarr answered, relaxing on his bedroll. "We left it behind long ago. This is the Icewode."

"How--how did we get here?" Oliver asked, trying to keep his teeth from chattering.

"The northern end of Threshold Forest runs into the Icewode, where the season never changes. It's always winter here. The animals who live here are... different. Because it's always cold, their fur is thicker and heavier than usual, much prized by fur traders. We're heading for a trading post called The Rendezvous. I need to get some information there, and we're supposed to meet up with the *Foressa* and the other Questors. If our luck holds. If not--"

Another unearthly howl pierced the night. Despite himself, Oliver shivered and imagined piles of bones picked bare, shining whitely in the moonlight. His bones.

"Listen," said Pavarr. "They're singing. It's when they don't sing that we need to worry. But we're inside a safe-hill, and Firemark can hear an eagle breathing beyond the Great Mountain of Zund. We're secure. For now."

Oliver tried to keep that in mind. "Why is it always winter here?" he asked.

Pavarr frowned and looked aside for a moment, as if weighing in his mind how much he ought to reveal. "It's because of the Ash," he answered finally. "The Ashes of Waste from the Desolation have invaded other parts of the Labyrinth World. The balance of Nature has been disturbed, and the seasons have changed beyond our capacity to predict them. The earth has grown unstable, Friend Oliver, and more dangerous than I can say.

"Later, when we meet the other Questors, I can tell you more about the consequences of the Great Disturbance. Then you will see why it is imperative to find Flavia and take her to the Abbey of Saint

Amber. She must be restored to health, for in her is the life of the world. But now I want to hear your story. All of it. Anything we learn may be valuable to the Quest."

Oliver duly recounted his adventures from the moment that Great-Aunt Belvedine had swept into his office to his first sight of Flavia. He didn't describe his feelings for her, of course. They were too precious... and he was ashamed to share them. He didn't need to: Pavarr guessed everything, and in sympathy said nothing. He simply listened keenly and asked questions about details Oliver wouldn't have considered worth mentioning.

"So you actually met Old Sal!" the prince commented with a chuckle when Oliver described his encounter with the cave serpent (significantly abridged to get through it as quickly as possible. The memory of Old Sal's snake-ish breath was still with him.). "She's known as the Terror of the Tunnels, and her reputation is twice as big as she is. I doubt if she would have bitten you; her venom sacs must have dried up years ago. She can still do constriction, though... I don't blame you for getting out fast!" He paused for a moment. "Do you know what happened to the other Questors?"

Oliver shook his head.

"They didn't tell you where they were headed. Did they mention The Rendezvous?"

Oliver nodded. "But they didn't tell me what it was, or where," he said, hoping to elicit an answer. None was forthcoming.

The prince pondered what Oliver had told him, gazing into the embers in the firepit as if seeing things beyond Oliver's ken.

"I'm told you have a special Gift," he said at last, "something you can use to assist the *Sendara*'s return to the Graelands. I won't ask you what it is. But if you want to tell me anything else, it's all right as long as we're inside here. And I might as well give you this."

He reached inside his shirt and brought out the ivory-colored envelope. It had a peculiar stamp of unknown provenance, and Oliver's own name on the cover in spidery handwriting. Official-looking marks on the face of it said Address Unknown; No Forwarding Address; Deliver to Ravenhome; Delivery Refused, Party Not in Residence; Return to Sender; Sender's Name Illegible; Forward to Keeper's Inn; Not Here Any More; and finally, Forward to Lightning-Struck Oak, the Icewode.

Oliver Medley flushed crimson from the roots of his hair to the soles of his feet.

"It's--it's a letter from Great-Aunt Belvedine," he admitted.

Pavarr made a sound between a laugh and a snort. "Belvedine de Montfort? Belvedine's your great-aunt?"

"Er--yes. I--I never got around to, ah, actually reading her letter. She was, ah, somewhat disappointed about that. What does it say?"

Pavarr grinned, white teeth gleaming in the firelight. (Oliver had a thought about a panther, but it was gone almost before it manifested. Pavarr, he realized, might not be an entirely *safe* person.) "It's not addressed to me, and I didn't read it, so I can't tell you. Judging by all the forwarding directions, the Raven Express had trouble finding you."

"I--I left it on my porch swing at home. Why didn't they just leave it there? I'm sure I would have remembered it the next day."

Pavarr eyed him for a moment and shook his head. "Friend, you do not know what evil surrounds you in your own world. Even there the servants of the Desolation have been watching you. If the Raven Messenger hadn't taken it, the letter would be in their hands now. Why don't you open it?"

Oliver didn't particularly want to do that, but he couldn't think of any more objections. Pavarr took the envelope from him, pried off the purple beeswax seal on the flap with his dagger, and gave it back. Reluctantly, Oliver unfolded the ivory-colored linen paper and read it. The contents, in nearly illegible spidery penmanship, were what he might have expected.

Great-Aunt Belvedine ordered him (with numerous adjectives, adverbs, underlines, and exclamation points) to attend her to Ravenhome, date and time named, there to embark on a Perilous Adventure involving a distant relation whose welfare was of the utmost importance to (the word was hidden beneath a smear of ink). Most particularly, Oliver was ordered to use his special Gift in the service of this distant relation. The special Gift was not named, nor was the distant relation; it seemed Great-Aunt Belvedine assumed he knew all that. Everyone he had met in this world, Oliver thought glumly, assumed that he knew a great deal more than he did.

". . . and avoid the Mire!" he made out at the end. The phrase told him nothing.

Enclosed with the letter was another document, smaller and much folded. As far as he could make out, it was something of a legal nature. As archivist of the Willoughby-Smythe Collection of Ancient Music, Maps, and Manuscripts, Oliver had a considerable amount of experience deciphering old documents, and he studied this one as best he could by firelight. But the parchment had been crunched and refolded many times until its creases had partially worn some of the letters beyond the point of decipherment. It also had several wet spots on it from being carried in a raven's beak through a snowstorm, and some of the ink had blurred.

"What is this?" Oliver asked, giving up. "I don't understand." He handed the paper to Pavarr, who took it to examine in the flickering light.

"It's your entry permit," he said at last.

"Entry permit? You mean—like a visa? Was I supposed to bring my passport? Nobody told me!" As far as Oliver knew, his passport rested securely in a safe deposit box in his credit union back home—wherever that was.

"Your permission to enter the Labyrinth World," the prince explained. "You can't get one of these in your world. It has to come from here, and you have to be examined and recommended by the proper authorities in the Labyrinth. Their signatures are at the bottom."

Oliver peered at the scratchy writing, which looked as if a wind had blown ink across the lines. "But I've never been examined for this, ah, entry permit! I don't know who would have recommended me. And why did Great-Aunt Belvedine send me this?"

Pavarr frowned a little. "That ought to be obvious, Friend. She expected you to use it to enter the Labyrinth. If you had, you might have avoided going through the Mort-Mire."

"I—I thought we had to go through there because of the fallen oak across the highway!"

"Things are not always what they seem in this part of the world," the prince answered.

"But no one asked for my passport at Ravenhome! No one mentioned it!"

Saint Amber's Rose

Pavarr considered. "They probably felt sorry for you. The *Sendara* would have known you didn't have it and told her attendants not to mention it lest they hurt your feelings. Believe me," anticipating Oliver's question, "if Flavia asked her to, even Belvedine wouldn't have said anything, no matter what she really thought.

Oliver steeled himself to face the awful truth. "Do you mean," he asked, "if I had opened the letter when I received it, even if I had just taken it with me, sealed as it was... then we wouldn't have had to go through the Mort-Mire at all?" *Or the Tunnels,* he added in his mind, but didn't say aloud. *Then it* was *my fault that Flavia was taken.* "We might be at the Abbey of Saint Amber right now with Fl--with the *Sendara,* if--"

"We can't be sure of that," said the prince, tucking himself into his bedroll. Out of kindness he avoided meeting Oliver's eyes. "Belvedine didn't include much relevant information in that letter, like how you were supposed to get into the Labyrinth in the first place, with or without an entry permit, so it's partly her fault. Better get some sleep now. We start again before dawn."

Oliver rolled into his blanket on the packed-earth floor. In case of sudden alarms in the night, he kept his spectacles on. Left to his own musings, he stared through the smoke-hole in the ceiling toward the eerie shimmer of Aurora Borealis, a celestial waterfall of emerald green and white satin. Behind it the stars of Ursa Major glimmered, spectral and remote.

Unwelcome images of shame and remorse arose in his mind, and his tender conscience made sleep impossible for a long time. It hadn't been all his fault; he understood that, but the beginning of it had been. And the end result of his procrastination had been the abduction of the lady of his heart.

When he finally fell into slumber, the singing of the White Wolves of the Icewode echoed through his dreams.

Charleynne Gates

Chapter Eleven

The Rendezvous

Cautiously the four Questors emerged from the Zemora tunnel into the Icewode again. Hera Vespasia, her feathers white with a light dusting of snow, waited for them on the branch of a tree next to the lightning-struck oak. Down she flew on silent wings as Mil, in the lead, crawled out and looked around. Landing on Mil's shoulder, the owl whispered, "Over there! Do you see the tracks?"

Mil waved the other Questors back to the entrance and went toward the trampled snow around the lightning-struck oak. "A stallion," she said under her breath. "Carrying two riders. One got off and walked over here, and then here." She crouched down, examined the snow more closely, then returned to the tunnel entrance. Ducking through, she spoke softly.

"Pavarr has been here! On Firemark, carrying another rider. Pavarr dismounted and went to the lightning-struck oak while the other one stayed on the horse. Then they rode east in the direction of The Rendezvous."

"Who was the other rider?" demanded Great-Aunt Belvedine.

"Can't tell. No footprints."

"Then how do you know there was another rider?" Great-Aunt Belvedine challenged.

"The *Foressa* knows what she's doing, Belvedine," said Tipp.

"I know Firemark's hoofprints, and he was carrying more weight than usual," Mil responded, keeping an even tone.

"It may have been baggage," Great-Aunt Belvedine objected.

"Baggage like this?" asked Mil, and held up what she had found in the snow around the hoofprints.

"A white owl's feather!" exclaimed Tipp. "Friend Oliver had one in his hat, like ours."

"How do you know it belonged to Medley?" demanded Great-Aunt Belvedine. "It could have come from Hera Vespasia, or any owl in the Icewode! It's ridiculous to assume--"

"Such a feather did not come from an owl of the Icewode," said Hera Vespasia quietly, and something in her voice stopped Great-Aunt Belvedine in mid-sentence. "No member of the *Norrengild* flies here by choice except messengers of the Raven Express, and they avoid it whenever possible. I recognize that feather because I chose it especially for Friend Oliver and asked the Mage Dandriel to set a tracking charm on it. I see that it has functioned perfectly."

"Also, Belvedine," Mil continued, "I found the feather on top of the horse's hoofprint."

"Meaning that it fell down when they were here," Tipp added.

Great-Aunt Belvedine sniffed, but made no further comment.

"By the condition of the tracks I estimate they're half a day's march ahead of us," Mil went on. "Pavarr will go on to The Rendezvous. We'd better--"

Just then Tapp, leaning heavily against his brother, gave a half-stifled groan. Tipp lowered him to the dirt floor of the tunnel entrance, and Mil went to his side, taking out her medallion.

"Wait!" Tipp bent over his brother, signaling Mil not to give him another drop yet. "He's trying to tell us something."

Tapp lay with half-closed eyes, his head turning restlessly from side to side. He muttered strange words mixed with low, growly noises which made no sense to his hearers.

"What's he saying?" Tipp whispered.

Mil shook her head and frowned. "I can't understand him."

Hera Vespasia flew from Mil to Tipp's shoulder and looked down at Tapp, studying his condition. The stricken Dwarvian's eyes rolled back in his head, showing the whites beneath shadowed eyelids. His skin had a grayish cast, making him look corpselike, and a trickle of black foam trailed from the corner of his mouth. He tried to sit up, only to collapse again.

"He speaks in the evil tongue of the *wyrg*a," the owl announced, clicking her beak. "I cannot distinguish the words, but I recognize the sound."

"*Wryga!*" exclaimed Great-Aunt Belvedine. "How does he know their foul speech?"

Charleynne Gates

"He doesn't!" Tipp defended his brother. "We never--"
"The arrow point," said Mil.
"Tipped with *wyrga* poison," said Hera Vespasia. "It has begun to work in him."
"What can we do for him?" Tipp pleaded.
The owl pondered. "Another drop of healing oil would ease his pain for a time, but nothing can halt the progress of the poison."
"What will happen to him?" demanded Great-Aunt Belvedine.
"Will he die?" asked Tipp desperately.
"No," Hera Vespasia said slowly. "No--though it might be better if he did!"
"What!" Tipp held his moaning brother's hand tightly. "What do you mean!"
"Arrows tipped with *wyrga* poison do not always kill," said the owl. "They can change the injured one so that--" She hesitated. "So that eventually he becomes a *wyrga* himself!"
"No! No!" Tipp shouted, oblivious to Mil's warning glance. "I won't let that happen!"
"Hush!" Mil cautioned him. "He hasn't changed into one yet. There may be something we can do to save him." She looked toward Hera Vespasia, a silent appeal in her eyes.
The owl considered, drawing her brows together. "There may be," she said slowly. "But only if we get him to a medicine woman before more damage is done. Before the poison hardens his heart. If that happens, there will be no hope for him!"
"Where is the nearest medicine woman?" asked Mil.
"Possibly in the Rover encampment," said Hera Vespasia. "If old Mother Asunta is still alive. If we knew where their winter camp is."
"We have to find her!" begged Tipp. "We can't let my brother..." His voice trailed off.
Hera Vespasia left Tipp's shoulder and flew back to the entrance, nodding to Mil to follow her. Mil let one more droplet of liquid from her vial fall on Tapp's wound, watching until his writhing movements calmed somewhat, then joined the owl where they could speak alone.

Saint Amber's Rose

"If we cannot find a healer among the Rovers," began Hera Vespasia, "and there is no other nearby, then it will be almost impossible to save Tapp from turning into--"

Mil glanced sharply at the owl. "And if he does become one?"

"Then it would be better for brother to slay brother! Death would be better than life as a soulless slave of the Lord of Desolation!" said Hera Vespasia.

Mil made a swift secret sign. "Creator prevent it! We will have to--"

A low shussshing sound came from outside the tunnel, followed by the crunch of a heavy weight stopping on the packed snow. Mil hastened to the entrance and peered out.

"Vladir!" she called softly, and signaled the others. As quickly as they could, with Tapp sagging against Tipp and Great-Aunt Belvedine shouldering Tapp's pack, the Questors crept out of the tunnel and into the never-melting snows of the Icewode.

The sullen sky was darkening to dusk before Firemark halted in a clearing in front of a ramshackle cabin built of split logs and splintery planks. A weather-worn roof over the porch sheltered a trio of rough-looking men in leather and skins who slouched against the posts. One of the men, a tall, scraggy-haired beanpole, grinned at the travelers, showing blackened teeth, but he had a half-crazed glint in his eye that Oliver didn't think went with a smile of welcome. Another one spat a stream of brown juice onto the dirty snow, squinted up at them, and emitted a low growl. The third ducked inside the cabin, letting the door swing shut behind him.

"This is The Rendezvous," Pavarr muttered over his shoulder to Oliver. "Don't say anything. I'll do the talking. And don't show your face. Evening, gentlemen." Nodding to the men, who did not return the courtesy, he eased himself out of the saddle and onto the ground. "Trader Skulk around?" he asked, after surveying the area. The squinting man jerked his head toward the cabin door.

Unexpectedly a small, hunched person with spindly legs and an unruly mop of straw-colored hair came running around the corner of the shack toward horse and riders. Panting with exertion, he pulled his forelock in Pavarr's direction and bobbed his head several times.

"G'd evening, sirs both, g'd evening, a fine day for travel, eh, sirs? Take your horse to the stables, sir? Bran mash and a rubdown and a drink for yourselves, sirs? Trader Skulk'll be happy to see you again, sir. Anything I can do to serve you, sirs both, anything at all--"

"That'll do, Nodd." Pavarr cut off the flow of welcome. "Your best care for my horse, and there'll be something more for you when we leave." Pavarr tossed a coin to the bowing hostler, who grabbed it out of the air so fast that Oliver wasn't even sure he had seen it done.

"Eh-heh-heh-heh, thank you, sir, thank you. Right this way, sirs." The hostler stretched out a pale, long-fingered hand to take the reins, but Pavarr shook his head and gestured for the little man to go ahead. Pattering over the slushy path, Nodd led them toward a tumble-down stable in back of the trading post. The outer building was in even worse condition than the main cabin and seemed in danger of falling down completely at any moment.

Nodd skittered across to one of the stalls, which was spread with a layer of sodden straw that stank of mildew. Firemark inhaled, snorted, shook his head, and locked his knees, refusing categorically to move into the stall.

"You'll need to muck this out first," Pavarr ordered. "Go fetch some hay, and mind you get it fresh. And bring some clean water in a clean bucket."

Nodd scurried out of the stable as fast as his spindly legs could carry him.

Pavarr helped Oliver down from the saddle, where he was still securely fastened. Oliver slid off the great horse's back, biting back a groan and landing on legs that had turned to jelly.

"Don't make a sound," Pavarr warned him.

Pavarr crouched down beside the pile of rancid straw and, unbelievably, scrabbled about in it. As Oliver watched, hardly able to breathe in the malodorous air, Pavarr brought out a small oilskin pouch, brushed it off, and swiftly tucked it inside his tunic.

"We'll go into The Rendezvous now," he said to Oliver barely above a whisper. "Remember: Don't make yourself conspicuous. Say nothing. Above all, don't name any names. We're in a very dangerous situation."

"Why are we here?" Oliver whispered.

Saint Amber's Rose

"For information," Pavarr muttered, keeping his face toward the horse and busying himself with saddle and tack.

"What information? Oh! You mean--"

Pavarr cut him off with a gesture.

By force of will, Oliver mastered the quivering of his thigh muscles and strode stoically beside Pavarr as they returned to the cabin and walked in the door.

The interior was too dim for Oliver to see very much at first, partly because, following instructions, he had arranged the hood of his cloak so that it shaded his face. Only a couple of narrow, grease-smeared windows gave any light, and what did filter through was too dim to make much difference. As his eyes got used to the dimness, he began to discern crudely hacked tables and benches about the room. Men dressed in animal skins and furs lounged around them and leaned against the walls, smoking foul-smelling pipes and drinking from large tankards.

Oliver wondered about the purpose of the gleaming knives slung from their belts. Hunters, he decided, or trappers, out here in this frozen wilderness for the fur trade. One of the men was carving on a stick of wood, making slow, even strokes, and the shavings curled off in perfect order at his feet. His knife must have a very keen edge. Oliver reminded himself to be extremely circumspect in his behavior.

Pavarr strolled to a scarred wooden counter at one end of the room, and Oliver made haste to follow and not stumble over anything. On the other side of the counter was a man so big and bulky that he blocked out most of the light from the window behind him. His thick, gray-streaked black beard straggled down to his waist, with beads and feathers and small bones braided at random through it. Oliver fervently hoped they were chicken bones rather than human, which was his first impression.

The man's face, with strings of long, unkempt hair hanging around it, was almost completely hidden. He was concentrating on the whetting of a long-bladed knife that looked, as far as Oliver could see, already as sharp as it was ever going to get.

"Skulk," said Pavarr, acknowledging the trader.

"Prince. Yer outta yer territory," the man returned in a grumble.

"Does that trouble you?" Pavarr inquired mildly.

Charleynne Gates

The man laughed once down in his throat. He didn't sound amused. "Not me. You here to sell yer horse?"

"No one touches the horse," said Pavarr, perfectly calm. "You know that."

The man--Skulk--grunted, whether in agreement or not, Oliver couldn't tell. "Git yew a good price fer it. Got a buyer interested."

"You don't have a seller interested."

"Who's yer friend?" said the trader, jerking his head toward Oliver.

"This," answered the prince, as if it were a matter of no importance, "is Mr. Riddle."

"Ain't seen 'im afore," returned Skulk, never ceasing to whet. "Fur buyer?"

"Tourist," said the prince, examining with great care a price-tagged necklace of fangs he had picked up from the counter.

"Don't get many o' those. Not much sightseein' in these parts," stated Skulk after a moment or two.

"He's just passing through," said the prince with the utmost indifference. "You serve anything fit to drink in this place?"

"W'iskey," replied Skulk, "if yew pays fer it."

"No, I'll decline the rotgut, if it's all the same to you. Give us a couple of your delicious hot appledores instead." Pavarr put the necklace back on the counter and started toward the other end of the dirt-floored room. "Come, Friend Riddle. We'll take advantage of Trader Skulk's kind welcome and warm ourselves at his blazing hearth."

Oliver followed as inconspicuously as possible, gritting his teeth in the effort to keep his legs steady.

Pavarr went toward a table made of a couple of knothole-dotted planks set upon uneven tree stumps. Beside it a stone chimney ran up crookedly from a cinder-filled fireplace where a lone ember was doing its best to give off a little heat.

"*Heketu,* Old One," Pavarr remarked pleasantly to the other side of the table, to a corner so ill-lighted that nothing in it could be seen. His breath made a vapor in the chill of the room.

"*Heketu, Domor,*" answered a shadow in the corner, startling Oliver so that he nearly emitted a squeak of surprise, but restrained himself with a gulp. The voice was only a breath, like the last echo from the bottom of a well.

Saint Amber's Rose

"We'll sit here," Pavarr decided, and eased himself onto a rickety stool. Oliver sat on one nearby and kept perfectly still, attempting invisibility as well as anonymity.

The room grew chillier. The single ember in the hearth labored earnestly at its daunting task, to little avail. Oliver glanced at Pavarr, who gazed into the distance, apparently absorbed in his own thoughts. What light there was outlined his dark silhouette with its hawk-like profile. On one side of the prince's face, the thin slash of a wound ran from his hairline to the corner of his eye. It looked fairly fresh, not yet completely healed over.

Oliver wondered what had made it. Saber? Dagger? Tooth or talon? Was it a battle scar, as Mil's appeared to be? *What kind of world is this, where people still fight with swords?*

Waiting for something to happen, concentrating on remaining as inconspicuous as possible, Oliver kept his eyes glued to one of the knots in the knife-gouged table. After a while its outline wavered. Oliver blinked, but the knot wavered even more and began to resemble the hooded face that he had seen back in the Mort-Mire... and again in Threshold Forest, when he had balanced, mesmerized, on the windowsill outside his room. As he stared, fascinated, the image stopped wavering and a face limned in front of him, a face with eyes yellow as flame and burnt black slits for pupils.

The face looked directly at him. Oliver tried to draw back, but found that he could not. The face willed him to stare into its eyes... His head drooped forward.

"Hot appledores for gentlemen both," said Nodd, and banged down on the table two chipped pottery mugs with steaming-hot liquid in them. Startled, Oliver jumped a little on his uncomfortable stool. The face dislimned and became a knothole again. Pavarr tossed a coin across the table; it disappeared into Nodd's palm, and the stablehand-turned-waiter scuttled away. Pavarr picked up his mug and drank. Oliver did likewise, doing his best to ignore a suspicion that the mug hadn't seen much soap and water since its last use.

The appledore disseminated heat to his insides, warming him thoroughly for only the second time since he had left Keeper's Inn. It tasted something like mulled cider (with the addition of a few unidentifiable spices) and began to revive him.

-- 209 --

They continued to sip in silence. The only sounds were the feeble crackle of the ember in the fireplace and the smooth slide of wood shavings from the man carving with his hunting knife. After a while Oliver's eyes began to get used to the darkness (he carefully avoided looking at the knot in the table again) so that shapes began to appear in the room.

Skins of animals hung on the walls, most with the heads still attached. Their open eyes glistened in the gloom, eyes full of terror and rage, the last expressions they held before the hunters brought them down. He couldn't identify the animals; their shapes and markings were unfamiliar to him. *Icewode creatures. They belong to this place of icebound trees and perpetual snow.*

More skins lay stacked in piles around the counter, their pelts thick with fur. How many hapless animals had the hunters slaughtered to satisfy the vanity of people in the outer world? He shuddered and felt depressed. There was a taint of evil in the atmosphere here, an odor of violence, of unclean death and old, crusted blood.

Pavarr held his mug between both hands, warming them, looking down into the murky fluid as if he were seeking an answer in its depths. He said something in a tone so low that Oliver barely made out the words. Then he realized that Pavarr wasn't speaking to him but to the shadow in the chimney-corner.

"When Wasting to the Graelands goes," Pavarr murmured, "And naught abates the dreadful snows."

Oliver thought that an odd thing to say.

After two or three beats of silence, the shadow gathered itself together like an inkblot, becoming a figure with a hidden face. Its outline was so misty that probably no one but Oliver and the prince would have realized it was there.

"Then seek one who no guile knows," it returned, the sound no louder than the hush of snow falling on a leaf. "Whose Gift awakes Saint Amber's Rose."

Quite a long time passed after that, while Pavarr continued to warm his hands and sip his appledore.

"Have you seen her?" Pavarr asked, his lips barely moving.

The gray form said nothing, but Oliver thought it wavered just a little from side to side in negation.

"Do you know where she is?"

Saint Amber's Rose

After another pause, the shadow-voice spoke.

> *To the Ruined Chapel go,*
> *Center of the endless snow.*
> *Where the Unsoul'd Warder keeps,*
> *Lies the Rose in death asleep.*

All of a sudden the lonely ember in the fireplace exploded like a firecracker, and in a burst of yellow flame, fire roared out again among the ash-blackened logs. Oliver's nerves, already stretched to the breaking point, snapped entirely, and he sprang up with a shout. Pavarr, who hadn't moved, glared at him. Greatly ashamed of his outburst, Oliver huddled into himself and sat down. When he dared to glance back at the chimney-corner again, the shadow was gone.

Oliver began to wish they might leave The Rendezvous. *Soon.* While Pavarr had been drinking his appledore, deep in thought, Oliver had been casting surreptitious glances around the gloomy chamber, and what he saw did not reassure him.

The men sitting and standing around the room all seemed to be very big, with huge muscles bulging under their animal-hide clothing. The women among them didn't look much different, not particularly... well... feminine, Oliver thought, if that was the correct term in the present milieu.

Two of the men had shaven heads, their scalps painted with some substance that glistened blue in the gloom. One man's ear had been half torn away--or bitten off. That must've hurt, Oliver sympathized, immediately forgotten when the man aimed an ear-to-half-ear grin at him. His yellow teeth had been filed to sharp points.

Unable to repress a shudder, Oliver turned back to the table and pretended to be absorbed in finishing his drink. When he looked up, Pavarr signaled with the least perceptible movement of his head to keep quiet and especially not to stare at the cluster of men gathering in front of the counter, coincidentally blocking access to the single door.

Pavarr moved away from the fire's heat and leaned closer. "We may be in for it now," he murmured. "If anything happens, stay out of the way and get outside. I'll try to hold them off."

What does he mean by that? Oliver wondered. *Not a fight, I hope. I really don't think I--*

Pavarr spoke a little louder, so that anyone beyond their table who was interested might hear him. "We're past our time," he said. "We need to be on our way."

The atmosphere in the cabin had changed since the ember exploded in the fireplace. Now there was a tangible threat in the atmosphere, unmistakably directed toward Pavarr and himself. Squinting eyes stared at them. Hoarse, sneering laughter--if you could call it laughter--came from two or three men talking over the hatchet-scarred counter to Trader Skulk. A single word detached itself from their conversation. It floated across the room to Oliver and crawled into his ear like a spider.

The word was "kill".

His stomach somersaulted. His skin turned cold and hot by turns; little hairs stood up on the back of his neck. His throat dried. His mind froze on the picture of himself as a blood-spattered corpse sprawled on the filthy floor, no one back home ever learning what happened to him. He glanced sideways at Pavarr, but the prince merely picked up his mug, tossed back the last of his appledore, and set it upside down on the rough-hewn table.

His gesture seemed to have transmitted a signal to the horde of barbarians at the counter, for one of them began advancing slowly down the middle of the room toward Oliver and the prince.

"Git 'em, Scourge," sneered one of the barbarians.

"Teach 'em a lesson, Scourge," said another.

"You show 'em, Scourge," a third joined in.

"Come in here like they owned the place."

"'Spectin' ta git served ahead of the reg'lars."

"Scourge'll take care of 'em."

"Nobody messes with the Scourge."

The man designated "Scourge" lumbered toward them, grinning evilly all the while. Pavarr paid no attention, kept his focus on the scratched bottom of the mug as if his greatest concern was whether to order another appledore. Oliver felt a trickle of cold sweat run down his temple, but was much too nervous to wipe it away. Desperately he dedicated the remainder of his life to being a better person, supposing there was a remainder to his life.

The Scourge stopped short at their table and hooked his great thumbs in his studded leather belt. "Don't like seein' strangers in The

Rendezvous," he rumbled. "Upsets the reg'lar patrons. Wot kinda bizniz you got here?"

Only then did Pavarr casually glance upward to the massive menace. To Oliver's astonishment, an expression of utter delight spread over the prince's face. He sprang up from his seat. "Why, as I live and breathe!" he exclaimed. "It's Marmaduke Prettyfoot! Marmie! What a pleasant surprise! It's me--Junior! Junior from Taraman! Don't you remember our boyhood pranks at Camp Ottawattie?"

Before the Scourge could react, Pavarr opened his arms wide, wrapped them around the brawny bonehead, and squeezed, lifting the man completely off the floor before setting him down again with a thunk.

The Scourge--or Marmie--staggered backward a few steps, then stopped, goggling at Pavarr. "Junior?" he said at last. "Pavarr o' Taraman? Wot you doin' here?"

Behind him the other savages crowded closer, their hopes for a stress-relieving scrap fading.

"Marmaduke?" one of them said disgustedly. "That yer real name? Marmaduke Prettyfoot?"

"Not 'The Scourge'?" asked another, sounding betrayed. "I always thought it was 'The Scourge'."

"Marmie!" said another hulk, and made a loud kissing sound. "Ain't that a sweet name!"

The Scourge whirled around. "Wot's it ta you, ya punk!"

"Oh, Marmie!" squeaked a gap-toothed hunter in a high falsetto. "May I have this waltz, Marmie dear?"

"Keep yer trap shut!" the giant roared, and let fly a powerful punch that sent Falsetto sprawling halfway back to the counter. The next instant fists and feet flew about the room to the sound of grunts and blows, the cracking of bones and sinews, the splintering of various tip-tilted benches and tables in the way.

Pavarr backed away from the melee, beckoned to Oliver, and began edging along the log wall toward the door. Oliver followed, holding his breath and sucking in his stomach to stay out of range of any misplaced punches.

Not counting a few close calls, they made it to the door without further incident. Passing the counter, behind which Trader Skulk sat on his upturned barrel and calmly polished an ax-blade, Pavarr bade the proprietor a good evening.

"Skulk," he said, "your hospitality beggars description."

Skulk growled something unintelligible and went on with his polishing. Pavarr slipped out the door, dragging Oliver by the sleeve.

The night was black and starless, the full Wolf Moon pale and sinister in the sky. As they ran outside, a shushing sound came over the snow, and a Rover caravan pulled up in front of the trading post. It was painted canary-yellow, neatly trimmed in red and black, and set on sleigh runners. A team of white-footed chestnut horses with steaming breath drew it, and on the driver's seat was a real-life Rover, swarthy of skin, with drooping black moustaches. He wore a sheepskin coat and hat and a leather belt with a wicked-looking curved dagger stuck in it. A small gold earring hung from one ear, and a curiously carven pipe was clenched between his teeth.

Seeing them, the driver removed the pipe from his mouth and grinned. "Get in," he said. At Pavarr's direction, Oliver climbed hurriedly up a short ladder toward a little black door on the back of the caravan. Pavarr remained outside as the spindle-shanked stablehand Nodd hastened forward, Firemark's reins in his hands. Pavarr inspected the horse quickly and tossed Nodd a coin which the stablehand caught in the air, then made several rapid little bows.

"Thank you, sir, thank you. A pleasure, sir, always a pleasure."

Pavarr mounted Firemark, rode up close to the driver and spoke a few words in an undertone--"*wyrga*" was the one puzzling word Oliver heard--then took off on his own through the Icewode.

The driver made a clucking sound and shook the reins, and the team started off at a run. Soon The Rendezvous was behind them, well-hidden by close-growing, black-trunked trees.

Oliver squeezed through the black door at the exact instant the driver urged his horses to full gallop. He tumbled down three stair-steps, saving himself from several hard knocks by landing on a lump softer than the floor.

"Hey!" protested the lump.

"Watch out!" said someone else in the narrow interior, which was so dark Oliver couldn't see his hand before his face.

"Medley!" hissed another voice, only too familiar to him. "Stop rolling around on the floor and sit up straight! We've had quite enough trouble because of you."

"Hush!" Mil interjected. A tiny flame appeared between Mil's hands, just enough to give a faint illumination to their quarters, and Oliver saw that the other four Questors--no, five, counting Hera Vespasia, perched on a wooden rod near a pot-bellied stove--were seated inside the caravan.

The interior, though small, was tidily arranged, with bunk beds strapped to the walls, a folded-up table, stools, cupboards, and a shining copper basin. On each side was a single shuttered window. Oliver noticed that the Questors were all sitting on the floor beneath the level of the windows, so that no one was visible through the least gap in the shutters. He also noticed that no one greeted him with joyous acclamation, as would have been natural in discovering that someone they had thought lost forever was found. Depressed at this lack of welcome, he wrapped himself tighter in his cloak and leaned back against a bunk bed next to Tipp, who had unintentionally broken his fall down the stairs. Mil snuffed out the flame, and darkness settled again as the caravan glided onward.

After a while Mil made her way to the front of the caravan and whispered something through the small porthole behind the driver. In response, he urged the horses faster until their hooves fairly skimmed over the snow.

"Excuse me, ah, where--" Oliver tried to inquire, only to be glared down by Great-Aunt Belvedine. He could feel her disdain even though he couldn't see her face in the dark.

Oliver gave up, figuring that no one was going to tell him anything anyway. What was he but a pawn in a dangerous game that he didn't understand, in a world to which he was not born? He hoped Great-Aunt Belvedine finally realized the consequences of her crack-brained idea of whisking him off to this world, with all of them crammed into a Rover caravan (if that's what it was) on sleigh runners, galloping at breakneck speed through an alien wilderness to who knew where.

Really, Great-Aunt Belvedine must have lost her mind, to have landed us in such a predicament! And--apparently--in a radically different space/time dimension, too, where he still didn't comprehend how things were supposed to operate. *If I hadn't met Flavia... If it weren't for my vow...*

Mil returned to her place, being careful not to show herself at any of the windows, shuttered though they were.

"It's about time!" Great-Aunt Belvedine's harsh whisper filled the caravan. "Perhaps now we can find out the information we need. If Medley has managed to obtain it! What is--"

"Belvedine," said Mil wearily. "Be quiet. If there are *wyrga* around, they can hear us talking. And have a little patience. Friend Oliver, did you and Prince Pavarr find out anything at The Rendezvous? Whatever you can tell us is valuable."

Oliver considered, trying to think back before the bar-fight. There was that shadow in the corner by the hearth...

"Well," he said at last. "There was a shadow in a corner by the hearth. Pavarr spoke to it briefly and--"

"What did they say?" interrupted Great-Aunt Belvedine. Mil leaned over and spoke to her, too quietly for anyone else to hear. Great-Aunt Belvedine subsided.

"Why, they just... Pavarr started to recite a poem. It sounded like a nursery rhyme."

"Do you remember it, Friend Oliver?" asked Mil.

"Yes, I think so, although I didn't understand what it meant. He said, 'When Wasting to the Graelands goes, and naught abates the dreadful snows,' and then the shadow said--if I heard correctly--'Then seek one who no guile knows.' I don't recall any more."

Mil drew in a breath. Tapp, whom Oliver hadn't seen before, groaned from his makeshift bed on the floor. Tipp got to his knees and bent over his brother, pulling the rumpled blanket over Tapp's shoulders and listening to the jumbled words coming from within his agony.

"We need not fear for him unless the wound closes," Mil said. "Shall I look?"

But Tipp shook his head. Tapp quieted down, apparently drifting off to sleep.

"I don't know what to do," Tipp lamented in an undertone, pressing his work-hardened palms together. "I can't let him die, but I can't let him be changed into one of those..."

"Soon we will be with the Rovers," Mil reassured him. "If old Mother Asunta is there--"

"If she still is," said Great-Aunt Belvedine. "I heard she was ailing badly last winter--"

Immediately Mil interrupted and muttered swift words in a language unknown to Oliver. He did not understand their import, but Great-Aunt Belvedine evidently did, for she shut her large mouth like a trap.

Mil faced Oliver again and concentrated intently on him. "Friend Oliver. Can you remember what happened after the 'nursery rhyme'?"

Oliver felt her projecting energy to him, helping him to remember. "I think I can... Yes! The shadow said--" and he repeated the rhyme he heard in The Rendezvous.

"Ruined Chapel?" queried Tipp. "Where is that?"

"I don't know," Mil answered. "I've never seen it."

"'The endless snows,'" Great-Aunt Belvedine remarked. "That would be the Icewode, I suppose. The chapel must be somewhere in this wood."

"The Icewode is enormous," replied Mil. "No one knows its extent. Even if the chapel is somewhere inside it, we would need a map to find it."

Oliver pondered the last two lines of the rhyme. "But who or what is the 'Unsoul'd Warder'? The 'Rose' might be Fl--"

"Do not speak that name here!" cautioned Mil. "I do not know of the 'Unsoul'd Warder'."

"And 'in death asleep'?" asked Oliver. "Does that mean--?"

"It means 'entranced'," responded Mil. "The sleeping death. It can be given--or taken away--by one who is its master."

"A Mage?"

"A true Mage would never use such a spell in an unlawful way. And the rhyme means that the 'Rose' is a prisoner guarded by the 'Unsoul'd Warder', whatever that may be. More I cannot tell. We'd better be quiet now. Pavarr told Vladir that there are *wyrga* patrolling this area of the Icewode. He saw one before you got to The Rendezvous."

The steady whisper of the sleigh runners punctuated a silence that filled the whole caravan. Sleep-deprived, disoriented, overwhelmed equally by self-pity and anxiety about Flavia, Oliver drew his elven-made mantle closer about him and lay down upon it to try to sleep. If he snored a bit every so often, no one said anything about it.

Whiss-whiss-whiss-whiss... whiss-whiss-whiss-whiss...

Oliver dreamed of footsteps running over the snow, and awoke. Rubbing his eyes, he sat up, but the footsteps didn't vanish; they kept on running. He tried to peer through a crack between the shutter-boards in the window, but so narrow was the gap that he saw very little of the outside. The whole limited field of his vision was a solid mass of white. Once in a while the black trunk of a tree cut through the whiteness like an inked line on a blank page, but otherwise it seemed to him that the world outside had been erased.

Whiss-whiss-whiss-whiss...

The footsteps ran beside the caravan, right below the shuttered window where he watched. He ought to be able to see what made them. It wasn't the wind: There was no wind. It wasn't any large animal: He would have seen its head or antlers. It wasn't the team of horses in front, or the sound of the sleigh runners in the snow.

Craning his head around to take the greatest advantage of the little crack, he peered as intently as he could. By straining, he got a glimpse of the place where the footprints ought to be. *There!* He hadn't been dreaming them after all. There were definite marks in the snow beside the caravan, prints not made by boot or hoof, paw or claw. They were eerily like a human footprint, only far longer and narrower than any human's could be. And barefoot! with a toe-end that tapered to a sharp point.

Wyrga? Is that what ran beside them?

Oliver blinked and stared. He could actually see the indentations being made in the snow, but not what was making them. No one seemed to be there! But against all reason, the running footprints kept up with the caravan, even as the driver, apprehending danger, urged his team faster.

Horror struck Oliver speechless. He pressed his lips together to keep from screaming aloud. How could an invisible being, *wyrga* or not, run as fast as a swift team of horses, and leave footprints? And why did he sense that the maker of the footprints was playing with them, as a cat plays with a mouse before killing it?

He turned to warn the others, only to find them also sitting up in postures of tense readiness. Mil moved quickly to take his place at the window, warning him to silence. For several seconds she peered through the gap at the running footprints.

Whiss-whiss-whiss-whiss.

"Not *wyrga*... It is the *Erl*-king!" she whispered urgently. "He'll want to take one of us. I fear it may be you, Friend Oliver!"

The *Erl*-king! Now Oliver was truly afraid. He shook with fear until the elven-cloak rippled, for *Erl* was a word he knew from the Maze World.

GOBLIN!

Fragments of an old song wound through his mind, a song about a goblin-king who easily outruns a horse at full gallop. A goblin-king who feeds on the terror of human mortals. Who steals their souls.

Whiss-whiss-whiss-whiss ran the invisible feet, leaving their unnaturally elongated prints in the snow. The whisper of *whiss-whiss-whiss-whiss* overlay the steady *ssssh* of the sleigh runners.

All at once Mil tore open the shutters. Oliver's first instinct was to stop her, but she moved too swiftly, and the deed was done before he could react. He saw the whole countryside laid out around them, for the snow made a covering like a sheet pinned to the ground by black stakes.

Mil leaned out the open window and turned her face toward the pallid moon. A sudden cry broke from her throat, an inhuman wail of infinite sadness and yearning, and shivered away into the dark forest.

Oliver held his breath, feeling his heart thump like drumbeats inside his rib cage. An answering howl came from deep in the woodland, and after that more howls, coming closer and closer. Soon Oliver saw what was making those cries, and his fear of the invisible running feet was eclipsed by another, greater by far:

Wolves.

A living stream of White Wolves burst out of the Icewode, a great pack of them running in the moonlight. Like quicksilver, they sped silently over the snow toward the caravan. They surrounded it, ran beside it, their hot breath rising in plumes. Hundreds of them, like a horde of ghosts, fanned across the snow from the forest to the caravan. Their leader, a huge male with silver-tipped fur, leaped and dived to attack the goblin king that the wolves alone could see.

A fury of barks, snarls, crunching of bones in a whirl of snow! Then a scream like nothing ever heard under heaven, and a long-drawn-out, quavering echo that vanished in the depths of the night.

And then nothing.

The driver slowed his team to a stop. The horses stood still in their traces, snorting and blowing steam from their nostrils. Oliver marveled that they showed no sign of fear at being so near their hereditary enemies, for the wolf pack now surrounded the caravan completely.

The king of the pack came forward to the caravan's unshuttered window, rose up to his full height, and placed his paws on the sill. Mil leaned out toward him and fondled the great head. "Grace to you and thanks, O Friend of the Night," she said. "We will meet again in the Graelands. *Va'in 'a moru'!*"

As if they were one being, the wolves arced around toward the forest... And then they were no longer there. The snow lay smooth again, as if neither goblin nor wolf had trodden upon it.

Oliver may have passed out after that, for he knew nothing more until much later, when the driver pulled up his horses again. As the sleigh slid to a stop, he woke up with a start and gawked out the open window of the caravan to the shore of a broad lake gleaming like a mirror under the moon. On its edge, where the shore met the bleak woodland, a ring of caravans circled around fires that flickered redly against the last remnant of night.

They had come to the Rover encampment.

Chapter Twelve

Incident at Nether Lake

Pavarr appeared beside the caravan as it headed toward an open place in the encampment. He rode up to Oliver's window and called in a low voice, "Friend Oliver!"

When he figured out where his name was coming from, Oliver leaned out the window.

"We're at Nether Lake," said Pavarr, nodding toward the dark body of water off to their left. "This is the Rover encampment. Keep your eyes and ears open. The Rovers wander everywhere in the Labyrinth World, sometimes even into the Desolate Lands. Listen more than you talk, and you should be all right."

Oliver nodded glumly and squinted out at the early dawnlight. *What really happened back there in our headlong dash away from The Rendezvous?* Had he dreamed them, or had the caravan actually been surrounded by wolves? And that invisible *erl*—goblin--whatever it was, making barefoot prints in the snow. He even thought that the White Wolf king had attacked and destroyed the goblin. *Of course none of it was real. Erls don't exist, and neither do goblins. Must have been a bad dream.*

No, it wasn't, his Inner Voice insisted. *You know perfectly well it was absolutely real.*

Oliver chose to ignore the voice.

Pavarr rode away, and the caravan took its place up in the circle. A few Rover men were already at work in a corral of horses, and several women, with bright kerchiefs binding back their long hair, bent over cooking pots. A few sleepy children wandered around, munching on bread that their mothers gave them. The smoke of rekindled campfires rose in the chilly dawn, giving the whole scene an air of having materialized out of the fog.

As soon as the caravan had settled in its place, two young men ran up to it, bringing a makeshift stretcher. Carefully they lifted Tapp out of the wagon, laid him on the stretcher, and brought him to a fire in the middle of the encampment. An ancient woman bundled in shawls, placidly smoking a pipe, sat beside the fire.

The two men laid the stretcher gently on the ground in front of the old woman, who at first did not appear to notice it. After a few meditative puffs on her pipe, she stretched out a wrinkled hand from under the folds of her shawls and moved it slowly in the air over Tapp's inert body, muttering to herself as she did so.

Oliver, watching from the window, found that he was holding his breath, as if he actually expected something miraculous to happen, Tapp to rise from the ground and begin walking and talking normally. He knew the idea was absurd: Tapp was seriously ill from the poisoned arrowhead and needed to be in a modern hospital where he could get proper care. Unfortunately, Oliver hadn't seen any medical facilities, as such, in the Labyrinth World thus far.

When the old woman had drawn three circles in the air over Tapp, she threw something into the embers of the campfire, which flamed up suddenly and died down again.

Probably some kind of trick powder that produces a harmless dramatic effect.

Despite the pyrotechnics, Tapp did not get up and walk; he remained motionless on the stretcher, his cloak tucked over him. Oliver thought he saw Tapp's chest rise and fall once, as if he had taken a deep breath, but there was no indication of an instantaneous cure.

The old woman said something to a younger one standing beside her, and then to the two men. The young woman went to a small cauldron over the cooking fire and began ladling hot liquid into a bowl. The men picked up the stretcher again and took Tapp to another wagon. The young woman followed them with the steaming bowl in her hand.

Great-Aunt Belvedine now appeared beneath the window where Oliver was looking out, his mouth hanging open. "Medley!" she hissed, her eyes on a level with his. "Come at once and pay your respects to Mother Asunta!"

Obediently Oliver climbed down the narrow ladder to the ground. His knees were more than a little stiff from traveling cooped up for so long, but he tried to hide it as best he could as he went forward with Mil, Great-Aunt Belvedine, and Tipp (whose face was crinkled with worry). As they approached the old woman, Great-Aunt Belvedine drew to one side and Mil and Tipp to the other. Oliver inadvertently found himself standing in the open space directly in front of Mother Asunta.

"So," she said after a long spell of smoking her blackened pipe. Oliver wondered if he ought to be feeling a bit nervous.

"This is the Gift-Bringer." She laughed quietly to herself and knocked out the ashes of her pipe over the fire. "Come closer! I want to look at you." When she raised her face to his, Oliver saw that her eyes were completely whited over with cataracts.

He hesitated.

"Medley!" hissed Great-Aunt Belvedine. "Where are your manners! Mother Asunta is Queen of the Rovers. Go up to her!"

Thus savagely prompted, Oliver took the last steps toward the old woman until he was uncomfortably close to her chair. "How do you do?" he ventured, hoping she wasn't going to run her fingers over his face, as he understood blind people do--and ashamed of his hope. But she didn't do what he expected.

"Let me see your hand," she said. Thinking she meant to shake hands, Oliver offered his.

"That's not what she means," Mil whispered. "You're supposed to cross her palm with silver. Then she'll tell your fortune. Do you have any coins on you?"

Oliver was not in the habit of consulting fortune-tellers, and he felt rather dubious about the prospect. Reluctantly, he felt in his pockets for loose change. There was none.

"It doesn't have to be money," Mil told him. "Do you have anything silver with you? Anything at all?"

Oliver searched his pockets again, this time including the inside pocket of his tunic. There he found his billfold, which he had inserted when he changed into his new garments at the inn. He opened it on the off-chance that a stray dime or two might have remained. No luck there, but in rubbing his thumb over the corner of a small triangular pocket, he found a lump and took out the object inside. It lay on the palm of his hand; firelight struck flashes from it.

It was the silver key his father had given Oliver years ago.

Mil and Great-Aunt Belvedine gasped in unison. "The key!" they exclaimed together.

"Give it to me," commanded Mother Asunta, and beyond his conscious control Oliver's hand, with the key on it, extended toward her. "Yes," she whispered as her fingers closed over it. Oliver imagined that her blind eyes saw through him into remote distances of time and space.

"Now let me look at your palm."

Again, as though it didn't belong to him, Oliver's right hand went out as he bent toward her. Unerringly she grasped it and turned his palm toward her unseeing eyes, then put her other hand over it. For several minutes she moved her fingers over the lines and mounds, humming to herself in a minor key.

"You will love once and forever," she said at last. "For love of her, you will pass through terrible dangers. You will have one chance-- only one--to save her. If you are willing to lose yourself, you will succeed. If you save yourself, you will lose her."

Mother Asunta pressed the key back into Oliver's hand.

His "fortune"--if it was that--seemed so general, and so enigmatic, that Oliver simply couldn't take it seriously. *Superstition!* he thought. Prudently, he didn't voice his opinion, but bowed and expressed thanks before stepping back with the other Questors.

"But the key!" exclaimed Great-Aunt Belvedine. "You can't entrust him with the key! He doesn't realize what it means! If I'd known he had it--"

Mother Asunta's clouded eyes glared at Great-Aunt Belvedine. "Belvedine de Montfort! The key belongs to this one." She pointed her pipestem toward Oliver, though how she knew where he was standing was a mystery. "And he alone must use it, for it will unlock his Gift. Remember my words!"

At this awkward juncture Pavarr appeared and murmured respectfully in the old woman's ear. He led the Questors to another campfire where a pot of savory stew simmered. Oliver realized that he was famished, and ate everything that was placed before him.

Drowsy after a full, hot meal, he returned to their caravan and composed himself to sleep. As he waited for slumber to overtake him, two voices from outside came clearly to his ear as he drifted off.

"Have you told him why you brought him into the Labyrinth?" asked Mother Asunta.

Great-Aunt Belvedine sniffed contemptuously. "He doesn't need to know. He will do as he is told."

"Better that he know," returned the old woman. "The knowledge will strengthen him."

"I will tell him what he ought to know when he ought to know it," insisted Great-Aunt Belvedine.

"Your pride will prove your downfall, Belvedine de Montfort," Mother Asunta warned.

"I don't need advice from you, Asunta," Great-Aunt Belvedine returned sharply.

The Queen of the Rovers took a long draw of smoke. "Did he ask the Question?"

"Of course not," Great-Aunt Belvedine snapped. "It wouldn't have occurred to him. He is without guile; he understands nothing. He doesn't even dream--"

Oliver huddled under his cloak, feeling vaguely offended, but when Great-Aunt Belvedine said the word "dream," something like a little window opened in his mind, and he remembered the dream he had had back at Keeper's Inn, the dream of Flavia lying on a marble bier in the... in ...

He slept.

". . . in the time we have left," Pavarr was saying as Oliver awoke from another confused and vivid dream. He heard voices, Pavarr's and Mother Asunta's, talking with two others near the main campfire. Shivering a little, Oliver got up and peered out the window.

"If... wound healed... Transformation... Guard well!"

"You are certain?" asked Pavarr, but Oliver couldn't hear the reply.

Pavarr, the old woman, and a Rover man were sitting on three stools beside the fire, now burning steadily. The morning sun, already halfway toward its noon, shone palely behind the glaring expanse of sky like a lighted lantern reflected in a cloudy mirror.

The encampment seemed virtually deserted except for the three people speaking quietly beside the campfire.

Perhaps the Rovers were off trading horses or mending pots and pans or whatever else they did for a living. Fires were banked to embers, and only a wisp or two of steam drifted up from the cooking cauldrons. Beyond the camp some hobbled horses pulled at a bundle of hay. Firemark, unhobbled, chomped at grain in his feedbag.

Charleynne Gates

Belying its dark name, Nether Lake beyond the encampment
seemed not so much to reflect the sun's rays as to swallow them in its
blue and sparkling depths. Little cream-curled waves lapped the shore
with small slapping sounds and retreated. On the farther edge
snowbanks reached down nearly to the lake itself, but on this side the
gray sand lay bare.

Oliver had a sudden inspiration. He leaned out the window and
tested the air, which wasn't really very cold. It wasn't exactly warm,
either, considering it was a winter day, but quite tolerable. No one
seemed to be about except the three people beside the main campfire,
and they were absorbed in their conversation.

His skin, as he stretched and yawned, felt dusty and unscrubbed.
How long had it been since he had had a proper bath? There didn't seem
to be any shower facilities in the camp, or none that he could see.

Why not have a nice, bracing swim in the lake? The water
would undoubtedly be cool, but the sun might have warmed the surface
to a bearable temperature.

There might be other factors worth considering before one
ventured into a foreign body of water, but strangely enough for the
rational person he was in normal life, those factors didn't occur to Oliver
Medley at the moment. In fact, the sight of that clean-looking lake grew
more alluring the longer he viewed it. He could almost feel the slither
of cool water along his back and thighs, imagine his cramped muscles
awakening as he stretched out in a crawl.

It was just too tempting.

He climbed down the ladder at the end of the caravan and
walked briskly to the edge of the water, where fine-grained sand spread
an inviting carpet for his feet. A flat-topped boulder made a convenient
place for piling his clothing while he bathed.

Exactly as he had anticipated, the water was chilly, but nowhere
near hypothermic levels. Oliver waded in quickly, treading on a smooth
bottom until he was waist-high in the water, then leaned forward and
began an exploratory breast-stroke, keeping his head above the surface.

Wonderful!

He turned onto his back and floated for a few seconds, but the
lake was a little too cold for that. Rolling over again, he swam freestyle
until he was farther out than his toes could touch. *How good it is to feel
really clean again!* A pitcher and basin were all very well in their way,

-- 226 --

but they couldn't compare with immersing oneself in water. *If I only had a bar of soap my bath would be perfect, but one can't have everything.*

He decided to try a shallow dive and see what might be down below the surface beside a few waterweeds. And he was curious about what fed the lake: *Is it snowmelt or a hidden spring?*

He dived where he was, peering nearsightedly through the crystalline depths to the bottom of the lake far below, not expecting to see much because he had left his spectacles on top of his pile of clothing.

But he didn't need spectacles to make out the thing that was down there. Either the water magnified it or it really was that big.

It was monstrous. And it was moving toward him.

He surfaced--to find an arm thrown roughly around his neck from behind, nearly choking him. Automatically his hands flew up to it, trying to pull the arm away from his windpipe, but the more he struggled, the tighter it grew. Oliver kicked out wildly and connected with a pair of legs, but after that first kick the legs wrapped themselves around his torso. He felt himself being pulled underwater, and thrashed around even harder. The two of them went under and bobbed up several times, sputtering and gasping for air, as a second arm went around Oliver's neck and fastened as tightly as the first.

The weight of the being on his back pulled them both down into the lake. Oliver had only half a second to take a last gulp of air. As they went down, the thing that had attacked him rolled underneath, and its hold loosened. Oliver seized his chance, flung his fists and feet out as hard as he could and managed to free himself. He shot up to the surface and swam as fast as he could for shore. Glancing back over his shoulder, he saw his attacker for the first time.

It was Tapp! But a Tapp he had never seen before. His normally plump, apple-cheeked face had changed into a hollow-eyed, beak-nosed caricature of his normal self, with mottled, mange-encrusted skin. There was only a nominal resemblance to the Dwarvian smith Oliver had known. And Tapp had murder in his eyes!

Scared nearly out of his wits, Oliver struck out again for shore, swimming faster than he ever had in his life. It wasn't fast enough--a clawlike hand grabbed his ankle. Oliver twisted around desperately to free himself, but the hand held on and pulled him back.

-- 227 --

Then all of a sudden the hand wasn't there any more. Adrenaline rushing through his body, Oliver trod water and looked over the lake, his head swiveling in little jerks. But the water was calm again except for ripples spreading outward from the point where Tapp had disappeared.

Without thinking twice, Oliver dived. Not far under the surface, Tapp, or the creature that had been Tapp, writhed in the grip of the monstrous entity from the bottom of the lake. The thing had multiple tentacles ending in snake-like heads that changed shape again and again even as Oliver peered through the roiling water.

He surfaced, took in a quick breath, and dived down again to the bubbling tumult. He barely saw what he was going toward, but he knew what he had to find, and by a miracle he found it.

A hand poked out of the boil. Oliver grabbed it and jerked as hard as he could. Whatever was holding Tapp must have been startled at the resistance, because all at once its grip loosened. Oliver pulled the hand with him as he fought his way through the churning lake to the surface, bursting out of the water like a porpoise. Tapp came up with him, eyes closed, head hanging back, his skin turning blue.

"Help!" Oliver yelled hoarsely as he wrapped his arm around Tapp's neck, keeping the unconscious Dwarvian's face out of water. He kicked out frantically toward the shore. "Help us!"

He kept on calling "Help!" even though Pavarr and a Rover were already running down to the lake and wading out to meet them. The two men lifted Tapp's limp body out of the water and bore it to the caravan, leaving a shivering Oliver to blot himself partly dry with his cloak. He put on his spectacles with shaking fingers, dressed hurriedly, and trudged across the gray sand after them.

Sunset was half over in the Icewode, and a single star shone in a green sky before Oliver was able to find out what happened to Tapp. One of Mother Asunta's attendants gave him a bowl of savory stew from the cauldron and flat bread baked on a stone by the fire for his dinner. He ate hungrily while he listened to Pavarr and the Rover chieftain and answered their questions.

"Everyone in the Icewode knows there is something evil in the bottom of Nether Lake," said the Rover chief, whose name was Gregorio. "But you, Friend Oliver, you are the only man within living memory who has dared to confront it. And to save your friend from a terrible death! We have never seen courage like yours--never!"

If Oliver's mouth hadn't been full of bread, he would have set the man straight on the matter of courage versus spur-of-the-moment foolhardiness, but he couldn't speak without choking. A low murmur of admiration went around the men and women gathered about the campfire. Pavarr grinned broadly and translated what they were saying in Rover language. Oliver's face turned red. One or two of the younger women standing nearby swished their skirts and flashed their dark eyes at him. Oliver turned even redder, if possible.

"Tomorrow night we will have a *porrach*, a celebration, in your honor, Friend Oliver!" Gregorio continued. "We will sing and dance. Constantine over there--" he nodded toward a man in a black shirt, with gold earrings in his ears, who looked so formidable, with arms folded across his massive chest, that Oliver gulped and swallowed his half-chewed bread--"is our finest singer. He will make a song about what you did today. I have sent Raven Messengers to all the encampments in the Icewode. Hundreds of our people will come, from our clan and many others. And you will dance for us, Friend Oliver, like the hero that you are!"

Oliver tried to say that he was constitutionally incapable of making his feet move in any kind of coordinated dance step, but the words wouldn't emerge. He shook his head instead.

"Bah!" exclaimed Gregorio. "That is not possible! Everyone dances! Lola and Paquita will teach you." The two young women smiled enticingly and began to move their feet and hands in a dance.

"*Hota!*" a man called out. "*Hota!*"

Someone strummed a guitar while others clapped their hands in an intricate rhythm.

Pavarr and Oliver walked back to their caravan as music and laughter rang out from the impromptu gathering. "Tell me, Friend Oliver," said Pavarr, "what were you really doing out on the lake?"

Oliver felt a blush rising to his cheeks and was thankful that the pale green twilight had darkened to deep blue, making his scarlet face less obvious. "I was thinking I'd like to, um, bathe, you see," he explained. "Wash off the dust of travel. The water looked perfectly calm and, well, inviting..."

Charleynne Gates

Pavarr chuckled. "I figured you wouldn't have heard about the thing at the bottom of the lake. The Rovers wash their clothes at the water's edge, but they never venture out any farther. You're a hero, my friend, regardless of why you were in the water. Gregorio and I saw you two struggling, but we were too far away to help you.

"Evidently Tapp sneaked out of the caravan when Carlotta and Bruno thought he was asleep. Tapp had already begun changing into a *wyrga*, as Mother Asunta warned. She was able to remove some negative energy from the wound last night and throw it onto the fire. But the arrow-point had already gone in too deep, and when the wound closed, the *wyrga* poison was trapped inside his body.

"Tapp wouldn't have known what he was doing when he attacked you. The poison drove him to try to kill the first living creature he saw--you. But you saved his life instead, rescued him from the thing in the lake. Why?" Pavarr asked suddenly, stopping and facing Oliver. "Why did you save him when he tried to kill you?"

Oliver thought for a moment. "I suppose it was instinctive. Or maybe not just that," he added. "I recognized Tapp in spite of the way he looked and the stench that came from him, an odor like burning oil."

Pavarr's eyebrows lifted. "Gregorio and I weren't close enough to him to smell anything. When we took him out of the lake, there was no odor. Burning oil, you say?" He frowned. "There are pockets of natural gas and sulphur in the marshes. Sometimes they catch fire, and there's a distinct odor when they burn. And there's another place where a stench like that pervades everything." He paused, his gaze far away. "But go on, Friend Oliver."

"Well, I... I liked Tapp. He never said much, but I thought he might come to like me, too. In fact," he went on, blurting out the feelings he'd kept inside too long, "I thought the other Questors liked me, except of course for Great-Aunt Belvedine. She thinks I don't measure up to my father. She's right; I don't. But I thought we were all getting to be friends together, taking the same vow and everything, only I suppose I was wrong about that since they left me alone back in the *Forbeodan* Tunnels. I managed to get out, and you saved me from dying of hypothermia. I never did thank you properly..." His voice trailed off.

Pavarr stood very still, studying Oliver as if he'd never seen him before.

"They left you alone?" he repeated. "You mean they didn't come back and try to find you?"

Now Oliver felt guilty for speaking ill of the other Questors. "It must have been my own fault. Somehow I wandered into the wrong passage. No, I remember how it was! I fell, and must have blacked out for a while. When I came to, everyone had disappeared. I couldn't see anything, so I crawled on my hands and knees for hours and hours, it seemed. Somehow I got into that place with the giant snake..." He shuddered and broke off.

Pavarr remained motionless. "How were you able to see it was a snake?" he said, almost in a whisper.

"Its eyes glittered green, like the finding-stones in the cave. I was never so terrified in my life." On Pavarr's questioning, he relayed the whole story as best he could.

Pavarr considered the information. "Friend Oliver," he said at last, "we have badly underestimated you. Not only did you rescue Tapp Whackitt from a grisly death, but you also managed to outwit Old Sal, the Terror of the Tunnels. I had a run-in with her myself, years ago, so I know how formidable she is." He massaged the scale-scars on his wrist reminiscently. "She's so old her venom sacs dried up years ago, but she keeps up her constricting practice."

He laughed suddenly and clapped Oliver on the shoulder in a friendly way, propelling him toward the caravan. "You're a nine days' wonder, Friend Oliver," he said, shaking his head. "You are indeed!"

Oliver didn't fully comprehend the reason for Pavarr's amusement, but he gathered that the prince approved of what he had done even though he hadn't actually done anything, at least not deliberately. He had simply fallen into some difficult situations by chance and gotten out of them by sheer luck, although to tell the truth, he wasn't at all sure that such things as "chance" and "luck" existed. If there was a greater plan behind surface appearances, then he, too, must be an infinitesimal part of that plan, and was grateful that he had been able to make a positive, if temporary, difference in its outcome.

"What will happen to Tapp?" he asked as they walked back to their caravan.

Pavarr became serious. "Tapp has fallen into a strange kind of trance," he said. "Did you realize he was stung by the lake monster? That's why he was unconscious when you got him to shore. Mother

Asunta says the venom from the monster may counteract the poison from the *wyrga* arrow. If it does, and Tapp survives the crisis, then he'll live and be his old self again. If he doesn't..."

"Can I do anything for him?" asked Oliver anxiously.

"Beyond saving his life?" said Pavarr. "No, Friend, nothing more. Bruno and Carlotta are keeping close watch over him. We will know by sunrise whether we'll have a celebration tomorrow night--or a funeral. Get some sleep now. You'll need it. Oh, by the way..." He reached into a pocket and retrieved the small oilskin packet from the stable at The Rendezvous. "You'd better take this. It has something to do with your Gift; I don't know what. Keep it safe."

Oliver tucked the packet inside his tunic and went into the caravan to a well-earned rest. When he awoke, he had forgotten all about the packet.

That had been two days ago. Since then the *porrach* had taken place, with uninhibited rejoicing for Oliver's heroism and Tapp's recovery. The two poisons had met in the Dwarvian's system, battled it out, and neutralized each other. Tapp had come within a hair's-breadth of dying, but had miraculously survived. And not only survived, but regained strength enough to join in the dance in Oliver's honor and to down a generous mug of the Rovers' fiery brew.

Oliver had been feasted and toasted until he almost began to believe he was worthy of it all. He felt quite proud of his new sheepskin vest, a gift from Gregorio, which made him look (he thought) very dashing indeed--more like a real Rover than a ragamuffin.

Lola and Paquita had worked with him through the afternoon, patiently teaching him some rudimentary dance steps. At last Oliver caught the spirit of it in his blood, and when it came his turn at the feast, stood up and danced in perfect rhythm around the fire to cries of encouragement and congratulation.

It was a night to remember.

The next morning the *porrach* was only a memory. The Rover caravans had vanished at sunrise, moving on to their next encampment. They left no traces but the blackened ashes of their campfires and the blue-shadowed tracks of sleigh runners in the snow.

Oliver's head felt like a pumpkin... the morning after Hallowe'en.

Mil, with Hera Vespasia on her shoulder, Great-Aunt Belvedine, Tipp, Tapp (fully restored to health, but bleary-eyed) and Oliver Medley stood beside the cold central campfire, chewing their last pieces of flatbread as Vladir, the driver of their van, fastened his horses in the traces and prepared to depart. Pavarr stood beside the Rover, listening to the driver's careful directions until Vladir, pipe clenched between his teeth, climbed onto the seat and took up the reins. He said something more to Pavarr, then with a flash of white teeth beneath his black moustache and a wave of his whip, sped off to join his clan. Pavarr walked back to the other Questors, frowning thoughtfully.

"Vladir says the only road to the Ruined Chapel that he knows of begins on the other side of Nether Lake," he told them. Last evening before the *porrach*, Pavarr had explained to the other Questors what he learned at The Rendezvous. All agreed that the mysterious chapel should be the next step on their journey to the Abbey.

The Ruined Chapel. That reminded Oliver of something; he couldn't think what. He looked across the lake, which once again seemed deceptively placid, its surface a mirror under the glass-gray sky. One would never suspect what lay in its depths.

"It isn't a large lake," he ventured. "Perhaps we could simply walk around it?"

"Can't be done," replied Pavarr. "I've tried it. The Rovers told me some kind of binding-spell was put on it in the last Age. I wanted to test its limits, so I started to ride around the lake, but the farther I rode, the longer the lake became. It wouldn't let me get to the opposite shore. There's no way we can go around it; it just keeps expanding."

"A spell?" Oliver echoed. "You mean--a magical spell?" Even though he had realized back at Ravenhome that he was in a world where genuine Magic was operant, Oliver's mind remained essentially that of a conventional rationalist. The idea that the laws of physics might have a Dark Side was still difficult for him to grasp, despite plentiful evidence to the contrary.

Pavarr explained patiently. "It's always difficult for people from the Maze World to accept the way things work in the Labyrinth. There's an explanation for magical phenomena, but we haven't time to get into it right now. Mil can tell you about it when our mission is accomplished. It involves calculations of a higher order than I've studied. In fact, I doubt if any Maze World mathematicians have even dreamed of them."

Dream! That's it! His dream at Keeper's Inn came back to him, every detail clear as sunlight.

"The Ruined Chapel!" he exclaimed. "I've seen it! I know where it is!"

"What!" shouted everyone else.

"Explain yourself, Medley!" demanded Great-Aunt Belvedine.

"I, well, I suppose I shouldn't have spoken," Oliver backtracked, regretting his outburst. "It was only a dream."

"We take dreams very seriously in the Labyrinth World," Mil remarked. "Why don't you tell us about it?"

Oliver took a deep breath and told them about the dream, how he had seen the Ruined Chapel with most of its roof gone and only its columns remaining, and inside it the marble bier with Flavia's body on it. "I saw it in a place with snow lying deep on the ground, and bare black trees all around."

"The Icewode," nodded Pavarr.

"Somehow I knew the ruined building was exactly in the center of the wood," Oliver continued. "There was a red road leading to it through the snow, and this odd-shaped, high rock standing beside the road." More and more images came to mind as he described them. "The red road started at the edge of a lake. It came out of the lake, I believe."

"That would be Nether Lake," said Great-Aunt Belvedine acidly, "where we are now. The red road is on the other side. Why didn't you tell us before? You've delayed us over and over, and who knows what has happened to Flavia in the meantime. It's all your fault, Medley!"

Tapp took a step toward her, folded his arms across his broad chest, and scowled at Great-Aunt Belvedine. "You leave him alone, Belvedine," said Tapp sternly. "From what I understand, you're the one who was supposed to explain to him how the Labyrinth World works, and you never bothered to do it. Did you expect Friend Oliver to figure it out on his own? He didn't cause the delay; it was all of us--especially me."

"Me, too," Tipp put in. He frowned, looking down at the ground. "Friend Oliver, I should have helped you more in the *Forbeodan* Tunnels instead of leaving you to fend for yourself."

"As leader," Mil said, "I should have watched out for you, set a slower pace."

"So I don't like anyone blaming my friend here," Tapp finished, looking directly at Great-Aunt Belvedine. "I don't like it at all."

"Why--why--well!" Great-Aunt Belvedine blustered. "Of all the--!"

"Ahem," said Pavarr before the situation escalated. "Sounds like you're a true dreamer, Friend Oliver. That means you can do remote viewing in your sleep! I have a better idea now where we're heading, although I've never been as far into the Icewode as the Ruined Chapel. Have you, Mil?"

Mil shook her head. "No, I haven't."

"In the meantime," said Tipp, "we'd better be deciding what to do, because somehow we have to get to the opposite shore, where the road to the Chapel begins. We need all the daylight we can get."

"I remember its other name," inserted Mil, snapping out of a brown study. "The Ruined Chapel used to be called Hermit's Repose. It's deep within Center North Icewode. The old rumor is that there's a Hermit still living in it."

"My informant at The Rendezvous mentioned an 'Unsoul'd Warder'," Pavarr mused. "But I don't know if the Warder is the same person as the Hermit. There's another thing, too. Back at The Rendezvous, Nodd told me there's a rumor going around that something is wrong with the Ruined Chapel. Something evil has gotten into it, but no one seems to know what it is."

"Nodd said that?" asked Oliver, startled. "When did he--?"

"He scratched some runes on the bottom of my drinking mug," Pavarr replied. "Nodd's one of us, loyal to the *Sendara*. He's been working in that highly dangerous position for years, passing on a great deal of useful information. There's a brave heart in that stunted body! Grace be with him!"

"Grace be with him," murmured the others, making the Sign of Protection.

"Can we be certain the *Sendara*'s in the Ruined Chapel?" Tapp asked. Oliver agreed, but didn't say so. He didn't want to delay them any longer by bringing up his doubts about this "true dreaming" business. The others knew more than he did about how such things worked in the Labyrinth; he'd have to take their word for it, at least for now.

"Nothing's certain until we find her," replied Pavarr, "and Friend Oliver's dream is the only clue we have so far. If there's an evil presence in the Ruined Chapel, then the Hermit may be guarding her against it."

"Or keeping her prisoner, if he was the one who abducted her," said Tipp. "But to return to the matter at hand: How do we get to the other side of the lake?"

Hera Vespasia, perched on Mil's shoulder, cleared her throat with a soft burr. "There are tunnels," she uttered in an owlish whisper, "running underneath the lake. I heard it from a rabbit some years ago. Considering that the information might be useful one day, I let her go."

"Tunnels!" exclaimed Great-Aunt Belvedine. "Excellent! We'll use them!"

"Tunnels?" repeated Tipp. "Tapp and I are used to those."

"Hmm," said Pavarr, rubbing his chin reflectively. "Firemark can go around the lake and meet us on the other side. The lake won't react to him if he's by himself."

"We'd better start, then," said Tapp. "*Gnaarx*'ll probably be looking for us if we stay out in the open much longer."

"*Gnaarx*?" asked Oliver.

"They come out of the Desolate Lands," said Tipp. "I hope you never see one."

"To the tunnels, then," decided Pavarr. "Hera Vespasia, you know the entrance?"

The owl gave a soft *whoo* and lifted her wings. The Questors picked up their knapsacks and prepared to follow her.

Except Oliver. He locked his knees and stayed where he was. "No," he said, not loudly but firmly. The others stopped their preparations and looked at him blankly.

"What is it, Friend Oliver?" Pavarr asked.

"No," Oliver repeated, "and I mean it. I will not go into another tunnel. I have been in a tunnel, and I will not go there again." And he folded his arms and stood his ground.

"How dare--!" Great-Aunt Belvedine began.

Saint Amber's Rose

"I understand," said Mil. "You are in the right, Friend Oliver."

"I don't blame you," said Tipp. "'Tis no shame to be doubly cautious when you've been in a situation like--well, like the one back there."

"We can't swim across," Tapp pointed out. "We know what's down there now."

"What about a boat?" said Tipp. "If we had a boat, and kept close to the edge of the lake, we'd get around to the other side without arousing the--the thing at the bottom."

"I did swim out quite a ways before I saw the, er, thing," Oliver stated, conscious of Tapp's sensibilities.

"Where would we get a boat?" asked Pavarr.

"There's a boat," Tapp said, sounding confident. Everyone turned toward him. "I just remembered. It's hidden."

"How do you know there's a boat?" Tipp asked, his tone wavering between surprise and envy.

"I know things," his brother answered with an enigmatic air. "While you were out courting that Fernlily gal over at Mugwort Glen, I went places. I've got friends, too."

"So you've been here before," said Pavarr, cutting off a fraternal dispute in the making.

"Not here," replied Tapp. "But I know a Dwarf who knows a Rover who knows a Riverman who has a boat, and--"

"Is this going to be a long story?" asked Tipp, rather sarcastically.

"And we rented his boat one time to go to the Marshmallow Festival at Marsh-Fell," Tapp continued, ignoring the interruption, "and I happen to know that the Riverman stores one or two of his boats on this side of Nether Lake. I know where one of them is, if no one's taken it in the meantime."

"Where would it be?" asked Pavarr.

Tapp thought for a moment. "Over here," he said, and trotted around the shore to a grove of black oak trees. There a snowdrift lay piled high between two treetrunks. Tapp swept away the snow with his hands, and an artifact shaped like a rowboat took form as the snow flew to either side. Tipp went to help him, and soon they found a whole boat in a waterproof covering, which they removed, disclosing two oars.

Charleynne Gates

Pavarr inspected it carefully. "The wood's old," he said, "but it looks pretty solid. It's a good size; I think it'll take all of us in one trip."

"We'd better hurry," said Mil, scanning the sky.

"Right," Pavarr agreed. "Let's get it down in the water. Don't make any more noise than you can help. We don't want to attract *gnaarx*."

"I'll see you on the other side," said Hera Vespasia, and flew away.

Pavarr and Mil, Tipp and Tapp and Oliver gripped the sides of the boat, heaved it free, and hauled it down to the lake. Great-Aunt Belvedine, umbrella at the ready, kept watch, peering sharply in all directions.

Mil directed them with gestures to get in and sit quietly, for the rowboat was filled to capacity. Then she gave the boat a shove, and it slid into the water. No one said a word; no one moved more than necessary.

Pavarr rowed, dipping the oars so carefully that he made no splash at all. Mil navigated and Pavarr steered toward the far shore, staying among the reeds and rushes as close to land as he dared.

Oliver, looking toward the center of the lake, inhaled sharply as a large bubble formed exactly in the place where he and Tapp... The bubble grew as if something was about to break the surface. Oliver's breath caught in his throat, and he reached over to Pavarr, pulling at his sleeve.

The bubble broke abruptly, as bubbles do, leaving behind nothing but a fine mist. If something had been about to surface in Nether Lake, it evidently changed its mind. The water became smooth again.

Nothing else disturbed their progress. Great-Aunt Belvedine kept a close watch on the surrounding shore. Mil and Oliver surveyed the lake. Tipp and Tapp made binoculars of their hands and scanned the overcast sky.

At last the rowboat grounded on the opposite shore. They clambered out of the boat and dragged it over the gravelly sand onto higher ground. Mil and Pavarr conversed in low tones, then Pavarr directed the others to haul the boat under cover. They hid it as well as possible, turning it bottom up and covering it with brush until it faded into the landscape.

"What's that?" asked Oliver, looking back over the lake and catching a shadow moving along its surface.

"Where?" said Pavarr as a sudden harsh cry in the distance made him glance at the sky. They all saw the three black dots in a vee-shape heading for the lake.

"It's too late," Pavarr hissed. "They've seen us. Get ready to run."

"What are they?" Oliver gasped.

"*Gnaarx*," Tipp whispered.

The black dots grew larger, with elongated, sharply-angled wings. They flew like birds, but didn't look like any birds Oliver had ever seen. The *gnaarx* had reptilian heads with fanged beaks, taloned feet, and snakelike eyes--red, unblinking eyes.

"Run!" Pavarr ordered, and gave Oliver a shove toward the shelter of a thicket as the *gnaarx*, with unbelievable speed, dived straight for them. A spray of wet droplets rained down on the Questors as they ran for cover, droplets that burned like fire when they touched bare skin.

They reached the shelter of the thicket and scurried underneath overhanging branches that blotted out the sky. Oliver fell on the ground, writhing and clutching his hand, which had caught several drops of the burning fluid. Never had he known such agony! So horribly painful was it that his voice caught in his throat, and he couldn't utter a cry.

The *gnaarx* flew over their shelter and headed off into the distance.

"They'll be back to try another pass at us," Pavarr muttered, "if they see us move. We'll have to stay here until we're sure they're gone." Then he noticed Oliver in convulsions on the sodden ground. "Look!" he whispered to Mil. "He must have caught some *gnaarx* spit! Does healing moss grow around here?"

Mil darted to a nearby yew tree and scraped something off its trunk. In a moment Oliver felt something cool, soft, and blessedly soothing being wrapped around his hand. In another moment the agony of the burning saliva diminished until it was only a warm spot on his skin, but he would bear three white scars on the back of his hand for the rest of his life.

"You're lucky, Friend Oliver. All-heal moss doesn't grow in many places in the Icewode, and it's the only thing that draws out *gnaarx* poison," Mil told him when his breathing calmed. "Otherwise, it's almost always fatal."

Oliver turned pale and sank back against the trunk of a tree. "Are they coming back?" he asked, trembling all over.

"We don't know yet, so stay under cover," Pavarr warned. "They'll probably leave the area if they don't spot us right away. They're not very bright. In the meantime, we need to keep absolutely still."

They settled into their hiding places again while Tipp crept forward to the edge of the thicket and peered out from between the branches. "Can't see any of them," he reported. "Looks like they've given up--at least for now."

Pavarr crawled up beside Tipp and scrutinized the gray sky. Three winged dots appeared in the distance, almost impossible to see, but Pavarr's keen eyes spotted them. "Back! Get back! And don't move!"

The Questors obeyed at once, scurrying farther under the trees and burrowing under the brambles. They listened intently, not daring to twitch a muscle.

The *gnaarx* made another pass over the lake. This time they dived much closer than before, so that the Questors heard the slicing hiss of their razor-edged wings. Two of them were larger, mature adults; the third was smaller, apparently their offspring.

The young one had the mindless audacity of youth, for it suddenly broke formation and in an act of pure bravado, dived toward the middle of the lake, almost touching the surface before it unfolded its wings and dashed off into the sky with a scream of glee.

The two older ones, distracted by their youngster's antics, turned around and circled back over the lake, uttering scolding cries. The adolescent ignored them and continued to make his rapid dives, each time ending lower and lower before pulling out and climbing. The older ones, their search for the Questors forgotten, darted over the water, avoiding the center, and chattered angrily.

Then the young one, too exhilarated to listen to the voices of reason, climbed higher, folded its wings, and dived for the water faster than before, so fast that Oliver could scarcely follow it. It plunged toward the lake's center, turning sharply upward half a second before impact--but the tips of its talons brushed the water, making feathery ripples.

Instantly a monstrous nightmare of a head burst through the surface and grabbed the young *gnaarx* before it cleared the water. Once, twice, the head gnashed its fangs together, and the little *gnaarx* was gone. The monster vanished beneath the water, and the lake again became as smooth as a mirror--all before Oliver's heart could beat twice.

The harsh cries of the older ones circling above changed from scolding to shrieks of rage and pain. So terrible was their anguish that he ached for them, momentarily forgetting his fear. No parent, even creatures like the *gnaarx*, should have to endure, much less witness, such a dreadful loss.

At last the bereaved *gnaarx* flew off in the direction they had come, and their despairing cries grew fainter until the Icewode was quiet once again.

"They won't come back now," Pavarr said after a long moment.

"Whew!" said Tipp, standing up and shaking snow from his cloak. "That was close!"

"Too close," said Tapp, exhaling a pent-up breath.

"Are we safe now?" asked Oliver.

"My friend," Pavarr answered, "we have a long way to go before we're anything like 'safe'." He skirted the underbrush and went toward a darker shape beneath the trees. The dark shape whickered softly, and Firemark stepped out of the wood. Pavarr mounted, bent low in the saddle to consult with Mil, and took off through the wood with Hera Vespasia flying over his head. Peering after him, Oliver saw the outline of a narrow path of dark-red dirt running through the snow like a trail of blood.

"All right, everyone gear up," Mil commanded. "And if you value your life, don't make any more noise than you can help. *Gnaarx* aren't the worst things in the Icewode."

They obeyed, shouldering their knapsacks, and fell into formation behind Mil: Great-Aunt Belvedine, Tipp, Oliver, and last of all Tapp, who insisted on bringing up the rear so Oliver wouldn't get lost again.

The Icewode closed in behind them. If a hooded face watched their departing backs from between two ice-splintered trees, none of the Questors noticed.

Charleynne Gates

Nether Lake, serene and secret under the leaden sky, dreamed its malefic dreams... and waited.

Chapter Thirteen

Origin Dust

"When the dung beetle moves," Hosteen Nashibitti had told him, "know that something has moved it. And know that its movement affects the flight of the sparrow, and that the raven deflects the eagle from the sky, and that the eagle's stiff wing bends the will of the Wind People, and know that all of this affects you and me, and the flea on the prairie dog and the leaf on the cottonwood." That had always been the point of the lesson. Interdependency of nature. Every cause has its effect. Every action its reaction. A reason for everything. In all things a pattern, and in this pattern, the beauty of harmony.
> --Tony Hillerman, *Dance Hall of the Dead*

"Dust you are, and to dust you shall return."
> --The Book of Genesis

"We will camp here," said Pavarr, returning out of the icebound forest. Oliver lost track of how far they had come, for they had plodded steadily onward over the red path for hours and hours. White vapor came out of their nostrils as they exhaled frigid air, as if the path itself were sending up smoke signals. Mil allowed few breaks and made them short, and forbade much talk. Even Great-Aunt Belvedine hadn't said a word.

The prince dismounted a little way off, so only Mil noticed that he had a thin line of blood across one cheek and was keeping his left arm pressed tightly against his side. Quietly Mil tended to him, and their whispered conversation did nothing to reassure her of their safety.

"No, I did not see him," Pavarr replied, "but I have felt Ab'addon watching us since we left The Rendezvous, and I believe he knew through his spies when you fled Keeper's Inn. I found signs of *wyrga* camps nearby. They leave their foul odor wherever they have been."

"How were you injured?" Mil asked, dabbing ointment onto a long scratch on his arm. She worked quickly, using her body as a shield to prevent the other Questors from noticing that anything was wrong.

"I ran into a *wyrga*, left behind because of some infraction of their servitude. The others had hamstrung it, then abandoned it. I meant to avoid it, but the thing heard or scented me. It stood up, Mil, dragged itself upright on its feet to fight me! It slashed at me with its talons a couple of times, but it was weak from starvation and didn't last long."

"It didn't bite you, then?" asked Mil. "Their venom is deadly."

"No," said the prince, frowning. "It didn't bite--even when it had the chance."

"You killed it before it could reach you?" Mil tied a knot in the bandage on Pavarr's arm.

"No," answered the prince. "It was--"

"What?" said Mil, giving her full attention to what he was saying.

"I don't understand it. The *wyrga* didn't try to keep fighting. It raised its hand and tore open the vein in the back of its own neck--deliberately! It died in seconds. But before it died, it looked at me--not as I've seen a *wyrga*'s eyes before, mindless and full of rage, but questioning, I'd say even pleading with me. It mumbled a few words in their war-tongue, and it was gone."

"What did it say?"

The prince repeated what he had heard from the dying *wyrga*.

"Something about 'Saurian'," Mil summarized. "That's all I get. He must have meant the Saurian River, but that's half a world away in the Desolate Lands, and we're headed in the opposite direction. What did the *wyrga* mean by that?"

The prince shook his head. "I don't know. I had the feeling that he might have been trying to warn me, or at least tell me something."

"Warn you? Why would a *wyrga* warn one of us?" responded Mil.

"I don't know," the prince repeated. "I don't understand it." He thought for a moment, then told Mil about the finding of Ildranna and Vord, of the destruction of Ildranna's village, and about the *wyrga* Andis discovered digging through the ruins of their home.

"A *wyrga* acting on its own, independently of the others?" Mil questioned. "*Wyrga* are not created beings; they don't have the gift of free will. They're made in the Lord of Desolation's factories, or so the rumor goes."

"The rumor is true. I've seen it. The minds and emotions of their human captives are removed in the process of making them into *wyrga*. When they are refashioned into slaves of Ab'addon, their only functions are to obey their master and to protect the *wyrga* collective."

"So they can't act independently," Mil concluded. "And they can't--" She stopped abruptly, and she and Pavarr stared at each other with a growing suspicion.

"Rebel," Pavarr finished. "They can never rebel against their lord."

But at least one of them may have done just that, was in both their minds.

"Do you think it's possible for a *wyrga* to be transformed?" Mil asked. "Into something... less evil? Can evil ever become good?"

Pavarr thought a moment. "I'd have to see it before I'd believe it. But the possibility for transformation is built into every living being, or so the ancient writings tell us. I'm no expert in the theology of evolution, but I guess that would have to include *wyrga*."

"Even though they're made, not created?"

The prince nodded slowly. "Even then."

Leaving aside these difficult questions, Mil asked, "Are you all right now? We ought to go back to the others. Are you going to tell them what happened?"

The prince shook his head. "Hera Vespasia knows, but I see no need to frighten them unnecessarily. There's nothing we can do about it anyway."

Pavarr and Firemark stayed some little distance from the others, "standing watch," Mil explained when she rejoined them.

The Questors ate a bite of journey-bread and a swallow of water. No fire, lest heat, light, and the crackle of flames attract unwanted observers. As soon as they had eaten enough to permit sleep, the Questors wrapped themselves in their gray elven-cloaks and became, to all appearances, stones lying in a rough circle inside a grove of leafless birches. Pavarr remained on first watch while the rest of the exhausted Questors plunged into slumber.

Charleynne Gates

Oliver awoke to Hera Vespasia's soft *hoo-hoo* a couple of inches from his right ear. His eyes flew open, but before he dared to move, he took the precaution of peeking around the edge of his cloak to see what the others were doing.

If the owl's call was meant to be an alarm, no one else was stirring. The other Questors remained asleep, camouflaged and covered with a fine white down of snow.

An object entered his vision: The owl, perched directly in front of him, stared into his face at close range, her eyes round and golden as twin harvest moons. Her head swiveled almost completely around to speak to someone at her back. "He is awake, Nemetona," she announced, "sufficiently for our purpose."

The two golden moons went away, and Oliver cautiously put his head outside the hood of his cloak. Right before him was a tall and ethereally beautiful woman. Dark hair twined with silver leaves fell about her slender shoulders and down her long white gown, which had green and silver birch leaves scattered over it in profusion. She looked as if she might have stepped from behind a tree, or from within a tree, for there seemed to be a veil between her and Oliver Medley. It was as though he were seeing her through a transparent layer of birchbark.

"Friend Oliver," she said, soft as a sigh of wind through the trees--not the frozen black branches of the Icewode, but living summertrees spreading out their mantles of light-washed green. "I am Nemetona. Rise and walk with me."

At her invitation he did, though how he did, he never could say afterward. Through the Icewode they went, treading so lightly upon the snow that they left no footprints. His hand was in hers, and although it looked like a woman's hand, it felt like a budding leaf.

Oliver asked no questions, for everything that was happening to him felt as if it had all happened to him long ago, before the memory of his present life was born.

They walked away from the sleeping Questors, away from the narrow red road and between close-crowded treetrunks whose naked branches stuck out at sharp, tormented angles as if they had been tortured into their anguished positions. Hera Vespasia flew above them. Occasionally her wingtip brushed the hood of his cloak, as if to remind him to keep his attention focused.

Together Oliver and the woman glided over the white ground, and he heard the subtle sounds of the night as they passed: ruffling of feathers, quick slap of wings, crunch of paws on crusted snow. Out of the corner of his eye he glimpsed ghostly forms of night-deer poised behind thorn trees like statues made of glass.

Gradually he became aware of eyes, yellow and unblinking, all around them, then of other forms, vague as mist at first, then clearer: warrior-women of the Owl Guard, tall and powerful, walking in darkness beside them; White Wolves of the Icewode silently encircling them; and around and about them in the breathing night, the manifold creatures of myth and legend: unicorns, winged horses, elves and fauns and faery-folk, children of the wood and wild, all white with rime, phantoms in a long parade that is passing... and has passed.

At last he saw an open space among the thorn trees, and within it, a black silhouette against a dark-gray sky, the shadow of a great stag, its antlers etching runes against the sky. Closer they came to it, and closer...

"Well met, Friend Oliver!" The Mage Dandriel appeared in the clearing.

"Remember what you see this night, Friend Oliver," said Nemetona, and Oliver was alone with the Mage, not knowing when or where his guide had vanished.

"Come with me, as you will to do so," said the Mage. As he had done before, Oliver willed, and the two of them walked over patternless snow deeper into the Icewode. A cloud drifted over the gelid moon, and darkness was absolute.

The Mage spoke, his voice blending with the night, and Oliver saw the story of his words as he had done when he was treading the labyrinth circle in Threshold Forest.

"Oliver Medley, child of human mortals, hear me. Once, long ago, when we were all the same, there were those among us who could, if they *willed*, change their forms, one into another. A wolf, so desiring, might become a man, or a man, a bear or fox or leaping fish. A woman, so desiring, might transform herself into an eagle, a tree, or a cloud upon a mountain. Thus did the Elder Ones learn wisdom from living in different forms of Nature.

"The old stories of your Maze World tell of these things, but now they are considered merely tales told to children, for the peoples of your world have become too dark of heart to believe in them. But you, Friend Oliver, ought to know that the oldest stories often tell the greatest truths.

"When humans became bent, their forms hardened into one shape, resistant to change, and they forgot the wisdom they learned in Elder Days. They began to believe that the Creator, who in the Beginning had made them guardians of the Earth, had instead given them license to rape, torture, enslave, and exterminate other life forms as it pleased them.

"And worse: Human mortals discovered how to transfer the seed of life from one species to another, for the benefit of neither species but to dominate all of them. Thus were made the mythologicals--fauns, satyrs, centaurs and all the rest--the unnatural melding of human mortals with animals. It was the scientists of Atlantis who first performed that great wickedness, then, when that island was destroyed, bequeathed their evil legacy to the ancient Maze World.

"As human mortals have extended their mastery over the Earth, so have they also continued to descend into a Hell of their own making. And the deeper they descend, the more alluring it seems to them. They are in love with Delusion, for Pride has blinded them; Greed has enslaved them. Eventually they will destroy themselves."

They stopped. The full moon reappeared, pale and gleaming, and its light showed that they were standing on the brink of a high cliff. It plunged so far down that Oliver couldn't see the bottom.

"Look there," said Dandriel, and his sleeve of his robe swept toward the vast space before them. "Behold the Great Waste, the place of nothingness. It is the realm of the Lord of Desolation, the kingdom of Ab'addon."

A hush fell over the Icewode. Below them, the restless wind roamed across a barren desert reaching as far as the eye could see. No variation appeared on the featureless surface, not a single mountain, lake, or river.

Oliver stared and stared again, straining until his eyes hurt. Nothing moved in that desolate place. Under the coldglass moon no green and growing thing sparkled into view; no nocturnal animal or bird or insect ran or flew or crawled upon it. The land was dead, empty and dead. Only the slightest outline of a large dark square in the distance indicated that something might once have been there. Sinuous ridged lines undulated toward and away from the dark outline, as if serpents moved beneath the surface.

He shivered, repelled by the sight.

"What is that?" he whispered.

"The ruins of the City of Dead Souls," the Mage replied.

"How did it come to be this way?" Oliver asked. "And why does nothing grow here?"

"You yourself should know," returned the Mage. "For it was your own kind, men and women of the Maze World, who wrought this devastation. Once the land was rich beyond measure, abundant with life and beauty. It was *your* people who imprisoned the wilderness and killed its green life, who felled the ancient trees and choked the flowing waters, who wounded the Earth so that it may not recover. It is your people who throw away grace as they throw away trash."

"But I did none of that!" Oliver protested. "When have I--"

"No?" asked the Mage. "When did you strive to prevent it, Oliver Medley? Did you not close your eyes to the evil around you and seal yourself in your own garden?"

"But..." said Oliver, grasping for a reason that eluded him. "I can't do anything! The problem is too big for me alone."

But the Mage didn't answer. Instead, Oliver began to hear whispering again, murmurs in the distance. Gradually they grew louder, more insistent, heavy with portent.

"Extinction is contagious!"

"EXTINCTION IS CONTAGIOUS!"

"EXTINCTION IS CONTAGIOUS!"

"But--but what can I do by myself?" he pleaded. "I'm only one person!"

"Use your Gift," he heard as the whispers spiraled around him.

"I don't know what it is!" he protested, turning around and around, trying to see who was there.

"Use your Gift, Oliver Medley."

"Tell me what it is! Tell me, please!"

"Use your Gift. Use your Gift!"

Out of the mythic wood a centaur came, with the body of a powerful horse and the head and muscular torso of a golden-bearded man. A quiver of arrows was slung over his shoulder, and a golden bow was in his hand. Long did the centaur regard Oliver Medley with calm, dark eyes under a brow gleaming like marble.

"I am Chiron, beast and man," spoke the centaur at last in his deep voice. "Look upon me, Brother, and be wise! As I am now, so once were you--and more beast than human! So shall you be again unless you heed the lesson of your dream. Remember everything when you awaken, for we, the people of legend, depend upon you to testify to all that you see and hear. We who are dying ask you to bear witness for us, that our fate might not be forgotten."

The centaur bent his bow and shot an arrow high into the sky, where it winked and flashed, a star shining against the night. "Remember us!"

"We must return now, Friend Oliver," said Nemetona, once more at his side. "For your hour of greatest need, I will give you my own gift. It may help you find yours."

A softness of her kiss upon his cheek, and the spirit-woman of the birch grove was gone.

Hera Vespasia's wing brushed across his eyes, and he slept.

Waking in the hours before dawn, the Questors followed the red road in the waning moonlight, trudging after Pavarr and Firemark. The owl flew ahead, then back to them, reporting to Pavarr and Mildrith. Preoccupied with his own thoughts, Oliver heard nothing of what they said.

Twice they stopped to refresh themselves with journey-bread and a drop of Mil's golden liquid, but never for very long at a time. Mil wouldn't let them sleep again, not even a catnap. "Sleep can mean death in the Icewode, even in daylight," she cautioned. "Keep alert."

And so they sat upright, not even daring to lean against a tree or boulder to ease their weary backs. When they had eaten enough to take the edge off their hunger, Mil made them put away the remainder of the journey-bread. "Not too much," she cautioned. "A full stomach makes you sleepy--and careless."

On and on with measured pace they trod, trying not to make more noise than necessary. Mil walked soundlessly. Great-Aunt Belvedine occasionally crunched a pebble beneath her French-heeled combat boot. Tipp and Tapp stepped on a dry branch, which snapped beneath their heavy boots. Oliver jumped at the sudden crack, thinking he heard gunshots. Then he remembered that he was in a world where, according to the two Dwarvians, there were no guns. *Which doesn't mean that there can't be worse things.*

Oliver himself had an unfortunate tendency to stumble over small obstacles. Once he almost went down, saved only by Tapp's strong hand catching him before he fell and propping him upright.

Soon Oliver lost all track of direction. The uniform landscape, the dense, monotonous wood, the seemingly endless path... on and on and on. When day faded into darkness, luminous eyes peered out at them, eyes of nocturnal hunters and their prey.

At last they came to a gigantic stone chiseled into a perfect cube, higher, wider, and thicker around than any of them could reach. The red path ran up to it and stopped, completely blocked.

"How are we getting past that?" Tipp inquired.

Mil pondered the massive boulder. "There ought to be a way, a door or an entrance of some kind."

"A door in a stone?" wondered Tapp. "Stones don't have doors that I've ever heard."

"Can't we just go around it?" asked Oliver

"No," Pavarr answered abruptly. "I've heard of this stone barrier. They call it the Skullmouth. No one following the red path can go around it or over it or underneath it, and it can't be moved out of the way. The path goes straight through it, so that's what we'll have to figure out how to do."

Oliver shivered as if a cold breeze had snaked up his spine, and hoped no one had noticed. "Go through a--a big stone like that?" he queried to cover his nervousness. "It looks as if it might be granite."

"Mm." Pavarr examined the obstacle, estimating its measurements by sight.

"I'm sure there's an entrance somewhere," said Mil. "The question is how to find it."

"It might open to a Word of Power," said Pavarr.

"Who knows one any more?" asked Tipp. "Weren't most of the Words of Power lost after the Third Age?"

No one answered. The immense boulder remained unresponsive to their plight. The languid moon shed just enough light to reflect off patches of snow. It gave no answers either.

Charleynne Gates

Hera Vespasia, gripping Mil's shoulder, suddenly fluttered her wings and *whoo*'d softly. "Wait! Not all the Words of Power were lost. The N*orrengild* keeps custody of some of them. I might remember one." The owl closed her moongold eyes, thought a moment, and uttered a word in Old Boreal. "*Merrendanor!*"

The Questors held their collective breaths and waited. After an interminable time (during which Oliver's lungs nearly exploded) a deep groaning began underneath their feet.

"What's happening!" Oliver gasped as the ground began to shudder and rumble and bits of dirt tumbled off the stone.

"It's an earthquake!" shouted Tipp. "Run for cover!"

"It's not an earthquake!" Pavarr called as Firemark backed nervously. "Stand your ground! It'll be finished in a minute!"

"So will we!" Tapp cried out.

But they kept their places while the earth beneath them behaved as if it were stretching itself awake after a long slumber. Not knowing which way to run, they had no choice but to stay where they were, flailing their arms and stumbling around crazily to keep their balance. Soon the shaking stopped, and the groaning faded away.

When they could see through the dust again, they saw that the massive cube of rock had been transformed into a gigantic skull with a cavernous opening like a mouth. The red path ran like a long tongue straight between its grinning jaws, to disappear in the darkness beyond.

"The sooner we move on, the better," Mil pointed out. "By now those *gnaarx* at Nether Lake have reported to the Desolation that they found us. And he would have sent out more of them by now."

"The Desolation!" Oliver exclaimed. "You mean--"

"Hush!" Mil cautioned, cutting him off. "That is where the *gnaarx* live. We know who sent them. Do not speak his name! Light the torches!" she continued. "Finding-stones will be no use here."

Quickly Tipp and Tapp produced thick branches they had cut on one of the rest breaks and lit them with flintstones. As they held the flaming torches high, Oliver saw that inside the Skullmouth was another tunnel.

Oh, no, he groaned inwardly. *Not another tunnel! I really don't think I can take it.* "That wouldn't be another tunnel, would it?" he asked.

Pavarr darted a glance at Oliver and recalled his personal issue. "Ah--no, it isn't," Pavarr reassured him. "Not really. More of a... passage."

"That's right! A passage," Mil echoed hastily. "It goes *through* the stone, you see, not underneath. We'll be on the other side in no time."

Tapp muttered something in his beard. "Tunnel. Passage. What's the difference?" But nobody heard what he said except Oliver, who peered into the dim interior and felt doubt rise within him. He wished he could get more clarity about the situation before they ventured on, but a sharp poke in the middle of his back from the point of Great-Aunt Belvedine's umbrella made the decision for him. Propelled forward whether he liked it or not, he scrambled to follow Tipp, Tapp, and Mil into the Skullmouth. Pavarr dismounted and walked with Firemark ahead of the others.

Their torches threw strange, wavering shadows as the group crept cautiously along the passageway. Oliver couldn't see much in front of him, but he dared not go any slower for fear of Great-Aunt Belvedine's umbrella, which was quite capable of delivering more than a gentle reminder. Nor did he wish to be left behind in another tunnel. *One giant cave serpent is more than I want to encounter ever again.*

The path through the Skullmouth stretched longer and longer. At last Mil signaled a halt for rest, and Oliver had a chance to look up and around... and wished he hadn't, for he saw that they were in a cavernous space as deep and wide as a canyon. The quiet drip, drip of mineral-laden water had made columns of stalactites and stalagmites which disappeared into the high shadows. Between the columns were skeletons, rows and rows of skeletons articulated as if they had died where they stood, with a skull delicately balanced atop each one. Flames from the torches lit up the grinning faces, and the wavering light gave them an uncannily lifelike expression.

After a minute or two of staring at the grisly relics, Oliver realized that they were Earth-creatures of the past, staring back at him out of their eyeless sockets. He thought that he recognized a few of them. Towering over him was a *tyrannosaurus rex*, and next to it stood or crouched other saurian remains. One of them was female, for inside the protective cylinder of her skeleton was another shape of bones, small and curled up: a baby dinosaur, forever safe inside its mother.

Farther down the line was a saber-toothed tiger, poised in the act of springing on its hapless prey, and then a huge woolly mammoth, its leathery trunk uplifted. Beyond it, as far into the blackness as he could see, was a multitude of skeletal artifacts, a vast boneyard of extinct life.

As the Questors went on, scenes of lost life played like reels of film against the curtain of darkness ahead of them, and Oliver saw a plenitude of creatures, alive and flourishing as once they had been in the dreamtime of the Earth. Aurochs and tarpan strode the land again. Silver trout and blue pike swam in rivers, gray whale in unpolluted ocean. Song sparrow and black tern flew familiar skies. The Yangtze freshwater dolphin and Fender's blue butterfly thrived. Red wolf, Cape lion, Atlas bear roamed their unfenced territories. Tiny Eohippus, early horse, galloped past them and disappeared into the future. Last of all, a passenger pigeon, a bone-bird clothed in an illusion of feathers, fluttered over their heads and imploded in a sprinkle of dust.

"How did they get here?" he whispered, wary of starting an echo. "What happened to them?"

"They're out of Time. Move on," Mil ordered.

Oliver moved on, but not before he sensed the answer to his question. It was the long parade of extinction they were passing, as in his dream he had witnessed the long parade of mythical beings. One by one, by thousands and tens of thousands, the great hosts of Earthborn species had been hunted to their deaths, hounded out of their habitat, gone to dust and lost to memory.

Whispers followed the Questors, echoing eerily around the huge chamber. *Extinction is contagious...*

EXTINCTION IS CONTAGIOUS...

EXTINCTION IS CONTAGIOUS.

As they went by one of the last skeletons, Oliver's cloak brushed against it, knocking the bones a fraction out of balance. Down from its perch rolled a skull, humanoid in shape, bumping its way over protruding bones until it slid to a stop on the floor. The other Questors ignored it, stepping around its wide, incongruous grin, but Oliver halted. The skull looked pitiful, lying there tilted on the side of its hollow jaw, as if it felt humiliated at being brought so low. Feeling sorry for the poor old thing, Oliver carefully picked it up and stood on tiptoe to replace it on top of its component parts. Then he hurried to catch up with the others, who had gotten some way ahead of him.

He didn't see the tiny crack that appeared in the ceiling when he replaced the head on its bone-pile, nor did he notice the little shower of dirt that cascaded down behind him. In his haste to rejoin the Questors, he slipped on a smooth pebble in the path. His foot shot out from under him, and he fell hard in a sitting position, the wind knocked out of him.

"Say! What's this?" Tipp exclaimed as a little clump of dirt fell on his head. Before anyone could answer, more dirt fell on all of them. Pavarr looked up and saw a widening crack in the ceiling traveling from the far end of the tunnel directly toward them.

"GET OUT OF HERE NOW!" he shouted, slapping Firemark on the rump. The horse immediately galloped, riderless, to the end of the passage.

The Questors ran as fast as their feet would move, but the crack in the ceiling kept pace, showering them with debris which battered their heads and shoulders. The horse exited the tunnel just as the line of skulls on either side began spewing dust into the Questors' faces.

Dust billowed into their lungs. They gasped, choked, and stumbled the rest of the way out of the tunnel. Blinded by unbreathable clouds, they failed to notice that Oliver was no longer with them.

Once again he was lost in a tunnel, and he couldn't see his way out.

Chapter Fourteen

The Ruined Chapel

The dust settled. His diaphragm came out of its state of shock, and Oliver was at last able to take a breath. He hated having the wind knocked out of him. It had happened to him once or twice before, usually when attempting some athletic endeavor for which he was totally unsuited. The only thing to do during those episodes, he had found, was to sit and wait patiently until his wind came back.

Furious with his own clumsiness, he got up and brushed dust off his clothes. He couldn't see the other Questors, but he could see daylight, and figured the end of the tunnel was not far ahead. Retrieving his knapsack, he trudged the last few yards to the exit and looked around.

The red path emerged between banks of snow, running straight to a shelter not far away. He could see one corner of a wall and part of a roof overhang above the hard-packed snow, so he trotted down the path toward it, thinking the other Questors would be inside waiting for him. At least he hoped they were waiting. If they had abandoned him--again!--as they had in the Tunnels...

He came up to the structure and stopped in his tracks. The Ruined Chapel! Like a temple of Elder Days, its elegant, carved columns supported the sky, for time and inclement weather had crumbled much of the roof, and its interior was open to the elements.

It was exactly as Oliver had dreamed back at Keeper's Inn!

Approaching cautiously, he stopped to listen before venturing inside, but heard nothing. No movement, no familiar voices. *Are the Questors here, or have they gone on without me again?*

All senses alert, he crept up to the doorless threshold and peeked inside. The room was dim even though the sky had lightened, as light as it ever got in this world of perpetual winter, and at first he couldn't see anything. Then, as his eyes got used to the change in light, he spotted the Questors. They were lying sprawled about the room, as limp as five bags of sawdust.

Saint Amber's Rose

His breath caught in his throat. *What's the matter with them?* *Are they sleeping, unlikely as it seemed, or... or dead?* With great care he advanced into the room, making no noise in case some hostile force was about.

Nothing stirred, and he leaned over the bodies. There weren't any wounds that he could see, no blood spilling out over the floor. The Questors were apparently alive but deep in slumber, for they were breathing normally, eyes closed, their cloaks tucked securely around them. Mil, Pavarr, and Great-Aunt Belvedine had evidently decided to make their beds on the floor, which was marble, hard and cold to the touch. Hesitantly at first, then urgently, Oliver shook each of them by the shoulder, to no avail. They didn't stir.

Tipp and Tapp were propped against a wall, leaning against each other like big rag dolls, their bearded heads drooped on their chests. From time to time Tapp emitted a snore, and Tipp made a kind of childlike bubbly noise with his lips.

A couple of Sleeping Beauties, Oliver thought, and stifled an impulse to laugh hysterically. He bent down to shake Tipp by the shoulder. As he did so, the Dwarvian gave a violent twitch. His booted foot jerked out and kicked Oliver sharply on the ankle, right on the place where it hurts most. "Ow!" Oliver yelped, and clapped his hand over the injured spot. Despite his outcry, Tipp and the others didn't move or awaken.

Oliver came to his senses at once, fearing that the noise might have alerted unknown entities he had rather not face alone. *Why didn't they wake up when I yelled? Should I try to get them up again? And where did Hera Vespasia go? And Firemark?*

At a loss for answers, he began to examine the room, which was narrow and shadowy in the corner where part of the broken roof remained in place. Three stained-glass windows in the wall gathered light and concentrated it in deep, brilliant colors.

A rectangular shape stood directly in front of the windows. It looked like a stone slab, or perhaps it had been an altar. Or--a bier! A great shining sword, hilt upward, stood at its head. (It was *Greenhallow,* famed of old, consecrated at its forging to respond only to the hero of the Graelands' ancient prophecies--but Oliver knew nothing of that.)

A body--or an effigy--lay upon the bier. Softly Oliver tiptoed toward it, holding his breath, as if breathing would disturb whatever rested there. As he approached, light from the windows shone on the bier, and he saw clearly what rested upon it. The scene was exactly what he had dreamed back at Keepers' Inn.

Flavia's body lay in repose on the bare white marble, slender hands crossed over her breast, eyelashes black against her pale cheeks. The skirt of her emerald-green dress covered her down to her small, slipper-shod feet and swept over the sides of the bier. The gemstones in her browband glittered faintly.

Oliver stared at her motionless form, shocked to find dream and reality thus brought together. *How did she come here?*

He tried to see a pulse in her throat, or to see her breast rise and fall. Hesitantly he touched her wrist, seeking a pulse, but there was no sign of life, although her skin wasn't completely cold to the touch. There seemed to be no rigor in her limbs, although it might have passed off by now.

As in his dream, he had found her, but she had gone into an infinite distance where he could not follow. In utter despair, Oliver sank to his knees on the cold stone floor and rested his head against the marble.

He did not see light travel across the three windows and illuminate the jewels in the sword's hilt, making the outline of a cross. The cross elongated, casting a net of rose-colored light over Flavia's body and Oliver's bowed head.

After a while he got up from his knees and looked down at her. There had to be some explanation for her unnatural condition, because surely it wasn't death. It must be a deep trance, something beyond his skill to detect. The more he thought, the more resolute he became. *She's still alive. She has to be!* There must be a way to bring her back to consciousness.

If only the other Questors would wake up and tell him what to do! Had the same thing happened to them, to plunge them into that abnormal repose?

What do I do now? Desperately he searched his memory, reaching for some previous experience that might yield a clue to what he ought to do in this situation.

Nothing came up. There was no similar experience, certainly not in his former uneventful life.

He scoured his mind for possible answers, no matter how far-fetched. In the meantime, his external vision was left free to drift to the radiant figures depicted in the windows. In the center window the stained-glass portrait of a lithe and beautiful tabby cat faced him, its golden eyes returning his stare with interest. A tiny silver key hung from its neck on a chain. At the bottom of the window were letters in antique script: **Saint Amber**. He had never heard of a saint by that name and had no idea what the words signified, as there was no human figure in the glass.

The window to its left showed a rose in bloom, a variety unfamiliar to Oliver. Its petals took on the colors of dawn, changing and deepening as light intensified in the gray sky. He contemplated the rose, and an itch of memory made him think he had seen something like it not long ago. He leaned in to study it more closely and was almost positive that he heard music, a soft, sweet melody, coming from inside the window. He held his breath, straining to hear more clearly, but the sound died away.

The window to the right showed a landscape with a fortress on a crag jutting from the side of a colossal mountain. Beneath it a sheer cliff plunged down to a river roiling with white foam, and beyond the river was a glimpse of blue ocean. Its topmost towers were bathed in the rose-gold light of sunset, and Oliver couldn't quite make out if the gleaming spires indicated a walled town or a castle. Whichever it was, the place appeared to be virtually inaccessible.

Oliver shook his head and gave up on fruitless speculation. Returning to the bier, he began to pace slowly around it. *If nothing else, I can at least watch over Flavia until the Questors wake up and let me in on the plan of action. If they have one, which of course they must have. Someone must have.*

Fatigue fell away as he kept vigil and mulled over the irony of the situation. Here, at last, he had found the lady of his dreams, but she was completely oblivious to his presence. He wished with all his heart that he was anything like the hero she thought him to be. Then he might be able to do something actually heroic, like rescuing her instead of walking around and around, feeling as useless as an old cobweb.

The other problem that occurred to him was that this situation felt--well, rather anticlimactic. He was embarrassed even thinking such a disloyal thought, but there it was. *This is the part in the story where the hero wakes the sleeping princess with a kiss. They get married and live happily ever after.*

The problem was, Oliver wasn't any kind of a hero, and he would never dare to kiss the *Sendara*, sleeping or not. *What am I supposed to do now?*

He paced around the bier several times, brooding on the question. Maybe now was when he was supposed to use his Gift, the Gift that people kept talking about, that Flavia was so sure he had. *But what do I possess that could possibly be necessary to Flavia and her mysterious realm?*

He glanced idly at the stained-glass windows again and was surprised to find that he had miscounted. There were actually four windows, not three. The one he had overlooked showed a small man in a gray monkish robe with the cowl folded over his shoulders. In one hand he held a water pail; in the other, a twig from a green-leafed plant. He looked out at Oliver in a friendly, inquiring sort of way.

"I wish you could talk," Oliver murmured to himself, pausing in front of the monkish figure. "I wish you could tell me what I ought to do."

He returned to his vigil at the bier, but now there was a small black dot dangling in front of his eyes. Oliver blinked, but the dot didn't disappear. It was a tiny spider (*Aranea diadema*) descending on a single silken thread attached to a remnant of roof-beam. In another minute it would reach the corona of Flavia's hair, for it was dropping down toward it straight as a plumb line.

Oliver's first impulse was to reach out and crush the little creature between thumb and forefinger. His second, more humane, was to reach above the spider and pinch off a length of silken line. The spider, sensing detachment, froze in mid-air. Oliver carried it, hanging on the end of the thread, to the near window, the one with the painting of the dawn-colored rose. He deposited the creature gently on the sill and turned to go back to his vigil.

But there was something blocking his way, a kind of haze that gathered itself and became an indefinite form, a hazy figure in a hooded robe. Its back was bent over the bier, its face close to Flavia's. Oliver could almost, but not quite, see through the figure; it wavered between transparency and opacity.

It's going to attack her! Oliver's heart stopped for a beat; he couldn't move. Then he thrust out a hand to push the thing away. "Stop!" he shouted, but the word came out as a choked whisper.

The mist-formed figure whipped around. Malice streamed from the thing. Oliver saw its dark energy shoot toward him like a flight of arrows.

The wavering form expanded, grew taller, looming over him. The folds of its hood fell open. To his horror, Oliver saw that it had no face. Only a black hole showed above its cowl.

Without a second to think about it, Oliver leaped past the thing and grabbed the sword at the head of the bier. One panic-driven pull, and it came out of its resting place, singing as it sliced through the air. With a strength he didn't know he had, Oliver whirled the shining blade in a circle. In one revolution the sword cut completely through the hooded figure, then grounded itself on the stone floor in a burst of sparks, nearly impaling Oliver's foot.

Then the thing was gone--vanished--as if it had never been there, and Oliver was not sure that he had seen anything after all.

"Well done, Brother!" said a jolly voice behind him.

Oliver jumped, spinning toward the sound. Peering to one side of the chapel, then the other, he saw nothing corresponding to the voice. *Hallucinations,* he decided. *I'm having auditory hallucinations.* After a few minutes his adrenaline levels returned to normal, and he felt the full weight of the ponderous weapon. Sweat dripping into his eyes, he struggled to lift the sword again and drag it back to its resting place. *This weapon was never meant for me,* he decided.

Panting, he stood back and stared at the sword's cross-bar, now as high as his head. *To think that I actually hefted that massive blade— even once--and used it to defend the Sendara!* For a moment he felt almost heroic.

After a brief interval of self-congratulation, he remembered that he still didn't know what he was supposed to be doing, and so resumed his slow perambulation around the bier. He wished that Pavarr, especially, would wake up and decide what to do next. They couldn't stay here much longer, where Flavia had already been exposed to the elements from the damaged ceiling.

Charleynne Gates

What if it rains, if it ever rains in the Icewode? What if it snows? That was more likely. *And it isn't any too warm in here. I ought to cover her with my cloak.* He took off his mantle and spread it gently over her motionless form.

"You mustn't worry so much, Brother," said the voice behind him. "Worry never helps."

Oliver's head swiveled around again, finally facing the window with the little monk and his pail and twig. Was someone talking to him from outside that window? *Is this a trick to lure me away from Flavia?*

"I am speaking to you, Brother Medley," the voice said again, and this time Oliver met the eyes of the man in the stained-glass window. "Yes!" said the monk, smiling and nodding. "I have been watching over the *Sendara* Flavia since Brother Klone brought her into the chapel. I am the Hermit of Hermit's Repose!"

"You!" Oliver exclaimed. "But you're in a window! How can you be speaking? And who is Brother Klone?"

The Hermit sighed and answered the last question first. "Brother Klone is the shadow-form you found bending over the *Sendara*'s body. Do not be concerned about slicing him in two; he was merely startled, for he cannot be killed by the sword. Brother Klone," the Hermit went on, "is, unfortunately, my creation. He often believes himself to be me. It was he who imprisoned me in this window, or so he thinks. In fact--"

The Hermit took a step out of the window and put his foot on the ground. The rest of him followed as a matter of course, and there, unmistakably, was the figure from the stained-glass window standing three-dimensionally on the floor of the Ruined Chapel, smiling at Oliver. "As you see," the Hermit continued, "I am perfectly free to move about as I please. I've never let Brother Klone know; it would hurt his feelings."

The Hermit advanced toward the marble bier. Immediately Oliver stepped closer, ready to block his way. The Hermit halted, looking kindly at him.

"Do not fear," he said, "I will not hurt the *Sendara*. I know all about you and the Countess de Montfort and the *Foressa* Mildrith, the Whackitt Brothers, Great Chief Hera Vespasia, and Prince Pavarr. Oh yes, I have known of your Quest for a considerable time." He stopped, appeared to be listening to something Oliver couldn't hear. "We'd better make haste."

"To do what?" said Oliver. "I cannot leave until the others are awake."

The Hermit glanced toward their sleeping forms and smiled all over his wrinkled face. "Ah, yes! We must do something about that. They are sleeping because of the Origin Dust that blew into their faces when you came through Skullmouth Passage. They couldn't help themselves, you know. It put them in a Trance of Extinction. That's what happens when you breathe in Origin Dust. You sleep, then you become extinct. I wonder"--he eyed Oliver keenly--"how you managed to escape its effects. Hmm... That's a tale for another time, I suppose."

Before Oliver could stop him, the Hermit dipped the green twig he was carrying into the pail of water and sprinkled the two Dwarvians with it. Both of them bounded upright on the instant.

"Who! What! Where!" they shouted, dazed with sleep. Then they assumed a defensive posture, scowling ferociously at the alien person in the monkish robe.

The Hermit ignored them, moving on to sprinkle Pavarr, Mil, and Great-Aunt Belvedine. With muted expressions of surprise the three awoke and scrambled to their feet, looking befuddled. Even the two warriors seemed unsure whether to draw their swords.

"Go out into the clearing," the Hermit told them calmly, as if he expected to be obeyed, "and wait. Prepare the horse to bear the *Sendara*." At once, moving like sleepwalkers, the five Questors went out through the window near the bier upon which Flavia lay--but they didn't appear to notice her.

"Wait!" Oliver protested, trying to stop them, but the Questors brushed by him as if he were invisible. "Don't leave! We can't abandon the *Sendara*!"

"Nor shall you," replied the Hermit. He dipped the green twig into the pail of water and brushed the wet leaves gently across Flavia's forehead, leaving the faintest trace of water like dewdrops on her alabaster skin. "*Sendara*!" he called softly, as if speaking to someone far away. "*Sendara*, awaken and arise! Your interrupted journey must resume!"

As Oliver watched, wide-eyed, Flavia's white cheeks began to tint with pink, and she drew in a deep breath. Her eyes opened, and they were once again a clear gray, mirroring the sky, as she returned from the remote place where she had been. Oliver's heart overflowed; he couldn't speak for joy.

"Help her to rise, Brother Medley," said the Hermit, and Oliver sprang to obey. With his aid, she rose to sit upright, her small feet drooped over the side of the bier.

Oliver held her hand and thought that, despite the circumstances, he had never been as happy as he was at that moment. Even so, an annoying little voice in his head cut through the romantic haze like a spray of vinegar. *Don't you wonder what's really going on here?*

Oliver ignored it.

"Cousin Oliver," Flavia said, as if she were not quite awake. "Where--?"

"We are in the Ruined Chapel in the Icewode," he replied. "Hermit's Repose."

Flavia noticed the gray-robed Hermit nearby, holding his pail and twig. "Where are my friends?" she said.

"They are outside, waiting for you, *Sendara*," the Hermit replied, bowing deeply. "You had better leave now. Brother Klone, who abducted you from the Mort-Mire, will be returning soon. He must not find you here."

"How can I leave?" Flavia asked. "My chair..."

Oliver had one of the worst moments of his life. *I'll have to carry her! There's no other way for her to get outside the chapel!* Flavia might not weigh very much, but he, Oliver Medley, was not in sufficient physical condition to carry her! Shame crept across his skin like little flames; embarrassment shortened his breath. He wanted to crawl under something and never come out.

"Come along," said the Hermit. He waved his green sprig, walked swiftly back to his window, turned and beckoned to them... and walked into the window and through it.

"Cousin Oliver?" said Flavia, turning toward him with questioning eyes. All at once she was in his arms, and she weighed no more than a small bird. He went toward the window... stepped into it... encountering not a pane of glass but a shimmering mist. In his brief passage he caught one glimpse of undreamed marvels, and then he was

Saint Amber's Rose

on the other side of the window, and Pavarr was there to take Flavia from his arms.

Back in the Ruined Chapel, Tipp and Tapp slowly relaxed from their defensive postures and rubbed their eyes.

"What just happened?" asked Tapp.

"I don't know, but I don't trust that Hermit," Tipp remarked in an undertone.

"Me neither," Tapp replied. "He looks like someone's idea of a hermit in a storybook."

"The *Sendara* went through the Hermit's window," said Tipp. "But she isn't fully awake. I don't feel totally awake myself. Something's wrong here."

"What about Friend Oliver?" asked Tapp. "He carried her through that window. Maybe he knows something we don't."

"He's in love with the *Sendara*," answered Tipp. "Wherever she goes, he will follow. He does not yet understand the evil that dogs our steps."

"Did you see that twig the Hermit doused us with? And the water pail?" asked Tapp. "He probably didn't think we'd recognize a branch of *riparia morta*, which triggers a hypnotic reaction in any creature that touches it. And I'm sure there was poisonous *bendor*-bush powder in the water. Good thing we Dwarvians are immune to it."

"The Hermit must not have known that," mused Tipp.

"The others acted like sleepwalkers!" said Tapp.

"Then we need to stay alert," said Tipp, buckling on his knapsack. "Why didn't he waken the *Sendara* when she first got here?"

"That's what I wondered," said Tapp, "and who is this Brother Klone he said abducted her from the Mort-Mire?"

"Quite a few things I don't understand about this place," said Tipp, "and I don't like the feel of it."

"Me neither," said his brother. "Finding the *Sendara* was too easy."

"Makes me think someone wanted us to come this way," remarked Tipp.

The two Dwarvians passed through the window, joining the Questors on the other side. Flavia sat on Firemark, and Pavarr stood beside them, holding the reins. All of them except the Dwarvians stood with closed, sleepy faces in the gloom of a hemlock grove outside the

Ruined Chapel.   A little distance away, virtually invisible to those below, Hera Vespasia perched on a limb in the canopy.

"What's the matter with you, Medley?" said Great-Aunt Belvedine, with less than her usual asperity, "you were supposed to watch over--"

"I have not been harmed," interrupted Flavia.   "I heard everything while I was lying in the chapel. Cousin Oliver defended me against the shadow."

"What shadow..." Mil began, a little groggily.

"Why were we sleeping?" asked Pavarr with a yawn.

"You inhaled Origin Dust when you came through Skullmouth Passage," the Hermit informed them. "'Dust you were, to dust you will return,' you know, like the extinct creatures you passed. If I had not awakened you, you would have slept, like them, until the end of the world."

"And where were you, Medley?" demanded Great-Aunt Belvedine, glaring at him. "You were supposed to be with us!"

"I, ah, slipped and fell," Oliver said, red-faced. "Got the wind knocked out of me. By the time I could breathe again, the dust had settled."

"A likely story!" Great-Aunt Belvedine snorted. A cloud of leftover dust blew out of her nostrils, reminding Oliver of a bull about to charge. Automatically he took a step backward.

"Do not blame Cousin Oliver," Flavia interjected quietly. "He has done well."

"True, *Sendara*," the little Hermit put in, nodding. "Brother Medley could not have awakened you without my help. He did not know that he had to ask before help could be given. Or whom to ask."

"Hmph!   Don't blame me," said Great-Aunt Belvedine irrationally, taking out her umbrella-sword and swishing it through the air in her morning calisthenics. "It wasn't my idea to bring him with us."

"It's never your fault, is it, Belvedine!" Mil snapped. "Put that away before you hurt someone."

"They're not behaving like themselves at all," Tapp whispered to his brother.

"It's either that Origin Dust," Tipp whispered back, "or the water he sprinkled on all of them."

Saint Amber's Rose

"Friends!" said Flavia, with uplifted hand. "We have far to go. Friend Hermit, will you give us directions?"

"I will, *Sendara*," replied the Hermit. "It is better for you to separate now and to continue in four different ways to your destination. That will confuse your adversary for a while, although you must still be wary, for his minions are all around us. Prince Pavarr and the *Foressa* Mildrith will escort the *Sendara* through the Icewode; Countess de Montfort and Great Chief Hera Vespasia will fly reconnaissance over the Icewode; and the Whackitt brothers will descend to the mines of their ancestors under the Icewode. You will meet at the Abbey of Saint Amber at the next full moon."

Flavia bent her head. "Friend Hermit, your words are wise, and we will obey them. Friends, let us go."

And they were gone.

"What's happening? Why are we doing this?" muttered Tapp to his brother as they trudged along one of the four shining paths leading away from the Ruined Chapel and the hemlock grove. No sooner had he said this than his feet began to move faster, as if they had minds of their own—or if the path itself were hurrying them along.

"I don't know, but I--I can't stop!" Tipp hissed as he also tried in vain to stop himself from marching forward. "It can't be the Origin Dust! It's this path, Brother! It's pulling us away from the others!"

"You're right, Brother!" said Tapp, struggling like Tipp to make his feet turn in the other direction as the sinister road sped them through the close-crowded trees. "Ow! Hey! Stop! Tipp, it won't let us go! It's taking us farther from the *Sendara*!"

"This must be happening to the others, too!" Tipp gasped.

"I knew there was something wrong with that Hermit!" Tapp groaned.

Back in the hemlock grove, Oliver stared after them as each group disappeared separately into the depths of the Icewode. *They're abandoning me again*! "Wait! Wait!" he called out in a panic. He ran a few steps toward the four gleaming paths where trampled snow was already smoothing itself out. In another minute there would be no trace of the Questors ever having been here.

Which way should I go? "Wait!" he shouted again, but the heavy air swallowed his words.

A momentary fit of hysteria shook him like falling leaves. He fell on his knees, beating the palms of his hands together. "Why did they leave me again?" he moaned. "Why?" But the episode passed, and Oliver heaved a deep sigh and pulled himself to his feet.

"Brother Medley, you fret too much!" The Hermit, twig and pail resting on the ground, sat comfortably on a tree stump, watching him.

"They've all gone! They've left me alone again!" Oliver mourned, not heeding the Hermit.

"Yes, they have, but you have a path to follow also."

"I can't go wandering around the Icewode by myself! I'd never survive."

"Indeed you would not," the Hermit assured him. "Come, sit down on that log over there. I am going to tell you my story before you leave. Oh, dear," he said sadly, "it has been a long time since I told my story to anyone. I hope you will be kind enough to hear it. You might as well. I will not give you directions until I have finished."

"But what about my friends?" Oliver moaned. "I'm supposed to be with them. I can't go on alone. I just can't." The picture of dejection, he put his elbows on his knees and his head in his hands and gave way to despair.

"You can generally do what you put your mind to doing, Brother Medley," said the Hermit severely. "Now listen: Brother Klone will return soon, and you must be gone by then."

Unable to do otherwise, Oliver resigned himself to this turning of his fate and composed himself to listen.

"Once, long ago," the Hermit began, looking not at Oliver but into the frozen tangle of the Icewode, "I was a young friar at the Abbey of Saint Amber. I was happy there, loving the quiet life, learning everything I could. The Abbey is famous for its medicinal gardens and its herbalists; I assisted them. I discovered a talent for the cultivation of healing plants and became the Abbey Herbalist. Word of my skills spread about the countryside, and the sick and injured began to come to me for relief until my days were filled with diagnosing illnesses and dispensing medicines. Little time had I for prayer and contemplation, and at last I felt a great weariness descend upon me, as well as a growing need for a life of solitude.

Saint Amber's Rose

"After a season the former resident of Hermit's Repose died. The Abbot, who had the governance of Hermit's Repose, needed a successor to watch over it and to succor the occasional traveler. At my request, he appointed me. I was glad to go. Here in the Repose--the Ruined Chapel, as those in the Outer World call it--I lived a solitary life, reading, writing, meditating. I planted my garden of vegetables and herbs, sharing my bounty with the rare traveler or pilgrim. Thus I lived in peace for many years.

"Gradually I became aware that something was lacking in my life. I am ashamed to say that I was... bored. Yes, my son," though Oliver had not spoken, "boredom is the chief danger of a peaceful life. Certainly it is a danger to those who love solitude, for solitude walks hand in hand with loneliness. I had wanted to be the Hermit of the Repose, and my life was useful and fulfilled. But I became too intimately acquainted with loneliness, and I knew I needed more... adventure in my life.

"One day as I was sweeping out the chapel, my broom dislodged a small piece of chipped marble in the corner. In retrieving it, I found the outline of a trap door. Curiosity overcame me! Although the door clearly had not been disturbed for years, I managed to drag it open. Imagine my amazement when I discovered a staircase leading to an immense space below the chapel, a chamber I didn't know existed. Oh, how infinitely better it would have been had I sealed the door again and left that room in darkness forever!

"But I was ignorant. Taking a lantern, I descended the staircase--a rough one hewn of wood. My light illuminated the entire chamber, and to my astonishment I saw that it was an alchemical laboratory! My predecessor had equipped the room with everything needful for his studies, including books and his own journals, in which I read the notes of his experiments and observations.

"Here was the answer to my prayer for relief from boredom! I studied, I experimented, I taught myself the alchemical arts. After many years, I mastered them.

"Then I determined to achieve the great goal of alchemy: I decided to create an homunculus. Do you know what that is, my son?"

"Yes," Oliver murmured, recalling the goal of artificially creating a humanoid life form.

"I wanted a companion," the Hermit went on, "for you see, although working in the alchemical arts alleviated my boredom, my loneliness remained. I wanted someone to talk to. Also, my years were beginning to tell on me, and I needed someone to share my labors--the gathering of wood for the fireplace, re-thatching the roof of my hut, searching for herbs to dry.

"I studied endlessly and performed many experiments. All of them failed, until at long last one succeeded. I made a true homunculus, a miniature human being, a replica of myself! A pure creation of my own mind... and my own vanity.

"It grew quickly, abnormally so, because that is the nature of homunculi once they are released from the glass incubator. I named it Brother Klone. Soon he attained my height and more, and gained the ability to counterfeit my appearance. I thought it amusing--at the time. I taught him everything I could. He was a voracious student! Soon he had absorbed nearly all the contents of my mind.

"He became a great help to me in doing the heavy work, fetching and carrying and the like. And when my limbs grew stiff and tired after little exertion, I turned over some of my other duties to him. I even made him Warder of my chapel.

"But I became aware that I could not trust him, for he had no feeling toward me, either of love or of hate, but only a hunger to possess. I realized he wanted not only to learn from me but also to *be* me, to absorb me into himself, and by absorbing me, acquire all my powers. He understands neither good nor evil; he has no capacity for mercy or pity. Despite all his learning, inside himself he is a monster without conscience. Alas! Although I could make an homunculus, I could not give him a soul.

"At last, after agonizing for many months, I decided to destroy the product of my studies. He is very strong physically, far stronger than I, and ferocious when aroused, so I had to work secretly lest he discover what I was doing and rend me in pieces. He is invulnerable to pain, but he can be returned to his original elements by means of magical arts. Time after time I began to work the spells that would dissolve him into his constituent elements, but always, at the last moment, I held my hand. Brother Klone is my own unnatural child, and I... I love him!"

Saint Amber's Rose

"Is there no other way to destroy this--I mean, your--'child'?" asked Oliver with less sympathy than he might otherwise have felt, remembering the faceless entity looming over Flavia on the marble bier.

"No. The duty--and the ability--are mine alone. He cannot be destroyed in any other way. Brother Medley! It is my son you are speaking about, my only son, and I am his only parent. How can I set my hand against what I have created? All I can do is watch over him and try to diminish the effects of the evil he may do." The Hermit hung his head and was silent.

Oliver couldn't think of anything to say, and so said nothing.

"The longer I let him live," the Hermit continued after a while, "the more his power grew. He determined to destroy me and absorb my energies, but that he could not do! He succeeded only in imprisoning me in that stained-glass window in the Ruined Chapel, although I soon discovered how to leave it at any time without his knowledge. Oh yes, I knew when the *Sendara* was brought into the chapel and laid upon the bier. It was my son Klone who abducted her from the Mort-Mire! He saw her beauty and sensed her power and wanted her for himself.

"Now about you and the other Questors. When my son brought the *Sendara* here, he believed that all of you would be trapped in the Ruined Chapel, and he could absorb your vital energies when he wished.

"That is why I was very concerned lest you keep marching around that marble bier until my son returned. It would have been impossible for the other Questors or the *Sendara* to awaken without my intervention. Only you had the ability to request assistance of me."

"But I didn't know that!" Oliver exclaimed indignantly. "Or I would have asked you as soon as I got here! How could I have known?"

"It is unfair," agreed the Hermit. "The fact is, no one could tell you because you are the Gift-Bringer."

"But what Gift am I supposed to bring?" cried Oliver, nearly beside himself with exasperation. "Can you tell me?"

"No," said the Hermit calmly. "I cannot, even though I know what it is."

"You know!" shouted Oliver. "You know! Oh! Why... why..."

The Hermit lifted his hand. "When I took my vows upon entering the Abbey, I promised to observe silence upon all matters

Charleynne Gates

concerning the Repository of Saint Amber. And that includes your Gift."

"Respository? What Repository? What does it have to do with me?"

"I may tell you only one thing," the Hermit replied. "Do you recall the rhyme you heard at Threshold Inn? The last line?"

Oliver pondered. "I think so. It was--'the pure in heart unlocks the Rose'."

"Exactly," said the Hermit. "The line refers to the one who possesses the key."

"I have a key," said Oliver, fishing out his little silver key and holding it on his palm. He studied it carefully, thus missing the sudden glint in the hermit's eyes. "I wondered why people kept asking me about my key. It doesn't unlock anything as far as I'm aware. My father gave it to me simply as a remembrance of him."

"It is far more than that, Brother Medley," the Hermit went on. "Your key will unlock the Rose. More than that I dare not say."

For a while afterward they sat in silence, and Oliver realized that another whole night had passed, and the first signs of dawn were appearing in the wintry sky. To his surprise, he wasn't at all tired. He had had no sleep in a day and a night, but listening to the Hermit had in some mysterious way revived him.

"'Rosy-fingered dawn', as Homer sang," murmured the Hermit. "You see, I know the classics of your world, too. Now, Brother Medley, you must be well on your way before my son returns. I will show you your path."

"Am I to go on alone?" asked Oliver.

"Solitary is your path," replied the Hermit. "You may meet others on it, but be judicious in your speech. Not all tales are for all ears. Now gird yourself for the journey. Ready? Follow me." The Hermit led him to the last of the four shining paths—the only one not yet blanketed with crystalline snow. "There lies the way," he said.

"But where does it go?" Oliver protested.

"I've forgotten to give you your walking staff!" said the Hermit. "How remiss of me." He hastened to a nearby hemlock and reached out a hand to caress its trunk. Oliver didn't quite see how he did it, but when the Hermit returned, he bore a freshly-carved stout staff. "There

-- 272 --

will come a time when you no longer need it," he explained. "Then return it to a tree. Any tree will do."

Oliver didn't think to ask how he was to manage that assignment, and took the staff without further protest. "But where am I going?" he asked.

"To the Abbey of Saint Amber, of course," replied the Hermit with a touch of impatience. "You will proceed by this path to Purple Valley. It is not far, and in the valley is a village where you may inquire how to get to the Abbey. Someone will help you. And now, goodbye."

Oliver had more questions, not to mention doubts, and he made no move to go. "Wait, please! I need more inf--"

"*Enthara!*" said the Hermit mildly. Before Oliver could finish his sentence, he found that he was already walking away from the Ruined Chapel and along the solitary path. The staff pulled him along, setting a steady pace that didn't allow dawdling. He tried releasing his grip on the staff, but it refused to let him go, and at last Oliver resigned himself to being led on the road to another unknown destination.

The Hermit waited beside the Ruined Chapel, seated on the tree-stump Oliver had left.

"I cannot tell how his journey will end," he murmured to himself, gazing after the retreating Questor. "He may not survive the ordeal that is coming to him. Likely he will die—quite horribly, if I know the villagers. But there is a Fate I do not see..." His head drooped, and for a moment the lines of guile and cunning on his face smoothed, and something of nobility that had once been there became visible again.

"Why did I ever enter that laboratory of unholy arts? Why?— when I knew all too well who enticed me therein. Ab'addon! who saw my untamed pride and used my own vanity to entrap me. Well, now I have done what he wanted, and it will destroy me. Who can tell—it may destroy him at the last, too!" He smiled a little ruefully, shook his head, and lifted his shoulders in a resigned shrug.

"Come, my son," he said. "You've been a good boy, and you shall have a treat."

The Hermit arose slowly from the tree-stump and went back into the chapel, his back bent as if he carried a terrible weight. A thin, hooded shadow crept obediently after him.

Charleynne Gates

Fool! I will *destroy you!* said the Voice in the Smoke, and the Mirror shook with the force of his wrath. *I will destroy the* Sendara--*the Labyrinth—and all worlds that are or will be!*

Chapter Fifteen

Purple Valley

The staff dragged him along briskly, but not fast enough to make him breathless. It allowed him to take a brief break every *kephan* or so (according to Oliver's reckoning, which was none too certain). The path, though scarcely a foot-stride across, was more or less straight, and it led him without much difficulty into a different part of the Icewode than he had previously seen. There was less snow on the ground and on the tree branches; much of it had melted into the earth. At any rate, he didn't feel as cold as formerly. In fact, he worked up something of a sweat as the staff marched him along, one-two, one-two, as regular as drumbeats.

If it weren't for the staff pulling him, he would have had a difficult time getting through the forest, for the trees crowded much closer together here than in the other part of the Icewode. It was darker, too. The dim light from the listless sun shone only on the path, and the staff kept him steadily in the middle of it. Once in a while he caught a peripheral glimpse of a shape or a face ahead of him on the path or darting behind a tree, but he tried not to look directly at it. What he could not see frightened him more than what he could see clearly.

If I just pretend I don't see it at all, maybe it'll go away.

He realized, in a vague way, that the thought wasn't very logical, but he couldn't help himself. The unseen and unknown stimulated and challenged some people; it had always frightened him.

After a while, he discerned a brighter light in the wood off to his left, as if there might be an open space in that direction. *I wish I could see what it is.*

No sooner was it wished than granted: Instantly the path swerved to the left. The staff turned him too sharply around the corner; his feet got entangled with each other, and he nearly fell on his face.

The staff waited stolidly until he regained his footing, then picked up its pace and marched him on again.

A sound came to him from a far distance, like ocean waves or a wind tearing through the topmost tree boughs. The staff seemed to hear it too, for it let him stop while he held his breath, concentrating on it.

Shhh, shhh, shuush, shuush, shlomp, shlomp. It didn't really sound like waves at all, now that he heard it more clearly. It was more like a regiment of cats licking their fur with sandpaper tongues.

The sound moved through the wood, coming closer toward him. He would like to have moved on at this point, but the staff stayed glued to the spot. Having no choice, Oliver stayed where he was, and an odd impression began to grow that something was eating its way toward him. The staff kindly allowed him to edge back a few steps.

Chchomp, chchomp, slurp-chchomp. Closer... closer. He made out a kind of moaning between the chomping noises, and soon words became audible between the moans. "O, the burning, the burning! O, the burning, the burning! O, the burning feet of fire!" On and on went the grotesque chomping, interspersed with moans and anguished cries.

Torn between fear and curiosity, Oliver tugged at the staff, which ignored him, and strained to see what was making the racket.

A being emerged from behind one of the trees, a small, human-shaped entity whose thin, gangly arms ended in stumpy tentacles with sucker-like protuberances at their ends. The tentacles wrapped around a tree-trunk, and the misshapen head bit at the bark, tearing it off piece by piece. The mouth must not have had any teeth, for it appeared to be crushing the fibrous material in its mouth parts and swallowing the pulp. Between slurping gulps it moaned again and again, "O, the burning, the burning! O, the burning, the burning! O, the burning feet of fire!"

The creature worked itself around the tree, gumming a ring of bark, then swiveled its spongy head and looked directly at Medley. Strings of black moss and woody fiber dripped from its wide slit of a mouth. It was repulsively hideous, yet Oliver thought he discerned an expression of suffering in its eyes.

"O, the burning!" it moaned, and his heart melted with pity. Impulsively he took a step toward the bark-eater, not realizing that the staff was allowing him to, and reached out toward it.

"Can I help you in some way?" he asked, on the presumption that it might understand him. "Have you been injured?"

Saint Amber's Rose

It immediately darted behind the tree and peeked out, rolling its protuberant eyes from side to side and sniffing the air suspiciously.

It's afraid of me. Oliver halted, not wanting to scare it away. "Is there anything I can do for you?" he said gently. "My name is Medley. May I know your name?"

"M--m--m--Med-el," repeated the bark-eater through its broad slit of a mouth. "Med-del-ley."

"Yes, that's it. And your name?"

"We... are... we are," it said in a hoarse, rough voice, as if it hadn't spoken anything other than moans for a long time and wasn't sure how to make his mouth shape forgotten words. "We are... *Wyndyg. Wyndyg.* We are."

"*Wyndyg,*" he echoed, trying to imitate the pronunciation. "Your name is *Wyndyg.* Very pleased to meet you. You said 'we'? Are there more of you here?"

Close up, the little bark-eater seemed more pitiable than terrifying. Oliver had an urge to go nearer, but the staff, intractable again, kept him within speaking distance but out of reach.

He began to hear louder chomping noises, and perceived in the shadows of the wood that more Wyndyg were hiding behind nearby trees, wrapping their tentacle-arms around the trunks and gnawing the bark. They ate steadily even as their frog-like eyes darted toward him warily, and Oliver saw that they were consuming the bark in a complete ring around the tree, exposing a wide swath of bare cambium and depriving the tree of the nutrients that sustained its life.

"Oh, wait!" He tried to take another step toward the *Wyndyg,* only to be jerked back by the staff. "You're not going to eat all the bark off that tree, are you? Don't you realize it will kill the tree? You don't want to do that, do you?"

"O, the burning, the burning! O, my burning feet of fire!" replied the first *Wyndyg,* and all the others responded, "O, the burning, the burning!"

"I don't understand!" said Oliver. "Are your feet injured? Can I help you in some way? Please don't keep eating the bark off those trees!"

"We are *Wyndyg,*" the first one answered between bites of bark. "We eat... we eat... all trees. We eat... everything. Cannot... stop.

Charleynne Gates

Have to eat... Our feet... always... on fire. Eating tree... only thing... make us better."

"How dreadful!" said Oliver, shocked to his soul. "How did this happen?

"We made... ourselves," answered another *Wyndyg*. "Once we... did not... look like this... We... made us... like... this. Had much... Wanted more... Feet on fire... Never let us rest... Have to eat everything... Eat the whole world. Cannot... stop. O, the burning, the burning! O, my burning feet of fire!"

While he was concentrating on what the *Wyndyg* was saying, Oliver hadn't noticed that many *Wyndyg*s--dozens, perhaps hundreds of the spongy beings--had circled around him, stripping bark in a ring around every tree, dooming everything they touched to an inevitable death.

"Lor... Des-late... make us... eat," moaned the *Wyndyg*. "Once... land behind us... all green... Now... never ... again. We ate... the light... out of the land. O, the burning, the burning!"

What wretched little creatures they are, thought Oliver, torn between revulsion and pity.

All at once he realized that he had let them come too close, for the first *Wyndyg* touched his sleeve with the sucker at the end of its tentacle. Oliver shrank back.

"Come with us," the little thing said. "We eat. . . everything. Then... we eat each other. Come with us... or we... eat you!"

Why didn't the staff let him escape? What's the matter with it? In a panic, Oliver shook the staff, willing it to speed them onward, but it remained stubbornly in place, and his hand remained glued to the shaft despite repeated efforts to free himself.

The *Wyndyg* crept closer. "Come with us," they whispered. "Let us eat you... Then you are free..."

The awful thing was that Oliver realized he had an acute desire to join them, despite knowing, deep in his heart, that he really wanted no such thing.

"O, the burning," the *Wyndyg* moaned. "Destruction... is... ecstasy!"

By now, Oliver was avid to get away, but he also wanted to stay, to become one of them, to kill and eat, eat and kill as they did. He felt their terrible resentment of life flood over him like a torrent of raw sewage, and it repelled him utterly. And yet the desire grew to yield himself completely to them.

All at once an otherworldly noise cut through the *Wyndyg*'s moaning, a strange, sad sound like the complaint of cattle lost in the fields of Time... a skirling sound that stirred the soul. Oliver recognized it, felt it reverberate in every bone in his body, for it was the drone of the Highland bagpipe! A lone piper, playing afar and marching nearer! The *Wyndyg* shrank back, retreated toward the dark, dying trees and vanished behind them as the insistent call of the pipes grew louder.

The piper, resplendent in a tartan of black and gold, appeared out of a swirling fog. He strode up to Oliver and removed the chanter from his mouth. The music faded with a protesting sob. Towering over Oliver, the piper fixed him with a stern eye.

"Do ye understand what ye hear, mon?" he demanded.

"Er," said Oliver, nonplussed. "I, ah, I've always enjoyed bagpipes, but I don't recognize the tune. What was it, may I ask?"

"'Twas the gathering song of my clan!" replied the piper. "Often did I play it, and ever did the lads answer the call to defend our freedom. Och, they were the brave lads!"

"What happened to them??"

The piper bent his head and frowned at the black ground. "We were separated in a fog during a battle on foreign soil. I couldna find them, and somehow they couldna hear me. Since then I've walked alone in the world, playing my pipes. One day the lads'll hear me, and we'll gather on the mountainsides and in the glens, and we'll be free again. It's a great thing, freedom. Do ye understand that, mon?"

Without waiting for a reply, the piper took the chanter in his mouth, filled the bag with air, and began playing again. He marched away along the solitary path where Oliver had come until he vanished from sight, leaving behind one last, lonely drone until it, too, faded into silence.

As if lost in a dream, Oliver stood still, forgetting where he was. The staff gave an impatient tug and dragged him onward. The path became twistier, curving around and back in a zigzag pattern.

After a while, when Oliver was breathing hard and perspiring heavily, the path took a right-angle jog, and the staff swung him around so sharply that he almost fell again. The staff planted itself firmly in place and didn't budge, and when Oliver regained his balance, he saw a sight in front of him that stopped him in his tracks.

A man clad in jester's motley hung from a tree-branch upside down. The man's hands were clasped behind him, and although one foot was suspended from a loop of rope, the other foot was free and bent behind the stationary leg to form a triangle. Seemingly unbothered by the sudden appearance of a total stranger, the hanging man stared back at Oliver and slowly closed one eye.

Oliver's jaw dropped. "Good heavens!" he gasped.

"Indeed! Agreed!" responded the hanging man, quite as cheerfully as if he weren't suspended in that uncomfortable position. "My dear sir, I concur!"

"But you're hanging!" Oliver exclaimed. "You must be in great distress! Let me help you down!" He tried to rush forward, but the staff refused to allow him to move. "Let go!" Oliver snapped.

"Never mind, Brother!" said the hanging man, with the hint of a brogue. "I'm neither hurt nor dying, except in the way of all flesh. I'm simply temporarily suspended! I'm taking time out to look at the world from a different point of view. Everything looks otherwhere when you're upside-down! A frown is a smile, and a smile's a frown! Try it sometime! Try speaking in rhyme! Be daring! Be bold! Question what you're told!"

"What do you mean? Who are you?" Oliver's eyes nearly popped out of his head as the hanging man winked again, first with one eye, then the other. Despite his eccentric position, he seemed to be in perfectly good health.

"Fly like a bee! Go climb a tree! *Hear* what you hear, and *see* what you see!" said the man, smiling although his upside-down expression looked sad.

Oliver shut his eyes tightly and shook his head to clear his vision. When he opened his eyes again, the man was gone as if he had never been there at all. The staff refused to let him linger, and Oliver continued along the path, whose zigzag curves had mysteriously straightened.

This section of the Icewode ended abruptly on the brow of a high hill, and Oliver came to the edge almost before he realized it. The staff stopped, kindly allowing him to keep his balance on the edge of the precipice while he peered about.

Saint Amber's Rose

Spread before him was a broad valley, free of snow and covered entirely with lavender and heather. Sunshine poured like rain on meadows curving around the low hills, changing color from purple to blue to lilac to lavender and every shade in between. So beautiful was the sight that it made his heart turn over. *I never knew there were places like this in the world*, he marveled, then remembered that he was no longer in the world he had once known.

He made a telescope of his hands (the staff, in a momentary lenient mood, permitted him to do so) and focused on something small and square at the nearer end of the valley. *Surely that's a house! And another one across the way!* It had to be a village, and the path led right through it. He couldn't see any people moving about, but of course he was too far away.

He squared his shoulders, grasped the staff again, and started down toward the purple valley. Someone in the village might help him on his way. The Hermit said so, but there was no telling how far one could trust the custodian of the Ruined Chapel.

The cozy little hamlet was only one street wide, lined with thatch-roofed cottages with flower-filled window boxes. Oddly, no one seemed to be up and about even though it was broad daylight. One expected people to be going about their business, doing their marketing and visiting, the children in school, cattle and sheep in the pastures cropping grass.

But absolutely no one was visible. The place seemed to be deserted. Oliver strolled on through the village, and the staff obligingly slowed down so that he could peek through the windows of several shops lining the street. All the buildings appeared to be empty. One of the shops, a bakery, had its half-door swinging open, as if someone had run out only a moment ago and forgotten to close it.

Oliver ventured inside. "Hello?" he called hesitantly. "Hello! Is anyone there?" But no one answered. He picked up a bell on the counter and rang it; the silvery tone echoed in the room.

No one appeared. *How strange.*

Even more puzzling, the counter had several warm loaves lying on it. Fresh bread! He took a deep breath of the yeasty aroma. Someone must have been here to bake these loaves. *Why isn't anyone minding the store?*

The scent of new bread made his stomach growl. "Forgive me," he murmured aloud, taking hold of the smallest loaf. He tore off a corner and put it in his mouth. How good it was! after weeks and weeks of almost nothing but journey-bread, which, while strengthening, had no particular flavor to speak of. He wolfed down half the loaf and felt infinitely better. Then he scrabbled about in his pockets for loose change to leave in payment, but found nothing. Once he found someone to talk to, he'd find out where the baker went and explain his situation.

A greengrocer ought to be around somewhere, too, where he might obtain a bit of cheese to go with the rest of the bread, and maybe an apple or some grapes. *And what I wouldn't give for a nice cup of tea!*

On the other side of the street was a shop that looked hopeful. It had a couple of bins standing outside, one full of red and yellow apples, the other with purple grapes practically bursting out of their skins. The shop was straight across the road from the bakery, just past a spreading chestnut tree. Oliver stepped outside the bakery, looked both ways before crossing the empty street (an ingrained safety habit), and walked briskly toward the greengrocery.

WHOOSH! A net closed around him; a rope jerked him high in the air before he realized what had happened. He swung back and forth in his woven cage, suspended between earth and sky. The staff lay where it fell on the ground, no more good to him than a dead stick. "Help!" he shouted feebly, "Help!" and struggled to extricate himself, but his fingers tore uselessly at the knots that enclosed him.

Suddenly an unseen rooster let out a triumphant crow, and an aged man in farmer's clothes and a veil-draped sun hat hobbled out from between two cottages at the end of the street. Cautiously he advanced toward the chestnut where Oliver dangled like a Christmas-tree ornament.

"Help! Can you help me out of here, please?" Oliver called out as soon as he spotted the man. "I'll pay for the bread! I didn't intend to steal it, I assure you! Please help me!"

But the old man waited until he was directly in front of Oliver's netted cage before he answered. "Well, now," he said in a high, rather squeaky voice. "'Twon't do you any good to make all that noise. You walked straight into a *wyrga* trap."

"*Wyrga*?" Oliver exclaimed. "No, I assure you I'm not one! I'm innocent of any crime, except for the bread, and I give my solemn word of honor that I'll make full restitution! Won't you help me down?"

The aged man considered for a moment, but shook his head. "I'm sorry, stranger," he said at last. "I'd help you if I could, but it wouldn't do you any good. Nope." He turned to walk away, shuffling his rheumatic feet slowly over the cobblestones.

"Wait!" Oliver called desperately. "Wait, please!" But the last glimpse he had was of a bent back disappearing between two cottages.

Now the villagers began to emerge from wherever they had hidden themselves, edging warily closer to the tree where Oliver hung imprisoned in mid-air. Despite his pleas, they said not a word in reply. They simply gathered around the tree and glared at him, muttering to each other.

One woman, the baker, to judge by her white toque and powerful, flour-dusted arms, raised her forefinger and pointed at him. "That's one of 'em fer sure," she declared. "That's one of them nasty, thievin' *wyrga*! Stealin' the bread outta the mouths of our chillern! I seen 'im with my own eyes!"

"That's right, Elsie Flourhands," someone chimed in. "We got 'im this time!"

"Let's take care of 'im right now!" shouted someone else. "No sense wastin' a trial on that sort!"

A group of boys and girls on the outskirts of the mob picked up stones and began lobbing them toward the net. No one moved to stop them.

"No! Wait!" cried Oliver, wrestling hopelessly with the knots of his woven cage. "Please, ladies and gentlemen! Madam Flourhands! I am not a *wyrga*! I admit that I took possession of a loaf of bread from the bakeshop over there, and I--I must compliment you highly! It was delicious, superior in flavor, texture, and nutritive value to any other loaf of bread I've tasted. I took it only because I was desperately hungry and couldn't find anyone to pay! I'll make restitution--I long to make restitution--twice over--three times over--if only you'll let me down!"

"'Ear 'im talk!" jeered another voice. "It's almost like a reg'lar person!"

"It's a disguise, I bet! He's a *wyrga*! Didn't I tell you I seen one a-sneakin' away from my south forty yesterday, leavin' one o' them burnt-over circles on it?"

"He's a *wyrga*! Let's git rid of 'im!"

"Cain't let 'im go, he'll be up to more of 'is evil tricks!"

"What'll we do with 'im?"

"Hang 'im!"

"He's a-hangin' already, Jem Doaks! Cain't you see that?"

"Boil 'im in oil, then!"

"Yeah! Let's get the cauldron and lower 'im into some boilin' oil!"

"He'll be talkin' outta the other side of his mouth then, I'll say!"

"Tryin' to make like we don't know a *wyrga* when we see one!"

Oliver's stress level now exceeded, by far, any scale of measurement ever devised. "No! Please! Let me explain!" he shouted over the rising anger of the villagers. "I'm truly not a *wyrga*! I've never been in your south forty, sir! I've never been here before at all! I came from--from Keeper's Inn!" Unsure how much he ought to reveal, even at this delicate stage in his journey--which could end abruptly at any moment, he decided to mention the inn first. The villagers must certainly have heard of it.

"'Ow do we know that?" was the question, stated with a sneer. "Anybody can say that!"

"But I really am!" Oliver yelled over the uproar. His words were drowned out as more and more people came out of their hiding places to see the fun. Already two men were piling up kindling directly beneath him, enough for a bonfire. Two others ran to a nearby smithy, crying, "Fetch the cauldron!"

Oliver's contortions agitated the net, bouncing it up, down, and sideways. The thought occurred to him that if he could make the net swing far enough to the side where it hung from the tree, maybe he could grab a branch and pull himself up. He didn't see how he could get out of the net, but he might at least be able to avoid plunging into a cauldron of boiling oil.

He strained to one side, then the other, trying to make the net swing a little farther each time. He did get it going a little way, but the villagers who noticed him only laughed, grasping at once the futility of what he was doing.

Swing... swing... swing. His self-made pendulum described a greater and greater arc out and back, out and back. *Almost had it that time!* Swing again, harder, harder! He squinted down below: They were indeed making a fire right underneath him! A wisp of smoke curled up, teasing his nostrils. The enormous black cauldron, now in place over the blaze, looked like a bottomless well. People ran to it, pouring buckets of cooking oil into its depths until it was filled almost to the brim.

Oliver redoubled his efforts. He had stopped shouting, realizing that it wasn't doing him any good. Better to use his remaining energy to grab that branch tantalizingly close to his fingers. "*Va'in 'a moru', Sendara. Va'in 'a moru',*" he whispered, unaware that he was doing so and unaware of its meaning. At that point he was past caring.

"Fire! Fire! Build it higher!" chanted the mob below. "Pour in oil! Make it boil!"

Swing... swing. The branch holding the net creaked and groaned with his weight and the force of his movements. Another fear popped into his overwrought mind: *What if the branch breaks? I'd plunge into the boiling oil!*

Swing... swing... SWING! On the last swing, he stuck his hand as far as he could out of the net, groping for a branch, leaves, even a twig. Instead, another hand, distinctly human, clutched his and held on.

"Don't worry, sir!" cried the hand's owner. "Just hold on tight! I'm going to give you a branch to grab onto while I swing the net up where you can get a purchase. There, that's right! You've got to help me now, sir! Roll your weight forward, can you, and then you'll be on the platform!"

One last heave, fueled by the power of fear, and Oliver bumped onto the floor of a treehouse built like a boat and anchored in the tree's canopy. He lay trembling and wheezing inside the net, unable to summon the strength to move.

"You there, *wyrga!*" called one of the mob. "Don't be thinking you're safe from us! We'll git you when the pot's hot!" Hoarse laughter arose from the crowd.

"Don't mind them, sir!" said Oliver's rescuer. "They can't get up here and they know it! I hauled up the ladder. Now we've got to get you out of that net. Let me see if I've got something to cut the ropes with. Oh, say! That's a dagger you've got on your belt! I guess you can't reach it yourself, can you. Here, I'll get it. Oops, excuse me, sir! There. Oh, it really is from Keeper's Inn! *Severnet*, it says. I've heard about the fine swords and daggers they make there. Wish I had one! What? Sure, I'll cut you out of that net before you can sing a chorus of 'A-Rowing Down the Sunder'." He fell to work, and the knots parted before the shining blade like tow. Soon Oliver was free of the entangling skein.

"Oil's a-boilin'!" cried a man in the mob. "You come on down here, ya evil *wyrga,* and git what's comin' to ya!"

"He ain't comin' down there, Eff Dibble, and you can put that fire out! You won't be needin' it today!" yelled the rescuer.

"That ain't fer you to say, Bertie Mossgrower," replied the man. "It's fer yer elders and betters to decide. You jist send that *wyrga* down here, and we'll take care o' the rest."

"I ain't a-goin' to do that, and you ain't a-comin' up here neither," replied the rescuer. "This ain't no *wyrga,* I tell you. You-all ain't never even seen a *wyrga,* which is why you don't know what you got a-hangin' in your *wyrga*-trap! This here's a gentleman from Keeper's Inn, and he's got one of their daggers. See!" And he brandished the slim weapon at them, catching the sun's rays and flashing them into the villagers' eyes.

"That don't prove nothin'!" scoffed another man. "He coulda got that anywhere. Prob'ly stole it. We ain't heard any news from Keeper's Inn fer years. You cain't trust a stranger just 'cause he says he's from there."

"You tell 'im, Snert Fardle!" said a voice at the edge of the crowd.

"Talk! Jist talk! That ain't gonna git us nowhere!" shouted another man from the outer edge of the mob. "We gotta git that *wyrga* down here, and I'll show you how we're a-gonna do it!" With that, he rushed forward through the crowd, scattering villagers left and right. He ran to the magnificent old chestnut tree, an axe glittering in his hands, and drew the weapon back to strike at the trunk.

But that was too much for the villagers. A concerted gasp of horror broke from them, and in a twinkling the mob transformed itself into a community.

"Hold on there, Tam Bludgeon! Stop!" they cried. "Think what you're doin', man!"

"You cain't hurt that tree!"

"Why, that chestnut's pert' near as old as the Great Mountain o' Zund!"

"It's got roots goin' to the bottom of the world!"

Two burly men dashed to the axe-wielding fanatic and pinioned his arms before he could deliver the fatal blow. The villagers, once again a reasonable citizenry, breathed a collective sigh of relief.

"Whew! That was a close one!"

"Aw, that Tam Bludgeon's always been impulsive."

"Needs a wife to settle 'im down."

"He cain't find a woman that'll marry 'im! That's the problem."

Much laughter at that observation.

"Anyways, our tree's all right."

"Yeah, but we still got that *wyrga* up there."

"You mean, if he really is one."

"Mayhap we don't egg-zakly know fer sure, one way or t'other."

"Why don't we ask Bertie Mossgrower? He's the one up there with 'im."

"How would Bertie know? He's just a boy!"

"He's smart, though."

"Right, that he is."

"Mayhap he kin find out what that *wyrga*--er, gentleman--is up to."

"Hey there, Bertie Mossgrower!" came from a large man with a flaming red beard.

Bertie's brown-eyed, impish face peeked through the leafy canopy. "What?" he answered as Oliver cautiously stretched his cramped limbs.

"What's that *wyr*--er, gentleman--up to? Kin you ask him?"

"I might," said Bertie, perfectly aware of his advantage. "Depends."

"On what?" inquired the man persuasively.

"On if you was to behave yourselves and take away that cauldron and stamp out the fire. But I already found out w'ile you was plannin' your wickedness. He knows the *Sendara*. He said the Secret Words." (This in a loud whisper.)

"He knows the *Sendara*! He said the Secret Words!" This was repeated, also in whispers, among the villagers.

Charleynne Gates

The inquirer looked up again to the boat-shaped treehouse where Bertie Mossgrower sat dangling his legs over the side, calmly munching an apple. Oliver Medley had managed to crawl into the cabin of the tree-boat, keeping well out of sight should anything happen.

"Well now, Bertie Mossgrower," continued Redbeard, "you and the gentleman up there know that anyone kin make a mistake." The villagers murmured assent, nodded heads. "Mayhap there was some mistakes made here today. We, ah, we'd like to 'pologize if we gave offense to the gentleman. And, ah, if the gentleman would like to step into my pub and have a nice cool pint of cider to refresh hisself, on the house o' course, why, he'd be very welcome."

Many willing hands came forward to assist Oliver down from the tree. He needed the assistance, for his legs were shaky and his balance unreliable after his near-death experience. Other hands brushed dust from his clothes and set his hat on his head again, and at last escorted him to the public house across the street, whose illustrated sign proclaimed it "The Flying Pig".

(The hemlock staff, unhappy at being thus callously ignored, picked itself up, hopped to a neighboring tree, and folded itself therein. Before the bark closed over it entirely, a few last words issued from the interior of the tree, to the effect of "ungrateful... didn't even invite me... see if I ever...")

The cider flowed like a cooling stream down Oliver's parched throat. Gradually his shaking limbs relaxed and his confidence returned.

"That's better, ain't it!" said the host, pleased at Oliver's appreciation of his brew.

"Ought to be," remarked another villager. "Bull Biggles here, he serves the best cider in Purple Valley."

"Best anywhere," declared someone else.

"I must thank my rescuer," Oliver said over the hubbub. "His name is Bertie Mossgrower, did you say? Is he here?"

There was some hemming and hawing. "Um, well, he ain't old enough to be in a pub," said someone in an embarrassed kind of voice.

"Oh?" said Oliver. "If it weren't for him I would have met a dreadful fate! I must go and find him. Can someone tell me where he lives? Or did he return to school?"

Saint Amber's Rose

"Bertie Mossgrower in school?" someone jibed. "He's the biggest truant in the valley! That lad's skipped more school than all of us put together!"

"I wouldn't say that, Flint Snipperson," someone else remarked. "You and Snert and Tam missed more school than you ever went to, that's fer certain!"

A laugh broke out. "No, you won't find Bertie in the schoolhouse."

"He's prob'ly gone down to Sunder Spring."

"They's some nice mosswort grows there. He picks it to take home to his grandmother, what he lives with down at the end of the common."

"Ah!" said Oliver. "Then if someone would kindly direct me to Sunder Spring--"

"Nothin' easier," said pub-owner Biggles. "You jist go down Chestnut Street, that's the main road what goes through the village, which the chestnut tree grows on, the same as you was--er, anyway, down Chestnut Street. When you git to the end of the cobblestones, you turn right once and left twice--"

"No, that ain't it a-tall!" a woman exclaimed. "You turn left once and right twice, where Old Puddin'ton's got his rabbit hutch."

"That ain't right either!" a man yelled. "You turn left twice and right once after you pass the oak grove!"

"Right twice and left once!"

"Right once and left twice at the well!"

"Left once and right twice!"

"No, you gotta turn left three times after you git to the well--"

The argument looked to continue interminably, and Oliver began to wish he were already on his way, if he ever found out which way that might be.

"They're all wrong, sir!" piped up a voice close to Oliver. Glancing up, to both sides, and finally down, he found its owner scrunched in a dark corner under the bar, the same Bertie Mossgrower who had saved him from a horrible death. "You come with me, sir," Bertie said in a stage whisper. "I'll show you the way out." With that, the youngster led Oliver unnoticed past the throng of debaters and outside into the sunlit day.

-- 289 --

"This way, sir," said young Bertie. "No need to thank me, Mr. Medley. It was kind o' fun! O' course I know it wa'n't fun fer you, a-hangin' in that there ol' *wyrga*-trap. Beggin' your pardon, Mr. Medley. I didn't mean no offense. It's just that it was almost like an Adventure, you know. Usually nothin' ever happens in this one-horse town, so I'm glad you happened to drop by. I like the way you talk, Mr. Medley. You sound just like a book."

"Thank you," Oliver responded, correctly interpreting the remark as a compliment.

"I wish I could talk like that," Bertie said, admiring. "I think it's real elegant. Oh, and"--reluctantly--"here's your dagger back, Mr. Medley. I didn't want you to think I forgot about it. It sure is a beautiful dagger! Never thought I'd get to see a real one from Keeper's Inn, let alone hold it. Look how the blade flashes in the light! Well... here it is, Mr. Medley."

"Why don't you keep it, Bertie," said Oliver. "I'm sure you'd be far more proficient with it than I ever would."

"You mean it, Mr. Medley?" Bertie's face lit up like the noonday sun. "Thanks! But--won't you be needing it yourself? On your journey?"

Oliver tried and failed to imagine himself actually wielding a dagger, or, for that matter, any weapon deadlier than a gardening trowel.

"I don't think so," he said. "I doubt if anything on my journey will come to that pass."

They walked to the far end of Chestnut Street (away from the fateful tree) and through a gate in a picket fence in front of a whitewashed cottage some distance from the village. "The Quarterdeck" was the name painted on the mailbox, with a design of a befouled anchor with leaping dolphins. A tall pole like the mast on a ship stood in front of the cottage, and upon it a red pennant fluttered freely.

Bertie went rapidly along a path of white gravel raked to perfection, with a tidy border of clam shells on both sides. The path guided them to the back of the cottage, where a well-tended garden of herbs, vegetables, and flowers was laid out with geometrical precision. Two sun-browned men who were hoeing cabbages looked up and grinned at Bertie. Several beehive boxes were lined up in strict formation in a glade behind the garden, tended by a beekeeper in protective clothing and a veiled hat.

"We're straight on course, Uncle Nunks," Bertie called to him. The beekeeper took off his hat and waved, and Oliver recognized the old man who had first spotted him hanging from the chestnut tree. "When Uncle Nunks saw you, he knew right away you wasn't no *wyrga*. He came and got me, and I shinnied up the tree where they couldn't see me from below and hauled up the rope ladder. We figured I could help you better that way.

"Uncle Nunks ran away to sea when he was a boy," Bertie chattered as they hurried along. "That's how he knows all about ships. He helped me build the treehouse just like a boat. He'd still be on a ship 'cept he got the rheumatics from climbing the rigging in wet weather and had to come back and live here. He don't--doesn't like the gossipy ways of the village and the people so afraid of anything new and different. He's goin' to go back to sea one of these days, and I'm goin' with him. We're bored with bein' stuck here in the village.

"I live with my grandmother and help her with the moss crop. It's slow work, doin' the same thing over and over, year in and year out. Uncle Nunks says it's no place for a boy with spirit. We're buildin' a real ship in the barn out back, and someday... Here he is, Uncle Nunks!" he finished as they came up to the beekeeper. "This is Mister Medley, Uncle. He's come all the way from Keeper's Inn. And--and he's goin' on an Adventure!" he finished, unable to hide his excitement.

Before Oliver could ask how he discovered that, Bertie turned to him, hope shining all over his face, and said, "Oh sir, you are going on an Adventure, aren't you? Please, sir, take me with you! I'm desperate for an Adventure!"

Chapter Sixteen

The Sundering

"So you've undertaken an Adventure, Mr. Medley! How I envy you! Many's the time I've sailed on the *Grand Adventure* before rheumatism caught up with me. Tell me about your plans!" said Uncle Nunks (actually Admiral Sir John Horatio Nunkins (ret.)), proprietor of the impeccably neat cottage, garden, barn, and beehives). His voice was much stronger, his grammar more educated, than when Oliver hung in the *wyrga*-trap. The three of them sat comfortably in the parlor, having an excellent tea with hot buttered muffins from which appleblossom honey dripped golden tears.

"Honey," Mr. Nunkins declared as he handed them delicate bone china cups, "is Nature's most valuable food. Since I've been keeping bees and enjoying the products of their industry, my aches and pains have diminished considerably. I don't let on, though, not in the village. Best not to be too conspicuous hereabouts."

Mr. Nunkins had pointed out his helpers in the garden as they passed. "Mr. Steward and Mr. Boatswain are working among the vegetables"--the two men paused in their work and touched forelocks to Oliver--"and Mr. Carpenter is out in the barn. We've been shipmates for more years than any of us can remember." ("Uncle Nunks was a sea-captain," Bertie whispered solemnly. Oliver was duly impressed.) "Come in! Come in!" continued their host, waving them inside. "You're most welcome. We have few guests from the world outside Purple Valley."

Oliver gratefully took advantage of plentiful hot water, soap, fluffy white towels—and a spare razor. He felt much better after he had sloughed off the last traces of Origin Dust.

Mr. Nunkins was well advanced in years, to judge by the network of seams and wrinkles in his face and his white hair tied back in a neat club, but his blue eyes sparkled, and his movements, as he poured tea from a Georgian silver teapot, were economical (as befits an old salt), and his hand perfectly steady. He listened with complete concentration as Bertie, with due modesty but barely concealed excitement, recited the details of how he had rescued Oliver from the villagers who were about to boil him alive, having mistaken the innocent wayfarer for a *wyrga*.

Mr. Nunkins shook his head soberly over the story. 'They're not a bad lot," he remarked to Oliver, "but being superstitious and virtually uneducated--few of them stay more than two or three years at school-- and generally uninterested in reading anything but the almanac, they're easily stirred up. I've seen them change from a cooperative community into a mindless mob in the twinkling of an eye simply because they won't apply reason to a given situation." He looked weary as he spoke, as if he had seen it happen far too often.

"Bertie here," he continued, "had as much instruction as the village school could give him--his grandmother and I saw to that-- although he played the truant a few more times than was absolutely necessary. Didn't you, lad?"

Bertie hung his head, but soon brightened up as his uncle went on.

"He advanced quickly beyond the other children, so I began to teach him what I know about ships and sailing. We may have neglected his grammar to a degree"--Bertie blushed--"but he took to trigonometry and celestial navigation like a whale to the open ocean, and the shipmates have taught him about lines and shrouds and sailors' knots. Young Bertie, before you get too puffed up for the likes of your old uncle, would you run out and invite the shipmates in for tea."

Though pleasantly phrased, it was not a suggestion. Bertie stood up immediately with a cheerful "Aye, sir!" and ran outside, leaving Oliver alone with his host.

"Now then, Mr. Medley," said Mr. Nunkins, leaning forward, his sky-colored eyes alight with interest, "I'd like to know your whole story. I've sailed all over this world and touched the shores of a few others in my time. I've seen marvels beyond imagining, so you needn't think I won't believe you. How did you get into the Labyrinth World, and what is your real purpose here?"

Sensing Mr. Nunkins' keen intelligence, Oliver decided to unburden himself. What a tremendous relief it was, to trust another person without any niggling fear that he might be divulging secrets to someone unworthy of his confidence! During his whole narration, from the day Great-Aunt Belvedine burst into his office back in the Maze World (he still couldn't recall the proper name of the place, although it was on the tip of his tongue) to the moment he stepped into the *wyrga* trap beneath the chestnut tree, Mr. Nunkins focused steadily on him. Oliver felt that piercing glance go through and through him, as if his every word were being carefully weighed in the scales of truth.

Mr. Nunkins allowed a few moments of considering silence to pass between them when Oliver finished. "I think you've done well, Mr. Medley," he said slowly. "Very well indeed, under the circumstances. I'd have been proud to have you as one of my officers."

Oliver flushed at the praise. Maybe he hadn't been quite as idiotic as he thought. Maybe there was still a chance to get to the Abbey of Saint Amber and to use his Gift, whatever it was, to help Flavia.

"--best for you to stay here for a few days," Mr. Nunkins went on as the footsteps of Bertie and the shipmates were heard on the walkway. "And be on your way when you're well rested. Don't worry about the villagers; they don't bother us here. Now then, Mr. Medley, Bertie, we'll plot your course. You'll be able to take the Sunder River as far as the Great Mountain of Zund. Bertie has a boat, small but serviceable, and he can take you at least part of the way. If he's up to the task."

"Uncle Nunks!" Bertie cried, beside himself with anticipation. "You mean I can go with Mr. Medley? On an Adventure? Hooray!"

"If Mr. Medley will have you," Mr. Nunkins said severely.

Oliver professed himself grateful for both advice and companionship, for otherwise he had no idea how to get where he was going.

Mr. Nunkins hoisted himself out of his chair and went toward a room leading off the parlor. "We'd better take a look at the charts, then," he said. "I haven't been on the Sunder since I was a lad younger than Bertie, so I'll have to remind myself about its twists and turns. Bertie, ask Mr. Boatswain to come into the study, if you please."

Mr. Nunkins' study was lined with bookshelves crammed with volumes on mathematics, navigation, astronomy, medicine, surgery, and ichthyology, together with that well-thumbed old standard, Clarke's *Seamanship*. Works on naval warfare were interspersed with biographies of distinguished fighting sea-captains such as Aubrey,

Hornblower, and Nelson. Celestial and terrestrial globes covered the tables, and spyglasses, sextants, compasses, and other instruments lay about the room.

"Here's a chart of the Sunder." Mr. Nunkins selected one of several scrolls and unrolled it across the desk. "It's old, but the most recent one I have. As I recall, the river is navigable for most of its length."

Mr. Nunkins' finger traced the course of the Sunder from nearby Sunder Spring where it had its birth, down its manifold meanderings on the way to the massive Mountains of Zund.

"As you see, the river circles the Great Mountain of Zund, passing by the cliff where the Abbey of Saint Amber sits. There is, or used to be, a dock for small boats directly beneath the Abbey. You can tie up there and ascend to the Abbey by means of stone steps spiraling up the mountain. The journey will probably take you a week or more. It's a very long river, is the Sunder, and doubles back on itself frequently. Yes, Mr. Boatswain?"

"One of the Raven Express messengers stopped by last week, sir. Mentioned something about a new obstruction in the Sunder between Purple Valley and the Mountains of Zund, before you get to the place where the river forks. He didn't say what it was. Seemed in a big hurry to get wherever he was going."

Mr. Nunkins frowned thoughtfully. "Hmm. Probably a downed tree or a rockslide into the river. You may have to make portage around it. Could it be some device of the Lord of Desolation? No, I'm sure I would have heard if his infernal *wyrga* had encroached this far. The messenger said nothing more?"

Mr. Boatswain shook his head. "Nothing, sir. As I said, he was in an awful rush. Didn't seem very happy about whatever it was that he saw."

"The raven is not a happy bird at the best of times," Mr. Nunkins observed. "But your reports have always been on the mark, Mr. Boatswain. Take notice, Mr. Medley, Bertie."

For the next few days Oliver was glad to bide his time at Mr. Nunkins' cottage, eating well and often and strolling along rose-bordered lanes around the bee-loud glade.

I wish I could stay here in this peaceful garden. I could so easily forget about the bad things--the Forbeodan Tunnels, that monster in the lake... the darkness I feel around me, that no one else seems to notice. I could so easily forget about this Gift I'm supposed to have. It was probably just someone's misconception in the first place. And Flavia--what chance is there that I'll ever see her again? She left the Ruined Chapel with Pavarr. He'll protect her. He--he's better for her than I am. Why break my heart over what I can never have?

An unseen bird chirped softly, and from deeper in the wood its mate answered. Oliver took no notice. He walked to the end of the lane, where a patch of purple-flowered thistles barred his way farther.

I didn't ask for any of this. I only wanted a little adventure--not all these dangers and trepidations! What I really want is my pleasant, peaceful life back. I'd be content to stay in my own garden 'til the end of my days.

I don't want to go on.

He turned away from the barrier of thistles and walked back toward the cottage.

I'll ask Mr. Nunkins. He knows things; maybe he can help me find a way back to my own world. Yes. That's what I'll do. I've come as far as I can in this one, and I haven't done anything but damage as far as I can see. After all, it was my fault that Flavia was abducted.

There was that incident at Nether Lake, when Tapp... but anyone would have done the same. I just happened to be there. Pavarr can take Flavia to the Abbey quite well without me. I'd only be a burden to them. Pavarr and Flavia... They don't need me.

Thus, sinking ever deeper into a quagmire of self-pity, Oliver reached his decision and set off to find his host.

But before he could carry out his recreant intent, Mr. Nunkins himself appeared, his beekeeping labors over for the day, and invited Oliver to sit with him in the garden and have a pipe and a cup of tea. Oliver declined the pipe but accepted the tea, and for the rest of the afternoon enjoyed the company of a man he grew increasingly to respect.

Not since his boyhood, when he and his father had talked about anything and everything that interested them, had Oliver known easy and unassuming companionship. Mr. Nunkins, with his broad and intimate knowledge of this and other worlds, supplied what Oliver had lacked for all those years. Much did he learn from Mr. Nunkins'

Saint Amber's Rose

wisdom and experience, and of the risks of opening one's heart to all that life has to offer.

"When I lost my dear wife, and our child with her, I thought my life would never be worth living again. I was like a dead man. My heart dried up and became a stone in my breast. But as I sailed on the *Grand Adventure*, I discovered that life went on despite my sorrows. As we touched different lands, I met different peoples, learned new things, and my heart began to heal. I took courage and decided to live again." Mr. Nunkins drew on his old churchwarden pipe, and as the white smoke curled around his head, looked into a far-away landscape in his mind's eye.

"It was my fault, you know. It was I who started all the--the troubles," Oliver said after a while, gazing intently into his teacup as if the assurance he sought would be revealed in the dark leaves. "Because of me, the Quest will come to a bad end."

"No one can know the end from the beginning," the older man remarked. "The only thing we can do is to go on, even when there is nothing but darkness around us."

"I'm afraid of the dark," said Oliver humbly. "How can I go on?"

"By finding the courage to believe in what you cannot see."

And with this enigmatic remark Oliver had to be content. Nor did he again muster the resolve to ask Mr. Nunkins how he might get back to his own world.

Mr. Nunkins repeated his careful directions on the morning of departure over a hearty breakfast of eggs and sausage, bowls of berries and cream, buttered hotcakes with wildflower honey, and plenty of hot tea. Not knowing when he would have the opportunity to eat a proper meal again, Oliver tucked away all the food he could manage.

"You'd best take one of my spyglasses, Bertie," said Mr. Nunkins. "And I've marked an area on the chart that may be questionable. It is an old chart, you know, and does not reflect recent changes in the river. The rapids may be more treacherous than formerly, and that could mean a longer expanse of whitewater to navigate. Have you any experience with whitewater, Mr. Medley?"

The image wasn't clear, but Oliver had a vague recollection of himself long ago, floating helplessly down a river--the Mc, McSomething--amid foaming swirls of icy water, his hand clutching the side of a large, inflatable raft. He had no idea where the image came from, but the feeling wasn't at all pleasant, and he shut the door of his memory firmly against it. "I... think I've seen some," he replied.

Mr. Nunkins may have had misgivings, but he kept them to himself and bade the two adventurers a cheerful farewell. "Remember: Keep a sharp lookout. Take your bearings several times a day, Bertie. One of you should stay on watch at all times. A good voyage to you both."

Bertie led the way toward Sunder Spring, spyglass and rolled-up chart in hand. "It's not far, Mr. Medley," he called over his shoulder. "We'll be there in no time. And then--Adventure!"

Oliver stood on the muddy bank and stared down at the sluggish, weed-infested trickle that was the River Sunder at its source. Tied to the dock--one splintery plank stuck in the mud--was a small rowboat with a few streaks of red paint on its weathered sides and a couple of beat-up oars in the bottom. The name *Venture For--* was painted in faded black letters on its side, except that the *th* was missing. Oliver couldn't figure out how the boat even floated, so shallow was the stream at this point.

"There's my boat!" Bertie pointed out with pardonable pride. "Ain't--isn't she a beauty?"

Oliver's heart sank. This was supposed to carry them the length of the Sunder? This little rowboat that looked as if it might sink if it got into water deeper than a foot or two?

But he didn't want to hurt his new friend's feelings, and managed to arrange a smile on his face. "Yes, indeed!" he said as heartily as he could. "It's a fine boat!"

What was Mr. Nunkins thinking? Surely he hadn't realized the present condition of this puny craft. And where were the flotation devices?

"Is there a flotation device aboard?" he asked.

"What? Oh, you mean one of these?" Bertie reached under the seat and dragged out a small floater attached to a frayed rope. The floater looked inadequate. Oliver looked doubtful.

"We'd better get going," said Bertie. "You can't trust those villagers. I've seen it before: One minute they're aiming to boil you alive, and the next they're pouring Bull Biggles' cider down your throat. When they get frightened, they turn into a mob, you see. They change their minds according to whichever way the wind's blowing. Once they think it over, they might take a notion to come after us. But they probably won't. People in Mossy Dell Village don't usually bother with Sunder Spring. They think it's insig--insig-nificant, and they go to Big Lake on t'other side of the village for boating and stuff. Anyway, they would've figured we were at my grandmother's. Uncle Nunks won't say nothing--anything. He's on our side. Besides, Mossy Dellers are kind of afraid of him. He's way smarter than them and they know it."

"I tell you, Mr. Medley," continued the boy seriously as he loosened the painter and brought the boat nearer. "These are strange days. Things been seen in this valley ain't, I mean, haven't never been seen before. Ashes where no fire's been. Perfectly healthy crops of moss shrivelin' up and dyin' for no reason. Trees disappearin' overnight, whole groves of them. Somethin's happening, and it ai--isn't good. We won't need to worry, though. I've got my slingshot in case of--well, just in case. Step on down, sir, that's right. It'll take your weight."

To Oliver's surprise, the boat took not only his weight but also the small oaken cask of good well water which Mr. Nunkins had thoughtfully provided. Mr. Steward had carried it down to the boat before breakfast. "Don't you go drinkin' any of that Sunder water, Master Bertie," he admonished. "No one knows what's in the river any more."

With Oliver, Bertie, and the cask sitting on the bare plank seats, the *Venture For--* was within an inch of getting mired in the mud of the stream bottom, but Bertie gave a firm shove against the dock with his splintery oar, and away they floated.

"Yessir," Bertie went on, pushing away stringy waterweeds that tried to entangle the oars in a close embrace. "I'm real glad you happened on this valley, Mr. Medley. I was about to die of boredom, being stuck here in ol' Mossy Dell Village. I mean, there's all kinds o' great things outside Purple Valley just waiting for someone to come and do them. I always wanted to be somebody, like them, I mean those heroes back in the Olden Days."

"Ah, yes," said Oliver, clutching both sides of the rowboat until his knuckles were white. "I know what you mean. Like King Arthur and his Knights of the Round Table."

"I don't know who they might be," replied Bertie, "but I'll take your word for it."

They drifted for a while in silence, with Bertie fending off the waterweeds. After a while Oliver felt secure enough to loosen his glue-like grip of the rim.

"Bertie," Medley began, speaking softly lest a sudden loud noise inadvertently cause the boat to upset. "You're sure your uncle's chart corresponds to--er--the Sunder River? This seems more like a creek than a river."

"Don't you worry, sir!" replied Bertie confidently. "This end of it ain't--I mean isn't--nothing. Pretty soon we'll come to a pond made by an old beaver dam, and after that it gets to be a real river. It'll take us out into the big world as far as we want to go!"

"If we get to the Abbey of Saint Amber, that will do just fine," said Oliver. "My sworn purpose depends upon arriving there by whatever means possible."

"Purpose, Mr. Medley? What might that be?"

Oliver hesitated. Bertie Mossgrower had certainly rescued him from a most unpleasant death, and he was, to all appearances, a clever-headed, good-hearted young person, innocent of guile. Oliver found it impossible to believe that Bertie was anything other than what he seemed. And his uncle, Mr. Nunkins, and the three shipmates exhuded seamanlike integrity.

Before he could answer, Bertie went on. "Might you be one of the hermits that lives together in the Abbey?"

"Hermits? Ah, you mean the friars. No, no," Oliver replied. "This is my first excursion there."

"Ex-cur-sion!" repeated Bertie. "Ex-cur-sion! That's a new word to me. I like the sound of it. Does it mean adventures?"

"Well, yes, I suppose it does," said Oliver. "Travels and journeys. And adventures."

"Hurray!" crowed the young man. "It's my first ex-cur-sion too!"

"Oh? You mean you've never been out of your valley before?" Oliver tensed inwardly. He hadn't thought of that possibility.

"No," Bertie admitted. "But I've wanted to for ever so long!"

"Then how do you--that is, are you certain that you, ah... hm... definitely positive that this is the correct route to the Abbey of Saint Amber?"

"Oh yes, sir!" said Bertie, with a confidence so shining and transparent that Oliver was filled with foreboding. "Uncle Nunks showed us on his chart, which is the best they make, even if it is kind of old."

"Just how old is it?" asked Oliver, feeling more concerned with each passing second.

"About a hunnert years, I guess," said Bertie proudly.

Oliver's spirits sank. If the chart was that old, then any new obstacle in the river--such as the one the Raven Express messenger warned about--wouldn't have been entered on it, nor would any changes of course in the waterway. Before he could make further inquiries, Bertie added, "If I'm not being too nosy, sir, would you be intending to enter the Order they have up at the Abbey? Going to be a friar, I mean?"

"No, not at all," said Oliver. "I wonder," he went on, neatly avoiding Bertie's potential follow-up question, "if you could tell me something about the Abbey. That is, what order of friars lives there, and what do they do?"

"What do they do!" Bertie laughed. "Everyone knows that! They're all Whiltians"--(What is a Whiltian? was on the tip of Oliver's tongue, but Bertie went right on)--"of the Order of Saint Amber, and they've lived on the Great Mountain of Zund ever since it rose up out of the sea. They're magical gardeners, so they say. There's supposed to be two of every tree and flower in the whole world planted in the Abbey gardens. They're famous healers, too. They say that anyone who's sick or injured can go there and be made well again. Birds and bears and all the wild creatures go to the Abbey when they get hurt. Even snails and spiders! They say that if a friar's shadow falls on you, you get well just from that. It must be a wonderful place! Are you sick, sir?"

"No, but Flavia is," said Oliver. The unguarded words spilled out while his mind wandered in the imaginary gardens of the Abbey.

"Who is Flavia, sir?" asked Bertie.

What have I said? thought Oliver. Had he inadvertently betrayed too much? *But Bertie must be the one the Hermit of the Ruined Chapel said would help me. He certainly has so far. I have to trust someone, and I like this young adventurer.*

He drew in a deep breath. "I have to entrust you with a great secret, Bertie," he said solemnly. "I am--that is, I was--traveling with a

-- 301 --

Charleynne Gates

group of--of friends toward the Abbey. We were taking a lady there to
be healed of a wasting illness. And this lady is... well, you would know
her by her title." He paused, then said in a whisper, "The *Sendara.*" He
thought it best to keep his explanation short and simple and not mention
anything about his Gift.

The oars stopped working and plopped on the water. Bertie sat
upright on the plank, openmouthed and staring. "The *Sendara!*" he
breathed. "You've seen her? Is she--is she really real?"

"Why, yes," Oliver replied. "I thought you knew her! When I
was caught in that trap in the village, you said I said the Secret Words. I
wasn't aware of saying them, and I don't remember what they were, but
you told the villagers that I knew the *Sendara.* And they let me go."

"Sure they did," said Bertie. "Everyone's heard about the
Sendara. And you did say the Secret Words. 'Course nobody in the
valley knows what they mean, and no one here has ever seen her. I
always thought she was somebody high up and far away somewhere. I
never imagined she was really real, not like us down in the village."

He was silent for a moment, letting the little boat drift and the
oars flirt with the waterweeds again. "But," he resumed as Oliver was
about to mention the waterweeds, "a few of us, like me and Uncle
Nunks and the shipmates, we know about the Secret Words. They're
kind of a code that shows you're on the right side of things. *Va'in 'a
moru', Sendara*, is what it is, you see."

"But what do they mean?" asked Oliver. "The words just came
out of me. I don't remember hearing them before."

"I don't rightly know," replied Bertie. "But it makes me feel
good to say them. It's like they make me believe I can do bigger things
than I ever figured I could. They open up something inside of you, like
the whole wide world is out there waiting, and--and everything you've
ever dreamed of is just over the next hill. I guess I'm not doing a very
good job of explaining."

"I think you're doing an excellent job," said Oliver sincerely.

"Anyway," Bertie went on, flushing pink at the compliment,
"when anyone says those words, we know he's not one of them, those,
ordinary-type Mossy Dellers, only thinkin' about what they're goin' to
have for dinner that day, and doin' every single day what they did the
day before, and never wantin' anything different than what they've had
all their lives. Never wantin' to go on ex-cur-sions and find out what

Saint Amber's Rose

life is like beyond Purple Valley. They don't know what it means to
want to have High Adventures! No sir, they don't know and don't care,
and I've had enough o' them!"

Having made that point, Bertie was silent for a while, teasing
the oars away from the affectionate weeds as Oliver mulled over what
the boy had said. *High Adventure. Noble Deeds. And Flavia. Above
all else, always and ever, Flavia. Where is she?* He hoped she had
arrived safely at the Abbey by now. Disconnected figments of
imagination drifted around his mind, entangling themselves like the
waterweeds around the oars.

The boat floated on, more smoothly now that the stream was
wider from bank to bank. The stream bed was still shallow, and every
now and then he felt the boat scrape the muddy bottom lightly. Bertie
kept on fending off the long, trailing weeds, and soon they became
fewer and fewer until the tops of the trailing plants were completely
underwater and could only wave woefully at the boat as it drifted over
them.

Cautiously Medley leaned over the side to take a look at the
stream, and discovered not only that he could no longer see the bottom,
but also that there were distinct objects deep down in the water. Faces...
human-looking faces, bodiless, not those of the drowned, as was his first
thought, but live, impish faces with wide-open eyes that stared at him
and mouths that mocked him with rude grimaces. And there was
another face, too, one that seemed oddly familiar. It had eyes like
yellow flames, eyes that commanded him to lean farther over the boat,
and *he wanted to obey...*

A bird of some kind swooped in front of him, and the tip of its
wing brushed against his head, breaking his trance. He jerked upright,
white to the gills. Not that he was afraid of falling in the water, it was
simply that he didn't know what forms of aquatic life were present in the
depths of that odd rivulet, and after his experience at Nether Lake, he
thought it best to be cautious. He glanced over at Bertie, wondering if
he had seen the same faces in the water, but that young man seemed
oblivious to anything but steering away from the last of those pesky
waterweeds.

At last Bertie shipped his oars and sat upright, wiping
perspiration from his brow. "Pretty warm work!" he said. "Want to
take a turn at the oars, Mr. Medley?"

"I've never done much--" Oliver started to say, then took a second look at the hopeful face of his new partner in adventure. "Certainly," he said, and the two of them changed places. Oliver moved slowly, for not only did he want to insure that the boat remained steady, but also the condition of the floorboards, patched and worn thin, was not such that he really wanted to put his full weight on them.

He managed the transfer without incident and took the oars, trying to imitate what Bertie had done. Taking a firm grip and bending radically forward, he swung them out wildly, first rowing a great swath of air and then dipping much too deep down in the water, where the weeds once again clasped them in a tender embrace. Oliver expected the oars to come along with him as he tried to complete the stroke, but the weeds had other ideas. Due to the violent stoppage of his efforts, he fell over backward.

"Uh-oh," said Bertie to himself. "Not much of a sailor. Maybe his other adventures were mostly on land."

They rowed on. Bertie instructed him as they went, and eventually Oliver learned to handle the oars less like eggbeaters and more like instruments for propelling a boat. He began to enjoy himself. The day was pleasant, the air summery, and the scenery changed with each bend in the river. As the channel grew deeper, the luxuriant crops of mosses, ferns, mugworts, and mushrooms raised by the farmers of Purple Valley gave way to fields of wild grasses and trees, some of which were new and strange to him.

"We're in country now, sir," Bertie remarked, and Oliver opined that it looked that way to him also. One tree he did recognize: an overhanging willow that trailed its pale green leaves in the water and murmured with every breeze. As they floated underneath, dodging the gracefully bending branches, Oliver thought he heard words in the willows' murmurings, but although he concentrated, he couldn't catch what they said.

To pass the time, he explained to Bertie about King Arthur and the Knights of the Round Table. With shining eyes, the lad peppered him with questions about what you had to do to be a knight. Oliver told him everything he could remember about Arthur and Lancelot, Gawain and Galahad until his memory ran dry.

After several hours of rowing shared between the two of them, they floated quietly into a large beaver-dam pond, placid and dappled with light and shadow. Bertie said they could rest a while under the willows, out of direct sunlight, and have something to eat. Oliver was glad to ship oars for a while, for the novelty of rowing had worn off. His hands were stiff and rather sore, and his stomach was making insistent noises. After lunch would be a good time to plan the further details of carrying out his--their--mission of getting to the Abbey of Saint Amber.

Bertie made a loop in the painter and tossed it expertly over a smooth hump of rock on the bank. They ate luncheon from Bertie's knapsack, bread from the Mossy Dell baker--excellent bread, too--and a pungent cheese, with leeks and pickled peppers on the side and a crimson apple apiece for dessert, all washed down with sweet water from Mr. Nunkins's well. As the food soothed Oliver's hunger pangs and spread contentment through his body, he began to feel more like an Adventurer. *Why not do some fishing here?* he wondered, oblivious to the fact that he had never fished in his life. *A nice bit of trout--or salmon--or whatever grew here--wouldn't come amiss.*

"Fishing in the Sunder?" Bertie said. "I don't think I'd try it, sir. Nobody exactly knows what lives in the Sunder any more. The villagers don't use water from Sunder Spring, and they fish over at Big Lake."

"It was just a thought," said Oliver, relieved.

The sun warmed them on the outside; lunch warmed them on the inside. Brown water lapped lazily against the side of the *Venture For--*, and the boat with its two passengers drifted back and forth, back and forth on its painter, bobbing gently in the slow current. Oliver yawned, basking in the pleasant afternoon. Both heads fell forward onto their chests at the same moment. Bertie and Oliver dozed.

The sun moved on, at one point hiding coyly behind a fluffy white cloud. A tiny breeze slithered through the willow branches. It didn't waken the two slumbering boatmen, but it did tickle a black nostril protruding from the lump of rock where Bertie had looped the boat's painter. The rock--in reality not a rock at all but a one-humped Sunder stonecritter (*Petroanimus sunderensis*)--opened a baleful moss-green eye and rose to its feet in the manner of a cat stretching after a nap. Noticing that an unwelcome constraint fettered its movements, it wriggled its slate-y skin until the loop slid onto the grassy bank. Its freedom restored, the stonecritter ambled away, intent upon its private business.

Unmoored, the *Venture For--* drifted slowly until it reached the other end of the pond. There, time and weather had forced a small breech in the dam that the long-vanished beaver colony had painstakingly constructed. The boat rested against the log-and-branch barrier, bobbing a little in the slow current, before the spilling water nudged it gently through the breech and onto the river on the other side.

None of this disturbed the sleepers, but as the river widened and deepened, the current ran faster. Soon the scenery began to change: Trees became fewer; riverbanks became rocky cliffs looming higher and higher, forcing the river into a narrow vise between them. The little boat rode smoothly over the water, too smoothly to waken either of its passengers. Swiftly the current bore the rowboat down the canyon, whose bare, dark walls grew and grew until their height nearly blotted out the sun.

The first rough ripple passed beneath the boat, waking Bertie. He opened his eyes and looked around sleepily, then with mounting panic. "Mr. Medley! Mr. Medley!" he cried, and sat up so fast he almost upset the boat.

"What? What?" Oliver mumbled, pulling himself out of his dream with difficulty. He stared uncomprehendingly at the landscape passing rapidly by them. It wasn't at all the way he remembered. "Where are we?" he asked. *How long ago did we eat lunch?*

Bertie's eyes stayed glued on the towering cliffs. "This is the... real River Sunder," he faltered. "I--I've never been this far before."

"You haven't?" Oliver gasped. "I thought you were familiar with the whole river!"

"I've never been beyond the beaver dam," Bertie confessed. "And... and this doesn't look like Uncle Nunks's chart said. The river's all changed. Yow!" he yelped as spray from a wave splashed him in the face. "We're in whitewater! We're heading for the rapids!"

A submerged object bumped them on the bottom, tilting the boat and almost spilling them overboard before it let them go on again. The current raced faster and faster as the canyon continued to narrow, and the brown water, deprived of direct sunlight, turned black. Only the foam dashing against the rocks glinted white in a single shaft of light from the very top of the canyon.

"Quick! Man the oars!" Oliver shouted, forgetting in his panic that he was the one who had been rowing last and was thus closer to the oars than Bertie. The two of them dived for the oars at the same instant, bumping into each other and sprawling onto the bottom of the boat. Bertie reacted quicker, scrambling up on the plank seat and grabbing the oars.

"We've got to get out of here! I'm heading for shore!" he yelled as he began pulling frantically against the speeding current.

What shore? wondered Oliver as he straightened his spray-dotted spectacles and peered at the cliff walls rising out of the black river. He wished--much too late--that he'd insisted on both of them having proper flotation devices. That deflated little object under the seat wasn't going to be any use at all.

Despite Bertie's best efforts, the rowboat made no headway against the fast-moving bulges of water that blocked them from moving crossways to the shore. Oliver managed to crawl forward to sit beside Bertie, taking over one of the oars and doubling the power of their pull.

But their efforts were useless. The River Sunder, far removed from its origin in a meek and muddy little trickle, had become a mighty battering ram digging its own channel through the formidable cliffs. The tiny *Venture For*-- was no more to the Sunder than a leaf riding its surface, and as easily sucked under, never to be seen again.

"Harder! Pull harder!" shouted Bertie, but he might as well have saved his breath, for nothing could have won against that overpowering current.

Suddenly a huge, storm-uprooted tree, its passage downriver blocked by a pile of debris, appeared directly in their path. Its splayed-out roots, like many-fingered hands, waited to snatch at them.

"Larboard! Pull larboard!" Bertie screamed, but Oliver, having no idea which side "larboard" was on, simply rowed harder.

They nearly made it past the wasted tree--but not quite, for one of its thin, thorny root-ends reached out and pierced a fold of Oliver's tunic like a skewer. For an instant the boat stood still, held captive against the roots of the tree.

Oliver tore at the root-end, trying to free himself but only becoming more entangled until Bertie clambered over him and wrestled it out of the cloth. The rowboat stayed where it was for a second or two until the rush of water sent it onward, but not before the tree-root, irked at being deprived of its catch, wound its strong, crooked finger around an oarlock and pulled, lifting oarlock and oar clean out of the boat.

"Not the oar!" cried Bertie, vainly reaching for the oar waving triumphantly overhead in the tree-root's clutches. He tried valiantly to row with the one oar left, but it was impossible. The *Venture For--* was at the mercy of the river.

"Get down!" Bertie yelled, and both of them crouched in the bottom of the boat and clung to the sides as the little craft bumped and jumped over rapids. The current ran them into a spout of boiling whitewater and spun the boat around and around, making Bertie and Oliver dizzy before spewing them into the mainstream again.

Water spray spotted Oliver's glasses so badly that he couldn't see ahead at all, but Bertie, peeking over the bow, realized that they were now heading at lightning speed directly for a gigantic sliver of black rock right in the middle of the river. The rock had an edge like a knife-blade. There was nothing they could do to avoid it.

"AAGH!" they shouted together as the *Venture For--* crashed against the blade rock on the point of its bow and split apart, half of it careening madly down one side of the river, half down the other. Each half carried one of the boatmen, clinging desperately (in Oliver's case, blindly) to whatever kept him afloat.

Struggling to keep their heads above water and not to be smashed against any other obstacle, Oliver and Bertie hurtled along, unaware that the sliver of rock had not only sliced their boat in half but had also divided the river. The gap between the hapless adventurers grew wider and wider as the two forks made a vee, each heading in a different direction.

Bertie held on tightly to his ragged half of the boat, whirling away from the rock, away from his erstwhile excursion partner, and very far away indeed from his life in Purple Valley. All he could do was hold on as the Sunder bore him to places beyond his ken.

Oliver's fork of the river rushed faster and faster through cliffs as high as mountains. The river ran like a long black tongue between them.

He clung to his fragment of the boat with all the strength that was left in him, fighting panic, fighting the bone-chilling cold of the water, fighting not to think about what might be ahead of him. Then he heard a new sound over the noise of water, a sound like a giant mouth sucking in great gulps of the river.

He hadn't long to wait. The Sunder shot him around the next bend toward the edge of a maelstrom, an immense whirlpool stretching from one cliff to the other. There was no way around: He was headed straight for it.

By instinct he snatched the empty oaken water cask, last remnant of the little red rowboat, and wrapped his arms tightly around it as the current bore him to the brink of the howling funnel. A short, swift wave washed over his glasses--miraculously still on his nose--and smoothed away the droplets of spray. Then he saw all the way down to the bottom of the whirlpool, and wished fervently that he hadn't. Masses of bones lay there, white bones... heaps and piles of white bones littering the riverbed.

Oliver Medley knew that he was going to die. His life flashed before his mind's eye like a falling star across the sky.

Still clutching the cask, he slipped over the rim of the maelstrom and plunged into it.

I'm lost!

It was his last conscious thought.

Charleynne Gates

Part III

Ancient Paths

Stand at the crossroads, and see, and ask for
the ancient paths, where is the good way,
and walk therein, and you shall find
rest for your souls.
> --The Book of the Prophet Jeremiah

Chapter Seventeen

The Longlost

"Brother, how'd we get ourselves into this position?" Tapp Whackitt grumbled as they trudged along the trail through the Icewode. "We ought to be back at Keeper's Inn right now, doing our proper work at our own forge. I could have been working on my metal art project. It's at a critical stage right now, and I was averse to leaving it. Inspiration doesn't strike twice in the same place, you know."

"You mean lightning," Tipp corrected, "not inspiration. 'Lightning doesn't strike twice in the same place,' is how the saying goes."

"No difference," Tapp muttered. "Inspiration. Lightning. Both of 'em strike."

"Besides," Tipp went on, not heeding. "You wanted to go on this Quest. You'd do anything for the *Sendara* if she but lifted her little finger. So would I."

"Oh, well," mumbled Tapp, glad that his brother was walking ahead so Tipp couldn't see him blushing. "'Twas only our plain duty."

They hiked along for some time without speaking. When they took a break to rest, "What are we doing here, Tipp?" Tapp asked. "I mean--" as his brother frowned in puzzlement, "why are we here? Why did that old Hermit divide us up? Doesn't make sense to me. Does it to you?"

Tipp thought it over. "No, now that I think about it. What was so bad about traveling in one group? We were supposed to stay together to protect the *Sendara*. Now she's got only Pavarr and the Foressa. Not that they're slackers, either one of them, but--"

"Exactly," replied Tapp. "And what about that other fellow, you know the one I mean. There was someone else with us, wasn't there?"

Tipp squeezed his eyes shut and concentrated. "Yes... Yes, there was! Wait a minute. Wait... Say! That old Hermit deceived us! He must have put a forgetting spell on us after all, but it's going off now! It was a name like Med... Med. Lee. That's it. And some kind of fruit, like an olive."

"Oliver Medley!" Tapp chimed in. "That's his name! Where is he?"

"I--I don't know," said Tipp, peering about as if the person mentioned might be found behind a bush. "I think we left him at the Ruined Chapel."

"I think a fog is starting to lift off me," said Tapp, rubbing his head briskly.

"Me, too," responded Tipp. "We're probably far enough from that chapel for a forgetting spell not to work any more. I remember the Hermit sprinkled us with water—"

"Right," agreed Tapp. "And we figured the water had *bendor-bush* powder in it."

"I thought we Dwarf-kin were immune to those things," Tipp said.

"Maybe there was something else in the water."

Tipp pondered the possibility. "The only thing that could compromise our immunity to those substances is... is... Tapp!"

"What?"

"The only thing that can override our immune systems is dust from the Grimmerund!" Tipp exclaimed.

"You mean--"

"The Hermit has been there, or sent someone to get it!" replied Tipp.

"You mean the actual Grimmerund? The big black mound in the middle of the Icewode? The place where Arkon went in to the bottomless cavern to battle the Ab-ardzs and didn't come out for seven years? I thought it was just mythical!"

"No, it was never just mythical," Tipp responded, "but I assumed it had gone to ruin by now. Evidently it hasn't, because Grimmerund dust is the only thing in the Labyrinth World that could have made us forget what we were doing!"

"You think we ought to go back, see if we can find the others?"

"They'd be way ahead of us, wherever they went," Tipp reasoned. "And who are we supposed to join? Pavarr and Mil went with the *Sendara* through the Icewode, and Belvedine and Hera Vespasia went over it, which means they flew. They may already be at the Abbey."

"Then we'd better go on," said Tapp. "Right?"

"Right," Tipp agreed. "Nothing else to do now."

"I wish we hadn't trusted that Hermit," Tapp complained as they took the trail again. "Seems like he put one over on us after all."

"We should have been more wary. And do you remember us sleeping in the middle of the day, as we did in the Ruined Chapel? We practically never do that."

"But at least the *Sendara*'s going on to the Abbey, isn't she?" Tapp queried. "She'll be safe once she gets there."

"I hope so," said Tipp. "I just wish I had a better feeling about this whole thing."

"By the way, where are we going?" Tapp inquired.

Tipp stopped again and took his bearings. "We're heading for the Longlost Mine. It's got the only tunnel that goes under the whole Icewode."

"That's the oldest mine outside the Mountains of Zund, isn't it? The one the Dwarves tunneled back in the First Age?"

"Wait," Tipp said slowly. "Let me check my mind-map. I thought so. The Longlost Mine is supposed to be near the Grimmerund. I haven't looked at this part of the map since... Come to think of it, I never have. Hmm. Brother, I don't like this at all. I think we've gotten onto a perilous path."

"Maybe someone doesn't want us to get where we're going."

"I don't know," Tipp replied, frowning. "But we need to keep especially alert from now on. And I wonder if we shouldn't take another route. I don't like the idea of anyone being able to trace us."

"But the Longlost Mine tunnels go clear to the other side of the Icewode, don't they?" Tapp argued. "Which is where we want to go. And we can't come to any harm in a Dwarf-dug mine, even if it is near the Grimmerund. After all, Dwarves must still be living there, right?"

Tipp pondered. His brows drew together. "If there are, nobody's heard from them in quite a while. And there are others beside the Hermit who would mislead us if they knew where we're going."

Charleynne Gates

Ab'addon was in both their minds, although they did not speak the name.

They left the path and pushed on over a secret trail that only Dwarf-kin know. No map exists or needs to, for all Dwarf-kin are born with mental maps, and they never forget how to use them. Deep into the Icewode to the west they went, at times having to stop and clear their way through debris-laden snowdrifts. It was slow going, given that night was falling fast and very little light came through the wood's thorny canopy. At one point Tapp wanted to light the lantern they had brought from the Ruined Chapel, but Tipp dissuaded him, not without a debate.

"Best not," said Tipp. "The Twilight People might not like it. I can hear them breathing beside us, soft as snowfall."

"I don't hear nothing," said Tapp sullenly.

"You would if you'd stop crashing around like that and talking to yourself. Walk softly, can't you?"

Tapp continued to grumble, but quietly. Neither of them felt entirely comfortable intruding so far into the territory of the Twilight People. Not that the Dwarvians expected any trouble, for the Twilight Tribe did not have a warlike reputation. All the same, it was good to be cautious, as they were a secretive race. Few dwellers in the Labyrinth World could claim to know them intimately.

At last the two Dwarvians reached their intended destination, a hidden place deep in the Icewode known to their ancestors and to few others. There they halted inside a grove of tangled thorn trees.

"Fangs of Frondor!" Tapp exclaimed. He peered through a gap in the ice-coated trees and grabbed his brother's sleeve.

"What's the matter?" said Tipp, scrutinizing the path on which they had come in case anyone had followed their tracks.

"Look at that!" Tapp pointed at the gap, which revealed a towering mound, a ziggurat of black stone in the distance. It was wrinkled all over with ice-grooved fissures testifying to its great age, and its pyramidal apex blotted out the sky. The monstrous mound swallowed any light that struck it and returned no reflection, as if it were a black hole become solid. In fact, the Dwarvians recalled from their ancestral traditions, you could see it only if you already knew it was there. Even as far away as it was, the thing radiated a constant negative energy that made them reluctant to move into its force-field.

"It--it's incredible," Tapp whispered. "Is--is that the actual Grimmerund?"

Tipp didn't answer immediately. He stared at the mound, took the measure of its immensity. "Yes," he whispered back after a while. "But we shouldn't be talking. We might be overheard. We'd better be about our business. The Longlost Mine ought to be nearby. I wish I had--"

But Tapp didn't hear what Tipp wished he had done because Tipp turned aside and began to pick his way along the invisible boundary of the force-field. He went a quarter of the way around the mound, intently examining everything he came across.

"Aha!" he exclaimed when they were outside the thorn grove but still within sight of the Grimmerund. "There it is!"

The two of them stared at a slight indentation in the ground. Snow blanketed the frozen earth, making the outline invisible to the eyes of anyone but Dwarf-kin.

"It must be more than an Age since anyone used it, but the Longlost mineshaft is still here," Tipp observed as they brushed away the snow. "The place is so overgrown with scrub brush, I can barely make it out. But it's a trapdoor, all right, and here's the iron ring that lifts it." He touched the ring gingerly, then gripped it and gave an experimental tug. The trapdoor didn't budge, didn't even tremble.

"Might take a Word of Power to open it," Tapp suggested.

"I think our pickaxes would do it," Tipp answered, "if we had them. If the earth around it were loosened, the door would probably open by itself."

"I knew we'd need our tools if we didn't bring them with us," Tapp grumbled. "Rushing off like that on a wild goose chase. No wonder we didn't take anything useful with us. No hammers. No pickaxes. What's a blacksmith without his tools? I ask you."

"We're not on a wild goose chase, Brother," Tipp reproved. "We're on a Quest."

"Don't know why," Tapp answered glumly. "Oliver Medley's supposed to be the one with the Gift or whatever it is, going to save the world. Not that he looked like he could! But he's a good fellow, anyhow," he added hastily, recalling the incident at Nether Lake.

"Never mind him now. Here, I did bring something useful after all." Digging in his knapsack, Tipp brought out a compact rod that unfolded to a stout hole-digger. "My own invention. I threw it in at the last minute when we were packing. It's no pickaxe, but it'll do the job."

The two Dwarvians took turns using the hole-digger to loosen as much of the packed grit around the trapdoor as possible. After a great deal of effort, they managed to clear a narrow edge around it. They united their considerable strength to pry it up by using the tool as a lever, then let the heavy trapdoor fall backward onto the ground with a dull thud. Tipp cocked a wary eye toward the forest in case the noise had been heard, but nothing came back to them.

The smiths stared into the black hole revealed by their lantern. Quite by accident, Tapp kicked a small pebble into the space. They listened, holding their breaths, for the sound of it landing, but though they waited for a long time, not the slightest echo of a plop rewarded them.

Tipp lowered his lantern into the hole to get a better view. The yellow lantern-light shined on earth and stone walls cut straight down... and down... and down.

Tipp moved the lantern away. The brothers squatted on the ground and looked at each other.

"Must be near bottomless," Tapp whispered. "Are you sure that's the entrance to the Longlost Mine?"

"Positive," Tipp whispered back. "And look there." He squinted down one side of the square hole. "See? Steps cut in the rock, like a ladder. And iron handholds! And--what's this? Here's some runes carved on the underside of the trapdoor! Hold the lantern up. I think I can make them out, although worm has gotten into the wood pretty badly.

I seal this door with the Runes of Binding.
An Age and two Ages let them hold fast.

I can't read the next line. Then something *Tal--* something. Can't read the name. Then -- *the last.*

That's all."

"What's it mean?" asked Tapp.

"I'm not sure, but we'd better lower the door again while we figure it out. I don't like the sound of those runes at all."

Saint Amber's Rose

Between them they pulled the ice-encrusted trapdoor back over the shaft and went to sit under a nearby ledge of rock that made a shelter more or less free of snow. Scrounging in their knapsacks, they found end-pieces of journey-bread and ate them to restore their strength.

"What do you think about the runes?" Tapp asked when their simple repast was finished.

"The Binding was designed to last for 'an Age and two Ages'. That's three Ages. We're in the beginning of the Fourth Age now, so..."

"But it doesn't say in which Age the Binding was put on the door," Tapp pointed out. "Could have been in the Second Age, which means it's got one more to go. Or in the Third Age, and have two more Ages to go. Or--"

"I get your point," Tipp replied. "But I think it's more likely that it was done in the First Age."

"Why?"

"Because sealing with runes is a terrible spell, one of the most dangerous to perform. Remember when we had Labyrinth History under old Professor Ironhand? He said the Runes of Binding were used only seven times, all in the First Age when the Earth was full of monsters that Chaos made. Most of them died out or were killed when human mortals came, but Professor Ironhand said that some of them couldn't be killed, so they were caught in special traps and sealed in hidden places with the Runes of Binding."

"I know one that wasn't caught," muttered Tapp, recalling what had happened at Nether Lake when he had gotten entangled with the thing at the bottom of its dark waters.

"Therefore, I'm guessing that somewhere at the bottom of that mineshaft--" Tipp resumed.

"--is one of the monsters," Tapp finished.

The two Dwarvians looked at each other.

"But," Tapp added, "is it likely? If there's something down there, it might not have survived this long. What can it find to eat in an empty mineshaft? The Dwarves may have abandoned it long ago. There's nothing in our mind-maps to say anything's still alive down there."

"True," Tipp responded, "but I wish I knew for certain."

"You know, we did break that seal when we opened the trapdoor," Tapp remarked. "I wonder if--"

"Not much use either of us wondering," said Tipp. "Let's just hope that whatever the Binding-Runes sealed in is dead. We've gone too far to turn back now, and the Longlost tunnels will get us closer to the Abbey. Besides, we've more or less run out of options."

Tapp agreed. "I guess nothing's likely to come out of the shaft now that we put the door back in place. If there's even anything down there."

"We need some sleep anyway before we go much farther," said Tipp. "This is a fairly good shelter here; it's out of the wind and snow. Let's get some rest while we can. I'd rather sleep here than in the mineshaft."

"Right," said Tapp, wrapping himself up in his cloak. "Say, what do you think is the matter with that Hermit? I mean the way he sent us off, like he was trying to confuse us."

"Not quite right in the head, maybe," replied Tipp.

"Two digs and a delve short of a hole in the ground," said Tapp, trying to ease his looming fear with a little humor.

Tipp ignored him, huddling into a small space for warmth.

"Two spokes short of a wheel," Tapp went on. "Two rungs short of a ladder. Two nuggets short of a gold brick. Two tweaks short of a twitch." The last one sounded particularly witty to him, and he enjoyed it several more times, muffling his chuckles in the hood of his cloak.

"Stop snorting like that," said Tipp crossly. "I'm trying to sleep here."

Dwarvians need little sleep at any time, but when they do, they plunge very far down into slumber. Some people, who don't know any better, say they turn into stone when they sleep, but that's just ignorance. Stones don't snore. Tapp was a whole orchestra unto himself.

The ghost of a moon floated overhead. A tawny forest cat, a seasoned hunter, came upon them and edged closer, scenting prey. The winter had seen fewer kills than usual, and he was hungry. Slaver dripped from his jaws. He set his paws silently on the earth and crouched, tense and ready to spring. A stray moonbeam picked out Tapp's bare throat where his tunic had slipped awry.

Just then Tapp inhaled, a long, loud, grinding rattle, and exhaled with a groan worthy of a horde of unquiet spirits. Startled nearly out of his skin, the cat sprang off all four feet at the same time, twisted in midair, and sped back into the forest. There, quite unintentionally, he started a nest of hares and had a full meal for the first time that week.

Tipp slept on, being accustomed to his brother's night noises. Later, at moonset, the trapdoor over the mineshaft trembled with a hidden agitation. The brothers merely turned over, unawakened.

"Wake up, Brother." Tipp shook Tapp by the shoulder. "It's the false dawn. We have to try going down the mineshaft now."

"Uhrr! Foo!" Tapp surfaced out of a vivid dream of lions and tigers. "What? Oh, right. Got to go down the mineshaft. Lead on, then."

"It's your turn, Brother," Tipp countered. "You lead."

Having eaten a bite of journey-bread out of their diminishing supply, the two Dwarvians returned to the trapdoor and examined it once again.

"Funny," Tipp mused. "The dirt around this door looks looser than we left it last night. Wonder how that happened?"

"I don't see any difference," said Tapp, hiding a yawn. "We must have dug deeper than we thought. Let's get on with it."

"Pull, then," said Tipp, and together they grasped the cold iron ring and pulled the door up. It came free with many a creak and groan.

"Huh!" Tapp peered into the black hole. "Looks like it goes on forever."

"Better light the lantern," said his brother. "And we should leave the trapdoor open. Let some air in."

"Besides, we might need a quick getaway," Tapp remarked.

"I don't think anyone's still living down there, not after this long," said Tipp.

"You never know," Tapp replied darkly. "Remember the runes."

With the lantern swinging from the crook of Tapp's elbow, the Dwarvians descended into the old mineshaft step by careful step, using chinks cut in the stone and iron handholds set in the walls. From time to time a foot, groping for the next groove down, dislodged a clump of dirt or a pebble, but although they strained to hear it hit bottom, never a plink or a thunk came back. Once or twice Tapp held the lantern out over the shaft, but even with its light they couldn't see far enough down.

"There's probably no bottom to this thing," he said softly.

"Hush!" Tipp cautioned, and sh-sh-sh-sh came the echoes from the invisible depths.

On and on they went. They could still see a patch of sky from the open trapdoor, lightening as the dawn rose but getting smaller and smaller the farther they descended. At last the sky-patch disappeared entirely, and they were enveloped in blackness which even their lantern-light barely penetrated.

After seven hundred steps straight down, "wait," Tipp said, careful not to let the echoes hear him. "We're not getting anywhere."

"What'll we do, then?" asked Tapp. "Go back up? Admit failure?" Inadvertently he spoke too loudly, and *ailure-ailure-ailure* caromed around the walls.

"That's not good," Tipp muttered, but whether regarding the idea of failure or the echo of it wasn't clear.

"Hey, look here," said Tapp, lifting the lantern higher. The light-beam revealed a smaller hole, possibly the entrance to another shaft, beside the handhold where they rested.

"Where do you think that goes?" Tipp asked.

"... *ailure... ailure... URE...URE,*" the echo continued, not falling into the depths, but coming back up!

"Who cares!" Tapp gasped. "Let's get out of here!" He swung himself and the lantern into the hole, landing expertly on hands and knees (Dwarf-kin have an inherited ability to maneuver in small spaces), then leaned out to give a hand to his brother.

But at that very moment one of the handholds Tipp was using expired due to centuries of accumulated rust. It crumbled into fragments, leaving Tipp dangling from the other. "Ay!" Tipp shouted, awakening more echoes, which doubled and redoubled down and down.

The shadows down there moved...

A shape appeared far below, a shape unlike any human or animal on the surface of the Labyrinth World. It had no limbs, but it climbed--or crawled, like a gigantic worm--up the wall of the shaft. In the lantern-light they saw that it was toadstool-pale; it gave off a malignant odor, nauseating as a rotting corpse.

Tipp screamed.

"Hang on, Brother! Swing over here! Grab my hand!" Tapp called out. Tipp obeyed just before the other iron ring he was clutching also self-destructed, being unused to the weight of Dwarf-kin after so many centuries.

The Dwarvians huddled together, backing as far into the smaller shaft as they dared, unable to do anything but wait.

The worm-shape crawled to the level of their hiding place and stopped. Its eyeless, misshapen head swiveled from side to side, as if it were sniffing for the invaders.

It found them.

The eyeless head turned toward the shaft as if it could see them. It moved toward the opening, started to thrust its head inside--and stopped. It tried again, twice more. The head was too big! It couldn't fit into the opening of the small shaft. Once more it tried to get at the shivering Dwarvians, to no avail. Enraged, the thing ran its head against the opening until dirt and loose pebbles fell in a small shower into the shaft.

Tipp and Tapp clung to each other, shivering, but the monstrous worm couldn't reach them. Then its mouth parts protruded, and a black substance oozed out and dribbled toward them. Steam rose from the black trickle, and the Dwarvians felt its heat sting their faces. They edged farther back into the shaft.

The substance stopped just inches away.

At last the worm gave up, redoubled on its enormous length, and went back down the main shaft.

"Whew! That was close!" Tapp exhaled a long breath and crawled rapidly ahead of Tipp to get as far away from the vertical shaft as they could.

"Let's rest here a minute," Tipp said, panting as he sat down in a wide place in the new shaft.

"Wh--what was that thing?" Tapp asked through chattering teeth.

"Probably whatever was sealed in here by the Binding-Runes," replied Tipp, wiping his forehead with the kerchief around his neck. "All the more reason for us to get out of here. But I can't locate this side tunnel on my mind-map. I see the shaft we came down, but--"

"We can't go back there!" Tapp exclaimed. "Those handholds are probably all eaten through with rust! Not to mention that monster down below! I don't know how we managed to get as far down as we did without it coming after us. We're stuck now!"

"We can't stay here," said Tipp. "Look at the lantern! It's almost burnt out. Do you want to stay in the dark until we really do turn into stone?"

"I guess not," Tapp mumbled. "What do we do?"

Tipp picked up the lantern and prepared to crawl forward. "I think we'd better keep on going along this shaft. There has to be a way to the other side of the Icewode."

"I hate tunnels," Tapp grumbled under his breath as he followed Tipp. "I hate them. I knew there was a reason we Dwarvians left the mines. Give me sunlight and fresh air any day."

"Don't waste oxygen," said Tipp over his shoulder.

They crawled for what seemed an interminable time. Knees and hands grew sore and dirt-encrusted from the shaft floor. The odor of dank earth was so thick that it became difficult to breathe. Tapp tried not to cough from the mustiness, but he couldn't help it.

"Wait!" Tipp stopped suddenly. "What's that?"

"What?"

"I felt an air current! Come on! We must be getting near an exit!"

They crawled faster. The air current grew stronger, filling the shaft, which soon widened and deepened. Tipp cautiously stood upright, finding that he could do so without hitting his head on the ceiling.

"Hold the lantern up!" Tapp urged. "Let's see where we are."

Tipp turned the lantern to full power and raised it above his head.

Tapp inhaled sharply. "Arrows of Arkon!"

"It's the Great Diamond Hall of the Dwarves!" Tipp gasped. "To think I've lived to see it!"

Light--blinding, brilliant--flashed and coruscated, reflected a million times from a million diamond facets. Diamonds were everywhere in the stupendous chamber. It was completely surfaced with diamonds large and small, cut and polished, darting points of radiance around the room. Diamonds formed its throne, its pillars and columns, paved its floor.

"I thought it was only a grandmother tale," Tapp said slowly. "But now--"

"Who's there?"

"What?" Tipp asked.

"I didn't say anything," Tapp replied.

"Then who did?"

"I don't know," said Tapp.

"Who's there?" Tipp called. "Is someone there?"

One there? One there? The echo came back multiplied.

Tapp shivered. "This is creepy!" he whispered. *Eepy... eepy... eepy*, the echo answered. "And cold! It's like the inside of an iceberg."

Tipp moved the lantern in a slow arc, illuminating the whole interior. Stalagmites rising like giant candles met stalactites descending hundreds of feet from the ceiling, every inch endiamonded.

"Are you Dwarves?"

"Yah!" Tapp jumped sideways, knocking against his brother. By misadventure the lantern landed on the diamond floor, smashed, and went out. At once the blinding darts of light vanished, swallowed up in darkness.

"Look what you did!" said Tipp angrily. "Now what'll we do?"

"Are you Dwarves?"

"Listen!" Tipp whispered. "Someone's here."

"Dwarves?" repeated the voice. "Are you... Dwarves?"

Tipp gathered his courage. "We are Dwarvians," he called into the darkness. "Who are you?"

"Dwarf," was the reply. "Help... me."

"Where are you?" Tipp called, louder this time. "I can't see you."

"Over here. I have... fire. Come... over behind..."

"Let's go," said Tipp.

"Right," said Tapp, and the Dwarvians began feeling their way into the intense blackness.

"Keep bearing right," Tipp directed. "Hello! Keep talking! I think we're getting closer."

"Come... fire," repeated the voice, closer but wispier, as if the speaker were using his last store of energy.

"I see something!" said Tipp. "A spark! There, behind that stalagmite."

They crept forward as quickly as they could, rounded the stalagmite, and saw the little flicker of a miniscule fire. It appeared to be made of a few thin sticks of kindling the size of toothpicks. Beside it sat a tiny figure hunched as closely as he could to the flame. A hood hid his face, and a ragged, torn cloak covered the rest of him. He rocked back and forth, shivering.

"Come closer," he spoke in a faint voice. "Are you... Dwarves?"

"Oh, sir," said Tipp in wonder and pity. "Are you alone in here? Is no one with you?"

"Alone, all alone," said the tiny man. "Dwarves used to... live here. All gone now. Gone away. Left alone." And he rocked and rocked, moaning softly.

"He's starving!" Tapp whispered. "Must have run out of food and been too afraid to go outside to hunt. Too weak to find any now."

"Sir, we are Dwarvians. Dwarf-kin," said Tipp. "Can we help you in any way? Do you have food left? Let me take a bit of fire on this stick here, and I'll look." He peered around for signs of anything that had been eaten--eggshells, empty bottles, breadcrumbs, anything. There was nothing but a couple of dried-up vegetable rinds and a few seeds and pits strewn about the floor.

"Here's a bit of journey-bread," said Tapp, taking it out of his pouch. "And water. Let me give you some water."

But it was too late. The little Dwarf pitched forward, only just missing falling into the fire because Tipp's strong hand caught him. Gently Tipp laid him down on the thin pile of rags that served as his pallet and dribbled a few drops of water onto his parched lips. The old Dwarf swallowed painfully as a trickle ran down his throat.

"Ah... good!" he rasped. "You are... kind."

"Where are the other Dwarves?" asked Tipp. "You must have been here for quite some time. Why did they leave you alone?"

The old one swallowed again. "Water," he begged. Tipp gave him another sip, then more, until he was able to breathe easier. Closing his eyes, he relaxed against Tipp's supporting arm. "I am dying," he said clearly. "You are Dwarf-kin. I will tell you all I can." He took a few more breaths; they sounded raggedly in his throat. "Dwarves... all dead. They came. The *wyrga*. Last year, up old mineshaft... under Grimmerund. Awakened the *Talgg*."

"*Talgg*? What's that?" Tapp whispered.

Tipp shook his head. "What is *Talgg*?"

"*Talgg! Talgg*!" The old one labored to say the word. His eyes opened wide; he stared fearfully at nothing. "The *Talgg*... ancient evil... Chaos-born... cannot die... Help me!" His voice rose to a shriek.

Tipp and Tapp exchanged a long look and nodded. Without speaking, they realized that the thing they had seen in the vertical mineshaft was what the old Dwarf called the *Talgg*.

Tipp held the old one tighter to ease his fears and tried to project some of his own energy into the withered body. "It's not here any more," he said, sounding more confident than he felt. "It's gone away. We're the only ones here. We're Dwarvians. I'm Tipp Whackitt. This is my brother, Tapp. We won't let anything hurt you."

"Ahhh," sighed the old Dwarf, and sank back again. "Dwarvians. I knew Dwarvians once. Good people." One clawlike hand reached out and grabbed Tipp's mantle. "Don't awaken the *Talgg*!" he begged. "You must go soon, or it will find you. The Grand Staircase will take you to the other side of the Grimmerund. Don't go back the way you came!"

"We won't. Just rest now," said Tipp, and Tapp murmured agreement. "Can you tell us what happened to the other Dwarves?"

"Long ago... Dwarves dug Longlost Mine. Carved the Hall of Diamonds... for our kings. But we dug too deep... disturbed the Talgg. Then *wyrga* invaded... killed all Dwarves. I wanted to fight, but... friends made me hide back there--" he pointed a wavering finger--"under the throne. Secret place. Hid 'til they... went away. . I ate what food I could find here. Afraid to go outside. Danger still in Icewode. No more food... Too weak to climb out... Friend Dwarvian." He clutched Tipp's cloak again. "I beg you, when I die, lay me with my fathers in the way of the Dwarves, as I did for those the wyrga killed." His red-rimmed eyes watered; tears trickled down his shriveled cheeks. "All gone to ashes. Dust and ashes."

"We will," Tipp promised. "As our ancestors did, so will we do for you."

"We promise," Tapp added.

"It... is... done," said the old Dwarf, and died.

"Poor old one." Tipp set the body gently down and covered it decently with the few rags the Dwarf had kept beside him.

"What do we do now?" Tapp asked. "We're supposed to be at the Abbey by the full moon! Shouldn't we be going?"

"He was a Dwarf," Tipp said slowly, considering. "And we are Dwarf-kin. We have always honored our dead with the Vigil of Remembrance. It is our most sacred obligation."

"Our most sacred obligation," repeated Tapp. "But are we not also obligated to the Quest? Which is the higher obligation--the Vigil or the Quest?"

"We are vowed to the Quest by our word freely given," Tipp mused. "But we are obligated to the Vigil by birth, blood, and breeding. He was the last Dwarf of the Longlost Mine. There is no one else to do this duty for him. If we abandon him, he will lie unmourned 'til the end of the world."

The brothers gazed at each other across the body of the old one, then nodded once, briefly, at the same moment.

"We will perform the Vigil," said Tapp, and together they set to work. Tipp blew up the fire, nursing the flame on scraps of kindling, and they began to arrange the old Dwarf's limbs, straightening the legs and folding the hands across his chest. With a strip of cloth they bound his eyes and ears that he might rest from the sights and sounds of the world he had left. With other strips they bound the feet together that he might rest from treading the world's wearying paths, and his hands that he might rest from the world's work. Finally, Tipp enshrouded him in his stained and tattered cloak.

While he did this, Tapp took a small lamp they found among the old man's pitiful belongings and searched the area, looking for any kind of tinder. When he had collected a scant armful of fuel, he and Tipp built a funeral pyre. It was a very small one, but the old Dwarf's body was very small, too, and after death seemed to have shrunk even more.

The brothers placed the body on the pyre. Standing one on either side, they stretched their hands over the old Dwarf and began to sing the Songs of Departing in the age-old language of the Dwarf-kin, a tongue that was old when the rocks were young. Then they walked four times around the pyre in a sunwise direction, once for each stage of a Dwarf's life.

Singing the last song, they stood at head and foot of the pyre. When they finished, "Fire of the Great Forge, take our brother," they spoke together. With a rush of heat the pyre ignited, and lashing blue-white flames leaped again and again from the diamond walls until the whole immense space seemed to be a whirlwind of blue fire.

Saint Amber's Rose

In no time at all the fire burned away all the sticks and scraps of kindling, mingling ashes of wood with the ashes of the old Dwarf.

"Now," said Tipp, "we must keep the Vigil here beside him for three days."

"Keep the first watch, Brother," said Tapp, "and I will go outside. We must know where the moon is in her monthly journey."

"We already know," Tipp rejoined sadly. "Luna is three days before the full. But go. See what is happening in the Icewode."

Tapp climbed out through the nearest vertical shaft, one so high that the Old Dwarf could never have used it, and returned at the end of the first watch, panting a little. "The Icewode is quiet, just as we left it. Except"--he hesitated--"except for a queer kind of thrumming noise, low and deep. It comes from the direction of the Grimmerund."

"What would make such a noise?" Tipp asked. "Not birds or animals, not here."

"No, nor was it the crackling of ice or the shushing of snowfall. It was almost like... like drumbeats, deep underground, but nothing I have ever heard before."

"It's your turn to take the watch," Tipp said. "I'll take a look outside."

But in none of the watches in all three days did either Dwarvian discover what made the thrumming noise.

On the third day the brothers carefully swept together the old Dwarf's ashes and picked through the remains of the pyre, searching. At last they found it: the heart of the old one, transformed into a glittering diamond in the pyre's blue-white heat. The two Dwarvians bore the heart to the Great Hall of Diamonds and placed it in the throne's high arch. The niche at the very top seemed made to hold it, and as Tipp guided it into its place, the diamond heart came to life, radiating light upon light in every color of the rainbow. Thus did the last King of the Longlost Dwarves go to his final rest.

"Farewell, Old One," Tipp pronounced. "Your Vigil is complete."

"Come, Brother," said Tapp. "We must make haste to reach the Abbey."

They took a last look at the magnificent Great Hall of Diamonds, whose wonders will never again be seen by mortal eye, and left to climb the Grand Staircase. The radiance of the diamonds flickered and went out, and the Longlost Mine was left in eternal night.

Chapter Eighteen

Skull Bottom

"What's this?" Tapp asked. He stopped in the act of adjusting his knapsack and went over to a round stone basin nearby. Silver-blue water in a shallow pool rippled gently in the lantern light. A little waterfall fed into the basin, which drained away to an underground channel. In the middle of the basin floated a crumpled-looking object.

"What do you mean, 'what's this'?" asked Tipp. "What's what?"

"This here," replied Tapp, "in the middle of the pool. Looks like it didn't ought to be there."

"What is it, then?" said Tipp, rather impatiently. One particular knot in the rope Tipp was coiling was proving stubbornly unpickable, and he didn't appreciate his concentration being disturbed.

The two Dwarvians were taking a break from the strenuous climb to the surface of the Icewode. They had decided not to follow the old Dwarf's direction after all, that they take the Grand Staircase back to the Icewode. *Wyrga* may have discovered it, Tipp thought, and be on the lookout for them. Instead, they went by the Secret Steps, a dark, narrow corridor with a number of twists and turns designed to confuse an enemy but easily navigable by Dwarf-kin.

Roughly halfway up, the Secret Steps widened onto a broad landing where a basin--actually, a wide pool--held water from the Sunder. The river water had been filtered so many times through dirt, gravel, and rock that by the time it reached this chamber, it was as clean as spring water.

"Don't know," said Tapp, standing at the edge of the basin and watching the object drift slowly toward him. "Might be a carcass."

"Of an animal, you mean?" said Tipp. "Probably got swept away in the river and sucked down here. Must happen once in a while."

"Doesn't look like an animal to me," said Tapp, studying the object intently. "Wrong shape."

"I'll take a look," said Tipp, using his teeth to pry open the knot, which finally yielded to persuasion and fell apart. "Arrows of Arkon!" he exclaimed, peering at the floating object. "That's a human body! Help me pull it out!"

Tapp reached out with his staff and hooked a fold of sodden cloth, using it to tow the body toward him. The two Dwarvians heaved it over the edge and laid it gently on the ground. Water streamed from every part of it, running off in little rills. The body had neither cloak nor tunic, but only pants and a corded thong for a belt, and was naked from the waist up. The skin was blue with cold and entangled in long skeins of green waterweed which wound around the face and wove into limp strings of dark hair. Whatever it was, it didn't appear to be breathing.

"Is it dead?" asked Tapp.

"I don't know," answered Tipp. "We'd better make sure. Let's turn it over and get some of the water out of it."

"Looks pretty near drowndead to me," said Tapp, "whatever it is." But he helped his brother turn the body over, and Tipp began trying to resuscitate it. At first there seemed to be no result, although water came out of its mouth and nose. But they kept on pumping in a steady rhythm, muttering, "Come on, now. Don't give up," as they alternated working on the waterlogged body.

"I think it's gone," Tapp pronounced after a while. But Tipp didn't stop, although perspiration, even in that chilly mine, poured down his face.

"No," Tipp replied, panting. "I think... it tried to take a breath... that last time. Why don't you take over for a while?" He sat upright to let Tapp take his place.

"Ehh," said the body, and coughed.

"It's alive!" the Dwarvians exclaimed together. Tapp fell to work, pumping harder to make the body disgorge any remaining water. Soon it coughed again and vomited up waterweed and a very small fish, which quickly swam away in one of the rivulets of water.

"Ugh!" said the body. "Et...ee...up!"

Tapp got off the body's back and helped it turn over again, removing some of the weedy strings over its face. "Why," he said, "it's a human boy!"

Saint Amber's Rose

The boy opened his eyes and stared into the two Dwarvian countenances looming over him. "Who... are you?" he whispered. "Where... am I?"

"You're in the Longlost Mine under the Icewode," replied Tipp, cautiously answering the last question first. "And who might you be?"

"I'm... Bertie... Mossgrower," said the boy, struggling to sit up. Tapp helped him lean against the stone basin.

"Mossgrower? Sounds like a name from over in Purple Valley," said Tipp.

"That... that's where I'm from," said Bertie, coughing and shivering. "Mossy Dell Village."

Tipp dug into his knapsack and produced a blanket, which he wrapped around Bertie's wet shoulders. "Wrap up in this. You need to get warm."

"Th--thanks," said the lad through chattering teeth. "D--do you have anything to eat, p-please?" he begged. "I haven't had any f-food for ever s-so long."

"Of course," said Tipp, digging into his knapsack again for a piece of journey-bread, which Bertie devoured almost in one gulp. Tapp found a rind of hard cheese, a handful of nuts, and half a dried apple. Bertie ate everything, hardly waiting to chew.

When the boy had wolfed down the scanty bits of food, Tipp began to question him, slowly at first. "Mossy Dell's quite a distance from here. How'd you happen to wander into this territory? I've heard Mossy Dellers don't like to go outside their valley."

Bertie took his time answering, studying the faces before him. "I--I don't remember very much," he said at last. "We--I mean, I took my rowboat out on the Sunder--"

"The River Sunder?" Tapp interrupted. "A rowboat on the Sunder? How did you manage that? Are you sure you mean the River Sunder?"

"Of course I'm sure!" exclaimed the boy. "The River Sunder starts in Purple Valley, in Sunder Spring."

"I didn't know that," said Tapp, surprised. Tipp studied the boy keenly.

"That's where we started," Bertie continued. "We--I mean, I was just rowing down the stream to the beaver pond. And then we ate lunch under the willows, and it was a real nice day, and the sun was warm, and I guess we--I mean, I took a nap or something. And the next thing I knew I wasn't in the beaver pond any more, and we were going awfully fast, and the whitewater... the rapids... That's the last thing I remember." He shuddered, then leaned back against the stone basin and closed his eyes, exhausted from his ordeal.

The Dwarvians moved a little way apart from him and conferred in low tones. "What was he thinking, trying to go down the Sunder in a rowboat?" Tapp asked, shaking his head.

"I'm more interested in what he meant by 'we'," Tipp returned. "Did you notice he kept correcting himself every time he said 'we'? I'm thinking he may have had a companion on this boating excursion. And did you notice the lad has a Dwarvian dagger on his belt?"

Tapp nodded. "So if you have yours, and I have mine, the only other one I know about was the one we gave Friend Oliver."

"Exactly," said Tipp. "I'm thinking the boy might have seen Friend Oliver. If so, what happened to him? And why was the lad reluctant to mention him? Do you think he stole Friend Oliver's dagger and killed him?"

"The boy doesn't look like a thief or a murderer," Tapp opined. "Maybe Friend Oliver gave it to him. But if Friend Oliver was with the boy, then Friend Oliver's prob'ly drowndead. Couldn't've survived that kind of whitewater, not on the Sunder. The boy was lucky. But I s'pose if there was somebody else with him, we ought to try and find him," said Tapp.

"Yes, if there's any possibility he's still alive," Tipp replied, "but I never heard of anyone getting out of the Sunder rapids alive. And we have to remember where we're heading and why we're going there. We can't leave the lad here in the mine; he'd never be able to find his way out. But do we dare take him with us?"

"We could take him up to the surface and point him in the direction of Purple Valley. Maybe he'd find his way home."

"Purple Valley's too far from here. He wouldn't make it alone, not without more food. Or warmer clothes," Tipp asserted.

Both of them glanced over at Bertie, who had fallen asleep. His head had rolled forward onto his chest, where journey-bread crumbs dotted his borrowed cloak.

"No," Tipp decided. "We certainly can't leave him here, or expect him to find Purple Valley by himself. He has no idea how far he has come, and the way back is too dangerous. He'd never get there."

"We'd better take him with us, then," said Tapp. "I've got a spare shirt he can have. I think it might be big enough for him."

Tipp nodded. "We'll have to build a fire and dry out the clothing he has left. He still looks pretty cold, too."

"He's not used to being underground like us Dwarf-kin," said Tapp. "And what about shoes? He'll have to have shoes, and where do we get shoes big enough for human feet?"

Tipp sprang up from the ground and began pacing in a small, tight circle. "Delays! Delays! We're already three days late meeting the *Sendara* at the Abbey!" The two Dwarvians stared soberly at each other.

"You know," Tapp mused, "whoever lured us here probably thinks we're already out of the way on account of the *Talgg* in the mineshaft."

Tipp thought that over and nodded slowly. "That could be to our advantage. It's just as well, I think, that we're not going all the way underground to the other side of the Icewode. That's what the Hermit would have anticipated, if the *Talgg* didn't get us. But to a more immediate matter: We have to leave here, and we'll have to take the lad with us, but we can't tell him where we're going or why. I hope he's up to the journey.

"We'll have to find the Dwarves' storage closet first. They must have had a place near the surface where they kept outdoor equipment. Might be a pair of shoes there that will fit him. Some of the Dwarves had pretty big feet. And let's hope the Dwarves had a pantry there, too, maybe one the old Dwarf forgot about or couldn't get to. We need to replenish our food stores before we go on."

"I'll go," said Tapp, "see what I can find."

"Right," said Tipp, "but let's build a fire first. Can't let the boy stay in wet clothing. Catch his death o' new-*mony*, as Granny Whackitt used to say."

A few hours later, awake, warm, dry-shod, and newly outfitted, Bertie Mossgrower proceeded single-file between the two Dwarvians as they went up the Secret Steps that led to the outside world. They spoke not a word, all breath being required for the thousand-step climb, but thoughts tumbled around Bertie's mind like whitewater in the Sunder rapids.

"We didn't introduce ourselves," said Tipp as they huddled around their campfire, waiting for Bertie to warm himself thoroughly and ward off the ill effects of his recent immersion in the Sunder. They had eaten a full hot meal salvaged from the pantry where the Dwarves stored their dried and preserved food. "I'm Tipp Whackitt. This is my brother, Tapp. We're Dwarvians." He waited a moment to see if Bertie recognized the names.

"How do," said Bertie, and pulled his forelock politely.

It was evident to the Whackitts that Bertie had either never heard of them or of Dwarvians in general, or else was a more practiced actor than he looked. The possibility that he might be a spy from the Desolate Lands had occurred to them, but nothing that he had said or done so far verified their suspicion. Bertie Mossgrower seemed to be exactly what he was: a boy on the verge of young manhood, fresh from the country and eager to see more of the world outside Purple Valley.

"Now I'll ask you another question," said Tipp, observing Bertie closely. "Any idea what happened to your companion?"

"My companion?" Bertie echoed. "I didn't--oh. I guess you figured it out." He shook his head slowly, gazing fixedly into the fire. "I don't know what happened to him. I just remember the whitewater. My rowboat must've got smashed up. Mr. Medley must've got drowndead."

Tipp and Tapp glanced at each other, the same question in their eyes.

"Mr. Medley?" Tipp asked. "He was in the rowboat with you? Is he a friend of yours?"

Bertie snapped out of his brown study, remembering too late that Mr. Medley hadn't wanted word of their journey to get around. "I'm on a Perilous Quest," he had warned his young companion as they started down the river. "And now, so are you. My mission--our mission--is to rejoin the *Sendara* and help her to reach the Abbey of Saint Amber. And no one else must know where we're going. No one at all!"

"Oh, sir!" Bertie had cried, nearly speechless with joy. "This is a real Adventure! And I'm on it! Hurray!"

But the perils of their glorious Adventure had proved too much for them, and Bertie had found himself in a cave deep underground where it was darker than darkness except for light from the little fire and the Dwarvians' lanterns. He couldn't think very well either: It was difficult to get things straight in his mind. Maybe he'd been hit on the head before he got whirled down to the cavern under the Sunder.

He couldn't have known, as did the Dwarvians, that the Dwarves of old had cunningly devised a drainage system from the rushing river to bring themselves fresh water for drinking as well as to power the engines they used for mining. It was the drainage outlet that had carried Bertie down to the basin and nearly drowned him. Now the mining engines were silent, as were the Dwarves who once manned them, but the waterfall remained, falling ceaselessly into the stone basin until, long Ages hence, the mighty Sunder should run dry.

"Um," Bertie began, feeling his way as to how much to reveal to the two Dwarvians. They looked all right, but you never knew, especially when you weren't in Purple Valley any more. Of course he'd heard of Dwarves in stories his grandmother told, but he'd never actually met any, and he hadn't known about Dwarvians at all. This isn't the kind of thing you'd expect to happen to you back in Mossy Dell.

He took in a deep breath and plucked up his courage. Might as well tell them the story--at least some of it. He didn't want to get Mr. Medley in trouble, but maybe these two Dwarves--Dwarvians, that is-- could help him find the poor gentleman. If there's any chance of finding him alive. Of course, if he was drowndead, then Bertie had a duty to go on to the Abbey himself and tell the *Sendara* what happened to Mr. Medley, so she'd know and wouldn't worry about him any more. What an adventure that would be, to meet the *Sendara*! Actually see her and talk to her! That would be worth any amount of danger! *Why, I'd row down the Sunder ten times just to see her!*

Bertie's lively imagination pictured the scene: the Lady herself, beautiful as the stars in the heavens, smiling upon him as he knelt before her. A tear would flow down her alabaster cheek as he told her of the sad demise of Mr. Oliver Medley. But then she might reward his valor with a knighthood (Sir Bertram of the Dell sounded impressive). How all this was to be accomplished, he had no idea.

"Um," he said again, and plunged ahead. "His name is--or was--Mr. Oliver Medley, is what he told me."

Again the two Dwarvians glanced at each other. "How did you happen to meet him?" Tipp asked, keeping his voice carefully casual.

Charleynne Gates

Bertie realized he might as well tell the whole story. "Mr. Medley came to our village on the road that comes out of the last bit of the Icewode. Just a traveler, such as we sometimes get passing through, especially in the summertime, walking along the main road. But those Mossy Dellers, they've been pretty spooked lately. Strange things have been happening in the valley, crops failing, blight killing ferns that never had a disease before, ashes found in fields where there wasn't no-- any fire or lightning-strike. Farm animals going missing, and no explanation to any of it. And all the newborn babies in the village last year had cauls over their faces. It made everybody nervous and jittery, always going around looking over their shoulders. They started getting afraid something real bad was going to happen. And then a couple of hunters that went over into the hill country came back and said they seen--saw signs of *wyrga* closer to the valley than they'd ever been before.

"Some Mossy Dellers got this idea to set a trap in the middle of the village square, where you'd have to pass over it if you was walking through. They put this big net on the ground and covered it over with dirt and leaves so you couldn't see it, and they tied the ends to the big chestnut tree in the square. Everybody in the village knew to avoid it, but Mr. Medley came walking in, all innocent and everything, and he sprang the trap. They was going to boil him in oil on suspicion of being a *wyrga*, but I seen *wyrga* before when I was out exploring by myself in the Icewode. They look scary and they smell bad, and he didn't look or smell anything like them.

"My Uncle Nunks told me about Mr. Medley caught in the trap, and we worked out a plan to rescue him. Uncle Nunks's seen the big world outside Purple Valley, and he knew Mr. Medley wasn't a *wyrga*. So I shinnied up the tree and used his dagger to cut him out of the net, and we stayed up in my treehouse until the people started remembering their manners. They let us go, and Mr. Medley said he was on an ex-cur-sion, and I asked him could I go along because I always wanted to get out of Mossy Dell like Uncle Nunks did when he was young. And he said I could, and he gave me his dagger 'cause he figured I could use it better than him." (Tipp and Tapp exchanged quick glances.) "He's prob'ly right, 'cause he don't--doesn't--look like much of a fighter. But"--loyally--"he's real smart. He talks just like a book! So I took him down to Sunder Spring where I keep--used to keep--my rowboat, the

-- 336 --

Venture Forth, and he said it was a fine boat. It's prob'ly smashed to pieces by now.

"See, the Sunder's just a little crick when you start out from Sunder Spring, muddy and lots of weeds in it, but pretty soon there's other cricks flowing into it, and it gets to be wider. It moves kinda slow, though, and there's an old beaver dam in one place that makes a nice quiet pond.

"I remember we got tired rowing--it's quite a ways from the spring--and the sun was warm, and we ate our bread and cheese under the willows at the edge of the pond. I guess we musta fallen asleep or something, because the next thing I knew, we were in whitewater. There's a little opening at one end of the beaver pond, and we musta floated through it while we were asleep. I never been farther than the beaver pond before, so I didn't know the Sunder got as wild as that.

"We were trying to keep afloat, I remember that, and get to one bank or the other, but the current wouldn't let us. And the rapids were coming up, and the water was a-boilin' up and... and... we were going faster and faster..." His voice spiraled higher with remembered terror, and he stared over the fire into the darkness as if he were seeing not the cavern where they sat, but the mad black river with its raging white foam. "I remember it all now! No! No!" He thrust out a hand to ward off a danger only he could see. "The big rock! We're headin' straight for it! We've hit! My boat's smashed up! Mr. Medley! Mr. Medley! The river's carryin' him away! I can't see him any more! He's lost, and I'm drowndead!" With that, Bertie put his face in his hands and burst into tears.

The Dwarvians looked at each other solemnly. "Poor lad! He's been through more than most grown men could take," said Tapp.

Tipp nodded. "They don't call it the Sunder for nothing," he declared in an undertone. "It's been a graveyard for many an unwary traveler." He put his hand gently on Bertie's shoulder. "It's all right now, lad. Rest a while."

The brothers went a little ways away from the fire. "Sounds like Friend Oliver got as far as the Sunder," Tipp said quietly, "and got drowndead. So there's an end to him and his Gift, whatever it was."

"I s'pose we'll never know," said Tapp. "Say, did you figure out what Bertie was talking about? Must've been the Blade Rock."

"Aye, but it's been a while since I was anywhere near it."

Charleynne Gates

"You remember what comes past the Blade Rock?" asked Tapp.

Tipp thought for a moment. "The Blade Rock splits the Sunder into two forks. One of them carried the lad down here and spewed him into the basin over there."

"And the other fork?"

Tipp frowned. "Let's see. It goes to..." His eyes opened wide, and he stared at his brother, horrified. "The Maelstrom!" he exclaimed. "It goes straight into the Maelstrom! If Friend Oliver made it that far, he's done for!"

"But wait!" Tapp interrupted. "What about the old tale about Arkon? They say he was once caught in the Maelstrom, but he grabbed an barrel and held onto it, and it floated him back up! So maybe there's hope!"

Tipp considered. "If there's hope, there's life, you mean? Maybe you're right. We shouldn't give him up for dead until we know for certain." He pounded one fist slowly into the palm of the other hand. "Delays and more delays! But we'll have to go to the Maelstrom and see if we can find him. If he came back up at all. If there just happened to be a barrel for him to hold onto. If." He shook his head. "The Maelstrom's a two-day journey on foot," he stated. "Might be longer if Bertie can't walk as fast as we do."

Tapp went over to Bertie and sat beside him. The possibility of a barrel in the rowboat was soon settled. No, Bertie told them, there wouldn't have been room in such a small craft for a big barrel. "The only barrel we had was a little oaken cask of sweetwater from Uncle Nunks's well, so we wouldn't have to drink out of the Sunder."

The Dwarvians and Bertie climbed the rest of the way out of the Longlost Mine and began the trek to the Maelstrom, despite having little hope of finding Oliver Medley. They went rapidly, for Bertie, being young and healthy, soon recovered his strength and easily kept up with the Dwarvians.

After two days' travel they came to the cliff edge, where below them the dreaded Maelstrom spun with evil force in the middle of the River Sunder, reaching from one bank to the other. Here the river was so wide across they could barely glimpse the opposite shore. Staring down into the terrifying whirlpool, Tapp wondered how even the legendary Arkon could have survived a plunge into its depths.

Saint Amber's Rose

Carefully the three picked their way along the edge of the cliff that rose sheer above the water. No sandy shore was down there that they could tell, and the moon gave enough light that they would have spotted something if the least bit of dry riverbank had been there to see.

"Keep going," Tipp urged, and on they walked, skirting the whirlpool, peering down occasionally, though never for very long at a time lest they grow dizzy from the towering height.

Not until they had gone past the Maelstrom did they spot a thin sliver of gravel beside the river, and on it an object different from its surroundings. They couldn't tell what it was, but inched their way down a treacherous path Tipp and Tapp recalled from their mind-maps. When they were closer, they discovered the remains of a solitary shoe, so battered and waterlogged that it was impossible to tell who the original owner might have been, although Bertie insisted it must have belonged to his late companion.

There was no other sign of Oliver Medley.

The three of them searched the area until the dim moon disappeared in the west and they could see no more. No other trace of man or rowboat did they find. With heavy hearts they returned to their vantage point, made a campfire, and considered what they ought to do next.

"What else can we do?" Bertie sat on the hard ground, legs crossed, shoulders hunched, head hanging down. He looked as dejected as it was possible for anyone to look. A tearstain had traced a dusty trail through the dirt on his cheek, but the tear was dried now. The boy and the Dwarvians had been sitting around the campfire for more than an hour.

Tipp drew in a breath and blew it out, then leaned against a boulder. He exchanged a quick glance with his brother, then looked back at the boy with compassion. "I'm sorry, Bertie; I can't think of anything more to do. We've looked high, and we've looked low. We've hiked up and down until we can't go any more. There's just no-place we haven't been."

"Brother's right," said Tapp. "We have to accept what most likely happened. Friend Oliver's gone, sucked down the Maelstrom. He... he's gone for sure."

But Bertie shook his head. "No, he ain't," the boy insisted. "Isn't. I don't mean to argue with you gen'l'men, but I've been thinking, and--and I'd know if he was dead. I know I'd know. It just feels like he's still alive. If--if you don't want to go on, that's all right, but him and me, we're pals, and pals stick together. I ain't goin' to desert him now."

"I admire your loyalty, Friend Bertie," said Tipp, "but--"

Bertie wasn't listening any more. He stood up and swung his knapsack onto his back. "I'm going to have another look around," he said, and started back down the trail to where the howling of the Maelstrom tore at the sky.

"Wait up, lad," said Tipp, and gripped Bertie's arm as they peered straight down into the gaping hole made by the thunderous waters. The rock chimney in front of them made a kind of shelter against the noise of the whirlpool, but they still had to shout to make themselves heard. "You see? It's hopeless."

"I dunno that it's hopeless," Tapp panted. He had rejoined them after making a sortie down another one of the nearly invisible trails snaking along the escarpment. "When I got down closer to the Maelstrom, it looked to me like there might be something we didn't see before."

"What is it?" Tipp asked.

"What?" Tapp said, taking little screws of cloth out of his ears.

"WHAT IS IT!" Tipp yelled.

"You don't need to yell," Tapp said crossly. "I'm not deaf yet, though I probably will be if we stay here much longer. I found some steps going down below the surface of the Maelstrom," he went on. "They're cut into the cliff wall. I'd guess they were carved out in the First Age."

"Where do they go?" asked Bertie.

"Don't know," said Tapp, "but I'd guess they parallel the Maelstrom, maybe even go down near the riverbed. Might be some clue there about what happened to Friend Oliver."

"Doesn't sound like much of a chance to me." Tipp looked doubtful. "We don't know where it leads or how far down. There'd still be a wall of stone between us and the river, so we wouldn't be able to see anything in the river."

"But what if there was something!" Bertie objected. "There might be a piece of my rowboat. Or something of Mr. Medley's, even if it's just another shoe. We can't leave without knowing. He might of got out of the Maelstrom somehow. He might of got tossed out on land and wandered off, not knowing where he was. He might of got carried downriver. He might of--"

"That's a lot of 'mights,' lad," Tipp interrupted. "We can't be sure of finding anything. This is pretty much unknown territory to us."

"And we'd have a very small chance of finding him," Tapp put in.

"But it's a chance!" Bertie pleaded. "We've got to go! Leastways, I've got to. Please, sir," to Tapp, "show me where the steps are."

Tipp exhaled. "I suppose we'd better go ahead, Brother. The lad'll never stop searching otherwise, and we have to get out of this place. We're nearly five days late getting to the Abbey."

Tapp darted a warning glance at his brother, but too late.

"The Abbey!" Bertie exclaimed. "Are you going to the Abbey, too? That's where Mr. Medley was going! He said the *Sendara* was there. I'd give anything to see her! She--"

"Hush, lad," Tipp cautioned. "Yes, that's our destination, but you'd best not mention that name again. We don't know who hears what we say."

"Come on, then," said Tapp impatiently. "We can't stop here."

The other two followed him as he led the way back down the escarpment, picking his way along a broken trail no more than three inches wide, where only the hardy mountain sheep dared go. One or two of the big rams poked their spiral-horned heads over the boulders to inspect the adventurers, but never did they discover what the trio was doing in their territory. From time to time Bertie stumbled and almost fell as loose pebbles rolled beneath their feet and bounced down the slope to the black maw of the Maelstrom. One slip...

"Here it is," said Tapp, pointing to the carved steps leading down beside the whirlpool. The others couldn't hear a word he said because of the tremendous noise and the twists of cloth stuffed into their ears, but his gesture was sufficient. They descended after him with extreme care because the stairway was narrow and the stones were worn to a slick surface.

Tapp held his lamp as high as he could to guide them, but the ceiling grew low as they made their way below the surface and into a stone-lined tunnel paralleling the river. Bertie, being taller than the Whackitts, had to crouch down quite a bit.

"Dwarf work," Tipp decided, examining the carvings along the yellow walls where drops of moisture pebbled the stone. Tapp nodded, not replying. The sound of the whirlpool was muted now that they were underground, but the roar was still audible, reminding them that the wall separating them from the river was thin.

At last they came to a landing, taller and wider than the passage, where they stopped. There was nothing particularly remarkable to see as Tapp shined the lantern around, just more stone of a mottled grayish color mixed with dull yellow. The original stair split into several different stairs at the four corners of the landing, and each led downward. Tipp moved his lantern over all the stair-holes, but they seemed to be exactly alike.

"What now?" asked Tapp. "Go back or go down one of these other stairs?"

"Which one do we start with?" asked Tipp.

"Wait! Look at this!" Bertie had wandered away to look at the flat stone wall at the widest part of the hollow chamber.

"What?" said Tipp. "Oh, I see what you mean. There's a chiseled line here"--tracing with his finger as Tapp held up the lantern--"that makes a big circle. It'd be a window if it were glass."

"I'm remembering something." Tapp frowned, concentrating. "What our great-great-great-grandmother told us when we were children. You know, that bit of rhyme about how to open strange doors."

"We don't want to open any door, strange or otherwise," Tipp pointed out. "The whole River Sunder's on the other side of that wall. If we opened a door in it, all that water'd rush in and we'd be gone in a flash."

"Well, I know that," said Tapp. "I meant what if the poem applies to windows, too. Maybe there's some way to see inside the Maelstrom."

"Doesn't sound likely," said Tipp.

"Oh! Oh!" Bertie squeaked. "Look what's happening now!"

The Dwarvians turned to the wall in time to see ripples begin to form in the stone circle and cascade from ceiling to floor, as if the wall were turning to jelly. Faster and faster the ripples came, then the wall inside the chiseled line became translucent. Gray light poured through it, grew brighter and brighter. All at once the stone stopped shuddering, and where the wall had been was a transparent round window like a porthole on a ship.

"See that?" Bertie whispered, going right up to the window and staring wide-eyed through it. "I knew there'd be something here! I knew it!"

Open-mouthed, the Dwarvians joined him. Outside were the thundering waters of the great whirlpool, but the chamber in which the three stood was level with the river bottom. Here the Maelstrom descended to a bed of rocks and boulders, but a few feet from the bottom it lost its force, leaving only a lazy current caressing the riverbed. Scattered among the rocks, as far as eye could see, were bones, heaps and piles of white bones, together with skulls that slowly bounced and rolled about on the sand, grimacing as if still in the agony of drowning.

And in that graveyard of bones, half-buried in the gravel but close enough to the window that they could see it quite clearly, was one side of a little red rowboat that had been sheared in half. That half still bore, in faded black letters, the name *Venture For--*.

"That's my rowboat!" cried Bertie. "That's the half Mr. Medley was in!"

"But that doesn't mean Friend Oliver's anywhere around here," said Tipp reasonably. "It's more than likely that his body's been swept away by the current." The look the other two turned on him would have melted the rest of the wall. "Or," continued Tipp, hastening to correct himself, "he might have managed to escape. Although I don't see how," he added in an undertone.

"But he might have," Bertie insisted. "Isn't there any way to find out?"

The Dwarvians had no answer, nor could they offer the least crumb of hope at this point. Tipp took a step forward until his face almost touched the melted-stone window. He brooded on the skulls floating in front of him. "Friend Oliver, where are you now?" he asked them, as if they were capable of answering.

Click-click! Click-click! Click-click! Three double taps, very distinct. CLICK-CLICK! CLICK-CLICK! CLICK-CLICK! The Dwarvians and Bertie glanced quickly around the chamber, but saw nothing behind them, no one in pursuit, and only themselves in the room. Then they looked out the window and down. One of the rolling skulls had come to rest directly in front of it and was staring up at them with its big empty eye sockets. Its large teeth clicked together.

"Whew!" said Tapp. "It's only that skull there. Nothing in here with us."

CLICK-CLICK! CLICK-CLICK! CLICK-CLICK! went the skull, sounding a trifle impatient, if such a thing were possible. Then, with a sudden motion, the skull bounced up so that it faced them squarely in the middle of the window.

"YAH!" the three yelled, and backed away several rapid steps from the window. Startled, they stared at the outlandish thing, which they saw wore the bicorne hat of a naval commander.

"Well, doesn't that beat all!" Tipp chuckled, laughing at their initial panic. "It's the current makes them jump around like that. And see? One of them rolled right into that old captain's hat. Makes it look almost alive."

The skull continued to click its teeth.

"No, wait a minute! I've heard of Sunder Skulls." Bertie and Tipp looked at Tapp. "The old stories say they belong to drowned sailors, but here in the river they really can come back to life--more or less. Bein' out there under water, they can't hear us, so they must be able to read lips. They saw what we were talking about! And they don't have tongues any more, so they talk by clicking their teeth!"

The skull nodded up and down and clicked its teeth madly.

Tapp snapped his fingers. "Hey! I think he's using the Seekers' Code! Remember? We learned it in Dwarflings Club when we were boys!"

"Is that it, Friend Skull?" Tipp approached the window again.

The skull nodded vigorously and chattered at them.

"Slowly, please!" Tapp pleaded. "It's been a long time since we used the Seekers' Code."

"Permit me... introduce myself... Captain Ezekiel Bones, at your service," clicked the skull more slowly, bowing. "My officers." A row of skulls bobbed up behind the captain. "And crew, late of His Majesty's Sloop Albatross." More skulls, some with a gold ring or two attached to their ear-holes, joined them, until the window was filled with staring eye-sockets.

Bertie crowded past the Dwarvians so that he was directly in front of Captain Bones. "Please, sir!" he begged. "We're trying to find Mr. Oliver Medley. Have you seen him at all?"

At once the skull began to chatter more rapidly, with breaks for Tapp to translate. "Man was here... Only one we've seen since we came... Maybe your friend... Looked dead, like us... Face gray as river water... Didn't open his eyes. Landed on riverbed... with a little oaken cask and broken-up old rowboat... We had many boats... on board our ship... 64-gun ship of the line... All of us... sailed in her... gone now... sank in storm."

"I'm very sorry to hear it." Tipp delicately deflected a tangential reminiscence. "If we might return to the subject of Oliver Medley?"

"Thought he might be one of us at first," clicked the skull. "But he still had flesh on him. He landed on river bottom... oaken cask in his arms... Cask floated him back to the surface, then he drifted away... in direction of... Saurian River."

"The Saurian River?" Tipp leaned closer to the window.

The skull chattered faster than ever, faster than the Dwarvians could follow. Other skulls joined in, all clicking and clacking as hard as they could.

"Wait! Slow down!" Tapp called, frantically motioning. The skulls fell silent while the captain continued.

"Goes to Desolate Lands... Ruler... evil... took us from our clean quiet graves under deep green sea... put us here on watch and watch..."

"Watch for what?" Tapp interrupted.

"Watch and watch... watch and watch... watch and watch..." echoed the skull-seamen.

"What do you mean?" said Bertie urgently.

"You don't understand," clicked the captain. "Watch and watch is how he made us keep lookout... Cruel and unusual punishment... Never mind," recognizing utter blankness on the faces of the three landsmen. "He made us look out for Bringer of Gift... If he should come this way... Never knew what he meant."

"Bringer of the Gift!" said Tipp and Tapp together. "That's Oliver Medley!"

"Do you know where Mr. Medley is now?" Bertie asked.

Charleynne Gates

"If the one we saw was your friend, he's in the Desolate Lands by now, most likely," clicked the captain. "Maybe even in the City of Dead Souls."

Tipp struck his hand against his forehead. "Desolate Lands... The Desolation!" he whispered to himself. "Why didn't I recognize it at once! Tapp, Bertie: Friend Oliver's worse than dead!"

"What do you mean?" asked Tapp.

"It's the Lord of Desolation he means." Tipp frowned. "Friend Oliver's on his way to the very place where the Lord of Desolation rules! It's in the opposite direction to the Abbey of Saint Amber!"

"Then I've got to find him and get him out of there!" cried Bertie. "Captain, sir, can you tell me how to get to that place?"

The captain nodded, bobbing up and down in the current. "We cannot go to the Saurian River," he clicked. "It's not navigable. But come in to us and we will take you as far as the Sunder goes, to the edge of Threshold Forest. From there you may find your way to the Saurian River. If you follow it, you will come to the Desolate Lands."

"But how can I get where you are, inside the river?" said Bertie.

"Put your hand on the window and think hard of your friend," the skull instructed. "Then close your eyes and push."

"Now just hold on there." Tipp's big hand clapped down on Bertie's arm and gripped hard. "I don't know what you skulls think you're up to, trying to get this lad in the river. Why, you'd be luring him to his doom! Don't you know he can't live in water the way you can? He'd drown!"

"He wouldn't at all," clicked the captain decisively, "and we can help him find his friend Mr. Medley."

"How can we be sure of that?" Tipp didn't try to hide his suspicions.

Another skull bounced up to join the first, a bo'sun with a black eyepatch and a jaw you wouldn't want to argue with. "Permission to speak, sir," he clicked to the captain.

"Go ahead, Mr. Brinefish," said Captain Bones, and the bo'sun turned to the window.

"We was mutineers before a big storm sank our ship," he clicked. "We shouldn't never've planned to do such a thing. We was mostly drunk at the time, y'see, besides which it was the natch'ral meanness in us come out. The officers was agin it, but we tied 'em up

-- 346 --

and took over the ship. Sailed right into a monstrous storm, which the cap'n here coulda got us through all right, him bein' a prime skipper, only we'd already knocked him on the head and locked him in his cabin. The ship broke to pieces and we all got drowndead fer our wickedness. That's how the Lord o' Desolation got us: through our wickedness."

"The men had a rightful grievance," insisted the captain. "I flogged too many hands too often. Life's hard aboard ship, and I made it harder for them than it ought to be."

"We're learnin' to get along now," said the bo'sun. "Ain't that right, Cap'n?"

"It is, Mr. Brinefish," agreed the big skull.

"Very touching." Tipp was unconvinced. "But I don't know about young Bertie here going in the river with you. Doesn't seem natural."

"Maybe they're right," Tapp put in. "Maybe the lad ought to at least try what he said."

"I don't think," Tipp began, but Bertie slipped away and scurried to the window.

"I'm going to find Mr. Medley!" he said, pressing his hand against it. Closing his eyes, he thought hard of his former companion and pushed. The transparent stone melted into a kind of mush, and Bertie fell or floated through; they never knew which. Suddenly he was in the river and gone.

Tipp and Tapp rushed to the window, pressed their hands against it, and pushed as hard as they could, but it had turned back into stone again the instant Bertie went through it. The two Dwarvians were left alone, staring at a blank wall.

"What'll we do now?" Tapp asked.

"We'd better go back up as quick as we can," said Tipp. "If we get to the surface in time, we might be able to rescue him."

"If there's anything left to rescue," Tapp mumbled, but he followed his brother as they ran back up the stair. They popped out of the entrance and gazed down into the Maelstrom. Nothing recognizable swirled around in the funnel, not Bertie or the skulls or anything else.

"We're too late," mourned Tapp. "Now we've lost them both, young Bertie and Friend Oliver."

"Wait," said Tipp, shading his eyes to look down the mighty Sunder.

"What?" said Tapp.

Tipp pointed; Tapp strained to see. Far down the swift, dark river was a floating object, a whitish-colored raft rigged with a single sail made of odd patches of canvas. The craft was--Tapp could hardly believe what he was seeing--formed of rows of skulls packed closely together, with Captain Bones beside Bertie. The boy was sitting with his knees pulled up to his chin and his arms clasped around them.

The little craft was making fair speed away from the Dwarvians. It was headed for a wide bend in the river, but before it was lost to sight, above the roar of the whirlpool came the steady cadence of a sea chantey.

> *Yo, ho, ho! Yo, ho, ho!*
> *'Round the Sunder bend we go,*
> *Off to the Darkness down below.*
> *Yo, ho, ho! Yo! Ho!*

sang the skulls as they bore Bertie down the River Sunder.

"Lively there, lads!" called the captain. "Look lively, now!" which was the last thing Tipp and Tapp heard as the craft disappeared from sight.

"I don't like what they were singing," Tipp frowned. "'Off to the Darkness' doesn't sound encouraging."

"Looks like we don't have any choice but to trust them now," said Tapp.

"They said the Lord of Desolation put them at the bottom of the Maelstrom deliberately," rejoined Tipp, "to watch for Friend Oliver. They may be taking the lad right into the Desolation."

Tapp shook his head. "I think they meant what they said. They wouldn't have any reason to love the Lord of Desolation. After all, he stole them away from their clean quiet graves under the deep green sea where they were resting in peace. I think they've been waiting for the Gift-Bringer, all right, or any friend of his, but not to betray them to the Desolation. What if they've been waiting for the chance to betray the Desolation? Get some of their own back?"

Tipp pondered the idea as he stared in the direction where the skull-boat had disappeared.

"Besides," added Tapp, "young Bertie himself wanted to go. We couldn't have stopped him."

"True," Tipp agreed. "We'd better get a move on, then. We're late meeting the others at the Abbey. I hope the boy'll be all right."

The Dwarvians hitched up their knapsacks, gripped their walking sticks, and trudged off in the opposite direction of the Sunder's flow, hiking over jagged rocks jutting out between them and their destination.

Bertie stared ahead and shivered, as much from dread as from the icy wind bearing down on their craft. He'd done it now, cast his lot in with the skulls who were taking him only they knew where. *I hope I did the right thing, going into the river like that.* At least he hadn't had time to swallow any water before the skull-crew grabbed his garments with their teeth, dodged him past the Maelstrom, then dragged him to the surface and bumped him aboard the raft.

Too late for regrets now.

"Don't be downhearted, lad," said Captain Bones, well aware of Bertie's mood. "You're a good friend to Oliver Medley. That's no small thing, believe me. Look here: We've got quite a distance to run before we put in to port. Why don't you tell me about your adventures thus far? It'll keep you from brooding over things we can't foresee."

Glad of any distraction from his worries, Bertie gave him a full account, omitting all mention of Oliver Medley's secret mission.

"Your 'Uncle Nunks,' you say?" asked the captain. "What might be that gentleman's proper name?"

"Admiral Sir John Horatio Nunkins," Bertie told him. "He used to be a sea-captain himself before he got the rheumatics."

"You don't say," said the captain thoughtfully. "That's very interesting. Very interesting indeed. Now then," becoming official again, "we'll put you off at Fool's Point, and we cannot get closer to the Saurian River than that. The Point is an old river-port abandoned long ago. Part of the dock has collapsed, but there's a trail of stepping-stones that'll take you to land. You'll have to walk for a few *kephan* through Threshold Forest to get to the Bordering Cliffs, which overlook the Desolate Lands.

"That's where you'll find another river that runs into the Sunder and swallows it up, you might say. That river is the Saurian, and it doesn't carry water, but a black poison. There's a stench coming off it that'll make you sick just breathing it, so keep your distance. And be careful of fire: One spark falling on the surface will set the whole river on fire, and there's not water enough in the Labyrinth World to put it out. In the olden days they called it the Dragonsblood River, and it's pure evil. If you follow the Saurian to the Desolate Lands, you might find your friend Mr. Medley. Heave to!"

In a trice Bertie was out of the boat and onto the wave-washed stepping-stones leading past the rotting dock. Two or three weather-worn, tumbledown shacks were scattered haphazardly on the riverbank behind it. One of them had an old, cracked sign hanging by a single rusty nail over the door. Fool's Point Bait and Tackle, it said in crude lettering.

Bertie thanked the captain as best he could through trembling lips.

"*Va'in 'a moru'*, young Bertie. *Va'in 'a moru'*," replied Captain Bones. The echo of "yo, ho, ho" hung briefly in the air as the skull-boat sailed back to the Maelstrom.

Bertie turned and faced the shore where the trees of Threshold Forest towered in the distance. The only moving things he saw were two black birds with vast wingspreads making wide, slow circles in the sky, high up and far away.

Vultures. Waiting for me?

But he pushed that thought away, set his jaw, and put his foot on the first slick stepping-stone, barely visible in the lapping curls of the Sunder River.

If a hooded face with yellow eyes watched him from the shadows inside the deserted bait shack, Bertie didn't see it.

Chapter Nineteen

The Desolation

I am a brother of jackals,
and a companion of ostriches.
My bones burn with heat.
     --The Book of Job

A viscid wetness dribbled onto his face and pooled in sticky little patches. He heard breathing near him, hoarse and irregular. His eyelids were heavy, as if weighted with damp sand, but slowly, slowly, he forced them open--and stared directly into a pair of alien eyes. Yellow eyes with brown gummy matter running out of the corners. The pupils were black and held no expression at all.

"Aah!" the man shouted instinctively. He rolled over on one arm; with the other he swept the space in front of him, meaning to strike at the yellow eyes, but making no effective contact at all.

The jackals--if that's what they were--jumped back and loped away, vanishing into the flat, featureless landscape. He watched them go, his heart thumping, his body shaking with weakness.

Gingerly he levered himself into a sitting position. His head ached; he put a hand to his forehead and discovered that he was hatless, his hair wet.

Where am I? Has it been raining?

He began feeling himself from head to toe, finding a number of painful bruised spots and--*ouch!* Probably a wrenched shoulder. *Where have I been? My clothing is wet through, and what's that smell? Is something dead?* He sniffed his tattered sleeve. "Oh! It's me! How did I--!"

The sound of his own voice seemed harsh and loud in his ears; at the same time his words fell onto the ground like cold iron. No echo, no reverberation, as if the air around him were dead.

He looked up at the blurred expanse before him, blurred because his glasses weren't in place, and somehow he knew they ought to be. He grabbed for the lenses, then for the earpieces. *Gone!* No wonder he couldn't see a foot in front of him. Everything within range of his vision ran together like a child's finger-painting.

He gulped and fought down the beginning of a panic attack. Without his corrective lenses he was, as it were, enclosed in an opaque glass box, and he could see nothing beyond its panes but shapes of indeterminate fuzziness.

Maybe the lenses were still here somewhere, caught in his clothing. "Please, please," he muttered to himself, "let them be here. Let them be here. Let them--"

He fluttered his hands over his clothes, which he found tattered and torn. You could hardly call them garments at all now: They were more like shreds of cloth held together by a belt. Hat gone, one shoe gone, cloak gone, pants and tunic in rags. Only a belt... *Wait! Is it still here?* Eagerly he groped around his waist. And there it was!

Relieved to find that, at least, he continued more calmly to search for his spectacles and found them, caught by one curved earpiece in the left side of the belt. He eased them free and restored them to their proper place, nothing gratefully that the lenses hadn't been damaged, aside from a few minor scratches. The other earpiece was, unfortunately, missing, having been snapped off at the point where it joined the frame, but the glasses stayed on his face, even if they tilted a bit.

His vision restored, he peered around again--and found absolutely nothing there. He was alone, except for the vanished pack of jackal-like animals--some type of scavenger, undoubtedly--in a featureless space that stretched onward to infinity.

Nothing broke the terrain, not mountain, mesa, valley, or bump on the ground. No vegetation greened the earth: no tree, no blade of grass, no flower of least renown. The ground, a dull, indeterminate non-color, ran on and on and on, unbroken by trail or print of hoof or paw, despite the jackals which had awakened him. A desert, the man guessed, and looked down for evidence of sand.

It wasn't sand, or not exactly. Whatever was beneath his feet looked more like ashes caked to the hardness of marble and reaching as far as the eye could see. What caused such a phenomenon? Some inferno that had scorched the earth to its bare bones? But he had never heard of a forest fire where not even a burned-out tree stump survived. Surely the ashes left from such a conflagration would be black?

He scuffed at it tentatively with his shoeless foot. Nothing came up. It was cold to the touch of his bare, bruised toes, but not unbearably so. In any case, the rest of his body felt uncomfortably warm.

A memory, remote and vague, drifted to the surface of his mind, of a kind of explosion that matched the sun in searing white brilliance. He couldn't recall what the thing had been, but he had the impression that it was something that men had made, and that its legacy was death.

Was this, then, the wasteland which that thing had left in its wake, a landscape totally devoid of life?

He turned to his left. Exactly the same landscape spread out before him. Behind him, the same thing. To his right--there's something at last! A gap in the featureless terrain, a scar in the earth, and in it a narrow river flowed. A few fragments of splintered wood lay scattered nearby on the hard-edged riverbank. Driftwood.

The current in the river ran swift and silent, without the smallest noise of ripple or splash, and its water was as black as a mineshaft. No white foam marked its inky surface; a hot, heavy odor emanated from it, stinging his nostrils and making his eyes water. The odor reminded him powerfully of something in his distant past; he couldn't think what.

There was something on the surface, something that glimmered slickly in flashes of dull light. Colors like a rainbow, rose-red, blue, green, silver... Pretty colors... Hard to turn his eyes away from the pretty colors on the dense dark water.

But he turned away at last. He recalled that he had had companions, or maybe it was only one companion, not so long ago, and they seemed to have been rowing down a river, but it didn't look at all like this one. What had happened to them? What happened to their little rowboat, their little... red rowboat, the... the *Venture Forth*, that was it!

His elation on recovering the name lasted only a second. What was his companion's name? Speaking of names, what was his own name? *I have a name; it's on the tip of my tongue. I just can't quite say it.*

Charleynne Gates

Across the desert--or plain or steppe, whatever it was--he spied a group of moving objects, possibly a herd of animals. They ran swiftly across the caked-ash ground as if they were fleeing--or hunting. They ran directly toward him, and he saw that they were long-legged, sharp-beaked birds with wicked talons that appeared to be capable of tearing a man apart. The sight of the creatures triggered a recollection of someone he had once known... No, it was gone.

Ostriches! That's what they are! He stared at the ungainly birds--skinny legs with plump black bodies bordered with white feathers--unable to move as they sped toward him. They swerved at the last instant before running him over and passed into the distance.

Now why can I remember "ostrich," but not my own name?

He became aware of a raging thirst and turned toward the river. Even if it was an uninviting black in color, that was probably silt carried from faraway fields. *A little earth won't hurt me.*

He had to lie flat on the ground to reach the water. It was about two feet down from the riverbank, and there wasn't any other way to get closer to it. Even in this position he couldn't see anything below the surface--not a fish, not a minnow. The acrid odor was so strong that he had to hold his breath to keep from choking. Rivers did have odors. He knew that down in his marrow, where memories of a greening earth dwelt. They smelled like wild water, like algae and wet pebbles, like brown beavers and swift, wriggly fishes.

This river didn't smell like any of those things, but it looked like water and flowed like a river, and he was so thirsty he didn't care about the details. He reached down and dipped his hand into the river up to his wrist.

The hand disappeared. Horrified, he jerked his arm out and stared at it. The hand was still there. He wiggled his fingers. They worked, but no water dripped from them: They were coated with a dark film, and they were warm from the liquid in the river, whatever it was.

This water's not for drinking, he decided, and tried to ignore his cottony mouth. He wiped his hand on the remains of his pants, got to his feet with difficulty, turned in the direction of the river's flow, and started walking. The hard, unfeeling ground had no give to it, and very soon what little energy he possessed drained away. The one shoe he had left dropped off after a while, but he didn't notice. On and on he trudged, his arms hanging heavily down. He thought about nothing.

Saint Amber's Rose

After a while, he didn't know how long, he noticed a difference in the terrain. His dulled senses hadn't taken it in; it was his feet that responded to the difference in texture of the colorless ground. It was gritty now, like fine gravel, but at least it didn't hurt to walk on, as real gravel would have. His toes stirred up tiny puffs of dust which spiraled up as he plodded on. They looked like little dust devils, miniature tornadoes.

He kept on walking, kept on walking. Kept on. And on. A wind came up, made a bellows to blow the dust devils into bigger funnels. He inhaled the wind. It smelled like nothing. Even the dust smelled not like ordinary dust but like nothing, as if this dust were not made of earth.

The dust devils whirled around him until he couldn't see very much out of his slanted spectacles, but it didn't get in his eyes. That was another mercy. What the twisting devils seemed to be doing was leading him in a direction of their own choosing, as if they were herding him. They pressed against him on one side or the other so that he had to move right or left as they directed, because he couldn't resist. At the same time he began to hear a curious grinding sound, like teeth clashing together very fast and far away.

When they had steered him where they wanted him to go, the dust devils died down and down, became nothing more than little puffs of powdery grit stirred up by his tread.

The landscape before him had changed. Something felt different in the atmosphere, something his beclouded mind couldn't put a name to. He halted for a moment, feeling an unexpected relief in the weary soles of his feet. Glancing over his shoulder, expecting to see a few of his own footprints leading back to his point of origin, he saw only unmarked grit. The wind had blown away all signs of his passage.

He looked as far ahead as he could, trying to discern some geographical feature that would give him information about where he was, or that might be a potential residence of mortal beings. He was beginning to feel his solitude acutely, and to be concerned about being marooned in an alien setting with no other human life.

What he saw didn't help. There was no horizon.

There was no horizon.

The sky was a glaring leaden hue with no break in it, like the cover of a coffin seen from inside. Leaden sky and leaden ground never came together in the distance; they simply vanished beyond where his vision could reach.

But surely there ought to be a horizon line that marks the curvature of the globe?

His mind couldn't grasp the idea of the absence of a horizon line. What he thought he was seeing must be the fault of his scratched spectacles. Maybe he had a concussion. Or else had plunged into sudden madness. *Or else I'm dreaming.*

At last he gave up fruitless speculation and simply trudged onward because he couldn't think of anything else to do.

The air gradually became smoky, like a cloud he had walked into without noticing. Breathing made his lungs sting, as if the air held some kind of unidentified chemical. He slowed down, sniffed at it delicately as if it were fine wine or perfume, which it definitely was not. He coughed as his lungs rejected the toxin, then scrabbled in his torn pocket and found a rag to cover his mouth and nose as he walked.

Sulphur. The air smelled like sulphur. *But how did I know what it's called?*

He stopped, squinted to peer through the increasingly murky air. Afar off, he saw a shape he hadn't noticed before. It was enormous, like a tower or a pyramid or something similar. Its shape wavered in the smoke, which seemed to be coming from it. On its apex a light shone, a fitful neon-orange glow flaring up and dying down, flaring and dying. Was it on fire? He couldn't tell, and his eyes were watering badly from the smoke.

He walked on, and walked on. The hard floor of the desolate plain did not vary, not in the smallest detail.

After a longer time he thought he saw a grouping of black dots in the distance ahead of him. It was difficult to figure out what they were through the haze, but he felt encouraged. Maybe they were houses! A village, or even a city. A city with people! They'd give him water! There, he might find out where he was or... possibly... who he was. He stepped faster, eager to get someplace. Anyplace.

He was terribly thirsty. The temperature of the thickening air was rising steadily, and the heat seemed to have gotten into his bones. The black river flowed along in eerie silence a few yards away, but it didn't tempt him to go nearer. *Something is very wrong with that water.*

Dust clouds once again began to billow in front of him, adding to the haze of smoke and making it impossible to see very far ahead.

Then he walked smack into a standing rectangular stone, invisible to him because it was the exact color of the ground. The rectangle writhed at his touch, as if it were trying to defend itself but couldn't move from where it was planted.

He stumbled backward and put a hand to his chest, staring at the rectangle. It was at least three heads taller than he was, and it seemed to be moving.

"I beg your pardon!" He choked an apology, coughing through the dust in his throat. "I didn't mean to... I couldn't see you for the dust clouds."

The stone ceased writhing. As soon as it was calmer, he saw that a figure of some kind was etched on its surface, a human-looking figure.

He edged around until he stood directly in front of the rectangle. Now he saw that the figure wasn't carved on the surface but was, instead, inside the stone. It was moving in a very limited way, as if it were a living creature trapped in a stone cage.

A dry wind soughed around the stone, sighing and groaning as it slid over the edges. *Why do you come here?* he heard in his mind, as one might hear a voice through a snowstorm.

"I don't—I don't know why," he stammered. "I don't remember how I got here."

Then go away! Run! This is no country for the living! Again the wind--or the stone--spoke inside his mind.

"What? Run where? What do you mean?"

The stone began to writhe and twist again, as if the being inside were impatient with his answer. *Get out of here, I tell you! Get out!*

"I don't know how! Please, if you can, show me!"

Go back! Go back along the river! the stone repeated, bending from side to side as far as it could, twisting violently as if it were trying to wrench itself free from the ground? *Go quickly, son of human mortals! As fast as you can!*

"But that's what I want to do!" he cried. "I just don't have the strength to walk all the way back along that black river! I've walked so long, I'm exhausted. I need water... real water, and rest. Please tell me who you are and why you keep telling me to go back!"

Charleynne Gates

The stoneman groaned, redoubling its efforts to escape from its entrapment. Its limbs--hand or paw--pushed at the stone barrier, and once he thought he could discern the shape of a face, but as though it were wrapped in a thick gray shroud.

I will tell you our story so that you may understand and flee from this place, said the stone face. *We are Stonemen.*

He saw that behind the first standing stone were many others, close but not touching, and facing every which way, without order.

As you are now, so once were we. Once we lived in freedom; once we had parents and wives and children. We were friends, families, neighbors. We worked on the Earth; we helped each other. We planted and harvested the Earth's bounty. We fished in the clear rivers and pastured our cattle and sheep in the hill meadows. We celebrated our great festivals at the turnings of the year.

We gave our free allegiance to the Sendara, *Guardian of the Graelands. At her behest, we band of brother knights, Companions of the Noble Way, kept watch and ward along our borders, lest any intruder disturb the peace of the Graelands. Truth and Freedom were our watchwords then; Faith and Honor kept us strong. We were happy in those days, but did not know it.*

"What happened?" The story drew him in; he forgot his thirst.

A shadow came into our minds, and we began to want more than we had. We wanted more land, bigger houses, more things to fill them. We wanted to be wealthier than our neighbors, more powerful, more feared. We wanted more and more and more. We sold the produce of our land--more than it could replace, and then we began to destroy the land itself. We built houses, villages, cities on the very soil that had given us our food. We cut down our ancient trees, our life-givers that had stood in their forest sanctuaries for thousands of years. We killed the animals, first only as we needed for food, then purely for sport, believing the wild creatures inferior to us. We stripped the Earth of timber, then of minerals: gold, silver, all its treasures, and left it wounded and scarred.

We ignored the Covenant of Creation and sold the land where our clans had lived since the days of our first ancestors--despite knowing that no created being can own the Earth itself. We sold and bought, sold and bought. We sold even our own children, for we gave them over to the merchants of delusion and death. Buying and selling, getting and spending, compelled our lives. Greed became our god. 'Having more' became our worship. Thus we gave our souls to the Lord of Desolation. Our hearts, and then our bodies, became stone.

"Who is the Lord of Desolation?"

He is the lord of this land, lord of all the desolate lands. He is destruction! Beware of him! If you keep following the black river, you will come to the City of Dead Souls, and he will take your soul as he did ours. Go back where you came from! Go back! Go back!

But how could he "go back" when he didn't know how he got where he was? All about him--front, side, back--was unrelieved monotony, except for the smoke-belching tower across the river. No landmark gave him direction. Only ahead of him were those dots that strongly suggested--at least to his mind--the hope of human habitation. He longed to come closer to them.

I need to go on. But how can I abandon this poor fellow, trapped the way he is? But the Stoneman hadn't asked him for help, only warned him to return whence he came.

"I'm very sorry about your plight," he said finally. "I wish there was something I could do, but I'm afraid I must go on despite your kind concern. You see, I really can't go back. I don't know quite how to... Well. I--ah, goodbye. Thank you very much. Thank you. Goodbye."

Oh, dear, he thought, turning away. *I'm sure the poor man believed he was giving me good advice. But how can I possibly go back to where I came from when I don't remember it? He did say there was a city ahead. I'm sure I can straighten things out there. I don't think I'd be in any danger of, ah, losing my soul. All I really want is to find my way back to wherever I came from. I'll just keep a low profile and avoid this "Lord of Desolation" person. What an odd title. Have I heard it before?*

Thus he passed between two long rows of Stonemen, carefully averting his eyes from the writhing forms inside their stone cages.

Go back! Go back! they called to him, nearly overpowering his intention. *Turn away from the City of the Dead!*

Shatter your glass! cried one of them, louder than the others. *Shatter your glass, and look at the face of your neighbor! For we cannot!*

But he did not understand what the speaker meant and kept on walking, not daring to look directly at the Stonemen lest he lose his resolve. Their wails grew more urgent as they moaned and howled at him. The wind blew aside some of the smoky haze, and he saw that the whole vast plain was filled with standing stones, all trying futilely to reach out and hold him back.

He hurried by, relieved when he finally passed the standing stones and came again to a clear space. By now the sulphurous haze had diminished, and the distant city became, by degrees, fully discernable.

Much sooner than he had anticipated, he reached the outer wall of a city whose impossibly high, glittering buildings stabbed like spears at the sullen sky. Beneath the wall was a body of black water, still as a pool of ink, gleaming like a gigantic mirror. Upon the water was a tall ship rigged with black sails, unmoving.

Nearer and nearer he drew to the city, walking like a ghost in a dream. His feet trod upon a wide walkway that looked like glass, but felt soft as moss. His feet sank down in it as if it were cool water.

He went forward slowly, drawing refreshment through his soles, and closed his eyes to savor the sensation.

When he opened them, he saw the figure of a man at the far end of the walkway. At first there was only a silhouette outlined against the glare, but coming closer, he saw that the man was perfectly proportioned and of a commanding stature, as if he were the resident god of the city.

The man was waiting for him.

It didn't occur to him to question whether the man was friend or foe. He trudged on as the grayish light began to illuminate the man's features.

The face, unlike that of most deities, showed not a smooth and sculpted countenance, but one graven with the lines and marks of experience. He had obviously known life, had fought his battles and garnered his victories, his defeats. A man who understood how the world worked.

The man was smiling at him.

Mesmerized, he approached, slowed, stopped. His mouth hung open.

The man stepped forward.

"Welcome, Oliver Medley," the man said, and extended his hand. His voice was deep as darkness. "Welcome to my city."

Saint Amber's Rose

"Thank you," Oliver croaked through a parched throat. Grasping the hand, he fell forward into unconsciousness.

The black-sailed ship sank slowly beneath the glassy surface of the water.

Charleynne Gates

Chapter Twenty

The Abbey

Old sins cast long shadows.
--an old saying

Night. A hooded shadow passes from darkness into darkness. A candle bursts into flame, illuminating half of the shadow's face inside its hood. Candlelight grows, and the shadow becomes a gentle morning face. The candle moves out of the small room in which the hooded one lives and lights its bearer's way up the many steps of a winding staircase to the top of a tower. There the candle is set to rest on the stone floor, and the hooded one goes to a rope hanging down from high overhead. The Whiltian friar (for such is the person inside the hood) begins to pull the rope, and the dawn bell of the Abbey--the *Belle Aurore*--sounds its sweet call across the cliffs and crags of the Great Mountain of Zund.

As it rings, the first rosy streaks of sunrise creep up the sky, and the residents of the Abbey emerge from their cells and file toward the Grand Sanctuary. As they come forth, their song merges with the ringing of the *Belle Aurore*. "Awaken! Awaken!" they sing. "Awaken, O glory of the dawn! Fill the world with your light. To every heart bring joy. Awaken! Awaken!"

"Alleluia! Alleluia! to the Giver of dawn, the Giver of grace!" respond the choirs of the Order. "Alleluia! Awaken!" as they descend to join the procession. At the very last, an insignificant figure emerges from behind a stone column and falls in line. No one appears to notice the addition.

Singing, the friars enter the Grand Sanctuary and stand to give praise. The Abbot takes his place in front and turns to face the eastward-looking rose window. "Alleluia! to the Giver of grace, Giver of truth, Giver of life!" he intones.

Saint Amber's Rose

"Alleluia! Awaken!" answers the chorus of Whiltian friars of the Abbey of Saint Amber. The sun rises over the Great Mountain, and the rose window glows with a many-colored radiance, as if from the heart of a rainbow.

Father Thyme, Abbot of Saint Amber's Abbey, sat behind his desk in his study after morning prayer. A thick pile of parchments lay before him, and sharpened quill pens and a filled inkstand had been placed near at hand by his clerk. The three-branched candelabra had been cleaned of old wax and refitted with sturdy white candles fashioned to burn steadily for many hours. Everything that his secretary, Brother Basil, could do to facilitate the Abbot's work had been done, and now the little clerk had retired to his desk outside the Abbot's door to attend to his other tasks.

Outside, the sun rolled smoothly across the lightening sky, bringing out the hidden colors of the deep canyons in the Mountains of Zund. Light bathed the ancient walls of the Abbey, burnishing them to a warm gold. Inside, the brothers and sisters of the Whiltian Order of Saint Amber went about the duties of the day. But the Abbot did not glance at the papers on his desk or lift his hand to pen and ink. Instead, he gazed out the open mullioned window, which looked toward the distant plains and forests of the Labyrinth World.

Ignoring his paperwork, Father Thyme rose from his chair and went toward the window. Even with his long sight he couldn't see the borderland of the Desolation, but he knew it was there, remote and menacing. He knew, also, that the ashes of the Desolation's Great Waste were advancing inexorably toward the Mountains of Zund. In his mind's eye he saw forest after forest falling before the remorseless march of death sweeping over them. He envisioned the terrified flight of the forest-dwellers and their helpless young, all smothered at last under an enveloping blanket of utter desolation. He foresaw the Labyrinth World at its end, a graveyard without a single green and living thing left upon it, a burnt-out planet hurtling through the black expanse of the cosmos.

The Abbot bowed his head. "Creator, let this fate pass from us!" he murmured. "Where is the Gift-Bringer? When will he come?" He left the window and, deep in thought, began pacing slowly about his study.

Charleynne Gates

Our oldest prophecies tell us that after a thousand years of peace in the Labyrinth World, the Lord of Desolation will arise and make war upon the earth. His desire is conquest; his aim, the ruin of the Graelands and the enslavement of the Sendara. *Destruction is in his heart, and no one will be strong enough to withstand him--no one except the One Without Guile, whose name we do not know, who does not know himself that he is meant to save the world. It is he who holds the key to Saint Amber's Rose, and it is he alone who must unlock the Rose. Only then will he discover his Gift and, under grace, bring it into the light before Darkness overwhelms us.*

"Creator," he pleaded aloud, "where is he?"

For a long time the Abbot walked the bounds of his study. In this terrible moment, none of his many tomes of wisdom or intricate star charts or far-seeing crystal globes could tell him what he wanted to know: Who is the Gift-Bringer? When will he come?

His perambulation brought him again to the window, where he stopped. The whole landscape of the country beneath the Great Mountain was spread out before him: first the vast, fragrant medicinal gardens of the Abbey, then hill and dale, stream and meadow far below, field and farm making a painterly scene of beauty and tranquility.

How long will these things last?

A layer of gray cloud moved above the mountains, temporarily blotting out the sun. Against a somber sky the Abbot spotted wisps of black, oily smoke drifting in from the Desolation. The smoke stretched its tendrils closer to the Abbey, spiraling around it with the stench of burning oil.

The Abbot touched a medallion hanging around his neck. His lips moved in prayer as he gazed steadily out at the darkening heavens. A wind blew up out of the north, whipping the smoke into momentary, unearthly forms. The Abbot watched and waited, knowing the dark vision would come, dreading its manifestation.

Four Horsemen limned themselves out of the smoke, galloping through storm-wracked skies. The first, gold-crowned, with features sharp and thin as knives, rode a white horse and bent a bow to full tension, a quiver of deadly arrows on its back. The second, an armored warrior, sat astride a monstrous scarlet mount, half horse, half dragon, and brandished a bloodstained sword. The third horse was black. Its skeletal rider held a pair of scales in which he weighed a pennyworth of

Saint Amber's Rose

grain against a pile of gold coins. The last horse was sickly pale; its black-enshrouded rider bore a gleaming scythe.

The Four Horsemen passed by; the storm clouds sailed on, and sunlight poured once again onto the Abbey of Saint Amber.

The Abbot bowed his head. "Pride. Envy. Greed. Revenge," he whispered. "Our old sins--to be unleashed once more if the Gift-Bringer does not come. How are we to defend ourselves in the coming battle against the Lord of Desolation?"

Suddenly the door to the Abbot's study burst open. Sister Celeret, Third Assistant Undergardener, stumbled inside, followed closely by Brother Basil, protesting at this unseemly intrusion. The young sister's robe was snagged and torn, her cowl awry, her hair hanging loose and tangled around her face. She ran to the Abbot, tripped on the hem of her robe, and fell to her knees.

"Father Abbot! Father Abbot!" she gasped. "Sister Valerian of the Forest Gate! She's been killed! She's dead!" And she collapsed, burying her face in her hands, sobbing wildly.

"Poor child! Poor child!" said Father Thyme softly, looking down at the body of Sister Valerian. It lay near the wrought-iron gate that divided the Abbey gardens from Threshold Forest. In death her small, childlike face was smooth, unmarked by care. Her little hands with their plump, short fingers lay outflung from her body, a handful of herbs and grasses scattered alongside. It seemed to the watchers that she merely slept--except for the straight thin gash across her throat.

"She died at once," said Brother Persil, the Infirmarian, kneeling beside the body as he examined the wound. "A knife or dagger with a keen edge, as far as I can tell."

"Has such a weapon been found?" asked Father Thyme. But no one knew of any.

"I cannot imagine that Sister Valerian would have done this to herself," said the Infirmarian. "There must be signs here, around her body and in the garden, to tell us what happened. She ought not to be disturbed until we check."

"But we cannot leave her like this, to lie out in the open!" Sister Clova, the Prioress, spoke quickly.

"Of course we will not, Sister," the Abbot reassured her. "Brother Burdock, when Brother Persil has finished his examination, will you and Brother Bay take Sister Valerian to the chapel?"

"I will carry her myself," said Brother Burdock, the Abbey Carpenter. "She was my friend." Tears coursing down his face, Brother Burdock knelt, lifted the tiny body into his arms and bore her into the Abbey. The Infirmarian followed, together with other Whilts who had hurried to the garden.

"Can you tell who--or what--killed her?" the Abbot asked a friar who still knelt beside the flattened grasses where the body had lain. "Could it have been a *wyrga*, Brother Constant?"

"Possibly," replied the friar, whose inconspicuous figure blended with the garden background of brown and green. As a member of the Abbey Council and Chaplain to the Abbot, Brother Constant was Father Thyme's chief confidante.

Brother Constant's eyes and hands searched the surrounding area for anomalies. He noted the displacement of an apparently insignificant twig or two, the lie of a swath of grass, and shook his head. "I do not detect their characteristic odor, but that may not tell the whole tale. I can't say definitely until I examine the ground farther out, but I'd assume the worst. Hm." Brother Constant picked up a shred of something stuck on a nearby bush, cloth fibers perhaps, and scrutinized it closely. After turning it over several times, he put it in the pocket of his robe.

"In the meantime, Father Abbot, let no one come near this part of the garden until we know definitely what happened to Sister Valerian. Also, it might be as well to have the Captain of the Watch keep a careful record of all who come in and go out of the Abbey, including the local villagers. It is a pity, but in these troublous times even those familiar to us cannot always be trusted. And," he went on as the two of them turned from the place of sudden death and started up the path to the Abbey, "neither can the people we know and love best--not always. I say this with reluctance, Father Abbot, but too often I have found it to be true."

"I know it, Brother Constant," said the Abbot with a troubled frown. "I have suspected for some time that--well, I can scarcely formulate my thoughts. There is a restlessness among us that was not always here. For some considerable time I have sensed a disruptive energy building. This very morning, my old friend, I saw the Four Horsemen riding the sky. And now--a murder committed within the grounds of our beloved Abbey! No longer is this a place of refuge, a sanctuary of safety and peace!"

Brother Constant nodded. "These are dark times, Father Abbot, very dark indeed. Who can say whether we shall survive them?"

They walked for a while in meditative silence.

"Father Abbot," remarked the Chaplain, "I did notice something that puzzles me."

"What is that, Brother Constant?"

"The Forest Gate at the end of the garden: Supposedly it has been locked for centuries."

"I believe that is so."

"Then how is it," asked the Chaplain, "that the gate has been recently opened--and closed again?"

The Chapel of the Silver Chalice was a small room, simply furnished and quite different from the Grand Sanctuary. In the front wall was a tall, slender window illumined by a single brilliant star in the night sky. The uncovered altar was a cube of dark, polished wood upon which rested a silver chalice. Its soft gleam reflected the halo of candlelight over a pinewood coffin wherein lay the earthly remains of Sister Valerian.

Sister Clova had received the body when Brother Burdock carried it in and had seen to its proper placement in the Chapel. When those who had escorted Sister Valerian had paid their respects and gone back to their appointed duties, the Prioress was left alone with the dead. Inside the coffin she put sprigs of sweet-smelling rosemary, a specific against evil, and then, dry-eyed, knelt in prayer beside it.

Father Thyme entered. He paused inside the door, his head bowed. After a long moment, he looked up again and straightened his shoulders, then slowly approached the kneeling woman.

"She was beautiful, Sister Valerian was," said the Abbot quietly. "How serene she looks in the candlelight. A pity I did not know her better. I believe you were closer to her than anyone else. It was you who had her assigned to care for the garden at the Forest Gate, the one farthest from the Abbey. She tended certain rare medicinal plants that bloom only at night, did she not? I was told that she slept by day. Few of the friars ever saw her."

Sister Clova was silent for a time, giving no indication that she had heard the Abbot's words or even realized he was present. "Father Abbot," said the Prioress at last, and her voice was old and sad and weary. "Will you hear my confession?"

The Abbot seated himself on the wooden bench behind her and composed himself to listen and understand. "Let me help you bear this burden," he said quietly. "You have borne it alone far too long."

There was silence in the Chapel for a time. Twice the abbot urged the kneeling Prioress to rise and be seated; twice she shook her head. The penitent's posture, she indicated, was the only right one for her in this dark hour which she had dreaded for so long.

"As you will, my dear friend," said the Abbot. His face obscured by the shadow of his hood, he attended so closely to the silence that it seemed to him there was no other sound in the universe but the wordless agony of the soul before him.

Sister Clova gazed steadily at the star outside the tall window. "It was many years ago," she began at last, "and I was newly come to the Abbey. How blessed I felt, being admitted here! It was the only home I ever wanted. How young I was then--and how naive! I thought that here in the Abbey I had entered into Paradise. I did not know, then, that evil hides even in Paradise--or that I might be the instrument of its desires!

"My first assignment as a postulant was to work under old Sister Mentilia. Do you recall her?"

Father Thyme nodded. "Yes. She was Head of the Infirmary Gardens for over a century, was she not? And perhaps had lived too long at the Abbey to remember how it feels to be young, or how to give wise direction to a young girl!"

Sister Clova bent her head and said nothing for a moment. "She was kind, but in a distant way. She lived only for her gardens. She loved the plants there, every leaf and flower, as if they were her children, and we who worked under her were almost invisible to her except as we tended our garden plots well or ill.

"She gave me the small plot farthest from the Abbey, where night-blooming medicinal plants live in an area of deep shade at the outer border of the gardens. I was proud that she entrusted me with those rare and precious blossoms. It may have been that pride ate into my heart and made me think myself a bit above the other postulants.

"One summer night I was sent to gather moonlilies, which bloom only once a year at midnight. They grow near the gate that opens into Threshold Forest, the gate we were taught never to touch. Indeed, at the time it was locked with three iron padlocks, although they had been there so long they had rusted almost to nothing. No one ever thought of replacing them with new ones, for no one imagined any danger.

"On that night the trees whispered things to me that I had never dreamed of before. It was all so beautiful that I rested from my work and gazed up at the moon. I made a wish... When I opened my eyes he was there, standing in shadow on the other side of the gate. I saw his golden eyes in the darkness. He wanted inside the garden; I felt it. And--he wanted me! I broke the rusted locks, and I--I opened the gate."

The faint hiss of an indrawn breath underscored her words. The Abbot stretched his hand toward her bowed head, but did not touch her.

"He came in. And I... and I... It was as if all the world's darkness wrapped around me like velvet, and I gave myself to him, body and soul. When I awoke, he was gone. The gate was open. I became frightened. I closed the gate and fixed the locks so that no one would see they had been disturbed.

"I returned to the Abbey before dawn. No one saw me. I tried to persuade myself that it was all a dream. But in time, I knew it wasn't. I went to Sister Mentilia; I told her my mother was ill in a distant village, and I needed to go and care for her for several months.

"Sister Mentilia didn't notice anything different about me. She blessed me absent-mindedly and let me go. I didn't return to my home village; my parents had died when I was a child, and I lived with a married sister before I entered the Abbey. Instead, I went to a cousin in another village. There I had my baby. We saw that she... was different, but I loved her! Nothing mattered to me except being with her.

"When I recovered, I knew that I had to return to the Abbey. I had no way to support my baby, young as I was, with no skills and no prospects for marriage. My cousin was married to a man who didn't mind that she kept my baby for me. I went back to the Abbey and asked Sister Mentilia to give me a different assignment. She did, without even questioning me, and I never went back to the moonlily garden again.

Charleynne Gates

"After ten years, my cousin fell ill and died. Her husband soon married again, and he wanted no more of my child, what with his other children in the house and those of his new wife. He sent her to me--and I was at my wits' end, not knowing what to do with her!

"Then I thought of a solution. The child was sweet and biddable, even though slow to learn, and she did not remember me as her mother. I presented her to the Abbot as an orphan cousin of mine, and asked that she be accepted as a ward of the Abbey. This was done, and when she became of proper age, she joined us as a postulant. I knew that she would never be able to take the final vows of our Order, but she was happy here and could do useful work for her keep.

"She became my special charge. She loved the flowers, and I asked the new Head of the Gardens to give her work where she could be by herself. The Head Gardener assigned her to the moonlily garden. But my daughter met no danger there, and my fears were quiet for all the years she lived here.

"But now she is dead, and I--I am the one who opened the gate of death for her! She was killed in the very place where I... O my child! My child! I gave you to the Darkness!" At last the wounded heart relieved itself in tears.

The Abbot waited. "Did you love him?" he asked.

The Prioress lifted her head and looked at him, puzzled. "Love him?"

"Yes, my daughter. Did you love the man?"

The Prioress looked back at the starlight shining through the window. "Yes!" she whispered. "Oh, yes! I loved him with every bone in my body, every drop of blood in my heart. And--oh, Father Abbot, I still do!"

Father Thyme nodded slowly. "Then there is hope. Love was at the beginning; love will be at the end. Love never fails."

Long did Sister Clova and Father Thyme remain in the Chapel of the Chalice. Forgiving and forgiven, the two of them spoke softly together until the star outside the tall window set in the west.

Sister Arvest, the Almoner, came to relieve the Prioress's vigil, and Father Thyme sent Sister Clova to rest for the remainder of the night. He himself paced slowly back to his own cell, wondering about the being who had hidden outside the Forest Gate. What manner of man had so easily seduced a Whiltian sister of the Abbey? Surely not some local farmer's lad. The residents of the valleys below always had the greatest respect for the Abbey, and none of them came into its gardens except by permission. As for the wood beside the Forest Gate, in general the farmers and herdsmen avoided its precincts, not even gathering kindling there. Some old belief about it, the Abbot recalled, though exactly what it was escaped his memory.

What was that mysterious entity Sister Clova had encountered? The Labyrinth Wood was an ancient part of Threshold Forest, which reached for many thousand *kephan* northwest of the Abbey. Incalculably old, it contained myriad creatures never seen outside its boundaries. Having no particular need for its products--wood was gathered on the other side of the Abbey--few of the friars ever ventured inside it. Since long before Father Thyme's rule, the Abbey had generally ignored the Labyrinth Wood. *Perhaps that has not been wise.*

"If only I understood why Sister Valerian was killed," the Abbot muttered to himself. He stopped short as a new thought occurred to him. "Why was our little Third Assistant Undergardener Sister Celeret so far beyond her usual station as the Forest Gate? How did she happen to find the body? I wonder. Yes, I wonder."

The Abbot shook his head. There was one person who might be able to shed light on the mystery: his old friend the Mage Dandriel, far away in Keeper's Inn. But it was rumored that the inn had been destroyed in the last earthquake. That area of Threshold Forest, being close to a portal between dimensions, was unstable and subject to earth tremors. But Dandriel surely would not have gone to destruction together with the inn. He had many secret ways about Threshold Forest, indeed, throughout the Labyrinth World, and very likely had escaped by one of them.

Father Thyme shut himself into his cell and opened a window. A raven landed on the sill, awaiting instructions. The Abbot spoke to it; the raven took off into the night and soon was lost to view.

The Abbot lowered his old bones onto his narrow bed and touched the medallion beneath his cowl. Is it possible that the man who came out of the Labyrinth Wood had some connection with the Desolation? Had the influence of the Lord of Desolation encroached this far, and as long ago as the conception of Sister Valerian?

Charleynne Gates

Father Thyme closed his eyes and concentrated on closing his mind firmly against the blighting fear of evil. "Light," he whispered. "Creator, give us light. *Va'in 'a moru'. Va'in 'a moru'.*"

But I am Darkness, and I am here, said the Voice in the Smoking Mirror. *I am Desolation, and I am with you always, even to the end of the Age.*

Chapter Twenty-One

The Grimmerund

Slowly Firemark walked beside Pavarr as they made their way along the path through the Icewode, away from the Ruined Chapel. Gently the great stallion bore the *Sendara* on his back. Low she bent over the saddle, her head drooping like a golden lily on its green stem. Her pale lips opened; her breath issued laboriously. From time to time a shudder of pain passed over her, and she bit back a moan. Pavarr, his brow furrowed in concern, glanced up at her, but she shook her head. Not for her the luxury of rest.

They went on.

Pavarr turned toward her at intervals, putting his hand over hers to comfort and reassure, and ever did she look down at him, wan and smiling.

"Fear not, my dear," she whispered. "It is not yet my time to die." Then a bluish shadow of agony clouded her face, and she turned away from him so that he would not see her suffer. But he did see, and his heart grew bitter and afraid.

High in the evening sky, charcoal gray clouds masked the moon. On the ground the trees stood grim and black, each encased in its chrysalis of ice. Snow fell, now only a few flakes, now in billows and gusts. Pavarr reached up to pull Flavia's mantle more snugly about her; he cautioned her to keep the hood pulled close over her shining hair.

Firemark's steady pace made nothing of the many *kephan* they had to cover. The horse followed without hesitation the unmarked path that led through the Icewode, for he and his kin had the sense of it bred in their bones. Pavarr was fully aware of Firemark's wisdom and allowed the horse to find his way unguided, for not to human mortals was this instinctive knowledge granted.

A hastening of light footsteps, and Mil came running to them, javelin in hand, sling of javelin-heads across her back. Anxiously she peered up at Flavia, but seeing that the *Sendara's* eyes were closed--in sleep or in pain, Mil could not tell--she fell in step with Pavarr. The two of them conversed in low tones.

"*Gnaarx* have been near here, and not long ago," said Mil. Her breath made almost no vapor in the cold air. "I tracked their foul odor and found one of their roosting places in a lightning-blasted tree. None of them are there any more, except..." Her voice trailed off, and she glanced keenly around, making certain they were not overheard.

"Except?" Pavarr prompted.

"Except for two of them, both infants. They had been wounded by the other nestlings, torn up so badly that they could not be healed, and then pushed out of the nest. You know the *gnaarx* abandon their sick and wounded. They leave them to die without care or comfort, not even a morsel of food to sustain them." She frowned and looked aside, exhaling sharply as if to banish any lingering residue of their stench.

"Did you--?" Pavarr asked.

"Yes. No living thing, not even a *gnaarx*, should be left to die by inches, in pain and isolation. The adults did not lay them together so that they might have at least some comfort in their dying! I severed a vein in the back of their skulls, the one that entraps them in their monstrous lives. As with the *wyrga*, it is the only way they can be killed. It was over in less than a breath. But--"

"But when the adults return, they will know at once what happened," Pavarr continued. "They will recognize the straight, clean cut of a Dwarvian-made dagger, for no blade is thinner or cuts a finer line. By this act of mercy, you have made the *gnaarx* aware that we are still in the Icewode--and the *Sendara* with us. Their master knows you are her gallowglass and are always near her."

"True," said Mil, frowning. "And if they return--when they return--they will find us and attack. I ought to have left them alone."

The two of them considered the implications of their worsening situation.

"'Mercy is the first imperative'," said Pavarr, quoting from the ancient *Book of the Labyrinth*. "'It should never be regretted.'"

Behind them, Flavia drew in a half-sobbing breath, which she tried to stifle by pressing the hem of her mantle against her lips.

Mil glanced up. "She is growing worse," she whispered to Pavarr. "We must get her to the Abbey quickly."

Saint Amber's Rose

"The slaves of the Desolation surround us in this wood," Pavarr replied. "We have to move with greater caution."

"I have been thinking about that Hermit of the Ruined Chapel," said Mil, falling into step beside him. "I am not sure we were right to trust him. I remember something like smoke, or a gray mist, in the Chapel, and a voice coming from the stained-glass window... and then we were walking into the Icewode, and he was gone. I think he may have been an agent of the Desolation."

"We are of one mind, then," said Pavarr. "But now we have gone so far on the way he sent us that it is too hazardous to go back. I've been planning our route as far as I can. The River Sunder must be near here. It flows through the Mountains of Zund. I have heard it runs beneath the Abbey on its high cliff. We can leave the Icewode path when we get to that black mound in the distance and head directly for the river."

"You mean the Grimmerund?" asked Mil, surprised. "Do you really want to go toward it?"

"Why not?" replied Pavarr. "It seems to be a landmark, and I thought by climbing to the top I'd get a better idea of exactly where we are."

"You would, certainly," said Mil, "but the risk is too great. The Grimmerund has an unsavory reputation. I once heard from the ravens that *wyrga* use it as a gathering place--and maybe more."

"More?"

"It is said to be a place of sacrifice," said Mil, "where the *wyrga* meet with--him."

"You mean Ab'addon?"

"I have been told so. And look: The trail is leading us straight toward the Grimmerund."

"I noticed," said Pavarr, "but I think we're being not led, but forced, toward it."

They looked to either side of the track. Thickets of briars, icicle-coated down to their long, shiny thorns, lined the trail on either side and reached far back into the wood. Even if the Questors used their swords to hack away the brush and carve out an alternate path, the task would delay them far too long, and Flavia's need for rest was urgent.

"You're right," said Mil. "We can't go back to the Ruined Chapel; we can't turn aside. We have no choice but to go on to the

Grimmerund. Wait," she added. "I'm picking up a scent. *Gnaarx*--
coming toward us from the north. They must have found their two dead
young and detected our presence. Firemark is turning eastward toward
the Grimmerund; we cannot escape it now. There's a small birch grove
near it, said to be under the protection of a woodland spirit. Flavia may
be safe enough there to rest for a while. I'll go back and decoy the
gnaarx off our trail, then meet you at the birch grove."

Pavarr nodded, and Mil took off running like wind over the
snow, leaving no footprints.

Flavia lifted her head and opened her eyes as Pavarr and
Firemark turned away from the main path and headed toward the
Grimmerund.

"Pavarr," she whispered, "I am very thirsty."

The prince stopped and reached into his knapsack for a flask of
goldenwater, which he handed up to her.

"Where are we?" she asked after she had sipped from the flask.
A little color crept back into her cheeks. "And--oh, Pavarr, where is--
where is Oliver Medley?"

Pavarr frowned, considering. "Oliver Medley? The Gift-
Bringer! I had nearly forgotten him."

"What has happened to us?" Flavia said, bending down. "Why
did we not remember Cousin Oliver?"

"I believe," said Pavarr slowly, "that we must have been under
some kind of enchantment that the Hermit put on us. I remember being
in the Ruined Chapel, and the Hermit talking to us through some kind of
mist, and then we were here in the Icewode. I don't know what
happened to Friend Oliver and the Dwarvians who were with us."

"And Belvedine," Flavia continued, sitting straight on
Firemark's back and looking keenly around for the first time. "And
Hera Vespasia. Where are they?"

"I don't know. But Mil thinks we ought to get off this path that
the Hermit put us on."

"But where would we go?" asked Flavia. "Didn't the Hermit
give us directions to the Abbey?"

"I doubt it," he replied, "but the briars are closing in behind us
and on both sides, forcing us where they want us to go, and now we
have no choice but to keep going eastward, toward that black mound.

The Grimmerund, Mil called it. We'll meet her there. When you've rested, we'll go on to the River Sunder and follow it to the Abbey."

"The Grimmerund!" whispered Flavia.

"What is it? What's wrong?"

"The Grimmerund is a dark mystery," Flavia answered, gazing into the distance. "It has been here since the beginning of the world. Many Icewodes have grown around it and died and grown again."

One slender hand stroked her forehead, as if to soothe away a headache, then pulled the collar of her cloak closer about her throat. "The Icewode itself has never been allied with any other realm of the Labyrinth World. Always it has stood alone, and few have ever known what lives inside it. Only..." Her head drooped forward again.

"We're going to find a place for you to rest," Pavarr told her. "Soon," he muttered to himself.

The grove of white birches appeared not far away, standing in its own little clearing west of the Grimmerund. He went toward it, hoping for a safe, if temporary, refuge.

Inside the grove the air was warm; no snow fell to the ground. Even in the middle of the Icewode, green mosses covered the earth, and deep in the curls of moss tiny white flowers bloomed. Summer reigned inside the grove; outside was perpetual winter.

"How beautiful! Let me rest here," said Flavia. She took a deep breath. "Why, I recognize this grove!"

"Then let's get you down." Pavarr lifted her from Firemark's back and carried her to a bed of soft, deep moss, letting the horse wander as he pleased.

"You know this place, Flavia?" Pavarr sat beside her and took her pale hand in his. "Have you been here before?"

Flavia closed her eyes and inhaled the green fragrance. "No--but it has the air of an old and sacred place. It is... a nemeton--a sanctuary! Good and holy spirits have walked here. That is why it is always summer within its boundaries. And look! Over there... See how the light dances!" His eyes followed her hand pointing to a young birch nearby, but he saw nothing unusual.

"I don't understand, Flavia, but all that matters is that you feel better here."

Firemark walked toward the other end of the nemeton, perturbed about the place where they had stopped to rest. The birch grove seemed harmless; he detected nothing inside it but the serene presence of invisible beings. That black mound they called the Grimmerund was different. He sensed nothing good coming from it, quite the opposite, in fact. A miasma of menace streamed from it like smoke. The horse felt it, smelled it, tasted it... and in the recesses of his ancestral memory, identified it. Lifting his head, he neighed suddenly, loudly enough to ring from the rocks all around.

"Ho, Firemark! Hush, my friend!" Quickly Pavarr came to the horse and stroked the massive head. "What's the matter?" He bent his ear toward the horse's mouth as Firemark whickered.

"It's something about this mound, the Grimmerund," Pavarr reported to Flavia. "Firemark senses danger around it, or inside it. I ought to go and find out what it is, but I don't want to leave you alone."

"Have no fear," said Flavia, her head resting against the tallest birch trunk whose branches, despite the cold and snow outside the grove, were full-leaved and shimmering in pale green light. "Nothing will harm me as long as I am here, and Mil will return soon. Go if you will, but do not put yourself in danger. If you find an opening into the Grimmerund, I pray you, do not enter."

Pavarr murmured something indistinct, took a last look around the grove, at its cushion of emerald mosses, its circle of white-barked trees, and went out into the snow. Drawing his dagger, he moved cautiously toward the black mound and vanished from sight of the little nemeton.

Now he heard what Firemark had reported: a sound like muffled thunder coming from underground. A hidden watercourse? No, it was deeper, more rhythmic, like drums or the tread of iron-shod feet weighted with darkness.

He followed the vibrations around the rock, all his senses on high alert. An odor came off the rock, not of earth or wet stone, but of something repellent, unclean. There was the scent of snow, too, not covering the ground here but lingering invisibly in the air, as if it were loath to touch the surface of the Grimmerund.

He crept forward, unable to see around the curve, and put his hand lightly on the mound. It felt spongy to the touch, like the tissue of a putrefying wound, and a dribble of fluid, like a rivulet of blood, trickled between his fingers. He snatched his hand away and examined it, but no stain tainted it, neither blood nor water. He looked at the

Grimmerund again and saw that it pulsed slightly, as if it were not rock at all but an immense, unnatural growth with a life of its own.

Mil ran on, chasing shadows that swooped down to the forest canopy and up again before she could aim against them. Once or twice a distant cry, sharp as a dagger-stab, echoed from the leaden sky, but as skilled a hunter as she was, she couldn't pinpoint it.

At last she halted, fitted javelin to thrower, and defiantly sent the silver weapon soaring high to and through one of the circling silhouettes. The spear-point struck into nothingness and went to ground in the far reaches of the snowbound wilderness.

She regretted the impulse at once, for her spear-points were of elven-make, unmistakable in their markings. Whoever found it, for good or ill, would know definitely where the Questors were in the Icewode.

I've let them lure me away from Flavia, she realized with a flash of anger at herself. *And wasted a spear-point. And given this part of the Icewode a clear sign that we are here. So pervasive is the evil in this place--and so easily have I lost self-control!*

Mil turned on her heel and began running back toward the Grimmerund, toward Flavia and Pavarr, hoping she was not too late.

Firemark paced nervously inside the boundary of the little nemeton, concerned about Pavarr's prolonged absence. Occasionally he cropped the grasses growing between the birches, keeping an ear pricked for the least alien sound. He realized much more clearly than Pavarr what perils surrounded them this near the Grimmerund. When he had neighed that once, and so loudly, he had a purpose the prince had not perceived, but those who heard him at a distance understood his meaning.

Flavia, alone and unafraid, leaned back against the birch. The tree was as great with wisdom as a woman with child, and it gave her freely of its strength. After a while, Flavia began to sing an old lullaby about the moon, one she had learned in childhood:

> *Softly the moon rises over the hill.*
> *Softly the breeze whispers,*
> *Then all is still.*

Caras, the Evening Star,
Shines in the west.
Night settles down.
Nature calls us to rest.

They were simple words, and she sang it simply, as her mother had sung it to her. When the song faded, the slender birch nearby began to shine within its white trunk, as if the tree were filling with moonlight. Brighter and brighter it grew as gradually the figure of a woman began to form inside it. At the base of the tree stood an oaken water-cask and a silver libation dish, attributes of the spirit of the birches. As the spirit took radiant form within the tree, cask and dish glimmered in the dark moss beneath the shimmering leaves.

The whispering of the leaves gathered and became the voice of the goddess of the grove.

Sendara, Guardian of the Graelands, our ancient home. Whither bound, Sendara?

"Is it you, Mother Nemetona? O Mother Nemetona, help us, I beg you! We are meant to take the Gift-Bringer to the Abbey of Saint Amber, but the Hermit of the Ruined Chapel separated us, and now we are lost."

Only the Gift-Bringer and not you yourself, child? For you are ill!

"I am, Mother Nemetona. I am ill of the poison of the Lord of Desolation. Even now I feel its deadly effect working within me. I must go to the Abbey if I am to live. But it is more important for the Gift-Bringer to be there, for in his Gift is the life of the Graelands and the Labyrinth World."

What is his Gift, child?

"No one knows, not even he."

What is his name?

"Oliver Medley."

Medley... whispered the birches in the grove, their leaves winking silver in the moonlight.

Oliver Medley, echoed Nemetona. *The name has music in it. Tell me.*

Saint Amber's Rose

"He is one of the seven Questors sent to search for me when I was held captive at the Ruined Chapel. From there we were to go on to the Abbey."

Where are the other Questors? asked Nemetona.

"The Hermit of the Ruined Chapel sent us in four different directions," replied Flavia, "saying that thus the Lord of Desolation would find it more difficult to track us. The Dwarvians Tipp and Tapp Whackitt were to descend into the lost mines beneath the Icewode; Belvedine de Montfort and Hera Vespasia were to fly over the wood, and Prince Pavarr, my cousin Mil, and I were sent riding through the wood."

And what of Oliver Medley?

"I--I don't remember clearly... I think the Hermit held him back until the rest of us had left the Ruined Chapel. He may have sent Cousin Oliver on the road to Purple Valley. Someone there was to help him on his way."

O my child! My child! mourned Nemetona. *How poorly you have been served! You do not know that the Hermit of the Ruined Chapel is no longer what he once was. His soul became bent when he fashioned an homunculus—his unnatural double. The Lord Ab'addon lured that unsouled being to his own evil purpose, which was to rule the Hermit, and through him--you! Thus did the Dark Lord separate the Questors, believing that none would ever reach the Abbey. Thus, isolated from one another, they might be more easily destroyed--and you with them!*

Flavia sank back against the white birch tree, and her face grew paler than the moonlight. "O Mother Nemetona!" she implored. "Show me a way to help them!"

I cannot show you how, but I can let you hear what my trees tell me.

She blew her soft summerbreath over Flavia, and the wisdom of the night opened to the *Sendara.*

Far away in the Icewode, the sound of Mil's footsteps came to Flavia's ear, footsteps running in the air above the snow, leaving no prints. Fast, faster she ran, darting like lightning-flash around tree and bush, over hillock and across gully, rapid in flight as a messenger of heaven, but ever did the Icewode stretch ahead, and little ground did she gain in her desperate race.

The sluggish ripple of muddy water came to her as Oliver Medley stood beside Sunder Spring, where the river began. Its waters trickled into an inconsequential little pool where waterweeds grew so thickly that the stream was nearly choked a-borning. "There's the River Sunder!" she heard Bertie Mossgrower proclaim proudly, "and there's my boat!"

Pavarr's stealthy footsteps came to her as he stole around the curve of the Grimmerund. The faint slap of his hand came to her as it met the alien substance of which the mound was made. The stamp of iron feet came to her from terrifying depths below the mound.

The voices of the Dwarvians came to her. Far beneath the Icewode, in the twisting tunnels of the Longlost Mine, Tipp and Tapp kept the Vigil of Remembrance and sang the Songs of Departing.

The breathing of the giant spider who dwelt on the Grimmerund's summit came to her. The soughing of the night breeze ruffled the hairs on its attenuated legs.

The soft beat of Hera Vespasia's wings in the night came to her.

And at last, the low, unnerving chant in the abyssal caverns of the Grimmerund came to her. She knew, then, that this was the place where the slaves of the Desolation gathered to make the Sacrifice of Darkness.

Flavia shuddered and put her hands over her face. "O Mother Nemetona," she mourned. "This wicked, wicked evil! And we have been driven directly to it! How can we get away?"

You must not think of getting away, child! No matter that you were tricked into coming here; this is where you were destined to be. It is your task to stop the slaves of the Desolation from performing their unholy sacrifice. You must free the sacrificial victim!

"Free the victim?" asked Flavia. "But where is it?"

Listen again, said Nemetona. Again she breathed among the leaves, and in that breath was the sound of wind brushing the silken strands of a gigantic cobweb on top of the Grimmerund. A captive trapped in its net of sticky filaments struggled valiantly to escape.

"Is that the sacrifice?" whispered Flavia. "But how--?"

It was unlucky enough to fly into the spider's webtrap, said Nemetona. *The Lord of Desolation intended the Gift-Bringer to be the victim, but because another one blundered into the web instead, the* wyrga *beneath the Grimmerund take it to be the one they were waiting for.   They will not move out until moonset, but then, in the utter darkness soon to come, it will be cut from the web and tortured until its terror and pain reach their peak, and then it will be killed, and the soul ripped from its body.   The energy of its death agony will be fuel for their engines of destruction, and its spirit will be enslaved to the Lord of Desolation, bound to do his bidding whether it will or no.   And then the Secret of Saint Amber's Rose will belong to Ab'addon!*

"What can I do?" Flavia whispered.

You must set the victim free, replied the spirit of the grove. *There is no one else who can.*

"I cannot walk!" exclaimed Flavia.   "O Mother Nemetona, I cannot free anyone!"

But the glow of moonlight within the white birch had faded, together with the oaken water-cask and the silver libation dish.   Flavia was alone.

Pavarr felt his way along the edge of the mound, avoiding touching its surface again.   The night wasn't yet absolutely dark; enough grayish light illuminated the rock to allow him to make his way to where a nearly invisible cleft exposed a narrow passage.   Pavarr edged inside cautiously, listening intently.   Eventually his ear caught the low vibration he had heard outside, a heavy, metallic beat, and over it the monotonous repetition of a dread name.   He recognized the name, one of many belonging to the Lord of Desolation.

The farther inside the cleft he moved, the faster the pounding vibrations rushed along the walls of the passageway, like the slithering of a demented snake.

A killing, he realized. *They're preparing for a killing. It can't be Flavia; she's safe in the birch grove.   But whatever they've taken, it will die soon,* Pavarr estimated, gauging by the growing intensity of the chant.

Another ninety degree turn in the tunnel, and he came upon it before he could stop himself: an immense hollow in the bowels of the Grimmerund, a cavern where masses of *wyrga* shrieked and howled their ritual chants before an inferno of black fire.   Its flames leaped up to a ceiling hidden by a roiling cloud of smoke.

Pavarr shrank back behind a protruding ledge and crouched to observe the scene, his heart beating wildly, his mouth dry with horror.

Here was the center of the evil they were fleeing, and they had come--by accident or deception--straight to it! How had they been so misled? Is one of the Questors a traitor? Not Flavia or Mildrith: He had known them since all three were children. Not the Dwarvian smiths with their tribal enmity against the Lord of Desolation. Not Hera Vespasia. Who else?

Medley! Oliver Medley, the unknown factor from a strange world, supposedly some remote relation of Flavia's. But who really knew anything about him? Did Belvedine, who had brought him into the Labyrinth? And where was she?

The pounding tread below him, and the relentless chant, doubled and redoubled in volume.

Got to get Flavia out of here, was his last thought before the *wyrga* guard sprang onto his back.

Hera Vespasia and Great-Aunt Belvedine found themselves in a tiny clearing in a copse of frozen trees, the Ruined Chapel out of sight behind them.

Great-Aunt Belvedine unfurled her umbrella, turned it upside down, and stepped inside. Taking a firm grasp of the crook of its handle, "Ready!" she said, and pointed her sharp nose in the general direction of the Mountains of Zund.

Hera Vespasia perched on a nearby branch, looking askance at these expeditionary preparations. "You may be ready, Belvedine, but in my opinion it would be as well to figure out exactly how to get where we're going! I do not trust that Hermit's instructions, not at all!"

"Really, Hera Vespasia, how can you ask such a question at the moment we ought to be taking off!" snapped Great-Aunt Belvedine. She scowled at some undefined point beyond the owl, who noticed that her eyes were glassy and unfocused.

She's still under the Hermit's spell, the owl realized. No use trying to talk her down. *She'd never believe she was under a spell in the first place! I'll try an appeal to reason—if she has any left.*

"I assume, then, that you know the way to the Abbey?" asked the owl.

"What Abbey? What are you talking about?"

"The Abbey of Saint Amber," Hera Vespasia replied patiently. "Our destination. You remember: where we were escorting the

Sendara before we were sidetracked into the Ruined Chapel. You do remember the Ruined Chapel, don't you?"

Great-Aunt Belvedine turned toward the Great Chief of the Norrengild, her eyes beginning to return to their normal frosty glare. "Of course I remember! I never forget anything! The Abbey is located on... or behind... or somewhere in the vicinity of the Great Mountain of Zund. I assumed you knew the way."

Hera Vespasia lowered her eyelids to half-staff. "It is common knowledge that the Abbey is located on a cliff halfway up the Great Mountain of Zund. But the Abbey, not to mention the Icewode itself, is outside my territory. As a matter of fact, so are the Mountains of Zund. I have never been to the Abbey. I thought you had."

Great-Aunt Belvedine narrowed her eyes. "It was your responsibility to secure the correct route! I'm quite positive that Amatilda Keeper told me so!"

"I wasn't told any such thing!" retorted Hera Vespasia. "Had I been told, I would have devised an appropriate itinerary prior to departure."

At this impasse, a moment of icy silence ensued while both parties gave serious consideration to the paucity of options for their immediate future. Then the owl cleared her throat and continued.

"I have heard that there are powerful downdrafts in the canyons between the mountains, as well as certain pseudo-mirage effects which render accurate visibility difficult, if not impossible, at higher altitudes. Even so, I have no doubt that I shall be able to plot a true course. Using the nutational values of the Jovian moons in combination with the magnetic fields of Labyrinthine ley lines--"

"Of course, of course," interjected Great-Aunt Belvedine soothingly. "I have the greatest respect for your powers of orienteering, Hera Vespasia, but if I might make a pertinent observation, time is fleeting, and we still have before us the problem of how to find our way with the least amount of risk to ourselves. If you could briefly--"

The owl condescended to explain in simpler terms. "We head in the general direction of the Great Mountain and fly low. We maintain a maximum distance of ten wingspans between us, keeping each other in view at all times. And--"

"How low do you mean?" Great-Aunt Belvedine interrupted.

Charleynne Gates

"I am explaining," said Hera Vespasia. "Please do not interrupt."

"Well!" said Great-Aunt Belvedine.

"First, I'll make a brief reconnaissance flight. Be so kind as to remain where you are until I return." Hera Vespasia rose above the Icewode with a silent movement of her wings and a short while later returned to her branch.

"The canopy looks fairly even from an aerial perspective. There is only one outstanding obstacle: About halfway between here and the Great Mountain is an immense black mound surrounded on all sides by thorn hedges, and some sort of swirling dark mist hanging over it. I thought of going in for a closer look, but something held me back. I suggest we take care to avoid the place. Other than that, I believe we have a clear airway to the Mountains of Zund."

"And where exactly is the Abbey?"

"On the opposite side of the Great Mountain."

"*Formidable*!" exclaimed Great-Aunt Belvedine in the native tongue of her latest deceased husband. "How are the others ever going to meet us there? They can't fly!"

"I expect they'll think of something," replied the owl. "The Hermit assigned them—"

"Hermit? What hermit?" said Great-Aunt Belvedine. "The *Sendara*'s safety depends solely upon the two of us, as I always thought it would. My great-nephew never was any good in situations requiring nerve! I've never understood why Flavia insisted on bringing him along. Well, come along! There's not a moment to lose!" She gave the handle of her umbrella a violent twist and shot into the air.

"Wait!" Hera Vespasia exclaimed. "That black mound--we mustn't go anywhere near it! It's--wait!"

But Great-Aunt Belvedine had already risen above the forest canopy and was bearing west northwest by north, give or take a degree. The owl gave a resigned shrug and took off in the same general direction.

Because it was now full night, an indigo night with threatening clouds driving across a white moon, Great-Aunt Belvedine couldn't see much below her. At intervals her umbrella grazed the treetops, bumping her uncomfortably until she regained altitude. Starshine was minimal. Having no altimeter or compass, she had to steer by sight, swooping low to try to orient herself by distinguishing one ice-coated tree from a virtually identical one next to it.

Great-Aunt Belvedine's temper wore thin. She wished in vain that she'd obeyed her impulse to trade in her old umbrella for a newer model (with a celestial positioning system built into the handle) when she had the chance, instead of wringing every last bit of mileage out of the old one, as was her invariable habit. Her last late husband, Jules, Comte de Montfort, used to say she could squeeze water out of a stone, she was so tight-fisted. *Dear Jules!* Sometimes she almost missed him.

The thought of her late spouse led to that of a more distant relative: her great-nephew Oliver Medley. Not for the first time, she wondered if bringing Medley to Ravenhome had been a really sound move. *I can't blame myself for whatever happens; it was all Flavia's idea.*

Belvedine peered about as the umbrella sped on. The air was becoming dense, with swirls of mist enveloping her and obscuring the moon. How inconvenient! And how she missed the navigational accessories in her new-model umbrella--that is, if she had actually purchased one. How exhilarating it would have been to drive a Super-10 Jupiter Pluvius XL with custom interior! How satisfying, the envy of her dearest friends!

Savoring the prospect of one-upping her entire social set, Belvedine lost all sense of time and place and flew deeper into the thickening cloud. Scarlet, she mused, scarlet with silver trim, or perhaps the Medley tartan with gold ribs and handle. On the other hand, lime green with magenta racing stripes would be daring but oh-so-chic. So many choices...

Whoosh! The cobweb trap on the Grimmerund sprang shut as she flew headlong into it, wrapping around her with thousands of soft, incredibly strong filaments, cradling her and her umbrella in an unbreakable cage. She hung suspended between the craggy points of two rock chimneys jutting from the very mound she had been warned to avoid.

"Whuh!" she puffed as the handle of her umbrella jabbed her painfully in the abdomen, and "pfff!" as the cobweb silk draped itself mummy-like across her face. "Mmm! Mmm!" she protested as she thrashed about, struggling to free herself.

Flashbacks of memory assailed her as she heaved and twisted, images of her second-to-last late husband, Sir Fotherham Fendrip, who always told her, "Bellie, one of these days your cheeseparing ways will get you in trouble."

"Oh, be quiet and go away," an unengaged corner of her mind told Sir Fotherham, who obligingly vanished as he had done for most of his married life.

"Mrr! Mrrr!" she called, but the silken threads had fastened her mouth so nearly shut that only a narrow slit between her lips remained. "Mehh! Mehh!"

The silken cocoon deadened any sound she made, but she continued to shout between bouts of flailing against the strands. At last, fatigued and panting, she ceased her useless struggle and dangled helplessly, swinging to and fro at the end of a single, steel-strong filament.

In the top left corner of the gigantic web Aranea slept. She slept in the correct arachnidian manner (as she did everything), head down, eyes open, claws fastened securely to the knots in her intricate and beautifully symmetrical web. Not for nothing had she taken her degree *summa cum laude* in Weaving and Architectural Design. No flies on her, no indeed! Any flies around Aranea were in one of her webs. Had she not won the Annual Arachnid Fly-Tying Contest for the past two hundred years straight?

In her dreams Aranea replayed not only her many past glories, but also those she expected in the future. Hundreds of centuries were yet to pass before her, as many as had already passed into oblivion. Just look at the number of spouses she had wed, the multitude of children she had given to the arachnid community. How glorious had been each of her nuptials! How magnificent the bridal feasts, every bite prepared by herself, a *cordon noir* chef of the first rank! How fitting the *piece de resistance*, whose appearance at table was always greeted with a standing ovation. (One can hardly imagine the volume of applause generated by eight spider legs multiplied by thousands!)

Occasionally she felt a pang of regret as she prepared the dish, for, as was the custom among spiders, the *piece de resistance* was the recent bridegroom. One or two grooms in the past had courted her most ardently, and she sometimes regretted their necessary demise. But stern

Saint Amber's Rose

Duty was the watchword of her soul, and she allowed no sentimental considerations to interfere with doing what was right.

She awakened instantly when Belvedine hit her web, for she felt its least twinge in her inmost being. The filaments had been spun out of her own body, and every strand vibrated with meaning.

A big one, she estimated, accurately translating the vibrations of the filaments, *big but skinny. Mostly bone and hardly any fat, but possibly enough nourishment for a few dozen eggs.*

After her brief respite, Belvedine resumed pitching and yawing, struggling futilely against the encompassing threads.

A lively one! thought Aranea. *Thrashing about like that, it's managed to wrap itself in its own cocoon. Saved me the trouble.*

The musty odor of the great spider wafted under Belvedine's nostrils, although Aranea kept her distance. The spider circled cautiously around her prey, gauging weight, heft, and degree of activity. Calculating the precise dosage of venom was crucial for a victim of such an awkward size. Too much, and her infant spiders-to-be would get a toxic overdose from eating the meat. Too little, and the captive might be flailing in her self-made cocoon for days, even weeks on end, wasting web time and interfering with the visual perfection of Aranea's architectonic design.

The spider edged closer. Her eyesight wasn't good, but her other senses were extremely acute. She scented the creature's emotions, a mixture of rage and fear and something else she couldn't readily identify. *Hmm!* This wasn't one of the species that usually hit her websites. *What can it be?*

Aranea circled around and around the cocoon. Not an insect: too big. Not a bird or a mouse: It didn't squeak. Not a worm. Not a beetle. Not a slug or snail. Some sort of four-legged mammal? It did have fur of a kind growing out of its head, but the rest of it was hidden in the silken mummy-wrap.

She extended her delicate sensors. The creature seemed to have a kind of covering beneath the cobweb strands, some sort of plant fiber. Aranea couldn't detect any other normal growth. What possible use is an animal without fur, feathers, or scales? How did it protect itself? Aranea shook her head over the foolishness of creatures who failed to adjust sensibly to their environment.

What's that long, shiny thing poking out of the cocoon--a talon? Maybe the creature has some means of defense after all. The talon seemed to be attached to the body, which gave the creature three, four... five appendages! A totally new species! Or maybe it had started out with six legs and lost one, or even eight and lost three. *But how does the thing keep its balance with an odd number of limbs?* Maybe it didn't, and that was why it had crashed into her web.

Aranea crept forward. She extended one slender leg and ever so gently touched the cocoon with a perfectly-manicured claw. The cocoon stopped moving--froze, in fact, as if the creature inside were processing information. Then it redoubled its fervent acrobatics, which only served to entangle it further.

Perfect! thought Aranea. *A trophy catch!* No doubt she'd be written up in the *Arachnid Times*, with her picture on the front page! Savoring her future success--never wise before one's chickens are completely out of their shells--Aranea moved in for a more detailed examination.

The moon sailed tranquilly over the expanse of forest known locally as the Icewode. It was always unearthly cold there; the chill rose even to her sphere. She never found out why, but the season here remained unchanging: The wode was icebound all year around. She wondered why going over it was always so much colder--a hateful, stabbing kind of cold--than any other place over which she passed.

The moon peered down at the tremendous mound in the middle of the wode. No matter how brightly she shone in her monthly course, and no matter how energetic Brother Sun was on his hottest days, the mound—Labyrinth dwellers called it the Grimmerund--never reflected the least amount of light back to them.

Tonight, for some reason, there was something reflecting light back to her, little shimmery strands of silver on top of the black rock. Curious, she descended a bit out of her orbit to examine it. (Cosmologically speaking, that wasn't strictly legal, but a lady of her years and experience was allowed a few liberties.)

Shades of the asteroids! The shimmery thing was a spiderweb! Biggest one she ever saw! Who could have woven that? The moon ran through her millennia of memories. *Why, it must be Aranea! Has to be! I'd know that characteristic knotting pattern anywhere.*

Saint Amber's Rose

And look! Some poor creature has gotten itself caught in the web. The silken cocoon enveloped the victim completely. Might be a bird--a tall one, like an ostrich from its size. It wouldn't be there much longer, that was certain. If Aranea had grown big enough to weave that huge cobweb, then she'd have to be getting a lot of red meat in her diet.

There she is, in the flesh! creeping around her prey. Aranea has definitely grown by leaps and bounds. In fact, she's gargantuan!

Reluctantly the moon went on her way, pulled by irresistible gravitational forces. But soon another light--or rather two, reflections of her own golden eye, attracted her. She bent closer.

"Hello, Luna," said the owner of the twin lights, perched on a branch several *kephan* from the Grimmerund, on the opposite side to Belvedine's prison.

"Hello yourself, Hera Vespasia," replied the moon. "I thought that was you. Aren't you a little out of your territory?"

"Only about three thousand *kephan*! But it wasn't my idea. I'm supposed to be on a Quest."

"A Quest! Whither to?" inquired the moon.

"For your ears only," said the owl, "we're looking for the *Sendara*. She was abducted and taken to the Ruined Chapel!"

"No!" gasped the moon, shocked. "Not the *Sendara*! I hadn't heard. Tell me more!"

Hera Vespasia narrated a condensed version of the story. "So the Hermit of the Ruined Chapel sent us out in different directions--"

"The Hermit did that?" interrupted the moon. "Hera, I wouldn't trust that Hermit an inch! I've seen some very strange goings-on in that vicinity. I could tell you a few things... But go on with your story."

The owl frowned, perturbed. "You don't mean the Hermit has gone over to the Dark Side? And we followed his instructions to the letter! This could be extremely serious. But to continue: He sent Belvedine de Montfort and me by air. You remember Belvedine?"

"I do indeed," said the moon glacially.

"We set out together, but she got off course. You know Belvedine--stubborn as a full-blood human mortal, always has to have her own way."

"How true," said Luna.

"Absolutely will not listen to directions."

"Believe me, I know," said Luna. "Where were you heading?"

"The Abbey of Saint Amber," replied the owl.

"But that's quite far away," said Luna, "deep in the heart of the Mountains of Zund."

"Don't I know it!" exclaimed the exasperated owl. "But I have to find Belvedine before I can continue to the Abbey. I don't suppose you've seen her? She'd be driving an older-model umbrella."

"No, I--wait!" replied the moon. "You know, I did see something odd a while back. Have you seen that big black mound in the middle of the Icewode?"

"You mean the Grimmerund? It has an evil reputation. That's why I set our course to give it a wide berth," said the owl.

"But that's exactly where I mean!" said the moon. "When I went over the Grimmerund, I noticed something different about it. There was this enormous, and I mean *enormous*, cobweb on top of the rock. I couldn't figure out who could possibly have woven it until I saw her. Aranea's back!"

"No!" exclaimed Hera Vespasia. "I thought she eloped with one of her relationships."

"Well, I don't know what happened with that, but she's back now," replied the moon. "And she's as big as a house. In fact, she must have eaten one to get as big as she is. She was creeping toward some poor creature caught in her web. Her victim was longer and thinner than Aranea's taste usually runs to. Do you think it might be--?"

"Belvedine!" exclaimed the owl, not pleased. "It would be just like her to fly straight into a webtrap. I told her to keep away from the Grimmerund! I'd better get over there and see what I can do. Thanks, Luna!"

"Good luck, Hera!" cried the moon, beginning to roll away. "Let me know how it turns out! Dear me," she murmured to herself, "everything's in such a turmoil in the Labyrinth World these days. I declare I don't know where it's all going to end!"

Hera Vespasia swept toward the Grimmerund. Her heightened senses picked up an oppressive fume, like greasy smoke. It clung to her feathers; the odor stung her nostrils like old mold.

She circled, keeping a sharp lookout for anything that moved. In the distance the moon traveled toward her setting, leaving only the faint, cold stars for illumination. The owl rounded the last arc of the mound exactly when a departing moonray shone on silver strands thinner than a hair. In the light they shimmered like fish gliding through clear water. Hera Vespasia spread out her wide wings, braking an instant before she ran into Aranea's cunningly engineered webtrap.

Holy Saint Amber! That was too close!

She spotted the cocoon in the center of the web, and no sooner did she spy it than the cocoon began thrashing about. *Can that be--* thought the owl. "--Belvedine," she decided, and moved cautiously closer to the web.

"Now what's this?" Aranea wondered, seeing a shadowy form, probably a big flying insect of some kind, heading for the middle of her exquisite web. She couldn't immediately place the species, and moved to investigate. One long, hairy leg after another extended itself across the web's interstices, not hurrying. After all, what could threaten her, the Mother of All Spiders?

The cocoon flung itself about wildly as the owl came nearer. Hera Vespasia approached with great care, for hundreds of sticky filaments awaited her least error in judgment. She inched as close to the cocoon as she dared and uttered a soft *hoo-hoo* to reassure the occupant. A muffled voice inside the cocoon cried out angrily, "MEWA? IFF AT OO? MMET! MME! MMOWT! MMV! MMR!"

"I'm trying to think how to do that!" whispered the owl hastily. "I suppose I could pinch off those filaments with my beak, but you've got so many wrapped around you it would take hours, and if I did, you'd be too heavy for me to carry by myself."

"Do mmit ammywwy!" argued the silk cocoon.

"Don't be ridiculous, Belvedine! You're hanging over a cliff, and it's a sheer drop. I can't even see the bottom."

"Who's there?" demanded Aranea, straining her octet of myopic eyes to bring the owl's shape into focus.

"Aranea!" hissed Hera Vespasia, turning her head halfway around to look the great spider in the face. "It's Hera Vespasia of the *Norrengild*! Don't you remember me?"

"Hera Vespasia?" exclaimed the spider. "What are you doing here?"

"I came to tell you whom you've got in your webtrap," replied the owl. "It's Belvedine de Montfort!"

"Belvedine! If I'd known that woman was anywhere near my web, I'd have--"

Charleynne Gates

"I'm not saying I'd blame you," Hera Vespasia interrupted, "but the thing is, we've got to free her. Not that she deserves it, but she's part of our Quest to rescue the *Sendara*--"

"The *Sendara*! In that case, I'll help you," said the spider. "The Icewode is all a-buzz with rumors about what happened to her. What's really going on?"

"All I can tell you is--what's that?" snapped the owl, returning her head to its front-facing position. "Did you hear a noise?"

"What noise?" asked the spider.

"MM! MM! MM!" came from the cocoon, more desperately than before.

"Not that one," said the owl. "The other one. I just heard it, like a humming or a drumming. I think it's coming from inside the Grimmerund."

"But that's impossible!" returned Aranea. "I'm sure there's nothing there but solid rock. I've built websites on the Grimmerund for Ages, and I've never heard anything inside it."

"Mm! Mmm!" expostulated the cocoon. With a terrific effort, it managed to rub off a few of the strands muffling its mouth. "Watch out behind you!" Belvedine shouted as a crack in the mound appeared directly behind Aranea and Hera Vespasia. It widened slowly with a terrible groaning noise, as if the very bowels of the earth were ripping open. Black smoke spiraled from its depths. A low, hypnotic rumble issued from the invisible caverns below.

Unable to see where the danger lay, the spider backed hastily to the topmost edge of her web, while Hera Vespasia hovered in the smoke-fume above the widening pit. She stared downward, horrified, before dodging swiftly back to Belvedine's cocoon.

"*Wyrga!*" she hissed. "A horde of them down there! This must be their secret gathering place!"

"Then go!" Belvedine rasped. "Fly to the Abbey and tell them!"

"But I can't leave you!" the owl protested. "If they'll find you, they'll kill you!"

"Never mind me!" insisted Belvedine. "Just go! The Abbey must be warned!"

"Wait there!" commanded the owl, out of patience. "I'm going to circle around and try to find help! The Pegasus Patrol might be--" With that, she lifted her wings and soared into the night.

-- 394 --

Saint Amber's Rose

Pavarr crashed to the ground under the weight of the *wyrga* guard. Its fetid odor nearly overcame his senses, but he steeled his will in that half-second and hung on, one hand pulling at the thick arm that choked him from behind, the other hand scrabbling for his dagger. He tried to roll the guard over on its back, but its huge bulk prevented much movement. The blow had knocked the breath out of him, and he knew he couldn't keep himself conscious much longer. Then the guard shifted its weight, and Pavarr seized the chance to draw his weapon and plunge it into the stinking, scaly arm.

Black fluid spurted over Pavarr; the guard gave a howl of agony and jerked its arm back. The momentum carried it off Pavarr's back, and Pavarr sprang upright, crouched and ready to attack.

The guard, maddened by its wound, charged blindly, striking at Pavarr with its savage *thringa* weapon. Pavarr ducked, darted in close, and stabbed his dagger deep into the *wyrga*'s gut. The guard stood frozen for an instant, then fell like a giant boulder on its face.

Pavarr ran forward, ready to sever the pulsating cord at the back of the monster's skull, but even as his weapon sliced through the vein, the guard turned its head toward him. With its last effort, the *wyrga* spat saliva directly into Pavarr's face.

Pavarr dropped his dagger and staggered back against the rock wall, his hands clutching at his eyes. The pain was greater than anything he had ever known or imagined. He felt as if his eyes were on fire, that no amount of water could ever cool them. Death would be a mercy compared with this agony.

He gave one cry, like a wounded animal, which echoed through the corridor, but so loud was the rhythmic pounding in the cavern that it was lost.

Suddenly the pain vanished as utterly as if it had never been. Panting heavily, shaking with shock, Pavarr crouched on the floor, thinking hard.

He waited. The pain did not return. Even the memory of it began to fade almost immediately. Gingerly he touched his face and eyes. The skin was whole; he felt no scars or burned flesh.

Cautiously he opened his eyes--to complete blackness. Naturally the tunnel was dark. The wavering illumination which had guided him this far had been from the black fire in the cavern far below.

Charleynne Gates

The fire must have died down. Is that why I can't see anything?
One hand fumbled inside his tunic and brought out a light-source, which
he switched on and shielded with his hand. Slowly he brought the light
in front of his face and stared at it. He couldn't see light or hand. He
couldn't see anything.

He was blind. The guard's venom had destroyed his sight.

Rising, he turned in each direction, seeing nothing. His other
senses, beginning to compensate, brought him the stench of the *wyrga's*
rapidly decomposing carcass beside him, the relentless pounding of the
drumming in the cavern, the touch of the tunnel's frigid walls, where
trickles of cold, oily moisture dripped continually to the floor and
patches of spongy stone felt like open wounds.

Resolutely controlling his repulsion, he felt his way back along
the passage where he had come, listening intently.

Got to get Flavia out of here!

Flavia sat upright, thinking fast. *How can I free the one
trapped in the web? I cannot walk, and I am sick with the poison of the
Desolation. But I must do it! I will!* She pushed herself away from the
white birch and began to crawl painfully toward the end of the grove
nearest to the Grimmerund. She hadn't moved far when she felt warm
breath ruffling her hair, and glanced up to see the black stallion standing
over her.

"Firemark!"

Rolling over onto her back, she unbound the green cincture tied
around her waist. Uncoiled, it made a long, thin rope. Knotting a loop
in one end, she threw it over the saddle. The first time it missed, and the
second. Then, her heart in her throat, she threw it a third time and felt it
catch on the saddle horn. She tied the ends of the cincture around her
wrists and gripped hard. "Go, Firemark!" she whispered, and the great
horse began walking slowly out of the nemeton toward the
Grimmerund, dragging Flavia through the grass behind him.

Firemark pulled her close to the face of the mound. There an
old birch tree stood, one that had nobly held its place against the
creeping contamination of the Grimmerund. There the horse stopped,
and Flavia loosened the cincture and wrapped it around her waist again.

A rush of wings stirred the sky! Beghed, Daughter of the Wind,
hovered lightly in the air, in position for Flavia to pull herself, with the

aid of the birch, onto the mare's back. "Firemark called us, *Sendara*," Beghed explained. "We are to take you to the Abbey."

"Wait! Someone is caught in the web at the top of the mound. We must free the victim before it is discovered!"

"As you wish, *Sendara*," said Beghed reluctantly. "But let us hurry!"

Beghed lifted into the air, and the pair spiraled around the Grimmerund. Flavia looked over the top ledge onto the summit, directly above the cocoon pumping itself back and forth, first over the rock, then out to the night sky. Belvedine! Her angular form was unmistakable even in the multiple swaths of her self-made cocoon. But her strength was flagging, and each effort to free herself took longer than the one before.

"Belvedine!" Flavia called.

The cocoon jerked to a stop in mid-air. "Flavia?" came the reply, less muffled this time because the resident had been gnawing at the strands, enough to free its mouth. "*Sendara*! You must not be here! You are in terrible danger! Go! Go!"

Her body wracked with pain and cold, Flavia couldn't help but let a gasp of laughter escape her. "Oh, Belvedine!" she said. "I have come all the way up here to free you. I will not leave without you!"

And now Flavia heard the low rumble within the Grimmerund growing louder and louder. Dhom, dhom, dhom went the metallic beating inside the cavernous rock. She had to free Belvedine, and quickly! But the cocoon hung in mid-air, beyond Flavia's reach. Most of the filaments suspending the cocoon had broken during the prisoner's persistent struggles, so that she swung by only a few remaining strands. But those would not break, no matter how hard Belvedine fought.

Desperate for help, Flavia scanned the mound's summit, and in horror beheld the cleft at the other end of the rock. It split wider, inching toward Belvedine as she dangled helplessly. Black smoke coiled up, and the rhythmic pounding grew louder.

"Belvedine!" she called again. "I am going to throw my cincture around you and pull you away from the web. Beghed can bear us both to the Abbey!"

Once more she unwound the green cincture from her waist. She made a loop in the rope and began trying to throw it to Belvedine, aiming for her silk-wrapped torso, but time after time the lasso fell short of the mark. At last she had to stop for rest.

"Don't worry about me, my dear," Belvedine called from where she dangled. "Save yourself! Your life is more valuable than mine!"

"No, Belvedine," Flavia insisted. "I will not leave you for the *wyrga*!" Once more she threw the lasso toward the cocoon, but her arm trembled and she couldn't send the rope as far as she had before. "I can't," she whispered. "O Mother Nemetona, I can't!"

"Flavia! Over there!" Belvedine screamed.

Flavia turned her head, seeing the cleft in the Grimmerund creeping closer, thickening smoke billowing out of it. Black flames flared through the smoke, and far beneath, the deep dohm, dohm pounded incessantly. "Help!" she tried to call out, but her words were only a faint rasp. "Mother Nemetona, help us!"

The crack reached the opposite side of the rock, and with a hollow roar the Grimmerund split in half. Hordes of *wyrga* spewed out amid smoke and black flames, howling in triumph as they saw their victims trapped on the mound.

One more time Flavia tossed the loop of rope toward the cocoon. It caught! The noose fastened tightly around Belvedine's waist, and Belvedine, sensing imminent freedom, pumped herself energetically until she swung like a pendulum to the outermost point above the Grimmerund.

Out of the night swooped Hera Vespasia, straight to the last few strands attaching the cocoon to the web, and severed them with her beak. The cocoon arced over the ziggurat and plummeted down, the tail of the green cincture whipping about in the air like magical writing.

Belvedine landed with a whump! on the back of Sornor Star-Rider as he dived underneath her. The cincture whipped itself several times around the horse's girth, anchoring Belvedine firmly to her rescuer, who at once flew in the direction of the Mountains of Zund.

"Now we must find Pavarr!" Flavia urged, and Beghed turned toward the flame-spewing crack in the mound. Over it she soared, her white wings flashing like starbursts, with the Sendara's red-gold hair streaming in the wind like the coming sunrise. And those of the *wyrga* that retained a dim consciousness of their lives as human mortals looked up--and were afraid and glad at the same moment.

Saint Amber's Rose

Far below, at the base of the mound, Pavarr emerged from the tunnel into a world completely dark to him, but no sooner did he put his head out of the entrance than Firemark's velvet nose pushed against his neck. At once Pavarr mounted, and Firemark took off in the same direction as the flying horses as *wyrga* poured from the cleft opening. Fast as a comet's fall did Firemark run, keeping pace with Sornor, Beghed, and Hera Vespasia as they sped over the Icewode.

In the remote reaches of the wood, Mil heard the dohm, dohm from the Grimmerund and halted, her gaze scanning the sky for the vee-shapes of *gnaarx*. There they were, in the distance and coming rapidly closer, and from many different directions, heading straight for her! But they couldn't have detected her presence that soon unless--the Icewode itself was working against her!

She turned the bezel of the ring she wore into the palm of her hand. Remembering the warning of the mentor who had given her the Vindr Talisman ("Use the ring three times only, and then release it"), she breathed on the gemstone for the last time and murmured a Word of Power.

She began to run again. Her feet skimmed over the snow with supernatural speed, faster than any wild creature in the Icewode, faster than the *gnaarx* could fly. Onward she ran until her path and Firemark's converged, and she leaped onto the horse's back behind Pavarr. The pounding hooves never slowed as the tireless horse galloped toward the forbidding Mountains of Zund--and safety.

Clinging to the topmost filament of her web, Aranea at last figured out what was going on. Squinting her eight nearsighted eyes, she managed to bring the advancing *wyrga* into focus. A smile of gustatory anticipation lit her features. "Come, children!" she called. "Fresh meat!"

A battalion of her offspring, each as gigantic as herself, appeared out of the numerous nooks and crannies in the Grimmerund. As one, the arachnids marched against the *wyrga* horde, forcing them to retreat until they were pushed back into the flames leaping out of the cleft. Howls of triumph turned into shrieks of agony as the spiders caught and stung to death those that escaped the fire.

And the day's battle ended with a glorious feast.

Chapter Twenty-Two

Merry Meet... and Part

Bertie Mossgrower stood on the shore of the River Sunder, wondering what he was supposed to do next. The skull-boat had disappeared, and no one seemed to be living in the tumbledown shacks on the waterfront. Not a sound disturbed the air except the faint rush of wind through the dark treetops and the lap of river-water against the pilings of the rotting dock. Bertie thought of calling out, just in case someone might be around, but decided against it. You never knew who--or what--might answer.

The problem is, how am I going to get directions to the Saurian River? Captain Bones hadn't said which way to go after he got on shore, and there weren't any signposts. *I have to move on somewhere; I can't stay here. That tree, the big oak up the bank: Why not climb it, see if I can make out some features of the landscape, maybe even see where the Saurian River is?*

Finding himself--again--in unknown territory, he took the precaution of untying the thong around his waist. With a deft knot, he made it into a slingshot. Smooth pebbles of the size he needed were plentiful on the shore, and he picked up a few for the pocket of his tunic.

He began walking up the little rise to the tree, but before he had taken half a dozen steps an arrow shot past him, not quite grazing his left ear. In no more than a second, he had loaded a stone in the slingshot and hurled the missile in the direction of the unseen archer. He hit something in the canopy of the big oak; a muffled cry and the sudden violent rustle of foliage told him that. The next instant a body fell out of the leaves, landed on a pile of brush underneath, and was quiet.

Bertie ran up the rise to the tree, trying to get to the enemy that had shot at him before it regained consciousness. It might be dead, though he doubted it. Stunned was more probable. As he ran, he felt for the handle of his Dwarvian dagger, ready and willing to use it if necessary.

He rounded a bush--and stopped short, eyes wide, mouth open. The body on the pile of leaves and grasses was alive; that was good. It was definitely not a *wyrga*; that was good, too. What it was, was something he hadn't expected to find shooting arrows at him, certainly not in a place like this!

It's a girl! That was obvious, even though she wore old hunter's clothes that must have belonged to her father or a brother. She looked about the same age as Bertie, maybe a little younger. Her chestnut-brown hair, thick and shiny, was short and ragged, as if it had been chopped off, and her face was pale, with no color in her cheeks at all. She lay moaning on the brush-pile, eyes closed, with her bow several feet away from her on the ground. It must have been knocked out of her hand when she tumbled down. Her quiver of arrows was underneath her.

Bertie had no idea what to do in this situation. The girl didn't look like someone who wanted to kill him, Bertie Mossgrower, specifically; on the other hand, she had definitely loosed an arrow at him and just about taken his ear off. *Who is she, what's she doing here, and why did she try to kill me--if that's what she was doing?*

The girl stopped moaning and opened her eyes. She rubbed a hand across her forehead. Then she saw Bertie, goggle-eyed and with his dagger halfway drawn, and sat upright very fast--too fast, because she gasped and swayed.

"Who are you?" she choked, and coughed. "Don't come any closer, or I'll--" Her sentence trailed off as she looked around for her weapons and saw the bow just beyond Bertie, out of her reach.

The boy snapped out of his frozen perplexity. "Who are you? Why were you shooting arrows at me? No," deliberately moving to block her access to the bow, for she had made a swift movement toward it, "not 'til you tell me why you tried to kill me."

"Kill you!" said the girl. "I did no such thing! I was aiming for that *wyrga* behind you, but it dodged my arrow and ran away."

"*Wyrga*?" repeated Bertie, justifiably suspicious. "I didn't hear anything behind me. Are you sure?"

"Of course I'm sure!" returned the girl, offended. "It was about to spring on your back, but I shot at it."

"Too bad you missed," said the boy, still skeptical.

"I didn't miss!" shouted the girl hotly. "I told you, it dodged the arrow! Don't you know how fast those things can move? Haven't you ever seen a *wyrga*? Or smelled one?"

"Yes, I've seen a *wyrga*," said Bertie, more thoughtfully. "I've smelled them, too--like burning swamp gas. I guess I didn't notice this one. I was thinking about getting to the tree so I could climb it." He grinned ruefully and sheathed the dagger. "I guess maybe you did save my life. Um, thanks." He extended his hand tentatively toward the girl. "Want a hand getting off that brush pile?"

"No 'maybe' about it!" the girl grumbled. "That *wyrga* would have finished you!" Then, startling Bertie, she grabbed his hand and sprang up to stand directly in front of him.

There was a pause. "I'm Bertie Mossgrower of Purple Valley," he said rather awkwardly, staring down into a pair of leaf-brown eyes.

"I'm Andis of Centerpole Village," she said, "I mean--" remembering that there was no longer a Centerpole Village--"Andis, daughter of Tirgon." She wondered later why she had named her father instead of her mother, for among the people of the Forest Villages it was the custom for sons to count themselves in the lineage of their fathers and daughters to claim that of their mothers. But at the time she didn't remark it.

"Centerpole? Doesn't that belong to the Forest Villages?" Bertie asked as Andis walked past him to retrieve her bow. "That's pretty far away from here, isn't it? Aren't you a little young to be so far from home?"

Andis refused to rise to the bait, although her lips pressed together in a thin line when her back was to Bertie. "Maybe," she said, vague as to which question she was answering. "But I'm a hunter, like my father and uncles. I'm used to being away from home for days and weeks on end. Beside, I'm on a quest for--" Aware that she was about to say too much, she bit off her sentence in the middle, bending her head to concentrate on brushing dirt and leaves off her bow.

"A quest for what?" Bertie asked, watching her quick, efficient movements as she restrung the weapon.

"Oh, just a quest," she replied. "Come on, I'll show you where the *wyrga* was. Then maybe you'll believe me," she flung over her shoulder, and led the way back to the edge of the riverbank.

"Phew!" said Bertie, wrinkling his nose. "That's the *wyrga* stink, all right." Andis gave a little toss of her head. "Hey, I already said I believed you. Wonder how I happened to miss it before?"

"Here are its tracks in the dirt, and there's my arrow," Andis pointed out. "Look! It ran off that way."

"If it's still around, I'd better go after it," said Bertie, drawing his dagger again and shouldering his way past Andis. "I don't want it stalking me again."

"I don't think you need to worry," the girl responded, ice in her tone. She made no attempt to catch up with him but stayed where she was, arms folded, gazing down the riverbank.

"Why not?" Bertie asked, looking back at her.

Andis nodded toward the narrow shoreline where the river met the bank. "Looks like it won't be stalking anyone now."

Bertie joined her, and together they stared down at the body of the *wyrga* lying half in and half out of the river.

"Seems to be dead," Bertie observed. "Must have run along the bank here, then fallen and rolled down there."

"It did dodge my arrow," said Andis, retrieving it. "Even if it hadn't, the arrow wouldn't have killed it--just stopped it for a moment. *Wyrga* can only be killed by slashing the great vein on the back of their skulls."

"I know," Bertie replied. "Maybe this one isn't dead."

"You think it's faking?" asked Andis. "To get us to come down where it can reach us?"

"Could be," said Bertie. But the more they looked at the body, the less alive it seemed.

Moved by one impulse, the two of them started cautiously down the riverbank, Bertie with his dagger at the ready, Andis with an arrow notched in her bow and ready to fire.

The *wyrga* lay on its back, unmoving. Its soulless eyes reflected the sky. Carefully the two circled around it, keeping out of its reach just in case. The *thringa* that all *wyrga* carry was still fastened on its belt. Apparently the *wyrga* hadn't intended to use the weapon, or hadn't had time to get to it.

"Look!" Andis whispered, crouching where she could see the edge of the great vein in its neck. "The vein's been cut!"

Bertie saw it also, the blackened, jagged slash-wound. How could it have been killed like that, when Andis saw the thing about to leap on Bertie's back, and no one else nearby?

"Whoever actually killed it," said Bertie slowly, "might still be around here. Why don't they show themselves?"

"I don't know," said Andis, "but I'm getting a bad feeling about this place. I keep seeing shadows out of the corners of my eyes, but they vanish whenever I try to look at them directly."

"So do I," said Bertie. "I'd like to thank whoever killed the *wyrga*, but--"

"Maybe they don't want to be found," Andis finished.

"Right," Bertie agreed. "And maybe they don't want us here."

"We should go, then," Andis whispered.

"Good idea," Bertie whispered back, and together they crept up the riverbank and merged with the forest.

In the shadows of the deserted bait and tackle shop, a pair of unblinking yellow eyes stared after them.

Down on the rock-strewn shore a wave swelled around the *wyrga*'s body and washed it into the river. It sank immediately and never reappeared.

They went westward on Andis's advice. She had no more idea where they were going than Bertie did, but at least (he reasoned) she was familiar with Threshold Forest--except for the part where they were right now. When the light began to dim, they made camp in a glade that seemed to be relatively protected. Andis thought they might make a small fire so they could heat their food and have some warmth as the chill of the night settled down.

Afterward, talking in low voices, they told each other about themselves, exchanging information in cautious bits and pieces, figuring out as they went along how much to trust each other. Bertie asked about the Forest Villages, and Andis told him about how life was lived in Threshold Forest--things commonly known anyway, and geographical features readily found on any map of the area. In turn, Bertie described Purple Valley and his boring life in Mossy Dell, and what they grew in the fields around the village—mosses and mushrooms, mostly. Andis was interested because she had never seen or heard of Purple Valley, although everything Bertie said could be found in the *Comprehensive*

Atlas of the Labyrinth World, 500th edition. A foxed and ink-stained copy lay on a reading stand in Mossy Dell Village School. Bertie used to like to turn over its outsize pages--when he happened to be in class.

When they ran out of ordinary things to say, the moon had risen, and they fell silent. A different kind of darkness drifted through the trees. A night-bird called, and was answered. The two young people saw each other's faces illumined fitfully by the light of their miniscule campfire, and somehow that made them feel more companionable. By unspoken consent they moved closer to one another and began talking about the things that were nearest their hearts.

"Why do you have to get to the Saurian River?" Andis asked. "It's a terrible place, I've heard. Smells worse than *wyrga*."

"Because I've got this friend, and we were in a--in my boat rowing down the Sunder--"

"The Sunder's awful swift, and treacherous, too," Andis interrupted. "What were you doing rowing down it?"

"It's not that swift back in Purple Valley where it starts," said Bertie. "It's calm there. Just a trickle, really. Not like later on, after the beaver pond..."

"What happened after the beaver pond?" Andis asked as Bertie's voice trailed off.

"It gets to be the real River Sunder, and then it gets running fast. We were running too fast when we hit the rapids, and then--"

"Then?"

"I--my boat hit a rock and broke up. The last I saw of Mr. Medley, he was being swept away down the other fork of the Sunder, toward the Saurian River, where it joins the Sunder a long way down."

"Oh..." Andis's sympathy showed in her voice; the night was too dark to see her face. "Your friend must have gone under. He, well, he couldn't have survived very long, could he, not in water like that. It's whitewater, isn't it?"

"Yes... I guess you're right. Except the skulls said--"

"Skulls?" Andis repeated.

"Sailors, I meant." Bertie realized he really couldn't explain skulls without bodies, let alone the skull-boat that had dropped him off at Fool's Point. "They said this was the nearest place to the Saurian."

"So--they think you have a chance to find your Mr. Medley?"

"If they didn't, I guess they wouldn't have brought me here," Bertie decided. "Anyway, I'm going to the Saurian River and find him. And I will find him." He set his jaw against looming fear.

"How do you know he's still alive?" Andis began before realizing that wasn't the best thing to ask under the circumstances.

"I just know," Bertie said, and Andis didn't pursue the matter.

"Where were you going?" he asked after a pause, while leaves rustled overhead--a nocturnal predator on the hunt.

"I'm going to fight *wyrga*," she answered firmly, and touched the bow at her side.

"All by yourself?" asked the boy, smiling a little.

"I scared yours away 'all by myself,'" Andis retorted. "And that's not the only one I've shot at."

"You've really killed *wyrga*?" Bertie questioned, half in admiration, half in disbelief.

But Andis suddenly found that she didn't want to talk about that other incident, when she'd loosed an arrow at the evil thing digging through the remains of her family home. Something about what happened back there troubled her, and she didn't know why. It wasn't fear. She hated all *wyrga*, but hadn't been afraid of that one: There hadn't been time for fear.

"Yes. I--I guess so. Anyway, I might have. It was at Centerpole..." Her voice trailed off as memories of the ravaged hamlet swept over her.

"Where are you going to find them?" Bertie's question cut in. "Are you just going to wander around Threshold Forest and hope to come across one or two?"

"Of course not!" Andis replied, stung. "I'm going where there are lots of them, whole armies of *wyrga*. There's going to be this big battle, see, and I'm going to be there and fight with Prince Pavarr because of what they did to my sister--" A sob came into her throat, and she choked on it, hating her own weakness and embarrassed because she was crying in front of Bertie, whom she had wanted to impress since the first moment she saw him without knowing why.

"What happened to your sister?" Bertie asked softly. He leaned in toward her--to hear her better, as he thought.

At this point, feeling in need of sympathy from someone of like flesh and blood, Andis let down her guard and confided her story, only leaving out the part that puzzled her, the *wyrga* she had wounded at Centerpole.

If she had wanted Bertie's complete attention, she had it now. He was wholly drawn in to what she was saying, and wouldn't have noticed if a dozen *wyrga* were surrounding them at that moment.

"--and Prince Pavarr brought us to Seventree Village, where my uncle and his wife and children live. My aunt is a midwife, which Ildranna will need in a few months. She's going to have a baby, and I won't be there to help her. Then I hid where I could hear Pavarr and my uncle talking. Pavarr said my uncle ought to make weapons for everyone in the village and hide them because the Lord of Desolation is massing an army of his slaves to take over the whole Labyrinth World. And Pavarr's going to Saint Amber's Abbey because the battle's going to start there, or something, and I'm going to join him and fight *wyrga*!" she finished.

Their little campfire was down to embers now, and they couldn't see each other's faces very well. For a while they kept silent, each thinking his and her own thoughts.

Saint Amber's Abbey! Mr. Medley said that's where he wanted to go, Bertie realized. *Did he know there's supposed to be a battle? He said he was going with the* Sendara. *Is she there, too? And who's Prince Pavarr?* A pinprick of jealousy made him frown at the dying coals.

Andis yawned and shivered, wrapping herself closer in her coversack (an Elvish invention, lightweight, waterproof, and warm).

"We'd better get some sleep," said Bertie. "We'll want to be on our way by dawn."

But Andis was already asleep.

It'd be best for her to come with me first, Bertie decided. *We can find the Saurian River, and then Mr. Medley, and it'll be easier with two of us. She's a good archer--for a girl--and she can get around in the forest. After we find Mr. Medley, I can take her to the Abbey, where Mr. Medley wanted to go anyway. If there's going to be a battle, I'd like to be there--to protect the* Sendara. *And--the girl. Andis. She's awfully young to be out here in the wilderness by herself. Hardly more than a child. I'd better keep her with me.*

With those weighty matters on his mind, Bertie never suspected that he had just made several grave errors. They were understandable, considering that he had never met anyone like Andis. The only points of comparison he had were the girls of Mossy Dell--and they were as different from Andis as sparrows are from a free-soaring hawk.

His first error was to assume that Andis needed--or wanted--his protection.

His second error was to assume that Andis would see the logic of looking for Mr. Medley first, rather than proceeding to the Abbey-- where (Bertie suspected) Prince Pavarr awaited her.

His third (and worst) error was to assume that Andis would do what he wanted her to do.

Thus deluded, Bertie's head dropped onto his chest, and he slept.

"Come on, wake up! We've got to get moving!"

Andis shoveled dirt over the embers to smother any remnant of fire and to disguise the fact that anyone had been there. It wouldn't fool a skilled tracker, but someone else might not notice that the ground had been disturbed.

Bertie opened his eyes and saw that Andis had already broken camp, or what little of it there was. She had folded up her coversack and brushed away the traces left on the ground where she had slept. With her quiver of arrows once again slung on her back and her bow in hand, the girl was nibbling a crust of journey-bread and peering around the glade.

"I've already climbed that tree over there." She pointed to the tallest oak in the grove. "But I couldn't get any bearings. The forest is too thick here. I think your best plan is simply to follow the River Sunder westward. Too bad the Saurian's so many *kephan* from here. I don't even know how far it is."

Bertie, not wholly awake, rummaged in his knapsack and found journey-bread. It was plain that Andis had beaten him to the draw this morning, and he couldn't think of a polite response.

"I had another idea," she continued. "We've already come a long way from Fool's Point and those creepy abandoned shacks there. You said you can row a boat. I didn't see any boats tied to that rotting dock, but I think there are more docks along the riverbank farther down. You could see if there's a rowboat at one of them and take it. I wouldn't worry about paying for it. I think this whole area's deserted anyhow.

Saint Amber's Rose

People moved away when the Lord of Desolation started invading Threshold Forest.

"Rowing down the Sunder would be a lot faster than walking along the bank. If I were you, that's what I'd do. 'Course I have my doubts about finding your friend Mr. Medley. I've heard about that Maelstrom, and I don't see how anyone could survive it. But--" she added hastily--"he might have, and gotten out safely somewhere."

Bertie, hearing his entire expedition neatly worked out for him, didn't trust himself to make a suitable reply.

"Unless," Andis continued thoughtfully, "you're ready to give up that idea and come with me to the Abbey. I'm sure Prince Pavarr can use you when the battle starts. You're good with that slingshot."

Bertie was wide awake now, and none too pleased with the eminently sensible plan Andis had suggested. He was supposed to be making the plans, not a girl younger than he was! He had a serious purpose; she just wanted to be off chasing imaginary *wyrga* with that prince or whatever he was.

"I'm not giving up any idea," he said, with frost in his tone. "I'm going to look for Mr. Medley. And--" he took a breath--"I think you should come with me. You're good with your bow and arrows, but you shouldn't be out in the forest alone and unprotected."

"Unprotected?" Andis shouted, then quickly lowered her voice. "I can protect myself, thank you very much! You're the one who needs protection! I seem to remember a *wyrga* that would have killed you if I hadn't scared it away!"

"I just meant--" Bertie started, with an apologetic gesture.

"What?" said Andis, folding her arms tightly across her chest. Her lips pressed into a grim line.

"--it might be better if we went together. We could look out for each other. If we look for Mr. Medley first--and find him--then all three of us could go to Saint Amber's Abbey. He's as smart as a book, Mr. Medley is. He could probably think of things that--that we can't. You should come with me."

Andis kept her arms folded and her lips prim. She considered the question, looked around the glade, considered again.

"I promised I'd go to the Abbey. Pavarr is probably waiting for me, so I can't go with you. You'd better come with me. And we'd

Charleynne Gates

better be going." And with that, she shouldered her quiver of arrows and started walking eastward. She didn't look back.

It was obvious to Bertie that she intended to have her own way-- and expected him to follow!

"Andis!" he called. "I'm going to find Mr. Medley! You'd better come with me!"

But she didn't return, and all he saw was the quiver on her determined back as she strode away from him.

Stubborn! he thought as he made his way down the riverbank on the chance of an abandoned rowboat being tied up at the dock below. He didn't want to admit that her idea might be their best option at this point... but she couldn't see him any more, so he didn't have to admit anything, at least not to himself.

To his surprise, three rowboats were tied to the dock, all with oars, all looking as if they hadn't been used in a while. He chose the one moored farthest out--it looked reliable--and pushed off down the river.

If she'd just been reasonable and seen things my way...

A pair of leaf-brown eyes gazed after him as the current pulled the rowboat into the middle of the river. *He's going to need help later,* the owner of the leaf-brown eyes decided. *He just won't admit it. Tsk! I can't leave him to do this by himself. He'll never make it. Boys! Why do they always think they know better than girls?*

Chapter Twenty-Three

The Lord of Desolation

They had for their king the angel of
the abyss, whose name, in Hebrew,
is Abaddon, and in Greek, Apollyon,
or the Destroyer.
--The Revelation 9:11

Oliver Medley swam to the surface of consciousness out of an abyss of nightmare. He opened his eyes--reluctantly--to a metallic glare filtering through filmy gray draperies drawn over narrow windows. Blinking several times, he studied what he could see of the room, and slowly, very slowly, he decided that the chamber in which he lay was totally unfamiliar to him. That might not be an accurate deduction: His spectacles were not on his nose. Stretching out an arm, he groped for them and found a nightstand beside his bed. On the nightstand--made of a transparent material ice-cold to the touch--were his spectacles, neatly folded, in front of a crystal bell.

He struggled to sit upright, and at the same moment grabbed for his glasses, knocking the bell over on its side. It tinkled faintly in protest. Hastily Oliver jammed the glasses onto his face and examined the bell, relieved to see that it didn't seem damaged. *Where am I?* he wondered as his mental processes began to work. *How did I get here?*

As if in answer to his thought, or to the bell, a door at the far end of the chamber opened. An entity entered.

"Good morning, sir," said the entity, setting a linen-covered silver tray upon an adjacent tabletop and opening the draperies to let in undifferentiated gray light. "Does the gentleman wish coffee? It is freshly made by my own hand."

Oliver stared, openmouthed. It wasn't only that the individual standing at the foot of his bed was habited in formal morning clothes and speaking like a well-trained butler, it was also that the individual reminded him strongly of a Wraith! *But how did I know what a Wraith looks like?*

He didn't, of course. *I have encountered an impossibility. My lenses must need cleaning.* He whipped them off his nose and wiped them surreptitiously on the bedsheet.

"Allow me, sir," said the entity, deftly removing the spectacles from Oliver's hand and polishing them to a high gloss.

"Thank you," Oliver stammered. "I--I would like some coffee. Oh... thank you very much." Taking a bone china cup from the entity's transparent hand, he gingerly took a sip. *It really is coffee!* His taste buds remembered the flavor and aroma from a place just beyond the reach of his memory. A pleasant sensation coursed through him, waking his mind and warming his limbs.

"The gentleman's bath is ready," the entity announced. "I have taken the liberty of laying out a change of clothing for the gentleman's interview. Would the gentleman wish assistance with his bath?"

"Er... no," Oliver replied at once, his modest soul taken aback. "Thank you, I... no. Could you tell me--"

"Very good, sir," said the entity, preparing to depart. "My name is Gloom. A touch upon the bell will summon me at any time." He left through the door, which, Oliver noted, was closed.

That was odd! But I still don't know where I am! And how did I get here? I wonder who that fellow Gloom thinks I am. And how did I know that he is a Wraith?

And, after a minute, *What interview?*

But no one was around to answer. "I suppose I'd better have a bath," he said aloud.

The bathing-room, which he entered through an open connecting door, was, to his surprise, a vaulted chamber in pink marble, a classical Roman bath of august proportions. It held three capacious pools filled with lovely blue water. He tested all three, finding that one was as hot as he could bear, one was pleasantly warm, and the last was cool.

The temperate pool was perfumed with the aroma of citrus groves. Oliver removed his glasses (useless in this atmosphere), cast off his metal-gray silk pajamas (forgetting to wonder how they came to be on him), and descended the tiled steps. He tackled himself with a convenient bath-brush, swathed away the residue of creamy lather in lemon water, and paddled around, emptying his mind of everything except the sensation of absolute and utter cleanliness.

The enticing scent of spices arose with the steam from the heated pool. "I must be dreaming!" he murmured, easing himself in. Enveloped in scented clouds, he leaned back against the bath-cushion and closed his eyes in ecstasy.

The cold pool welcomed him with the invigorating fragrance of snow-dusted balsam fir trees. He jumped in, feet first, and swam rapidly from one end to the other, reveling in the teasing slither of cool water rippling past his arms and legs. The sensation came close to reminding him of something in his past... something not nearly so pleasant. He shut his mind against the memory.

Not wearing his glasses, he was nearly startled out of his skin to find Gloom waiting for him as he climbed out of the cold pool. Decorously turning his head aside, Gloom held out a dressing gown of soft, white toweling.

"It is almost time for your interview, sir," the butler said. "Perhaps I might assist with dressing? His lordship has chosen the costume for the day."

Lordship? Before Oliver could inquire further, Gloom turned to lead the way back to the bedchamber. He moved along the curiously icy corridor in a swift, smooth glide on the balls of his invisible feet, never quite seeming to touch the floor. Much bemused at this unique method of locomotion, Oliver hastily trotted after.

The bed was now neatly made, and not a trace of previous occupancy was to be found. On the bedcover a suit of clothes was laid out, and Gloom at once began the process of robing him. So efficiently was it done that Oliver didn't realize what sort of garment he wore until Gloom turned him to face a cheval glass.

The reflection was not the Oliver Medley he was accustomed to seeing, but (so it seemed) someone else entirely. Gone were the remains of his tattered habiliments. In their place was a costume straight out of an eighteenth-century drawing room: black velvet knickers, a ruffled shirt of lily whiteness, a velvet vest, and a coat of salmon-pink brocade. His hair had been covered with a powdered wig neatly clubbed into a black-bowed peruke, and upon the wig was a black tricorne trimmed with silver. The wig and hat didn't quite cover the silver earring in his left ear. The ornament seemed incongruous with his new outfit, and he glanced at the valet, about to ask if it ought to be removed.

"I wouldn't touch it, sir," said Gloom. "If I may say so, it adds a certain degree of *je ne sais quois* to the ensemble. And," he added almost inaudibly, "a certain degree of protection, which might become necessary."

Oliver forgot about the matter immediately and automatically "made a leg," pointing his right foot forward and bending the opposite knee, to examine his feet, finding that he wore white silk stockings and high-heeled court shoes, black with silver buckles. Rising from his bow, Oliver discovered that he held an ebony walking staff in his right hand.

Astonished at his transformation, Oliver looked at the butler for an explanation, but the imperturbable Gloom volunteered no information.

"If the gentleman is ready, I shall conduct him to the dining hall. His lordship does not like to be kept waiting." The butler hesitated for an imperceptible instant, and something that might have been called an expression flitted across his features. "If I might venture a cautionary word, sir? The gentleman would do well not to ingest the comestibles served tonight. There are circumstances in which a fast is as good as a feast."

Oliver looked an inquiry.

"At least," the butler continued, "until the gentleman has become... ah, seasoned to the climate hereabouts."

Oliver gripped the ebony staff to adjust his balance as he followed Gloom, wobbling in unaccustomed shoes. Exiting the bedchamber, they came into a vaulted corridor whose gilded walls were hung floor to ceiling with gigantic oil paintings in ornate frames. Oliver blushed furiously when he realized what the subjects were: groupings of fat little cupids with tiny wings hovering over reclining full-fleshed goddesses basking in the gaze of rampant gods and satyrs. One particularly enticing image was of a rosy-cheeked nymph fleeing from a goat-footed faun. The nymph had golden-red hair and reminded him of someone; he couldn't think of whom. Oliver forced his eyes to stay on Gloom's transparent back for the remainder of their progress.

The butler opened a gilded door at the opposite end of the long corridor. "This way, sir," he murmured. Thus encouraged, Oliver took a cautious step forward, put his left foot over the threshold, and entered the dining hall.

The room was the very replica of the swollen-beamed, lantern-lit belly of a full-masted ship of the line, one in whose cabined confines Oliver had spent many an imaginary hour with a book, indulging in youthful fancy. It was also extremely well heated, and his brocade coat and velvet vest began to feel uncomfortably warm. A trickle of perspiration inched from his hairline into his collar.

"Mr. Medley, my lord," the butler announced. Bowing slightly, he disappeared through the closed door.

His host stood at the extreme end of the room, and all that Oliver could discern was a black silhouette in front of a wall of concave windows. The windows were undraped, and through them Oliver discerned cloudy swirls of dark waters with a few loose fronds of seaweed that brushed lazily across the glass, as if the vessel were not riding the surface of the waves but had long ago sunk fathoms deep under the sea. A skeletal form with humanoid skull attached drifted by just as Oliver looked away, and he couldn't have said later whether he actually saw it or not.

The silhouette's back was toward Oliver. A peculiar bump rested upon its left shoulder. The nature of the bump soon became evident, for the silhouette raised a bow and drew it across the strings of a violin. Singularly haunting tones issued forth, twisting at last into a melody oddly familiar but not precisely identifiable.

The music ended on a tri-tone, and the violinist turned to face him. "Oliver Medley." His voice was a warm and pleasant baritone. "Again, welcome to my city and to Castle Mormorion, my humble abode. May I present two of my assistants, *Madame la duchesse* d'Ophidian and *Madame la marquise* DeCair."

The silhouette gestured, and two beautifully painted and pompadoured ladies emerged from the dusk. They swept low curtsies, their teasing fans only just failing to conceal their décolletages. Oliver concealed his scarlet face by returning their bows in his best drawing-room manner. The ladies seemed familiar, too, if only he could place them in context.

"*Enchantée, Monsieur* Medlee. *Enchantee*," they murmured together, rising gracefully. Oliver choked coming up from his bow, trying his utmost not to look where he shouldn't, and never afterward remembered if he made any response at all.

"I want him," the shorter one, a blonde in pink silk garlanded with masses of pearls set in gold, whispered behind her fan as they backed elegantly away.

"*Mais non, ma petite!*" (No, little one!) hissed the taller, a brunette in black velvet draped with an abundance of diamonds. "He's mine."

Overhearing their whispered competition, Oliver didn't feel particularly flattered. On the contrary, his sole sensation at the moment was a shiver of apprehension and a strong desire to remove himself from the vicinity of the two aristocratic ladies as quickly as possible.

The silhouette came forward, dismissing the ladies with an abrupt nod, and became a man dressed in the costume of a bygone era: a sea-captain's blue uniform coat with ruches of lace at collar and cuffs.

"Don't be concerned about my servants. You are under my protection here," he said genially. "I hope you will give me the pleasure of dining with me. Too often I am forced to dine alone. Your company would be a great boon." He swept an arm toward a long table in the middle of the room, a table laden with gleaming silverware, translucent china, and cut crystal set upon bone-white damask. Atop every plate lay a blood-red pomegranate. A rather curious centerpiece, a single large, ornately-worked silver spoon, lay flanked by pots of some pale, bulbous flower whose botanical name Oliver couldn't recall at the moment.

He stared at the flowers, whose cobra-like heads nodded solemnly to each other as if they were conducting an interminable board meeting. And lo! Serving dishes appeared as if by magic along the length of the table, and upon them rested the most succulent food Oliver had ever imagined. Entrees baked, roasted, and sautéed to perfection sang their siren songs. Wisps of steam, delicate as nymphs, danced in white spirals above the ambrosial fleshpots.

Temptation beckoned. Resistance vanished. For the longest time Oliver had eaten only nourishing but monotonous journey-bread and drunk nothing but earth-tasting water, and now his fasting stomach, stimulated beyond endurance by the enticing provender before it, beat to quarters with a loud roll of drums. Oliver's feet carried him straight for the laden board as if they had minds of their own.

Saint Amber's Rose

A chair moved out by itself from the table at the man's right. Oliver sat--or fell--into it. Now he was close enough to see his host full-face, but by this time his vision was so blurry with hunger that he couldn't put the features together in any way that made sense. A certain distortion of reality was, of course, concomitant with voracity.

"Fall to, my friend," invited the man. "Eat of my bounty, as much as you desire."

Promptly forgetting his usual good manners, his customary grace before meals, and the veiled warning of the Wraith-butler Gloom, Oliver fell to. What viands! What delicacies! What alimentary allurements! He couldn't begin to count the masterpieces of culinary art arrayed before him, nor did he try. He ate and ate and ate again. As fast as he emptied the plate before him, he found another gourmet delight filling it. And the wines: Never had such vintages come from mere grapes! No, these were the pressings of the first fruits of Temptation.

One miniscule corner of his mind remained detached from his disgusting exhibition of gluttony, and it wondered how he could eat two, three, four times more than his usual quantity in a single meal, but it had insufficient strength to stop him.

At last, when the waistband of his trousers threatened to split asunder and his stomach could hold no more, Oliver desisted, crossing knife and fork over his plate--missing the fleeting expression of distaste on his host's face--and leaned back in his chair with an involuntary sigh. He was satiated, stuffed like a fattened goose... or believed he ought to be, and did not understand why the more he ate, the less his stomach thought he had eaten. *That is irrational; I ought to be far more than satisfied; therefore, I must be.* He eased his waistband a bit to prove the point to himself.

His host being occupied in conferring with an obsequious attendant, Oliver took the opportunity to study him surreptitiously.

The man had eyes like chameleon crystals in a face both experienced and good-humored. He cut a far more elegant figure in his costume than did Oliver, and his movements were the assured gestures of one accustomed to command. With all the self-confidence of a pumpkin, Oliver had always admired—and envied--that quality in others.

Oliver glanced at the man's right hand, resting on the tablecloth. On the index finger was a massive gold ring set with a strange, glittering gem, black as the pupil of a cat's eye. Oliver could scarcely take his eyes off it. The pulsating glitter was hypnotic. Staring at it, he felt a warm drowsiness steal over him. His eyelids drooped; he nodded.

The man dismissed the attendant and turned to Oliver with a smile and an apology. "You have dined well, my friend?"

"I have indeed, I thank you," Oliver replied, blinking himself awake. "It was a glorious repast. Truly a Barmecide feast." He meant to say "Olympian feast," but the other slipped out. He hoped his host didn't notice.

"You don't mind the costume?" the man went on. "It's from one of my favorite historical periods. I rather fancy dining in costume, though I'm afraid I tend to overdo it."

"Not at all," Oliver responded. "Quite abominable." He meant to say "admirable"—thought he had said it—didn't notice the substitution. "May I ask the name of my host?"

"Why, how remiss of me!" the man said. "I'm afraid I've lapsed into shocking bad manners. It comes from being so much alone. My name is Ab'addon; I rule the City of Dead Souls and all the country around it." The man looked directly into Oliver's limpid brown eyes with his own intensely blue ones and smiled. The ice-blue of the irises glimmered into silver as Oliver returned Ab'addon's gaze, and Oliver couldn't tear his eyes away. He felt compelled to keep on staring until he all but tumbled into those widening pools of silver light...

His belly emitted a digestive rumble. Oliver shook his head. The man leaned back in his chair and took up his wineglass.

"I am sometimes known as the Lord of Desolation."

He broke off to sip the red wine.

Oliver, in a state of near-torpor, couldn't think of a suitable reply and so said nothing. The Lord of Desolation didn't seem to expect one and continued the conversation by himself.

"You honor me by staying as my guest. You cannot possibly realize what it means to me, having you come here so--miraculously, one might say, although I was distressed to learn of your misadventure in my--in the Maelstrom. It's one of the ways to my realm, though not the easiest, to be sure. Would you tell me how you managed to survive it? If you feel sufficiently recovered."

"I'd be delighted, your lordship. Your highness. Your grace. Hic," said Oliver, stifling a small belch.

Saint Amber's Rose

"Ab'addon, please," said the man pleasantly. "I have no other name, and need but one title. About the Maelstrom?"

Befuddled as he was by fumes of wine and post-carnivorous lethargy, Oliver tried his best to recall how he had arrived in Ab'addon's dominion. *What Maelstrom is he talking about?* A maelstrom was a sort of whirlpool. What did a whirlpool have to do with his arrival?

"I'm terribly sorry. I--I don't seem to recall it just now."

"Not at all?" his host inquired, his eyes bright as polished coins.

Oliver pondered. "No. I really cannot recall. I must have suffered some short-term memory loss. Perhaps it'll come back to me, but at the moment..."

Ab'addon smiled warmly. "I understand. A few days of rest and relaxation will see you as good as new. You'll spend them here, of course. No, I absolutely insist on it. I do enjoy good company, and I get so few visitors since--the Harrowing." He broke off for a moment, looking into the distance.

Poor man. He seems so vulnerable. Oliver felt sorry for him, surrounded as he was by all that grandeur and with no one to share it. *Must be a terribly lonely life.*

"I'd be most grateful for your hospitality," said Oliver Medley. "If I wouldn't be putting you to any trouble."

"No trouble at all, I assure you," replied his host. "Would you care to see the rest of my home? It's been some time since I had the privilege of escorting a guest on a tour. I work on the place constantly, trying one thing and another. I like to show it off. Come!"

Even as he spoke they were walking out of the dining hall. Oliver cast one backward glance at the groaning board behind them and realized that he may have had a drop too much, for it seemed to him that the serving dishes held not lavish foodstuffs but only piles of stones. An optical illusion, no doubt.

They strolled through a corridor crowded with more gilt-framed paintings and marble statuary. A great many doors opened off the corridor, giving enticing glimpses into rooms filled with treasures of artistic genius. As they passed the entrance to a grand ballroom, Oliver glimpsed a splendid company of women and men in satin and lace and powdered wigs, all laughing, flirting, and dancing to crystalline notes from harpsichord and violin. *How delightfully civilized!* Oliver wanted very much to join them, but such a blast of frigid air came from inside the room that he shivered as they went by.

The last room on the floor, unlike the others, was very small, bare as a prison cell. There was nothing inside it except a spinning wheel with a great heap of green vines and tangled flowers beside it. A woman sat at the wheel, a woman with a cascade of golden-red hair and eyes like the sea under sunlight, under storm. She seemed to be spinning the vines and flowers into bright gold, which fell into piles of coins beside the wheel. The woman never glanced up, never ceased her work, and he had the impression of some great sorrow that bound her to the wheel. Instinctively he wanted to stop and ask if he might be of service to her, but "Come, my friend," said his host, and took his arm.

At last, having climbed--or floated, Oliver never figured that out--up a great number of stairs, they emerged onto a wide balcony enclosed by a wrought-iron railing. Ab'addon, still talking (he was a mesmerizing raconteur), walked them to the railing and with a wave of his ruffled sleeve, indicated the broad landscape below.

"This is my country," said the Lord of Desolation. "My kingdom."

Obediently Oliver looked down, which was a grave mistake. A wild vertigo clutched him in its claws. The undigested remnants of his recent bout of crapulence threatened to erupt in a most shameful fashion. Only by an extreme exertion of self-control did he restrain himself from hurling the contents of his stomach broadcast over his host's domain.

The effort of mastering both vertigo and nausea made drops of perspiration burst out on Oliver's forehead. Surreptitiously he took out a lace-edged handkerchief from his sleeve and wiped them off, making himself breathe deeply to regain composure. White-faced but steadier on his pins, he peered over the railing again.

They stood atop a tower, surely the highest tower that ever was. A cloud drifting low in the leaden sky enveloped his head like a turban, and he realized how high off the ground they must be.

"Do you know," his host remarked with a wry smile, "if one or the other of us happened to fall off this tower--or jumped off, as the case might be--my servants would catch us before we hit the ground? I assure you they would, at any hour, day or night. Their devotion to me is absolute."

"How wonderfully reassuring," Oliver murmured, thinking that he wouldn't care to test even the most devoted attendant in that manner. What if the servant happened to be on break at the critical moment?

"And there is my city," said Ab'addon, "with her towers and spires. All mine."

From beneath the turban of cloud Oliver saw a sparkling city of spires spread out as far as the eye could see, a multitude of black needles glittering with a myriad cold lights pricking the sullen sky.

Oliver saw no sign of life.

"My city," repeated Ab'addon. "I am its lord. Its residents serve me well. Indeed, I am almost too well served. Sometimes one wants to fly away, to be free of everything that binds one to duty, to responsibility, to... other lives. Have you ever felt that way?"

"Oh, um," said Oliver. He couldn't honestly say whether he had ever felt that way, having been accustomed to fulfilling his responsibilities without complaint all his life. On the other hand, he had never had to bear the awful burden of ruling over a realm. "I can see how that might be tempting," he agreed, more from politeness than conviction.

"I believe you really understand," said his host seriously. "I can't tell you how greatly I appreciate that." He clapped a powerful hand on Oliver's shoulder.

The blow was firm enough to propel Oliver forward a step or two so that he stood tight against the railing again. So far below was the ground that he might as well have been standing on a distant star.

And where was that mighty city he had just seen, with its towers and pinnacles and myriad points of light? It had vanished, leaving only a gray and gritty land around Ab'addon's tower. Before he swayed away from the railing, Oliver caught a glimpse of a faint outline under the surface, as if a great city had once existed there and now lay buried. Undulant lines of sand wavered around the outline like serpent guardians of the dead.

"You know," said the Lord of Desolation, keeping his grip on Oliver's shoulder, "sometimes I get so lonely here. You might not think it, but even with my servants around me, I really have no one to talk to. It's depressing, you know, having no companionship with a compatible mind."

Charleynne Gates

Oliver murmured something; he didn't know what. Feeling the iron clutch on his shoulder, and dreadfully aware of the sickening height upon which he stood perilously poised, he didn't dare to venture an opinion. It might be the wrong opinion.

"My friend," Ab'addon continued, as if the idea had just occurred to him, "I would be foolish indeed not to take advantage of the opportunity Fate has brought me. Here you are, an answer to prayer, as it were. My kingdom is vast beyond measure; I need a friend--a confidante--to share its burdens. Stay here! Rule my realm at my side. Create the world as you would have it. Nothing shall be impossible to you, if only you remain as my guest. Think about it. Consider it for a while. But I warn you," with a laugh of such joviality that Oliver shook in his silver-buckled shoes, "that I won't take No for an answer."

Oliver found himself alone in his bedchamber. The crystal bell stood on the nightstand table, but there was no sign of Gloom.

He sat on the edge of the bed, holding his head in both hands. *Where am I really? Who is my strange host? Why can I not remember how I got here? I must have come from somewhere.* He massaged his head absently, concentrating. "A boat. A small... red... boat. On a river. Going fast, faster... no! NO! I don't want to remember! I won't!" Springing up, he ran to the door leading to the hallway and yanked it open--and stopped, not believing his eyes.

The long hall with its gilt-encrusted ceiling had changed completely. Gone were the massive paintings hung on the walls. Gone were the scenes of splendor and debauchery, of peach-toned nymphs and dark-furred fauns revolving in the greenwood. Now there were only mirrors everywhere he looked--mirrors large and small, tall and wide, smooth and speckled. As he watched, astonished, he saw beams of intense light begin to flash from one to another, as if the mirrors were alive and signaling to each other. Then the light-beams turned, as if they sensed an enemy, and attacked, aiming directly at him. Fiery darts of pain stabbed at his eyeballs and exploded in agony in his skull.

Clutching his head, he stumbled back into the bedchamber and fell at full length on the thick carpet. But as he lay writhing in excruciating torment, one clear glimpse of truth and despair flared in his mind. Before he blacked out, he understood that he was not a guest but a prisoner in that palace of desolation.

Chapter Twenty-Four

Council

The Assistant Infirmarian entered the emerald bedchamber on swift, silent feet. She bore a tray with a pitcher of light-green liquid which she set on the nightstand and poured into a glass before taking Flavia's pulse. Flavia closed the antique volume in which she had been reading and lifted her head.

"Better," the Assistant Infirmarian pronounced, "but your ordeal has taken its toll, *Sendara*, and you must have more rest."

"Thank you, Sister Linden," said Flavia, sipping the medicinal drink. The Assistant Infirmarian bowed and departed. "Has Cousin Oliver come?"

Great-Aunt Belvedine shook her head and continued pacing restlessly back and forth before the windows of Flavia's bedchamber. A pair of sandals had been found for her unusually large feet, for her absurd high-heeled combat dress boots had been lost in the wild flight from the Grimmerund. No trace remained of the cobweb cocoon, which had been carefully unwound, strand by strand, by two novice Infirmarians. Those precious silken strings were now stored in a medical supplies cabinet for use in the binding of wounds, should the need arise.

"I wish I knew where he is," Flavia said. "I am certain he is in danger because he pledged his fealty to me." She put the book aside. "There is nothing in here that tells me how to protect him."

"Or what his Gift might be," Belvedine finished sharply. "If we only knew what it is, I'd figure out how to use it myself!"

"His Gift is less important than he is," Flavia insisted. "I would happily forego his Gift to have him safe with us."

Belvedine muttered something uncomplimentary to her great-nephew. "You care too much about him, Flavia. It is not wise. Medley was included in the Quest only because of his potential usefulness,

-- 423 --

which appears less and less likely to be fulfilled." She drew her brows together in a scowl. "You will remember I was always against bringing him into the Labyrinth World," she said darkly.

Flavia was prevented from replying by the urgent ringing of the great Summoning Bell. "Listen!" she commanded, holding up her hand. "That bell has not been rung in four hundred years. The Abbot has ordered all members of the Abbey and families of the community to gather within its walls. The outer doors will be shut and barred after them--no one allowed in or out. Because of me! My coming here has put them all in peril."

"But you will be safe, *Sendara*!" Belvedine emphasized.

"Nothing is certain now," Flavia replied, looking toward the window and out, where the once-broad River Sunder's flow was being forced into a narrower and narrower channel.

Below the Abbey's walls, farmers and fisherfolk, artisans and merchants, all with families and children and carts with bundles, streamed inside the Abbey. They assembled in the courtyard in an orderly fashion until the Abbey's officers could assign them to sleeping-places and find stables for their animals. A low murmur arose from the crowd, but no one pushed or shoved another or raised a voice in protest. Even among the children no loud noise was heard, and babies' cries were gently hushed. The Summoning Bell had not been heard since before the oldest of the Community's elders had been born, but all of them recognized the peril that approached, and they waited patiently while the Whiltian friars took care of them.

"The walls of the Abbey cannot be breached," Flavia continued, "but they can be climbed. An enemy could easily be killed by archers on the towers, but the Abbot forbids such a defense--and so do I. The Abbey's ancient Rule is one of peace, and it will be honored."

"Then we will be at their mercy--and they have none!" cried Belvedine, wringing her hands and pacing ever faster. "Nothing can prevent the *wyrga* armies from scaling the walls. The Lord of Desolation is determined to get you in his power."

"I know it," Flavia answered softly. "And it may be that he will do so in the end. But Ab'addon has not captured Cousin Oliver--or his Gift. I would sense it, if he had!"

"Medley may be forced to yield to him," warned Belvedine. "The Lord of Desolation has ways of taking what he wants. If Ab'addon manages to entrap Medley in some way... My great-nephew is not a person of strong will. Unlike his parents, he has always been placid and irresolute, too timid to initiate anything adventurous on his own. I had hopes that he would outgrow his natural meekness, but alas! I have been greatly disappointed in him. He has always been a misfit in the family, and now he is nothing but a burden to our Quest. I do not believe that he has done us any good at all!"

"He has done so and will do more for us, Belvedine!" Flavia insisted. "He is the one whose coming was foretold--the One Without Guile. I was certain of it as soon as I met him. His Gift will be the salvation of the Graelands--and the Labyrinth World. We must believe in the prophecy!"

The door to Flavia's chamber swung open, and the *Foressa* Mildrith, clad in silver mail that gleamed like fish scales, walked rapidly into the room and nodded to Flavia. "*Sendara*, word has come from one of Hera Vespasia's *Norrengild*, who was able to speak with the vultures on the borders of the Desolate Lands. They have seen Oliver Medley!"

Belvedine stopped pacing and stood stock-still, her mouth ironed into a line. Flavia sat up straight against her pillows, shadows forming under her wide green eyes. "Where is he?" she whispered.

"They say Cousin Oliver has disappeared into the City of Dead Souls," Mil replied.

"Was he captured?" Belvedine demanded. Mil paid no attention to her.

"Is he... Ab'addon's prisoner?" Flavia whispered. "Surely he did not go there of his own free will?"

Mil hesitated. "We... do not know, *Sendara.*"

Father Thyme, with Pavarr on his arm, entered the *Sendara's* chamber and spoke of what they had learned of the *wyrga* armies and the damming of the River Sunder. Flavia's eyes darkened to the hue of storm clouds as she listened, although her cheeks once more grew deathly pale.

Not a word did she speak until they finished. "My illness has delayed us far too long," she decided. "Our company of Questors is divided. We do not know where Cousin Oliver is. If the Dwarvians did find the lost mine beneath the Icewode, we have heard nothing from them. Hera Vespasia has not been seen since we fled the Grimmerund. And now the armies of the Lord of Desolation have nearly surrounded the Abbey. If they overcome us here, the Graelands will have few defenses left!"

"Father Abbot!" said Pavarr, tense in every muscle. "It is imperative that we have a council of war! Grant us this before it is too late!"

"Yes!" Belvedine joined in. "Let the members of the Abbey hear this! They should have a voice in our plans, too!"

"I agree," said Mil, more respectfully but as firmly. "We must plan our defense--and our counterattack!"

But Father Thyme held up a restraining hand, and the three fell silent. Gravely he shook his head. "No, my children, in our Abbey we do not speak of making war."

Though his eyes were bandaged, Pavarr gripped the hilt of his dagger. Mil did the same. Belvedine opened her mouth and might have said something regrettable had not Flavia glanced severely in her direction.

"I ask your pardon, Father Abbot," Flavia said. "My friends think only of my safety."

"I understand, my daughter," the Abbot replied. "Their loyalty to you does them honor. But our mission at the Abbey of Saint Amber has always been to heal that which is wounded, to restore to wholeness what has been broken, and to live in harmony with all beings under the Creator. We are vowed to peace 'til the world's end."

"Then how do we combat the invasion of the *wyrga*?" Pavarr demanded. "Their attack must come as soon as they can ford the Sunder."

"We shall have a council indeed," said the Abbot, "but let it be a Council of Restoration. We will speak of ways to return our Labyrinth World to health--to wholeness--and to peace."

"Yes!" said Flavia, her face alight from within, her voice strong and sweet. "To restore what the Lord of Desolation has destroyed! That must be our sole purpose! So let it be!"

Brother Persil knocked at the door and came into the room. "Father Abbot, Friends," the Infirmarian said firmly, "I must ask you all to leave. In three days' time, not before, the *Sendara* will be well enough to attend a council. Until then, she must rest." Brother Persil swept a graceful gesture toward the door. The others made their reverences to Flavia and left the room, Belvedine with a quick backward scowl to make sure no enemies lurked behind the tapestries.

"I detect movement in the Desolate Lands," said Mil. "There!"

"I thought it couldn't pick up anything past the Bordering Cliffs," said Pavarr. Unable to see where she was pointing, he leaned over Mil's shoulder toward the crystal globe in the Abbot's study. It rotated slowly about an invisible axis, and pinpoint lights sparkled inside it as the Questors' united wills brought into focus what they strove to see.

Gradually neighboring parts of the Labyrinth World appeared, finely detailed in their true colors except for the Desolate Lands, which were a colorless blank. In his relentless advance across the Labyrinth World, Ab'addon had covered his expanding territory with a blanket of sorcery, making it impenetrable to oversight. Even Mil's expertise in the physics of cyberspace had not been able to open a window into what the Lord of Desolation wanted to hide.

"This kind of movement does not come from anything belonging to the Lord of Desolation," Mil replied. "If it did, I would not be able to see it; therefore, it must be from something alien to the Desolation."

"Is it one of the Questors?" asked Pavarr. "Could it be Friend Oliver?"

"Possibly. Wait!"

"What? Where?" Great-Aunt Belvedine interjected.

"Right here! See that?" Mil answered. "This is from several days ago--or weeks. An indefinite time past. I cannot tell precisely when. I see two objects moving. There is a considerable distance between them. I estimate that both are heading toward the City of Dead Souls. It does not appear in the crystal, but I can approximate its location. One might be Friend Oliver, but who the other is, I cannot tell."

"We are still missing the Dwarvians," answered Pavarr. "Can you find them in the crystal?"

"I'll try," answered Mil, her fingers working over an apparatus resembling the strings of a harp doubled and crossed. "Here's something: a third object alien to the Desolate Lands! It also moves toward the City of Dead Souls, but not like the others. This one meanders. Now it seems to be resting."

"Are you sure they're not *wyrga*?" Belvedine rapped out. "Or *gnaarx*? They might be letting you see them deliberately, to mislead us."

"I doubt it," Mil replied. "*Wyrga* and *gnaarx* act only at the command of the Lord of Desolation. They are incapable of deception because they cannot plan ahead or predict the outcome of anything they do."

Belvedine sniffed. "Outcomes cannot be predicted in any case," she stated flatly.

"Not so!" said the Abbot, who entered the room with Hera Vespasia, newly arrived, on his shoulder. "The Web of Life connects all things. A tug on one filament is felt throughout the web. Anyone with sufficient patience, humility, and a steady intent can learn to sense the movements of the intertwining strands. Those who do, may see the shadows of things to come."

The Questors and the Abbot returned to Flavia's chamber and reported what they had discovered.

"Shadows of things to come," Flavia repeated, and put down the scroll she had been studying. "But shadows shift," she whispered, lost in thought.

Father Thyme inclined his head toward her. "Yes, and they can be made to shift by one who *wills* it," he responded. "He who discovers the power of his *will* may conquer the world--if he first conquers himself. But Hera Vespasia has come to tell us more about the *wyrga*."

The owl saluted Flavia and quickly went on. "After the *Sendara* and Belvedine were rescued from Aranea's webtrap atop the Grimmerund, I circled back to see what the *wyrga* would do when they lost their intended sacrifice." She told in full how Aranea and her gargantuan children had destroyed the *wyrga* in the Grimmerund.

"I intended to fly to the Abbey right away, but I saw more *wyrga* from the Desolate Lands gather about the mound when Aranea's brood had gone. Hundreds of thousands of *wyrga*-slaves, more than I realized the Lord of Desolation had made. All were armed with *thringa*-weapons, and when they saw the gruesome remains of the Araneans' feast they became enraged, howling for vengeance!

"I flew under cover of night, invisible to those below. I watched them gather to the summons of their dark drums until the whole Icewode around the Grimmerund was filled with them. They shrieked war cries in their misbegotten tongue, and in their frenzy some even skirmished among themselves. I saw other beings come out of the deep Icewode and join them, monstrous things I have never seen before in the Labyrinth World. Their *wyrga*-leader stood on the summit, urging them to war against the Abbey."

"A leader!" Mil exclaimed. "The *wyrga* have never had a leader from among themselves. They are nothing but mindless slaves! How is this possible?"

"The Labyrinth World is changing," said Father Thyme. "I am not surprised to hear of a leader arisen from the *wyrga*. Slaves they were made and slaves they are, but in the hearts of all living things is the desire to be free. And not even the Lord of Desolation can suppress it forever!"

Father Thyme turned to question the owl. "Great Chief, do you believe the *wyrga* intend to storm the Abbey before the Lord of Desolation discovers their intention?"

"That is what I surmise," Hera Vespasia replied. "Their leader said, why should they help the Lord of Desolation capture the *Sendara*? If they took her themselves, they would gain all her power, and thus become mightier than he!"

"Impossible!" exclaimed Pavarr. "Ab'addon made them and can unmake them at will. When he discovers what they are plotting, he has only to speak a word, and they are ashes! Their scheme will never succeed--though I almost wish it would!"

"Unless--" murmured Father Thyme, tapping an index finger against his chin. The others focused tensely on him.

"Unless what, Father Abbot?" asked Mil.

"Unless the Lord of Desolation already knows what they intend!" he said slowly. "That may be part of his strategy, to let the *wyrga* believe they are capable of invading the Abbey and capturing the *Sendara* on their own. It may be that he will use them and their greed to create a diversion. He is very skilled at using the greed of his victims-- even his allies!--for his own purposes. While our attention is all on guarding against an attack by the *wryga* and protecting the *Sendara*, the Lord of Desolation may be planning something else entirely!"

Charleynne Gates

"But what?" Belvedine gasped.

"In our concern for the *Sendara's* safety, have we not forgotten someone else, one whose presence here is of equal importance?" the Abbot reminded them.

"The Gift-Bringer!" Mil exclaimed, with a hiss of indrawn breath.

"You mean my great-nephew?" huffed Belvedine. "We already know he's not here. Flavia has nearly made herself sick again with worrying about him. When he does show up, I'll have something to say to that young man!" She shook her fist in the face of the absent Oliver.

"He was my responsibility," Pavarr claimed. "I gave my word to protect him, and I failed in my duty. He may be lost--or dead."

"If he is, it's his own fault," Balvedine snapped. "He ought to have kept up with the rest of us."

"But he couldn't have," Mil interjected. "Remember, we were separated when we left the Ruined Chapel."

"Separated? How?" inquired the Abbot.

"By the Hermit who lives there," Mil replied. "When Flavia awakened from her trance, he told us we should go in three different directions to the Abbey, so there'd be a better chance of at least some of us getting here. Pavarr and I escorted Flavia, riding Firemark through the Icewode. Belvedine and Hera Vespasia went by air. The Whackitt brothers took the path to the Longlost Mine of the Dwarves, and Cousin Oliver--" she hesitated.

"Yes?" prompted the Abbot, leaning toward her.

"He was sent off by himself," Mil went on. Her brow creased with the effort of remembering. "To Purple Valley, I think. As we were leaving I heard the Hermit say the way was short, and when he reached a certain village--Mossy Dell, it was called--someone there would help him get to the Abbey."

The Abbot sank back in his chair and bowed his head. "The Hermit of the Ruined Chapel! If I had known you would encounter him--"

"What is it, Father Abbot?" Pavarr asked quickly.

Father Thyme took a deep breath. "The Hermit of the Ruined Chapel was once a Whiltian friar here at the Abbey. He wanted to replace the old Hermit who had died, and our previous Abbot let him go. As Assistant Prior at the time, I was not convinced that he was wise

-- 430 --

enough to bear the burden of solitude, but we had no one else to send, and my doubts were overruled. He seemed to be getting along satisfactorily, and we forgot about him, for he gradually ceased to make any report to the Abbey. Eventually he was corrupted by elements within himself that he knew not how to master. Loneliness and arrogance of intellect overcame him, and he succumbed to the lure of the Desolation."

"What did he do, Father Abbot?" Pavarr inquired.

"He fashioned an homunculus--a human-like being--by means of the Dark Arts. When I became Abbot, I had occasional word about him from travelers who passed by the Ruined Chapel, and when I heard about this entity that followed the Hermit like a shadow, I knew that something was terribly wrong. I was on the point of summoning him to appear before the Abbey Council when the present crisis arose. The homunculus, I fear, has become more than his shadow. I believe the Lord of Desolation has used it to ensnare the soul of the Hermit."

"Then he must have sent Cousin Oliver to his death!" Mil exclaimed. Flavia said nothing, but her face turned pale, and one hand went to her heart. Belvedine hastened to her side.

"Perhaps not," the Abbot replied. "I do not believe that the Gift-Bringer can be lost to us so soon, and in such a fashion. We must believe that he still lives, and will yet bring his Gift to us." He rose from his chair. "Now, my friends, we are needed in the Grand Sanctuary. Even in the midst of troubles, we may not forget our duty to the dead. Sister Valerian waits for us to send her to eternal joy." He moved toward the door, but Pavarr stopped him.

"Father Abbot!" said the prince urgently. "I beg you, allow me to station my Taraman warriors at the battlements. Our longbow archers can keep the *wyrga* at bay. We cannot let the enemy think we are undefended!"

The Abbot shook his head gravely. "No, my son. No one will fire a weapon from these walls. Your warriors may keep watch, but nothing more."

He strode purposefully from the room as the tolling bell began to ring, counting the number of years Sister Valerian had passed at the Abbey of Saint Amber.

The friars of the Abbey and the Whiltian families of the community gathered for the funeral of their sister. The great space of the Grand Sanctuary, with the soft light of its rose window diffused throughout the pillared room, reverberated with hushed whisperings. Tall white candles with tapering yellow flames made points of light in the perpetual dusk.

On the main floor, in front of the rows of wooden stalls, rested the casket that enclosed the earthly remains of Sister Valerian. A cloth of emerald-green samite, richly embroidered with twining leaves and flowers in gold thread, draped the casket, small as a child's, and swept the tiled floor in graceful folds around it.

Father Thyme paced slowly up the center aisle, paused with bowed head before the casket, and went to stand at its head, facing the congregation. The faint sonorities in the Grand Sanctuary gathered and became a muted chant.

The Abbot began the Service of Departure and Remembrance. "Dear Friends, we gather to honor a sister of our beloved community. As the sparrow flies out of a winter night into the banquet hall of the king and out again into the dark, so do we come from darkness into the light of present day, and soon return to the dark. But beyond all darkness is Light, and in that Light we will dwell in peace forever."

The murmured chant softened until it became indistinguishable from the whisper of candle flames.

The Abbot continued. "We now commit the body of Sister Valerian to the elements of *Terra, Ayr, Fyr*, and *Watyr*, and we commend her soul to the eternal Light. So be it ever!"

The low, sweet chanting of the friars grew louder. As the music reached its climax, a beam of rainbow-hued light from the rose window engulfed the casket. The light became blinding, and the congregation hid their eyes from its radiance.

Then as suddenly as it had appeared, the rainbow light vanished, and with it the casket, leaving only the gold-embroidered cloth sinking slowly to the floor. The singing died down as well, and the hush of the Sanctuary descended.

Father Thyme had pronounced the dismissal, and the friars had begun to file out of their stalls, when the Officer of the Watch rushed in, ran to Pavarr, and whispered something to him in great haste.

Saint Amber's Rose

"Father Abbot!" said Pavarr at once, "one of my Taraman warriors has been hit by a poisoned *wyrga* arrow! The enemy are drawn up in full battle formation beyond the Sunder, which is shrinking rapidly. Give us leave to attack now, while we have the advantage!"

The Whiltian friars, hearing this, began to talk among themselves, but the Abbot raised his hand and silence fell. He drew Pavarr aside and spoke in a low voice.

"My son, each of us is born to a duty, and you must do yours as we do ours. I wish that Oliver Medley were here to use his Gift, but we must continue without him. I cannot command you to attack, because the Abbey of Saint Amber may never be an aggressor. But go, prepare your defense, and grace be with you!"

Pavarr, with the Officer of the Watch, hurried to the outer walls.

The congregation filed out until no one remained in the Grand Sanctuary except a lone figure in a Whiltian friar's robe--a robe disarranged and smeared with dirt. Slowly the figure approached the gold-embroidered cloth lying on the floor, all that was left of Sister Valerian.

Hesitantly the figure knelt, reached out a hand to touch the cloth--and snatched the hand away as if the cloth had burned it. Then the figure sprang up and fled from the Sanctuary, fled from whatever imaginary forces pursued it.

Sequestered in his study, Father Thyme conferred with Hera Vespasia. "Tell me what else you have seen, my daughter," he begged the owl.

"The situation is very grave, Father Abbot," she replied. "Even worse than the Questors believe. They made their journeys here through terrible obstacles. Overcoming them riveted their attention on each danger in turn, and they have necessarily lost, to some degree, their sense of what looms over us. In my flight under the moon I soared over everything that impeded them and oversaw a vaster space than they could.

"The Desolation's forces are much closer than they realize, closer than even Prince Pavarr thinks. Ab'addon's engines of mass destruction are poised to render all the world a wasteland. He has bought and sold the souls of countless human beings. They dance along his golden path blindly, gathering up glittering trinkets that he strews before them, neither knowing nor caring that they dance to their deaths.

"The Desolation's siege engines are stationed at these points." Using the tip of her wing, the owl indicated on the map spread over the Abbot's desk where the *wyrga* had advanced into the Labyrinth. Its defenses had indeed been penetrated to a far greater extent than the Abbot realized.

Father Thyme sat perfectly still in his chair when Hera Vespasia departed, his head hooded and bowed so that his face was entirely in shadow. For a long time he pondered, considering every possibility of resistance... of defeat... of surrender. He thought of the march of time upon all worlds, of the rhythms of creation and destruction, life and death. He thought of the necessity for that which is built up to be pulled down and once more rebuilt, emerging in new forms, for such is the nature of the cosmos within the fabric of time and space.

As the ocean's tides ebb and flow, so does life within the Labyrinth. Such is the Creator's will.

Was it then beyond his duty to interfere with that age-old pattern? Many Ages had seen the building up of existent forms: Was it now their turn to be destroyed? *Is the world's end closer than I thought?* This very Abbey had stood upon the Great Mountain of Zund since it had risen groaning from the earth. It seemed as if it would last forever, but the Abbot knew that even the mountains will crumble one day and the Abbey with them. *Has that time drawn near, and I did not see it?*

He had offered shelter to the Questors and to everyone who knocked at the Abbey's door, for here at least they would be safe until the Desolation conquered everything. He could protect the *Sendara* for the time being, but what about the Graelands, the heart of the Labyrinth? That land was far away, out of the Abbot's sphere of influence. Was it better not to actively resist the coming--perhaps inevitable--destruction?

Father Thyme's head sank lower on his chest, his shoulders bowed under the weight of his burden. Many years had he ruled as Abbot: He had grown old in the service of the Abbey and the people of the Labyrinth. He sensed that the present Age was drawing to a close, and he was weary.

Saint Amber's Rose

If the Lord of Desolation and his evil are permitted within the grand design of the Creator, then who am I, old Thyme, to presume to alter the destiny of the world?

"I am no longer worthy to lead the Abbey," he whispered, and Darkness coiled serpent-like around him. "Doubt assails me. I fear what may come. I fear the Desolation."

Hold on, hold on, said a still, small voice in the center of his soul.

Through the open window came the sudden, joyful song of a bird, a cascade of trills pouring from its throat. Again and again it called out, oblivious to the dark decisions pondered in the Abbot's study. It paused, and from the wood beyond its mate's reply came, clear and sweet.

Within the penumbra of his cowl, the Abbot heard and smiled. *So shall the small and innocent teach the great and powerful. Thus be it ever!*

"Joy shall be our watchword!" the Abbot proclaimed, pushing aside his heavy cowl and rising from his chair. "Joy! which the Desolation does not know and never will!"

The Abbot took his place on the abbatial chair in the Council Chamber. Before him were the assembled friars; beside him were Flavia in her silver chair and the Questors Hera Vespasia, Prince Pavarr, and the *Foressa* Mildrith.

"Sisters and Brothers!" The Abbot rose to address the company. "Great Chief Hera Vespasia of the *Norrengild* brings us news: The agents of the Desolation draw near. You have seen for yourselves how the River Sunder has been dammed, with a great lake forming behind it. Soon the river will dwindle to a level where the *wyrga* armies can cross without hindrance.

"Their incursion is no work of Nature. It has been caused by evil in the minds of human mortals, their unrelenting greed with which the Lord of Desolation has entrapped them."

He bowed his white head. "I, too, was drawn into his deceit, for I was close to surrendering my will to him. I would have enclosed us in this Abbey and waited passively for the Desolation to overcome us even though I know that if Ab'addon triumphs, the world will plunge into chaos. Courage and compassion alike will vanish from the hearts of human mortals, and none will have a care for any but himself. Destruction and death will sweep across land and ocean; plague and famine will consume all living beings, even to the stones. The whole of the Labyrinth World, aye, the green Earth itself, will end in Ashes of Waste."

Father Thyme straightened his shoulders and looked squarely at the congregation. "This must not happen! Not while Saint Amber's Abbey endures! As long as we have the secret of Joy, we can resist the evil of the Desolation!"

"So be it ever!" chorused the friars of Saint Amber, and began discussing the means of joyful resistance.

"Father Abbot! Councilors!" interrupted the slow, heavy voice of Brother Burdock, the Carpenter, which quieted the Whilts with its power. "Have you all forgotten Sister Valerian? That she was murdered in our own garden, her throat cut open? I was her friend, and I have not forgotten! I say that evil is already inside our Abbey! Someone here killed Sister Valerian! Councilors, a traitor sits among us!"

"A traitor! Who is it? Who could it be?" broke from the Whilts. "Surely not one of us! No Whilt would act against the community!"

"It must be one of the strangers!" someone cried out. Later, no one in the Abbey was able to identify the voice. All agreed it sounded familiar, but no one could say exactly who it had been.

"The strangers! It must be the strangers!" the Whilts began shouting, and surged out of their seats, milling around the room. Mil and Pavarr quickly moved to stand beside Flavia's silver chair, their hands on the hilts of their swords. Belvedine stepped behind Flavia, her blade-thin height and deadly umbrella defying anyone to come closer.

The commotion increased. Hera Vespasia took off from her perch and flew about the Council Chamber low over the heads of the Councilors, who ducked to avoid her whirring wings and dangerous beak. She landed on the crest of Flavia's chair and opened her golden eyes to their widest extent.

The Abbot was about to call for order when three loud knocks came from a door leading to the Upper Abbey. Startled, the friars stopped their excited talk and stood still, waiting... for what, they did not know. No one had knocked at that door in a great many years.

-- 436 --

Saint Amber's Rose

The heavy old door creaked open. An aged Whilt stood in the doorway, a cane in each hand, flanked by two attendants. She was dressed in blue robes of antique pattern, with a white wimple covering her head. Despite her great age, her face was clear and unwrinkled, and in her eyes shone incalculable wisdom.

Amid the sudden hush, the aged one walked slowly into the Council Chamber. Awed whispers ran about the room. "Sister Hesperia! It is Sister Hesperia, the Oldest Whilt! She hasn't been out of her room for over a hundred years!"

The old one advanced until she faced the Abbot. "What is this unseemly clamor that has disturbed my rest?" she demanded, and although her voice was as one who speaks out of the past, there was no quaver in it. "Whilts of Saint Amber! Sisters and Brothers! Have you no respect for your Abbot? Or for our guest, the *Sendara* of the Graelands? For shame!"

Profound silence filled the room. No eye dared meet the Oldest Whilt's. Every head was bowed.

"Forgive us, Father Abbot. Forgive us, *Sendara*." One by one the Councilors murmured their apologies.

Flavia smiled at them, and moon and stars dimmed in the light of her face. "Forgiven, dear friends."

"Sister Hesperia," said the Abbot, "we are honored by your presence among us. I beg you to be seated in the abbatial chair once again, as when you were our Abbess."

Sister Hesperia proceeded to the abbatial throne and seated herself thereon. Murmurs arose from the Whilts. "She ruled our Abbey in days of yore, when peace dwelt in the land. Even the Great Waste was green then. They say she is the wisest of all the Whilts that have ever lived!"

"Honored Sister Hesperia," the Abbot began, "we have the misfortune to quarrel because--"

"I know, I know," the Oldest Whilt interrupted. "There is nothing that happens in this Abbey that I do not hear. I am distressed to learn that the Whilts of Saint Amber have surrendered to the worst enemy of all, worse than the Lord of Desolation himself!"

The assembled Whilts held their breath.

"FEAR!" she scolded, pointing a finger at the community. "Fear is your enemy! Faith is your ally! Believe in what you know to

-- 437 --

be true, and cast out fear! Now: Where is the heir to the Oaken Crown?"

The Whilts looked at one another, disconcerted. Who can that be? they wondered amongst themselves. We have never heard of such a person!

Pavarr stepped forward, turning his bandaged eyes in the direction of Sister Hesperia's voice. "Honored Sister, I am Pavarr, Prince of Taraman. I am heir-elect to the Oaken Crown. What do you require of me?"

Instead of answering Pavarr, the Oldest Whilt spoke to the Abbot. "Father Thyme, can you tell me where rests the sword *Greenhallow*, which once lay before the altar in our Grand Sanctuary?"

The Abbot hesitated. "*Greenhallow* disappeared years ago. None knows where it lies now."

"Wait!" said Mil, and came forward to stand with Pavarr. "*Greenhallow*, the Sword of Life! I remember--I saw it in the Ruined Chapel!"

"It must have been stolen by the Hermit," said the Abbot. "He could have taken it, under the influence of the Dark One."

"*Greenhallow* must be recovered," said Sister Hesperia. "It is the only weapon with the power to withstand the Lord of Desolation. And it can only be wielded in battle by the hero for whom it is destined."

"Do you mean Oliver Medley, Sister?" the Abbot asked. "He is the Gift-Bringer of the Prophecies--the One Without Guile."

"No, not that one," replied the Oldest Whilt. "The One Without Guile is meant to awaken the Rose. It is the heir to the Oaken Crown who must wield *Greenhallow* in single combat with the Lord of Desolation--against the Blackfire Rod!"

"But Sister Hesperia, I'm blind!" Pavarr protested. "How can I fight in single combat?"

Sister Hesperia rose from the abbatial chair with the assistance of her attendants, and walked slowly toward the door to the Upper Abbey. "Tell Brother Gall," she said over her shoulder, "to look on the third shelf of the seventh cabinet in the Apothecarium. He will find a small blue jar in the back left corner. I put it there myself when I was Apothecary to the Abbey, some eight hundred years ago. Inside it he will find an ointment called Balm of the Archangel. He must anoint you under the eyes for three days."

Without another word, she exited through the same door by which she had entered, and the door shut abruptly behind her. And long it was before the Community of Saint Amber saw the venerable Whilt again.

With the disappearance of Sister Hesperia, the Whiltian Councilors began to discuss, in an orderly manner, what they were about to face. So intent were they that only the Prioress noticed that one of the younger Whilts had slipped away. Wondering, Sister Clova watched as a narrow door obscured by shadows close slowly. Before it shut completely, Sister Clova made her decision and quietly followed.

Her footfall light upon the floor, the Prioress made haste to keep the hem of the other's habit in sight. Swiftly the two of them, pursuer and pursued, fled through winding corridors until the first one reached the open door of the Chapel of the Silver Chalice. Without stopping, she ran inside, straight to the altar. There she knelt, weeping, her face buried in her hands, shoulders shaking.

The Prioress stayed a moment in the doorway, watching, waiting... and at last understanding. Quietly, so as not to disturb the penitent, she walked up the center aisle until she stood beside the younger Whilt. Softly she spoke, and her voice was filled with tenderness and pity.

"My dear child."

The younger one shuddered, as if her body were collapsing into itself, but her hands remained over her face.

"Be not so distressed," the Prioress said. "Forgiveness is all around us, for Love never fails." And she bent to touch the trembling shoulder.

But on the instant Sister Celeret bounded up, away from the extended hand, and ran toward a side door. One wild look she gave the Prioress, and her face was desperate with terror and longing. "Not for me!" she cried. "I can never be forgiven!" Then she was gone, flying fast through the Abbey's twisting, spiraling passages downward, ever downward.

Charleynne Gates

Chapter Twenty-Five

Realm of the Stonemen

The River Sunder broadened, narrowed, broadened again. Streaks of a black, oily substance appeared in the water, writhing in the current like snakes. Bertie didn't like the look of them at all. He touched one with an oar; the paddle came out slimed with the stuff, whatever it was. He brought the oar in, sniffed it. It stank, almost nauseating him. Quickly he put the paddle back in the water; the river washed the black traces away.

The farther he rowed, the more black streaks appeared, until the Sunder became more than half tainted. Bertie frowned, wondering what the stuff was and disliking the thought of rowing any deeper into it. He grounded the rowboat on a shallow bank where the forest ran down to the river. Scrambling out, he turned to grab the painter... *Zing!* An arrow shot past him and stuck in a tree.

Bertie immediately crouched, poised his slingshot, and peered around to see what had attacked him. After a few seconds a slim figure stood up from behind the bushes several yards away, holding a bow at tension and a black-fledged arrow ready to let fly. Cautiously, the figure approached him, keeping the arrow at the ready--pointed not at him, but at something that fled into the forest. The crash of its passage through the brush faded out of hearing.

"Andis!" Bertie exclaimed, half in relief, half in exasperation. "What are you doing here? And why are you shooting at me--again?"

"Ssh!" Andis commanded. She stood for a full minute longer staring in the direction where her intended target had vanished. Nothing moved. She relaxed, allowed her bowstring to ease tension, and returned the arrow to her quiver. "Thank you, Andis," she said with more than a hint of sarcasm. "You saved my life--again."

Saint Amber's Rose

"Thanks, Andis," Bertie responded with as much grace as he could muster. "I guess you saved my life, even if I didn't see what you were shooting at. What was it, anyway?"

"Another *wyrga*, I think," said Andis. "Didn't I tell you this forest is full of *wyrga*? More and more of them, lately. You have to keep an eye out. Which you were not doing."

Bertie flushed. "I was busy. The river's tainted with something; I can't figure out what it is."

"You can't afford to let your guard down," Andis reproved. "I knew you'd need protection; that's why I followed you. I actually have more important things to do, but I really couldn't let you go on alone. You're just a babe in the woods."

"I'm n--!" Bertie bit back the words he desperately wanted to say. He had been caught off guard; she had saved his life, twice now. Maybe. "All right. What do you suggest we do?"

"I don't know," said Andis, suddenly out of ideas. "What's the matter with the river?"

"That black ooze," said Bertie, nodding toward the water. "I'd like to know what it is before I go on. Not that I'm going to stop looking for Mr. Medley," he added hastily.

"I think that black stuff's from the Saurian River," said Andis, scanning the water. "I've never seen it before, but I've heard about it. They say the River Sunder used to be clear, pure water from the spring to the sea, but that was a long time ago. The Saurian River has leaked into it somehow, and now this whole part of the Sunder is fouled by Saurian blackwater. It's poisonous, I've heard. It's bad enough if you breathe in the fumes, but worse if you fall into the river itself. The Saurian runs through the Desolate Lands to the place where the Lord of Desolation lives. That's what they say. I've never been there."

They both stared at the long fingers of slime inching up the River Sunder.

"There's where I have to go," Bertie decided, "but not on that blackwater. If we're on the river, we'd breathe it in; we couldn't help it." (Andis smiled to herself at the "we".) "We'd be an easier target for wyrga if we're on the water, so we'd better go by land, even if it's slower. We'll follow the river at the edge of the forest."

He went back to the boat and started to pull it up higher on the bank, out of the river's reach. "Come on!" he said over his shoulder. "I can use a hand here."

It took them several days of walking and camping, alternating watch, lacking sleep for safety's sake. Always wary, but not a *wyrga* seen or smelled. Over the days they became more at ease with each other, confiding things they would not have done in other circumstances.

And then, before either of them realized what was ahead, they came upon it, as suddenly as walking between two trees: the devastation of Threshold Forest, where the invading *wyrga* had crashed through the wood with their ponderous engines of mass destruction. Tree-stumps crudely hacked and burnt, deep gouge-marks wounding the earth, grasses ripped out, roots torn away, streams choked, habitat destroyed, animals and birds driven out to perish. Even the insects had fled. Desolate under a leaden sky, the ravaged earth lay unshielded from a pitiless sun.

The two young people stood at the edge of that boundless ruin and held their breath.

"What made this?" Bertie whispered after a time.

"He ordered it," Andis whispered back. "The Lord of Desolation."

Then they heard the unmistakable sounds of grief borne on the small wind, coming from everywhere... and nowhere.

"Someone's crying. Who's there?" Bertie looked around for the source.

Shivering, Andis moved closer to the boy. "I--I think," she said through her own tears, "it is the forest... weeping."

Bowing their heads, they listened. Hand sought hand, and in a little while they went back into cover again, following the River Sunder to its doom.

In the barren waste left behind, the Earth wept for her lost children.

At long last they came to the Bordering Cliffs and saw in the distance the turbid, stinking Saurian River which, having finally overwhelmed and drowned the River Sunder, wove a black channel through the Desolate Lands.

"There it is," Andis murmured. "But I can't see where it's going." For there was a dark fume over the land, and all they could see were indistinct shapes far ahead, shapes that wavered and changed and seemed to be in one place and then in another without having visibly moved between them. And one shape, straight as a needle and unmoving, had a strange, dark light in it that flashed and disappeared, flashed and disappeared with a slow, hypnotic pulse.

"Pavarr told me about that tower with the black light," Andis continued. "Maybe if we get close enough, we can find a way to get into the castle next to it."

Bertie didn't particularly like hearing that name "Pavarr" again. Andis had an annoying habit of emphasizing it. Besides, he could figure things out for himself.

"That's what I planned on doing," Bertie said. It was almost true.

"We'd better start down there," Andis told him. "Looks like there's kind of a trail." She started toward the edge of the cliff.

"No," said Bertie, and something in his tone stopped her.

"What do you mean?" said Andis. "You need my help."

"No," Bertie repeated, a little more firmly than he meant to. "Look: I'm--I'm glad you came this far. You're right; it probably was a better idea to for us to go together. But now I've got to go on alone. No, listen," as Andis started to protest. "I don't know what I'm going to find in that castle, if I can even get inside it. If you stay here, you can keep a lookout. And--and I might need backup. You know, help getting out. There'll probably be two of us, and I don't know what shape Mr. Medley'll be in. He might be sick or tortured or something."

Andis considered this possibility. "Hmm... Maybe you're right. I'll stay here." Unbeknownst to them, "here" was the exact spot where Pavarr and Ildranna had recovered after their ordeal in Castle Mormorion.

"That's good," said Bertie, relieved that getting her to stay put had been easier this time.

"I'll give you twenty-four hours," she declared, and set her bow and quiver down beside a flat rock made for sitting. "Not a minute more. You ought to be able to find him and bring him out by then."

Bertie didn't bother to argue.

He crouched beside the shore of the black river, uncertain what to do next. Once or twice he had had to cross an eddy of the river and had come so close to falling into the slick-surfaced ooze that he had almost been sick with nausea. Slipping and sliding, keeping his balance with difficulty, the boy made his hesitant way inland, in the general direction of the wavering tower-shape he had seen through the smokefall. Breathless, he stopped at the first of a long row of standing stones and sank down to rest, leaning against the nearest one.

This country looks awfully bleak. No recognizable landmarks anywhere, no mountains, hills, or rivers except the one he had followed here, and he'd hardly call that a real river. No water in it, just that thick black stuff with a swift current pushing it along. And that stench! Now that his senses weren't totally occupied with where he was putting his foot every single step, he became more aware of acrid fumes coming off the river. They made his head swim. He wanted to throw up.

Wash your feet! He heard it, but not with his ears. It was a command, and it was inside his mind.

"What? Who said that?" he asked aloud, coughing.

Wash your feet! Then he realized that the voice had come from somewhere nearby.

WASH YOUR FEET! This time it was the kind of command that when you heard it, you obeyed, no questions asked.

Bertie sprang up from his sitting position and looked around wildly for water to wash in, anything but the noxious liquid in the river. But there was nothing but gritty, grayish ground, more like hard-caked ashes than sand, unlike any soil he had ever seen.

"But there's no water!" he protested aloud, not knowing who had spoken to him.

Use the ashes, repeated the voice. *Not as good as water, but you'll have to use them to clean your feet. Scrub the Saurian poison off them, or you will die. Hurry!*

Obediently Bertie bent down and used his fingers to try to scrape some loose grains from the ground, but the ash was so firmly packed that nothing came up. Suddenly his feet began to sting, more and more with every second, until he felt as if they were on fire and burning up. "Ow! Ow! Help me!" he cried, falling back on the ground again and trying in panic to scrub off the viscid coating with his fingers.

Behind you, spoke the voice.

Bertie swiveled toward the huge boulder. At its base lay a large chip of rock with jagged edges. Quickly he grabbed it and began to stab the ground again and again with it as his feet kept on swelling and burning until tears streamed down his face from the pain.

At last he made a little mound of loose ash. Flinging aside the digging tool, he began to scrub his feet frantically with the grit, which absorbed the oily black substance as he rubbed until finally his feet were clean and free of residue. They were bright pink from the rubbing, but the agonizing pain was gone, and the flesh had no burn marks.

"Whew!" Bertie sighed with relief, leaning back against the boulder and wiping drops of perspiration off his forehead. "Thanks, mister... ah, mister?"

You are welcome, said the voice right in his ear, startling Bertie into leaping up again and backing away from the boulder. Now he saw that the great stone was moving, swaying slightly from side to side the way a rock oughtn't to be doing, and realized that the voice had come from the stone itself. That seemed improbable if not downright impossible, for in Bertie's rather limited experience boulders do not move and sway of their own volition, nor do they speak.

Do not be afraid, said the boulder. *We will not hurt you.*

Who is this young man? inquired a different voice, gentle and caressing. It came from the standing stone in a row across from the first one. *How handsome he is! He must be about the age our own boy was when we became stones. Is he looking for the other one who came here recently?*

The other one... the other one, echoed a multitude of standing stones. They extended as far as eye could see except where gaps, like missing teeth, appeared at random.

Someone like me? thought Bertie, regaining partial use of his wits. "Beg your pardon, sir," he said to the first boulder. "As it happens, I am looking for someone who might have come this way not long ago. His name is Mr. Oliver Medley. Did you see him?"

The boulder became very agitated, nodding its great head vehemently and twisting its body, as much as it could, from side to side.

Yes! Yes! We saw him! We warned him! He would not listen to us! He would not believe us!

Believe us! Believe us! the other stones echoed. They swayed from side to side, apparently in agony, and their suffering struck Bertie's heart.

"I believe you, sir!" he exclaimed, and in sympathy put a hand on a sloping shelf of the boulder as he would have on the shoulder of a friend. The stone sighed and drooped beneath his hand; startled, Bertie snatched his hand away and stepped back hastily.

You are right to wonder at what you feel, young Friend, said the boulder. *We are Stonemen. Once we were human mortals, men, women, and children living in a green and fertile paradise. Then we hardened our hearts and our souls; our bodies also hardened until now we are immovable stones, and our land is dust and ashes. But not all of us were changed completely. In some of us, hearts still beat and have not yet been crushed under the unrelenting weight we bear. It is that which you feel, Friend--the life which remains beneath the stone.*

"Oh!" Bertie exclaimed, at a loss for what to say. "I--I'm very sorry! Is there anything I can do for you?"

Take heed to what we say! replied the Stoneman.

Warn him! Warn him, Stonefather! insisted the other Stonemen while the complaining wind wrapped itself around them.

The Stonefather told Bertie how Oliver Medley had passed among them, but despite their warnings, had gone ahead into the City of Dead Souls.

"You mean he--he's dead?" Bertie gasped.

We do not know, replied the Stonefather. *We know that he went alive to the City, and that the Lord Ab'addon took him. More than that we could not see.*

"Lord Ab'addon?" Bertie asked. "Who is he?"

Be warned, young Friend! He is the Lord of Desolation, and rules all the country hereabout. The City which you see afar off--the Stonefather swayed to one side; Bertie peered over his shoulder and saw in the distance the outline of the tower he had seen before. It didn't exactly look like any city Bertie had imagined, but he wasn't inclined to doubt the Stonefather's word.

It seems like empty buildings, but in truth it is a warren of dwellings, and all who reside therein are dead souls. The Lord of

Desolation made that City. The Saurian River flows into it and is consumed there. Your friend was already suffering from the effects of being submerged in that river. Because of the poison which permeated his system, he was all the more drawn to the City. Nothing that enters it ever emerges, for the Lord of Desolation is Lord of the Wasteland, Lord of the Abyss, Lord of Chaos and Despair. BEWARE OF HIM!

BEWARE! BEWARE! wailed the other standing stones, and writhed and bent, struggling to escape their confinement.

"Oh, sir!" said Bertie, greatly troubled. "I hardly know what to say. It sounds like a dreadful place. But I've got to go there! Mr. Medley is my friend, and I can't abandon him. He might not be dead. He might be trapped inside there, trying to get out. I've got to try and help him."

The Stonefather straightened and spoke again. *Yes, you will go, young Friend. You have chosen your destiny with clear eyes. Will you tell us your name, that we may know one whose heart is brave and loyal?*

"Bertie Mossgrower of Purple Valley, at your service, sir!" Remembering his manners (taught him firmly and with great patience by Grandmother Mossgrower), Bertie bowed deeply from the waist.

The boulder bowed (as much as he could) in response. *I am Endorgon, Chieftain of the Stonemen. Across from me is the Stonemother Andrasil, my dear wife.*

Bertie turned and bowed to her.

I would welcome you to this land, continued the Stonefather, *but it is no longer our home, and we do not want to bid you stay. It is best for you to leave us now, to go forward or back, as you desire. Move quickly, for the Lord of Desolation keeps careful watch over his realm. Rarely does anyone enter or leave without his knowledge.*

Suddenly an alarm sounded from the Stonemen farther down *The Black Flame! The Black Flame!* they cried out. Bertie did not know what they meant and simply gawked around.

Then he saw it, and knew terror. From the top of the distant tower came a long spear of black fire that swept over the whole countryside around the tower.

"What is it?" Bertie gasped, fascinated by the thing that crept closer and closer to them.

Here! Behind me! the Stonefather ordered. When Bertie failed to respond, he reached out a stone finger and hooked the boy's shirt, dragging him back to the shelter of the boulder. *Crouch down! Hide from the Flame!*

Hidden behind Endorgon's bulk, Bertie instinctively made himself into as small a parcel as he could, whipping off what remained of his shirt and pulling it over his head. Shaking with fear--of what, he did not quite know--he curled into a shapeless lump, trying to seem like part of the boulder itself. With his eyes masked, he couldn't see what happened as the Black Flame passed among the standing stones, but he heard a faint hiss as it scorched the ground. At intervals he heard a scream, then several sharp cracks, then the sound of stone crumbling to pieces.

A high keening broke out among the Stonemen, and Bertie guessed that the Black Flame had struck and destroyed one of them. *That's why there are empty spaces among the Stonemen!* He felt a surge of anger against such cruelty. Equally with the anger, an overwhelming sense of compassion washed over him, pity for the Stonemen who couldn't move out of the way to escape or to defend themselves.

But after pity came fear again: *I have to go to the tower where the Black Flame came from!* What other horrors would be waiting when--if--he got there? And how, supposing he found Mr. Medley, was he going to get out again?

He held his breath and kept absolutely motionless as the Black Flame sizzled so closely to him that he could smell scorched ash. More horribly still, the evil thing stopped right in front of him and lingered there, as if it sensed that something alien was nearby. Through a tiny tear in the cloth of his shirt, Bertie managed to peek out and see the Flame, a dazzling, alluring black brightness that twisted and blazed with unbearable heat.

It wanted him.

And he wanted it! If he only reached out the tip of a finger, he could touch the unbearably beautiful light that seemed—that was--alive with a life beyond anything Bertie had ever imagined. To touch it, give himself to it... That was all he wanted, forever and ever...

He moved a finger the distance of a hair's breadth. Almost against his will it inched beneath the covering of his shirt.

Saint Amber's Rose

Va'in 'a moru', Sendara! Va'in 'a moru'! rang inside his mind. It was the Stonefather's voice! Bertie's finger stopped moving. As if it had heard the thought pass between them, the Black Flame hissed, flared, and struck blindly--not at Bertie but at the Stonemother, Andrasil. She split down the center and burst apart.

A howl went up from the Stonemen that reverberated beyond the farthest borders of the Desolation. *Aiee!* they cried. *Lost!*

Andrasil! Andrasil! roared the Stonefather, raging in grief. *My wife! Beloved!* He writhed his great body and tried to stretch out his arms, but the weight of flesh become rock was too much for him, and his effort collapsed. He could not move from his rooted place, nor touch the splintered body of his wife lying across the path beyond his reach.

No longer caring about his own safety, Bertie sprang to his feet and ran around in front of the Stonefather, stopping short at the scene before him. The boulder that was once the Stonemother lay broken, a light veil of dust rising from her shattered parts.

Guilt clutched at his heart as he looked at her, and tears ran unheeded down his face. *It's my fault,* he said to himself as his shocked mind worked to understand what he saw. *She died because I came here.*

In the distance, its lust for destruction satisfied, the Black Flame traced its way back to the tower. Raising his head, Bertie glared at the place where the Flame had retreated like a predator to its den. "I will go to your tower, Mr. Lord of Desolation," he said, clenching his fists. He spoke at first under his breath, then louder as his determination grew. "I will find Mr. Medley, and then I will destroy you. This is Bertie Mossgrower speaking, and I will destroy you."

The Stonefather mourned, stretching out his stony hands even though he could not touch his wife. Bertie looked at her, broken in bits, and knew there was nothing he could do, except--

He went to her and carefully lifted in his arms the one piece that had been her head. Reverently he bore it to the Stonefather and laid it at his feet, where, after years of cruel separation, Endorgon could at last touch the face of his beloved wife.

Bertie bowed again to the Chieftain of the Stonemen. "I must go now, sir," he said. "I'm sorry... I'm awfully sorry. If you could ever forgive me..."

The Stonefather made no reply, but lifted his face to the sky and cried in a loud voice, *Ehhemet! Hindren fallinomen darin!*

At once the shape of an enormous bird, black-feathered wings widespread, appeared in the north. It swooped down toward Bertie, its yellow beak gleaming, red-rimmed eyes staring straight at him.

Bertie panicked, not knowing which way to run. He braced himself for the snap of the pointed beak into his flesh.

But it never came. Instead, Bertie found himself dangling in mid-air as the vulture (*Cathartes aura*) bore him swiftly toward the tower. As they climbed higher and higher, Bertie saw the whole panorama of the Desolation beneath them: a featureless plain of gritty ash with the Saurian River slicing like a black wound through it. *Is it going to drop me in the river?* he wondered, helpless to do anything about it.

He did not wonder long. Before Bertie's numbed mind could achieve full panic mode, the vulture plummeted down to the tower top, stopping its giddy dive only when its talons touched the twigs of a nest set into the crenellated round top of the tower, which was thin enough to look like a spire when viewed from afar.

The vulture dropped Bertie onto the floor of the nest. Luckily, being slender and not fully grown, Bertie fit into it, though without a great deal of room to spare. In fact, he nearly landed on a sleeping egg, obviously the vulture's progeny. Standing up shakily, Bertie took a deep breath--and inhaled the fug of a vulture's living quarters. It reeked of leftover scraps of carrion, nearly overwhelming him.

"There now, my dear," said a female vulture in comforting tones. "You're safe. We're on top of the Black Flame Tower, but believe me, there's no better place for you to be. He'll never find you here. You see, just below us is the room where the Black Flame lives, and even he doesn't care to get too close to it, for all it is his own making. It's a good thing Endorgon called us to rescue you. If you'd stayed down there any longer, the Black Flame would have found you, and then he would have known about you!"

"He?" asked Bertie, disoriented from his wild ride. "You mean the Lord of--"

"Let's just say the L. of D.," interjected the male vulture, smoothing his feathers. "You don't want to be too free with his name in these parts. Names can be dangerous things, you know. There's power in them, so it's not wise to be calling people by their true names too often. Anything might happen." The gigantic bird glared at Bertie and clenched his talons. Bertie gulped.

"Now, honey, there's no need to be frightening the boy," said the mother vulture. "Why don't you go make a little reconnaissance flight, and I'll get this lad something to eat. He looks as if he hasn't had any food for a week! Luckily, I've been trying out a new recipe for *hors d'oeuvres*. Here, child--" holding out a leaf-dish dotted with oval-shaped white things that looked like hard-boiled eggs--"have a nice deviled eye."

Bertie's face turned green, but he controlled himself manfully and managed to express thanks, hoping that he wasn't giving offense. "I'd really just like a piece of dry bread, thank you kindly all the same," he croaked, and scrabbled around in his knapsack for any remaining crusts of journey-bread. Maybe that would settle his stomach enough to let him ignore the pervasive odor of animal intestines.

"Just as you wish, dear," cooed the mother vulture, and mercifully put the plate of hard-boiled eyes out of Bertie's view. "I suppose you're wondering why we brought you all the way up here on top of the Black Flame Tower." For a moment her eyes glinted redly, and Bertie wondered if he had mistaken the vultures' intentions. "The Stonefather was perfectly right to call us. Endorgon knew it was too dangerous to let you continue by land. You saw what the Black Flame did to Andrasil. Poor Andrasil! We all loved her. The Chieftain will be so lonely." A tear ran down her beak. "Grace be with him!"

"To continue," she went on, "not all the Desolate Land is under the control of the L. of D., just most of it. He does not know this; that is, he does not think about it. We vultures are charter members of the Ancient Order of Carrion-Eaters, and we have survived what he did to the land because we *are* survivors. That is why the Creator put us here: to clean the land. Many scavengers--jackals, cockroaches, and others-- also go about their hidden business across the realm, and among us all is a network of communication extending far beyond what he imagines.

"At the borders of the Desolation the great reptile clans are stirring into life again, creatures not seen in this world since the Dawn Age. It was the blood of their ancestors that he spilled to make that appalling Saurian River, and the new generation has not forgotten. Look there!"

Charleynne Gates

One huge wing gently forced Bertie to lean over the side of the nest and peer down the sickening height of the tower to its base, where the Saurian River disappeared beneath it.

"The L. of D. uses the river to fuel his infernal engines," said the mother vulture, releasing Bertie from the pressure of her wing (much to his relief). "It is those engines which he uses to make war against the Earth, to devour the forests, fields, meadows and marshes. Before he came, we did not hunt and kill each other, for in the Dawn Age plants and herbs sufficed for food. We lived in harmony, one with another, the wolf with the lamb, the lion with the newborn calf. Oh, how beautiful it was then, how very good, before the Desolation appeared and swept across it!" For a while she remained lost in thought as Bertie cudgeled his mind.

Were the old tales true, then, that they told me when I was a child? Was there really a Golden Age--or a Green Age before the sons and daughters of Earth became bent and greed-driven, befouling their own nest? Bertie was too young to realize fully what that meant, nor yet wise enough to guess at the truth. But he thought more deeply now than he ever had before, and he did not like what he learned from his awakening mind.

The mother vulture cast a considering glance toward the eastern sky. "Father is returning," she said. "He will take you where you need to go. I must hurry and tell you what else you should know. What is your name, child?"

"Bertie Mossgrower of Purple Valley, ma'am," he said, rising and bowing as low as he was able within the tight confines of the nest.

"Mossgrower! What a lovely name! I remember moss, so soft and cool. Well! That was a long time ago. The friend we heard you speak of--oh, yes, we hear very well, and from very far away! Oliver Medley: He is here in the City of the Dead. We saw him as he passed through the rows of Stonemen. Endorgon warned him of the danger, but he was already infected with the poison of the Saurian River and did not understand. We saw the L. of D. take him into Castle Mormorion, but your friend never came out."

Bertie shivered, though the stinking nest was warmer than was entirely desirable, given the redolent remains of the vultures' dinners.

-- 452 --

Father Vulture landed with a thump on the nest and settled his wings. Fixing Bertie with a stern glare, he inquired of his wife whether appropriate instruction had been given.

"Certainly, dear!" she answered. "I was just coming to what we had planned for Bertie and his friend. You'd better continue."

The father vulture scowled. "You've got to get into the Black Flame Tower by yourself, young man," he said. "We vultures do not go under roofs. Climb on my back--careful of my primaries, boy!--and I'll take you around the tower. I'll show you where the exits are and how to get out when you've found your friend Medley. The L. of D. is used to us vultures flying around, so he won't pay us any attention. Keep down low between my wings, and whatever you do, don't let any of his guards see you! Let's go."

With a beat of outstretched wings, the vulture and Bertie vaulted into the gray sky. "What!" snapped the father vulture, noticing that something was still anchoring him to the nest. Turning, he discovered his mate had a firm grip on one ankle.

"Hold it, hot stuff! I want to give this to Bertie." She handed him a bedraggled wallet. "I found it beside the Saurian River where Oliver Medley came ashore. I was too late to give it back to him; he had already disappeared into the castle. He'll be happy to get it, I'm sure. Goodbye, love!"

Bertie tucked the wallet inside his shirt, waved his thanks to her, and they took off.

Father Vulture traced a spiral pattern around the spike of the tower. The wind whistled past his ears as Bertie hung on for dear life to the bird's scrawny neck. Despite his fear, he concentrated hard on what he had been told, knowing that his life--and Mr. Medley's--might depend on it.

Down they swooped, near enough to view the entrance to Castle Mormorion, a ponderous iron double door. No knocker or keyhole was visible, but as they flew by, Bertie saw that on the facade were carved letters in a language he did not understand:

Abandon all hope, you who enter!

Charleynne Gates

If Oliver Medley had entered the castle through those doors, he would have been able to read the letters, and he would have been greatly troubled by them. But Oliver Medley had entered by another way.

"No one knows what those scratches mean," said the vulture. "We think they're some kind of evil magic that keeps the land in bondage to the L. of D."

"Look there," commanded Father Vulture as they rounded the castle and ascended toward the tower again. "You see those embrasures?"

Bertie did. The top of the tower, beneath the nest, had small slits like windows cut in it at regular intervals all around.

"That's where the Black Flame lives, inside that chamber," continued Father Vulture. "It sleeps until the L. of D. sends it out to destroy. When it's awake, its light passes through the embrasures, one at a time, but it goes dark when it travels along the walls between them. The Flame cannot penetrate the walls of the Tower, y'see.

"Now listen, boy: The only way for you to get inside that tower is by getting through one of those embrasures. The other entrance, as you saw, is the door at ground level, and you'd never break in that way."

"C-can I d-do it now, while the Flame sleeps?" asked Bertie through chattering teeth (not only because of his natural fear, but also because it was icy cold riding on the vulture's back, with the wind shrieking past his ears).

"No. The Flame would detect your presence in its sleep and destroy you in one flash. You will have to enter when it's awake, while its attention is elsewhere."

"B-b-b-but," Bertie began, gripping the vulture's throat tighter.

"When the Black Flame stabs through the embrasure nearest to us, we will dodge it. We winged ones are accustomed to tactical aerobatics. When the Flame gets to the other side of the tower, you will slip through the embrasure and into the room. Then, before the Flame finds you, you will have to discover the hidden door to the lower levels of the tower."

Hidden? thought Bertie. "But how am I supposed to find it?"

"When the Flame passes across the solid wall between the embrasures, it will illuminate the outline of the door, but only for an instant. The doorway is very thin, but you can probably squeeze through."

-- 454 --

Probably?

"You will find a stairway, or possibly a ladder--I have no information on that point--which will take you to the interior of the tower, where, I have been told, there is a passageway leading down to the castle. Somewhere in there you might find your friend Medley."

All at once the Black Flame wakened, bursting through one of the embrasures on the side where they were circling. It sizzled like the scorching tongues of Rumor. Father Vulture dodged it adroitly with a flick of his wing, and they dived underneath it. Numb with horror, Bertie watched the Black Flame touch ground in front of the Stonemen and begin to slither among them, occasionally blasting one of them to pieces. The Stonemen nearest their destroyed kinsmen began a high keening, setting the very marrow of Bertie's bones quivering.

"Pay attention!" ordered Father Vulture. "Here comes your window of opportunity. You will have only a few seconds to find the hidden door once you get inside. If you aren't through the door before the Black Flame comes round again, nothing in this world can save you from instant death. Now go!"

He swooped down again, kiting next to the embrasure. Unable to help himself, Bertie froze onto the vulture's neck. Father Vulture rolled toward the tower. Bertie slid off, tumbled through the embrasure, and found himself inside the room. The vulture soared off into the sky, and Bertie was left alone.

The room was bare, with a metal wall icy to the touch. The doorway! He had to find it before...

Across the small room the Black Flame flashed out through an embrasure, coming closer and closer.

Bertie looked around desperately, trying to find the outline of a door in the wall before the Black Flame found him. There! On the opposite wall, the faint rectangular outline of a door appeared in the reflected light of the Flame.

Now the Flame flared through the embrasure next to him. Bertie glanced at it, abandoned all thought of escaping back outside, and leaped across the room. As he touched the wall, the door slid back, and Bertie slipped through at the same instant that the Flame passed over the place where he had been crouching only a heartbeat before. The door shut behind him, and Bertie was in total darkness, balanced precariously on what felt like the rung of a ladder. He put his hand out and met a smooth cold surface, with no crack or groove to tell where the doorway into the room had been.

There was nothing else to do but inch his way down to depths unknown or else stay here, clinging to the ladder, until he rotted away to a skeleton. Bertie took a deep breath, wondering if he might never have another chance to do so. *Va'in 'a moru', Sendara! Va'in 'a moru'!* came unbidden to his mind, and courage rose within him. Lifting one foot off its rung, he began the perilous descent.

"A word with you, young master," spoke a voice out of the dark as a hand clamped around his ankle.

Bertie cried out--he couldn't help it--and let go of the ladder. Down he plunged--about four feet--into the arms of an entity standing beneath him.

"We must hurry," said the entity, setting Bertie firmly on the ground. "We have little time. Mr. Medley is in grave danger, and there is much I have to tell you before we reach him. Quickly!"

Chapter Twenty-Six

In the Garden of Smoke and Mirrors

And I have asked to be
Where no storms come.
--Gerard Manley Hopkins

If you wish to avoid seeing a fool,
you must first break your mirror.
--Francois Rabelais

Shatter your glass, and look on the
face of your neighbor.
--Sargent Shriver

"So I gave him twenty-four hours."

Andis sat on the sitting stone, hugging her knees, her bow and quiver of arrows lying beside her. Seated on a fallen log opposite were Tipp and Tapp, who had been listening intently to her story.

Their meeting had been something of a surprise, at least to Andis. Hearing footsteps in the underbrush (deliberate on the part of the Dwarvians, who realized she was there and did not wish to startle her more than they could help), she had immediately swung herself up the nearest tree and hidden in its foliage. Fortunately, she decided to interrogate before she loosed the arrow aimed at Tipp's heart. After a few rounds of question-and-answer, during which both parties revealed enough about themselves to understand that they were on the same side, the initial tension dissipated.

The three of them had come to the conclusion that they were going to have to help Bertie get Oliver Medley out of the City of Dead Souls. The problem was, none of them knew for certain if Oliver was indeed in that city, or if Bertie had managed to get inside Castle

Charleynne Gates

Mormorion and find him. Or if either one of them was still alive. And, most importantly, given that the two of them might be alive, how they would find a way out.

The Dwarvians pondered the problem.

"I believe you're right, Miss Andis," said Tipp. "That's why we came back: not only to help Bertie find Friend Oliver, but also to make sure the two of them find their way out of Castle Mormorion, and then out of the Desolate Lands. The lad's very young for such a dangerous mission. The Lord of Desolation is no one to trifle with."

Andis, younger than Bertie and having about the same degree of acquaintance with evil, nodded solemnly. "I know. I tried to tell him he doesn't have the experience for this kind of thing, but he wouldn't hear of me going with him. Now he's past his time getting back, so I suppose I'll have to go looking for him."

The Dwarvians glanced at each other.

"That's definitely a possibility," Tipp agreed quickly--and tactfully. "But before we take action, ought we not to formulate a plan of some kind? Some way to coordinate our efforts. We're all here to carry out the same mission."

"Three heads being better than one," Tapp added.

Andis admitted the wisdom of this suggestion, much to the relief of the Dwarvians. Though their acquaintance with the young lady was brief, they recognized the adamant determination at the root of her character. It wouldn't have been easy to argue her into a different frame of mind, but an appeal to reason found its mark.

"It occurred to us on the way here," Tipp began, and launched into a detailed explanation of a rescue-and-escape plan possible only because of the Dwarvians' hereditary mind-maps. Tipp avoided mentioning the mind-maps themselves, for twice in the history of the Dwarf-kin an enemy had captured a Dwarvian and put him to torture in order to extort the secret of the mind-maps. Never had an enemy succeeded in doing so, for the captives had died rather than betray their ancestral heritage. Neither Tipp nor Tapp suspected Andis of being in the enemy's camp, but in these troublous times you never knew. *Better safe*, as the Old Ones said, *than sorry*.

"It isn't difficult getting into the castle," Tipp continued. "The Lord of Desolation made it so. If you can pin it down at all, that is. Castle Mormorion's like a mirage--the closer you get, the farther away it seems to be, except for those the L. of D. wants to come in. The problem is getting out. There is a main entrance--a front door, so to speak. But it only opens inward--to let, ah, 'visitors' in. Not outward."

"Then how do they get out?" asked Andis, a bit impatient with the explanation.

"Mostly they don't," said Tapp, which halted conversation for several anxious moments.

Tipp cleared his throat. "Our best option is the old sewer."

"Sewer? Ugh!" said Andis, shuddering.

"Most people don't think of it," said Tapp.

"We're not sure it's used for sewage any more," said Tipp.

"Might be dry," said Tapp. "Or not."

"Wait a minute," said Andis, and quirked a suspicious eyebrow. "How do you know there's an old sewer if you've never been there?"

The Dwarvians didn't answer right away, and there was another awkward silence while the wind sighed in the evergreen boughs overhead.

Tipp took a deep breath and began rather pompously, "Well, you see, we have--"

"A lot of old maps," Tapp interrupted, finishing Tipp's sentence with a warning look at his brother. "At Keeper's Inn, where we're from. Lots and lots of old maps. In the library." Which was true, if misleading.

Andis nodded, having heard about the inn when they were introducing themselves. She seemed satisfied with that answer, which was, perhaps, a pity, for Andis loved secrets--and what's more, always kept them. Only an old owl (a distant relative of Hera Vespasia) who lived in a tree next to the hunter's hut ever heard a whisper of anything Andis said, and everyone knows that owls never tell secrets.

The question of the sewer passageway next occupied the discussion, and was finally settled, though not without argument. It took all of Tipp's eloquence (which was considerable, for he was a popular after-dinner speaker) to persuade Andis that the interests of Bertie and Oliver would be better served if Tipp and Tapp went to Castle Mormorion and Andis stayed right where she was, where the edge of Threshold Forest met the Bordering Cliffs. At first Andis was not at all agreeable to the prospect of being "left out of the action," as she put it, but soon saw the logic of the Dwarvians' plan.

-- 459 --

At last it was agreed: Because of their knowledge of how to get into--and, they hoped, out of--the castle, Tipp and Tapp intended to venture down the Bordering Cliffs to the Realm of the Stonemen, which could be seen as a faint gray mist in the distance. There, depending on the conditions they found, one of them would stay as backup, and the other would continue to the castle. After an agreed amount of time, the backup would follow in case the first needed help. Andis was to be in charge of communications. Tipp and Tapp instructed her in the manner of summoning the Raven Express messengers, "which," Tipp added severely, "few human mortals know how to do."

"Except for Prince Pavarr," said Tapp, observing the girl's cheeks flush pink at the name and deducing a partiality in that direction.

"And Belvedine de Montfort," Tipp added with a shudder. "Friend Oliver's great-aunt, who brought him into the Labyrinth World. But no one knows exactly what she is."

"Or wants to," Tapp muttered.

Andis, meanwhile, was to summon a Raven messenger and send dispatches at regular intervals to the Abbey of Saint Amber, giving their position and any other pertinent information. Tipp, who was growing more and more concerned about their being so long delayed getting to the Abbey, went over the instructions twice and made Andis (who had an excellent memory) repeat them. As an afterthought, he said she might as well send a Raven messenger to Bertie's Uncle Nunks in Purple Valley.

"'Uncle Nunks'?" Andis queried. "Is that his real name? I mean, could the raven find him?"

"Admiral Sir John Horatio Nunkins," Tipp corrected himself. "The Quarterdeck Cottage, Mossy Dell Village, Purple Valley. He'd be glad to have news of his nephew."

"And be careful yourself, lass," said Tapp, who had developed a fondness for the girl. "There's no such thing as a safe place in the Labyrinth World just now."

Andis watched as long as she could as the two Dwarvians made their way down the broken cliffside to the floor of the Desolate Lands, following ways known only to their ancestors. Even in the terrible Desolation there are secret paths unknown to Ab'addon, for the original Dwarf tribe had carved them out in the First Age. The Whackitts went so rapidly along them that an observer might conclude that the Hidden

Saint Amber's Rose

Ways are magical, but in reality they are simply the product of the Dwarves' superlative engineering skills. At length Tipp and Tapp disappeared into the grayish-white spume that perpetually veiled the Realm of the Stonemen from mortal eyes.

"Is that the place? Those big standing boulders over there?" asked Tapp, making a spyglass of both hands and trying to bring the dim shapes into focus through the persistent fog.

"Arrows of Arkon!" exclaimed Tipp, staring where Tapp stared. "They look like they're moving! Swaying back and forth!"

"Swaying stones?" asked Tapp. "I thought they were supposed to be standing still."

"They used to be human," said Tipp. "That's what I've heard in the old legends."

"Human mortals? How'd they get to be stones?"

"Don't you remember your Labyrinth History?" Tipp reproved. "It was because of greed--"

"What's that!" Tapp interrupted. "That thing there, darting down the rows of Stonemen! Is it lightning? No, can't be lightning. It's all dark, like a black flame... But that's impossible!"

"It is a black flame!" Tipp gasped. "A killing flame! Look over there! It split that boulder in half! What's that sound?"

For now they heard the wail of agony sent up by the Stonemen grieving the violence wrought upon the victims. It grew louder, borne by the wind blowing across the barren plain to the Bordering Cliffs, and the Dwarvians understood its meaning. The blood in their veins grew cold as they advanced deeper into the Desolation.

The Dwarvians found the Stonemen mourning the loss of their Stonemother. *Aiee! Aiee! Andrasil!* they mourned, and their sorrow tore at the Dwarvians' hearts.

Seeing the shattered body of the Stonemother and realizing what must have happened, Tipp and Tapp removed their hats and bowed low before the great standing stone, Chieftain of the Realm. In return, Stonefather Endorgon bent, as much as he could, over the face of his wife, whose expression, even in death, was one of sweetness and peace.

"*Aven ni moran te inndor*, Stonefather," said the Dwarvians.

Moran helfidor vandira, replied the Stonefather formally, receiving their courtesy as gravely as it was offered.

Charleynne Gates

"Please accept our sincere condolences for your great loss," Tipp went on with the traditional ritual of acknowledging bereavement. "May grace be restored to you, ever living in victory."

So may it be. So may it be forever, murmured the Stonemen.

"Sir," said Tipp, "we ask pardon for our intrusion in this time of grief. I am Tipp Whackitt, and this is my brother, Tapp. We are Dwarvians on a mission of the utmost urgency on behalf of the *Sendara* of the Graelands. We believe that our young friend, Bertie Mossgrower, came by here a short while ago. Have you seen him, and can you tell us where we may find him?"

The Stonefather nodded. *Yes. He was searching for his friend, Oliver Medley. I called a vulture from the Black Flame Tower to take the boy into the City of Dead Souls.*

"We seek Oliver Medley also!" said Tapp. "Is he there?"

We do not know, replied Endorgon. *He came here to us, and we warned him to go back whence he came, but he went on into the city. If young Bertie found him, perhaps they got out again, but they did not return here. If they found another way out, they would have to pass through the* wyrga *army, and we do not think that would be possible.*

"*Wyrga* army?" queried Tipp, looking around. "Where?"

Put your hands on my shoulders, said Endorgon, *and concentrate. Then you may see as we do.*

Tipp and Tapp put their hands on the Stonefather's shoulders and concentrated. Soon the haze over the plain began to quiver, as if they were looking through the air above a campfire. When the motion settled, the Whackitts saw a vast army of *wyrga* surrounding them. Their vicious weapons were arrayed as far as the Dwarvians could see, for there was no horizon in this dreadful land, and the *wyrga*, at a distance, simply melted into the dull glare of the sky. It was obvious to the two Dwarvians that the army was ready to move out.

The Dwarvians immediately made the Sign of Protection. When they took their hands from Endorgon's shoulders, the *wyrga* army disappeared as if behind a heavy curtain.

"How did they let us pass through their ranks?" Tipp exclaimed.

They act only at the command of the Lord of Desolation, said Endorgon, *and it is likely that they did not see you because you traveled here by the ancient Hidden Ways. The* wyrga *have no imagination; thus, they cannot perceive the secret signs and pathways of the true*

Labyrinth. As for Oliver Medley, we think he was deliberately lured into the City of Dead Souls. I called the vulture to take Bertie Mossgrower where the lad wanted to go, for the Lord of Desolation pays no attention to the comings and goings of the vulture-kin. They are neither slaves nor allies of the Desolation, but they and the ash-vrom serve his purposes by keeping his borders clean.

"Now we have to decide what to do next," said Tipp, frowning deeply. "Go on or go back."

"We have to find Bertie and Friend Oliver!" Tapp exclaimed. "We can't abandon them to their fate!"

"I know, I know." Tipp rubbed his forehead, thinking hard. "We'll find them. But we also need to warn the Abbey about the *wyrga* army. I had no idea there were so many, or that they were ready to invade the Labyrinth World in full force. We've been hearing rumors of war for a long time, but this means the real thing is closer than we imagined."

"Then one of us--" Tapp began slowly.

"--will have to go on and look for Bertie and Friend Oliver, and the other will go back where young Andis waits," Tipp finished. "And send word to the Abbey."

The Dwarvians looked at each other.

"We've always worked together before," said Tapp. "I thought one of us was going to stay with the Stonemen until the other came out with our friends."

"Yes," Tipp nodded, "but time is running against us. We don't know how long it will take to find Bertie and Friend Oliver--or if we will be able to escape together. Someone needs to warn the Abbey as soon as possible."

"Then let me be the one to go into the castle, as we planned," said Tapp. "I have an obligation to Friend Oliver. You go to the Abbey and tell them about the *wyrga* army."

To separate would be the best way, Endorgon interjected. *There is less likelihood of you both being detected and captured. We Stonemen cannot move, but we can pass a word to the vultures about what we see, and they, in turn, may be able to help you. I dare not call them here too often lest the Black Flame notice, for it spies for the Lord of Desolation as well as destroys. It is very dangerous, but it has no mind and cannot reason, and so may be outwitted.*

The brothers glanced at each other, recalling that the mysterious (and possibly evil) Hermit of the Ruined Chapel had also separated the Questors. But now, they agreed without speaking, their options had narrowed to one, and this was it.

"It's a long way to the City of Dead Souls, and Castle Mormorion within it," Tipp observed aloud, "and the plain is flat and bare, with no way to move without being seen. It's not so far back to the Bordering Cliffs, and whoever goes to the castle--"

"I'm going to the castle," Tapp interrupted. "That's settled."

"--will be in greater peril," Tipp finished. "We'd better stay here for the night and sleep on it. We'll have to figure out a way to dodge that Black Flame thing, especially if it doesn't operate on a regular schedule."

The sky darkened, not the way a sunset on Earth gives way to blue twilight and indigo night, but as black ink is poured out all at once from a bottle, drowning everything beneath it. With night came cold so immediate and extreme that the Dwarvians hastily wrapped themselves in their cloaks.

"Stay close to me," said Endorgon, "and do not move about."

The brothers huddled close to the great boulder, camouflaged in the cloaks that made them look like rocks. Unable to risk making a fire, they nibbled at cold crusts of journey-bread and wondered what was happening to Bertie and Oliver... if they were still alive. Sleeping fitfully, waking often, they heard sharp cracks all through the night as frost got into minute crevices in the Stonemen and further injured those who had survived the brush of the Black Flame.

From time to time the Dwarvians peeked out from the shelter of their cloaks to where the unseen *wyrga* armies were camped beyond the Saurian River and saw the eerie glow of their unnatural fires spread across the Desolation.

"I'm older; I'll find Bertie and Friend Oliver," Tipp decided in a whisper.

"You will not," Tapp retorted immediately. "You've always made the decisions for us, but not this time. Friend Oliver saved me from that monster in Nether Lake, and I owe him big. I've told you I'm going, and I'm going."

"But Mother always told me to take care of you," said Tipp.

"That was when we were children. I don't need a caretaker any more; you've just gotten into the habit," said Tapp.

"Well..." said Tipp, thinking it over.

"We don't need to waste our breath talking about this," said Tapp. "What we need to do is figure out how I'm going to get into the city and the castle, find the two of them, and get out again."

"You'd need to be just about invisible to get there in one piece," said Tipp.

Invisible! Struck by that sudden thought, the Dwarvians stared at each other in the darkness.

"There is that spell Father taught us years ago," Tapp remembered.

"The Talisman of Misperception," Tipp nodded. "But--"

"It might be dangerous to use," said Tapp.

"It is dangerous. Very much so," Tipp pointed out. "It takes away a certain amount of life energy--might make your life shorter than normal--but renders enemies unable to perceive us, Father said. You wouldn't really be invisible, because the true Tarnhelm of Invisibility was lost Ages ago. The Talisman of Misperception just misdirects others' vision, leaving you vulnerable to being heard or scented. Not to mention footprints. They wouldn't be invisible."

"That's a risk I'm willing to take," Tapp insisted.

"I'm not willing for you to take it," Tipp argued.

"You don't have a choice," responded Tapp.

And for the rest of the night Tapp wouldn't reply, no matter what his brother said. Finally Tipp gave up and endeavored to get what little sleep he could manage.

There was no dawn; the coffin-like lid of the sky turned suddenly from black to glaring gray. The Dwarvians awoke and made their preparations with the minimum of fuss.

"I will stay here with the Stonemen until nightfall to see what happens," Tipp decided after conferring with Endorgon. "You may need help getting back out of the castle with two more people, and we don't know what kind of shape they'll be in."

Tapp smiled to himself at his brother's tacit agreement with the plan he had insisted on. Always before, Tipp had been the leader in their joint ventures. Now Tapp was out in front. He found it a new and interesting sensation, and not unwelcome. As a matter of fact, he savored the thought of the upcoming test of his courage and perspicacity.

"All right, then. We'd better activate the Talisman," said Tipp. "The sooner you start, the sooner you return."

The brothers grasped each other's right forearm in the old manner, closed their eyes, creased their brows, and together recited the words of the Talisman in Old Boreal.

Tipp opened his eyes. "Where are you?" he demanded, looking about.

"I'm right here," Tapp answered. "Right where I was before."

"I can't see you," said Tipp. "At least, I don't think I can. Stonefather, are you able to see him?"

As a vapor, replied Endorgon. *But remember, we Stonemen can perceive things that others cannot. Friend Tapp, if you travel in a zigzag pattern and rest at irregular intervals behind one of us, you may escape undetected. You must guard against the Black Flame at all times, for if it finds you, there is no defense against it.*

"And the *wyrga* army?" asked Tipp. "Can they see him?"

I think not, answered Endorgon, *but I cannot be certain.*

"Then I will wait here for you," said Tipp, his voice rough to hide his emotion. "If you're not back by nightfall tomorrow, I'll assume--I mean, I'll go on to the Abbey."

"Farewell, Brother," said Tapp, and turned toward the City of Dead Souls, where the high towers and battlements of Castle Mormorion could be seen shifting and changing like clouds and smoke. The brothers knew they might never see each other again, might perish in the attempt to rescue Bertie and Oliver and to reach the Abbey, but they saw no need for a prolonged leave-taking that would only weaken their resolve.

"Farewell, Brother," Tipp answered, hearing Tapp's footsteps recede into the distance.

Oliver Medley basked upon a Regency chaise longue overlooking a pool of mirror-like water in the pleasure-gardens of Ab'addon's palatial estate. The scent of roses wafted to him on a tender breeze. Above him spread a sky whose azure brilliance was softened by painterly white clouds. Their forms melded lazily into shapes that sometimes reminded him of things half-forgotten, and sometimes didn't.

Saint Amber's Rose

It didn't really matter that he didn't quite remember how he got here: Nothing mattered here; that was the beauty of the place.

On a mosaic path on the other side of the pool his host strolled, deep in conversation with his estate manager, a Mr. Finbiter, a skeletally thin, black-clad individual whose bronzed skin appeared metallic in hue. The manager's expression seemed never to change nor his eyelids to blink, as if his face had been welded onto his skull. A greater contrast with the classically regular form and features of his master could not have been imagined.

Ab'addon is certainly a fine figure of a man, Oliver mused. In another time, another place, he might have been envious. But there was no need for envy here. Why would there be, when one's slightest wish was instantly fulfilled? When one's desire for worthy intellectual companionship had been realized to a far greater degree than one had ever thought possible? And without mess, without the tiresome bother of those things so frequently occurring in personal relationships: difficult meetings and rancorous partings, disagreements, jealousies, quarrels, and tardiness. Oliver particularly disliked tardiness.

But here, where everything ran smoothly, exactly in order and precisely to time, it was as if he belonged to the most exclusive men's club in the world. Whatever world this might happen to be. *Which doesn't matter anyway.* What mattered was that he was in it at last, a member with full privileges for life... and beyond.

And in this place his debilitating shyness in social situations, a defect which had plagued him from his earliest years, had utterly vanished like... like wherever he was going before he had been detoured into this wonderfully agreeable country. Really, he had just about ceased to care whether he ever got back. Life here was focused upon one thing and one thing only: Oliver Medley's perfect, unchanging contentment.

The tiniest sensation of thirst touched the back of his throat. Instantly an apricot-colored liquid in a goblet of the finest cut crystal was in his hand. From previous experience he knew that the contents would stimulate without intoxicating and propel his tongue to soaring flights of wit.

From the other side of the azure pool Ab'addon glanced Oliver's way, smiled with that charmingly wry quirk he had, and raised his own glass in a silent toast. Oliver returned the gesture and sipped.

Rather amusingly, when he swallowed, he seemed to hear Ab'addon say to two ladies in rustling skirts who accompanied him, "Get his key," and then nothing more until he quaffed the wine again. "Find out what lock it fits," the master added, but Oliver had no idea what they were talking about. Castle Mormorion didn't have keys and locks! Why, there was no place in the entire castle--indeed, in the whole of the realm--where he couldn't go if he wanted

"This is Liberty Hall," the lord of the realm had told him. "You must do exactly as you please. Go anywhere you like. Whatever you want, tell Gloom. Anything at all--yours for the asking."

To prove a point, Oliver set his empty glass on the air, where it was instantly whisked away by an invisible hand.

"I believe," he remarked to no one in particular, "I'll have a stroll about the gardens before I change for dinner."

His host's magnificent gardens were endless, or so it seemed, and Oliver had lost track of how many times he had explored them. Every turn in the path revealed some new delight, a flower he had never seen before in colors he barely comprehended.

At intervals trees overspread their shade and dangled ripe fruit before his eyes. That peach tree in front of him: It was laden with golden spheres whose rosy blushes seduced his senses. How good one would taste! That one dangling on a branch right in front of his nose, so ripe and full of juice that it was about to fall from the tree.

His mouth watered. He reached for the lovely globe...

A massive black shape swooped down and landed in front of him, startling him so that he stepped back, stumbled, and sat down abruptly on soft grass.

The shape, an immense vulture, glared at him. It didn't look friendly.

Cautiously, Oliver put a hand to the ground to lever himself up. The vulture unfolded its great wings and stretched its bald neck toward him.

Oliver stopped.

Behind the bird, the luscious peach Oliver had been about to grasp fell to the ground and splattered orange pulp over the manicured lawn.

The vulture, with a disdainful glance out of its red-rimmed eyes, flew off, quickly becoming a winged vee in the sky.

Saint Amber's Rose

Oliver picked himself up, took a quick, embarrassed look around, saw nobody, and assured himself that his dignity remained intact. Odd thing to happen! A vulture--a carrion-eater, of all things!-- landing in the middle of Ab'addon's meticulously-tended gardens. What did it think it was going to find--a dead body? Such an unattractive thing as Death would never be found here, of all places!

It did make one wonder, though, whether more unexpected events might occur. Not that he expected anything unexpected to occur, so to speak, it was just that he had supposed that life in his host's domain was too well-ordered to allow for the unexpected.

Absently he returned to the walkway and went toward his apartment, not noticing that behind him, where the peach lay in ruins, something black and wormlike emerged from its dark-red pit and crawled back toward the tree.

He passed a little walled circle-garden situated just behind his own chambers. Walking about the grounds in the company of the master shortly after his arrival, Oliver asked what grew in it, but Ab'addon brushed away the question.

"Nothing in particular. Just an experimental planting," the Lord of Desolation replied. "It didn't take root. That happens occasionally-- even here," he said, smiling. "But we'll try it again sometime."

Out of pure curiosity, perhaps stimulated by the encounter with the vulture, Oliver decided to venture through an entry-way of crumbling yellow brick into the enclosed garden plot.

Lord Ab'addon had been accurate: There was virtually nothing here. The ground was bare, with only scattered stems of dry grasses poking through the hard, cracked soil. A stunted apple tree scarcely bigger than a sapling grew in a corner where it couldn't possibly get any sunlight. Two or three withered pippins beneath it testified that the tree had once borne fruit, but not for many a season.

In the center of the circle was a neglected shrub that might have been a rather nice rosebush if someone had taken proper care of it. Ab'addon's gardeners must have forgotten about this quaint little retreat. The lord of the realm surely didn't realize what a deplorable condition the enclosed garden had fallen into, with so much of his time occupied with affairs of state.

Oliver walked around the rosebush, peering closely at it and considering whether he might be able to do something to nurse it back to health. That would be a modest return for his new friend's munificent hospitality. But to his surprise, when he got around to the back he found that the bush hadn't given up entirely, for it had managed to produce a single flower, a miniature rosebud tinted in the colors of a summer morning. Impulsively he reached out and plucked it from its branch. Inhaling its delicate scent, he strolled back to his rooms.

The valet, Gloom, was in his bedchamber, arranging the designated costume for dinner. Evening dress in Castle Mormorion changed daily, as the Lord of Desolation was fond of plays and masques to while away the long evenings. Delighted to oblige, for he had long cherished fantasies of treading the boards, Oliver had at once entered into the spirit of the thing.

Each night was different, with dinner corresponding to the setting. One evening Ab'addon had portrayed Henry VIII, with Oliver as Sir Thomas More. The *duchesse* d'Ophidian and the *marquise* deCair had charmingly represented two of Henry's queens, Ann Boleyn and Katherine Howard. Marveling at the accuracy of detail, Oliver simply couldn't figure out how the beheadings were done. With mirrors, he supposed, because the next evening one lady was an exquisite Titania and the other, Fairy Mustardseed. Ab'addon, of course, was Oberon.

Oliver had been cast as Bottom the Weaver. That had been delightfully amusing, except that his ass's ears had tended to itch at awkward moments during the play, and the temptation to scratch had proven, regrettably, impossible to resist.

Then there was the night--the many nights--that they had recreated *Les Miserables*--not just the play but the entire book, somewhat too realistically for his liking. He had been served nothing but hard, stale bread and moldy cheese, with sour wine to wash it down. Oliver grew so tired of the food, without daring to complain, that he was compelled to imagine what it must be like to have nothing else to eat in real life, as did many of the people in the book. *But this isn't real life, is it. This is...* He couldn't put a finger on what it actually was.

Theatre. Illusion. That was the nature of illusion, was it not? That you didn't know what was happening behind the scenes.

How long had these entertainments been going on? Days, months... years? Life in Castle Mormorion often seemed like a dream that repeated itself, with minute variations, over and over. Like everything else in his host's realm, time evidently didn't matter here, not in the way he vaguely recalled.

"Does the gentleman wish assistance in donning his costume for the evening?" inquired Gloom. As usual, the Wraith-valet had materialized at the exact moment his services were required.

"Yes, please," Oliver replied, and Gloom's indefinite hands began skillfully draping the garments, coincidentally blocking Oliver's reflection in the cheval glass.

"I beg pardon, sir," the Wraith began after a brief interval. A hint of tension appeared in his voice that Oliver hadn't noticed before. "If I might speak to you about a personal matter? Thank you, sir. Do you have any idea how long you have been with his lordship, Mr. Medley?"

"Not... exactly," Oliver replied after a moment of reflection. "Strange, I was just thinking of that myself."

Gloom's normal transparency became almost opaque with emotion.

"Mr. Medley, you have been here far longer than I believe you intended! Let me explain: I myself am not a slave to his lordship, as are the others here, but an indentured servant. I foolishly bound myself to him for the customary term of seven years. He deceived me, as I should have anticipated. I have served in this place many times seven years, but I cannot leave because time does not flow here in the same way as in the outer world, and my articles of indenture are still in force. I am trapped in Castle Mormorion, but you can leave, Mr. Medley! You can escape! I can show you how!"

"But why should I want to escape?" Oliver inquired reasonably. "I like it here." *Gloom seems quite beside himself tonight. Poor man probably needs a vacation.*

"Sir, you must listen! Look over there."

The Wraith turned Oliver's shoulders toward the nightstand beside the canopied bed. On it was a slender vase of blown glass so delicate that a harsh breath might shatter it. Standing in the vase was the rose Oliver had plucked from the bush in the little walled garden.

"Do you recognize that rose?" Gloom demanded.

"Why, yes," Oliver replied. "I brought it in myself."

Charleynne Gates

"That rosebush is his lordship's most prized possession," Gloom whispered urgently. "He took it from Saint Amber's Abbey. He calls it... *Flavia.*"

Flavia. That name... It belonged to someone he had known long ago. Someone important to him--then. But who was it?

An image began to take form in his mind's eye, shimmering like light on water, but he couldn't quite get it in focus. *Maybe if I just sit quietly and think for a while...* Taking a deep breath to clear the cobwebs from his mind, he set himself to the task.

It took a considerable time for the image to become focused, overlaid as it was with veil upon veil of oblivion, but at last it emerged into full clarity. But even as recovered memory came sweeping back, so, once again, did Shame, that sharp-toothed hag, riding high upon its crest. Oliver Medley bowed his head and squeezed his eyelids closed, unable to face the radiant silver light.

Here in Ab'addon's pleasure palace he had slipped into complete self-absorption. Here, because he had found placid contentment, he had forgotten where his true loyalty lay: to the Lady to whom he had sworn lifelong fealty.

He saw the truth clearly now, and named the truth he saw: *Love.* The one thing that wasn't here, that could never live in the City of Dead Souls.

For if I have not love, I am nothing.

"Exactly, sir!" exclaimed the Wraith, discerning his thought. "That is the truth that will make you free!"

The deep, rolling tone of a gong sounded through the halls of Castle Mormorion.

"Sir, you are summoned to dinner!" said Gloom. "If you would escape, it must be now! Come!"

Filled with renewed determination, Oliver arose and followed. Drawing aside a tapestry of unicorns in a field of golden flowers, the Wraith showed him the outline of a small, narrow door.

"This door will take you to the Hall of Mirrors. You have seen it when the mirrors were awake, but they are dormant now, and you will be safe until they awaken again. You must count the mirrors quickly, beginning with the first one on your left. The exit is behind the seven hundred and seventy-seventh mirror. When you find it, shatter the mirror!"

Saint Amber's Rose

"Do not listen to any voices you may hear in the Hall: They are merely a reflection of your own thoughts. And, sir, if you happen to encounter any of my brothers in the outer world--their names are Grimtread, Dour, and Gall--please tell them that Gloom is alive but confined in Castle Mormorion. *Va'in 'a moru'*, sir! And here—take the rose with you!"

The Wraith gave him a push, impelling Oliver through the door (which disappeared from view as soon as it closed behind him) and into the shadowed corridor, where he stood stock-still, too astonished to be afraid.

He didn't remember ever seeing this place before.

There were only mirrors here--multiple mirrors large and small, all fly-specked and dull but swirling inside with smoky images.

He couldn't see his reflection in any of them. Quickly he secreted the rose underneath his tunic and tightened the laces again.

"Oliver... Oliver!" Voices called his name--voices inside the mirrors, beyond the wavering smoke. Tantalizing, seductive voices.

They seemed to want him. He turned toward the nearest mirror, where columns of brown smoke writhed and shifted, assuming first one shape, then another, too rapidly for him to discern what they were.

"Who... who is it?" he called, not seeing anyone.

"Oliver! Oliver! Come to us!"

"Where are you?" he replied, coming closer to the mirror until he was touching the spot where his own reflection ought to be, but wasn't. In its place were drifts of smoke.

"In here, Oliver. Come join us, Oliver." Two voices, women's lovely, laughing voices. "Come with us, Oliver."

"Come dance with us, Oliver!"

"Come play with us, Oliver!"

"Come see what you've been missing, Oliver!"

Teasing laughter, a duet of silver flutes in the distance.

"It's beautiful inside the mirror, Oliver. Come and let us show you!"

Was there a warning of some kind about voices? He didn't remember.

"I--I don't know how to come to you. I can't see you."

"Look behind the smoke, Oliver! Look hard! Look hard!"

-- 473 --

He looked--hard. Stared into the smoke. Through the smoke.
Yes--I see them now! Two dim figures, dark in the mirror.
"How do I--?"
"Step into the mirror, Oliver! Come into the Garden of Smoke
and Mirrors. Come in to us!"
He stepped into the mirror. Blinded by a swirling brown froth,
he stretched out a hand in front of him and felt it grasped by another,
soft, feminine, with tapering fingers. Lips like open flowers pressed a
kiss on his cheek.
"Welcome, dear Oliver!" the silver-flute voices said in unison.
"Open your eyes, Oliver!"
He hadn't realized they were closed, but obediently, he opened
them--and found himself in a garden more incredible than he had ever
thought possible. Everything in it--trees, flowers, birds, butterflies--was
made entirely of precious gems!   The prospect was even more
breathtaking than the Lord of Desolation's gardens.
He turned, and there were the ladies who had called him, and
each was more beautiful than the other. Clad in diaphanous gowns,
crowned with pearl-encrusted wreaths, they smiled upon him, and he
was lost.
"*Madame la duchesse d'*Ophidian," he said, recovering, and
bowed and kissed the hand entwined with his. "*Madame la marquise*
deCair," bowing and kissing the hand of the other.
Delighted laughter.
"*Mais voici*, Louise, we have here *un homme très charmant*!"
exclaimed the marquise.
"*Mais oui*, Blanchette. And, I'll wager, an opponent *très
formidable*," returned the *duchesse*.
"Opponent?" Oliver murmured, dazzled by the aspect of so
much beauty so close to him.
"You will play our game with us, won't you, *cher* Oliver?"
whispered the deCair into one ear. The delicious fragrance of her breath
stole under his nostrils and made him lightheaded. Without quite
realizing how it began, he found himself moving in the quaint steps of a
minuet with the two aristocrats to the accompaniment of a solo violin.
"Certainly, if you wish it," he replied rather groggily. "But I
don't know how to play the game."

"*Eh bien, mon enfant*," laughed the Ophidian, "do not worry about that."

"We are going to teach you," said the deCair, "about everything."

"First we need a key to begin the game," said the *duchesse*. "Blanchette, did you bring the key?" The tiniest of frown lines appeared in her flawless forehead.

The *marquise* gave an enchanting little gasp. Her pretty cheeks flushed. "O la, la!" she exclaimed. "I have forgotten it! *Que je suis stupide!*" A miniature tear formed in the corner of her eye, and her carmine lip trembled.

"*Non, non!*" Unable to bear the sight of her distress, Oliver hastened to clasp both her hands to his heart. "Absolutely not, my dear *marquise*! You must not say such things! Wait! I think--I think I might have a key."

He patted the usual places about his person where one might secrete one's valuables. Nothing felt familiar, and for some reason, he couldn't locate where his pockets ought to be.

"Now where did I put it?" he asked himself as the ladies promenaded around him in circles, crossing and re-crossing until they became a blur. "I'm sure it's here somewhere."

Louise and Blanchette danced round and round him, faster and faster, as the unseen violinist spun the melody higher and higher. Oliver had to keep turning and turning to follow them, and quickly grew dizzy.

Then he felt hands patting him all over, swift, relentless hands searching for something.

"Oh, I say--"

But the dance went on and on, the music played higher and faster--and the hands that patted were no longer soft and lissome. They pinched and slapped and tore at his garments.

"Don't--don't do that! Please stop! Get away!"

But abruptly the ladies changed into something monstrous-- things of nightmare, things of death, as their names foretold. The Ophidian became an enormous, gray-coiled snake with open mouth and gleaming fangs lunging toward him, while the deCair turned into a decaying corpse. Her skeletal fingers, dripping with strips of rotted flesh, reached out for him.

"Give us the key!" they hissed. "Give us the key!"

"No!" Oliver screamed, flailing his arms uselessly. "Get away from me! Get away! I renounce you! I renounce your master! Help! HELP!"

All of a sudden a light appeared through the obscurity, a bright light that put everything in the dreadful garden in deep shadow. Someone stood inside the light, a figure Oliver couldn't see very well but that seemed familiar. He blinked and stared at it, and the light became the only thing he saw. The maddening music faded out of mind, and a great quietness was all he heard.

As if it were the most natural thing in the world to do, Oliver straightened himself and walked toward the light. Behind him, unseen, the nightmare ladies dissolved into dust.

He found himself where he had been before, standing in the Hall of Mirrors.

In a dusty corner of the Hall a frightened little figure scrunched itself into a ball and panted softly. He didn't want to wake up the echoes again, no, he didn't! They were terrifying! They had nearly driven him out of his mind. He had run and run, where he did not know, anywhere to get away from them, but they kept coming after him. Only by staying quieter than a mouse--a dead mouse, at that--could he make the echoes be still. The things they said to him! He wasn't really sure what they were because he couldn't quite make them out, but they sounded menacing, and he was afraid. He didn't really know why he was afraid, and that made him more afraid than if he had known why he was afraid.

A dagger of pain stabbed him in the middle of his shoulder blades. He moved, not more than an inch, to ease the discomfort, but somewhere a little bell rang out with an icy tinkle. He froze, waiting for the echoes to chase him again, but there was nothing. He listened for a long time, eyes and ears wide open, but nothing else broke the silence.

Cautiously he began to uncurl himself, one finger and one toe at a time, to ease out of his cramped position. He managed to push himself up without arousing any dangerous bell-sounds, and started once more to find an exit out of this place of endless echoes. *If there is an exit...*

He tried to move without setting them off, but as carefully as he crept along, the terrible little bells jingled like the laughter of devils. When they did, he halted, quivering, lest the echoes hunt him down like a fox before the hounds.

But this time nothing happened.

Slowly he tiptoed down one side of the corridor again, searching for the place where he had lost count of the mirrors. He squinted into every glass, wondering if this one was where he had started--or had it been that one?

But mirror after mirror reflected only smudges--until he passed, for the third time, a dusty, cracked mirror in a half-hidden alcove. A three-legged stool sat in front, as if someone had once used it as a vanity mirror. A hunch stopped him; he went closer to examine the glass, which was speckled with streaks of blackened silvering.

Is the exit here, and I missed it before?

Hesitantly he took the last step up into the alcove and put his face close to the murky surface. Deep inside the mirror was a shrunken little creature with ghost-white skin and big, staring eyes. Its arms flopped ludicrously inside checkered sleeves, and on its head was a curiously-shaped cap tapering to four points, each hung with a golden bell.

Bells and motley. The creature was a jester! A fool.

Oliver despised it on sight. Then he realized it was his own reflection.

"No!" he shouted. "No!"

The bells jangled crazily, multiplying their echoes down the corridor. Mocking him!

Driven beyond reason, he made a wild grab for the stool and hurled it against the glass. The mirror cracked; the lines radiated to the edges like a giant cobweb. Shards fell onto the floor.

"Mr. Medley?" came from the other side.

Bertie Mossgrower stepped through the empty doorframe and caught Oliver Medley in his arms as Oliver fell over in a dead faint.

Charleynne Gates

Part IV

The Way of the Rose

Surely thine hour has come,
Thy great wind blows,
Far-off, most secret,
And inviolate Rose.
        --William Butler Yeats,
                The Secret Rose

Chapter Twenty-Seven

Escape and Escapade

> I will give them a different heart and put a new spirit
> into them; I will take the heart of stone out of their
> bodies and give them a heart of flesh.
> --The Book of the Prophet Ezekiel

"Mr. Medley! Mr. Medley! Wake up! We've got to get out of here!" Bertie patted Oliver's pale cheeks rapidly.

Oliver's eyelids fluttered open. He stared up at Bertie with half-glazed eyes. "Wha--?"

"It's Bertie, Mr. Medley! Bertie Mossgrower! Don't you remember me?"

"Bertie... Moss... grower. I think I... remem..."

"That's good. Come on! We have to leave now!" said Bertie. Pulling and heaving, he managed to raise Oliver to his feet. "Let's go!" He grabbed Oliver by one checkered sleeve and yanked, forcing him to follow Bertie through the narrow doorway Oliver thought was a mirror.

The door led to a spiral stairwell made of black metal. The stairwell was dark as a tomb--Oliver couldn't see more than a foot ahead--but they immediately plunged down in descending circles, following the tight spiral. Bertie, active from his childhood, ran swiftly, and adrenaline shot through Oliver as he strove to keep up. He didn't have any choice: Bertie kept a firm hold of his sleeve.

Long past the time when Oliver thought he couldn't run another step, they landed on a level surface, and Bertie stopped. Here was a fraction more light than in the tenebrous stairwell, enough to let them see that they were standing on a stone slab with a viscid wash of liquid slapping quietly against its edges. Other stairwells branched off the slab, leading down under the surface of the liquid. A low, arched ceiling rose above them, and all around them was a broad stream. It might have been polluted river-water except for the texture, which was thick and oily, and the stench rising from it, which nearly choked them. (It was especially hard on Oliver, who was panting heavily from exertion.)

Bertie let go of Oliver's sleeve, and both of them covered their mouths and noses with folds of their garments. They had nothing with which to cover their eyes and still be able to see, and tears ran down their cheeks from the stinging fumes.

"Mr. Medley!" Bertie said hoarsely next to Oliver's ear. "I think we're in a sewer or something. The ghost told me we can escape to the outside from here."

"How?" Oliver coughed. "What ghost?"

"He said his name is Gloom," Bertie rasped. "He showed me how to get here, but he didn't say exactly how we're supposed to get outside. I guess we'll have to swim for it. You can swim, can't you?"

"Yes, but not in that! It doesn't look like water," Oliver replied, catching his breath.

"It's not real water. It's from the Saurian River, and the Stonemen told me it's poisonous. The Stonefather made me scrub it off my feet right away. He said the stuff'd kill me if I left it on." Bertie looked down anxiously at his feet, where the sluggish fluid dampened the soles of his shoes.

Gloom... Stonemen... Stonefather... Oliver thought, and somewhere deep in his mind a memory-bell tinkled.

"I wish we had a torch or something," said Bertie. "It's too dark to see very far."

"I don't think lighting a fire would be wise," Oliver suggested without knowing why.

"We need some kind of a light to show us which way to go," argued Bertie, squinting at several tunnels branching off in different directions. All seemed identical, and there was no indication which of them led to the outside, if any did. The minute amount of dull, grayish light that filtered through the dusk was of little use.

They stood on the wet stone slab, irresolute, realizing they would have to do something soon, but unable to figure out what that ought to be.

Saint Amber's Rose

All at once they became aware of a deep, muffled sound, a vibration coming from far beneath the black stream--a rhythmic pulse of crushing and grinding, as if a horde of unimaginable beings were gnawing iron bars. Startled, they listened intently, holding their breath.

"Mr. Medley!" Bertie gasped. "This stuff in the sewer--it isn't sewage at all! It--it's fuel! The Lord of Des--" he broke off in a fit of coughing. "The ghost man said he diverts the Saurian River down here and uses it to run his engines of destruction! They're right below where we're standing. There's *wyrga* operating them. They might come up here and find us. We've got to get out of here NOW!"

"What's that!" whispered Oliver, staring at something over Bertie's shoulder and gripping the boy's arm tightly.

Bertie whipped around. There, as far as they could see down one end of a tunnel, was the malformed imprint of a moving shadow against the wall. Even in the gray half-light they saw that it grew until the misshapen smear that was its head reached to the ceiling. With no other way to escape, Oliver and Bertie backed toward the spiral stair, waiting for the thing to close the distance as it inched toward them. Nearer it came... nearer...

"Friend Oliver?" whispered the shadow. "Bertie? It's Tapp!"

"Tapp?" croaked Oliver.

"M-Mr. Tapp?" stammered Bertie. "Where are you?"

"Oh, I forgot," said Tapp. "You can't see me. I'm standing right next to you."

"You-you're the shadow, Mr. Tapp?" Bertie asked, eyes wide, staring at hard at the blank space where the voice came from.

"Oh. Right," said Tapp. "I forgot about that, too. I cast a shadow even though I'm more or less invisible."

"More or less--what?" asked Oliver, more at a loss than ever.

"Just take my word for it," answered Tapp. "Now follow me, and we'll get out of this place."

"How?" Bertie questioned. "We can't see you."

"Um... Here, take a handful of my cloak," (Oliver felt cloth being pushed into his hand) and Bertie can grab hold of your sleeve. Don't let go, whatever you do. We'll follow this ledge next to the wall here. It's under about an inch of sludge, so don't slip! And don't worry: I'll get us out. All Dwarvians are born with mind-maps. They've never failed us yet. *'a-TORR!'* ("Let's go!" in Dwarvian).

Charleynne Gates

Bertie and Oliver did as they were told, edging cautiously after Tapp. *Kephan* after *kephan* they inched their way through the many-branched tunnels, guided by Tapp's unerring sense of which way was out. Fumes from the turgid underground fuel-stream burned their eyes and nostrils without letup, while the fitful, dirty-brown light concealed more than it revealed. The iron beat of the machines far below them kept up a rhythmic crush, grind... crush, grind until Oliver felt as if the relentless pounding was inside his own head.

They had been creeping along for quite a while before Oliver noticed that the air (what there was of it) had brightened imperceptibly, and concluded that they must have gone a considerable way from where they started. Tapp finally halted. After consulting his mind-map, he pointed toward the distance, where a tiny patch of brighter light cut through the murk.

"Look!" he whispered. "There's light out there! See?"

Oliver gazed at the light, and a mixture of memory and relief flooded through him.

He was really going to get out at last! Out of Ab'addon's pleasure palace! Out of that seductive garden of lies and delusions! *And, in the mercy of grace, out of perfect, unchanging contentment!*

Gratitude rose through him like water through a siphon. "Thank you," he murmured, and a tear inched down his cheek that wasn't from the fumes.

"What's happening, Mr. Medley?" whispered Bertie, who couldn't see the light as clearly.

"We're almost out!" Oliver squeaked.

Tapp shushed him, then sniffed the air delicately several times.

"Listen!" he ordered quietly. "Something's coming after us. We'll have to run for it. When I say 'Run!' you run! And when I say 'Jump!' you jump! Got it?"

"But where--" Oliver began, but didn't finish the thought because Tapp hissed "Run!" and took off. Oliver followed, maintaining a fast grip on Tapp's cloak.

Running sideways along a slick, narrow ledge isn't easy, but they managed. Oliver and Bertie were far too terrified of the consequences to allow themselves to make a mistake, but just as Oliver was certain that his next step would be his last, the ledge ended.

"Jump!" Tapp called, and leaped off. Unable to prevent themselves, the other two jumped after him, landing in the middle of the dark river. The toxic effluent closed over their heads.

They came up again quickly, only to find that an iron grating stretching from one wall to the other barred their way.

"Duck under!" commanded Tapp, and did so himself, pulling Oliver with him. Oliver grabbed Bertie and pulled, but Bertie didn't come up after them.

Tapp spat out black sludge. "Where's the lad?"

"I don't--Bertie!" Oliver shouted. Without thought of danger, he ducked back under the stream and felt around for the boy. Bertie was still there, but a tooth of the grating had snagged his shirt, and he couldn't get away. Unable to see anything in the thick liquid, Oliver tried to free him by touch, but the pointed tooth had pierced completely through the fabric and wouldn't let go. Oliver finally gave a mighty jerk on the cloth, and the shirt ripped apart. Bertie wriggled out of it, and the two of them surfaced beside Tapp.

"Th-thanks, Mr. Medley!" Bertie coughed.

"Come on!" Tapp called back. "We've got to swim for it!"

Bertie and Oliver could barely see where they were going, but they paddled after Tapp, following the noise of his splashing toward an unseen destination.

They would have made it, too, Tapp assured them later, except for a freak current that dashed down the middle of the underground river and swept them, helpless, out to the open sea. They hardly had a chance to realize what was happening before the relentless waves propelled them far from shore and into deep water, where they bobbed up and down like bell buoys among the foaming billows. Oliver, a respectable swimmer, had everything he could do just to tread water and keep afloat. He didn't have a hand to spare to help the others—if they were around to need help. Once or twice he caught a glimpse of Bertie in the distance, flailing around much as he was himself.

"Help!" cried Oliver as loudly as he could over the roar of the brine-laden waves. "Somebody HELP!"

"Don't make so much noise!" Tapp demanded, next to him and now visible (salt water neutralizes the Talisman of Misperception) and also treading water. "Do you want someone to hear us?"

"Pfft!" Oliver spat out a mouthful of cold sea-water as an errant wave splashed his face. "I thought that was the idea! Where's Bertie?"

"Don't worry. They've got the lad," Tapp said, and began swimming away from Oliver.

They? Not wanting to be left behind, Oliver followed, hoping Tapp knew where he was navigating, considering how they were being tossed about in the restless waters.

But in half a dozen strokes they did indeed bump into a floating structure of some sort. The night was moonless, showing few stars, so all that Oliver could make out was an elongated dark shape.

Tapp climbed up something on the structure and heaved himself out of sight. Oliver panicked, unable to see where Tapp had disappeared.

"The ladder! Can you see it now? Climb on up, sir! We'll help you," said two or three voices above him. He groped for the ladder and after two or three attempts, felt his way up with assistance from unseen helping hands as the structure he was climbing heaved and rolled, upsetting his equilibrium to the point of nausea. Gasping for air, he finally tumbled headlong onto some wooden boards and discovered that he was in a boat.

"Mr. Medley!" piped a familiar voice. "It's Captain Bones and the skulls! They were looking for us!"

Bones? Skulls? wondered Oliver as he took Bertie's hand and staggered to his feet.

Bertie presented Oliver, disheveled as he was, to Captain Ezekiel Bones, commander of the rescue vessel. To Oliver's dazed eyes, Captain Bones seemed to be an abnormally cadaverous individual, having a head with so little flesh as to resemble a skull--or at least it appeared that way in the faint starlight. His entire body matched his head, for it was as skeletal as a frame could be.

"Mr. Medley," said the captain, lifting his bicorne. "Welcome aboard the *Marrowbone*!"

Oliver murmured something and tried to orient himself as much as he could in the darkness. It looked as if--and he wasn't too sure about this--the whole crew were as lean in build as the captain, and all their heads were skulls. *That can't be right!* But it was. A focused ray of light from a nearby star momentarily illuminated the single mast and the sailors distributed at various points along the sides.

-- 484 --

They were skulls, with skeleton bodies. A couple of them had black patches over one eye; some had a gold ring or two fastened in their ear-holes. The skull-heads could be clearly seen, although the skeleton-bodies were less distinct. Salty shouts and rough-edged commands that Oliver couldn't quite distinguish filtered down from the rigging.

"This is excellent!" Bertie bubbled happily at Oliver's side. "The captain told me they decided not to go back to their clean, quiet graves under the deep green sea after all. They thought there might be some action, and they didn't want to miss the fun! They knew the Saurian River runs under Castle Mormorion, so they figured if we got out, we'd be swept out to the open sea, so they waited here for us!"

"Now here's what I have in mind, Mr. Medley, Mr. Whackitt," said Captain Bones, returning from conferring with the sailing-master and getting down to business. "Your destination is the Abbey of Saint Amber. I propose we set sail to another inlet, one farther from the Saurian River and the Desolate Lands. Then we sail up the Sunder to the Abbey. The *wyrga* won't be expecting you, and certainly not by the river. Wind and current'll be against us, and we'll have to beat up, but my crew can get us there in three days."

Oliver didn't doubt it, and agreed.

"Have you been anywhere near the Plain of the Stonemen?" asked Tapp, thinking of his brother waiting for him. "The Sunder flows near there, I think."

"No," answered the captain. "It looks that way on maps, but there's actually quite a bit of impassable territory between the Sunder and the Plain. It's the Saurian River runs into the Plain of the Stonemen."

Tapp said nothing more, but two vertical creases appeared in his forehead as he worried about Tipp, who he knew would be worrying about what might have happened to his little brother.

Will we meet at the Abbey--or ever again?

Tipp wandered back and forth among the Stonemen, absorbing what they told him about their dolorous situation but also keeping a weather eye out for danger. Twice he witnessed the death-dealing Black Flame trace its meandering path among the hapless boulders. Each time it struck at random, once mutilating its victim but leaving it alive. The second time it split a young Stoneman in half before his parents' eyes. Tipp took shelter in the nick of time behind an adjacent Stone, clenching his fists in frustration because he couldn't do anything to help them. *I will*, he promised himself. *I will find a way to destroy this evil thing.*

"Stonefather," he said, addressing Endorgon partly as a way to stop worrying about Tapp and partly to give the Stoneman some temporary distraction from his sorrow. "Stonefather, I have heard the old stories--the legends about how your people became stone. Are they true?"

Endorgon sighed deeply. *"They are, Friend Tipp. Once we were loyal friends of the* Sendara *of the Graelands. We were Companions of the Noble Way, and rode at her behest to make right whatever wrongs had been done in the realms of the Labyrinth World. We were free and happy then. If only we had been content! But greed crept in little by little. We had no thought of taking harm or giving it, but harm goes with greed like its own shadow. Our hearts hardened, little by little, and then our bodies as greed replaced comradeship... and freedom... and love.*

"We became stone, and now we cannot move. Eventually the Black Flame will destroy us all, one by one. I told this to Oliver Medley and to young Bertie Mossgrower, as I have to all travelers who pass by--not that there are many of those in the Desolate Lands. Friend Oliver did not heed my words; young Bertie did, but chose to continue to the City of Dead Souls. I could do nothing to persuade them otherwise. It is a terrible thing to want to help others and yet be unable to do so. Can you understand that, Friend Tipp?"

"I can indeed," Tipp replied. "But you have already helped, Stonefather, more than you know. And I am sure that you will do greater things when the final battle comes with the Lord of Desolation."

"How can we possibly do that, Friend Tipp?" asked Endorgon. *"None of us can walk one step from our rooted places. Do you truly believe we Stonemen can be of use?"*

Heedless of whatever might be spying on them, Tipp jumped up from the hard ash-ground. "Yes, I do!" he exclaimed. "Because that's it! That's the secret! *Belief!* Stonefather, I say, with the utmost respect, that you're wrong. Maybe long ago your hearts were hard--but no more! You mourn for those you love, you care for unwary travelers, you shelter the lost, you grieve over your own hard hearts. Truly, you have been transformed! Once again you have become Companions of the Noble Way. I know you can help fight the evil that the Lord of Desolation has wrought on the Labyrinth World. It's *believing* that will do it!"

The Stonefather listened closely, bending his great head to the Dwarvian. *"And you think this is possible, Friend Tipp?"* he asked, his mind divided between doubt and hope.

Tipp stood his ground, looking up at Endorgon. "I do, Stonefather. There is a saying written in the *Book of the Labyrinth*: 'I will take the heart of stone out of their bodies and give them a heart of flesh.' I believe those words were meant for you and your people."

"Hmm, hmm," said Endorgon. *"You have spoken well, Friend Tipp. It may be that we have become entrenched in our sorrows and have forgotten our great purpose. I will confer with my people, and we will consider what you have said."* He straightened and uttered a low rumble in a language unfamiliar to Tipp. A chorus of similar deep rumblings answered, and Tipp politely withdrew a little farther off so that he wouldn't intrude on the Stonemen's deliberations.

Settling down on a low rock while he waited, Tipp drew a fold of cloth over his nose and mouth to cut down on the effluvium from the nearby Saurian River. He didn't know if what he had said to Endorgon had done any good, but he had felt impelled to say it.

They've endured enough punishment for their greed, these Companions from the First Age! Often, as Tipp knew well, through suffering comes self-knowledge, and from self-knowledge comes wisdom, and from wisdom, transformation. If the Stonemen were able to ride again, what a boon they would be to the defense of the Labyrinth World!

Now for the Abbey: He ought to find out what was going on there. Tipp closed his eyes, searched his mind for the appropriate map, and activated it.

There was the Abbey, standing as it had for uncounted centuries. But what was this? The broad and mighty River Sunder, which had always protected the Abbey from hostile forces on its landward side, was diminishing before his eyes! It was scarcely half its former width. *And--do my senses deceive me?* A massive army of *wyrga*, encamped with their machinery of wholesale destruction, surrounded the Abbey in every direction, even to the edge of the ocean.

What should I do now? Should I go back to where Andis waits? Or is time too short? If I go on, can I get through enemy lines to reach the Abbey? Should I try going the other way instead, into the City of Dead Souls, to see if I can find Tapp and Oliver? Anxiously Tipp mulled over these dark matters, but no easy answers came.

At length, as the day was nearly over, Tipp returned to the Stonefather. "There is no sign of my brother Tapp or the boy Bertie or Oliver Medley coming out of the City of Dead Souls," he said. "I must head for the Abbey, which is under siege by the *wyrga* army. What have you decided?"

"Friend Tipp, you have shown us a new thing," said Endorgon. *"We think that it is good. But first we must work to energize our belief, making it grow strong so that we can move from our embedded places. When we are ready, when once more we live in victory, then shall the Companions of the Noble Way ride to join you!"*

Tipp bowed deeply before Endorgon and the Stonemen. "Farewell, Stonefather," he said. *"Va'in 'a moru'."*

Greatly troubled in his mind, fearing he would never see his brother again, Tipp turned away and once more trod the secret path above the Saurian River, toward the distant Abbey of Saint Amber.

Deep underneath Castle Mormorion, Bertie's torn shirt waved sluggishly in the fuel-stream, where it was caught against the grating. Gradually it came to rest across the iron bars, blocking two or three spaces. There it began to gather into its folds bits and pieces of debris, thorny branches, unidentifiable gobs of sludge. Slowly the openings in the grating grew smaller.

Even though the Hidden Ways made him nearly as invisible as Tapp was under the Talisman of Misperception, Tipp walked cautiously, keeping all his senses alert. Everything he saw convinced him, more and more, that war against the Lord of Desolation was imminent, not far in the future as he had once believed. He did not need the Stonefather's assistance this time to see the expanse of *wyrga* armies covering the bleak lands between the City of Dead Souls and the Bordering Cliffs-- and beyond.

Tipp decided to gamble on his skill at moving in a targeted area unnoticed. He wasn't certain how well informed Prince Pavarr was about the size of the enemy forces, so if he could gather intelligence--any kind at all--to take to Pavarr, who would surely command the defense, they would be that much better prepared. The Dwarvian's mind-map had shown him how closely the Lord of Desolation's invisible forces had encamped around the Abbey and how near they were to a full-scale invasion.

Seizing his opportunity, Tipp stepped off the Hidden Way and almost at once entered a zone where extreme danger was palpable in the air. A short distance ahead, herded into a huge penned yard, were Ab'addon's ominous instruments of annihilation: decimators, siege engines, crushers, grinders, eradicators. Cautiously he crept around the gigantic structures, realizing quickly that he had stumbled onto a secret weapons cache.

The night was deadly cold. As Tipp crept among the grotesque machines, keeping well behind cover, he glimpsed the tremulous glow of *wyrga* heating units and figured that the guards would have congregated around them, warming themselves and probably talking about the coming invasion. *If I can get closer to them, near enough to listen without being detected...* He huddled behind a monster eradicator, close enough to feel a faint warmth from one of the units.

"What we do?" asked one guard, a young one by the voice.

"Wait," answered an older one. "Lord Ab'addon say, go to Abbey, kill everyone. Get *Sen'da*."

"Why get *Sen'da*?" questioned the younger one. It must have been the wrong question, because his only answer was a cuff from one of the others.

"Lord Ab'addon order!" was the gruff reply. "We obey! No question!"

Quiet, except for the white buzz of the heating unit.

Another *wyrga*-figure joined the group. Tipp peered through the darkness, but he couldn't tell exactly where the new one had come from. Not from the guards' box in the middle of the enclosure. Tipp was certain of that. Did he slip in from outside? Not likely. To his knowledge the *wyrga* usually worked in pairs, to spy on each other. Ab'addon didn't trust even his mindless slaves.

"Not always obey," said the new voice.

"What you mean?" said the older.

"Heard from *wyrga* under Grimmerund."

-- 489 --

Another pause. Tipp strained his acute hearing to its utmost.

"What happen?"

"They want go against Ab'addon," said the middle voice. "Figure he want *Sen'da*, must be some power she got. He use us to get her--"

"Then he take her power!" said the young guard.

"Why he need us to get her?" asked another.

"We take her!" said the young one. "Then we get her power!"

"Hrg! Hrg!" growled the others, apparently in agreement.

Tipp hardly dared breathe. A potential mutiny brewing among the *wyrga* rank and file! *Does Pavarr know about this?*

The Dwarvian thought quickly. Here was a possibility that some of the *wyrga* might break away from the Lord of Desolation. *They might even try to take matters into their own hands, attack the Abbey without waiting for Ab'addon's order. I have to get that information to the Abbey fast!*

Quiet as a ghost, he edged backward around an angle of the eradicator's base. He moved slowly, testing each step, always keeping an eye on the clutch of guards lest they suddenly recall their duty to actually guard the premises. He could not have known about the metal tooth that had dropped earlier from the eradicator's mouth due to a careless repair job. He could not have helped stepping on it and stumbling. He made next to no noise, but that little was enough, for the *wyrga*'s hearing was unnaturally sharp.

They were after him in a flash! Tipp didn't even consider running, for he was fully visible, and the *wyrga*'s speed would have caught him in seconds. Instinctively he leaped onto the tall machine beside him and climbed nimbly up its skeleton to the control chamber. He slammed the door closed after him, locked it, and began punching any button that looked like a starter.

The guards began swarming up after him just as the eradicator awakened. Feeling an alien hand at its controls, the machine stirred, twisting its long neck to try to get at the creature interfering with it. Unable to reach Tipp, and becoming more and more irritated at the contradictory signals flooding its system, the eradicator spooked and ran amok. Blindly it charged into a nearby siege engine, cut its victim in half, and rolled over the corpse. On it ran, maddened by whatever Tipp was doing to the controls, and charged into other giant machines, which in turn awakened and began attacking each other.

In the melee, the *wyrga* climbing up Tipp's eradicator were shaken off, falling hard on the ground. Some of them were run over and crushed by grinding wheels and moving treads. Other *wyrga* guards, scrambling to the rescue, mounted their prodders--small, quick machines used to control the herds of mass-destruction engines--and gave chase, only to be overwhelmed by the stampeding eradicators.

At last Tipp discovered the controls which steered the thing and was able to assert some measure of command over it. Afraid the horde might turn in the direction of the Abbey, he maneuvered his eradicator out of the middle of the brawl. Crashing through the metal fence, he headed in the opposite direction--toward the Bordering Cliffs and the Desolate Lands, hoping the others would follow.

But the young eradicator had tasted freedom for the first time in its life. Now that it was out in the open, it ceased to obey any of Tipp's repeated orders. As if it had suddenly developed wings, it fled straight for Threshold Forest--where Andis, unsuspecting, waited.

Tipp pounded the control panel until he made the eradicator stop in its tracks and rear violently, like a terrified horse. Sweat pouring down his face, he wrestled with the joystick until he forced the ponderous machine to turn in the direction of the immeasurably high cliffs that look down on the Saurian River. The eradicator raced headlong toward them, and before Tipp could figure out how he had managed to stop it the first time, plunged off the cliff where the poisonous black Saurian meets the roiling, foam-tossed sea.

Chapter Twenty-Eight

Strategic Meeting

"Cap'n Bones!" called the skull-sailor on watch. "Off the port bow!"

Captain Bones pivoted to port as a giant black hulk appeared out of the night and loomed over the *Marrowbone,* apparently about to ram the smaller craft broadside.

"Hard a-starboard!" the captain shouted to the helmsman, who immediately gave a sharp turn to the wheel, maneuvering their craft away from immediate danger. "Battle stations!" to the crew. "Fire at my command! Get down!" he snapped to Oliver, Bertie, and Tapp, who, being landsmen, simply stood in the middle of the deck, mouths agape.

Nothing more happened in the next several moments. The lightless hulk stopped where it was, drifting soundlessly. The *Marrowbone,* barely clearing its prow, maintained a position close enough that cannon-fire would overshoot them.

"What in the name of Neptune--" the captain muttered, then stiffened as cannon-ports opened above them and sharpshooters' rifles poked out, pointed straight at the little *Marrowbone*'s captain and crew.

Captain Bones took breath and prepared to give the order to fire.

A gleam of light from a gun-barrel bounced off the water and illuminated a name painted across the big ship's bow.

Grand Adventure.

Bertie rushed to the railing and leaned over the side. "Uncle Nunks!" he screamed, heedless of caution. "Uncle Nunks! It's me-- Bertie!"

"Hold fire!" A voice familiar to Bertie and Oliver gave the order, and the long-barreled rifles disappeared from the cannon-ports. In a trice the *Marrowbone* was being towed behind the *Grand*

Adventure, and the skull-crew joined their mates aboard the larger vessel.

Both ships had been running without lights, lest a watchful enemy catch sight of them. Outside lights were still banned as they crept slowly along the coastline, keeping a careful lookout at the mist-enshrouded shore. Only inside the admiral's cabin was the low light of a lantern allowed, casting elongated shadows against walls and shuttered windows.

Admiral Nunkins's seamed, sunbrowned face grew solemn as he surveyed the group seated around his table: Captain Ezekiel Bones, known to him from the days when they had sailed together, master and mate, to off-world ports of call; Bertie, his nephew, whose tale poured out as fast as his tongue could talk; and Oliver Medley, who had gotten sidetracked from his original Quest in some way that seemed embarrassing to him as well as difficult to understand, but whom Bertie had rescued at risk to his own life. Tapp Whackitt from Keeper's Inn had been unknown to him until now, but further conversation elicited information that verified the Dwarvian's character and reputation.

"Ah, sandwiches! Exactly what we all need," the admiral pronounced as Bertie's tongue finally ran out of steam. A plate of salt beef, bread-and-cheese, and sardine-and-mustard sandwiches appeared on the table. "And more hot tea, if you please, Mr. Steward. We'll need all our wits about us tonight, for we sail in dangerous waters. We shall have a strategy session, for we must assume that the Lord of Desolation is considerably ahead of us. If I remember correctly, Mr. Medley, Ab'addon's purpose is the capture of the *Sendara* of the Graelands. And you were escorting her to safety in the Abbey of Saint Amber."

Oliver turned white to his ears; he sank back in his chair. He had endeavored to conceal the essential core of his mission when he and Bertie had stayed at Quarterdeck Cottage. *Have I been that clumsy after all?*

"Don't be concerned, Mr. Medley," the admiral continued. "Rumors of such doings have been rife in the Labyrinth World for a considerable time. We who protect the *Sendara*'s interests have made certain that those rumors are as inaccurate as possible; nevertheless, we have to assume that the Lord of Desolation has made the most of what he has learned."

"Uncle N--," Bertie burst forth, unable to contain himself any longer. "I mean, Admiral, sir, how did you find us? How did you know where we were?"

Admiral Nunkins smiled, tolerant of interruption under the circumstances. "A Raven Express message was received from a young lady, a Miss Andis danat-Tirgon, or daughter of Tirgon, as you would say, Mr. Medley."

Bertie's cheeks turned pink, a fact that did not go unnoticed among his fellows. Tapp at first hid a smile, then grew thoughtful. *Tirgon... Tirgon.* He rummaged through his mental files, for Dwarvians never forget a name, and that name recalled an order he and Tipp had filled at their forge some time past--an order for swords and lances with special properties. *But where is Tipp now?* Tapp wondered. *Still with the Stonemen? Or did he risk going to Castle Mormorion after Bertie and me?*

Bertie swallowed. "How did she--I mean, how did the raven know you were out at sea?"

"I wasn't, then, lad," continued the admiral. "The message reached us--you remember Mr. Boatswain, Mr. Steward, and Mr. Carpenter, Captain Bones?--at Quarterdeck Cottage. The note told us you went into the Desolate Lands to find Mr. Medley. We took counsel together and decided that, since the *Grand Adventure* was almost completely refitted, we'd give her seaworthiness a test. That's the story we put about, for there are spies of the Desolation everywhere, even in Mossy Dell Village.

"Of course we were really looking for Bertie here. We sailed as close to the Desolate Lands as we dared--and waited."

Tapp was about to bring up the subject of Tipp, and the urgency of finding him before he decided to risk going to Castle Mormorion, when a wave splashed over the side, and a cry sounded from the lookout's post atop the mainmast. The group inside the cabin couldn't hear it clearly, but something in the tone of it caught their attention, and they were already halfway out of their chairs as a sailor ran into the room.

"Admiral, sir! Lookout spotted a man falling off the high cliff with a big machine coming after him! Bo'sun's launched a rescue boat, sir!"

The admiral hastened out of his cabin, followed closely by the other four. They leaned over the bow peering at the bo'sun's crew, who heaved a short, limp figure into their rowboat.

"Tipp!" Oliver, Bertie, and Tapp shouted at the same instant.

A rescued Tipp, huddled in a spare blanket, sat in the admiral's cabin with a bowl of hot beef broth warming his insides. A cup of good strong tea stood near to hand. Even better than that, five pairs of eyes focused intently on him. He had an audience, which always brought out the best of his narrative powers. He wasn't disappointed: They were enthralled, though Tapp didn't seem to appreciate his masterful handling of the rogue eradicator as much as Tipp thought it deserved.

"That herd of mass-destruction engines was doubtless intended as reinforcement for the Lord of Desolation's invasion forces," commented Captain Bones. "They're useless to him now." He grinned, showing rows of square brown teeth, and a twinkle of admiration shone in his eye-hole.

"I concur, Captain," said the admiral. "Friend Tipp here seems to have decimated their rear guard--and Ab'addon might not yet be aware of it."

"Prince Pavarr won't be aware of it either," said Tipp. "I'd wager he's at the Abbey by now--as we ought to be, Tapp and I."

Unnoticed by each other, Bertie and Oliver both felt a certain lowering of spirits at the mention of the prince's name--for different reasons.

"I need to send a message to the Abbey," Tipp continued. "Right away. Pavarr needs to know about the *wyrga* army--and the mutiny brewing in the ranks. That *wyrga*, the one that joined the guards--"

"You refer to one *wyrga*," commented the admiral. "Do you mean it was alone?"

"It seemed to be, sir," replied the Dwarvian. "I could hear them talking better than I could see them, but that *wyrga* did appear to come out of the night by itself. I'd guess he was some kind of leader."

"Unusual, if so," said Admiral Nunkins. "They nearly always function only in groups, obedient to the group-mind. We believed them incapable of individual initiative."

"But I was attacked by a single *wyrga* at Fool's Point, after the skull-boat dropped me there," Bertie said.

"You fought him off?" exclaimed Captain Bones. "Good lad!"

"Well, actually," said the truthful Bertie, "it was Andis. She drove him away."

After that admission, Bertie had to explain his connection with the "young lady, Andis danat-Tirgon". He gave his report with complete objectivity--and fooled no one.

"By the way, Brother," Tapp asked later on, "did you happen to hear a name for this *wyrga*?"

"I didn't think they had their own names. I heard they're called by their position in the cohort," Tipp replied. "But come to think of it, I might have heard them call this one *tid* or *tir*. It sounded like a number in their language, ten maybe. Why?"

Tapp explained in detail why he had asked, and the more he developed his theory, the wider grew Tipp's eyes. Late into the night they conferred, fitting together far-flung pieces of a puzzle that grew more complicated as they explored it.

High over Threshold Forest, a *gnaarx* sped toward the Desolate Lands. It gripped a ragged bit of paper in its beak, taken from a raven messenger.

Scowling, Andis paced back and forth in the little clearing at the edge of Threshold Forest near the Bordering Cliffs. She was not a patient person in any case, and these unreasonable delays, coupled with the frustration of not knowing what was happening to Tipp, Tapp, and Bertie, gave her an angry energy that expressed itself in kicking piles of fallen leaves and occasionally jumping up to swing hard on a tree branch.

Why didn't they let me go with them? She was as good a tracker as Bertie, she was positive about that, and could have been in and out of Castle Mormorion in half the time. On the other hand, she didn't know what Mr. Medley looked like, and Bertie did. So did the Dwarvians.

It was the forced inaction that was getting to her, and she was honest enough to admit that to herself.

Saint Amber's Rose

This business of being in charge of communications had sounded important when she first agreed to it, but the thrill of it had begun to pall. *At least I got to call a messenger from the Raven Express.* That was exciting, to think that she was in on something that no other human mortal knew how to do, except Pavarr! And some lady she didn't know.

Per request, she had sent off a message to Admiral Nunkins in Bertie's home town, but had received no reply. Not that she expected one; she just wished she knew what the admiral--Bertie's uncle, evidently--decided to do.

Also per request, she had sent a raven to the Abbey of Saint Amber with a message for Pavarr to let him know the reason for the Questors' absence. Before departing, Tipp had outlined carefully what she was to say and how she was to say it, the difficulty being how to communicate sufficient information without being too explicit in case agents of the Desolation intercepted the message. Tipp didn't consider that a very likely contingency because by covenant among the Labyrinth Realms, the Raven Express was considered neutral and was allowed to fly unhindered through all regions, regardless of political or geographical barriers between realms.

It wasn't easy, thinking of a way to tell Pavarr about the rescue operation to Castle Mormorion without naming names, but I made it as obscure as I could manage.

She hadn't heard back from the Abbey, and the messenger certainly should have arrived there by now. Not that she had any right to expect Pavarr to reply to her personally... It was just that she felt she ought to be doing something, anything but stay in one place, not knowing what was going on.

I can send another message to the Abbey. The first raven might have gotten lost somehow. Or something might have happened to it.

She used her newfound knowledge to summon another raven, but now that one had arrived, Andis couldn't think of what else to say. The first message had exhausted her ability to encode information so that only Pavarr could understand it. Another one would only repeat the message and possibly increase the chances of the enemy intercepting it.

"Take whatever time you need, miss," remarked the raven perched on a nearby branch. "But I'm on the clock, you know. I can take my half-hour lunch break while I'm waiting, but then I have to get back to work. Either you'll need to give me a message or I'll have to report to my next assignment. Union rules. Messengers, Guides, Signalers, and Semaphorists Union, Local 7614." The bird dipped his beak in a thermos cup of *mekhash ban* and took a bite of road-kill on rye with mustard, hold the onions.

Andis blew out a breath and rubbed her forehead. "I understand." *I don't know what to do now. Why don't they come back? When I see that Bertie Mossgrower again, I'll--*

"I'd like to communicate with the Abbey as soon as possible, and Miss Andis as well," Tipp requested. "I'm afraid that if she doesn't hear from us, she'll take off on her own and follow us to the Stonemen and then to Castle Mormorion. No telling what'll happen to her there."

"Certainly," replied Admiral Nunkins. "But we won't be able to summon the Raven Express from here. They're land-based and don't work offshore. Along the coast we use the Seagull to Shore Service. I'll signal for one of them."

They hadn't finished their plate of sandwiches before one of the Seagull to Shore personnel landed on the foredeck.

"Assistant Chief Communications Officer Ephraim Bartholomew Seagull reporting for duty, Admiral," said the gray-winged herring gull (*Larus californicus*) with a smart salute.

Tipp quickly penned his message to Andis and pondered how best to alert Pavarr about the invisible *wyrga* army surrounding the Abbey without alerting enemy forces at the same time.

"Permission to speak freely, Admiral?" asked Assistant Chief Communications Officer Seagull. "Sir," he addressed Tipp at the admiral's nod, "I understand the need for haste, but a gull wouldn't fly directly to the Abbey from where the young lady is. Our service is strictly ship to shore, and a gull flying such a distance over Threshold Forest would arouse suspicion."

"What about flying in by a different route, from the open ocean?" asked Captain Bones. "We could take the *Grand Adventure* out beyond sight of land."

"That would involve another messenger service," replied Assistant Chief Communications Officer Seagull. "Albatross Air-Post operates the open ocean routes. They're a fine service and I can highly recommend them, but if time is a factor here, I'd say you'd be better off having me carry this message to Miss Andis. She can then summon a Raven Express messenger to go on to the Abbey. Ravens fly over the forest constantly and wouldn't be noticed. Or I could call another gull and have him fly directly to the Abbey with your message. Sir."

"Captain, sir!" interrupted the First Officer of the skull-crew, saluting. "I believe our ship is being watched from shore. I detected the flash of light off a spyglass lens. One seagull taking off from the deck might not be noticed, but two might be suspect. Sir."

"Good observation, Mr. First," Captain Bones nodded.

"Then I'd suggest that we have Assistant Chief Communications Officer Seagull here deliver both messages to Miss Andis danat-Tirgon," said Admiral Nunkins. "She can forward the message to the Abbey by Raven Express. And I believe I'll add something to your communication to the young lady, Mr. Tipp."

The gull came in for a landing at the exact moment when the Raven Express messenger drained the last drop of *mekhash ban* from his thermos cup.

"Well, miss, I've got to be on my way now, so if there's no message--hello! What's this? Why, it's Eph Seagull! Say, what're you doing in these parts? This is Raven Express territory, you know!"

"Assistant Chief Communications Officer Ephraim Bartholomew Seagull with a message for Miss Andis danat-Tirgon," the bird saluted Andis, for the moment ignoring the raven. "It's on my left leg."

As Andis bent to untie the paper, the gull turned a frosty glare on the raven. "Augustus Corax," he acknowledged with a stiff nod. "I am aware of the territorial boundaries of the Raven Express. This is a Seagull-to-Shore communication and as such, perfectly legitimate. As you know."

(There is a certain coldness in relations between raven and seagull operations. That is because ravens are Union and seagulls are Service, and thus have differing viewpoints on how things ought properly to be done--though both are thoroughly professional and have excellent reputations.)

"Hmp!" returned Augustus Corax, and flapped his wings preparatory to takeoff.

Charleynne Gates

"Oh, wait! Wait, please!" cried Andis, deciphering Tipp's note as fast as she could. The news that Bertie was safe (appended by Admiral Nunkins) put a blush in her cheeks, but the rest of the letter made her frown with concern. "I need to send another message right away. There's more, isn't there, Officer Seagull?"

"Yes, miss." Assistant Chief Communications Officer Seagull opened his beak to deliver the oral part of his charge.

A rustling in the underbrush nearby! The two birds flew to cover instantly. Andis dropped the letter and caught up her bow. She fitted an arrow to the bowstring and stood poised to fire as a handsome stag and doe with twin yearlings emerged from a thicket and stopped short at the sight of her.

Andis lowered her bow, indicating that she was not hunting and intended them no harm. Courteously she wished them good day.

"Good day, miss," returned the stag, panting as if he had run a long way. "Is this your--your home camp?"

"No, it isn't," replied Andis, wondering why the deer displayed a curiosity unusual in the forest. "Just temporary."

"Then you're not staying here? Permanently, I mean?" the doe asked, glancing nervously over her shoulder in the direction they had come.

"No, but why? Is something wrong?"

"Haven't you heard?" said the stag. "The *wyrga*--they've pushed all the way through Threshold Forest! They've mowed down a big swath of trees and left the earth bare down to bedrock. There's no shelter or food for anyone now, and the lakes and streams are clogged with debris. We cannot drink from them!"

"Our home is gone!" the doe burst out. "Destroyed by the slaves of Ab'addon!"

"But won't you be safer going in the other direction, to the Abbey?" Andis asked. "The friars give everyone shelter."

"We cannot get to the Abbey!" said the doe, taking a few steps closer to Andis.

"*Wyrga* armies have surrounded the Abbey," said the stag. "No one can get through. And worst of all," he said, joining the doe with their children, "the *wyrga* killed a raven messenger!"

"What!" exclaimed three shocked voices.

"Where? How?" gasped Ephraim Seagull. "You mean they broke the Covenant of Neutrality?"

"Yes! A messenger was flying to the Abbey, and the *wyrga* knocked it out of the sky with their *thringa*-weapons! The raven tried to get over the walls, but it fell outside and disappeared in the *wyrga* camp."

Andis turned pale and sat down suddenly on the nearest rock. A raven messenger shot--maybe even killed! *Was it the bird who was carrying my message?*

The deer family hurried on its way, although Andis couldn't imagine where they thought they might find safety. Usually, in times of distress, such as drought or a forest fire, the Abbey provided refuge. Now it was under siege!

"How am I supposed to get another message through?" she muttered to herself, gnawing at her underlip.

The raven squared his jaw. "I'll carry it, miss!"

Andis shook her head. "But the other raven--they said the *wyrga* killed him!"

"I'll find a way to get it through somehow," the raven insisted. "There's more than one way into the Abbey."

"Don't be foolhardy, Augustus," said the seagull. "The *wyrga* show no mercy."

Augustus Corax drew himself up and stood at attention. "A comrade may have fallen, but the Raven Express never fails in its duty. Give me the message, Ephraim. It *will* go through."

The seagull delivered its charge orally, in the clicking code-language of the bird messengers, and then--for the first time in the history of relations between Raven Express and Seagull to Shore--a gull saluted a raven.

"Good luck, Gus," said Ephraim Seagull.

The raven took off. It circled overhead, dipped its wings, and headed in the direction of the besieged Abbey.

"I have to get back to the ship now, miss," said the seagull. "They'll want to hear what's happened. Any message you'd like to send?"

Andis shook her head slowly, looking at the ground. "No, but thank you, Officer Seagull. Oh... Would you say hello to... I mean, um, I guess... No message."

Charleynne Gates

Assistant Chief Communications Officer Ephraim Seagull let the wind-current launch him into the sky. Andis was alone again in the clearing at the edge of Threshold Forest.

I won't be left out. I won't! Pavarr needs me--he can't fight all those wyrga *by himself! And what if the raven doesn't get through with the message this time? I'd better follow and make sure nothing happens to him.*

Strapping on her knapsack and picking up her bow and quiver, Andis set out for the Abbey, following the raven's sky-trail.

A wind came up and blew the leaves around the empty clearing until not a trace of bird or human mortal marked the ground where they had been.

She will die by the hand of her kindred, said the Voice in the Smoking Mirror.

Chapter Twenty-Nine

Reconnaissance

Ephraim Seagull flew through drifts of fog toward the dark, indeterminate shape that was the *Grand Adventure* lying out of sight of land. Even though he was as accustomed to land as he was to water, getting away from the brooding darkness of Threshold Forest made him feel lighter, as if a woolen blanket had been lifted off him. He drew a welcome breath of cold salt air deep into his lungs.

Something is definitely wrong back there. He sensed it, an indeterminate foreshadowing of doom that vibrated to the end of every sensitive feather.

He thought of the adolescent human mortal, Andis, and worried about her. She seemed too recently out of the nest to be on her own, but you never knew about these human mortals. Their family practices were strange to him. *Barely out of the egg and here she is, in the middle of a highly dangerous situation with no adult of her own species along for protection. Odd.*

And Augustus Corax: Mentally the seagull wished him well, then wondered about the other raven messenger, the first one the girl had sent to the Abbey. *Whatever happened to him?* The Covenant of Neutrality was supposed to cover avian messengers during Acts of War and Tumult, but in these troublous times the old rules had gotten all twisted around. For instance, there used to be a rule--a very old and respected one, too--called *habeas carcass*, which guaranteed the rights of any creature detained on suspicion of a crime, but since the spread of the Lord of Desolation's rule, had mysteriously disappeared.

The ship's bulk loomed out of the fog. The seagull banked sharply left, dived, and landed on the quarterdeck.

The Questors hurried into the admiral's cabin to hear the seagull report the news of a raven messenger assassinated by enemy forces.

"That would never have happened in our day," said Captain Bones, shaking his head.

"The Labyrinth World has grown more dangerous than ever before," Admiral Nunkins agreed. "If we--"

"Urgent message for the Admiral," said a signalman, running into the cabin and saluting. "Received by heliograph."

Admiral Nunkins took the message, perused it, and drew his brows together. "It's from my old friend, the Mage Dandriel, whom I believe you know," he said. All the Questors nodded except Bertie. "He says--in code--that Oliver Medley must go to the Abbey at once, without delay." He lowered his voice. "Ab'addon has discovered that Mr. Medley escaped from Castle Mormorion. It is imperative that you get inside the Abbey walls, Mr. Medley, before Ab'addon locates you. It is your Gift that makes him desperate. He must prevent you from using it at all costs."

"But--but I don't know what my Gift is!" Oliver protested.

The Admiral turned his intense blue gaze directly upon him, and Oliver wished he hadn't spoken.

"That doesn't matter now," said Admiral Nunkins. "All that matters is your getting safely to the Abbey."

A suspicion occurred to Tipp, whose mind, in nearly all cases, was a suspicious one.

"How did the Lord of Desolation find out that Friend Oliver got away?" he asked, carefully not looking at Oliver.

"You didn't tell him anything when you were in Castle Mormorion, did you?" Tapp looked straight at Oliver. A pleading note was in his voice. "You wouldn't have done that."

Oliver glanced at the faces of his fellow Questors around the table, at Captain Bones and Admiral Nunkins, and did not find the moral support he wanted--and had unthinkingly counted on up to this point. Horrified, he realized that they were actually considering the possibility that he had betrayed the Quest!

Oliver felt his face grow pale. He gulped and swallowed, as anyone, guilty or innocent, might do when confronted with an unjust suspicion.

"Did you promise him anything?" Captain Bones turned his eyeholes directly on Oliver, who saw no hope in their remote black depths.

Saint Amber's Rose

"Mr. Medley wouldn't do that!" Bertie protested. "You didn't, did you, Mr. Medley! Tell them you didn't!"

For a moment Oliver couldn't speak, couldn't force out even a word of protest. He hadn't betrayed them! He knew he hadn't! But he had been in that castle, in the garden of smoke and mirrors, for an awfully long time--or so it seemed--and the truth was, he didn't remember exactly what he might have said to the Lord of Desolation or his minions.

"I--I--I," he began, hating himself for stammering and thus sounding unconvincing. "I certainly did not promise the Lord of Desolation anything at all! At least," he went on miserably, "I don't think I did. I honestly don't remember much about the--the time I spent there. It seemed to last forever, but... Maybe I said... No, I don't believe I told him anything. I don't remember." He put his head in his hands as if he could squeeze some detail of relevant information out of it. "I don't remember."

The expression on his face was so stricken that, one by one, the others became embarrassed for him and turned their eyes away.

"Wait!" Oliver shouted as a sudden image blazed into his mind's eye. "I *do* remember how I got out! It was the Wraith Gloom! He was my valet while I was in the castle. He showed me how to get out. He opened a secret door and let me into the Hall of Mirrors--and--and then Bertie found me, and we escaped! That's it!"

The admiral frowned. "A Wraith serving in Castle Mormorion? That doesn't seem likely."

Tipp eyed Oliver askance. "The Wraith clan is a venerable one, with never a stain on its honor. Hard to imagine any of them mixed up with Ab'addon."

"He--he said he was an indentured servant," Oliver went on hastily as more and more of his immediate past scrolled down the screen of memory. "The Lord of Desolation tricked him when he signed his articles of indenture. He said it was when the Companions of the Noble Way were threatened. Ab'addon was planning to make them slaves. *Wyrga*, was what he said."

"The Wraith Gloom indentured himself to Ab'addon to save the Companions from that dreadful fate?" Tipp repeated. "You mean the ones who became Stonemen?"

Admiral Nunkins stood up abruptly. "I think we've heard enough to clear Mr. Medley of the charge of betrayal, at least temporarily. If further investigation is needed, it will have to take place at a later time. It is obvious that right now we will have to take him on trust--and get him inside the Abbey as soon as possible. I dare not ignore the Mage's report. Now," as they gathered around a chart unrolled upon the table, "the route I have in mind will be difficult as well as dangerous, but if the Abbey is surrounded by *wyrga* forces, then this will be the only approach that will be left undefended.

"As you see here, the cliff on which the Abbey stands is a sheer rock wall plunging straight down to the River Sunder. It has merely the thinnest strip of gravel for a shoreline. The ship cannot approach it, but the *Marrowbone* can take you up the Sunder. Then you will have to climb the crag to the Abbey, which also has a high wall rising from the edge of the cliff. From sea level to the top of the Abbey is over a *kephan*, but I believe with the proper climbing equipment you will be able to circumvent the *wyrga* guards. Mr. Steward and Mr. Carpenter can supply you with--"

Oliver stood back from the others, who were intently studying the chart. He envisioned in lurid detail the result of attempting to climb a towering rock wall in moonless darkness, in imminent peril of plunging to a watery grave in the cold, remorseless ocean. The prospect was not encouraging.

"No," said Oliver Medley, forcing the word past a choking sensation in his throat. "No, I really couldn't. I've never climbed anything higher than a kitchen stool in my life, and I don't think that now would be the appropriate time to start. There must be some other way into the Abbey."

The admiral, Captain Bones, Tipp, Tapp, and Bertie looked blankly at Oliver.

"Brother," said Tapp before anyone had a chance to expostulate, "turn on your mind map. Let's zoom in and see what else is there. We haven't come all this way to turn back now."

The two Dwarvians shut their eyes and concentrated while the others held their breath and waited tensely, all too aware that time and opportunity were rapidly slipping away from them.

"There it is!" exclaimed Tapp.

"I had no idea," Tipp marveled. "It must have been made in the First Age!"

"What! What is it!" everyone else shouted.

"It's a Hidden Way," Tapp explained, opening his eyes. "We didn't know about it until right now because it's so old and so well hidden that only the Dwarf-kin can detect it. Back in the First Age the Dwarves carved out many Hidden Ways all across the Labyrinth World. One of them ran from the Abbey clear through the Desolate Lands--only they weren't desolate then, but green and blooming. When the Lord of Desolation crept like smoke into the minds of human mortals, he turned them against their own land. The trees ... They cut down the beautiful trees..."

Tipp put a hand on Tapp's shoulder. "We can't think about that now." To the rest, "What this means is, we can get Friend Oliver up to the Abbey by the Hidden Way without doing any rock-climbing. It's a stairway--steep and narrow, but maneuverable. With Tapp and me to help him up, we can manage."

"And me!" exclaimed Bertie. "I'm going, too! I said I'd help Mr. Medley get to the Abbey, and I will!"

"I--I'll go," said Oliver Medley, plucking his courage out of the pit into which it had fallen. "I'm ready." Can't let the lad down, even if I--

"Hmm," said Admiral Nunkins. "In that case, we'd best send you on your way as soon as possible. Captain Bones, here's what I propose--"

As stealthily as a nocturnal hunter, Andis made her way through the crowded trees of Threshold Forest, following Augustus Corax. Sometimes she saw him, a black silhouette low in the sky, fluttering from tree to tree, and sometimes she had only the clues he left: a dropped feather or the screech of an angry pair of songbirds when he landed too near them. At other times he took a rest break and, well aware that she was tracking him, waited for her to catch up. Conscious of the potential presence of Ab'addon's spies, he tried to make as little noise as possible, but once, despite the danger, he had to croak "Nevermore" to call her back when she seemed to have lost his trail.

All too soon they came to the area of the Great Devastation. There they stopped at the edge of the trees and stared at what Ab'addon had done to the heart of the forest--deep, jagged scars made by the merciless engines of mass destruction. Nothing was left but blackened tree-stumps, lacerated layers of soil, and the glistening, rainbow-colored slick of Saurian fluid that had leaked from the machines.

The leaden sky mourned over the earth's nakedness, but contained its tears. There was no place for them to fall except upon open wounds.

"Why?" Andis whispered as slow tears edged down her cheeks. "Why are they so cruel to the Earth?"

"Human mortals have a terrible resentment of Mother Earth that we of the natural world do not understand," replied the raven, now perched on the girl's shoulder. "The Earth gives birth to us, nourishes and shelters us. She embraces us again when we die to this life. Why such hatred of her? I do not know the answer, but I know that the Lord of Desolation takes only human mortals--not us animals--to make into his *wyrga* slaves."

Andis could not stop staring. The stark, vicious evil of what was in front of her riveted her gaze to it against her will.

"Come, child," said the raven softly, and brushed the lobe of her ear with his wing. "Our duty lies in another place."

Together they withdrew into what was left of Threshold Forest and went steadily onward, and did not look back.

After several days they came within view of the towers of the Abbey, where it rose out of the sea on the lofty mountain-crag from which it had been carved. The two of them hid themselves in a stand of evergreens, the last grove before the open immensity of sky and sea.

"Look!" whispered the raven unnecessarily, for Andis's eyes were already wide with the wonder of her first sight of the Abbey of Saint Amber. Bright banners whipped from its spires in the sea-borne wind, and its crenellations gleamed golden in the setting sun. High in the air a half-dozen black vee shapes circled lazily over the Abbey.

"*Gnaarx!*" hissed the raven. "Get down!" as one of the black shapes broke formation and darted over the grove where Andis and the raven hid. Twice the monstrous thing circled the grove, then flew back to its group.

"I don't think it spotted us," said Augustus Corax, keeping a keen eye on the *gnaarx*. "But we won't be able to count on that for long.

We need to scout the territory. You see the wall nearest to us where that gnarled old tree grows against the side, almost to the top? There's a single window there, high up, hidden under the leaves. Now here's the plan: I'm going to wait until nightfall, when the *gnaarx* won't be able to see as well, and then I'll try to make it to that window. Can't take a chance going over the battlements 'cause the *gnaarx*'d spot me for sure. The window's our only option.

"If I make it, I'll tell them that you're outside here, and they'll get you in somehow. If I don't make it--well, don't stay around here. You head for home as fast as you can, child, and let whatever's going to happen, happen by itself. Keep away from the messes that other human mortals make. That's my advice."

But I'm already in this mess, Andis thought but did not say. *And Prince Pavarr is probably in the Abbey, and Bertie Mossgrower might be, too, and if he is, he'll probably need me to rescue him again. That boy can't handle all those* gnaarx *and* wyrga *by himself with his little slingshot*, thus ignoring Bertie's swift, unerring aim with his slingshot.

They waited until the night was dark enough to mask the raven's black wings. As Andis watched, bow and arrow in hand, Augustus took off and flew to the gnarled tree against the wall. But as he was about to land on the hidden branch nearest the window, a pair of *gnaarx* appeared suddenly from behind a high tower and dived with hideous shrieks to attack the raven.

Quick as thought, Andis let fly with deadly force. Her first arrow hit the *gnaarx* closest to the raven. The *gnaarx* plummeted down the sheer cliff, out of sight, and the other screamed defiantly and wheeled away, only to drop in turn as a second arrow found its vitals. The raven hopped or fell inside the open window. Andis wasn't sure if he'd been wounded--or worse.

I've got to go after him! She began running toward the Abbey, bent over as much as possible for concealment and zigzagging through patches of underbrush. Heedless of possible watchers, she scrambled up the gnarled tree, so concerned about the raven that she did not notice what followed her.

But something had seen her arrows' flight. Something had tracked her from the protection of the evergreen grove to the base of the gnarled tree and climbed after her without a sound until a scale of loose

Charleynne Gates

bark, disturbed by Andis's small foot, refused to bear the weight of the second climber. It tore from the trunk and slid to the ground.

Andis heard, turned--and saw the *wyrga* behind her. For one instant she froze in horror, long enough for the medallion she wore around her neck to free itself from her clothing and dangle freely with her sudden movement. A sliver of light from the crescent moon shined on the medallion's face.

The *wyrga* stopped when she did, seemingly held as immobile as she was. Later, Andis told the Questors that she thought the thing's eyes held recognition. Of what, she didn't know. But there was a spark there, a light that ought not to be in the eyes of a slave of Ab'addon.

Then the thing reached for her, but its iron talons missed, for the *wyrga* was all at once overwhelmed in a storm of beating owl-wings and talons that tore at the vulnerable vein in its neck. Hera Vespasia attacked again and again, giving her victim no rest. Trying to fight her off, the *wyrga* lost its grip on the tree-trunk and fell the whole way down to the rocky ground.

"Hurry, child!" the owl rasped. Andis needed no encouragement to move. She reached for the window where the raven had vanished, and with no time to think about what she might be getting into, swung herself over the casement and tumbled inside.

The girl had never been in a chamber like this one, had never even dreamed that such a room could exist. The ceiling was formed of living trees whose topmost branches interlaced so high up that they vanished in shadow. The healing fragrance of pine and fir permeated the air. Andis took a deep breath and felt--not lightheaded exactly, but expanded inside herself in some mysterious way. As if... as if there might be more to Andis danat-Tirgon than she herself had ever realized.

White flowers of every kind, visible as light in the indigo-shadowed room, stood in crystal vases on every surface, and great bowls of water lilies rested on the marble floor. Silver brushes and combs gleamed softly on the dressing table, and crystal knobs on the ornate wardrobe flashed in answer.

In the center of the room was a bed made of woven boughs, with coverings in shades of deep blue and dusky lilac. And in the bed, reclining against masses of blue and silver pillows, lay the most beautiful lady Andis had ever imagined. Her glorious hair tumbled in waves and curls across the bedcovers, and her face... In some way Andis did not understand, the lady's face seemed to be not quite part of this world. As if the lady were more alive than anyone Andis knew, even though she was sleeping.

But Flavia was not asleep. The raven's fall, then Andis's tumble into her bedchamber, had awakened her. She was not frightened, for she realized at once what had disturbed her slumber, and discerned also the innocence and courage of the girl, and loved her for it.

"Come here, child!" Flavia called, and the girl started and scrambled to her feet. Unsure what to do with herself and her weapons, she grasped her bow awkwardly, considered laying it down, then gripped it again. Not to use against the lady! No, but she didn't know what was coming next, and it was better to be prepared.

"There is no need to be afraid here," said the lady. "Come closer!"

Andis tiptoed to the side of the bed, where the most natural thing to do was to kneel so that the lady could see her and she could see the lady clearly. It wasn't easy, she found, to look directly into eyes so full of wisdom and kindness.

"What is your name, my dear?" the lady asked, and her voice was like a tender wind through harp strings.

"An--Andis danat-Tirgon. Wh--what is your name, my lady?"

"I am Flavia, *Sendara* of the Graelands."

Andis bowed her head, for although she had heard all her short life of the fabled Graelands and their Guardian, she had never quite believed the stories. Now she saw the truth of them, and the truth was more wondrous than the tales.

"I am at your service, my lady, for all of my life." The words tumbled out of her as awkwardly as she had tumbled into the room, but the lady did not laugh. She lifted a slender hand to caress the girl's cheek.

"I accept your service, Andis danat-Tirgon. Be filled with the power of the Light!"

A radiance like moonlight shot through Andis from her head to her feet, and at that moment she became a young woman. The expression of her face changed and deepened, and those things best left in childhood dropped away from her and were forgotten.

"And now, my dear, if you will ring that silver bell on the table there, the Infirmarian will come to tend to Friend Corax."

Andis gasped and reddened, for in her amazement she had forgotten about the wounded bird. Springing up, she rang the silver bell, which, although it made very little sound, was effective, for at once the Infirmarian and an assistant hastened into the lady's chamber. Carefully they transferred the raven to a small stretcher and hurried out again.

"Come, sit here." Flavia motioned toward a blue silk hassock beside the bed. "Tell me about your journey. I am glad that you have come to me, for we have much work to do together, and the end of night is near."

On the stony ground below the walls of the Abbey, the *wyrga* eased itself upright. It moved haltingly, stumbling from one step to the next. Its iron-caged chest rose and fell raggedly, as if it were in pain-- but *wyrga* feel no pain, or so it is said.

A harsh whisper spoke urgently inside its mind. *Find the Ruined Chapel. Bring me the sword. Bring me the sword!*

Slowly, as if resisting the voice, the *wyrga* went away from the Abbey. At intervals it stopped and looked back at the small window high in the wall where Andis and the raven had vanished. There it saw the faint glow of a silvery light. Long did it stare at that light.

At last it turned away and disappeared into Threshold Forest.

Chapter Thirty

Greenhallow

Deep under the dungeons of Castle Mormorion, Bertie's discarded tunic gathered more debris into its folds until the grating was almost completely covered. The Saurian River began to back up and explore alternate routes, and soon found the path of least resistance: the diminished channel of the River Sunder. The Saurian ran up to meet it, and the Sunder's course soon filled with thick black fluid crawling its way back to the source.

"I see the flame of a candle... two candles... three candles on the mantelpiece," Pavarr recited dutifully. "I see a cat crouching in the corner of the hearth. She has one blue eye and one yellow eye and five white hairs in her brindled tail."

"You are cured, Prince," the Infirmarian pronounced. Brother Gall, the Apothecary, handed the Infirmarian a small blue jar of ointment, and Brother Persil dabbed the last bit of it under Pavarr's eyes. "I was concerned about that left eye. *Wyrga* venom usually does permanent damage when it isn't immediately fatal, but your eyes have mended completely."

"I am grateful, Brother Persil, Brother Gall," replied Pavarr, rising from the examining chair in the infirmary. "Now, Father Abbot, I'd like to take a look through the telescope on your roof. We'll have to plan a strategy before--"

"The observation tower, then," said the Abbot. "Come." He opened a door, revealing a spiral staircase, and began to ascend it. The Infirmarian, having other patients to attend, nodded to Pavarr and hurried away.

"Prince," said the Apothecary when the others had gone. "A word with you, if I may."

"Of course, Brother Gall," said Pavarr. "What may I do for you?"

"I have three brothers. We know that Grimtread is in service at the portal of Ravenhome, and Dour is Personal Assistant to the Mage Dandriel. It is our youngest brother who has us worried. None of us has heard from him in some years, and we have been unable to locate him. I wondered if, in your travels, you might have seen him."

"His name?"

"Gloom, sir. Like my brothers and me, he is a Wraith."

"The Wraith Gloom!" the prince exclaimed. "Yes, Brother Gall, I have seen him! He serves in Castle Mormorion in the Great Waste."

"Mormorion!" gasped the Apothecary. "The fortress of the Lord of Desolation! How is this possible?" His face lost its color, and he sank into the examining chair Pavarr had vacated.

"Brother Gall! You are ill! Shall I call the Infirmarian?"

"No... No, I thank you, Prince." The Wraith took in a deep breath and exhaled, and a faint but healthy bluish tinge appeared in his cheeks. "It's only that the news is... We had hoped to hear better. Can you tell me anything more?"

"He told me that he serves under articles of indenture. The original seven years should have been over long ago, but Ab'addon manipulates time in Mormorion so that your brother fears he can never escape. But--" he lowered his voice--"this must be kept in strictest confidence, Brother Gall. I went to the castle and met him by arrangement, for Gloom secretly works for the High Council of the Labyrinth. He took me to the place where Ab'addon makes his human captives into *wyrga*-slaves."

"The most terrible of all his evils!" the Wraith gasped. "What can we do?"

"Alert your brothers," replied Pavarr. "Hold yourselves in readiness for the day when we must do battle with the Lord of Desolation!"

Pavarr followed the Abbot up a winding stair into a small circular room with a domed glass roof whose panels were open to the sky. A powerful telescope stood in the middle of the room, aimed at the landscape below the Great Mountain. A man peered into the eyepiece, making minute adjustments to the instrument. As Pavarr entered, the man turned to him, smiling.

Saint Amber's Rose

"The telescope is ready," said the Mage of Keeper's Inn.

"Dandriel!" Pavarr exclaimed. He grasped the man's outstretched hand eagerly. "But the earthquake! I heard the inn was entirely destroyed."

"It was," replied the Mage. "It stood at the vortex of several dimensions, and thus was subject to frequent disturbances in its energy field. The buildings are in ruins, but all therein returned safely to their own worlds."

"I thought only the Questors escaped! When they told me of the disaster, I assumed the enemy had caused it."

"Ab'addon could not have worked his evil at Keeper's Inn," Dandriel replied. "It was the combined powers of the Elder Ones, the constellations themselves, when they gathered for the High Council. No Earthly structure can contain those tremendous cosmic forces for long. Jon and Amatilda Keeper willingly consigned the inn to its inevitable doom, knowing that its sacrifice was necessary for the preservation of the Graelands."

"Friends," called the Abbot, standing at the telescope. "Time presses."

Pavarr hastened to join him, viewing the scene far below the Abbey: the once-swift River Sunder, the forests, woodlands, dales, and plains running many *kephan* down to Purple Valley. There, to his horror, he saw the remorseless engines of the Lord of Desolation advancing, crashing through shady groves and pleasant arbors, leveling the hills, befouling the streams with their effluent, tearing up the earth and turning everything in their path to dust and ashes.

The engines of mass destruction had surrounded the village of Mossy Dell, waiting to crush its little shops and houses to rubble. In the village square a masked and hooded rider sat on a horse shrouded in black from head to tail, without one speck of color. The faceless rider wore a glittering cloak that dazzled the eyes, and held a balance scales in one gauntleted hand. With the other, the rider passed down a heavy bag of gleaming gold coins to the mayor of Mossy Dell, Bull Biggles the publican.

Behind the mayor stood Elsie Flourhands, impatient for her gains, and after her a long line of villagers and their wives and families, all of them with avarice shining in their faces--even the children.

Charleynne Gates

Most of the Mossy Dellers carried empty bags and baskets for their anticipated share of the buy-out, and some brought their own scales to check the weight of the gold. Even old Midas McSkim, the richest man in Purple Valley, was there, driving a wagon with four big barrels in it. As he owned more land than anyone else, he expected the lion's share of payment and ignored, as he always had, angry glares and disapproving glances from the villagers.

But they were no better than he, for without a second thought they all had sold their farms and fields, woods and meadows, ancestral homes and native village itself, for nothing more than a pile of golden coins.

"The Desolation has come sooner than I expected!" the prince exclaimed. "All the while we Questors were trying to reach the Abbey, his forces were on the march--and we did not realize it. We might easily have run into them!"

"The Lord of Desolation does not see everything, even in his own realm," said the Mage.

"His forces will have to stop--at least temporarily--when they reach the Sunder," the Abbot observed.

"They can blast the Abbey to pieces from the farther shore," said Pavarr. "They will hurl missiles to breach the walls."

"I think not, my son," replied the Abbot calmly. "Our walls are not made of ordinary stone, but of star-fallen material. The Desolation's weapons cannot harm them. What he wants is not our Abbey but the *Sendara*, and he must have her alive. With her in his power, he can control the Graelands, and then--I need not tell you--he will command the Labyrinth World. But he can only come near her if someone in the Abbey betrays us. And I know of no traitors here."

"If your walls hold, and the enemy cannot pass the Sunder in spate, Flavia is safe--as long as she remains in the Abbey," Pavarr concluded. "And we still have time to arm the battlements. Give me your permission, Father Abbot, to summon reinforcements from Taraman. My warriors are ready; they will come by the unguarded Eastern Pass through the Mountains of Zund and be here in a matter of--"

"Wait, my son." The Abbot raised his hand. "Even in the face of invasion, the Abbey must never become a source of destruction. Summon your friends if you wish, for all are welcome here, but my oath of office forbids me to allow a weapon to be fired in anger from these walls."

The prince's jaw worked with tension, but he bowed his head before the Abbot.

"Prince Pavarr!" called the Mage from his position at the telescope, which he had turned so that it looked back at the River Sunder. "You have not yet seen this."

Far up the Sunder, where for centuries past it had roared down the flanks of the mountain chain, a horde of *wyrga* were erecting a massive barricade against the raging waters, a dam in two halves made of dark metal. The *wyrga* crews and the gigantic engines pushed the dam's two parts out into the river from either side. By mischance several *wyrga* fell into the roiling waters and went under, but none of their comrades made any attempt to rescue them.

The dam's construction advanced slowly, for the Sunder itself fought against it, but as Pavarr kept watch, the two halves inched steadily toward each other. The mighty Sunder was about to be imprisoned, and the river would shrink as a lake formed behind the dam. The prince knew that eventually the river would be reduced to the size of a stream, and then no natural defense prevented the *wyrga* army from crossing the riverbed and climbing the walls of the Abbey.

"Prince Pavarr!" Mil called, and came into the observation tower, Hera Vespasia on her shoulder. "You have seen? You know what we face?"

"I have seen, and I know," he replied.

"As Sister Hesperia told us, the sword *Greenhallow* must be taken from the Ruined Chapel," the Abbot reminded them, "and brought back before the entire Abbey is cut off."

"I will go, and gladly," said Pavarr. "Firemark will bear me."

"The distance is too great!" Mil told him. "The Ruined Chapel is almost half a world away in the Icewode. Even with Firemark's speed, you cannot go there and return before battle is joined. And that will be soon—I calculate another day and night at most!"

"Is there no other way?" asked the Abbot. "The Flying Horses--"

"Sornor and Beghed are on patrol near the Bordering Cliffs," said Hera Vespasia. "Swift as they are, they cannot be summoned in time. And their regiment is even farther away."

"Then--" the Abbot began, his brow creasing.

"There is another way," Mil said hurriedly. "My ring--the *Vindr* Talisman! Here," tugging it off the forefinger of her left hand, "wear this. It will give you supernatural speed--but you alone, on foot, not on Firemark or any other mount. It may be used three times only, then must be given to someone else, but it will take you to the Ruined Chapel and back. Speak this Word of Power when you use it," and she whispered the Word in Pavarr's ear.

Firemark objected to this plan in no uncertain terms, for he and Pavarr had faced every venture together, and no created being in the Labyrinth World could outrun the stallion. For the prince to go without him was, to Firemark, unthinkable.

"I am sorry, my friend," said Pavarr. "It is none of my liking, but the *Foressa* is right. I must go alone and on foot. I will be back by darkfall tomorrow."

Hera Vespasia flew down from a rafter to land on the stall door. "Go now, Prince! The way is clear. And grace go with you!"

Pavarr twisted the bezel of the ring into the palm of his hand, murmured the Word of Power, and vanished into Threshold Forest.

The Ruined Chapel was as the Questors had left it: cold, empty, ungiving of its secrets. The marble bier upon which Flavia had lain kept no trace of her. Pavarr barely glanced at the four stained-glass windows in the wall next to the bier. If he had, he would have seen the Abbey, the cat, the rose, and the Hermit exactly as they had been, showing no sign of life.

But the Hermit watched and waited.

Carefully Pavarr studied the space around him, testing air and ground, gathering whatever information he could before proceeding to his goal: the great sword *Greenhallow* standing at the head of the bier. Sensing no immediate threat, he went cautiously toward the bier--and froze. Outside the rose window--wasn't that a moving shadow? There!--and gone! Not bird or animal, but human-shaped and purposeful in its movement.

Quick as thought, the prince had his Dwarvian dagger out and crouched into a defensive stance. No place to hide in here. He kept silent and waited.

The shadow passed.

Pavarr pivoted to follow, anticipated where the shadow would emerge in a clear space between the ruined columns. He thought he knew what was coming...

The shadow appeared in the empty space--and Pavarr did not understand.

The thing was a *wyrga*! But a silver light radiated from it--a light no *wyrga* could ever contain! And--was that the faint outline of silver armor? But as quickly as the prince perceived it so, the *wyrga*-shape came back, iron-barred head and demented form, a *thringa*-weapon clutched in its hand.

For a long moment the two enemies stared at each other, taking the measure of each other, assessing the threat.

Then one of them moved--neither one knew which--and the *wyrga* struck out! Pavarr dodged easily, leaped sideways so that the marble bier was at his back.

The *wyrga* followed, closed the gap between them to within striking range. It stopped, the *thringa* aimed at Pavarr, ready to slash-- but it held fire.

Pavarr sidestepped slowly, nearer to the great sword, and wondered why the *wyrga* didn't charge when it had the advantage. A *wyrga* attacking from this short distance would be impossible to escape, for the iron exoskeleton made it practically invulnerable, and the great vein on the back of its skull was all but unreachable in a face-to-face attack. Pavarr's only hope was to get close enough to *Greenhallow* to wrest it from its place and use it in his own defense.

The *wyrga* took a stumbling step forward, raised the *thringa*-- but the silver light shone round about it again, and the outline of silver armor. A blurred face appeared for an instant behind the iron bars of the exoskeleton. The *wyrga* staggered, and the *thringa* fell to the marble floor. The *wyrga* sank to its knees, as if on the point of collapse. Its head rolled onto its chest; its shoulders sagged.

Pavarr stayed where he was, tense, dagger ready, for never had he seen a *wyrga* act in this way. Never did *wyrga* attack alone; never had the prince seen one weakening, as this one seemed to be. He took a cautious step toward it.

But all at once the *wyrga* began to change, and Pavarr stood still again, hardly believing the evidence of his own eyes. The outline of shining armor returned, solidified, melted into an iron exoskeleton again. The silver light reappeared, grew brighter, dimmer, brighter again, while the *wyrga* wavered back and forth from its hideous form into something entirely other--a shape resembling a knight in armor.

The face behind the iron exoskeleton became a human mortal's face--one that Pavarr recognized.

"Tirgon!" the prince shouted, and dropped his weapon to his side.

From behind him a Shape of Darkness sprang at Pavarr! The prince, all his instincts on alert, dodged away and struck back with his dagger—to no effect. The Shape pursued, opened its cloaked arms to engulf him--and suddenly fell back as a *thringa*-weapon tore through it. For an instant the Shape bent over as if in pain, then turned toward the source of its wounding: Tirgon, too exhausted from his transmutation to move out of its way.

Taking advantage of the thing's distraction, Pavarr leaped to the head of the marble bier and seized *Greenhallow*. With one mighty effort he raised it from its place and swung it in a shining circle. The blade cut through the Shape, singing as it whirled, and the Shape crumbled into nothingness.

The prince strode swiftly to where Tirgon knelt, lifted the sword again--and touched the wounded warrior's shoulder with the blade. "Arise and be healed, Sir Knight Tirgon, Commander of the Legions of Light!"

Pavarr raised the knight--no longer *wyrga*--and embraced his old friend, companion of his youth.

Behind the prince the Shape of Darkness reassembled, slowly and as if in agony.

Behind the Darkness, the Hermit in the stained-glass window waited.

The Shape grew to ceiling height. Now fully visible, it moved to attack, unseen by either man until the sudden clatter of a pail thrown on the floor alerted them to danger. In a flash both men swiveled and took postures of defense.

"Enough, my son!" the Hermit cried, and stepped out of his window.

The Shape whirled to face him, thrust out an empty sleeve.

"Enough!" said the Hermit again, and began the gestures of Disenchantment to undo the magical workings by which he had made his unnatural son.

The Shape wavered, became stronger, wavered again. It tried to move toward the Hermit, but the power of Disenchantment held it back by invisible chains.

"Do not resist, my son Klone!" the Hermit commanded as tears ran down his cheeks. "I made you a thing of evil, child of my own pride and arrogance! You stole the *Sendara* from the Mort-Mire; I knew it and did not stop you! I sent the Questors on divergent paths so that they might be destroyed. I betrayed my vows; I must make them right again!"

The Shape hurled itself against the magical barriers; they did not yield.

"Return to the elements, my son!" the Hermit cried. "Let us both be at peace!"

A face under the black hood materialized, livid with rage. All at once the Hermit threw up his hands. The invisible chains broke, and the Shape lunged forward. It was already beginning to dissolve, but it clasped its melting, empty sleeves around the Hermit's throat. Father and son struggled together, yielding at last to inevitable death.

Pavarr and Tirgon buried the Hermit in the little cemetery behind the Ruined Chapel. Inside its rusted wrought-iron fence were four or five graves of former Hermits, their headstones cracked and twined with withered brown vines. Of Brother Klone there was nothing left, for the Hermit's son had dislimned into its constituent atoms. These had returned to the mineral kingdom to be transformed to a greater purpose, for in the economy of the Creator nothing is lost, nothing is wasted.

The two men spoke the Word of Peace for the souls of the Hermit and Brother Klone. Afterward, they talked of the tasks awaiting them.

"I must take *Greenhallow* back to the Abbey," said Pavarr. "Only with it can we overcome the forces ranged against us."

"You mean to confront the Lord of Desolation," Tirgon declared, guessing his friend's unspoken purpose.

"It will be so," nodded Pavarr. "Will you come with me? You had no equal among the Companions in battle."

Tirgon was thoughtful for a moment, studying the ground. "My friend, as long as my Companions remain in the Realm of the Stonemen, waiting for release, I am bound to go there. I will seek a way to restore them to the life we had. When we ride together once more as Companions of the Noble Way, then we will join you, and nothing shall stand against us!"

"The journey to that Realm will take many weeks," said Pavarr. "How will you go? Is your horse nearby?"

Tirgon shook his head. "Astara escaped my fate. I sent her to the outer meadows of the Graelands before the *wyrga* captured me. I can call her with my thought, and she will meet me at the Bordering Cliffs. I know of many secret paths through the Icewode and Threshold Forest."

"Even so, the way is long, and will be harder now--"

"And I have lost my *wyrga* powers," Tirgon acknowledged. "They can run for days without tiring, and need no sleep. No longer can I do those things."

The two friends pondered their seemingly intractable problem.

"I have the *Vindr* Ring, the talisman of great speed!" the prince remembered. "If I give it to you-"

"But you need it to return to the Abbey," Tirgon protested. "The *wyrga* army may invade at any time!"

A whicker sounded in the wood beyond the Chapel cemetery, and Firemark walked toward them. He shook his head reproachfully at Pavarr.

"All the years we've been together, and I still don't know everything you can do!" Pavarr said, stroking the horse's neck. "Tirgon, take the *Vindr* Ring. Recall the Companions to their duty, and grace be with us all!"

"Grace be with us all!" Tirgon responded. Turning the bezel of the ring inward and speaking the Word of Power, he sped on foot toward the distant Bordering Cliffs.

Ab'addon stood before the stunted little bush from which Oliver had plucked its one rosebud. "Wraith!"

Saint Amber's Rose

"Lord Ab'addon?" replied the Wraith Gloom, appearing instantly, knowing that nothing could save him and glad in his heart that the last act of his life had been to place the Rose in Oliver's care.

"Where is he? Where is Medley?"

"I do not know, Lord."

"You showed him how to leave my castle. You gave him the Rose!"

"I did, Lord—but I did not *give* him the Rose. He found it by himself and took it in innocence, as the Prophecy said he would! And when he understands how to use it—your lordship's rule of the Labyrinth will be at an end!"

Ab'addon made no reply. He shuddered, and black flames shot from his eyes. His body dissolved into a fiery whirlwind, and his hands of fire stretched toward the Wraith... The Wraith vanished, swallowed up in darkness.

A howl of unappeasable rage exploded from Castle Mormorion. A Shape of black flame shot out of its topmost tower, heading for the remote Mountains of Zund.

Charleynne Gates

Chapter Thirty-One

The Way of the Great Mountain

The Gift is the power--not you, the Gift. The test of your
strength will be in your ability to bring the Gift to others.
Remember, the Gift is the power! Give the power to others,
when the time is right.
                    --David Morehouse, *Psychic Warrior*

Lap, lap. Sssh, lap. Little wavelets slapped against the rocky
shore of the Sunder as it rounded the cliff on whose towering height
stood the Abbey of Saint Amber. Rising behind the Abbey, blotting out
much of the night sky, stood the formidable Great Mountain of Zund.
Dark blue clouds veiled its summit and swallowed the faint light of the
scattered stars.

The keel of the *Marrowbone* scraped against gravel on a narrow
beach on the mountain's foot, just high enough to let its passengers
climb out. "Steady!" came Captain Bones's whispered command.
"Over the side, and don't make more noise than you can help!" to the
Questors, and "Cast off! Lively, now!" to the skeletal seamen, who at
once shoved away from the thin strip of crumbling rock. "Good faring!
Keep the wind in your sails!" came back as a fading echo.

With these encouraging words to buoy them up, Bertie, Oliver,
Tipp, and Tapp jumped off the retreating boat and landed on a shore
hardly wider than a footprint. Quickly they scrambled up the strip of
sharp-edged stones and took shelter under an overhanging ledge of the
mountain to regroup. They watched the boat with its skeleton crew
return down the diminished Sunder, its current still swift enough to bear
the *Marrowbone* all too rapidly out of sight.

Although his clothes were dry--more or less--and they were
temporarily out of the icy wind that blew perpetually around the Great
Mountain, Oliver shivered. Here they were, at the Abbey at last, but in

an apparently hopeless situation. *How are we supposed to get into the Abbey?* It seemed impossible, even though the Abbey's back wall was only a stone's throw away.

Beside him, Bertie shivered also. Much as he tried to suppress his fear, his teeth chattered like a fistful of loose pebbles. "Mr. Medley!" he whispered. "What do we do now?"

Feeling more at a loss than he ever had in his life, Oliver shook his head. "I don't know," he said unhappily, and wished the knot of anxiety in his stomach would untangle itself.

"Seems to me," said Tipp, "that we'd best follow the captain's advice. He said something about a stair nearby. And there is that Hidden Way—if we can find it. Don't know if our mind maps'll work in this territory."

"Feels like there's shadows all around us," muttered Tapp, to no one in particular.

"Well, if there is a stairway, it must go up into the Abbey," said Tipp optimistically, "otherwise, how would the friars be able to get down here? And they do: I detect the signs of their passing. And look up there, where the water line used to be: See that old post for mooring boats? But where might such a stairway be?"

"Can't see much," said Tapp, squinting in the opposite direction up the formidable Great Mountain, whose rough peaks loomed over the Abbey. "Too dark."

Oliver took in a deep breath of cold air and yawned wider than he intended. He lost his balance and staggered back a step or two. "Ow!"

"Ssh!" said Tipp and Tapp together.

Oliver tore his mantle free from a bush whose thorns had poked him cruelly in the back. Its scraggly black branches, camouflaged in the darkness, grew through cracks in the ledge and spread out across the cliff face.

"Say, what's that?" Tapp exclaimed, pointing beyond Oliver to something behind the thorns.

"What?" asked Tipp.

"I thought I saw a flash of light or something."

"Where? Oh! in back of these!" said Tipp. He approached the bush and began putting the branches aside, taking care to avoid their long, hard spikes.

-- 525 --

"What are you doing?" Tapp asked.

"I thought I saw it, too," Tipp replied, "just for a second, behind this bush. Ow!" as a thorn-point scraped his cheek

"Might be an entrance to the mountain behind that bush." said Tapp. He took out his Dwarvian dagger, which gleamed faintly in the darkness. "But I can't see anything from here."

He moved closer cautiously, dodging the thorns, and turned his dagger from side to side, trying to catch any least ray of light and reflect it against the back wall of their shelter. One flash illuminated a thread-thin outline which caught and held the light. "There's something. Can't tell what that is," Tipp observed.

"Could it be Dwarf work?" Oliver asked. "The entrance to one of their hidden passages?"

"No," said Tipp and Tapp simultaneously.

"We know the marks of Dwarf-kin," Tapp explained. "There aren't any here."

"How can you possibly..." know that, Oliver started to say, then abandoned the intention. It really was too dark to see much of anything, but for lack of any other explanation he had to accept their word in the matter.

Bertie thought it was about his turn to speak. He had been trained from his youth to be respectful of his elders and not to talk quite so much when grown-ups were discussing an important matter, but in this instance the grown-ups seemed to be veering rather far from the immediate concern.

"Maybe we should go up and see what it is?" he asked, pointing out the obvious. "If it's an entrance, maybe we could figure out how it opens."

Tipp, Tapp, and Oliver looked at Bertie, then at the glimmer of light.

"I mean, couldn't we cut away some of the thorns and get closer?" Bertie continued when no one answered.

"We might," said Tipp slowly, after some pondering. "But we'd have to be very careful how we did it. The Great Mountain of Zund isn't like other mountains. It's more... hmm... alive, I think. Whatever it keeps, it keeps til the end of Time. That's what they say. See, those thorns are growing there for a reason. It won't do to be prying into places we shouldn't. The Mountain might not like it."

"There's stories about them that tried to get inside it," said Tapp. "None of 'em ever came out the same way again."

Leaving that question unanswered for the moment, by unspoken consensus they considered other options. Craning their necks, they peered out from the sheltered overhang and gawked up the impossibly steep sides of the Great Mountain.

"Do you think it's climbable?" asked Tapp in a whisper.

"It's solid rock," replied Tipp. "Doesn't look like there's anything to hold on to, and we didn't bring the proper equipment." Without the proper equipment, it was obvious that such a climb wasn't to be thought of.

Straining to see across the dark strip of river, the four Questors tried to estimate the condition of the outer wall of the Abbey, but its stonework looked to be as unclimbable as the Great Mountain.

"Now what?" Tapp inquired. "There's no way to get inside that I can see—not the Great Mountain or the Abbey."

Tipp shook his head. "Doesn't look like it. I'm afraid we're at an impasse. Friend Oliver? What do you think?"

But Oliver had sunk down and stiffened in a crouching position against the wall. A bitter wind invaded the interior of their precarious shelter and slid its frigid fingers down his spine, but he hardly felt it. He wished he felt anything except this pervasive dread. After traveling countless *kephan* through forests, tunnels, lakes, and rivers in a strange and often terrifying world, having endured experiences he could hardly bear to remember, much less make heads or tails of, his limbs simply refused to function any more. He realized that it was a paralysis of will rather than of body, but it didn't seem to matter.

The Servant of the Desolation, who had followed Oliver like his shadow all the way from his own sunlit garden, leaned over and blew its Stygian breath around him. The Menace of the Dark fell upon him, and he went cold with fear. He couldn't have moved a step if Death itself had stood in front of him.

"Mr. Medley?" said Bertie. "What's the matter? Are you sick or something?"

Oliver formed words with his lips, but nothing came out of his throat except a dry rasp. He tried again: same result. He shook his head "no," but once he started, he couldn't stop until Tapp clapped him on the shoulder.

Charleynne Gates

"Steady on, Friend Oliver," said the Dwarvian firmly. "We've made it this far; we can make it the rest of the way. And look here: You're not the same person who showed up at Keeper's Inn. You've lost weight, walking this far across the Labyrinth World. You've toughened up. You're stronger than you think you are."

Tipp frowned in thought. "The captain said there was a stairway--"

"A Hidden Way, you said," Tapp pointed out.

"I know what I said," Tipp responded in an irritated tone. "I just can't locate it on my mind-map at the moment."

"I can't see any sign of a stairway where it ought to be," said Tapp. "They're usually on the outside of a mountain and go around it in a spiral."

"You're thinking of mounds," Tipp corrected. "Burial mounds, like the ones the Elder Folk built."

"Maybe the stair's inside the mountain," said Bertie. "Maybe it's hollow inside. Meaning no disrespect to the—the Mountain, maybe it wouldn't mind if we cut away a little bit of that bush..."

The Dwarvians paid him no attention.

"A Word of Power'd probably open that doorway," Tipp mused. "If we only knew the right one."

"Which we don't," said Tapp.

"Hcra Vespasia knows some of the old Words of Power," Tipp mused.

"She's not here," Tapp observed. "It's just us."

"I think we need more help than just us," Oliver ventured.

"Nobody around here but us," said Tapp, his voice rough to hide his emotion.

Tipp frowned and pulled on his lower lip. "I guess we need to start working on that thorn-bush," he said reluctantly, "even if the Mountain doesn't like it. Come on, Brother. It'll take both our daggers to cut through that tangle."

The two Dwarvians started toward the thorn-bush, daggers out and gleaming, but no sooner had their blades touched the first twig than a deep rumble sounded under their feet, and the Great Mountain began to shake. New cracks appeared in the cliff face, and a shower of pebbles and dust began to fall. The Questors huddled together as far under the ledge as they could, for larger rocks came next, and last of all a boulder or two crashed down and splashed into the river. After that, the Mountain quieted, as if it had made its point.

After a few more moments of fearful waiting, the Questors ventured out of their shelter, but stopped in their tracks as the light behind the thorn-bush began to shine brighter and brighter, and slowly filled in the outline of an arched door.

"Look!" Bertie gasped, his eyes nearly falling out of his head. He hardly needed to point, for Tipp, Tapp, and Oliver were already staring as hard as they could.

The thorn branches across the doorway moved aside by themselves, and a tall figure walked out of the door.

"Fear not, Friends," said the tall figure, and Oliver, who could scarcely believe the evidence of his eyes, recognized the Mage Dandriel in his indigo robes. He looked less substantial than Oliver remembered, hazier in a way, as if he weren't really there. But the next moment Oliver had forgotten the impression.

"W-who's that?" gasped Bertie.

"I am Dandriel. Do not be alarmed, Bertie Mossgrower. Yes, I know who you are. I know, as well, your steadfast courage and your loyalty to the Gift-Bringer."

Bertie's mouth gaped as he puzzled over the meaning of this pronouncement.

"Friends Tipp and Tapp."

The Dwarvians removed their hats and bowed low before Dandriel.

"Oliver Medley." The Mage turned and looked straight into his eyes, into the depths of his shivering soul. "Oliver Medley, your great task lies before you. Have you discovered the secret of your Gift?"

Oliver shook his head again. "No," he said sadly. "I really don't believe I have any special Gift."

The Mage's brows drew together like thunder; his eyes flashed under his deep hood. "If you had no Gift, you would not have been brought into this world!" he said sternly. "The time for doubt is past, Oliver Medley. The time for discerning your Gift is here. The time for using it is soon to come. There must be no more delay! The *wyrga* army has surrounded the Abbey. Soon they will cut off the Sunder's flow entirely. Then their forces will sweep over the Abbey and annihilate all life within its walls. Remember your promise to the *Sendara* Flavia!"

Oliver shivered and bowed his head.

"Bertie Mossgrower, come to me!" With a swirl of his cloak, the Mage beckoned to the lad. Bertie, impelled by a shove from behind (delivered by Tipp), stumbled forward to stand before Dandriel.

"One of you must climb the secret stairway into the Abbey and tell the Abbot and the *Sendara* that the time of battle draws near. Tell them that the Forge of Unmaking will be fired again." The two Dwarvians glanced hastily at each other and came to attention, ignoring the icy wind. "And say to them that Oliver Medley will ascend the Great Mountain to give the signal for battle.

"Bertie Mossgrower, will you accept this charge?" the Mage went on.

Bertie sensed the great opportunity of his life opening before him and took it. "I will, sir! I will!" he said, and put his whole heart into his promise.

"And tell the Abbot," Dandriel continued, "to gather the Community of Saint Amber into the Grand Sanctuary--and sing!"

"Sing?" Bertie questioned, not sure he had heard correctly. "But sir, if the Abbey is being attacked--?"

"Sing!" repeated the Mage. "They must sing down the light."

"Wait! Wait!" Oliver interrupted as the Mage's commands wove their way through his mind. "I--I'm ascending the Great Mountain? But I can't climb--"

"I will show you the way," the Mage answered, and returned his attention to Bertie. "Come!" The Mage walked swiftly back to the cliff wall, vanishing into the door in the stone. Bertie ran to catch up and also vanished into the doorway.

The Dwarvians waited imperturbably, as did Oliver. He didn't know what else to do. His mouth hung foolishly open.

"Take this stair," said the Mage to Bertie as they stood inside the Great Mountain. (Bertie's guess had been right: The Great Mountain's core was hollow!) "Follow it to the gate under the river. The gate will be above water now, and you will be able to squeeze past its bars. The river channel will take you into the Abbey. Remember your charge!"

And he was gone, leaving Bertie alone at the top of a dimly lit stairway carved into the wall of the cave. Bertie set his foot on the first step and began his descent into deeper shadow, with the odor of swift water coming to him more strongly. After a while the steps became damper, and cold beads of moisture dripped at random from the low ceiling. One icy pearl of water plopped on the back of Bertie's neck and inched down under his collar. He shivered and went steadily on.

The silver doorway vanished, locking Bertie into the cliff, and Dandriel returned to the remaining Questors. He beckoned to the Dwarvians. "Friends, as you know, deep in the heart of the Great Mountain lies the Forge of Unmaking. If it is your will, descend and awaken the ancient fires once more, that they may consume the evil of the Lord of Desolation. Will you accept this charge?"

"For this destiny we were born," Tipp proclaimed, with a touch of pomposity.

"And we will fulfill it," added Tapp.

"Come!" said the Mage, and strode back to the silver doorway. The two Dwarvians followed, leaving Oliver alone in the inadequate shelter of the ledge as icy air currents whipped around him.

"Now, Friend Oliver!" ordered the Mage, returning and walking swiftly in a northerly direction farther around the mountain. Oliver trotted after him.

When he caught up, the Mage was making magical passes at a crack between two boulders at the mountain's base. The crack widened slowly as Oliver watched. Given what had happened to Bertie and the Dwarvians, he had a sinking feeling that he too was about to be locked inside that looming eruption of earth and stone.

He didn't want to be. His blood ran cold with dread. Close to panic, he wanted nothing more than to leave these premises as fast as he could and forget everything that had happened to him, except...

Flavia. Lady of Light, to whom he had promised his life, his honor, and his fealty—his faithfulness--"'til the world's end," he recalled himself saying. His life at present probably meant little, but his sworn fealty? That was worth his life, his honor, and everything he had.

Because I love her. And without love, I am nothing.

When Dandriel had finished his mystic gestures, he turned again to face Oliver, who stood steadfast despite his trepidation. The thin crack behind Dandriel had widened soundlessly until there was a space

-- 531 --

just large enough for someone of Oliver's height and breadth to enter. Beyond was blackness.

"Oliver Medley," Dandriel began. "Before you lies the Way of the Great Mountain. At its summit you will find the chamber wherein dwells the Repository of Saint Amber."

"But what is the Repository, and what does it have to do with my—my Gift?" Oliver found courage to ask.

"No one now alive knows the answer to your question. I can tell you only that it was created in the First Age and placed inside the mountain by the Founder of the Abbey, who then sealed it shut. No one has disturbed it since that time."

"But why--" Oliver started to ask, but couldn't find the right words.

"Why were you chosen?" the Mage finished his question. "Simply because you are the Gift-Bringer, the One Without Guile, identified as such by our ancient prophecies. We are certain of it, or we would not have sent Belvedine de Montfort to fetch you."

"Great-Aunt Belvedine? But she didn't explain anything about it!"

A small sigh escaped the Mage. "We realize that, but there is no more time. Your Gift, Friend Oliver, is linked to the Rose of Saint Amber. In some way not known to us, you alone are able to make the Rose bloom again. Will you accept this charge?"

"I will," said Oliver. "But how will I know what--?"

"It will be made known to you," said the Mage. Putting his hands on Oliver's shoulders, the Mage gently pushed him through the crevice between the boulders. "Remember your promise. *Va'in 'a moru'.*"

The crevice closed, and Oliver was left unhappily alone in darkness so absolute that he couldn't see his hand before his face.

Bertie Mossgrower climbed down the stone stairway... and down until he felt as if he had been treading these steps most of his life. And it looked as if several hundred more steps went down from where he stood. Once in a while even he, young and active as he was, had to stop and rest. But at least there was a glimmer of light from above, a long, mist-laden sliver, as if from a crack in the stone somewhere. The stairs ended at an iron grating, as the Mage had said. The top half rose above the water, and the bottom half went down to the bottom of the river—or the sluiceway, as Bertie figured it was.

The place was too dark to see how far down the bottom was, but Bertie wasn't concerned about the possibility of swimming. It was the narrow space between the grating bars that worried him. Being an active boy, he was lean and lithe, but could he squeeze through, as the Mage thought?

If the purpose of the grating was to stop large river creatures from getting into the Abbey, Bertie reasoned, maybe it didn't go all the way to the bottom. In that case, he'd just dive down and swim underneath to the other side.

He took off his shoe and stuck his foot in the water to test it— and felt the spongy resistance of a living creature. A slug-like head reared up and groped for him with two of its taloned tentacles. Bertie jerked his foot back, and the tentacles, feeling around without result, vanished under the water.

No wonder they put up an iron grate!

Swimming obviously wasn't an option: He'd either have to squeeze through the grating above water or else give up and go back. Admit failure.

I'll never do that! I won't fail them!

Holding his breath, then exhaling, sucking in his stomach as much as possible, Bertie tried squeezing through the space between the last iron bar and the stone wall. It was a slow, painful business, but at last he got through. Going on, he began climbing up again by another tedious, winding staircase.

Doesn't it ever end? But it did at last, and Bertie saw a brighter sliver of light through the mist. It came from beneath a wooden trap door that did not quite fit into its place. There was a gap of half an inch or so on one side, and through it shined a faint, rather soggy light, as if beyond the door was a damp room.

A cellar?

Bertie crept up to the trap door, put his palms experimentally against it, and pushed. Much to his surprise, the door yielded--not easily, creaking in protest, as if it hadn't been opened in a long time, maybe centuries.

Bertie peeked out through the crack, squinting to make out through the dusk what those big round shapes were, lined up along the walls. After a while he realized that they were barrels... possibly wine-barrels. He must have emerged into the Abbey cellars!

He exhaled, relieved that he'd actually made it. Probably not many people came down here among the barrels holding the harvest of the seasons, quietly aging. Purple Valley had vineyards and wineries, too, so Bertie was fairly confident of what the barrels were for. (The Abbey vintage was as far superior to Purple Valley's as a waterfall is to a mud puddle, but Bertie was too inexperienced to know that.)

This place was most likely not disturbed very often. They might have someone check the barrels once in a while. All the better! Easier to get access inside the Abbey without being stopped before he got to the Abbot. *If I can find the Abbot.* He remembered that he didn't have any idea where anything was in the Abbey, and certainly no idea where the Abbot was likely to be.

No matter. His charge was to find the Abbot and deliver the message to him and to the *Sendara*. He had promised, and he would do what he promised, whatever might happen to him.

Once again he made himself as small as possible to edge through the slender opening (the trap door was very heavy, constructed of thick planks bound together with broad iron bands, and Bertie didn't want to let it creak any more than he could help) and found himself behind a shelf of casks. Quickly extricating himself with the least possible noise, he tried to close the door so it would look undisturbed. He nearly did it without any sound, but at the last moment the thing escaped him and fell into place with a muffled boom.

Bertie froze, fearing someone had overheard, but after several minutes no one appeared. It seemed that the cellar was deserted—at least for the moment.

Slowly, on tiptoe, he made his way through the rows of barrels. There were a great many of them, far more than he had imagined, and the rows wound through the cellars until, even with his keen sense of direction, he was thoroughly confused. Light was intermittent, filtered through a miasma drifting through the passageways.

At last he came into a different room, one with even more barrels than the first, and in one corner was a trap door. For an instant Bertie's heart leaped into his throat.

Did I walk in a circle and come back where I started?

Saint Amber's Rose

He was about to tiptoe over to the trap door to make sure, when he halted abruptly in the middle of the room. *It isn't the same trap door!* This one was chained to a large iron bolt in the floor and fastened by a ponderous padlock. It looked as if nothing could get in or out, not past that padlock and chain.

What are they trying to keep down here that they don't want to escape? Or is it the other way around? Is there something outside that they don't want to come in?

Curious, Bertie started to go closer to see why this trap-door was locked in such a manner, but just then he heard a tiny noise--a soft sound like a voice muttering to itself, asking itself questions and answering them in the next breath. He darted behind a row of barrels and hid, peering out between two of them.

Whatever he might have expected, it wasn't this: a young woman in a long green robe cinctured by a white rope that seemed to have been recently dragged in the mud. Her hair streamed in bedraggled strings down her shoulders, and her face--what Bertie could see of it in the dusk--was pale as old ashes. He thought she might have been crying, but he wasn't sure. At any rate, she seemed distressed about something.

Bertie's first impulse was to reveal himself and ask how he might help her--she was pretty despite her mud-spattered clothes and unkempt hair--but she appeared to be speaking to someone, and he had been brought up not to interrupt others.

The young woman came closer, meandering, to where he was hiding. Occasionally she stumbled over a chip in the stone tiles, but managed to catch herself awkwardly before she fell.

Now Bertie understood where the soft muttering had come from: The woman was talking to herself. There was no one else nearby.

"He loves me," Bertie heard. "He loves me. I know he does. He wants to come to me. He loves me. I know he does. He loves me." She repeated the words over and over, half-whispering, half-pleading, and at length Bertie understood.

The poor young woman had gone mad. Some terrible thing must have happened to turn her mind like that. *Should I go up to her? Or would his sudden appearance frighten her, make her condition worse?*

Charleynne Gates

As he pondered the question, she came nearer to the row of wine-barrels where he was hiding, so close that he could have reached out and touch the hem of her robe just by moving a finger. He held his breath, hoping she wouldn't detect his presence.

To his relief, she passed by his hiding place without noticing the extra shadow among the barrels. Bertie watched her walk hesitantly, stumbling occasionally, toward the padlocked trap door. Her back was toward Bertie, but he saw her stop in front of the trap door and take a big, rusty key out of a pocket in her robe, talking to herself all the while.

Kneeling, she fumbled with the padlock--too big for her small hands--and dropped the key. It slid away toward Bertie's hiding place, slipping across the slick tiles, heading in a straight line directly for his feet. With no time to get out of its path, he drew in his toes as much as he could and held his breath. The young woman scurried on hands and knees after the key, muttering as she crawled. Bertie's flesh crept as she neared him, her hands patting the floor ahead of her to find the key, and he was nearly sick with revulsion when he finally understood what she was saying.

"It wasn't my fault. I had to kill her--Sister Valerian. She wanted him! She was going to open the gate and let him in. But it's me the Dark Man wants. Not her. It's me he loves. I couldn't let her have him. I had to take my knife and cut her throat."

Only by the utmost self-control did Bertie keep himself from moving out of her way—and quickly. He bit his lips together to keep from screaming. That fragile-looking young woman was a murderer!

To his extreme relief, the woman found the key less than two inches from his little toe. Her fingers closed around it, and she gave a glad little chortle which made Bertie's blood run cold. Then she stood up and staggered back to the iron trap door. This time she managed to fit the rusty key into the rough old padlock. The key was difficult to turn, and Bertie automatically started to get up and help her. But he caught himself in time and stayed where he was.

After much struggle--Bertie actually saw blood trickle down her hand from where she cut it on a sharp edge--she got the key turned, and the shaft of the old padlock sprang from its hole. The woman slipped the chain off the padlock and took hold of the trap door by its handle. She tried to lift it, but its solid iron weight was too much for her. Again and again she made the effort, and again Bertie had to stifle the impulse to help her. Still the stubborn thing resisted.

Finally, exhausted, the woman dropped on all fours beside the trap door. After a few minutes, panting and wiping her brow, she stood up, and with shaking arms made another try. It was obvious to Bertie that she was using the last of her strength.

The trap door budged--not far, only the fraction of an inch--and groaned mightily as it was forced to yield. The woman couldn't lift the cover all the way back, but with a gasp she slid it aside, revealing a gaping black hole beneath it.

Bertie stared, wide-eyed, as a vapor emerged from the black hole, a faint gray mist with spots and flashes of iridescent color which rather bedazzled him. He had to tear his gaze away from it--which was harder to do than one would think.

The vapor grew taller, expanded, became the silhouette of a man. Sister Celeret dropped to her knees with a cry of joy and raised her arms toward it. "Lord Ab'addon!" she exclaimed. "Lord Ab'addon! You've come to me! I worship you--"

The man bent down, put his hands around her throat, and strangled her. It was over in a moment. He threw her body aside without a backward glance and stepped out of the black hole.

Bertie gasped. He didn't mean to; he couldn't have helped it.

The man looked up, saw Bertie staring at him--and smiled. "Come here, lad," he said, beckoning.

Despite himself, Bertie stood up, took a step out of his hiding place. Only a step, but it was enough, because then he had to take another step, and another, without intending to at all. The Dark Man drew him closer... closer...

"Go, Bertie! Run to the Abbot!" called another voice, and out of the shadows strode the Mage Dandriel. The spell broke. Bertie did not hesitate. He ran for his life, heading out the way he had seen the young woman come into the wine cellar.

"Mage!" Ab'addon defied him. "You are too late! You have no power here. Your presence is nothing but a thought projection. I will win in the end, and the Graelands—and the Rose--will be mine!"

Dandriel lifted his right hand, palm outward, against the Lord of Desolation. "Not by my power, but by the power of the Light, you will be defeated!"

Charleynne Gates

Ab'addon's form twisted, shrank into an indeterminate Shape of Darkness and glided so swiftly out of the wine cellar that he could not have been seen by anyone other than a Mage. Dandriel thought of following, but shook his head. His charge had been fulfilled; the final act must be accomplished by the One Without Guile. So said the Prophecy, and the Mage bowed his will before it.

Chapter Thirty-Two

The Forge and the Web

The stairway in the mountain spiraled down and around endlessly, or so it seemed to the two Dwarvians. The farther they descended, the warmer they became, "and it's not just from the exercise," Tapp remarked when they took a breather.

"No, the temperature is rising," Tipp agreed. "We are getting closer to the Forge."

"The Forge of Unmaking!" Tapp whispered. "I've always wondered if it was real, as the old stories said."

"It seems," Tipp responded, "that we're about to find out."

By the time they reached the bottom of the stairway, both Dwarvians had perspiration streaming down their faces.

"Look at that!" exclaimed Tipp, wiping salty droplets off his forehead.

"I am!" panted Tapp. Both of them stared straight ahead, where two gigantic iron doors blocked their way farther. Red-hot and glowing they were, putting out massive amounts of heat. The Dwarvians, experienced as they were in all kinds of metalwork, were hard put to it to figure out how the doors stayed red-hot without melting.

"Well, Brother, how do we get inside?" asked Tipp. "I'm assuming the Forge of Unmaking is behind those doors."

"Look up there, on the lintel!" Tapp pointed. "Aren't those words?"

"Aye, they are," said Tipp. Hand shading his eyes, he squinted at the raised symbols arched over the double doors. "They're written in an archaic dialect of Old Boreal. Proto-Zundian, as far as I can tell."

"So what do they say?"

Tipp read them with difficulty, one symbol at a time, translating them into Common Tongue.

Within the Forge, Unmaking Fire.
Count well the risk. Unmaker's ire
Unharnessed be: An ending dire,
When the world dissolves in fire!

"I don't like the sound of that," Tapp mumbled.

"Nor do I," said Tipp. "But we've gone too far to go back. The fate of the entire Labyrinth World may depend on us!"

"Um-hm." Tapp was accustomed to his brother's occasional outbursts of bluster. He understood that Tipp was trying to work up the courage to proceed, and frankly, so was he. "How do we open the doors? We can't get any closer; they're red-hot."

"Let's try an opening spell," said Tipp. Taking out his Dwarvian dagger, he pointed it toward the doors and made motions as if turning a key in a lock. Tapp did the same with his dagger. Together they spoke the spell in the ancient Dwarf tongue, hoping that the doors would recognize it and respond.

They did. As smoothly as if they were blocks of ice instead of molten metal, the two enormous doors opened slowly until they settled back against the interior walls, revealing a huge chasm inside.

Dancing flames leaped and writhed inside the vault of the Great Mountain. A narrow path led between the flames straight to a massive anvil, a black silhouette against the restless firelight playing on the wall behind it.

The two Dwarvians stared at the anvil and the hammers, tongs, and other tools of the smithy beside it.

"Here goes," said Tipp.

"Here goes," echoed Tapp.

"*a-TORR!*" they said together.

Taking a deep breath of overheated air, the Dwarvians walked without hesitation along the path to the anvil as the flames roared tall around them.

Behind them, the red doors swung shut again.

Darkness was total. Oliver stood where the Mage had left him, without a shred of light to show him where he was. *How am I supposed to climb if I can't see anything?*

Saint Amber's Rose

Having no choice, he waited. Waited for something to happen, for Dandriel to return, for light to shine, for the door to open and let him out. For answers to come.

None of those events took place.

He began to feel very apprehensive. *Is the Mage coming back? He must be; I can't see where to go. It's so dark in here... like the* Forbeodan *Tunnel... the cave where that serpent...* He cleared his throat convulsively. The sound went up into the vault of the mountain, echoing "hem-hem-hem" until it was lost to hearing.

Oliver turned around to face the direction where he thought they had entered and took a hesitant step forward, but immediately turned his ankle on the uneven, pebble-dotted ground and sat down abruptly. Now he did see light--little explosions of colored lights inside his eyelids.

Hyperventilating from the shock of his abrupt descent, he inhaled rapid gulps of air. Choking from the thick odor of earth, he had the acute sensation of hundreds of tons of dirt pressing down, crushing the life out of him. He was on the verge of panic when he heard a voice speaking to him from ground level, or so he thought.

"*M'sieur* Medlee!"

Whether the voice was inside or outside his head, he couldn't tell, but it repeated the statement.

"Y--yes?" he replied shakily. *Hallucinations... I'm having auditory hallucinations. Now I'm replying to myself.*

"*Permettez-moi* to present myself," said the speaker, with a distinct continental accent. "*Général Napoleon-Bonaparte d'Escargot* of the *corps militaire de gastéropodes*, at your service.*"

Oliver guessed, rather than saw, the accompanying bow.

"Oh... ah... *très heureux*," he responded with a gasp, having no time to consider the oddity of conversing in polite French in his present environment.

"We need, first of all," stated the *Général*, "a light. At your feet you will find flintstones. You may strike a light with them."

Obediently, Oliver felt around for the flintstones (the same pebbles which had caused his ankle to turn) and struck them together. A few sparks appeared and vanished.

"They won't... catch," he said, coughing in the musty air. "There's no tinder."

"*Encore*," came the inexorable command. "Again. You must try again."

Oliver kept striking the flintstones together, producing at last a series of sparks. They caught--not tinder, but thousands of shiny, winding lines of slime all over the walls. Snail-trails! As soon as they caught the light, they held it, and the whole interior of the mountain blazed out with uncountable candle-power. Oliver shut his eyes tightly, but couldn't escape the resulting headache.

When he felt that he might be able to bear the intense illumination, he opened his eyes to the narrowest of slits. What he saw before him was no illusion: He was inside the immense hollow core of the Great Mountain, and next to his feet was the source from whom he had been taking orders.

The voice did indeed belong to a snail. Not an ordinary garden snail, but one as big as a cat! He wore a military officer's hat in the style of Napoleon Bonaparte and possessed a pair of formidable black moustaches.

Perceiving that Oliver was able to see him, the snail levitated, raising its large single foot to its forehead in a military salute. Oliver bowed as best he could.

"*M'sieur* Medlee," the *Général* went on. "I desire to thank you, on behalf of the entire *famille d'Escargot*, for your *très généreux* act of clemency to my nephew, *Caporal* Gaston d'Escargot."

"Oh?" said Oliver, struggling in vain to decipher the meaning. "I don't recall... What act of clemency would that have been?"

"The lad was about to kill your so-beautiful rose, as he was assigned to do," replied the *Général*. "You permitted him to go free among the wild thyme instead of crushing him underfoot or eating him with garlic butter, as usually happens to us snails. We are all very grateful."

Oliver's cheeks turned pink. "Oh, well, please don't mention it. Happy to be of help."

"And so," continued the *Général*, "when our Command Center received intelligence of your Quest, we decided that we could be of assistance by lighting your way to the Repository of Saint Amber."

Oliver, still seated, snapped to attention. "*Mon Général*, do you know what the Gift of Saint Amber is?" he asked.

"*Je regrette, M'sieur,*" was the reply. "I do not. Everyone in the Labyrinth World knows where it is kept. It reposes itself in a sealed *chambre* inside the summit of the Great *Montagne*. That is all that we know."

Oliver pondered the implications of the *Général's* description and made up his mind that eventually he would have to stand up and do something. What that was to be, he could not imagine.

"Thus," continued the gastropod, "the matter of transporting you to the sealed *chambre* becomes of the utmost importance."

Oliver struggled to his feet and contemplated the now brilliantly-lighted interior. "I really cannot think how I am to get up so far. I was told there was a stairway, but there isn't one that I can see. And the Mage has locked me inside here."

Again he imagined the overwhelming weight of that mountain of earth and stone pressing down upon him... but by stiffening his will, mentally refused to allow the incursion of creeping claustrophobia.

"But the stairway, it has crumbled away long ago."

Oliver's spirits plummeted.

"But there can be more than one way to the top of a *montagne*," stated the *Général* enigmatically.

"Where are the other ways?" Oliver begged. "I cannot climb rock walls unaided, and I see no other way to the top."

"Mr. Medley! Mr. Medley!" cried a new voice at the level of his ear.

Oliver's head swiveled to locate the source. He found it directly before his eyes: a little black spider dangling from a nearly-invisible thread.

"Mr. Medley!" the spider repeated in a squeak. "Don't you remember me?"

Oliver stared at the black dot waving seven of its eight legs in an agitated manner. Reluctant as he was to believe in speaking spiders, he was forced to conclude that if snails had the ability to converse, there was no reason an arachnid could not do the same.

"I'm sorry... Have we met before?"

"Oh, yes!" replied the little creature. "In the Ruined Chapel. I was the Resident Arachnid at the time. You saved me from making a dropdown right into the *Sendara's* hair! Now do you remember? Oh, you do! I am so relieved! I was afraid you wouldn't, not that you had to, you're a very important person and I'm just one of the many, but I'm so thrilled that you do. Oh, my!" she continued, bobbing up and down on the end of her filament. "This is the most exciting day of my life. Imagine! I'm actually talking to the Gift-Bringer! My sisters will be green with envy! And--"

"Very happy to see you again," Oliver interrupted as courteously as he could manage, "but at the moment I am rather preoccupied with--"

"How to get to the top!" cried the little spider. "That's why I'm here! Mother Aranea sent me. Maybe you've heard of her? She's the Founding Mother of Clan Aranea. She stays mostly at her website on top of the Grimmerund, especially now that she's getting on in years. Rheumatism in her legs, you know. When you've got eight legs, that's a lot of aches and pains. Some of my sisters live near her, a few thousand of them, and they keep an eye on her. Not too closely, of course, on account of us spiders tend to eat our young if they don't move out of the nest when they're supposed to. I expect I'll do the same when I get married. Eat my young, I mean. I'm told they taste like chicken."

Oliver had no answer to this astonishing bit of information.

"Not that I've had the experience myself," she went on. "I'm still a single girl. Mother says I ought to be thinking about setting up a website of my own pretty soon. All my sisters are married, and I already have about a hundred thousand nieces and nephews. I just haven't met anyone who makes my heart flutter... Are you married, Mr. Medley?"

"No... no."

"Oh, dear, I am running on, aren't I?" the little spider ran on, with a touch of maidenly embarrassment. "I do get carried away and chatter a lot. My sisters are always telling me that. It's because I'm kind of nervous right now. I mean, it's such a big assignment! I've never had a mission this important before, but Mother Aranea said it was time for my mettle to be tested, whatever that means, so here I am."

"Assignment?" Oliver repeated, feeling left behind.

"Oh, I've completely forgotten to tell you! I've been appointed Acting Webmaster for Operation AmberRose. Me, Annie Aranea, Acting Webmaster! Oh, shame on me! I didn't introduce myself. What terrible manners! Please don't tell Mother Aranea. I'm Annie Aranea of the five-hundred-and-eighty-eight billionth Clan generation. I'm so honored to meet you officially at last, Mr. Medley!"

"Thank you. Very pleased to, ah, meet..." Oliver responded, wary of believing completely in the voluble arachnid dangling in front of his nose. "But if we might return to the subject at hand--"

"Which is getting you to Saint Amber's Rose!" said Annie Aranea. "That's why our clan mounted Operation AmberRose. If you'll just look up--"

Oliver looked up, shielding his eyes from the illumination produced by the silver snail-trails. There on the high walls were thousands--millions--of little black dots skittering to and fro, each one spinning strands of web filaments. As he watched, mesmerized, the strands began to weave together and form a rope ladder of cobweb silk, stronger than steel, which let down by degrees until it finally reached the ground where he stood.

"It's a ladder," Oliver said, stating the obvious.

"Yes!" Annie Aranea exclaimed delightedly. "It is! You can use it to climb up to the sealed chamber! Clan Aranea Spidersilk is the strongest thing there is in the Labyrinth World. It'll be perfectly safe."

Oliver stared at the delicate-appearing chain of loops and wondered how he might possibly decline the assignment. He certainly had never imagined rising to heights like those he faced at the moment. It was easier to imagine a precipitous descent in free-fall than to see himself arriving safely.

But he knew where his duty lay. No matter what fantastical or frightening events swirled around him, he had to keep the thought of Flavia foremost in his mind.

Oliver stepped hesitantly onto the bottom rung and grasped the strands.

Général d'Escargot once again swung his great foot up to his forehead and levitated rigidly at salute. "*Courage, mon ami!*"

"You're so brave, Mr. Medley!" the little spider said. "And don't worry! I'll be with you every step of the way!"

Oliver smiled uncertainly, replied, "*Merci*," in as steady a voice as he could, and began to climb the cobweb ladder.

Bertie darted up the steps on silent feet. Not for nothing had he explored the burns and braes all over Purple Valley in his boyhood, and learned to tread noiselessly. Many a young fox and squirrel had he startled nearly out of its skin by sneaking up behind it and clapping his hands. Now his very life, and the safety of the Abbey, depended on keeping out of sight and sound of the Darkness in the cellars behind him.

Straight up the stairs he ran, following the aroma of baking bread. It would have to come out at the kitchens, Bertie reasoned, thinking hard even as he ran. But would the Abbot be in the kitchen? Probably not. The Abbot would be in his study or a chapel or something. But at least he could ask someone where the Abbot's study was.

Bertie reached the entry to the kitchen and stopped, peering around. Food cooking in the fireplace ovens reminded him fleetingly that he was hungry, but he told himself sternly not to think about that.

There was no one in sight. Pots and pans stood on the counters next to piles of vegetables, waiting for someone to prepare them. *Where is everyone?*

Hesitating only a moment, Bertie made his choice and ran through the kitchen, hoping to find the refectory where the Whilts ate their communal meals. It was the next room, a long hall with a single table set with clean plates and cups, indicating that sooner or later a meal would be served. He decided against going in, for the refectory was empty also. Then he remembered that on the other side of the kitchen he had seen a little stairway that looked as if it went up higher.

On impulse, he turned and dashed back through the kitchen to a small archway and started up those stairs, not knowing if that was any better way to find the Abbot, but hoping against hope that it was.

No sooner had Bertie left the kitchen than four Whiltian friars-- the Steward of the Refectory, the Cellarer, and two young cook's helpers--returned from communal prayers in the Grand Sanctuary and began preparing the meal.

The Shadow serpentined up the winding cellar stairs, unhurried, tasting the air currents for the warm scent of young human flesh, the one who had been hiding in the cellar tonight watching as Sister Celeret died, and then had escaped. The Shadow traced the boy's scent, hunted among rows of barrels, poked its misshapen head into dark, dusty corners, but the scent there was fading, nearly cold. No one else was in the cellars.

In its cloud shape, the Shadow drifted through the open cellar door and into the lower quarters of the Abbey, passing behind the meal preparers. The two young Whiltian sisters peeling and paring vegetables for the pot did not see him, but the Steward of the Refectory noticed an unpleasant, musty odor definitely not emanating from the food being readied for service. He sniffed again, turned toward it--and missed the end of the darkness as it vanished into the refectory.

What was that odor? Brother Quorn couldn't put his finger on it, but something stimulated an archaic response in his brain: *Danger!*

"Sister Gwesta!" he called to the Cellarer, who was decanting a bottle of red wine. "Do you smell something odd?"

"What's that, Brother Quorn?" Sister Gwesta put down the decanter and looked toward the Steward. She sniffed--and her eyes grew wide. "Yes... Yes, I smell it!" Swiftly she walked toward the door to the wine cellar, which remained open after she had fetched the wine. She stood at the head of the stairs, peering down into the dusk below, inhaling the alien odor and puzzling over it.

"Do you know what it is, Sister?" asked the Steward.

"It's coming from the cellars. It--it smells wrong, somehow, but I cannot think why."

The two cook's helpers forgot their paring and peeling and came to stand behind the Cellarer, looking over her shoulder and sniffing.

"I don't like it, Sister Gwesta!" said one of them suddenly, and shivered. Nervously she wrapped her hands in her apron.

"I don't either, Sister!" said the other. Both young Whilts backed away, their expressions frightened.

Brother Quorn strode to where the Cellarer stood and took a long inhalation of the odor coming from the depths. He frowned, let it tease his memory... Then he and the Cellarer stared at each other.

"The Saurian!" Brother Quorn exclaimed in horror. "The river that flows through the Desolate Lands! It smells like the Saurian!"

Sister Gwesta's hand flew to her mouth. "How can that be possible! Nothing from the Desolation can get into the Abbey!"

"Something has gotten in, and brought the stench of the Saurian with it!" said Brother Quorn. "The Abbot must be told, and the Captain of the Watch. Sister Gwesta, will you send for them--and hurry! I'd better go down and see how the Saurian odor got in here."

"Come, Sisters! Find the Abbot and bring him here quickly! Quickly!" The Cellarer herded the young Whilts before her, and the two of them scurried out of the kitchen into the main part of the Abbey.

Brother Quorn took a lantern from a hook by the cellar door and lighted it. Pausing, he thought better of his impulse, extinguished the flame, and hung the lantern up again. Cautiously he began to descend the stone steps. Rows and rows of oaken barrels met his gaze, barrels and their shadows and implements kept in the wine cellars. Farther in he went, looking keenly about and listening for any alien sound. He sniffed the air every few steps, finding traces of the Saurian's odor but unable to pinpoint where it originated.

Still farther inside he went, until he was almost at the opposite end. Then a ray of mist-shrouded light fell on something that didn't belong in the wine cellars. It looked like a bundle of cloth, the dark green of a Whiltian robe. Why would a friar's habit be down here on the floor?

Cautiously, Brother Quorn went closer, rounded a stand of casks--and saw it all too clearly. A body lay crumpled on the floor, a body clothed in Whiltian green. And beside the body was an iron trapdoor--open. Its heavy padlock had fallen alongside, with its shaft sprung and a key sticking out of its lock.

And from the black hole beneath the iron trapdoor emanated the heavy, acrid odor of the Saurian River.

Coughing from the fumes, his eyes watering, Brother Quorn made his way to the body and reached down to give assistance. Then he saw the face.

"Sister Celeret!" Her expression held such agony that he could not restrain a gasp of shock. On her throat were the unmistakable bruises of strangulation. Once again violence had invaded their peaceful sanctuary, bringing bloodshed and death.

"Who has done this!" he whispered, then "HELP!" in a shout. "Sister Gwesta! Sister Gwesta! Sound the alarm!"

Oliver climbed until his thigh muscles shook from the effort of lifting his legs step after step. Being no athlete, and unused to cobweb ladders, he went slowly, making sure one foot was fully engaged before

Saint Amber's Rose

attempting to lift the other to the next rung. After a while he became quite warm, and not only from the exertion.

Climbing required extreme concentration in order to restrain his natural desire to look down as well as to put his feet in the right places. His need to *not* look down--versus his growing compulsion to do exactly the opposite--became more acute the higher he went, until perspiration poured down his face from the effort.

"I'm so warm," he whispered to himself. "If only a little breeze..."

Which actually began even as he formulated the wish—or the prayer: a tiny breeze. It cooled his fevered forehead and dried the sweat trickling down his neck and into his eyes. He glanced to one side and the other, curious about where that blessed relief had come from.

It came from many thousands of spiders. These weren't Clan Aranea spiders; these were daddy longlegs (*Pholcus phalangioides*), dangling from their sticky filaments and twirling in circles so fast they became invisible. From the force of their centrifugal motion came the breeze that made it possible for him to go on.

"Thank you," he whispered.

The Shadow drifted at its leisure through the corridors of the Abbey. It had no need to hurry. The Abbey was at its mercy--of which quality it had none. The invasion forces of the Lord of Desolation were in place, waiting only for the River Sunder to diminish to the point where the *wyrga* armies could cross. There was nothing to stop them, nothing to prevent them scaling the walls and overwhelming the inhabitants. Before the onslaught of the invincible *wyrga* not even the famed Taraman warriors had a hope of survival, let alone victory.

All was in readiness--on the Desolation's side. It seemed to the Shadow that nothing in the Abbey of Saint Amber was in readiness, either for defense or attack. Silently it glided past room after room, cell after cell, all with open doors and all empty.

Foolish, timorous creatures, these Whilts! Weak as water from Ages of soft living in their garden paradise. They are spineless, incapable of resistance. And their Abbot, old Thyme: useless. Senile. They should have cast him out long ago.

The Shadow considered both the openness and the emptiness of the cells. They were empty because everyone had fled, hiding

Charleynne Gates

somewhere, afraid even to breathe. *Let them hide.* The Shadow had no need of the Whilts or their ridiculous Abbot. It wanted only the *Sendara* of the Graelands. Finding her in this warren of rooms was all that had to be done. How can she escape now? A helpless cripple, confined to her silver chair, her "defenders" turned tail and gone!

A pity that Oliver Medley had escaped for the moment. His Gift, whatever it was, might have proved interesting. A pity the two ladies, *la duchesse* and *la marquise*, hadn't been able to seduce or scare it out of him. There were other methods of extracting information. *I'll deal with him later.* Medley, or his Gift, was not really necessary if he could trap the *Sendara*. Medley was a creature of no importance, not in this world or any other.

The Wraith Gloom had been inexcusably careless, letting Medley slip away like that, not that Medley could have gotten out of the castle. That would have been an impossibility. No, he was still wandering around the myriad corridors of Castle Mormorion, imagining himself lost.

The cloud-shape drifted past the infirmary, whose open door revealed only two shriveled old men wrapped snugly in shawls and propped up in their beds with several pillows. The Infirmarian was reading to them from a large book resting on a lectern. It was the holy *Book of the Labyrinth*, written in Old Boreal, first language of the stars.

If Brother Persil and his two patients were aware of the Shadow's presence, they gave no sign, for the Infirmarian's back was to the doorway. And although both Whilts were blind from age, their wrinkled old faces shone with joy, as if the words read in the Infirmarian's gentle voice brought them inexpressible peace.

The Shadow tasted the words of the Book and spat them out as if they were flames. It gave the infirmary a wide berth and passed on.

Oliver stopped to rest, panting in the currents of air swirling around him. His skin itched from the salty sweat that beaded his forehead and crawled down the back of his neck. His clothing was soaked with it, as if he had been standing in the rain. Never had he performed physical labor like this, or so continuously. He felt as if he had been climbing these silken rungs for days on end. Wrapping one arm around a rung, he scrabbled for the handkerchief in his inside pocket and wiped his forehead, then bent his head to reach for the back of his neck.

Inadvertently he looked down and wished he hadn't, because the sight immediately gave him vertigo and nausea. As he hadn't eaten in quite a while, there was nothing in his stomach to come out.

Below him looked like a bottomless hole. Anything he had seen when he started climbing had vanished--the snail, the little black spider, the rocky floor of the mountain's cone. Even the silken ladder disappeared into the darkness a few rungs beneath him. He felt as if he were suspended in the vast void of outer space.

Obviously he couldn't go down again. There was nowhere to go but up, where the snail-trails gave illumination, but "up" seemed to be as far above him as "down" was below.

Fear chilled him. His skin broke out in goose bumps. His mouth went dry. The calf muscle in his right leg tightened. *Don't let me get a cramp! Please!*

The cramp passed without much pain. He set his mind firmly on his mental picture of Flavia and kept on climbing. Time ceased to have any meaning. Eventually he got his second wind, and his protesting muscles, figuring they weren't going to get any attention, calmed down and let him do his work without further complaint.

Hand over hand, step after step... until he bumped his head--hard--on something that felt like solid glass. He stopped abruptly and peered at what had impeded his progress.

It looked like a trap door, improbably made of crystal. By the light reflected from the snail-trails he saw that where his head had hit was a circle engraved in the crystal, with several other marks inside it. It must be a symbol, he guessed, for the marks were more than random scratches. *If only I knew how to interpret them!*

"Mr. Medley! Mr. Medley!" whispered a little voice. Oliver started, nearly losing his grip on the ladder. He had forgotten Annie Aranea. "We've made it to the top! The Repository is on the other side of the trap door. Now don't worry," said the spider reassuringly into his ear. "I've been doing a web search to find the meaning of those symbols. Mother warned me something like that might be there. Did you know she almost saw the Repository before the room was sealed up? She didn't really, though, because all us spiders are nearsighted. Wait a minute... Wait a minute... I think I have something! There!

We've got it! The translation is 'S . NG A... ND EN . ER FR... ND BEH . .LD... LO .Y WIT . O . T... ND.' Oh, dear! Some of it's worn away, you know."

"Is that all?" Oliver asked after a pause.

"Yes," replied Annie Aranea. "That's all it says."

"I think I can decipher that," said Oliver, who had always enjoyed word puzzles. After a few moments of cogitation, "'Sing a (something) and enter friend behold a glory without end,'" he translated. "I don't understand. It doesn't seem to make sense. If it's asking for a song, which one does it want?"

"It doesn't say," replied the spider.

"There are millions of songs! Operatic arias, lullabies, sea chanteys, rock songs--"

"Do rocks sing in your world, too, Mr. Medley?"

"I--don't know," said Oliver, and hastened on. "Maybe it wants a folk song. Something from this region, perhaps. But I've no idea what the folk songs sound like in this country."

"I don't know the ones that human mortals sing," said Annie. "The only songs I know are from *A Little Golden Book of Spider-Songs* that I learned when I was small."

"Is there a missing symbol between 'a' and 'and'?" asked Oliver, studying the circle.

"Doesn't... seem to be," replied Annie Aranea, tapping frantically at her web with as many claws as she could spare.

Have I climbed all the way up here for nothing? Oliver rested his aching head on his hands, wishing he could just give it all up. But he couldn't do that either, for then he would have to live with the awful knowledge that he had failed the Lady of Light, and failing her would be worse than death.

"Nothing else here. Hmm," mused the little voice next to his ear. "I wonder if you really need to sing a whole big song? Couldn't you sing some little ditty?"

"But what ditty, Annie?" replied Oliver.

"Well, just something! I don't know how to put it, but just, you know... sing a note or two! Just try it!"

"But I don't know which notes they want!" Oliver began, losing patience. His head hurt, and perspiration had dried in rivulets down his skin, leaving him chilled now that he had stopped climbing. His arms ached from holding on to the rungs.

Then it came over him all of a sudden: *Sing A!* How simple!

He had been trying to make it complicated, and it wasn't in the least. The symbols must mean A above middle C, the note every symphony orchestra uses to tune itself. The answer was so straightforward that he had almost missed it.

From childhood Oliver had been blessed with perfect pitch, the ability to hear in his mind exactly what a particular musical tone ought to sound like before it was played or sung. That innate talent stood him in good stead now. Ignoring his discomfort, he took a deep, controlled breath from his diaphragm and vocalized an A in the tenor range. Then he sent it up an octave, to A over middle C, and held it.

The crystal trap door shivered and split down the middle! The two halves flew back, and radiance streamed out of the opening. Cautiously, blinking a bit, Oliver put his head through the doorway.

There, directly in front of him, was Saint Amber's Repository.

Then he understood, beyond all doubt, the meaning of his Gift.

Chapter Thirty-Three

The Repository

In quietness and in confidence shall be your strength.
--The Book of the Prophet Isaiah

Bertie raced up the stairs, pausing only to look behind him and to listen carefully for sounds of pursuit below or alarm above. None came, and he ran on. His breathing came easily, for all during his boyhood he had run races with his deer friend Fleetfoot in the meadowed hills above Mossy Dell Village. Everything that he had learned in the wild now served him well, for as he ran from known into unknown danger, he was leaving boyhood behind him. There was no more time or thought for play; all was now in deadly earnest. He had to find the Abbot, to tell him what he had seen in the wine cellar, and about Mr. Medley.

And tell the *Sendara* what the Mage had said! And hurry!

He reached a landing that led to a corridor. It looked as likely a place to start as anywhere, and he dashed into it without stopping.

Every door was open; every room was empty. Bertie glanced into each one as he ran past, but to his increasing frustration, found no one to ask where the Abbot might be. *Where are all the friars?* But no one answered his unspoken question.

At last he saw a ray of light at the end of the corridor. It was faint, but more than he had seen coming out of the other rooms. Maybe someone's there, someone who can tell me where the Abbot is. He ran toward it.

Oliver heaved himself up into the opening of the glass trap door and rolled awkwardly into the room that had been sealed since the First Age. It was full of light, soft and glowing rather than the bright, brilliant light of the snail-trails. The light-source, as far as he could tell,

-- 554 --

was invisible, for there seemed to be no windows in the enormous space inside the summit of the Great Mountain of Zund. Such a space was necessary in order to contain the Repository of Saint Amber, for its towering height swept to the summit of the mountain's dome.

It was carved of wood with a sheen like the colors of an autumn sunrise: rose... orange... amber... gold. Inside its panels were seven manuals--keyboards--which ordered its varied sounds. A grand array of gleaming pipes ranged around the entire chamber in standing rows, from the smallest high soprano to the tallest deep bass: the singing voices of the great instrument. Over the manuals lay a crystal cover with a small keyhole in the bottom right-hand corner.

Oliver struggled to his knees and stared open-mouthed at the creation of an unknown genius who had lived and died many Ages ago, and tears came to his eyes. Gratitude overwhelmed him that he had been allowed to behold beauty like this once in his lifetime.

For the Repository of Saint Amber was a magnificent pipe organ, the most wonderful musical instrument he had ever seen or imagined. Because it had been enclosed within an hermetically sealed chamber, it had remained in its original pristine condition. Not a grain of dust or rust or drop of moisture had come near it since the days of the Founder of the Abbey.

As if he were careful of disturbing its rest, Oliver got to his feet and tiptoed closer, looking for something he expected to find... and there it was, on the casework above the cover: the words *SOLI DEO GLORIA* inlaid in script of gold.

It's real. I'm not dreaming.

"Mr. Medley! Mr. Medley!" came a squeak from the region of his breast pocket. Oliver came back to himself and glanced down. "We're here! That's it!" cried Annie Aranea.

"I know," he whispered. "It's the most incredible pipe organ I've ever—"

"No, it's not; it's Saint Amber's Repository," Annie contradicted, "and you're here to make it sing," she went on. "I don't see how, but that's your Gift, isn't it?"

"Yes!" he said solemnly and happily. "Yes!" This was his Gift, he realized now, his high privilege and sworn duty: to awaken what the little spider called "Saint Amber's Repository". He did not comprehend how doing so could help the *Sendara*, but do it he would, even as he had promised.

"Oh, please hurry, Mr. Medley!" exclaimed the little spider, beside herself with excitement. "I can't wait!"

"Wait," he said, examining the crystal cover and trying without success to lift it. "I can't move this cover. It's locked."

"Well, use your key!" replied the spider with a touch of impatience. "That's what it's for!"

My key? The silver key my father gave me! With mounting anticipation and shaking fingers Oliver fished around in his pockets and found the little key, almost dropping it in the process. *He must have been here too!*

His heart in his throat, Oliver inserted the key into the tiny lock and turned until he heard a click as the wards slid back. At the same time he thought he heard another sound, a crack as if stone had split nearby.

He slipped the key back into his pocket and slowly, carefully, slid the crystal cover up and over the manuals. At the same instant, two massive doors at opposite ends of the chamber wall opened and swung inward, revealing a storm-clouded night, and a wind began to blow through the vault. The wind coiled into the organ and filled the bellows, which murmured in the bowels of the instrument.

With a certain amount of trepidation Oliver edged onto the organ bench and studied the array before him. Everything he could desire to create thousands of different sounds was there. He sat motionless, rapt in admiration of the organ-builder who had made and placed it in the sealed chamber.

The Shadow meandered along the corridors, in no haste. It had lost the trail of human boy for the moment, but no matter. Nothing could evade the Shadow forever. Not even in a refuge like the Abbey, with its cool green gardens of healing and peace. Memories haunted the Shadow's dark mind, images of a lost Garden where once, inconceivable Ages ago, it had walked in the full light of day...

No! Better to keep its attention on the present, in which its one goal was to discover where the *Sendara* had hidden herself. *She cannot escape me now.* The Shadow had been waiting since the Great Expulsion for this moment!

Saint Amber's Rose

It slithered up steps, explored branching corridors; it passed open doorways. No mortal scent came from any of them. Except... there was something emanating from the open room at the end of the corridor: a faint warmth, a ray of silvery light.

The Shadow moved toward it, tasting the air currents. A human mortal was inside that room! Not the boy, but a Whilt, a solitary friar. A Whilt would know where the *Sendara* hid. If the Shadow found an opening in the Whilt's mind, then the *Sendara*'s whereabouts would be open to it. *Ridiculous creatures, these Whilts!* Thinking themselves safe and secure from all alarms, and all the while their ancient Enemy roamed at will about their little paradise.

The Shadow found the strongest current of mortality and followed it into the Chapel of the Silver Chalice, where Sister Clova, alone, knelt in prayer under the tall window above the altar.

Night had fallen, and on the other side of the window the sky had darkened to indigo. Tiny points of light sparkled on high, ranging themselves in patterns familiar to the Labyrinth World. Their white light spilled into the chapel, making the Chalice on the table gleam, and thence out the open doorway.

After a time the mirror-like surface of the Chalice reflected the Shadow's sinister, fluctuating form as it appeared in the doorway. Sister Clova, her eyes closed as she whispered her prayers, did not see either the reflection or the reality. No noise alerted her, for the Shadow made no sound as it slithered toward her. Some instinctive warning made her open her eyes, glance at the Chalice, and realize what had entered their holy place.

She took a quick breath. Standing, she turned to face the menacing Darkness, the Shadow that towered above her, its monstrous head swaying slightly in the shifting light... and Sister Clova smiled. Smiled into its unblinking silver eyes as if she saw beyond the hideous outer form to the truth of what was inside it, a being to be loved and set free.

"Ab'addon!" she said with great tenderness. "Beloved!" And opened her arms.

Summoned by his true name, the Lord of Desolation materialized in place of the Shadow. He did not answer, but came closer and closer until, putting his hands around her neck, he began to strangle the mother of his child. Even as she struggled for breath, steadily she gazed into his eyes, and in her gaze was no fear at all.

Bertie hastened toward the doorway where light spilled out. He saw--or thought he saw--a drift of gray cloud enter the doorway just before he came up to it. He followed it, found that the doorway led to a room that looked like the inside of the little church back in the village, except it was very simply furnished, just some benches and a square wooden table with a silver cup on it, and above that a tall window with a constellation of stars shining through it.

But something else was in the room also: that Shadow Bertie had last seen in the wine cellar! And behind him was one of the friars in a Whiltian green robe. And--and the Shadow had wrapped itself around her, and it was choking her!

"Stop!" Bertie shouted at it. Forgetting the danger to himself, he ran up the aisle to help, if help he might. As he ran, he thought that the Shadow was shadow no longer, but a man with silver eyes that gleamed in the darkness like predators' eyes in the forest. For as Bertie cried out, the man turned to look at him. Then, as the boy froze, horrified, the man became Shadow again and flung Sister Clova's body away. She fell to the floor, unconscious.

The Shadow advanced on the boy, who retreated step by step as its stare caught and held his gaze. He could not turn his eyes away!

Closer came the Shadow, closer, and raised its monstrous head over Bertie. Breaking out of his trance with a tremendous effort, Bertie whipped out his Dwarvian dagger and pointed it toward the enemy. "*Va'in 'a moru', Sendara!*" he yelled, but where the impulse came from he never knew.

The Shadow lunged faster than eye could follow, wrapped itself around Bertie, and lifted him off his feet. The Dwarvian dagger dropped unnoticed to the floor and skidded along the stone flags.

"PUT THAT BOY DOWN THIS INSTANT!" ordered a voice that demanded obedience.

The Shadow twisted to face this new challenge and met the needle-sharp point of Great-Aunt Belvedine's umbrella stabbing into its throat. Blood dripped down its shape-shifting body and spattered onto the floor like flakes of rust.

Saint Amber's Rose

The Shadow screamed in pain and dropped Bertie on the stone floor. It swayed toward Great-Aunt Belvedine, who backed away as it advanced.

"Ab'addon's here!" Belvedine shouted, menacing the fiend with her lethal umbrella as she retreated toward the door. "HELP! HELP!"

But the Shadow, though forced to divert energy to alternate between its darkness and Ab'addon's man-form, still managed to take its opportunity. It darted again toward its attacker, wrapped itself around her, and reared toward the high ceiling. Enraged, the brute tightened itself around her, cutting off her cries for help. But her first shout of warning had been heard, and the pounding of feet on flagstones grew louder as the guards of the Watch scrambled to respond.

At the same moment, in the kitchens below, Sister Gwesta began to ring the alarm bell, and its clamor reverberated through the Abbey. DANGER! DANGER! it rang over and over, until every corner of the Abbey, from the cellars to the watchtower, was on high alert.

In the Grand Sanctuary, where the Whiltian friars were gathering for Prayers of Extraordinary Intercession, the Abbot heard the alarm bell and noises of tumult and shouting from the chapel. Nodding as if this was the signal for which he had been waiting, Father Thyme arose from his stall. Leaning on his shepherd's staff, he faced the congregation of Saint Amber's Abbey. They rose with him, standing straight and unafraid, as if unseen armor shielded them.

"Sisters and Brothers!" said the Abbot. "Darkness has broken into our Abbey. Let us make ready to sing down the Light!"

The Watchers ran to the doorway of the Chapel and stopped short at the sight before them: A huge Shadow, a mixture of cloud and darkness, towered nearly to the ceiling, and Belvedine lay limp and blue-faced in its embrace. Spilled blood stained its front from a wound in its throat, but its size and strength were obviously so much greater than theirs that, with their small, ineffectual weapons--staves and short daggers snatched up as they ran--they could do nothing against it.

Pavarr appeared behind the last of the Watchers, the sword *Greenhallow* shining in his hand, and understood immediately what had penetrated the defenses of the Abbey. He ran forward to confront it.

"HO! Mighty Lord of Desolation!" he called, taunting the Shadow. "Do you now make war against children and old women? I, Pavarr of Taraman, challenge you to single combat--if you dare to face me as a man!"

The Shadow hissed angrily. It let Belvedine drop beside Bertie as it swayed toward Pavarr. The prince kept his eyes on the monster and walked slowly backward, brandishing his sword as he goaded it.

"Come on!" Pavarr jeered, beckoning it toward him. "Quit hiding behind your Shadow and fight me in your true form! What! Are you afraid? The Lord of Desolation, the great Ab'addon, frightened of a human mortal?"

Mocking with his voice and feinting with the great sword, Pavarr lured the Shadow out of the Chapel and into the corridor. There, compelled by the calling of its true name, it changed form and became Ab'addon. In his hand was the Blackfire Rod, equal in length and power to *Greenhallow*.

Forgotten by the combatants, Bertie and Great-Aunt Belvedine, bruised and shaken, helped each other off the floor.

"The *Sendara!*" Belvedine whispered hoarsely. ""We've got to warn the *Sendara!* This way! Come quickly!" She grabbed Bertie's hand and dragged him with her to the front of the Chapel. They took the half-conscious Sister Clova's hands and hastened through a hidden door behind a pillar and onto a narrow, cobweb-encrusted stairway.

They fought, the two of them, Prince and Lord, surrounded at a cautious distance by the Watchers. And none who witnessed or heard of it will ever forget that combat, for it is told in *Chronicles of the Rose*, and the words writ therein will endure as long as stars burn in deep space.

The two circled around each other, their eyes locked, their weapons testing the air. No Watcher spoke; no one dared interfere, for none could have borne the consequences. Ab'addon swung out first. The Blackfire Rod darted perilously near Pavarr's face, but was blocked by *Greenhallow*. Pavarr struck straight, but his sword was swallowed in darkness as Ab'addon swayed aside, and the edge of the lord's black cloak deflected what would have been a mortal hit.

Again and again each one thrust and parried, not in haste but warily, each seeking the measure of his opponent. Strike and strike again! Only to feel one's weapon blocked in mid-descent, or to find one's enemy sidestepping the blow. Circling and circling, close in, then springing apart, the two mortal foes studied each other, learning each other's heart and mind as intimately as if they had been brothers.

Pavarr pressed his advantage when he had it, as did Ab'addon. They were nearly equal in strength and dexterity, but Ab'addon's Blackfire wove like swift snakes around Pavarr's sword, its flames licking the shining blade. Slowly, slowly, the Lord of Desolation drove Pavarr back toward a narrow set of stairs at the far end of the corridor.

Twice the Blackfire thrust dangerously close to Pavarr's face; he managed to parry. Once *Greenhallow* cut the air near Ab'addon's throat, where dark blood from Belvedine's umbrella-tip had dried; he dodged by the distance of a hair. They gave each other no quarter, these warriors who had no peer in the Labyrinth World save each other.

Pavarr sprang onto the first stairstep, determined to bar the way. Ab'addon halted, fighting in place, unable to advance. But then, mysteriously, Pavarr seemed to tire, only slightly, but enough for Ab'addon to close with him. The two struggled together, *Greenhallow* pressed hard against Blackfire. They stared into each other's eyes, Pavarr frowning, Ab'addon certain of victory. Pavarr's hand trembled; Ab'addon pushed against him, and as Pavarr stumbled off the step, Ab'addon darted past him to take Pavarr's position.

The prince lunged for the Lord of Desolation, who slipped past the thrust and mounted another step, and another and another, keeping Pavarr at bay below him. Pavarr backed away reluctantly, unwilling to risk the deadly Blackfire and unable to work his way past Ab'addon's offense.

Ab'addon glanced once, quickly, up the spiral stair, where light shined at the top. Then he returned his attention to Pavarr. Thrust and double-thrust, and the Blackfire Rod grazed Pavarr's shoulder above his sword-arm. Pavarr cried out and grabbed at the wound, for the Blackfire Rod gave the most terrible injury of all weapons. The merest cut from it could be fatal, for its unquenchable fire sank deeply into the victim, leading to an agonizing death over many days.

Pavarr quickly joined his other hand with his sword hand, and he swung out against Ab'addon's renewed attack. But Pavarr's efforts flagged as the Blackfire worked into his body from the wound site; the force of his blows weakened and diminished.

Charleynne Gates

Ab'addon smiled. Now he was certain! The *Sendara* must be cowering at the head of the stairway, guarded only by the weakling Whilts. The prince would not have fought so desperately if she were not hidden nearby. Ab'addon had not expected the Prince of Taraman to give way easily, but then no human mortal—save one--had ever been able to stand against him.

For one instant, in the arrogance of certain victory, the Lord of Desolation dropped his guard. It was a mistake--he realized it immediately, refocused, and guarded himself again. But the attack did not come. Pavarr, seemingly dazed, failed to take advantage of the opening.

Ab'addon whirled and dashed up the stairs. Pavarr stayed where he was, gripping his wounded shoulder, his blade's point resting on the stone tiles. He glanced at the Watchers who now gathered around him, received their silent tribute--and smiled, looking steadily up the stairs where Ab'addon had disappeared.

Bertie and Great-Aunt Belvedine, pulling Sister Clova along with them, panted up the long-unused stairway, which was thick with dust. Several times they stumbled over broken steps, adding to their already plentiful scrapes and bruises, but Belvedine refused to allow them time to rest.

"Faster! Faster! Got to warn them!" she muttered between gasps, and that was all she had breath to say. Twice Bertie glimpsed, out of the corner of his eye, indeterminate black forms, low on the ground, slipping past them down the stairwell. At first he feared they were unnatural creatures of the Shadow, but then he heard the skitter of their claws and caught the red gleam of their eyes and realized they were only rats--though that was bad enough. He was much more careful not to fall or to loosen his grip on Sister Clova.

At last they came to the top of the stairs, where a little splintery door barred their way. It was so small and narrow that when Belvedine pushed it, she had to stoop considerably to squeeze through, and even Bertie, not yet fully grown, had to duck so as not to bump his head on the arch.

When the three had gone through the doorway, and were able to stand up straight--*O glory!* thought Bertie. For they had reached the roof of the topmost tower of the Abbey, and night had painted the sky in deepest darkness, and star-twined constellations radiated their white light upon--

Her.

His inmost senses recognized her at once: the Lady of Light, and he knew, without a word spoken, that here were Beauty and Truth, living in victory.

She was seated in a silver chair with wheels on it. Beside her were two men, one with a long beard, clad in white robes and carrying a shepherd's staff, and the other in an indigo robe the color of the night sky.

The three of them seemed to be in solemn consultation. Bertie could not hear most of what they were saying, but the man in dark blue robes spoke two words which he did hear.

"Father Abbot," said the man, speaking to the other, and Bertie realized that here was the end of his mission. He could deliver his message!

Ignoring Belvedine's frantic clutch at his sleeve, "O sir!" Bertie called to the Abbot, and started toward them. He stopped abruptly before he had gone more than a few steps, for the three had turned to look at him, not as if they were startled or even surprised at his presence, but as if they had known all along that he was there.

The two men looked kindly upon him, and the *Sendara...* the *Sendara* smiled at him, smiled right into his eyes, and at that moment he realized that delivering his message was no longer necessary. From these three personages nothing was hidden, and in their wisdom and at their bidding, Truth would be proclaimed from the rooftops.

Belvedine managed to grab Bertie's tunic and pull him back beside her and Sister Clova, who had sunk down exhausted, leaning against the tower wall.

"Stay here! We're safe here," Belvedine whispered.

Bertie figured that although he longed to go closer to the radiant lady in the silver chair, at this point discretion might be more prudent than valor. He obeyed Belvedine's peremptory command and stood beside her and Sister Clova, his rescued dagger out to guard them just in case.

A cloud or a gathering of mist descended between Bertie and the *Sendara*. He saw and heard everything that went on, but it was as if he and Belvedine and Sister Clova were as far away as the moon.

Charleynne Gates

"Mr. Medley!" came a whisper from his front pocket. "You can make it sing, can't you?"

"Yes!" said Oliver. "I've always dreamed of--"

"Then I think you'd better get on with it," urged the spider.

"But the music! What music am I supposed to play?"

"I thought you knew!" replied Annie Aranea. "Don't you have it with you? Isn't it in a packet or something?"

Packet? The oilskin packet Pavarr gave me! I forgot all about it! What did I do with it? Desperately Oliver searched his mind and his person. *I never did open it... Pavarr said it was important. Where--Oh! It's in the lining of my belt!*

Oliver pulled out the oilskin packet and opened it. A many-times-folded, crumpled piece of ragged parchment appeared. By unfolding and smoothing it, then bringing it close to his eyes and squinting, he made out scratchings that vaguely resembled notes of music.

"I can't read this!" he protested. "It's too faded. Now what do I do? No, don't tell me. I'll try—it won't do any good—I'll try it anyway." And he placed the old, torn sheet of paper gingerly on the music rack. "It won't work. I can't—"

He stopped talking, staring as his mouth hung open. As if by magic (which it was), the single sheet of music began to expand, and the notes became blacker against the page, darkening until he could read them clearly. Then he saw the signature of the composer at the end and nearly fell off the bench.

"Why, that's—that's—"he gasped.

"Mr. Medley!" Annie Aranea interrupted. "The *Sendara's* waiting!"

Flavia! I will not fail her! Oliver concentrated his whole mind on the task before him. With a murmured prayer, he took a deep breath and placed his fingers on the keys.

Ab'addon sped up the narrowing spiral stair, meeting no one, despising the pathetic little friars who failed to protect their Lady of Light. As soon as he captured her, the Light would be his--his alone. Darkness would overcome the Labyrinth, Darkness utter and absolute, the Shadow of Chaos in which the Lord of Desolation lived and moved and had his being.

Not since the Great Expulsion had he come so near her. This time he would not fail! Her Light was his for the taking.

He rounded the seventh turning--and met the sole guard at the door to the tower roof. She advanced with drawn sword as if she had expected him: the *Foressa* Mildrith, the *Sendara*'s champion.

"Ab'addon!" she called, and the deep assurance of her command halted him in mid-stride. "Servant of Darkness! Consider well what you do, and enter at your peril!"

He snarled, struck her sword aside--but there was no sword, and no *Foressa*. She had vanished. The arched door was now unbarred and open, and a silvery light shined through it.

Victory was close--so close. All he had to do was go through the door, take possession of the *Sendara*... and all that she was, her realm of the Graelands, the Labyrinth World and all worlds after that, would be his.

He did not need Saint Amber's Rose.

He took the final step, crossed the threshold of the arched doorway, and strode onto the tower roof where Flavia herself sat in her silver chair, with the radiance of stars shining on her crown of silver leaves. On her slender fingers her two rings, set with blue and green gems, winked and gleamed in the starlight.

Beside her chair stood a young girl clad in a gown of green trimmed in silver, with a green band around her brow. (Bertie, in amazement, recognized Andis, utterly transformed from the girl he had known in Threshold Forest.) A white birchwood scepter, carven with symbols of Truth and Grace, lay on the cushion in her hands.

"I have you," said the Lord of Desolation, speaking softly in triumph. "Now I have you." Blackfire Rod in hand, he approached the Lady of Light, who regarded him calmly. Her glorious eyes met his, and in hers was nothing of fear, but only the clarity of immortal wisdom.

The girl at her side bent to offer the cushion. With her right hand Flavia took the white birch scepter and extended it toward him, opening her left hand in the gesture of peace. "Do but touch this scepter, and together let us heal this wounded world. For the Night of Shadows is passing, and dawn is soon to come."

"I think not, Lady," he replied, smiling. "*I* am still lord of this world. I will rule it--*and you*--until the end of time."

"Then return to your wasteland!" she answered him in sorrow. "Be forever diminished, for your hold on this world is at an end."

"Never!" said Ab'addon. "I will make all things desolate!"

But Flavia pointed her scepter toward the ground. "*Terra!*" she called.

A wind stirred, and Hera Vespasia landed on the back of the *Sendara*'s chair. "*Aer!*" spoke the Great Horned Owl, her wings outspread.

Ab'addon stared in disbelief as a figure clad in white and bearing a shepherd's staff stepped out of the night to stand behind Flavia's chair.

"*Fyr!*" pronounced the Abbot, lifting his staff.

Another figure, in robes of indigo, came forth. "*Watyr!*" proclaimed the Mage Dandriel, and swept his blackthorn staff toward the dammed-up Sunder.

Stunned by the Summoning of the Four Elements, Ab'addon roared in wrath and began to swing the Blackfire Rod against the white birch scepter.

"Ho, Ab'addon!" came a shout behind him. Ab'addon whirled to find Pavarr coming out of the arched doorway, the sword *Greenhallow* aimed at the Lord of Desolation's heart. Behind him stood the *Foressa* Mildrith, guarding the door against all possibility of escape.

Trapped, Ab'addon faced the prince, his silver eyes blazing with hate. He swung the Blackfire Rod at Pavarr, but *Greenhallow* struck the Blackfire Rod clean and true. The Rod burst out of Ab'addon's hand and leaped high in the air, spiraling end over end, its flames flaring scarlet and black.

As the Rod reached the top of its arc, streaking across the sky like a burning arrow, the massive army of *wyrga* encamped in the plain below spotted it. "Black Flame! Black Flame!" their guards cried out.

"Lord Ab'addon!" the *wyrga* shrieked in their hideous war-tongue, and began to move their earth-destroying engines across the riverbed toward the Abbey.

The Blackfire Rod plummeted, falling straight toward the channel of the River Sunder. But the *wyrga*'s dam had cut off the river's free flow, and the Sunder had been overtaken by a thickening stream of

Saurian fluid. As soon as the Blackfire Rod touched down, the whole channel, from the dam to the place where the river emptied into the ocean, exploded into flame.

Oliver Medley pressed the keys of the first chord.

Nothing happened.

"No!" he exclaimed, shocked. "What--happened? Why isn't there any sound? I--"

"Mr. Medley! Mr. Medley! It's the Rose!" shrieked the little spider, in her excitement bouncing up and down on her filament. "You forgot to put Saint Amber's Rose in its place!"

"What? What Rose? What are you talking about?"

"The one you've got! Haven't you got it?" demanded Annie, nearly beside herself with anxiety.

"I don't have any Rose! I don't understand!"

"Oh! Oh! Mr. Medley, you found Saint Amber's Rose! That's why the Lord of Desolation is after you! He wants it back. Now's the time to use it!"

"Found—what? Where?" Oliver cried out, wild with frustration. To be so near his Gift, and not to be able to do this one last necessary thing, was unbearable.

'Mr. Medley!" pleaded Annie, "you went into the Great Waste and took back the Rose that the Lord of Desolation stole from the Graelands! Please tell me you remember!"

Driven by the ominous sense of his impending failure, a current of emotion shot through Oliver. Anger like a red beacon radiated through him, and for an instant all the pent-up rage of his life threatened to erupt—anger that his father had died when Oliver was too young to lose him, anger at his utter ignorance of what he was supposed to be doing in the Labyrinth World, anger that necessary knowledge had been kept from him, anger at his own timidity that he had let Great-Aunt Belvedine bully him into this dilemma. It was because of her that he was sitting here, not having a clue what to do next!

But then the wave of wrath passed as suddenly as it had come, and in its place was the acknowledgment that he was here because he truly wanted to be. It was solely because of his love for Flavia--*not* Great-Aunt Belvedine's bullying--that he had persevered to this point.

Charleynne Gates

Well aware of the crucial moments flying past, he made himself stop his wrathful thoughts. He concentrated on breathing deeply and steadily, calming his mind and letting his memory take him where it would.

And there it was, tucked behind unwelcome recollections of the Garden of Smoke and Mirrors: the rosebush he had seen in Ab'addon's secret garden, the one planted in dead soil but bearing a living bud. He had plucked it, and the Wraith Gloom had insisted that he take it when he escaped from the Desolation.

I put it under my tunic... Is it still there, after everything I've been through—the Saurian's filth, the ocean's salt water, the interminable climb up here?

It was. Carefully, in wonder, he drew it out. Small and fragile as it was, a harsh look might have withered it—and yet it was alive, unmarred by adversity.

"That's it!" crowed the little spider. "That's the Rose I've always heard about!"

"But where do I put it?"

The crystal vase! The crystal vase on the Repository!

A myriad voices in his head spoke to him, voices he recognized: Aurelia Dawn... Jon and Amatilda Keeper... the Mage... the Dwarvians... Hera Vespasia ... even Old Sal! And many others, from Ages past and Ages yet to come, all urging him on.

You, Oliver Medley, have the Secret of Saint Amber's Rose. Place it on the Repository, and unlock its voice!

With no doubts now, Oliver reached up to the crystal vase and inserted Saint Amber's Rose. Glorious light streamed from it, and the bud began to open, unfolding shining petals tinted in the colors of a summer morning. And the sweet fragrance of the First Garden filled the chamber.

Then once more he placed his hands upon the keys--and sounded the first chord in quiet confidence. The music of Saint Amber's Repository, silent for many Ages, rang out in full voice, echoing beyond the Mountains of Zund across the world.

Chapter Thirty-Four

Singing Down the Light

Music is a means of grace--a way that you reach back into the world and create change.
      --Anton Armstrong, Oregon Bach Festival

And the great dragon was cast out, that old serpent, called the Devil, and Satan, which deceiveth the whole world: he was cast out into the earth, and his angels were cast out with him.
      --The Revelation of Saint John

      The glorious music rang out from the Mountains of Zund across the Fathomless Ocean. And thus was recorded in *Chronicles of the Rose*:
      The front line of the *wyrga's* engines of mass destruction had already advanced toward the Abbey, crawling over the riverbank and into the Saurian stream. The explosion blew them apart, sending pieces of red-hot metal high into the air. A gale of wind blew down and scattered the hot metal parts over the advance line of the *wyrga* army. Howls of terror rose to meet the death-dealing rain of molten iron, and its ranks began to break as confusion and fear struck at the same moment.
      Unable to see the disaster ahead, the rear army kept pressing forward, forcing the front lines to push against them as they tried to escape the conflagration in the riverbed. Panic! as the front line fought their own rear guard. Earth-destroying machines crashed into one another and fell, annihilating *wyrga* who couldn't get out of the way.
      The Whiltian friars in the Grand Sanctuary, hearing the chord as their cue, took breath and sang down the Light:

Charleynne Gates

Awaken, Light of the Dawn!
Awaken, O Glory!
O joy of life! O joy of creation!
Joy be our Light!

Thus did they raise their chorus in confidence, and their anthem echoed and re-echoed from the Great Mountain over the snow-capped Zundian chain, down to the Sunder riverbed where the *wyrga* armies roiled in tumult and desperation, trying to escape the devouring flames.

At the sound of the chord the great doors of the Abbey burst open, and a mounted troop of Taraman archers, Pavarr in the lead, galloped out, shooting volleys of flaming arrows into the writhing masses of *wyrga.*

Hearing the chord in the heart of the Great Mountain, in one swift motion the Dwarvian smiths brought down their hammers on the anvil, and the force of the blows reverberated through the vault and awakened the rainbow fire slumbering at the mountain's root.

And with that blow the dam across the River Sunder cracked and was riven through its center, and each half buckled and fell as the unleashed river poured through.   In freedom and fury the river thundered out of captivity, rolling down with the clash and clamor of a million swords.   The river's volume had multiplied while it was confined, creating a vast lake, and the colossal weight of accumulated water drove the Sunder forward like a flight of meteors across the sky.

The Sunder swept over the *wyrga* armies without pity or surcease, and as the fiery furnace in the riverbed destroyed the front lines, so the rushing waters claimed fully a third of the middle guard. Madness overtook the *wyrga,* and they fought each other to escape, but the foaming torrent plunged irresistibly over them and their engines and dragged them under.

Riding high on the crest of the flood was the refurbished eighty-six gun sloop *Grand Adventure*, with Admiral Sir John Horatio Nunkins on the quarterdeck beside Captain Ezekiel Bones, reclothed in humanity and gold-braided uniform.

"Uncle Nunks! Captain Bones!" Bertie screamed, leaning over the tower-roof balustrade and waving frantically.

The captain spotted him and yelled, "There's a good lad, Sir John!" into his admiral's ear over the deafening noise of the river.

Saint Amber's Rose

"That he is!" Admiral Nunkins yelled back.

"If he hadn't come around and stirred us up, we skulls'd still have been drifting around the river bottom with no purpose in life, instead of getting in on the action," the captain went on. "And we'd never have met up with our own admiral again and manned a spanking new ship."

"And arrived at the precise moment you were needed," the admiral complimented.

The two old sailors saluted the young man as they hurtled around the Abbey.

The skeleton crew--now fully fleshed and smartly outfitted in proper seamen's garb--held battle stations and manned the cannons, which fired continuous broadsides of radiant light against the Desolation's darkness. Down the old Sunder channel they ran before the wind, sails billowing white, pressing hard against the last of the invaders. Slowly the *wyrga* army retreated toward the end of the open plain where the frozen Icewode lured them with the seduction of safety.

But the plain was no longer open.

Oliver played on and on. A spectrum of tonal colors never heard before or since streamed from the organ, a mighty tempest descending to the deepest notes and rising again to the highest, swelling across mountain and plain, hill and dale, ascending into the storm-wracked sky until the stars themselves sang in harmony with the congregation of Whiltian friars, earthly and celestial choirs blending.

Deep under Castle Mormorion, in the black pit where captive human mortals awaited their dreaded fate, the Wraith Gloom heard the first chord and was recalled to life. Knowing that freedom was rising on the wind, swiftly he went to the cages and with a single merciful dart of light from his mind, put to rest those mortals who were too wounded and broken to recover. Those who could be healed he released from imprisonment, giving them water, food, and clothing, and sent them home. But he slew the *wyrga* guards and their soulless torturers and dissolved them into their constituent atoms.

Far away in the Desolate Lands, the Stonemen planted in their rows beside the Saurian River heard the first chord and began to awaken to life--to action--again. One of the younger ones, not so burdened as his elders with gnarling greed and ancient guilt, with a tremendous effort pulled his stone foot free of the layers of hardened ash in which it had been buried. His mates raised a resounding cheer. They tried it themselves and found that it wasn't impossible after all, despite what they had been taught to believe.

Other Stonemen, following this very clear example, set to work with renewed hope. By ones and twos and dozens, they freed themselves--not without pain--from their confinement in the past, and found that they could move about again. At first they lost their balance and stumbled at every other step, for they had forgotten how to walk, and as every young creature knows, walking takes practice.

But they persisted, clomping around and around on their stone feet, falling over and helping each other up until they began to get the feel of it again. They formed themselves into lines and rows and practiced walking in the same direction. Then a veteran Stoneman, who remembered what was good about the old ways, began to call out, *"Ho... Ho... Truth, Valor, Honor bright! Sword of Justice, live in Light!"*

The Stonemen began marching in step as the veteran called the cadence. As they marched, they joined in the chant, at first uncertainly, then with a growing belief in themselves. And they recalled the nobility of what they had been and the greatness of what they were going forward to be, and the energy of each Stoneman added strength to strength until the whole became greater than the sum of its parts.

For once, long ago, the Stonemen had been Companions of the Noble Way, and as that identity reawakened in them, their hard stone shells crumbled and fell aside, and the Companions resumed their mortal bodies, rejoicing in the truth of their being.

Abruptly they halted. Straight ahead, looming high and stark above the ashen land, was the formidable cliff that marked the boundary between the Great Waste of the Desolation and the rest of the Labyrinth World. Atop the cliff, a black silhouette against the perpetually leaden-hued sky was the form of a man with three stick-like protuberances reaching above his head. A bird perched on the man's shoulder.

A current of recognition stirred in the Companions, a rebirth of knowledge long absent. They waited...

Saint Amber's Rose

The bird unfolded its black wings and swooped down to the Companions, landing on the Stonefather's outstretched arm.

"Hail, Master of the Companions!" said the raven.

"Hail, Gabriel Corax!" said Endorgon. *"Long has it been since we have seen a Raven Messenger!"*

"Long indeed, Master," replied the raven. "And the message I bear is of greater importance than any I have brought you in the past."

"Say on!" Endorgon replied, and the raven told him of the Quest and the Questors, of the Abbey and the *wyrga* armies surrounding it. Nor did the messenger omit to tell of the *wyrga*'s appalling engines of mass destruction.

"Remember this: I only deliver the message," said Gabriel Corax. "I take no responsibility for the consequences. You number many Companions, Master, but the *wyrga* are a host more numerous than grains of sand on the shore." Spreading his midnight wings, the bird flew off.

There was silence among the Companions for the space of a breath... A white mare with shining mane came galloping to the top of the Bordering Cliffs. Upon it rode a knight, belted and helmed, who brought the horse to a halt at the edge of the precipice. It reared, and the knight drew sword and saluted the company on the Great Waste.

"Hail, Companions of the Noble Way!" the rider called. "I, Tirgon, greet you!"

"Tirgon! Tirgon our Commander lives again!" Glad words wove among the Companions, every face alight with joy.

"Who among you remembers the vows we made in fealty to the *Sendara*?" Tirgon asked. "Will you ride with me to her aid?"

"Companions! What say you?" Endorgon roared.

"Onward!" cried a young voice from the ranks, that of the first Companion to free himself from his stone imprisonment.

"To the Sendara*!"* shouted another.

"For Andrasil!" called another, and the Companions rent the air with cries of *"Andrasil! For Andrasil!"* They had not forgotten the Stonemother lying in pieces in the land they had left, called by some in the outer world *Kibroth-hatta-avah*, the graves of greed.

A noise like the groaning of beasts in agony came from the high cliff, and with a skirl of pipes the Piper of the Icewode summoned his long-lost Companions to the Great Battle between the defenders of the

Graelands and the invaders of the Desolation. With a shout the Companions ran forward to answer the call and discovered that they were no longer running but riding on powerful chargers as they had in days of old.

Once again the Companions were garbed in shining armor, knights bound by holy vows to the Lady of Light. Onward they galloped, and bright banners streamed from their lances. Joy was in their hearts as they advanced to meet their adversaries, and no tremor of fear dimmed their exultation as they hastened toward the overwhelming force ahead.

"Andrasil! For Andrasil!"

Forward the Companions sped, back to the world they had abandoned, riding with fullness of heart and clarity of purpose. The Piper led the Companions through the Icewode, over snow-laden ground between ice-coated trees, and those who dwelt therein marveled at the passing of that noble company with its fire-colored banners. This also was recorded in *Chronicles of the Rose*, and none who read therein will ever forget their tale of glory.

Melody poured through him to the organ. Oliver was transported by energies his mind did not understand--but his soul did, and compelled his heart and hands to its higher will. And as the anthem rose over the towers of the Abbey, so did Oliver's vision. The instrument he was playing faded from his sight, and he saw in the distance a Garden of green delight, a summerland of sun and shade, blue stream and fragrant meadow stretching as far as eye could see.

A lamb, awkward on its newfound feet, skipped, stumbling, into the clearing... stalked by a wolf pup creeping close behind. Oliver's breath caught from pity for the helpless prey. He ran forward--and stopped as the wolf sprang up and over the lamb's head, landing in a somersault and rolling on the grass. The lamb ran up to the wolf, butted it in the stomach, and chased it into the trees. *They're playing a game!* Oliver realized, like children, wolf and lamb together, and he wondered where he was, that such a thing could be.

He saw a kind of mist in the middle distance, and when he had blinked it away, there was the Lady of Light. She was seated, not in her silver chair, but on a stone covered with emerald moss, and around her creatures of the wild gathered in peace and patience, awaiting the benison of her hand upon them. A stag raised his antlered head behind her; a golden-maned lion lay at her feet. On a branch nearby perched an owl, its round eyes wise and serene.

Oliver saw a man sitting with her, a man wearing the plain robes in which He had walked the desert hills. The two of them talked intently with each other, laughing, happy in each other's presence as good friends ought to be.

Oliver stared. The man was somehow familiar. Suddenly Oliver knew who He was! In mounting excitement he began to run toward them...

But Mil walked unhurriedly to meet him, holding her sword before her. Silver flames coruscated up and down the blade, and its gleam blocked Oliver's view and prevented him from going farther.

Mil smiled at him. "You may not enter yet, Friend Oliver. Not until Time's End, and Earth be healed and whole again."

Oliver came to himself, still playing the wondrous instrument. On and on the ecstatic music rang until he no longer felt the difference between himself and it, for of such virtue was the Repository of Saint Amber that it opened the heart of any listener to the infinite music of the spheres.

In pandemonium, the mass of *wyrga* that had survived retreated toward the Icewode, running pell-mell to the frozen forest--

--only to meet the lowered lances of the Companions, resplendent in their armor. They emerged from the vastness of the Icewode, bright banners flickering like flames amid snow and ice.

In vain did the first retreating *wyrga* attempt to stop themselves, to avoid being dissolved in the unbearable light that streamed from the Companions' lances. Mad with fright and desperation, the first lines of the *wyrga* turned back and hacked their own troops down to get through them. Some of them scrambled aboard the few remaining eradicators, fought their drivers and threw the bodies out of the cabs, and rammed the machines straight into their own armies.

Nor were the Companions the only force ranged against the slaves of the Desolation. Flanking the knights, battalions of Dwarvid infantry marched steadily forward, each one swinging an iron mace by its chain. Their spiked weapons whirled overhead, sending out sparks of fire as the Dwarvid forces curved their lines into a pincers movement, trapping the maddened *wyrga* beyond help or hope.

A rush of wings in the sky, a strike of hooves on the air, and Sornor, Beghed, and their Skyborn kindred thundered out of the lightning-lit night and set upon the hordes of shrieking *gnaarx* and *wyrga*. A legion of flying horses charged the armored lines, devouring the ground and leaping up again, and wherever their sharp hooves struck was devastation.

None escaped, for after the Skyborn came the four Wraiths and their multitude of brothers. The remaining *wyrga* were so affrighted that their coward hearts gave out, and they dissolved into nothingness with the keening of the Wraiths tearing them apart.

All night long the noise of battle rolled. Not a drop of blood tinged sword or lance of the Companions, for as they advanced their light pushed back the *wyrga* army until it met the flooding Sunder. Then were the slaves of the Desolation utterly consumed, and the Labyrinth was free of them.

On and on the Sunder raced, bearing the *Grand Adventure* on its crest, until the river left the Abbey's demesne and poured between the stark Bordering Cliffs marking the boundary of the Desolation. There the waters spread over the plain, drowning the foul Saurian River, and swept on toward the Black Flame Tower.

The ship aimed its cannons directly at the Tower to coincide with the moment of passing. Black fire burst out of the Tower's embrasures, but the cannons' iridescent broadside met the deadly flare at midpoint and destroyed it. Then with a roar like the world ending, the bulk of the Sunder waters rose up and over the Black Flame Tower, crashing down upon it and submerging it. Down like stones in the sea the Tower sank, and its destruction was barely heard above the raging of the waves and the howling of the winds. The Sunder flowed on, and the Tower was nothing to it.

"Huzzah! Huzzah!" yelled the skeleton crew, waving frantically from their battle stations.

"I think, Captain Bones," said Admiral Nunkins with the courtesy for which he was famous, "we might indulge in a celebration."

"Certainly, Admiral!" the captain responded happily. "Mr. Steward! My compliments to the cook, and we'll want a feast for all hands tonight!"

Saint Amber's Rose

"Aye, sir!" the steward answered, grinning 'til his jaw cracked, and disappeared into the galley.

The ship sailed out into the Fathomless Ocean, and the night was dark as the underworld, and only the wave-tops reflected faint starlight.

"Cap'n!" the midshipman on watch called urgently halfway through the celebratory hornpipes. "Back there on the flood, directly astern. Something appears to be growing, Cap'n!"

Captain Bones took the spyglass and focused on the black shape silhouetted against the blacker night, a kind of dome barely showing above the Sunder where it left the land and flowed into the ocean. After some moments of study, he asked for Admiral Nunkins' opinion.

The admiral gazed for several minutes at the object before he spoke. Then he removed the glass from his eye and turned to the captain.

"I believe we would do well to beat to quarters, Captain Bones," he said in an even tone, but with such foreboding in it that the captain at once gave the order.

"Mr. First!"

"Sir!"

"Beat to quarters, Mr. First!"

"Aye, sir! BEAT TO QUARTERS!"

Merrymaking instantly forgotten, the crew scrambled to battle stations and aimed the guns toward the distant point on the shore where Captain Bones peered through the spyglass.

"Have you any idea what it is, Admiral?" he asked.

"I do, Captain. That is the Black Flame Tower, and in our haste to claim victory we assumed it was submerged under the flood. It is rising again!"

As quietly as possible the ship came around so that its full starboard battery was aimed at the tower on the shore. The gun crew bent over their weapons, ready to fire. All lights were doused to make the ship as nearly invisible as possible. Not a sound could be heard except for the low-voiced exchange between admiral and captain. Everyone on board watched the target, eyes straining to see through the dark. Slowly but without pause the Tower emerged from the settling waves and once again crawled toward the sky.

The Abbot went to the place where the Lord of Desolation had lately stood. Lifting his shepherd's staff and spreading his arms over the Labyrinth, he called to the night and the stars, the winds and the waters. "By *Terra, Aer, Fyr*, and *Watyr*, let the Labyrinth be restored! Return to the Noble Way!"

The crew of the *Grand Adventure* held its collective breath. The Black Flame Tower rose to its former height and stopped. A light showed near the top. It reached out toward the ship...

"Hold fire! Stand down!" shouted Admiral Nunkins and Captain Bones simultaneously.

Like a bolt from a crossbow, the Tower light sped across the water--but no longer was it the Black Flame! Now its beacon of white light made visible every rock and shoal. It swept up and down the coast in a slow half-circle, illuminating all dangers of the shore to ships at sea.

"A lighthouse! The Black Flame Tower is a lighthouse!"

No longer would its terrible fire destroy whatever lay in its path. The Tower had been transformed into a guiding light, and would remain so until Time's End.

Lantern-lights burst out again on the ship in answer to the lighthouse beam. A volley of huzzahs! erupted from the crew, who resumed their dancing with renewed rejoicing. Even Admiral Nunkins and Captain Bones, brimming over with high spirits, were seen to cut a fine figure in a hornpipe, much to the admiration of the sailors.

Back in the Maze World Oliver had left, a small green tendril pushed out of a hairline crack in the concrete floor of Vanity Fair Mall. The tendril grew and became a sapling, grew and became a slender trunk with branches. Other cracks formed, uprooting the mall's foundation, and lush foliage burst through. Concrete buckled into uneven slabs; storefronts toppled, spilling showers of glass shards and metal debris. Twining vines climbed up supporting columns and pulled them down.

Once again the forest took over Vanity Fair Mall, burying concrete, glass, and metal under layers of earth and stone. The small green tendril grew into a great tree planted by rivers of water, and all the birds of the air made their nests in its boughs, and beasts of the field sheltered under its branches.

Saint Amber's Rose

Oliver Medley played the last chord on Saint Amber's Repository and held it until the mountain resonated. A fountain of many-colored lights burst from the organ pipes and shot through the summit's opening, fanning across the brightening sky.

Over the Great Mountain of Zund a rainbow arched in the heavens, spanning from the north to the south.

And a new day dawned.

Charleynne Gates

Epilogue

Saint Amber's Eve

In the first hour after sunset, as the evening star shone in a lilac sky, the Companions of the Noble Way processed in solemn lines into the Grand Sanctuary of the Abbey, bearing their flame-colored banners and singing. With grave expressions they marched forward, and the deep-voiced melody of their anthem filled the immense room to the echo:

> *Be thou my vision,*
> *O Lord of my heart;*
> *Naught be all else to me,*
> *Save that thou art:*
> *Thou my best thought*
> *By day or by night*
> *Waking or sleeping,*
> *Thy presence my light.*
>
> *Be thou my battle shield,*
> *Sword for the fight;*
> *Be thou my dignity,*
> *Thou my delight;*
> *Thou my soul's shelter,*
> *Thou my high tower,*
> *Raise thou me heaven-ward,*
> *O power of my power.*
>
> *High King of Heaven,*
> *My victory won;*
> *May I reach heaven's joys,*
> *O bright heaven's sun!*

Saint Amber's Rose

Heart of my own heart,
Whatever befall,
Still be my vision,
O Ruler of all.

Filling the Grand Sanctuary, they halted before the chancel, where stood the Abbot's chair and Flavia's silver chair with Hera Vespasia perched on its back. Beside her the *Foressa* Mildrith Antara and the Countess Belvedine de Montfort guarded the *Sendara* of the Graelands, and young Andis waited in attendance on her liege Lady. The Mage Dandriel remained behind the Abbot. Inside the shadow of his hood, the Mage's eyes shone like gold--and no one cared to look into them for long lest he see reflected the secret content of his own soul. On the other side of the abbatial chair stood Pavarr, Prince of Taraman, who strode forward to receive the Companions.

The knights sang their hymn until its end, and the chorus of Whiltian friars joined in the descant until the sanctuary rang and rang again. At its conclusion the knights placed their clenched right hands over their hearts in salute to the Abbot, the *Sendara*, and the prince, and Pavarr returned their salute. Oliver Medley, exhausted from his labors on the pipe organ, was propped upright in the first row between two Dwarvids. Next to them, more Dwarvids marshaled the bewildered (and overawed) Bertie Mossgrower and their Dwarvian kin, Tipp and Tapp Whackitt.

The chamber hushed. No sound disturbed the air save for the whisper of flames on white tapers held by the Whiltian friars in their stalls. Candlelight danced and darted against the smooth stone of the walls, from whence it flickered into the vault above.

"Bertie Mossgrower!" the Prince of Taraman spoke in a tone that brooked no opposition. Bertie would have frozen on the spot had it not been for his Dwarvid escorts, who took his arms in a firm grip and brought him up the chancel steps to stand before the prince.

Pavarr eyed the boy coldly. "The *Sendara* of the Graelands summons you, lad. Attend her!" he said, and allowed no expression on his face until after Bertie had passed by, wide-eyed and shaky about the legs. Then a corner of the prince's lip twitched up in the beginning of a smile.

With considerable trepidation Bertie approached the Lady in her silver chair until, both by instinct and the sheer inability to walk upright any longer, he sank to one knee before her and bowed his head.

"Friend Bertie," said Flavia in her beautiful voice. He dared to lift his head... and the kindness in her eyes vanquished his conviction of unworthiness.

"You saved the Gift-Bringer's life and were loyal to him through many trials. With courage beyond your years, you have rendered a signal service to the Labyrinth World. I give you this in token of my gratitude, for upon it is set the emblem of the Graelands. Grace go with you always, Friend Bertie Mossgrower."

Andis bent toward her, offering a cushion of emerald samite. If the young woman's cheeks bore a rosier flush than usual, and if she cast a modest glance at Bertie from underneath her lashes, no one marked it save that young man.

Flavia took up a medallion from the cushion and hung it around Bertie's neck. The medallion was engraved with the Flowering Tree of the Graelands under the constellation of the Great Bear. Underneath it was written a motto in curving script: *Va'in 'a moru'*.

"Friend Bertie, the Prince of Taraman has asked for you to be his personal squire, to become, in time, a Knight-Companion of the Noble Way. We would have your free consent. Is this your wish?"

Joy spread over Bertie's features like a sunrise. He had to swallow before his throat worked, but at last he brought the words out: "Oh, yes, Your Majesty!" he croaked. "I mean, Your Highness. I mean..."

"I am called *Sendara*," said Flavia, and smiled at him again.

This is my great adventure! thought Bertie, and found himself standing at attention beside Pavarr without quite knowing how he got there. *Now it's really beginning!*

"Tipp and Tapp Whackitt!" called Prince Pavarr.

Their Dwarvid escorts promptly propelled the Dwarvian smiths up the steps of the chancel. Removing their caps, Tipp and Tapp bowed low before the Lady of Light.

"You risked your lives to enter the Forge of Unmaking," she said. "By your efforts the River Sunder was freed, and the imprisoned light at the heart of the mountain released. You have given extraordinary service to the Labyrinth."

Saint Amber's Rose

Flavia then invested each of them with the Badge of the Golden Oak, the Labyrinth's highest award of honor. Tipp and Tapp, pink-cheeked with embarrassment and pride, went to stand beside the Abbot's chair.

"Oliver Medley," said Pavarr, and looked darkly upon the stricken countenance of the erstwhile organist.

Two Dwarvids gripped Oliver's arms firmly, rendering escape impossible, and escorted him up the chancel steps--not to the *Sendara* but to Pavarr.

"Kneel," said the prince, unsmiling. Oliver fell to his knees. Mouth open, he gaped at Pavarr.

The prince of Taraman unsheathed his sword. *Greenhallow* rang out as it leapt from the scabbard. Pavarr held the glittering blade upright, inches before Oliver's face.

Oliver turned white as a scoured bone. *I failed her! I couldn't do what she asked of me... and now I'm going to die.* He drew in a deep breath. *Then let me die as one who did the best he could.* Summoning the remnant of his courage, he waited for the fatal blow.

The prince swept the great sword down in a half-circle so that its hilt was highest. "Will you defend the poor and oppressed?" he demanded. "Will you never draw sword save in the cause of justice? Will you be loyal to the *Sendara* Flavia, Lady of Light?"

A silence descended in the room. The congregation filling the Grand Sanctuary waited for him to answer.

"I will," said Oliver Medley, binding himself forever by his word of honor.

"In the name of the Creator and Saint Bran and Saint Amber, I dub thee knight," said Pavarr, tapping Oliver three times on the shoulder with the flat of his blade. And then, if Oliver weren't astonished enough, the prince delivered the *colée*, a slap to Oliver's cheek that knocked him sideways onto his rump and made him see stars. If there was a momentary wry smile or a twinkle in the eye of the Companions who recalled their own knighting, no one noticed.

"That's so you remember your vow," Pavarr informed him, and gave him a hand to help him to his feet. "Arise, Sir Knight Oliver Medley, Defender of the Graelands!"

Charleynne Gates

Two senior Companions invested him with the belt worn by every knight. His was bare of sword and scabbard, they told him, because he was expected to earn them in service to the *Sendara*.

Then the whole assembled company erupted with a tumultuous cheer, and the bells of Saint Amber's Abbey pealed until the Zundian Mountains rang again. Everyone rushed to congratulate him amid a swirl of merriment. Oliver had a fleeting impression that Great-Aunt Belvedine actually came up to him and said, "Well done, Medley. Your father would be proud." But there was such tremendous excitement going on around him that he never afterward could be certain of it.

Fireworks burst above the Abbey, spilling golden scintillations in the night sky. A shower of colors fell over the land to delighted shouts of children in the courtyard: a wizard with a wand shooting out green sparks... a pair of flying horses... a beautiful princess... and a wicked dragon who lashed its tail furiously before it slithered off in the direction of the Desolate Lands. Nothing like it had ever been seen in the Labyrinth World, but never before had there been such a cause for celebration. The Graelands had been saved! The dreaded Ashes of Waste had retreated back toward the Desolation and vanished before their eyes like snowflakes on the desert's face.

Alone, Oliver stood on the wide balcony off the Great Hall, watching a spectrum of sparkles flung against the dark. Nothing in his world--what the people here called the Maze World--could have prepared him for this adventure. Nothing could have prepared him for falling hopelessly in love with the Lady of Light.

After the feast, he had left the singing, dancing throng of merrymakers and made his way toward the balcony. Considering all that had happened to him, he needed to be by himself for a while to think, to realize how greatly recent events had changed him.

But nothing in this world or any other could have prepared him for what he saw here. Crossing to the balcony, he inadvertently caught a glimpse of Pavarr, also leaving the merrymaking. Pavarr's back was toward Oliver, and the prince did not see him. Oliver wondered where Pavarr was hastening, when from under a shadowed arch someone whose golden-red hair flew about in the wind of her motion came running to meet the prince. He caught her up in close embrace, and her face was hidden against his chest.

-- 584 --

Saint Amber's Rose

Flavia! Oliver's tongue refused to form the word. Quietly he stole past the two lovers to the balcony, his heart rent in pieces. He had no right to feel betrayed, for never had he spoken to her of his love, nor could he have expected any like feeling from someone so far above him.

I will be glad that the Abbey's physicians have healed her, that she can walk again, even run to meet the choice of her heart: Pavarr.

Oliver stared out at the star-sprinkled night, at the fireworks delighting the inhabitants of the Abbey, and a single tear slid down his cheek.

"Cousin Oliver!" The one unmistakable voice, the voice he loved, called to him from nearby.

He turned. Flavia was on the upper balcony, seated in her silver chair.

Oliver's face could hide nothing of what he felt. Wordlessly he knelt at her side.

"My younger sister, Falanna, has long been betrothed to Prince Pavarr," she explained. "Now that he has completed his mission against the Lord of Desolation, they will be married."

Oliver couldn't speak for a moment, digesting this information. "But I--but I thought..." He hesitated. "I thought," he whispered, "the Abbey physicians would... make you walk again."

Flavia smiled at him, but sorrow shadowed her face. "Oh, Oliver. The Abbey's healers and their medicines are the best among all the dimensions. If medicine could heal me, it would be done. As I told you at Ravenhome, we of the Labyrinth World possess the secrets of High Magic. If magic could heal me, it would be done. Not by these ways will I arise."

Oliver bowed his head, and her hand rested upon it. Then an idea, at first as small as a raindrop, grew in his mind until it became as irresistible as dawn. "My lady," he faltered, "I think I... may have what is needed. I pray it may be." He felt inside his tunic and brought out the Rose of Saint Amber, which he had taken from its crystal vase when the music ended and the Rose had again diminished to a bud. His heart in his throat, he gave the flower into her hand.

And watched, hardly able to believe what he beheld, as the Rose began to open to its full beauty. Golden light streamed from its heart and surrounded the *Sendara* in her chair until she was the center of its radiance. One hand she extended to Oliver, who took it, supporting her as befitted a dedicated knight.

And she arose from her chair, tall and beautiful as the Flowering Tree of the Graelands!

Flavia turned toward the balcony, toward the people of the Labyrinth who had gathered in the courtyard—the Questors, Knight-Companions, the Mythologicals from days of yore, and all beings of Past and Future who were and will be vowed to her service.

With both hands she raised the Rose above her head as if it were a Cup of Grace, and Light cascaded from it to all beings in all times and in all places. And they knelt before the splendid Light, which is Truth, and Goodness, and Love.

Flavia brought the Rose to her heart and spoke to her innumerable children.

"For your Courage, for your Fidelity, that you stood fast against Chaos and Old Night—for these things I love you and thank you. Not since the Beginning of All Things has there been as great a force arrayed against us. Not since the first star arose in the heavens have the living faced a doom such as this—and never have any in Creation shown more valor than you, my beloved ones.

"Let no one say that we will lose the last great battle against the Desolation, but rather that we will strive to live in the Noble Way until this world and all others are green with life and peace. Let the constellations burn out before we forget our vow!"

"So let it be!" came the chorus of all beings in all times and in all places.

Oliver found himself once again at the feet of the *Sendara* in her silver chair.

"Dear Oliver," she said softly, "it is your Gift of Perseverance that has saved the Labyrinth—and me. But now you must return to your own world. It is our Law, and I have no power to bend it. Tell me what gift I may give you as some slight reward for your great service."

Oliver looked directly into her gray-green eyes, changeable as the sea under sunlight, under storm. He put his hands together in an attitude of prayer, formally offering fealty, and Flavia covered them with hers.

Saint Amber's Rose

"My Lady," he said. "I am your liege man forever. I need no gift, for in serving you I have had my reward. Of your grace I ask only that I may remember... everything."

A swirl of moonlit leaves--oak, ash, and thorn--fell about them, and Oliver Medley awoke in his own garden. Of the Labyrinth World nothing remained—and his memories began all too quickly to dim, as dusk shades into darkness.

"Welcome home, Oliver," said Aurelia Dawn, leaning casually over the garden gate. "That's a nice belt you've got on. How was your adventure in the Labyrinth World?"

"Oh, Mr. Medley!" cried Annie Aranea, struggling out of his front pocket, "this is the most beautiful garden I've ever seen! I just know I'm going to be happy here!"

And Oliver remembered.

Charleynne Gates

Va'in 'a moru'

which means

LET YOUR LIGHT SHINE

The End of the Beginning
of the Chronicles of Saint Amber's Rose

About the Author

Charleynne Gates holds degrees in music, folklore, and English lit. She plays classical piano and organ and lives with a loud-voiced Siamese cat in a green city in the Pacific Northwest. Her most recent exciting adventure was seeing actual (and magical) flying carpets in Turkey.

About the Artist

Kathryn Nance (cover art and illustrations) is a long-time friend of Charleynne's and has spent many years in the theatre as a costume designer. With an MFA in Design, she has drawn designs for over forty of her own shows, including *The Barber of Seville* under the direction of the great Metropolitan Opera basso Renato Cappechi.

Charleynne Gates